JIMMY CARTER

THE HORNET'S NEST

A NOVEL

OF THE

REVOLUTIONARY WAR

SIMON & SCHUSTER

NEW YORK LONDON
TORONTO SYDNEY
SINGAPORE

SIMON & SCHUSTER
Rockefeller Center
1230 Avenue of the Americas, New York, NY 10020

This book is a work of fiction. Many names, characters, places, and
incidents either are products of the author's imagination or are used fictitiously.
The major events of the war are historically accurate.

SIMON & SCHUSTER and colophon are registered
trademarks of Simon & Schuster, Inc.

For information regarding special discounts for bulk purchases,
please contact Simon & Schuster Special Sales at
1-800-456-6798 or business@simonandschuster.com.

Designed by Amy Hill
Map copyright © 2003 David Cain
Illustration on part title pages copyright © 2003 Jimmy Carter

Manufactured in the United States of America

1   3   5   7   9   10   8   6   4   2

Library of Congress Cataloging-in-Publication Data
Carter, Jimmy.
The hornet's nest : a novel of the Revolutionary War / Jimmy Carter.
p. cm.
1. Southern States—History—Revolution, 1775–1783—Fiction.
2. United States—History—Revolution, 1775–1783—Fiction. I. Title.
PS3553.A78144H67 2004
813'.54—dc22
2003059094

ISBN 0-7432-5542-9

*In memory of
my parents, Earl and Lillian,
my brother, Billy,
and my sisters, Gloria and Ruth*

About the Author

Jimmy Carter, who served as thirty-ninth President of the United States, was born in Plains, Georgia, in 1924. After leaving the White House, he and his wife, Rosalynn, founded the Atlanta-based Carter Center, a nonprofit organization that works to prevent and resolve conflicts, enhance freedom and democracy, and improve health around the world. Author of numerous books, including the best-selling memoir *An Hour Before Daylight*, Jimmy Carter was awarded the 2002 Nobel Peace Prize.

Acknowledgments

This novel was begun more than seven years ago and, while writing three other books, I turned constantly to it with new ideas and information about my own ancestors and others who played a crucial role in achieving our nation's independence. Most Americans know very little about major events of the war in Florida, Georgia, and the Carolinas, and I wanted to present as accurate an account as possible of the complex and crucial inter-relationships among colonists, British officials, and the Indian tribes during the twenty years that led to the war's successful end in 1783.

I would like to thank the librarians at Emory University and others in Georgia and North Carolina for providing me with maps and more than two dozen history texts and biographies, written by both English and American authors. They also helped me understand how people traveled, fought battles, grew crops, made shoes, and what words were used during the eighteenth century.

My wife, Rosalynn, was my earliest editor, and her questions about the interrelationship of characters, both historical and fictional, were incisive and helpful.

The strong influence of Michael Korda and Alice Mayhew, editors at Simon & Schuster, provided the necessary incentive for me to arrange the text in a more logical fashion and, with some pain and reluctance, to reduce its original length.

As with all my other books, Faye Perdue provided easy and pleasant communication with the editors and librarians and handled the myriad details of a book's being born.

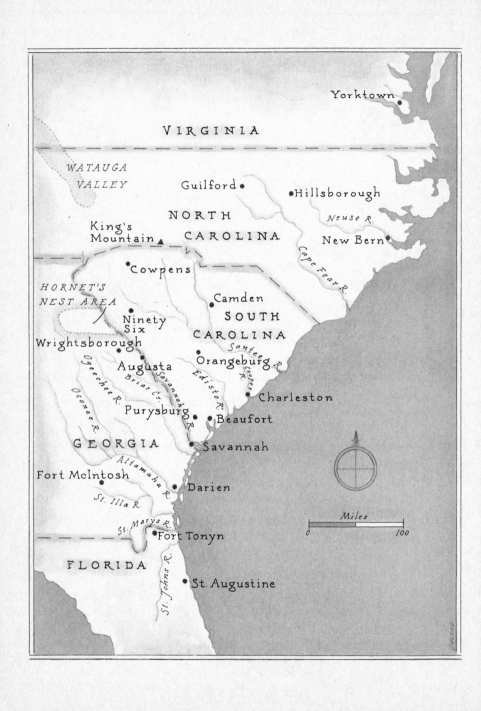

Yorktown

VIRGINIA

WATAUGA
VALLEY

Guilford

Hillsborough

NORTH
CAROLINA

Neuse R.

King's
Mountain

New Bern

Cowpens

Cape Fear R.

HORNET'S
NEST AREA

Camden

SOUTH
CAROLINA

Ninety
Six

Wrightsborough

Santee R.

Orangeburg

Augusta

Briar Cr.

Savannah R.

Edisto R.

Cooper R.

Ogeechee R.

Oconee R.

Charleston

Purysburg

Beaufort

GEORGIA

Savannah

Altamaha R.

Fort McIntosh

Darien

St. Illa R.

St. Marys R.

Fort Tonyn

FLORIDA

St. Johns R.

St. Augustine

Miles
0   100

Contents

Principal Characters

Ethan Pratt (wife, Epsey): frontiersman, later Georgia militiaman

Henry Pratt (wife, Sophronia): Ethan's brother, member of North Carolina Regulators

Joseph Maddock: Quaker leader

Kindred Morris (wife, Mavis): naturalist, neighbor of Ethan Pratt

Newota: young Indian, neighbor of the Pratts and Morrises

Elijah Clarke (wife, Hannah): organizer and leader of Georgia militia

Aaron Hart: aide to Elijah Clarke

Lachlan McIntosh: Georgia military commander

Button Gwinnett: Georgia political leader

Thomas Brown: organizer and leader of Florida Rangers

Quash Dolly: slave woman

OTHERS

Georgia militia leaders: James Jackson, John Dooly, William Few

South Carolina militia leaders: Andrew Pickens, Francis Marion, Francis Sumter

Continental military commanders: George Washington, Charles Lee, Benjamin Lincoln, Robert Howe, John Ashe, Horatio Gates, Nathanael Greene, Daniel Morgan, "Lighthorse Harry" Lee, "Mad Anthony" Wayne

British military commanders: Thomas Gage, William Howe, Henry Clinton, Charles Cornwallis, Augustine Prevost, Alured Clarke, Banastre Tarleton, Patrick Ferguson

Royal governors: William Tryon, North Carolina; James Wright, Georgia; William Campbell, South Carolina; Earl Dunmore, Virginia

Georgia's elected leaders: Council of Safety President Archibald Bulloch, Governors John Adam Treutlen and John Houstoun

Aides to Thomas Brown: Alonzo Baker, Chief Sunoma, Daniel McGirth, James Grierson

Chesley Bostick: a Son of Liberty, Brown's persecutor

Emistisiguo: distinguished Indian chief

Herman Husband: leader of North Carolina Regulators

John Stuart: Royal Indian superintendent

William Bartram: naturalist, explorer

William Henry Drayton: South Carolina firebrand patriot

Count d'Estaing: French naval commander

BOOK I

1763–1773

CHAPTER I

The Philadelphia Cordwainers

1763

The young girl stood quiet and unseen behind the trunk of a large walnut tree, its leaves and branches scarred on one side by a recent fire. Her demeanor and even her clothing would have indicated to a careful observer that she led a relatively protected life in a family of modest means. Although concealed, she didn't appear to be ill at ease, but quite sure of herself. Her high-topped shoes were polished but plain, like new ones designed for a long life, and her black dress was of good quality but without frills of any kind. She wore a bonnet that only partially concealed her thick and somewhat unruly hair, most of it twisted into a tight bun on the back of her head. Hers was almost but not quite the same as clothing worn by the many Quaker families in Philadelphia.

From her vantage point on the edge of a side street among modest houses and shops, she could survey most of a small vacant lot—or one that was almost empty. There were the remnants of a burned house, its outline delineated by a rim of scorched weeds and grass. The lone chimney was standing and some of the foundation pillars were still visible, flat rocks only partially held together by blackened mortar. When the unoccupied house had burned the previous month, the neighbors had been successful in limiting the blaze to the one structure, largely because the nearest home was twenty feet away.

There was a boy working just beyond where the house had stood. She knew his name was Ethan, and that his father was Samuel Pratt, the neighborhood shoemaker. Recently she had volunteered to carry her father's shoes to be repaired and was disappointed when only Mr. Pratt had been in the shop. This was the third time she had come to watch Ethan, and she felt somewhat guilty. Her parents would have been surprised to see her doing anything devious or surreptitious. She was not afraid or embarrassed, but only reluctant to confront another person her age, and especially the boy she was watching.

On previous days she had seen him use a pinch bar to remove the few remaining cut nails from charred boards and timbers, and carefully straighten each nail with a hammer and put it into an old bucket. Then he had gathered the wood debris against a leather apron that extended from his upper chest down to his thighs, and laboriously arranged the pieces in neat piles on the ground, each parallel to the others. Only after the ground within the foundation was cleared and swept smooth had the boy prepared his garden plot in what had been the backyard. He had cut down the weeds with a scythe, broken the ground with a pick and mattock, raked it level, and laid off rows with a hoe. He used two stakes and a taut string to make each furrow perfectly straight before moving to the next one. Now he was planting small pieces of white potato from a bucket in regularly spaced hills almost exactly a foot apart. The girl was fascinated by the care, persistence, and precision with which he labored, totally absorbed in his work. She noticed that there were no wasted movements of his agile hands.

Now she made a deliberate decision to move a few inches out into the open, and the boy looked up and saw her, she presumed for the first time. For a few seconds, they both seemed uncomfortable, not knowing what to say. She finally made a remark that she had carefully rehearsed: "It's interesting that those potatoes are akin to tomatoes."

Ethan, somewhat aggravated to be observed without knowing it, replied, "That's foolish. A potato grows under the ground, and tomatoes on a bush."

The girl thought for a while and said, "Then maybe my father's book is wrong."

"What kind of book?"

"It describes the different food plants produced in Europe."

Ethan was intrigued, but reluctant to continue talking with a stranger. He said, with something of a smile, "Well, you'd better take another look."

He turned to continue his work, and when he glanced up again, the girl was gone. This was one of the few times in his life that he had spoken directly with any girl other than his two sisters. He figured that she was probably about his age, since she was larger than his sisters. She was not unattractive, but dark eyebrows gave her face a somewhat brooding appearance. He was pleased that he had been able to correct her mistake, hoped that he had not hurt her feelings, and then forgot about her completely. He had no premonition that they would spend a good portion of their lives together.

Late the next afternoon he was watering some new onion plants and saw the girl approaching from across the nearby street. She had a book in her hand and walked directly toward the garden plot, without hesitation. When she arrived at the edge of the lot, she waited for him to speak first.

"Well, what did you find about the vegetables?"

Trying not to sound superior in any way, she glanced in the book and said, "Tomatoes and potatoes are both in the nightshade family, with a Latin name spelled s-o-l-a-n-a-c-e-a-e. They came from South America. My father has a special interest in the names and origins of plants." She paused for a few seconds and added, "And so do I."

She turned the book around and held it out to Ethan as he approached her, and without touching the pages, he read the text. Then he wiped his hands on his trousers, took the book, and thumbed through its pages, stopping to read a few sentences about corn, peas, okra, carrots, sweet potatoes, and other plants that he knew.

She said, "I told my father about your garden, and he said you could borrow the book if you wish."

When Ethan nodded and kept the book, the girl turned and began to walk away. He called after her, "I'm grateful. What is your name?"

"Epsey Nischman." She hesitated a few moments and then added, "My father is a Moravian minister, who teaches in our church's boarding school. We live about two hundred yards from here, and I have seen you working in the garden. My grandparents used to live in Savannah, Georgia, and my grandmother lives with us now."

They exchanged a little more information about each other, with Epsey describing a house "full of books" and parents interested in helping Indian tribes improve their lives with religious instruction and better farming practices. Epsey soon knew that Ethan was eighteen years old and he found out Epsey was two years younger.

Ethan said, "I've had a very small garden plot for several years just behind our house, but it's mostly in the shade. Only last weekend Mr. Parvey came in our shop to get his shoes repaired, saw me working in the backyard, and said if I would clean up this lot I could plant a garden. I'm to save the boards and nails for him and give him a third of the vegetables I grow."

"Why didn't you plant in the clean place where the house stood?"

"Because my father said that a hot fire would kill the ground for a year or two, so things won't grow on it."

Epsey offered to help him with his work, but he declined politely. She told him where she lived, and he promised to return the book the next Saturday morning.

As night approached, Ethan walked down a path behind the shops and small houses to the back door of the Pratts' home and entered the kitchen. His father and sisters were at the table, and his mother was preparing to serve supper.

"You're late again," she said. "We were just getting ready to eat."

"I've been in the new garden. I only have a couple of hours each day after the shop closes to work in it."

His father said, "You're not like Henry was. He always wanted to stay in the shop as long as he could."

Ethan decided not to reply.

The shop was not an unpleasant place. There were four workbenches in the center of the main room, spaced evenly around a lighting source that supplemented what came in through the windows and doors. A single high-quality candle burned in the center of four small globes filled with water, each the size of a large man's fist. Each created a prism that focused the candle's light in a small spot, and the shoemakers shifted their work to be in the brightest place. The soft leather for the upper shoe was stretched into proper shape, holes were punched with an awl, and strong linen or flax thread was used for sewing. Although steel needles were available, everyone preferred to use stiff hog bristles, which were enmeshed in the end of the thread and guided the fibers through the holes. The thick soles were often attached with small maple pegs. All the toes were square, and the shoes could be worn on either foot.

Samuel Pratt was from a Scotch-Irish Presbyterian family and had come from Ulster to Philadelphia as a young man. Most of his earlier friends had moved on into western Pennsylvania, but he had stayed in the city to ply his trade. He was a member of the Guild of Cordwainers, the older name for their craft. Mr. Pratt was proud of his shop and his trade, commenting often about its value to the community, the breadth of its contact with even the most elite members of Philadelphia society, and the fact that the Worshipful Company of Cordwainers had helped to finance Captain John Smith's first expedition to America in 1607, long before the Pilgrims came to Massachusetts.

The family lived in the heart of Philadelphia, where Mr. Pratt earned enough to support his wife and four children, somewhat crowded into two rooms above the shop. In the larger room upstairs, two old blankets hung from a length of rope, with a bed on each side. The boys used the space nearest the door and the girls enjoyed a window that looked out on the street. On the ground floor, a narrow room extended all the way across the house behind the shoemaker shop, with a long table surrounded by two benches and two chairs occupying much of the floor space. The fireplace at one end provided warmth and a place for cooking, and supplies of leather goods were stored in shelves along the walls. Mr. Pratt sometimes worried about the future, but the other members of the family took it for granted that they would never lack anything they really needed.

Although Henry was the one who seemed to be interested in his father's trade and loved to be at the shoemaker's bench, the making and repairing of shoes and other leather goods just made possible the camaraderie and political discussions with customers and loungers that he really loved. He was small for his age, loved to be with people, and had many boyhood friends. Even when quite young, Henry joined in the discussions about the exciting political life of Philadelphia and its cultural and economic affairs. He worked rapidly and with great skill but despised taking orders and keeping records. Competition from other shoemakers in the city was intense and his father showed no inclination to retire and permit either of his sons to run the shop, so from an early age Henry's ambition was to move away from home, own his own place, and live an independent life. Influenced by some broadsheets distributed by the Guild of Cordwainers, Henry planned to travel to Norfolk, Virginia, and later to settle in western North Carolina, where he'd read that a number of Quakers had established new homes. He was never insubordinate to his parents and didn't want to cause them concern, so he shared his plans only with Ethan.

Ethan was the youngest child, born in 1745, two years later than his brother. He had little love for either the work or the talk of the shoemaker's shop. He was interested in tools, machines, and how things worked, but was even more fascinated with plants and how to grow them. Even as a small child, Ethan had felt closed in and restricted, and wanted mostly to be alone. He had always been quiet and aloof, disappointing his older sisters when he rejected their efforts to cuddle and care for him. Ethan was now tall, thin, blond, and handsome in a rough way. There had been a time when Henry was dominant, but Ethan was larger even before they became teenagers, and after their first bodily contest they had learned to respect each other as physical equals. As soon as he could obtain his mother's permission, Ethan had begun moving his bedroll downstairs to a corner of the shop, but only for privacy during the night and not because he was attracted to the place during the working day.

He watched Henry with interest and sometimes embarrassment during busy hours in the shop. The conversations were often lively, and Henry would make loud, confrontational statements about political affairs, and was sometimes personally critical of prominent people in the city, including Benjamin Franklin and some of the more influential Quakers. The age or substantiality of other men in the shop never dampened his provocative opinions. Ethan soon realized that his brother would take diametrically opposite positions in subsequent discussions, obviously just to engender lively exchanges. Their father rarely commented except on matters that involved his own profession, and seemed to realize that part of his business was due to Henry's helping to provide a forum for the exchange of ideas.

Ethan realized that when his brother left home, he would be expected to become his father's apprentice, customarily a commitment of six or seven years. He was always uncomfortable around other people and, taking advantage of Henry's presence, he escaped whenever possible to visit a nearby blacksmith or a cabinetmaker, where he volunteered to help them and carefully observed them at their craft. Without explaining or really expecting to have a place to use them, he asked Henry to help him acquire tools of his own with which he could work with wood. Henry found a small collection for sale at a low price in the estate of an older friend of their father. For years, Ethan had enjoyed working behind their shop in a small garden plot, only about twice the size of their kitchen table. He had experimented with various kinds of seeds and cultivation practices, and was proud when his vegetables helped supplement the family's diet. During the growing season he had tended the garden while the shop was closed or without customers, and considered it a source of pride to be called "farmer" by the other children.

He had finished planting his new and larger garden when Saturday morning came, and was strangely excited as he walked toward the Nischman's house. He assumed it was from the possible chance of seeing the big collection of books. He knocked timidly on the door, which was immediately snatched open by Epsey. She introduced him to her parents and grandmother. Her father, Georg, asked Ethan how he had liked the book.

"Very much," the boy replied. "It has the kind of information I've always wanted but didn't even know was written down anywhere."

They moved into the library, a small room with walls covered by bookshelves filled with stacked magazines, old newspapers, and carefully arranged books.

"I inherited many of these from my father, the church has furnished me with others, and I have bought a few. Most of them are about religion and other practical subjects," Mr. Nischman said, then glanced at Ethan. He was pleased when the boy did not respond but acknowledged his small joke with a smile.

"You are welcome to come here anytime you wish, and there are some of these books that you can take home to read."

After that, Ethan visited the Nischman home often, and he and Epsey explored the library together. Ethan soon realized that she was thoroughly familiar with her father's work and assessed even the most mundane issue through its religious connotations. God was obviously directly involved in the characteristics of seeds and the plants they produced, and engaged in how they were grown and used. She soon found that the interests of her new friend were quite narrow, focused on subjects concerning farming, animal husbandry, handicrafts, and information about life in other parts of the New World. Although their motivations were unrelated, their involvement in farming overlapped because the Moravians were dedicated to sharing agricultural knowledge with native populations in the Caribbean islands and the more western regions of the colonies.

Epsey was soon working with Ethan in his garden, and Mr. Nischman helped them locate different varieties of seeds and seedlings with which Ethan had not been familiar. Ethan learned that Epsey was somewhat solemn but not unhappy and, unlike Ethan's, her parents were eager to gratify her modest wishes. She didn't talk much, which suited Ethan well, but they communicated without restraint on the management of the vegetable plots.

Neither Ethan nor Epsey had many friends, and both families obviously welcomed their growing friendship. Their courtship was just a series of small evolutionary steps of shared experiences, mostly involving the study of botany and geography and the planting and cultivation of the garden. The next summer, it seemed natural to everyone when they decided to marry. Much later, when their relationship had become formal and permanent, Ethan couldn't remember the first time he held her hand or when he had given her the first, dutiful kiss.

That summer, Henry Pratt announced his intentions to leave home after Christmas. Ethan and Epsey were married two weeks after his departure, and they moved in with the Nischmans. Ethan continued helping his father in the shoemaker's shop and received a small salary that was enough to meet his new family's needs.

One day Mr. Pratt surprised Ethan by offering him a larger portion of the profits and telling him that he would someday own the shop, but Ethan replied that he and Epsey planned to join Henry as soon as he was settled in North Carolina. The Pratts were disappointed and angry, but Epsey's father was delighted with the decision. The Nischmans were obsessed with evangelizing the American Indians, and they were happy for their daughter and son-in-law to be living and perhaps doing missionary work in the backcountry.

CHAPTER 2

Sons of Liberty in Norfolk

1765

When Henry Pratt left Philadelphia, he took with him only what he could carry on his back: his clothes, some shoemaker's tools and supplies, and forty-three silver Spanish pieces of eight he had been able to save during the previous five years. His ultimate goal was to settle in North Carolina, but he was not in a hurry. He followed a relatively good road down through Delaware and Maryland, paused to spend two days in Annapolis, and then crossed over the Chesapeake Bay to Virginia on a ketch that served as a ferry. After wandering around the town and observing the bustling trade in leather goods, Henry decided to spend a few months in Norfolk.

His first visit, early on Monday morning, was to the largest and obviously most successful shoemaker shop, where he insisted on speaking directly to the owner.

When Mr. Carlyle arrived shortly before noon, Henry judged him to be a serious businessman and explained to him that he had been a shoemaker in Philadelphia and wished to continue his trade in Norfolk. He added, to avoid any misunderstanding, that he was not an apprentice, but had years of experience.

The owner said that he had a vacancy and offered to take Henry on, on a trial basis. After some discussion, they decided that Henry would craft one pair each of men's and women's shoes, and they would then seek to reach an agreement on the terms of employment. Choosing the design of Philadelphia's latest styles, Henry quickly fashioned the shoes and presented them to Mr. Carlyle with a smile. He had to acknowledge Henry's skill and offered him a job as a regular employee, to be paid by the week as were his other workers. The young man politely declined this offer and said he would prefer to work with a fixed payment for each pair of shoes. After some careful assessment of how much he was actually paying his current shoemakers for each pair they produced, Mr. Carlyle made an offer, based on Henry's shoes being examined for quality before payment was made and the terms of their agreement not being revealed to the other shoemakers.

Henry accepted, pleased by an arrangement that would give him independence from the strict control of his employer, remove any limit on his maximum earnings, and permit flexibility in his working hours so that he could travel around the city during the daytime to learn about aspects of the leatherworking trade with which he was not acquainted.

To minimize his living expenses, Henry made arrangements with a nearby family to share two simple but ample meals each day, and got permission from his employer to set up a folding cot at night in the shoemaker's storeroom, where he would serve as something of a night watchman. When necessary, he worked there by candlelight to maintain an acceptable level of shoe production. Henry pleased his employer by producing shoes of good quality at a surprisingly high rate, sometimes more than two pairs a day.

He was able to work part-time at a large tannery, where he learned how to cure, dye, and finish the hides of cattle, unborn calves, deer, and horses, and the skins of sheep and goats. He accumulated a careful list of supplies he would need to produce leather for heavy belting for drive pulleys, saddles and harnesses, work shoes, and the finer grades used for jackets, hats, dress shoes, and other light apparel.

On his cot at night, surrounded by the reassuring odor of cured leather and sometimes the stench of the tannery left on his own clothes, Henry planned for his future in North Carolina. As he worked in the shop, he constantly accumulated information from customers who were familiar with the social and political situation in the western regions of the southern colonies.

Henry also visited a local tailor shop, which specialized in the production of fine leather purses, jackets, and other clothing. After he bought a pair of relatively expensive gloves, he obtained permission from the owner to visit the working area. There were several women cutting out patterns and sewing the soft and flexible leather, keeping their heads carefully averted as he walked down the narrow aisle between them, pausing on occasion to observe their work more closely. The last worker, relatively young, looked up at him from her task after he had watched her for a minute or so. Her eyes never wavered from his, they exchanged smiles, and that afternoon he waited outside the shop until she emerged.

Her name was Sophronia Knox but she preferred to be called Sophie, and it was immediately apparent that she welcomed the opportunity to become better acquainted with Henry. They walked to a nearby public area, found a bench, and exchanged information about each other. He quickly learned that Sophie lived with an uncle and aunt, and had never been to school but knew how to read, write, and work with figures. She had been apprenticed to the tailor since she was twelve years old and had begun to be paid a small hourly rate a year later. Sophie was satisfied that her wages were paid directly to her guardians. They treated her kindly, and she was pleased that for the past year she had been given four shillings a week to save or spend as she wished. She was seventeen years old and could not remember her parents, both of whom had died in an epidemic of fever when she was a small child.

Sophie, with her sparkling eyes, curly hair, white teeth, and full, voluptuous lips, aroused Henry in an intense way. She had an apparently unconscious habit of putting her fingers on him when they were talking to each other, and there were increasingly frequent times when her fingernail dragged across his chest or one of his biceps. She impressed Henry with her candor, and he was somewhat overwhelmed with the outpouring of opinions and information about every subject with which she was at all familiar. Although the scope of her life had been limited, she was obviously a keen observer and eager to learn from others. It seemed she would never run out of things to report about her employer, fellow workers, her aunt and uncle, their immediate neighbors, people she had met at church, or her other few acquaintances. Even the simplest and most innocuous conversations or events filled her with a great reservoir of memories that to her were worth sharing.

She was apparently interested in everything Henry had to say, and since exchanging information had always been one of his favorite pastimes, they got along well from their first meeting. They were never at a loss for words, both waiting expectantly for their next opportunity to speak. Sophie's family was from Scotland, and her uncle still worked in a firm where her father had also been employed. Their primary business was buying tobacco, grading its quality, packing it in large hogsheads, and shipping it to Glasgow. There seemed to be a deep antagonism between the Scots and the English merchants in Norfolk, so Henry heard only disparaging comments from Sophie about anything to do with London.

Henry was eager to meet her uncle and was soon invited to their home, where he immediately felt at ease. Mr. Knox was proud of his work and relished telling Henry of the firm's progress and its ability to triumph over English competitors in capturing the lucrative tobacco trade. His particular responsibility was to expand the exchange of goods with Virginia farmers, who increasingly depended on the firm's providing them with whatever was necessary to produce a crop and to survive during the winter. He was not at all ashamed of their techniques for forging an almost inseparable tie to these producers of tobacco and wheat, based on a liberal credit policy that almost invariably resulted in indebtedness that could rarely be settled with the proceeds from a single crop. The farm families were, therefore, obliged to continue the exchange of their crops and livestock for implements, consumer goods, household supplies, food staples, and a limited amount of cash during the growing season. Because of his religious beliefs, Mr. Knox was personally opposed to slavery, but his business obligations permitted him to be flexible on the subject. There were some families in the area who refused to purchase slaves and insisted on working their own land, but Mr. Knox told Henry that the average tobacco producer in Virginia possessed twenty slaves.

He explained that although otherwise highly competitive, the merchants in Norfolk usually refrained from competing with one another for business with a family that was already obligated to a firm. Since there was usually no other source of dependable credit, this permitted the merchants to "buy low and sell high," which produced maximum profit among them all. Factors and bankers in Glasgow and London backed Mr. Knox's company and others like it that provided year-round loans to colonial farmers. Interest rates were high, and the risks of losses were minimal. The danger of unpaid bills was offset by security deeds on land, property, and slaves, which more than covered the debts, and the merchants and factors frequently wound up owning plantations and smaller farms when the owners could not pay and faced foreclosure. As often as not, the bankrupt families simply abandoned their estates to move quietly to frontier lands for a new start.

The Knoxes were devout Presbyterians, and Henry attended services with them. He found that there was little formal ceremony there, but a strong dependence on the morning sermon. The clergyman was not reticent in expressing his views on current circumstances, finding little difficulty in connecting almost any political or social issue with an appropriate selection from the Scriptures. The sessions were filled with criticisms of the dominant Anglican Church, its closeness to the political authorities, and demands for the full independence of all worshippers. Members of the congregation seemed to be caught up in these issues, and they precipitated long Sunday-afternoon talks and sometimes mild arguments between Mr. Knox and Henry.

Although there were some political comments at church that were surprising and somewhat disturbing to Henry, Mr. Knox was even more outspoken in his home.

"I've always been a loyal subject of the crown, but King George the Third is so ignorant and incompetent that he has strained my confidence in the monarchy itself."

Henry had never heard such comments in his own family. Any negative references to the royal family would have been almost as unlikely as a personal criticism of Jesus Christ. In order to disassociate himself from Mr. Knox's opinions and, at the same time, to keep the conversation going, he replied, "Well, down through history we have often had monarchs who lacked perfect judgment. In fact, a few were known to be quite sinful and even mentally deranged."

Mr. Knox replied, "But this one has violated a long-standing principle that has been honored for more than a hundred years, when Charles the

First tried but failed to impose English worship services on Scotland. Since then, the king has acknowledged that Parliament has the power to govern. In fact, ever since the Magna Carta in 1215, citizens have been assured that there would be no taxation without representation. Otherwise, we Scots would never have joined with England sixty years ago."

Henry realized that he was at a disadvantage in this discussion. Mr. Knox was much more familiar with British history, and particularly with facets of it that applied to his own people.

"I thought it was Parliament that passed the Stamp Act earlier this year, and not King George?"

"The problem is that the king no longer stays aloof from the details of administration concerning the colonies, and injects himself into almost everything that is domineering and abusive. Instead of acting as something of a sea anchor, to provide stability and restraint while parliamentarians consider legislation carefully, he is in the forefront of wild and ill-considered decisions. His voice and influence are used to inflame the public and force Parliament to act against those of us in the colonies."

Henry replied, "But the final influence is with the people, and the leaders they choose to represent them in London."

"Henry, what you don't seem to understand is that in every colony, perhaps excepting Georgia, we have developed political systems that are much more democratic than anything Great Britain has ever known. Although the crown appoints the governors and their councils, all the colonies have some form of parliaments or assemblies that deal with internal matters. From town meetings in Massachusetts to legislatures in the Carolinas, the people have gained the right to make decisions about our own lives, including the levying of taxes. Until George became king in 1760, these rights were basically unchallenged, but since then he has encouraged Prime Minister Grenville to put the screws to the colonies. They've tried in every way to interrupt all navigation except trade that benefits Britain and is carried on British bottoms. We Scots will never forgive him. On top of that, the Stamp Act imposed on us from London is a direct violation of our freedom, and a departure from the ancient principle of no taxation without representation."

"Mr. Knox, I understand what you're saying, but I don't see that the Stamp Act is all that much of a problem."

"Son, aside from the legalities involved, it is an unbearable burden for my business and for anyone else that has to deal in contracts, deeds, bills of sale, wills, or any other kind of legal documents. The tax is even imposed on playing cards, marriage licenses, newspapers, and pamphlets. This is something we cannot accept."

"I don't understand why this has happened. Why wasn't London satisfied with the way things were going?"

Mr. Knox hesitated a moment and then replied, "The answer to that is complicated. With the end of the French and Indian War, England had prevailed over all of her historic enemies and is now dominant in North America and on the world's seas. At the same time, there is a tremendous debt that has to be paid off, accumulated from all the military action. The colonists have also been a financial burden, with few if any taxes collected over here ever sent to England."

"But why single out the colonies? Didn't we do everything possible to help in the war against France?"

"Well, to be truthful, the answer is no. Most colonial governments met the official requests from London for financial contributions, which rarely even covered the expenses of the colonies. But, in fact, a lot of merchants, including my own company, continued to trade freely with the French even during the conflict. It was very lucrative for us, and the British seem to resent it even more now than when the war was under way. This is one of the main arguments that the king has used against us. About ten thousand of the British troops that were fighting the French and the Indians are now quartered over here, and some hotheads in Parliament claim that our taxes should be used to pay this cost."

"Mr. Knox, I noticed that you said we can't accept the stamp tax. If you refuse to pay the tax, I don't see how any jury made up of your neighbors would ever punish you."

Knox nodded. "That brings up another problem, just as serious as the tax. Parliament has also mandated that any violators would have to be tried in British admiralty courts, appointed and controlled from London, and not by a jury of our peers. Many of our prominent men, including Patrick Henry and George Washington, have spoken out publicly against these threats to freedom in all the colonies."

"Then with so many British soldiers in the colonies, what can we do?"

"Some things are already being done, as I'm sure you have heard. There have been riots in some of the port cities, especially further north in New

England, and many merchants along the coast are trying not to buy British goods. I know for a fact that this has become a serious problem for my own home company in Scotland, and the financial and mercantile leaders are hurting much worse in London and are calling for a repeal of the Stamp Act."

Henry didn't respond further, but the conversation had a great impact on him. At the shoemaker's and the tannery, he repeated and even embellished on the points made by Mr. Knox. He found, however, that few of his fellow workers had any concern about the Stamp Act, since none of them had needed to use legal documents since the law was passed. Most of them were somewhat uncomfortable when Henry extended his criticisms beyond the Parliament and prime minister and referred personally to the king, and he soon had a reputation as a source of dissension against the government in England.

One afternoon, as Henry left the tannery, two young men were waiting for him at the gate.

The older one asked, "Are you Henry Pratt?"

"Yes. Why do you ask?"

"We have heard that you have spoken out against the Stamp Act. Is that right?"

"Well, that's really none of your business. Before I answer, you'll have to tell me your purpose in coming to see me."

"We belong to a small organization that is devoted to opposing this unfair and oppressive law, and we're looking to find kindred souls. We were hoping you could join us for a tankard of ale, or whatever refreshment you prefer."

"Well, I'm indeed thirsty after a hard day's work and would be glad to share a drink with you."

When seated at a nearby tavern, the men introduced themselves as Shelby Somers and Daryl Gethers, and they claimed that both their families were large landowners. Henry could soon tell that his new acquaintances were well educated and knowledgeable about political affairs in the Commonwealth, and they wanted him to join a group that they called the Sons of Liberty, also known as the Liberty Boys.

"We don't have much of an organization," they explained, "but we are dedicated to two basic activities. One is to help encourage and enforce an agreement among all merchants to avoid buying or using goods from England. The other is to induce British officials not to use the official paper with expensive stamps on it."

Henry was quiet for a while, took a long drink of ale, and then asked, "How could you do these things?"

"First of all," said Somers, "we have the backing of the gentry, which includes most of the political and commercial leaders in Virginia. Our own fathers are prominent and influential. The basic premise is that we are loyal citizens who only demand the same rights that have been guaranteed in Great Britain for generations and that have always been assumed in the colonies. We're not blaming the king. Prime Minister Grenville, who brought about all these problems, has now been removed from office, and we believe that King George will be looking for some way out of this confrontation with the colonies. We just want to encourage everyone in England to realize what a terrible mistake the Parliament has made."

"Why do you need me, if all you aristocrats are united in opposition to the Stamp Act?"

"We've heard about your strong opinions on this matter, and we need someone who is familiar with the good people who are shoemakers, tanners, and other artisans. And to be frank with you, we know of your close relationship to Mr. Knox. He is a good man, and as a Presbyterian and a Scot, he can be very influential among the merchants who are not tied directly to London. His company might be touched by the embargo against trade with England. It would be helpful if they would join us, and you might help us avoid hurting the merchants in Glasgow and concentrating on those in London. That's where the pressure needs to be applied."

"I'm inclined to help you all, but I'd like to talk to Mr. Knox first. He doesn't tell me what to do, and I know he's as opposed to the Stamp Act as I am. But maybe he could give us some good advice."

The young men quickly agreed, and they parted company.

Henry looked forward to his next Sunday-afternoon talk with Mr. Knox, who also relished having such an eager listener. This time, Henry took the initiative and described his conversation with Somers and Gethers, but without naming them. The response was immediate and clear.

"I've known about the Sons of Liberty for several months, and I agree with their basic purpose. All the leaders in our company, including those in Scotland, are strongly opposed to the Stamp Act in the colonies, considering it to be abusive and counterproductive. Many of us believe that the purpose behind it is not just to develop something of a trade monopoly for England and raise revenue, but also to keep the colonies in a weakened financial condition. Some London factors have deliberately encouraged landowners in America to accumulate a load of debt that they know can never be repaid.

"At the same time, we're concerned about an embargo, because we fear that our own merchants in Glasgow might suffer along with those in London. We have a number of ships in the Carolinas and Georgia right now loaded with rice and ready to go to Europe, and an embargo would cost us a lot of money. Although we are prepared to suffer some consequences, we would certainly like to see maximum pressure brought where it will do the most good, by inducing London to change its policies."

Without saying so, Mr. Knox clearly approved of Henry's joining the Sons of Liberty and proceeded to tell him how the effect of trade restraints might be focused on English merchants, manufacturers, and shipowners. Henry listened carefully and soon shared this advice with the Sons of Liberty.

After that, Henry maintained an acceptable level of shoe production but cut back on his work at the tannery. He spent all his spare time with the group. He learned that Somers was the leader and that his father was a large landowner near Norfolk and also a member of the House of Burgesses, the parliament of colonial Virginia. As had been originally explained to Henry, the members of the Sons of Liberty were divided into two groups. One, in which Henry was mostly involved, obtained information about commerce in the port city. They built up a list of all goods being imported and the national origin of each item. Some, like rum, came from the Caribbean. Others, like paint, glass, and firearms, mostly came from England. In these cases, the Sons of Liberty learned where they could be obtained from other countries. Where England was the only known supplier, they decided to urge Virginians to refrain from buying the item at all, a point that had been emphasized by George Washington, a prominent member of the House of Burgesses. Although the Commonwealth's only newspaper, the Virginia *Gazette,* refused to publish anything that was critical of the mother country's government, the lists were promulgated widely on leaflets and posters, and it was soon obvious that they were having an effect.

The other group, which Henry joined on a few occasions, organized demonstrations against officials who had custody of stamped paper, attempting to intimidate them against using the documents for the collection of the tax. Although there was news of riots and acts of violence against determined British officials in some of the colonies, most of those in Norfolk soon pledged not to distribute the stamps if the crowds around their homes and offices would disperse. Sophie was eager to join in the demonstrations, but both Henry and Mr. Knox objected that this was an improper role for a woman.

The activities of the Sons of Liberty were well known to the public, but Henry pleased Mr. Knox by informing him in advance about most of their plans. As a result, Henry received financial contributions that he was able to share with the Sons of Liberty to cover their expenses for posters and brochures.

The Sunday-afternoon conversations at the Knox home continued as usual and covered an increasingly broad range of subjects. With Henry's developing interest in political affairs, he looked forward to these sessions, and the older man was well practiced in expounding his rigid opinions and priorities. Although normally opinionated himself, Henry was able to admit his ignorance about many subjects, and both he and Sophie asked one question after another without hesitation. One afternoon Henry decided to explore a very basic question, which he was sure every educated person must understand.

"Mr. Knox, what is the difference between people who live in England and those who live over here? How can we have such conflicting ideas if we share the same history, speak the same language, and are loyal to the same royal family?"

"Henry, there is a natural difference between those who have stayed at home in England, Ireland, Scotland, and Wales and their kinfolk who decided to leave home and move here to America. Each group believes itself to be superior. Colonists think that those still in Europe lack initiative, are not courageous enough to depart on an unpredictable adventure, or don't have the foresight to take advantage of new opportunities. They seem to be docile, willing to accept encroachments on their political or religious freedoms, and to accommodate with little question the changing policies of their government. On the other hand, we have come to find freedom, to worship in various ways, to begin new lives, to challenge what is in effect an unknown continent, and to suffer hardship if necessary to achieve these goals. Does this describe the attitude of most of the people you know?"

Sophie replied, "That's certainly the way I see the situation. How can the folks back in Britain disagree with this?"

"There are different opinions on both sides. Some people back in the old country agree with our views, as many of the gentry, particularly in Virginia, still consider anything in London to be superior—even the people there. Some of these are what you might call the outcasts of the gentry class, including a lot of second and third sons who received no inheritance. You can observe them here in Norfolk attempting in every way possible to copy life as it is in England and considering themselves superior to the rest of us. They think that it was mostly misfits who left home, including radical worshippers like the Pilgrims, Quakers, Baptists, Mennonites, and even Presbyterians, all inferior in the eyes of the Almighty. In fact, we have to admit that a number of the settlers have come over here as paupers and indentured servants, having failed to earn a living back home. On the bottom, maybe, are a large group of criminals who have been paroled to provide a workforce in the colonies, although often their crimes were just the nonpayment of debts.

"In any case, when someone leaves a mother country, it is a case of separation or rejection, either voluntary or involuntary. This drives something of a wedge between people."

Henry considered this for a few moments and then asked, "But aren't the colonies very valuable to Britain, to provide things like cotton, timber, rice, indigo, and tobacco, and also a market for England's manufactured goods?"

"Well, I certainly think so, but there are prominent Englishmen who disagree. They believe there is a limited amount of wealth in the world, and as much of it as possible should be attracted to the mother country. Compared to the Caribbean, India, and Africa, the colonies in America have not been very lucrative in trade, and at the same time are too costly to hold. I noticed recently that some leading members of our Parliament were condemning the decision at the end of the French and Indian War to keep Canada, calling it just thousands of acres of barren wilderness. They thought one small island in the Caribbean would be much more valuable. Another problem is that our population over here has exploded, multiplying tenfold just in this century—now almost a third as many as there are back home—and we are becoming more and more difficult to manage from such a distance."

Sophie said, "Well, I can understand the advantages of India and the Caribbean, but don't see anything attractive about Africa."

Mr. Knox hesitated a moment before saying, "This is something not much discussed, but the slave trade provides a steady stream of money back to England, a lot of it through Liverpool. The colonies in tropical climates must have workers to accommodate the extreme heat, and the British have found that a few places to buy slaves along the West African coast are as good as gold mines. The British elite pretend to disassociate themselves from slave traders, but they are deeply and eagerly involved in the accumulation of the profits, even as they look the other way."

Mr. Knox had finally touched upon a subject that he usually avoided. With this one exception, he was able to correlate his political opinions with his interpretation of the Holy Scriptures. As an honest and devout man, he could not defend the involvement of his company in the slave traffic, but he attempted to rationalize what he was doing.

"We never buy slaves," he explained, "but sometimes become the unwilling owner when we have to foreclose on a farmer and he has Negroes as part of his property. Also, when we resell a slave that we come to own, we are careful to have him resold by responsible dealers."

Sophie asked, "But don't you lend money to them to buy slaves?"

It was obvious that Mr. Knox was uncomfortable with the logic of his explanations. Although he couldn't relate his actions to his basic religious standards, he was able to compare them favorably with those of other merchants.

"This is unavoidable when Negroes are necessary for the operation of a plantation. If there is any appreciable acreage, there is no way for a landowner to produce rice or tobacco, for instance, without a lot more labor than his own family can provide. We would have to go out of business if we were the only ones who refused to make loans to meet such a need, but we try to use our influence to minimize abuse by cruel and greedy owners, so it's probably better for the slaves to have us make the loan than most of our competitors. Although they deny it by having different names as owners of the slave ships, some of our British competitors are even bringing blacks from Africa over here to be sold."

Mr. Knox went on to explain that prosperous Englishmen dominated the Commonwealth government in Williamsburg, crafting laws that were almost invariably self-serving, and often to the detriment of lower-class Virginians and those like the Scots who competed in trade between London and the colonies. A strict man in his personal habits, Mr. Knox condemned especially the wealthy families who patterned their social lives after the aristocracy of England, and who, he said, often outdid the people "back home in London" in drunkenness, frivolity, and apparent obsession with their pedigrees. Henry was surprised to perceive the intensity of his older friend's animosity toward the landed gentry, some of whom were his firm's largest customers.

Later, Henry and Sophie agreed that her uncle was not completely logical in his explanations. His sympathies seemed to be with tenants, yeomen, and small farmers, but he had to admit that, as a merchant, he was forced to cast his lot with the dominant elite on matters that affected his own company.

The next Sunday, Henry somewhat reluctantly asked a question that revealed his relative ignorance about political alignments and the history of the mother country.

"Mr. Knox, what's the difference between Whigs and Tories?"

Mr. Knox laughed softly and responded, "Well, both names came about a hundred years ago from the other side as something of a curse. 'Whig' originally meant a horse thief, and later referred to people like me—a Scottish Presbyterian inclined to question the policies of a king. 'Tory' referred to an outlaw whose first loyalty was to the pope. Later, the Whigs were inclined to be those who placed their faith in business and commerce while Tories represented the Anglican Church and honorary titles—all tied to favors handed out by the crown. Nowadays, I would say that Tories and Loyalists are about the same, while Whigs are those that are emboldened to question some of the decisions made by King George the Third. As you can well imagine, there are radicals on both sides who tend to bring credit or discredit on the names, depending on the attitude of the observer."

Sophie and Henry spoke almost simultaneously: "I guess that makes me a Whig."

Mr. Knox said, "I may be one also."

Sophie was familiar with Mr. Knox's prejudices and was reluctant to probe them openly, but alone with Henry she analyzed their conversations with pleasure, humor, and objectivity. Although she usually agreed with her uncle, she could understand and empathize even with pompous aristocrats, slave owners, English merchants, and the laggard workers in the tailor shop. Henry, on the other hand, almost invariably had sharp and carefully defined opinions on almost every subject; there was seldom any middle ground for him. Inevitably, they argued often, but there was one subject on which they agreed: they would be going together when Henry was ready to depart for western North Carolina.

Sophie helped Henry with the next letter to his family in Philadelphia. It was an unusually long and friendly one, designed to make as good an impression as possible. Henry described what he had learned about the leather trade and thanked his father for the good training he had received as a shoemaker. He wanted Ethan to know about his plans to move to North Carolina the first week in October and wondered if his brother still planned to come to the frontier region. Henry hoped that his two sisters had found beaus and were soon to start their own families, and revealed the surprising news that he and Sophronia Knox were soon to be married. He and his wife-to-be both promised to write to their families after they arrived in their new home.

Both Henry and Sophie were eager to be married and on their way, and Henry announced that they would go to the courthouse and have the local magistrate perform the ceremony. Sophie thought longingly of her "bridal chest" and some of the fancy clothing that she and the Knoxes had accumulated since her childhood, but she kept her initial objection to herself. Somewhat hesitantly, they informed Mr. Knox of their plans as they prepared to eat their next Sunday meal in his home. Henry noticed Sophie and Mr. Knox murmuring to each other and was glad to see that both of them were smiling, obviously pleased with plans for the expeditious ceremony.

That afternoon, as the two men sat on the front porch for their customary discussion about affairs of the day, Mr. Knox said, "Henry, as you may know, Sophie has turned over to me a portion of her wages ever since she became employed, and she now has a tidy sum that will be helpful in setting up housekeeping in North Carolina."

Henry was surprised and responded, "Mr. Knox, Sophie has told me that this has always been her contribution to help pay her share of the expenses in your home."

"Nonsense! You will have unpredictable expenses, and Mrs. Knox and I are well able to help. We consider her to be our daughter, and we will add a contribution of our own to her dowry. In addition, we will purchase the required stamps for your marriage license."

Henry was startled and exploded in anger. "No, sir! I'll be damned if there will be a British stamp on anything of mine!"

Mr. Knox was very proper in his own speech, and this was the first time he had heard an expletive come from Henry's lips. Henry's face flushed, and he apologized for his outburst. Neither of them spoke for a while, until finally Henry said, "I know we can't go to the courthouse, and it might even be a problem with a public ceremony in the church."

Mr. Knox responded, "Maybe Sophie would agree to a nice, quiet service here in our home. I'm sure our pastor will not insist on a stamped marriage certificate."

Standing just inside the window behind a curtain, Sophie smiled to herself, went to her room, and began laying out the bonnet, veil, and lacy dress that she would be wearing during the ceremony in the front parlor, as she had been planning since the first day she had met Henry Pratt.

CHAPTER 3

A Corrupt Royal Government

Mr. and Mrs. Henry Pratt moved to Orange County, North Carolina, and set up housekeeping in the growing settlement called Childsburg in the late winter of 1765, the year before the town's name was to be changed to Hillsborough. This was the trading center for a community in the foothills of western North Carolina, lying almost equidistant from the Neuse and Haw rivers. Many backcountry farmers had moved in from Pennsylvania, to escape the restrictive Quaker oligarchy or just seeking new land. Some families had lost their previous jobs or property, and others were dissatisfied with their relatively inferior economic and social status in the coastal regions. They were a highly diverse population, who had come originally from England, Scotland, Ireland, Germany, Switzerland, and a few from Scandinavia. They paid little attention to organized religion, except for those in a nearby settlement of Quakers. All the newcomers considered themselves to be pioneers, establishing a new society whose overall premise was freedom and individuality. By choice and necessity, they were almost totally self-sufficient, importing just a few staples like iron, rum, gunpowder, and salt, and exporting mostly animal pelts and cattle. As soon as the farm families could meet their own needs for food grain and a garden, they cleared additional land for cash crops, mostly tobacco, and sometimes flax and indigo.

When Henry told the community officials that he was an experienced shoemaker, they welcomed him with enthusiasm and immediately offered him a choice of several empty lots near the center of town. But knowing the characteristics of a tannery, Henry suggested instead a site on the eastern outskirts of the village near a small stream so that he could wash his hides and the prevailing westerly breezes would carry the obnoxious odor of curing hides away from other residents. He and Sophie built a small shop with living quarters upstairs, very similar to what he had known in Philadelphia.

When it was completed, Sophie selected a broad and smoothly planed board and painted SANDY CREEK LEATHER SHOPPE on top, with HENRY PRATT, PROP. underneath, which Henry nailed over the front door. On the back of their property, he erected a large, open-sided shed for the curing of hides. The Pratts had no other competition in the community except for a Quaker shoemaker several miles away who served mostly other Quakers, so Henry was soon busy repairing and selling shoes, saddles, harnesses, saddlebags, and even leather fire buckets lined with pitch. Sophie was somewhat disappointed that most housewives did their own sewing, but there were enough unmarried men to buy the gloves, vests, and tunics she produced. One, a long, loose-fitting shirt called a "wamus," was especially popular, and she filled a few orders for leather caps and hats.

Both having come from the more stylish coastal area and having been involved in producing clothing themselves, they were interested in what the frontier people wore. All apparel was handmade, of durable leather or heavy woven fabric that could be taken apart and sewn back together. Some farmers and woodsmen had leather shoes, but Indian moccasins were more common, often stuffed for comfort or warmth with moss or buffalo hair. Their headgear was a slouch felt hat or, in winter, a fur cap of coonskin, bear, fox, or squirrel, usually with a tail in back.

Frontier women wore linen or linsey-woolsey dresses called "Mother Hubbards," often hanging straight down, or with a cloth belt around the waist in an attempt at style. The only undergarments were petticoats, made of the same material. Housewives usually wore aprons to protect the dress.

Woolen or quilted capes were added for warmth, and most preferred linen bonnets or shawls. Footwear was similar to that of men, except that a surprising number of women wore wooden shoes.

Emulating his father, Henry arranged for his shoemaker shop to be a place for customers and loafers to spend an hour or so, sitting on two long benches near his workplace and discussing the affairs of the day while he continued with his work. To permit the men to engage in their masculine discussions, Sophie did her work in their living quarters upstairs, where she could still overhear their arguments and ribald jokes when she chose to do so.

Although they had enjoyed a delightful and adventurous sexual relationship, it was only after they settled in Hillsborough that Henry and Sophie realized that they were deeply in love. They explored the community together on Sundays, and at other times, when the shop was closed, found it easy to share their most intimate thoughts, and yearned for each other when they were apart. Henry was even inspired, on occasion, to write a poem for Sophie, expressing feelings on paper that he could not otherwise put into words.

For the first few months Henry and Sophie concentrated their efforts on establishing a good business, and the discussions in his shop were somewhat restrained and cautious. He resolved just to listen until he knew his customers and the loungers better, but he was naturally loquacious among his peers and couldn't restrain himself for more than a few days. His first impressions were of how different life was in this frontier area, compared with what it had been in Philadelphia and Norfolk. Even though there was a clear distinction and natural incompatibility between the rich and poor families in Orange County, both groups seemed relatively satisfied with the status quo when the Pratts arrived in Hillsborough. The social and political divisions seemed secondary to a common scramble to establish new lives in a strange environment.

His impressions changed when a small group of regulars at the shoemaker shop began to stay for an hour or so after Henry quit working, to share a few pitchers of ale and enjoy a more frank and incisive discussion. Henry was caught up in the arguments and intrigues of the region and soon aligned himself with the small property owners, workers who had no businesses of their own, and farm families and tradesmen who wanted freedom to manage their own lives. None of them shared the social status or governmental authority of the more prosperous merchants, large landowners, and courthouse politicians, most of whom derived their wealth and influence from ties to their equivalents on the coast.

Henry's new friends combined their skills as raconteurs with an eagerness to learn as much as possible about the political situation in their own area. They were fascinated with Henry's description of his involvement in Norfolk with the Sons of Liberty, and he repeated some of the political opinions he had derived from them and from Mr. Knox. One of the group, Richard Pyle, was employed as a scribe in the courthouse and, despite the danger of losing his job, was willing to share with Henry and a few others information that was recorded there on wills, tax digests, and property transfers. It was clear that, as in other communities, the powerful families were using every device to increase their wealth and influence. In Orange County, their procedures were not always legal or proper.

Ethan had planned to follow his brother to North Carolina as soon as Henry was settled. However, their father was ill when Henry arrived in Hillsborough, and Ethan felt obligated to work full-time just to take care of the shop. Though Mr. Pratt recovered well enough to walk around the city and visit with friends, he still seemed to be reluctant to resume his duties at the shoemaker's bench. Ethan and Epsey soon began to suspect that this was a pretense to prevent their leaving home, and insisted that Samuel Pratt take on a young apprentice, who proved to be ambitious and competent. While he was being trained, the young couple delayed their departure and contented themselves with studying the increasingly eloquent and descriptive letters from Henry's new wife, who seemed eager to share information about their lives.

On occasion, Epsey responded to Sophie's letters, telling little about their humdrum life in Philadelphia. Instead, she mostly asked questions that she and Ethan wanted answered about their future home, which was obviously a rapidly changing community. They learned that the population of the settlement had increased greatly, just seven years after the first permanent merchants and tradesmen had opened their stores on the site. Farmers who lived in more remote areas, where Ethan planned to settle, could exchange produce for basic necessities in small hamlets near their homes or isolated general stores owned by some of the larger landowners.

But Hillsborough was the major center of commerce and trade and also the county seat of Orange County, and all legal affairs had to be conducted in the courthouse.

There was little ongoing relationship between most families in this frontier area and those who had occupied the coastal areas for more than a century. The backcountry was in the foothills, and the upper reaches of the fast-flowing streams were not navigable: only logs could go through the numerous rapids and falls, or small cargo that could be portaged around the difficult places. Farmers had to depend on packhorses to move their goods to the nearest barge sites, and development of road transportation was slow and spasmodic. There was a natural difference of interest and in wealth between the coastal plain and the hill country.

Epsey was relieved to learn that there were few slaves in the area. For instance, as late as 1763 in Orange County, fewer than one family in ten owned any slaves and most of those had only two or three, who worked in the woods and fields side by side with the landowner. Sophie knew from Mr. Knox that in the older settlements of the coastal region, half of the households had slaves, an average of about twenty each. Also, money was scarce in the backcountry and possessions were minimal. Henry relayed information from Richard Pyle that probated wills at the Hillsborough courthouse showed an average wealth of families to be less than £200, including land, implements, livestock, crops in storage, and all personal belongings. This was a relief to Ethan and helped him plan for his financial needs before leaving Philadelphia.

It was inevitable that the situation around Hillsborough would continue to change. The western land was productive, and with tobacco prices skyrocketing and little new land available, property values increased rapidly. Many of the original settlers, especially within ten miles or so of the county seat, found that their small land holdings would sell at a price higher than they had ever expected. Their more affluent and ambitious neighbors were eager to buy land whenever a small farmer was in financial trouble or ready to move farther west. There was a surge of transactions that required action by officials at the courthouse, including land titles, bills of sale, crop mortgages, deeds to secure debts, tax assessments, and liens.

The number of lawyers proliferated to handle these legal affairs and to interpret the stream of laws and directives that were coming from the royal governor and his council. New agreements were now being legalized among the more influential Carolinians to take advantage of opportunities opened to them, and punitive laws had to be enforced against both actual criminals and those who failed through ignorance or design to comply with the complex regulations.

Henry Pratt became increasingly knowledgeable about North Carolina political affairs as he and his friends shared ideas and information with one another. Governor William Tryon was loyal to the crown and, although unsuccessful in his efforts, used every means short of violence to suppress protesters of the British Stamp Act. A shrewd political tactician, he consolidated his hold on the colonial government, carefully maintained a subservient council, and spread a net of other loyalists throughout the colony, bound together by mutual advantage. Tryon consolidated his control over the remote areas of the colony by appointing all the sheriffs, judges, tax assessors, and clerks, and secured their loyalty through bribery, intimidation, or by tacit permission for them to enrich themselves at the expense of the general public.

Although he was criticized on the coast, the greatest outcry against Tryon's policies came from frontiersmen in the region around Hillsborough, including Orange and Alamance counties. Knowing this, and despite the rapidly growing population in the west, Tryon made sure that the eastern counties retained control by dividing favored counties into smaller units, each having its own allotment of delegates. There was no practical way to appeal these decisions, since respected British courts were thousands of miles away, and Tryon seemed to be one of London's favorite royal appointees. These concerns became an obsession with Henry Pratt and others, who shared their frustrations with one another.

Most of the Pratts' favorite customers were farmers, who came by on their monthly shopping expeditions to be measured for shoes, to buy harnesses and sometimes clothing, or to acquire tanned hides as raw material for their own handicrafts. Others who came to the shop more regularly were townsmen, who would sometimes buy an item but mostly enjoyed a congenial place for conversation. Jokingly, they began to call themselves the Sandy Creek Association, and would refer to their visits as "a meeting of the association."

Henry was one of the more aggressive members of the group. "We cannot afford to be timid, and nobody else is speaking out for us. We've got to grab everybody's attention, and the best way is to be strong and bold," he urged them.

Richard Pyle responded, "Well, I work in the courthouse and hear a lot of complaints and also some of the responses. The people are confused about what's going on, and don't understand what their relationship ought to be with the officials. Just going public with our criticisms won't be helpful or gain much support for our position."

Henry didn't like to be questioned so clearly in his own place and responded, "Richard, we are not in the business of protecting your courthouse masters from tough criticism. Everybody knows what is going on around there, so why shouldn't we just come out with it?"

Others joined in, somewhat cautiously. "We need to keep it simple." "Maybe the high ground would be better." "Are we going to put our names on the petition?" "We ought to make some good recommendations, not just criticize."

After a long discussion, Henry found a way to back down without losing face.

"Why don't you let me draft something, based on my experience in Norfolk? I know what worked there, and I'll try to catch what all of us seem to be saying. It certainly ought to be simple, clear, and keep us on a sound footing. When I get it done, in a day or two, all of us can go over it and change it around until everybody agrees."

With Sophie's help and strong advice, Henry worked laboriously over the statement. They talked back and forth for a while, and finally Henry said, "Why don't we just call for some kind of public meeting and let people bring up their grievances and also demand a citizen's right to give instructions to the courthouse crowd?"

Sophie exclaimed, "That's it! It's simple, clear, just calls for our basic rights, and is something that could be done."

The next day Henry was proud of their work, especially when everyone else agreed with the statement. With a few changes, they had it printed up, signing it "Members of the Sandy Creek Association."

Their decision was admirable and idealistic, but most of them soon came to realize that it was politically naive. The statement dealt almost exclusively with local offices and called for regularly scheduled public meetings in which the citizens could let their views be known and also issue

directives. If adopted, the proposal would have transformed the entire political system in the county and throughout the colony. It aroused some interest, but was ridiculed almost unanimously by influential citizens, and
ignored by the county officials. After a few days, Henry and the other men
decided that they had at least raised some of the issues, but that a meeting
would not be helpful until the general public was more interested.

As the only leather worker in town, Henry was thriving, and Sophie was
soon overrun with orders for clothing. Henry began asking some of their
customers if they knew of anyone who might be interested in helping her.
The Pratts were surprised when the apothecary's wife, Josephine, came by
the shop and offered to do some sewing of the soft leather. She could only
work four hours a day and insisted on just a small wage, considerably less
than Sophie had been paid in Norfolk. She said she didn't need the money;
she had no children, her husband didn't need her help in dispensing his
limited stock of medicines and advising customers who had an ailment,
and she was tired of being at home alone.

The apothecary, Dr. Railston, shared his responsibilities with Miss
Norma Hume, an experienced midwife who knew more about the practice
of general medicine than anyone else in the county. Although there was no
licensing requirement for concocting and dispensing medicines, Dr. Railston and Miss Hume had earned a good reputation around Hillsborough
during their months of practice. They spent several hours each week gathering and processing native roots and herbs, including sassafras, mayapple,
bloodroot, and slippery elm. They added honey, licorice, camphor, alcohol, paregoric, opium, saltpeter, and calomel to flavor and supplement their
medicines, always careful to remember that an evil taste was considered
commensurate with curative powers. As a team, they made a good living
treating both male and female patients. Either together or separately, as appropriate, they diagnosed ailments, bled patients, prescribed whatever
medication might be available, delivered babies, lanced boils and ulcerated
sores, set broken bones, and sometimes extracted teeth.

When not busy, Miss Norma joined the other two women in what they
called "stitching and chatting." They got along well together and found that
the work seemed to be quite enjoyable as they shared an ongoing conversation. Norma was almost helpless in dealing with leather and sewing, but
seemed to know everything about what was going on in the community,

both in the city and out in the countryside. She had a cousin in Norfolk whom she visited twice a year, and on her next trip took with her some orders for supplies that were not available in Hillsborough. Sophie sent a note to the Knoxes, which Miss Norma promised to deliver. While she was gone, for the first time in her life Sophie began to feel tired and sluggish. She seemed to be gaining weight and noticed things around the workplace that aggravated her. She found herself complaining to Josephine about little events concerning the shop, and then later apologizing. She resented, mostly without comment, having to fill customer orders and also cook and keep the house and shop clean.

Miss Norma returned from visiting her relatives on the coast, some of whom she had treated for "distemper," and reported that Mr. and Mrs. Knox were getting along well, but that he wanted Henry to know that there was indisputable evidence that the British government was slowly but surely taking away the colonists' rights.

Henry commented, "This has been clear to me for a long time. I thought we'd get away from it by settling way out here in the hills, but we may be worse off than the people in Massachusetts and Virginia."

With her knowledge of ailments, Norma quickly diagnosed Sophie's persistent nausea and sluggish feeling. All three women were delighted that she was pregnant. It was only after one more period was missed that Sophie informed Henry. He was euphoric, and announced that they should perhaps protect the new baby by not having sex. Sophie laughed and said that, on the contrary, this was a time for celebration, especially in bed. That night, they tried some things they had never done before.

About a week later, the doctor climbed the outside stair and knocked on the door where the two women were at work. He told his wife, whom he called "Mrs. Railston," "I just went by Miss Norma's house to pick her up in the buggy and found that she is too ill to get out of the bed. This is not like her at all, so she must be really sick. She wouldn't let me come in to see about her because she said she first needed a woman to help her get dressed and clean up around her bed."

Sophie volunteered to go with Dr. and Mrs. Railston, and they were soon at the little cabin on the edge of town. After identifying themselves, they could hear a weak voice giving the two women permission to enter. They found the midwife with vomit on her gown, and indicating that she was also "messed up behind." As the women worked to clean up the bed, they could tell that Miss Norma was gasping, her throat was inflamed, and she was burning with fever.

"I don't know what's wrong with me, maybe just the colic, but I'll see if Dr. Railston has some ideas," she said, as the women left the house and the doctor entered. When he emerged, he was obviously distressed.

"As soon as I saw her, I was pretty sure that Miss Norma might have the pox. I've seen a few cases, and I have a pamphlet at home that describes the symptoms and what they have learned to do in England and also in the colonies when any cases develop. It scared me half to death when I saw Miss Norma's rashes, knowing how bad y'all have been exposed, and I tried to protect myself as much as possible. Now I'll have to do all I can to safeguard you and also other people in the community. She said both of you were all over her and her soiled bedclothes. It will be necessary to burn those clothes you're wearing, and to wash off anything you might have picked up on your hands or arms in the house."

He paused for a while, and then turned to Sophie and added, "Maybe your husband will agree to let you come to our house and stay for a few days until we can see how Miss Norma gets along."

Sophie didn't like this suggestion at all and said, "I want to go home first and talk to him." But Dr. Railston replied, "We don't want your husband to be in contact with the pox, so it would be best for you and him not to be together just yet. Let me go and I'll explain the situation to him."

At the shop, Henry was finally convinced to accept the arrangement, and went upstairs, put together some of Sophie's things, and she got settled at the Railstons' house. While the women carried out his instructions, the doctor reread the pamphlet. It described how everyone in a contaminated house or ship could best be quarantined, how they must not be permitted to come into contact with other people, and what treatment was most effective. People who had previously survived the pox were not known to have it again.

Word of the illness swept through Hillsborough in an hour or two, and the community agreed to support Dr. Railston when he imposed a strict quarantine on Miss Norma and everyone she had contacted during the three days since she had returned from Norfolk. Sophie remained in the doctor's house, and he soon realized the possible consequences from the exposure of the two wives to the disease. This illness equaled in seriousness any case he could find in the texts he studied. The following morning, Miss Norma was worse off, and Railston began thinking about what he could do for Sophie and his wife. After cleaning himself and changing his own clothes, he went to the leather shop to talk to Henry.

"Henry, ever since I studied medicine I've seen cases of smallpox, and during the last few years we've learned a few new things. First of all, let me tell you that it's not a hopeless case; many people recover once they've been infected. It's true that entire Indian tribes have been wiped out by smallpox, and in Iceland and Greenland more than one-third of the population died in epidemics, but nowadays in England and the rest of Europe, about eight out of ten people recover from the disease. They've been exposed all their lives and those that didn't die may have had small cases. In fact, I may have been in contact with the pox when I was a boy.

"I never suspected it earlier, but now it's pretty clear that Miss Norma became infected while visiting on the coast, and it usually takes a couple of weeks before the first symptoms show up. Then there are a few days of headaches, high fever, and perhaps vomiting, following which the patient feels better. But after that comes a rash, something like fleabites, on the face, palms, and foot soles, and then larger and larger sores break out on the body with pus in them. In some cases, the sores just crust over and heal up, and this is what causes the scars we see on so many people's faces. But if the sores all run together or the infection goes inside the body, to the brain, heart, or lungs, that's when it can't be cured."

"Then when do people get the pox?"

"Well, I'm not really sure, but maybe the person can spread smallpox to others just a short time after being exposed, and before there are any clear symptoms. There is no doubt that our wives were in close contact with Miss Norma. Whether we like it or not, they might now be able to give the disease to others."

"Is there anything you can do for Sophie and your wife?"

"Henry, in the last few years some people have been given a light dose of smallpox, also called variola, in hopes that it might head off a more serious case, but this is something that hasn't been proven for sure. They call this procedure variolation, or inoculation. It's a hotly debated subject among doctors and especially among the general population, and is illegal in most cities along the coast, except Philadelphia. There was an outbreak of the pox there last year, and some people were paying three pounds for the procedure. In 1760 there was pox in both South Carolina and Georgia. A doctor in Savannah who tried variolation had his house and apothecary burned down and was, in effect, run out of the colony for trying to give smallpox to people who had been exposed. I've got a pamphlet on the subject at home that I've just reread, and considering how serious our exposure has been, I recommend strongly that the two women and I be inoculated."

When Henry objected, Railston reminded him that as they were probably infected already, inoculation wouldn't hurt anything, and it might head off a truly serious case.

"How would you do it?" Henry asked.

"What seems to get results sometimes is to collect some of the pus on a string, let it dry, and then put a little of it in the person we want to protect. It's supposed to give a milder case that won't be fatal, and after that they won't get the pox again."

"How would you put this in your body?"

"I have a description of what they've done in other places. You just cut a little slit in the skin of the upper arm, put the string in the slit, wrap it so it won't fall out, and that's all. The cut is not any bigger than when we bleed patients, and shouldn't hurt much."

Henry finally agreed, and Railston got some of the pus from Miss Norma and carried out the procedure on their wives and on himself. Within a few days Sophie and later Mrs. Railston had developed slight infections, but the doctor had not. The day that Miss Norma died, Railston had to inform Henry that Sophie had a high fever, and a deep red rash had developed on her face and neck.

"What does this mean?" Henry asked Railston.

"I'm afraid it's the most serious kind of pox. I think my wife is responding to the variolation and I probably had some pox as a boy. We'll just have to keep Sophie comfortable and pray that she'll be all right. Judging by how far it has already advanced, it's pretty clear that her disease came from the original exposure to Miss Norma, and not from the inoculation."

Henry wanted to be with Sophie, but the doctor induced him to limit his visits to talking through the window of the room where she lay. She struggled to talk and to keep his spirits up, but her throat felt clogged and, to Henry, her few words didn't seem quite rational. He carried a chair to the house and sat on the front porch, refusing to go home even to eat. The doctor brought him some biscuits, side meat, and milk, and gave him periodic reports on Sophie's condition, which grew increasingly serious.

When she finally died and was quickly buried, Henry closed the shop and stayed inside for three days, except for a brief burial ceremony that was attended by only a few of his customers. He refused to talk to Dr. Railston, who shared his grief. Then he forgave the doctor and plunged into an orgy of work, but the lighthearted discussions around his shoemaker's bench were missing. There was an unprecedented element of bitterness in his comments, increasingly concentrated on the government forces that tended to control at least a portion of his life. He finally wrote a disjointed letter about what had happened and sent it to his family in Philadelphia, not much caring whether it ever arrived.

CHAPTER 4

The Regulators

FALL 1766

During an extended period without any letters from Henry, Ethan sent several messages to his brother, asking for advice on when they should join him. After the family received the brief letter telling of Sophronia's death, Ethan decided to leave Philadelphia. As quickly as possible, and over the continuing objections of his father, Ethan and Epsey moved to North Carolina.

Henry welcomed them when they arrived in Hillsborough and invited them to stay with him in the shop. Ethan could detect a sense of both despair and bitterness in his brother, quite unlike his earlier exuberant spirit, and especially since his marriage to Sophie. Although Ethan wanted to proceed as soon as possible to acquire and settle on some new land, he saw that Henry needed him, both in his business and as a companion. He and Epsey decided to live with Henry for six months, before moving to the country during the early spring of 1767. Mrs. Railston, who was still working, showed Epsey how to do some of the sewing tasks, and the leather shop was soon operating again at almost full capacity.

In their private moments, Henry answered Ethan's first questions about the growing frontier community with just a few words, apparently not wishing to discuss anything that had happened to him or Sophie since they had arrived more than a year before. Also, the two brothers spent only a brief time recalling old times in Philadelphia and their relationship with other members of their family. But Ethan could never get enough information about anything that might affect his and Epsey's future lives as frontier farmers. He probed constantly for any facts about the local people, the structure of the colony's government, how local officials might relate to an application for a homestead site, and what kind of people he was likely to meet on farms farther west. Henry knew the answers to most of these questions and gave constructive advice, but it was obvious that he was almost unbalanced on the subject of fraud and corruption around the courthouse.

"We have two criminals who control our lives in Orange County, Governor Tryon and Edmund Fanning. The bastard Fanning is supposed to be just the register of deeds, but he makes all the final decisions at the courthouse and decides who will be appointed to other official positions. No attorney can even practice here without Fanning's approval."

Ethan asked, "But don't we have a right to elect members of the assembly, where all the laws have to be written?"

Henry responded with a bitter laugh. "The upper house is appointed by the council members, who are carefully chosen by the governor. The lower house is elected by us property owners, but the candidates are put forward by Fanning and the other big shots in the county, with the approval of the governor, of course. And the sheriff conducts the election. Even when there are opposing candidates, no one knows how many votes were put in the box or what the accurate count might be."

Ethan was silent for a while and then said, "Henry, the governor can't be all bad, or the king and Parliament would remove him from office."

"He's a shrewd man who wants two things: to keep peace in the colony and to enrich himself and his crowd. There are a lot of wealthy and influential people on the coast with close ties to London. Tryon is more careful there, and things are better even for average citizens. The big up-country population is demanding more influence in the colony's affairs, which is a threat to Tryon's control. From this region he wants money, total government control, and land.

"The original charter of the colony spells out how frontier land is distributed, and it's done fairly well when new settlers like you first arrive, but what happens after that is where the problem lies."

He was convinced that Ethan would find his warning to be justified when he applied for a grant, and urged him to learn all about the process before making an official application. He provided more and more detailed answers, filling in personal descriptions of community leaders, his own experiences, concerns about the government, and some guarded comments about the Sandy Creek Association. After a few weeks his conversation became quite lively and not so uniformly cynical, and he even laughed a few times. His old customers began to assemble as before, to debate current issues and to keep alive the streams of community gossip.

Ethan rarely took part in these sessions, but listened to Henry with close attention. He and Epsey visited some of the nearby families in the rural areas and learned everything they could about procedures for obtaining land grants, the sources and price of farm equipment and supplies, and agricultural practices. The obvious hardships of frontier life only strengthened their determination to begin work on their own place.

On most Sundays, Epsey stayed at the shop while Henry and Ethan rode out a dozen miles or so, mostly westward from the town. They visited the most remote areas of the county, where land grants were still available, and became acquainted with some of the farmers who had recently settled there. They learned that many of their potential neighbors would be Quakers, or Friends, who had been moving down into the region from Pennsylvania and New Jersey. Most of these men were experienced farmers and seemed delighted to offer advice to Ethan. They even described the few remaining farm sites that were set aside by law for new settlers, and the brothers examined them closely.

Excited about the prospect of having their own home, Ethan ignored Henry's warnings about living in such a remote region and finally decided on an area that he thought would be suitable. The following weekend, Ethan and Epsey rode to the frontier area alone and spent two days exploring and trying to envision the best place for a house, barn, areas to be cleared for cultivation and grazing, and some woodlands suitable for livestock to browse. Earlier settlers had chosen the flatter and more productive land, which was where the trading center had developed. What was left was at the northwestern boundary of the county, and although much of the cultivatable land was hilly and bordered on two sides by swamps, the homesite was at least blessed with adequate springs and creeks to provide a year-round supply of good water.

Ethan then went to the courthouse, somewhat worried by Henry's distrust of the officials and their issuing of land grants. In fact, they seemed eager to approve the one he had chosen and went out of their way to make the procedure easy for him. All that was required was a simple letter of agreement, signed by the county clerk, and a small plat of the land with boundaries described by the location of large trees, streams, a rock outcrop, and some corner posts of locust wood. A portion of the land had to be cleared, a home built, and crops planted, which was exactly what Ethan and Epsey planned to do.

As soon as possible, they loaded their belongings on two horses and two oxen they had bought, hauled them to their homesite, built a rough shelter under some pine trees on a small hill, and began clearing land. It would have been almost impossible to cut down the large trees, so Ethan girdled them by merely cutting through the bark all the way around the lower trunks. Each tree would die, still standing, but would no longer shade the crop or sap moisture and nutrients. He cut down straight trees, mostly ten or twelve inches in diameter, and dragged them with his oxen to the homesite to form the walls of their cabin. All the other undergrowth and tree limbs were piled and burned. Ethan realized that, for a few years, plowing would be difficult and that most of the cultivation would have to be done with hoes. He and Epsey worked hard on the farm, enjoyed the relative solitude of their home, and rarely visited their neighbors. Other than Henry's customers, they met few people in Hillsborough other than the merchants from whom they obtained supplies and who would later be buying their farm products.

Ethan was now twenty-one years old, quite tall, somewhat lanky, careless about his appearance, with his blond hair pulled back and hanging long down his back, tied in a pigtail with a leather thong. People's eyes were frequently attracted to his strong hands and extremely long fingers, with which he made small gestures when he spoke. He was slow to laugh aloud, but smiled often and usually had a pleasant expression on his face. His size and appearance were inclined to arouse a sense of jealousy or competitiveness among men, but his modest demeanor and reticence usually assuaged these attitudes after a few minutes in his presence. He was soft-spoken, primarily motivated to mind his own business, to be alone, and to develop his farm and property well. Ethan was at ease with himself, not threatened by others or obsessed with obtaining what they had.

Ethan had a natural affinity for tools, guns, knives, and almost any kind of equipment. As a skilled shoemaker, woodworker, and blacksmith, he was always willing to provide advice or assistance to any of their neighbors, most of whom were members of the Society of Friends. He demurred politely when asked to participate in their religious or social gatherings.

Epsey was taller than most women, and her body was strong and graceful. She appeared to be solemn and thoughtful, but she was not an unhappy woman nor did she have a tendency to be critical of others. Her movements seemed slow and methodical, but she was efficient and could accomplish tasks with surprising ease and swiftness. Like Ethan, she was very sure of herself as she dealt with the challenges of a frontier life.

During their first months together, Epsey observed Ethan quietly but with great attention. She came to understand and respect him, despite some early disappointment when she realized that he was strong-willed, rarely revealed his own thoughts or opinions, and obviously relished the times when he could be alone. He considered matters carefully, listened to her opinions when she offered them, and then made the final decisions for the family. As a couple, they were compatible and rarely had serious personal discussions or an argument of any kind. She and Ethan found it natural to divide their responsibilities neatly into three categories: hers, his, and those things that required them to work together. She looked forward to the hours during the day when she could be alone with her garden and housework. Epsey respected Ethan's gentle ways, his ability to accomplish almost any task, and his meticulous attention to obeying the law and doing what he believed to be right and proper. In fact, she and Ethan were surprisingly alike in many ways.

One difference was that Epsey was deeply religious and read the Holy Scriptures at some time every day. She had never discussed her parents' missionary ambitions with Ethan, but after their marriage she had been at first disappointed and, she admitted to herself, then somewhat relieved to find that his interests were not in religious adventures among the Indians.

Some of the verses in the Song of Solomon and about the various biblical families reminded her of one disharmony that had been of concern when they were first married, but it had also been resolved without disturbing their relationship with each other. Epsey had led a sheltered life in a strict and religious home and was uncomfortable about intimate relations. She had never been aroused sexually and looked upon lovemaking as something to be borne as an embarrassing duty to her husband, a masculine peculiarity that was best addressed with acquiescence and reserve.

At first she was afraid that he might be disappointed by her reticence, but found that this did not seem to displease Ethan. She considered the rarity of his sexual advances as agreement that her attitude was the correct one.

Despite their differences in appearance and interests, Henry and Ethan were compatible and became close enough friends to confide in each other and to share advice when a major decision was to be made. Ethan and Epsey always visited Henry's shop when they were in town and usually spent the night with him when they were together. Ethan preferred to return to his homestead, even late at night, when he was traveling alone. Once or twice a month, usually late on Sunday afternoon, Henry would ride out for a visit to the farm, where he enjoyed helping with the chores and expressing his political concerns. Ethan made it clear that he was not particularly interested in politics unless the issues had a direct effect on his family or his farm, and couldn't understand why his brother became so exercised about events in London, New Bern—where the governor held court—or even Hillsborough. As the months passed, he became concerned about Henry's increasing anger and distress. Despite all this, he and Epsey were polite listeners as Henry expressed his strong views.

One afternoon the brothers were sitting on the cabin porch, involved in a typical conversation. Henry was addressing a well-worn subject.

"The British Stamp Act was bad enough, and we thought the Parliament had learned its lesson when they repealed it last year. Even when it was implemented, it never did fall too hard on average farmers, artisans, and small merchants like us, because we don't have many transactions that call for stamped documents. It was the rich ones who had to pay, and I didn't mind this very much, but I was really proud that the Sons of Liberty and a lot of other colonists rose up in public opposition to it. I believe it was the trade embargo we organized against England that finally made both King George and Prime Minister Grenville back down."

Ethan responded politely, "I'm glad they learned their lesson and won't push us around anymore."

"That's just the problem. I've got a letter from Mr. Knox in Norfolk saying that the new prime minister, whose name is Townshend, is pushing for a tax on things that we have to have, like lead, glass, tea, paint, and paper, and Parliament may have passed it by now. If so, there will be the same kind of trouble we had with the Stamp Act."

"Well, it's not going to bother me. Let the people in Boston and

Philadelphia worry about it. And besides, we can just buy our glass and paper from the French."

"That sounds easy, but the British control the seas and are already enforcing trade regulations that let their ships haul the goods."

Ethan was silent for a while and then asked, "Henry, what does Mr. Knox say about England having a right to put a tax on its own products? Hasn't this always been the case?"

Henry was surprised, as he often was, by how much his brother seemed to know, even while claiming to lack interest in public affairs. He decided to give a short answer, and then change the subject to one on which he considered himself to be an expert.

"Maybe Parliament can regulate commerce at home and with all the colonies, but Townshend seems to be singling out the American colonies for special taxes, to be collected by British officers sent over here to regulate us."

Ethan was accustomed to Henry's outbursts and responded quietly, "Well, the Tories have always tried to take advantage of poorer people. We saw this in Philadelphia before we came here."

"I'm not talking about Whigs and Tories now, but about whoever has control over the markets and the political situation. Some of the worst ones are the Whigs, who are the loudest critics of London but the first to use their wealth or power to rob the rest of us."

"Henry, I think you're overly upset, and there's not much that can be done."

"I am upset, and there is something to be done. Some of us members of the little Sandy Creek Association have joined up with some other men, both in Orange and the other western counties, to form a group known as the Regulators. We've had a couple of meetings already, and if we can really get organized we're going to make some changes in the political system."

Ethan was quiet for a few moments and then said, "I hate to hear that. You're making a good living at the leather shop, nobody is bothering you, and most of the folks around here just want to be left alone."

Henry never liked advice contrary to his own inclinations, and he replied quite harshly, as he stepped off the porch and climbed on his horse, "You've become too much influenced by your Quaker neighbors. As long as you all are doing well yourselves, you don't care about anyone else in the colony. I'm glad that a few of us are willing to speak out and try to improve things, especially if it means protecting our freedom and our rights."

He whirled and rode away, and Ethan regretted this first argument they had had as adults in which the differences seemed to be irreconcilable. He pondered what his brother had said. Was Henry exaggerating the problems? Were he and the other frontier families too selfish or timid?

Epsey came out of the house and said, "I heard Henry raising his voice to you. What was the matter with him?"

"As usual, he was upset with the governor and the courthouse crowd and thinks we farmers are not doing enough to help him try to change things."

The Pratts' farm was shaping up nicely, and they had a good growing season. Epsey helped with the farmwork when she was not caring for the house. There was always enough for her to do around the yard, barn, feedlot, and garden, and she helped Ethan at planting and harvesttime, and with hoeing weeds in the open fields. Ethan did all the plowing, construction, repairs, and blacksmithing, and particularly enjoyed caring for the hogs and cows that ran loose most of the time in the woodland areas. He monitored their movements closely as they fattened on leaves, grasses, and acorns, and supplemented their diet, when necessary; they would come to the clearing at least once a day when he called them.

Most of Ethan's neighbors were members of the Society of Friends, whom many people called Quakers. Having begun to move down from Pennsylvania and New Jersey more than ten years earlier, many of the Friends had settled near the Eno and Haw rivers, in the north-central part of the state. Although independent in spirit and small in number, the group stayed together and were mutually supportive. Their faith was strange to some, but their general beliefs seemed admirable. They dressed simply, abhorred violence of any kind, spoke simply in what seemed to be both German and ancient English, and met at least once a month to worship.

Their history was well known to people who lived in Philadelphia, and therefore to the Pratts. They believed that something of God existed in every person, and that no officials, even church ministers, were needed to guide one to discover the truth or define what was righteous conduct. Refusing to pay tithes, take oaths, or remove their hats even in the presence of the king, the Friends were severely persecuted by officials of the government, the Church of England, and, in America, by the Puritans and members of other religious faiths. Some of the Friends had found refuge in

Rhode Island, where Roger Williams had established a colony based on absolute religious freedom, but their prime opportunity had come in Pennsylvania, where the charter obtained by William Penn had given them full
protection and equal treatment under the law.

Not having any deep religious commitment of his own, Ethan had
agreed reluctantly to accompany Epsey to a Quaker meeting when they
first moved into the community. He was somewhat startled when everyone
sat stiffly in one of the farmers' homes, in total silence, apparently waiting
until some kind of "inner light" moved one of the members to tremble, perhaps then to speak. Sometimes the entire service was spent in silent medi-
tation. At other times a general discussion would follow the statement of a
worshipper, usually about the application of Christ's teachings in the community life, the criminality of slavery, a concern about how children behaved or were treated, the use of alcohol, or some abusive action of the
government. Since anyone was welcome at the meetings, the leaders realized that some visitors were sure to report any critical comments concerning royal government officials.

The acknowledged leader of the Friends was a man named Joseph Maddock, who operated a gristmill on a creek about five miles from Ethan's
home. All families in the area carried their grain to Maddock's mill, knowing him to be an honest man—a rare thing for a miller—whose toll was always what he promised it to be. As did other Quakers, he posted his fees
for the various services he offered and considered it a violation of truth to
bargain or to modify these charges for a particular customer. Any busy
farmer in the area who wanted to continue working at home could send a
young boy or a slave to the mill and be sure he would get back the right
amount of flour, meal, or grits, ground the way he had ordered it. Although
silence often prevailed in the regular religious meetings, Maddock liked to
talk, so it was natural that most farmers preferred to carry their own grain
to the mill and catch up on local news.

To Ethan, the mill itself was a fascinating place, with the system of
shafts, pulleys, and leather belts driving the large grindstones, and the constant atmosphere of productive work being done there. The customers had
a natural feeling that they were fully and gainfully employed even while re-
laxing and enjoying themselves. It seemed that the hard work was done as
a free gift of nature—not by the effort of humans or animals, but by the
power of rushing water beneath the mill house. Everyone would watch the

careful weighing, and the division between the farmer and the miller, either of the whole grain or the final milled product. Overall, visits to the mill were pleasant adventures, a surcease from monotonous farmwork, a chance to socialize and hear the latest news—and the way back home fueled with visions of the biscuits, cornbread, and grits that would be served from the still-warm bags on the wagon.

CHAPTER 5

The Regulator Revolt

Ethan began to hear more and more about the Regulators, mostly expressions of concern among the Quakers that some of the hotheads might resort to violence. Even on his remote farm, he could sense that the community was becoming divided, with the large farmers, merchants, lawyers, and office holders all strongly condemning the increasing numbers of poorer and more alienated men who were known to be joining the group.

Ethan remained aloof from it all, and after their heated exchange Henry hadn't visited as often and seemed reluctant to discuss political issues with Ethan.

On one occasion, two rough-looking men stopped by his farm. They'd obviously been drinking and had lost their way home. The men said that they had been to a meeting of Regulators near Hillsborough and, when they heard Ethan's last name, asked if he was related to Henry.

"Yes, he's my brother," Ethan said.

"He's a good man, one of our most respected leaders, and knows more about what goes on in the Orange County courthouse than anyone else. He's not afraid to speak out and is always pushing for us to take more action and not just have meetings to organize."

After the men left, Ethan was worried about his brother and decided to learn more about what was happening. On Henry's next visit to the farm, Ethan described the men who had visited him and repeated some of what they'd had to say.

"Ethan, I know these two. They're from a settlement up the Haw River and are inclined to be a little rowdy every now and then. Basically they're good men, and seem to agree with me most of the time. I'm not apologizing for them, but want you to know that we have some smart and responsible men among us who know how to do things carefully and legally. Herman Husband is our overall leader, and he is a peaceful man—a Quaker, in fact—who is well educated and a prosperous farmer. Our approach is a peaceful one. We prepared a petition that has been signed by more than two hundred men here in Orange County, and the same one went to Anson and Rowan counties to be signed. We then sent copies both to New Bern and to London to express our grievances."

"That seems to be the right way to go, but I'll be surprised if anything comes of it. If not, what would be your next step?"

"This won't fail, because we're right and are accumulating a broad base of support. As you know, we in the western counties now have too big a population to be ignored any longer, and there're a few honest legislators that approve of what's being done. If nothing happens in New Bern, we'll just have to rely on the king's officials who come over from London."

"Well, I reckon we folks out here have a right to petition, and I'm glad to hear that the Regulators are trying to remain peaceful. How many do you think have joined up?"

"You would be surprised. Although our meetings are limited to twenty or so, more than half the men I know in Hillsborough are supporting us, and a good many of the farmers. There'll be a meeting at Joseph Maddock's mill during the afternoon of the first Saturday, and I hope you'll be there."

"I may or may not, but I can't believe the leader of the Quaker families out here is publicly supporting the Regulators."

"You're right about him not being involved, but Maddock has agreed to let us have a meeting at his place. In fact, one of the governor's men has been invited just to make sure that everything is legal and proper. I've brought you a copy of our petition, and I doubt if there's anything in it that would cause you a problem."

"Well, I'll think on it and then decide if I want to come to any kind of gathering."

After Henry left, Ethan read the document and assessed the situation in his careful and methodical way. Although he had not been bothered personally, Ethan could see the need for more representation for the small farmers both in the colonial assembly and in the county seat. He shared Henry's conviction that all the local officials were aligned with the governor and his council, and he felt that they should answer to the people in Orange County. One thing he particularly resented was the law that used his tax money to compensate slave owners if one of their slaves committed a serious crime and was imprisoned or executed.

This didn't happen very often, because slaves were valuable and their owners were influential enough to save the life of one they really wanted to keep. But there was always a fear of a slave uprising, and examples had to be made. On several occasions, after a slave was hanged, his head was cut off and placed on a stake for viewing for several days, and on four occasions in North Carolina, for particularly heinous acts, slaves were burned at the stake.

He could tell that, in all these matters, things were getting worse. So far he had been able to pay his taxes on time, but, as was the case in all rural areas, cash money was scarce, even rarely used. Lately, Maddock had told him that future taxes would have to be paid in hard currency, but this was hard to believe, since most trade was by barter, with certificates for stored produce used as legal tender.

As Ethan thought about the situation, he was more inclined to go to the meeting and size up what the Regulators were doing. He saw no need to discuss the matter with Epsey, since this was primarily a man's business. On the first Saturday, he just saddled his horse, said, "I'll be gone for a few hours," and rode off toward Maddock's mill, about an hour's ride from their farm.

Epsey watched from the front door as Ethan rode away. She was perplexed and somewhat concerned to see her husband do something that seemed out of character. She had overheard part of his conversation with Henry, but never expected him to attend any public meeting, particularly one that might lead to violence. Ever since she had known him, he had seemed obsessed with staying away from other people, minding his own business, and not becoming involved in any of the public issues or events that seemed important to most other men. He rarely talked to her about his brother, but had made a few gentle comments about his wish that Henry would just take care of his shoemaker's shop, and maybe find another woman, since his wife had now been dead for almost two years. Henry seemed to be exerting a greater influence on Ethan, and she had a sense of foreboding as she saw him riding toward the mill.

When Ethan arrived, he walked back and forth across the low dam and then went under the mill house to examine the waterwheel, now standing still with closed gates diverting the normally rushing water in the mill race into the main stream. Having spent many hours up in the mill waiting for his grain to be ground, he was thoroughly familiar with the topside system of flat belts, shafts, and pulleys, but there was a latticed fence enclosing the area beneath the house, with a small locked gate. The miller wanted to be sure that hogs and other animals didn't fall into the stream and jam the moving parts of his mill. Ethan had always been reluctant to ask permission to open the gate, but this afternoon it was open, and he stooped and entered the closed space. He felt more at ease here by himself than in the yard with the gathering crowd. He could see through openings in the fence that there were several dozen horses standing hitched in the yard, and small groups of men were talking quietly to one another. Some of the settlers seemed somewhat tense, and the customary ribald exchanges were missing. For some reason, he also felt a sense of impending trouble.

A few of the men looked at him as he emerged into the sunlight, and those who knew who he was were surprised to see him. Some of Henry's friends had always felt uncomfortable around Ethan, who rarely spoke and had never taken any part in politics or other affairs of the community. He was the tallest one there by several inches and was dressed as a frontiersman in leather breeches, Indian-style moccasins, and a long homespun shirt. Most of the men had never seen him, but the word quickly spread that he was the younger brother of Henry Pratt, the shoemaker in Hillsborough. He received several nods of welcome as he moved through the crowd toward four men gathered around his brother. Judging from their dress, they were all townspeople, and he recognized two of them as customers he had met when he'd worked in the leather shop. Henry was obviously glad to see Ethan.

"I was hoping you'd come, but didn't think you would leave the farm. How's Epsey?"

Ethan smiled. "She's fine, but she won't be too pleased to have me come here. Good afternoon, Mr. Milton, Mr. Ramsey."

Henry introduced the other two men. As Ethan expected, they were either workmen or owners of small shops. Ethan looked around at the crowd assembled in the yard; there were now more than a hundred men. Although the miller was a Quaker and more than half the rural families shared his faith, no flat black hats were visible. Also, none of the courthouse officials, lawyers, or large merchants was to be seen.

Henry said the assembled men were awaiting Herman Husband, the leader who would be addressing the group. He was from a Quaker family and one of the few relatively wealthy men who was openly participating in the Regulator movement. It was known that he didn't always speak and act as a Friend, except perhaps when he would attend their monthly meetings, but he was totally opposed to any acts of violence. Some said that he was trying to arouse support for a future political career, but his leadership was accepted because he had no challengers and was known to be fervent in his belief that changes were needed in North Carolina.

Ethan wanted to hear what Husband would have to say, but didn't wish to be seen as taking any initiative. In fact, he was still somewhat doubtful about the wisdom of letting Henry convince him to come. Finally, around two o'clock, Henry suggested that they move into the already crowded mill house, and they leaned against the back wall just inside the door. Ethan noticed that Joseph Maddock was now present.

He soon heard some commotion outside and the movement of feet toward the mill house and presumed that Husband had arrived. Ethan had no trouble looking over the heads of others and saw the leader of the Regulators walk in, accompanied by several other men. He was a stocky man, not much more than five feet tall but weighing about two hundred pounds. He had a florid face and piercing eyes, and paused just inside the door to become accustomed to the darker interior and to look around for familiar faces. One of those he recognized was Henry.

During this half minute or so, the crowd opened enough to form a passageway from the door to the sacking platform just below the main millstone. Then Husband moved forward with measured steps, not speaking but nodding briefly to several other men he seemed to know. Without hesitation, he mounted the three steps, turned, and looked down into the upturned faces of the crowd. With slow and deliberate movements he removed his slouch felt hat, exposing a snow-white forehead and a full head of reddish hair, wiped his face with a bandanna, and replaced his hat. When he finally spoke, it was with a surprisingly low voice, requiring that his audience be exceptionally quiet. He seemed somewhat timid and ill at ease, but was clearly in charge of the meeting.

"I'm glad to see so many of you here, and want to thank Brother Maddock for letting us use his mill house as a meeting place. Let me introduce Charles Robinson of Anson County and Christopher Nation of Rowan

County. They are substantial farmers and good men, as all those who know them will attest. Also, I want to acknowledge the presence of Mr. Edmund Fanning, a well-known local attorney, who I understand is here to represent Governor Tryon as his secretary."

Everyone turned to look at Mr. Fanning, a wealthy man who owned a large house in Hillsborough and was influential around the courthouse. Ethan and Henry had not noticed the nondescript man before, but now saw him in a corner, trying to look at ease as he leaned against a wall stud. He nodded his head slightly and ostentatiously opened a notebook, to indicate that he would be making entries throughout the meeting, taking note of each person and then apparently writing down his name or some description.

Husband continued, "We want it to be plain that we have nothing to hide and consider it advantageous for the governor to know what we have to say. I might add that most of what we will discuss has already been included in a written petition, which was signed by several hundred citizens of this region and adjoining counties, including many of you. So far, we have not had any response to our requests, either from New Bern or from London, but we hope that our representatives in the assembly will help us get our message across, and that Mr. Fanning will remind the governor of our requests."

Husband turned for a few minutes to talk quietly with the two other men on the platform, then nodded his head and resumed speaking to the crowd.

"I have listed some of the things that are of concern to us and will repeat them, mostly for those of you who may not be familiar with our petition. But there is no doubt that every one of you has been hit by these same things."

As he spoke, Husband's words remained low-pitched, but Ethan noticed the increased intensity of his voice. Feet shuffled and some of the men nodded, but there was no verbal response to these introductory remarks.

Husband glanced down at a folded paper in his hands and continued, "First, we want representation in the state government equal to our portion of the population. Although there have been some improvements in the assembly, most of the decisions that affect us are still made by the governor's council, who are all rich and powerful people who seem to be more interested in the eastern counties than in those of us out here in the Piedmont region. There seems to be special attention paid to big farmers near the coast, all of whom have large numbers of slaves. I don't know if you all have heard this, but there is a new law that makes us taxpayers compensate rich farmers every time one of their Negroes dies, even of natural causes— if they certify that the death was premature!"

Ethan heard Henry curse, and there were murmurs throughout the crowded mill house. The previous compensation had applied only to those rare occasions when a slave was given a long sentence or hanged for a capital crime. Some of the men looked at Fanning, who ignored them and continued to write in his notebook.

Husband waited a few seconds and then continued, "Second, I want to make it clear that our worst problems are not in New Bern, but right here in all three of our county seats. We want to have a hand in choosing the local officials who take care of things around the courthouses, and in monitoring and correcting how they perform their duties. We're tired of being cheated and overcharged by sheriffs, justices of the peace, tax collectors, recording officers, and judges. Their highest calling is to enrich themselves. We insist that, through public meetings, we citizens can help set the policies that affect our lives."

Henry whispered to Ethan, "Those were the main points we made in the Sandy Creek Association more than a year ago."

Husband's voice was becoming stronger as he went on with his discourse, and now there was no difficulty in hearing what he said. The crowd, in any case, remained deathly still as he paused and took a sip, perhaps of water, from a small flask carried in his hip pocket. Now he spoke very deliberately, with a slight pause after each phrase.

"Even worse in many cases are the dishonest lawyers who now stand between us and getting licenses, buying property, recording deeds, having our day in court, and even paying the taxes we are charged. When they can't find an honest case they encourage court suits to be brought against us, and then everyone in the courthouse eats up our fees and fines like hogs in a trough of slop!"

As he emphasized the final words, for the first time in the language of the assembled farmers, the men broke into cheers. There was a hubbub in the mill, as people turned to one another to recount their own grievances at the hands of the attorneys who, with licenses often obtained by bribery, had flooded into the county seat. There were now more than a dozen lawyers in the small town. The speaker waited a full minute before he raised his hand to obtain enough silence to continue. With the tension broken, there were loud expressions of approval and support after each of his statements.

"Now let me speak a word about taxes. We don't mind paying our share, but the laws are being changed every year to shift the burden from the ruling elite to the shoulders of peasants, small farmers, and honest workers. Many of them cost the poorest citizens the same amount as the richest ones, like the poll tax, work levies, and duties and fees on the necessities of life. I have to admit, as most of you know, that I have a good-sized farm and make a fair living—maybe much more than many of you. But I don't want to enrich myself or avoid my duties as a citizen at the expense of my less fortunate neighbors. The tax laws are a crime, and an embarrassment to every right-thinking citizen!"

Many of his listeners didn't understand much about the tax system and had accepted it as something immutable that had been and always would be imposed on them, but it was obvious that they appreciated a man like Husband pointing out its unfairness. He now continued with something they could understand better and was a sore point with every farmer.

"Also, not many of us have hard money, and we deserve the right to pay fees and taxes in farm produce, as we always have. The legal officials and money changers always twist the value of currency to our disadvantage, and we figure that this amounts to a twenty-percent extra levy on us when we have to trade what we produce for gold or silver coins before we pay our debts. The further we are from the coast, the more it costs us to buy money to pay taxes and fees to our own government.

"If we get just a little behind in anything we owe, more and more of our crops, livestock, and then farms are being taken without due process, or sold by the sheriff, often in secret and way below market value. And we notice that almost all of this property winds up in the hands of the very local officials who are charged with protecting our rights. In some cases, the proceeds of our confiscated property are not even applied to our debts!"

An early scattering of applause was hushed when Husband raised his hand, indicating to the audience that he was not through with this point.

"We also see that licenses to operate new mills, contracts to build roads and bridges, and permits to run ferries all go to members of the crowd who run the courthouse and manipulate the outcome of elections. These same officials control the nominating and electoral procedures, and use bribery and intimidation when necessary to get elected themselves as assembly-men—and even as vestrymen in our churches!"

Ethan found himself joining in the pent-up applause and cheers that re-sounded in the mill house. Henry was watching him, with a slight smile on his face.

Husband continued, "Although this is the final point I want to make, it is one of the most important, both for our protection and especially for those who live further west along the frontier. We want our own militia members to have a right to choose their officers, and we demand that they get out of their barracks in the east and stay out here where they belong, to protect us from bandits and from the infernal Indians."

This last remark brought a thunderous and sustained response, with every man in the room joining in the applause—except for Edmund Fan-ning.

Husband was now completely at ease, and he turned to the governor's aide and asked, "Mr. Fanning, would you like to make a comment?"

"Yes, I would. You can be sure that the governor will have a full report on the meeting."

Husband looked over the excited crowd and said with great force, "Men, if you agree with what I have said, I hope you and your neighbors will give the Regulators your support. Through peaceful means, we intend to make some changes in North Carolina."

He came down from the platform, and a number of the men crowded around Husband to ask questions, but Ethan and Henry walked outside and stood near Ethan's horse. Henry asked, "Well, what do you think?"

"I agree with most of it and trust that Tryon and the assembly will cor-rect the problems. What has been the response in town?"

"With the exception of the courthouse crowd and the big merchants, al-most every citizen seems to be supporting the Regulators. This is really the first open meeting, and we wanted to have it in the rural area of the county. You could see the response."

"Well, I don't want to join up with any group. Epsey and I just want to be left alone to mind our own business, but I hope you'll come out every now and then to let us know what's happening in Hillsborough and New Bern to correct some of the problems."

. . .

A few days later, one of the Friends, a man named Thomas Whitsett, rode up to the Pratts' cabin, dismounted, and approached Ethan, who was cutting firewood with a bucksaw. They exchanged polite greetings and then the Quaker asked, "Hast thou heard about Brother Joseph Maddock?"

"No, not since we were at his mill Saturday."

"A troop of militia came to his house, arrested him, and he is now in jail in Hillsborough awaiting trial."

"On what charge?"

"He is accused of inciting treason against the crown, because of the meeting of the Regulators."

"That's hard to believe. I was there and know that he never said a word, either against the crown, the governor, or in favor of the Regulators."

"None of us attended the meeting, so we can only testify to his character. We need thee to join us and others in providing testimony as to his actions when he is brought before the court. Although not one of us, thou art known to be an honest and peaceful man, and thy word will be very important on Maddock's behalf."

There were almost fifty families among the Friends, owning a little more than ten thousand acres of land around the Pratts' farm. Ethan knew the Quakers in his community to be good farmers, honest and dedicated to hard work, and without hesitation he agreed to join them as a witness for Maddock. Whitsett was to inform him when the trial would be held.

On the appointed day, Ethan rode into the county seat, where he found more than a hundred Friends assembled—men, women, and older children, all obviously concerned about their leader. He was one of the few non-Quakers who was to testify, although Herman Husband and a few other Regulators were there. As one of the listed witnesses, Ethan was seated near the front of the courtroom and watched as Maddock was brought in and placed in the defendant's stall. He refused to take an oath, simply stating that he would tell the truth. After some consultation with the attorneys, the judge ordered the questioning to commence. After Maddock had identified himself and described his role as a miller, he answered the prosecutor's questions as succinctly as possible.

"Did you organize a meeting at your grist mill on the first Saturday of this month?"

"No."

"Was such a meeting held?"

"Yes."

"Why was it held at your place?"

"It is a convenient and well-known site, and a number of groups have used it for meetings."

"Who called the meeting?"

"I don't know, but Mr. Herman Husband and two other gentlemen asked me if they could use the mill house for a meeting."

"Did you know it would be on behalf of the group known as the Regulators?"

"Yes."

"Did you know that their purpose was to disrupt the orderly government processes of the county and state?"

"No."

"Did you hear what was said at the meeting?"

"Yes."

"Did you not hear treasonous remarks made by Mr. Husband and others?"

"No. I understood that the comments were almost the same as those expressed in the petitions made last year to the state government and to the Parliament in London."

"Were there any calls for violence or illegal acts?"

"No."

"Was any liquor or other alcoholic beverage sold by you or anyone on your premises?"

"No."

The judge called the prosecutor to the bench, and they consulted for about five minutes. Then the prosecutor sat down, and the judge announced, "The court finds that the defendant is not guilty of inciting other citizens to commit treasonous or illegal acts, but permitted his premises to be used by men who stirred up dissension in the community. I have here an affidavit from Mr. Edmund Fanning, who is present in the court, certifying that inflammatory statements were made and that Mr. Maddock, as proprietor, did nothing to stop the proceedings or to ask the people to leave. Therefore, I find the defendant guilty of participating in disturbing the peace, and fine him fifty pounds." Pounding his gavel, the judge adjourned the court.

Among the spectators, this fine was considered both unjustified and excessive, equal to the total value of a Quaker's farm and equipment. Never-theless, within an hour the assembled Friends had collected enough money among themselves to pay it, and Maddock was released by the bailiff. As he left the courthouse, he passed by Fanning and several of the local officials. Fanning called out, "Maddock, you haven't heard the end of this."

As the months passed, Ethan heard from the Quakers that they were be-ing harassed by the governor's agents and by county officials. Almost all his neighbors' farms were visited repeatedly by the sheriff's deputies and the tax collectors, and on each occasion livestock and feedstuff were inven-toried, land and property value assessments were raised, and demands were made for immediate payment of current and back taxes—all in cash money. Assessors raised the value of Maddock's mill to an exorbitant level.

When Ethan carried some of his corn over to the mill, he found the miller alone, grinding meal and weighing it carefully in half-bushel bags. He greeted Ethan with a warm handshake and said, "I want to thank thee for offering to be a witness on my behalf. That was a neighborly thing for thee to do, and I hope it has not caused thee any trouble with the gover-nor's men."

"No, I've not been bothered, but I hear that the Friends have been hav-ing a problem with the tax assessors."

"Yes, two of the farmers have already had their places condemned, and they will be sold after three weeks of public notification. A goodly number of others are in danger of the same action, and it has only been my ability to sell reserve supplies of grain that has let me pay what they have de-manded on the mill."

"What can be done?"

"Governor Tryon has made it clear that he despises the Society of Friends and considers us a threat to political stability in North Carolina. Also, our opposition to slavery has caused the wealthier landowners to be concerned. Our pacifism makes us appear weak, and subject to abuse, so we tend to support each other as a group. I'm convinced that the governor and his associates have their eyes on our land, and see an opportunity to get it cheap through public sale."

Ethan was surprised to hear Maddock speak so frankly, and to be so openly critical of the officials. It was something of a compliment to be trusted in this way.

After hesitating a few minutes, the miller continued, "Those of our faith are accustomed to displeasure from others and even abuse, and until now I have encouraged those at meeting to stand firm. But last week a friendly merchant came to tell me that there will be increasing pressure on us, both by legal and illegal means, to give up our property here. I don't want this to be known, but I'll be traveling to Georgia in a few days to see about getting some new land. I understand that the governor, James Wright, is an honest man and is eager to have settlers move into the northern part of the colony."

"Yes, I've seen the public notices, but I understand that this is an isolated area exposed to Indian attacks, without protection, unserved by roads or other transportation, and with no nearby markets or trading posts. It's much worse than this part of North Carolina was when we moved here."

"Well, thy information may be right, but I wish to learn for myself."

CHAPTER 6

Quakers Move to Georgia

SEPTEMBER 1767

A few weeks later, Ethan was surprised to see Joseph Maddock ride into his yard. It was the first time he had been to the farm.

"Have you already made your visit to Georgia?"

"Yes, and I have obtained tentative rights to about twelve thousand acres of land, just west of Augusta and the Savannah River. Governor Wright enjoys a good relationship with both the Creek and Cherokee Indians and has a firm agreement that cedes the land. The treaty with the Indians was signed in sixty-three, after the governor assembled leaders from the Carolinas and Virginia to meet with all the Indian tribes. More than seven hundred people participated in the agreement, so we can be confident that there will be no dispute about our property. Thy information is correct about roads and markets, but we are willing to help develop what we need. I was planning to take all the Friends' families with me, but only forty are willing to go. The others will try to stay here or move back up north, where they came from. I've come to see if thou would be interested in joining us."

Ethan was surprised by the proposition, but hesitated only a moment before replying, "No, I reckon Epsey and I will stay here. We've about got our place in order and haven't been bothered by the officials any more than any other farmer in the Piedmont area. We're still hoping that the government will respond to the Regulators' petitions and that things will get better."

"Well, we wish thee well. We're convinced that once they set their eye on a farm, they'll use any means to get it. So far they've just concentrated in this region on us, but thy land is in the midst of a good bit of ours, and thou may be next."

Pressure on the Quakers continued, and by the fall of 1767 most of them had decided to leave after they harvested their crops. Those who were still financially solvent settled their accounts with local merchants and sold their homes, land, and other goods at prices well below the normal market value. Ethan attended the forced sale of a farm that adjoined his, but decided not to bid on any of the property, most of which seemed to change hands in a quiet and prearranged way among the public officials, lawyers, and large landowners.

Soon after this, Ethan rode by Maddock's mill and found that the miller had removed the pulleys, belts, and gears but had left the large millstones behind. A few days later, the Quakers going to Georgia loaded their belongings on packhorses and sleds and headed down the Cape Fear River toward the coast in a long caravan. Three families stayed in the Hillsborough area, and the others returned to their former homes in Pennsylvania and New Jersey.

The following year, most of the Quakers' farmland lay fallow, and Ethan rarely saw anyone on the formerly well-kept premises except a few hired caretakers who lived in the houses and prevented damage or theft of the property by Indians or passersby. The growing season was spent in a flurry of land speculation, with most farms ultimately being acquired by large planters who seemed to be closely associated with the governor. They, in turn, bought new slaves and hired overseers to manage the work on property that was spread throughout the county.

The Pratts soon found themselves to be one of the few families who owned just one relatively small farm and did all their own work without hired labor or slaves. They had a good season and a bountiful harvest, and seemed to be forgotten by those who had concentrated their efforts on driving the Quakers out of the territory. Henry came to visit them regularly and reported that the Regulators had increased greatly in strength and influence in the Piedmont area. He estimated that about six thousand westerners were supporting their efforts out of a total of eight thousand families who were on the tax rolls in the area. Herman Husband was elected to the assembly and was aggressive in raising the issues that had been covered in their earlier petitions and during the meeting at Maddock's mill. Henry and Ethan agreed that prospects were good for some reforms in the colony, and Ethan decided to clear more land for crops, buy more brood cows and sows, and to expand his woodland pasture areas.

Late in the fall, while Ethan was repairing fences, one of the bailiffs came to his house and delivered an official summons to the district courthouse, signed by one of the judges who served there. At first, Ethan was inclined to ignore the order and see what might happen, but after the next rain, when his fields were too wet to plow, he decided to ride into Hillsborough. Not wanting to alarm Epsey, he told her only part of the truth, that he wanted to trade some of his tobacco for horseshoes, cut nails, and bar iron for fabricating other metal instruments in his blacksmith shop. When he arrived in the county seat, his first stop was to show the paper to his brother.

After reading it carefully, Henry said, "A number of people, especially farmers, have brought documents like this to my shop. Since it only requests that you come to the tax office, there's no way to know the purpose of the visit. Sometimes it's to clarify something on the records, or the assessors may want to question the value you have placed on your property."

With a laugh, he added, "Maybe you have overpaid, and they want to give you a big refund! If so, be sure to stop by here and share some with your brother before you go back home and give it all to Epsey."

None of Henry's alternatives was troubling, so Ethan did his trading and then proceeded to the courthouse to see what the officials might want with him. He leisurely dismounted from his horse and entered the front door, confident that a mistake had been made in requesting his appearance. There, for the first time in his life, he was confronted by two men in uniform, holding rifles.

"Who are you?" one asked.

"I'm Ethan Pratt and have been asked to come here."

The soldier glanced at a paper in his hand and motioned toward the tax office. "You're wanted in there," he said.

"I've paid my taxes," he said.

"Shut your mouth," said one of the soldiers. "You can talk to Mr. Langhorn inside."

Ethan was taken aback. "I'll not be going inside," he replied, and walked out the front door. As he put one foot in the stirrup to remount his horse, he heard steps close behind him and a sharp command, "Halt there."

He looked around and saw both rifles leveled at his chest, with the flints cocked. He was ordered to stand down and put his hands behind his head.

A wave of anger swept over Ethan. He was half again as large as either of the men, and his first inclination was to attack them. But he realized that he was unarmed, defenseless, and that his life was at stake. He nodded, lowered his hands, rehitched his horse, walked rigidly to the tax office, rapped on the door, and entered the room. A man, whom Ethan had never seen, was sitting at a small desk and turned to look at him as he entered. Ethan was still, and the man shuffled his papers for a minute or so and finally spoke.

"Are you Ethan Pratt?"

Ethan nodded.

"Why don't you pay your fees and taxes?"

"I have always paid them, and on time."

"Let me see the receipt for the stamps on your marriage certificate, a copy of the title to your land, the inventory of your equipment and farm produce at the end of last year, and your license to operate a blacksmith shop. We figure you owe the government a substantial amount."

"You know I have no stamps. I was married almost four years ago in Pennsylvania, before the Stamp Act was passed and later repealed, and I estimated the value of all my equipment and produce last December, as do all farmers, and the inventory was approved by the tax assessors. And my forge is used just for my own benefit and as a favor for some of my neighbors. I've never charged anyone for smithing work. I don't owe any back taxes, and I'm not going to pay for a license to operate my own blacksmith shop just for farm use."

Langhorn again looked at some papers on his desk and then said, "Mr. Pratt, since you are obviously in arrears by at least ten pounds and have taken this attitude, I am hereby adding a penalty of two pounds to what you owe. Go two doors down on the right and pay the county treasurer."

"I'll never pay it," Ethan said and turned to leave the office. The Redcoats were lounging at the front door, and Langhorn shouted, "Arrest that man."

Ethan was soon in jail and stayed there the rest of the day and that night, in a quandary about what had happened to him and what he should do. On the next afternoon the cell door was opened, and he was motioned out. "You can go," the jailer said. "Your taxes and fine are paid."

When he opened the front door, he saw Henry standing there holding the reins of their two horses, with Epsey, who appeared uncharacteristically ill at ease. Ethan looked from one to the other, and then Epsey said, "Henry offered to lend us the money, but I decided to sell enough cows to pay what we owe," she said.

"We didn't owe it, and you shouldn't have given them the money."

"It was the only way to get you back home. The governor's men came to our house and told me you were in jail and were soon to be put in stocks in the town square. They called you a troublemaker and said we wouldn't long have our place. I went to see Henry, and he gave me advice on what to do."

Ethan realized that his wife had done the only thing possible and didn't comment further to her about his arrest. He said, "Henry, let's go by your place and talk awhile before we go back home."

The front door of the shoemaker's shop was locked, and Henry bypassed it even though it was his usual working hours and went up a back stairway and into his living quarters. "We'll have a cup of tea and spend some time discussing this mess," he said. While Epsey put water on to boil, Ethan told them about his experiences, describing how he had been treated as a common criminal. Henry listened until the tea was served all around and then said, "Ethan, let me tell y'all what I've heard. As you know, they've got all the land around you that belonged to the Quakers, and they want that farm of yours. This is just a first step, a warning, and they'll continue to look for some excuse to force you off of it."

"Well, I'm not leaving. I've still got some confidence in the government to treat me right. We should be hearing soon about the assembly's response to the Regulators' petition."

Henry glanced at his brother, whom he considered to be naive and overly trusting. Instead of further discouraging Ethan, he decided to emphasize the few reasons for optimism.

"With all the new assemblymen we got elected in our region this year, we have a chance to change things in New Bern. We turned out of office al-

most half the incumbents in the whole colony, and of the eight who won in
Orange, Rowan, and Anson counties five were Regulator supporters and
only two were the old county officeholders. The best thing is how bad Herman Husband defeated Edmund Fanning, who was Tryon's main man out
here. All of this should send a shot across the bow of people who might
have been aiming at you."

Ethan had never been in a predicament of this kind, when his own fate
was almost completely in the hands of others whom he hardly knew.

Somewhat weakly he said, "Well, I'm sticking it out anyhow."

"Ethan, you need not be involved personally, but the Regulators are
planning some direct action to express their anger with what's happening
and it's going to be close to home. I suggest that y'all go on back to your
farm and just mind your own business for a while. Let some of us see what
we can do."

"Henry, I don't want you to get in trouble."

"You don't have to worry about me. There are too many of us involved,
and there is no way we can accept Tryon's refusal to address the points in
our petition. We have waited a year, peacefully and with patience, and
there's nothing much the Regulators can do in New Bern. The solution to
our problems is at the courthouse in Hillsborough."

The couple rode toward home in silence, still somewhat uncomfortable
with each other. This was the first time that Ethan had ever let his wife see
him in a vulnerable position, or uncertain about what should be done. He
considered the discussion of an important decision with his wife to be an
indication of weakness. Having been arrested was a great embarrassment
to him, and his first resentment at her for bailing him out had turned to a
realization that she had acted properly. He finally decided just to explain
things to her, as recognition of her good judgment and a roundabout way
of expressing thanks.

"Epsey, I know and observe my duties as an Englishman, and also
know my rights. It is obvious to all of us that Tryon is not an honest man
and has been moved by a hatred of the Friends and a desire for their land."

He paused for a while and then added, "The fact is that those of us who
have come to this area from the Pennsylvania region have never been given
any say-so in any public office. A man has to own five hundred acres of
land and twenty slaves to hold a seat in the assembly, and just two or three
of the richest ones around here could qualify. Herman Husband is about

the only one of those who sees things our way. The judges and other county officials in Hillsborough have got their offices by paying bribes, and their purpose is to stay on the good side of the governor and to enrich themselves. I'm sure that King George and our representatives in Parliament do not know what is going on here in North Carolina, and I believe the situation will be corrected when they find out.

"I've met a time or two with the Regulators and found them to want just simple and fair government and to resolve our problems peacefully. We'll just have to hold what we've got and mind our own business until we get some action from London."

Epsey had never heard Ethan say so much at one time, and she quickly agreed with him, having full confidence in his judgment and his ability. She glanced at him now and saw that he was frowning and his jaw was clenched. The truth was that Ethan had some deep concerns, which he thought he was concealing from his wife. He couldn't forget the words of Maddock: "Thy land is in the midst of ours, and thou may be next."

Henry came out to the farm the next Sunday morning and gave Ethan a more complete and encouraging report on events at the colonial capital.

"Husband and his group have really been performing well in the colonial assembly, putting forward all the justifiable proposals that the Regulators have developed during the last few years."

Ethan asked, "Do you know what bills they have introduced?"

"Of course," said Henry, somewhat proudly. "We Regulators helped draft them all before Herman took them to New Bern, and each one deals with a different problem. One calls for judges and clerks to be paid a specific salary and for fees and fines to go into the county treasury. Another requires that sheriffs be replaced as tax collectors. We want a limit to be placed on lawyers' fees, and for six-man juries to try small-claims cases if either litigant requests it. A very important one for farmers is that produce be declared legal tender for the payment of fees and taxes, and for the head tax to be replaced with property taxes based on actual value. Our most popular proposal is that lawyers be prohibited from service in the assembly because they are intent on making their own fortunes and are blind to the interests of poor and industrious citizens."

"What has been the reaction so far?"

"It's too early to tell for sure, but our folks believe we have enough support to pass most of the legislation. These are the kinds of things that any reasonable person can both understand and support–probably even a good number of men who have been aligned with Governor Tryon in the past."

When Henry left, Ethan shared some of the information with Epsey, and they were more confident about their future than at any time since the Quakers had left. If just half the proposals were adopted, life in the colony for small farmers and others would be transformed for the better.

Henry didn't return the following weekend, and Ethan was surprised to see him riding up on Wednesday. He was obviously troubled, and Ethan joked, "Have you closed your shop and quit working?"

Henry dismounted and said, "Well, I may have to quit for good. Have you heard what has happened in New Bern?"

"No, we don't get any news out here except when you bring it."

"I wish I didn't have to come this time. The fact is that our legislation was making good progress in the assembly, and many citizens even in the coastal counties were speaking out in favor of it. But when the assembly finally began a serious debate on our grievances and the wide support became clear, the son of a bitch of a governor just dissolved the body altogether. He then announced that he and his council would make all governmental decisions until new elections could be held and a legal body constituted."

"I can't believe this. Now what can be done?"

"One answer is that our strength has grown too much, not only in the west but throughout the colony. There's a limit to what Tryon can do from New Bern when the great majority of the people don't support his policies."

For several months there was little political activity in the capital, and the Regulators proceeded to consolidate their strength. At the same time, Tryon and his supporters decided to go all out to elect a more favorable assembly in 1770. They adopted some of the more popular proposals of the Regulators as their own and cast their political appeal toward farmers. Also, there seemed to be a lot of money changing hands. The Regulators, on the other hand, were overconfident, deriding these new tactics of their opponents and predicating their expectations on their successes of the previous year.

When the votes were counted, political power shifted strongly toward the governor. Even in Orange County, two of the four new assemblymen elected were either merchants or county officeholders. Tryon announced that the new assembly would initiate reforms, but the Regulators denounced this statement as a dishonest attempt to weaken their cause.

In the summer of 1770, Henry received one of his rare letters from Mr. Knox in Norfolk, and after discussing it with his friends in Hillsborough, he brought it out to Ethan's home. Even before he could be invited into the cabin, he broke into a tirade.

"Ethan, I can see why our petitions to London have been wasted. The Parliament is as bad as Tryon's council. As you've probably heard already, they've suspended both the New York and Massachusetts assemblies and are making all of us pay for quartering British troops, and the Townshend Act has put a tax on almost everything we have to buy that comes from England."

"Henry, you know we've discussed this before, and the taxes are just on a few things that we can mostly do without."

"Well, the people in Massachusetts don't agree with you, and Mr. Knox says that the leaders in Boston have called on all the other colonies to join in opposing this oppression. Just recently, customs officials seized a sloop owned by John Hancock. When the good folks ran the tax collectors out of the state, London sent four thousand soldiers to protect the officials when they returned. Some of the citizens protested, and the Redcoats shot and killed five innocent people. In the letter, he says that almost everybody in Norfolk is supporting a boycott of British goods, even people that have always taken whatever London handed out."

"Maybe Parliament will back off if it hurts their trade."

Disappointed but not surprised at Ethan's equanimity, Henry added, "Well, the only reason I rode way out here was to let you know that we ain't going to get any support from London, so the only way to deal with the arsehole governor is by our own action."

Henry mounted his horse and rode away, without waiting for Ethan to respond.

Concerns in the North Carolina hill country about Tryon's intentions were soon justified, as abusive actions intensified in the county seats. One of the most troublesome decisions came when the sheriff of Orange County announced that he would collect taxes only at five locations and on certain dates, and that payments must be made in legal tender. This was especially disturbing to farmers, who had always made payments when and where they marketed what they produced.

The Regulators posted an announcement encouraging their members and others to continue to pay as before and, in response, Judge Edmund Fanning ordered the sheriff to seize the horse, saddle, and bridle of one of the Regulators who lived in the county seat and had signed the proclamation. When the property was sold for nonpayment of taxes, a group of armed men rode into Hillsborough, seized the horse, and fired several shots into Fanning's house. When the judge returned from a nearby county, he ordered the arrest of three of the men known to have rescued the horse. The influence of the Regulators became obvious when Fanning could not raise a suitable force to form a posse.

Colonial officials responded by posting notice of a new Riot Act in Hillsborough, branding anyone who refused to honor a court summons treasonous, and liable to be hanged. The law authorized the governor to recruit and arm a militia in order to preserve order throughout the state, and to pay forty shillings to each recruit. He announced the first week in May 1771 that he would be moving his military force toward Hillsborough, which he considered to be the focal point of lawless activity.

CHAPTER 7

The Battle at Alamance

MAY 1771

The Regulator leaders were fully informed about Tryon's activities, having made certain that a number of their key people had volunteered to serve in his forces. There was considerable discussion about their best response to the militia force. One more moderate group, including Husband, preferred that the dissidents lie low for a while, until the governor was forced to permit the militiamen to return to their homes because of inactivity. Henry and others believed that this was the time to demonstrate their overwhelming public support, and to force the colonial government to accede to what they considered their totally justified demands for reform.

The dispute became moot when the Regulators learned that Tryon was coming to Hillsborough. They decided to have a mass rally, to demonstrate peacefully both their political and military strength. It was scheduled for noon on the third Saturday in May, to be held on the banks of Big Alamance Creek, about fifteen miles west of Hillsborough. Governor Tryon condemned the assembly and claimed that it would be a violation of the Riot Act. But Regulators posted handbills and went throughout Orange County urging all men to attend, to "help secure through peaceful and legal means the just rights of poor Industrious peasants, honest industrious familys, and other poor Inhabitants."

Henry came by Ethan's home early on the morning of the meeting day, and Epsey served breakfast to the brothers. Once they were done, the two stepped outside. Ethan started the conversation. "Henry, I've heard what y'all are planning over on Alamance Creek, and I need to know what you have in mind."

"There are enough spies on both sides so we know what's going on as soon as a decision is made. Tryon is moving toward Alamance Creek with some of his militia, but we will proceed with our meeting and will make sure that it is completely peaceful. We're expecting more than two thousand to join us, and we're glad he's coming, so he can see how many people are sympathetic to our cause."

It was obvious that Henry was exuberant, totally convinced of the invincibility of the Regulators and discounting the seriousness of the situation.

Ethan said, "Public demonstrations are one thing, but a military battle is something else. I've heard that the militia are well armed, even with cannon, and are led by some of the best British officers. You won't have a chance against them if real fighting breaks out."

Henry smiled and replied in a confidential tone, "Well, let me give you some recent news. Tryon sent scouts out against us, led by Colonel John Ashe. We captured him, one of his captains, and several men."

"What did you do with them?"

"They're being held prisoner but will be released when Tryon moves back to New Bern, where he belongs. Some of our men roughed them up a little, so they won't forget the experience."

"Henry, I think you're making a mistake with the gathering on the Alamance and are exaggerating your strength. There is no way you'll ever get two thousand men to come out for anything, much less to an out-of-the-way place like that. The most important thing is to keep it all peaceful."

"Ethan, we're trying to get people to join us who are known to be in favor of a peaceful resolution of our differences. You saw the way we handled the meeting at the mill, because we had folks like you and Maddock there. I really want you to ride over to Alamance Creek with me."

"We stay pretty isolated out here, and that's the way I want to live, but if you can guarantee it's going to be a peaceful assembly, I'll go along with you."

Henry was obviously delighted and assured his brother that the Regulators would avoid any military confrontation.

Ethan went into the cabin and returned after a few minutes.

He said, "It's time for us to leave if we're to be there by midday. Epsey doesn't want me to go, but she's fixed some sweet potatoes, biscuits, and side meat to take with us."

They saw a surprising number of men on the trail as they approached the assembly grounds, most of them carrying a musket or rifle, as was the custom whenever there was any travel away from home. Even while working in one's own fields, there was always a weapon at hand, because of constant threats from bandit groups or Indians, and the chance of a good shot at a deer or turkey. Despite Henry's urging, Ethan had decided not to bring a gun in order to emphasize his desire to avoid any violence.

Henry said, "You can see already that we'll have more men here than you thought. There will be two or three speakers, who will mostly explain the situation in New Bern and pass around a new petition that will also go to London. We understand there have been some great changes in King George's ministry. Lord North has been made prime minister, and he is very much concerned about dissension in the colonies. Tryon knows this and is determined to prevent our communicating with Parliament."

Ethan looked around at the crowd and said, "I see a lot of guns, and some of the men seem to be in organized groups. Are they looking for trouble?"

Henry laughed. "No. They and the rest of us are trying to avoid trouble, but we want to make damned sure that Tryon sees that we are ready to defend ourselves, and to discourage any plans he might have to launch an attack. If we get our two thousand men, as seems likely, we'll have twice the number that he has. We've all agreed not to start any trouble, but we won't be scared off."

As they mingled among the other men and overheard a few belligerent comments, Ethan thought that Henry was overly optimistic, both about the peaceful intentions of the Regulators and of the governor's forces. He agreed that the local situation was bad, but it was unlikely that a few thousand dissatisfied farmers could change the existing order of things all the way throughout the colony and even in London.

There was a generally relaxed and confused atmosphere in the large clearing, with many of the men telling jokes and discussing farming, horses, and other frontier subjects. A few were gathered in a circle around two men who had removed their shirts and were wrestling with each other. Then word was passed, and the crowd assembled around a platform made of two barn doors laid across wagon bodies. Assemblyman Husband addressed them.

"This great gathering of interested citizens is a wonderful sight for those of us who have been feeling right lonely in New Bern."

A wave of laughter indicated that the men were in a good mood.

"I understand that the governor, with some troops, has moved this way and is not far from us now, this side of Hillsborough. We hear that he plans to go from here on into Rowan County, where his militia forces have run into a little trouble with some of our Regulators and decided to go back home to plow."

More laughter, and then Husband spoke in a more serious tone.

"There is no doubt that we mean to change things in this state, and we'll do it for three reasons. First, because our cause is right! Second, because our numbers are great and our resolve is unshakable. And third, because the king and prime minister have made it plain that they want to see justice done in the colonies.

"Tryon claims that we are rebels in a state of war, but the fact is that we are peaceful citizens, loyal to our king, who only demand justice."

It was obvious to Ethan that Husband had improved his skills as an orator since he'd first heard him speak at Maddock's mill. There was loud and sustained applause and cheers after he made each point, and he waited just the right amount of time to be most effective. Now he was interrupted by a man who approached the platform and called him over for a message.

Husband raised his hand for silence and spoke again. "Gentlemen, I have just been informed that Governor Tryon and his militia are approaching us from the east and have demanded that we disband this meeting. Are we ready to do so?"

There was a thunderous chorus of "No!" from the crowd.

"Do you think he can arrest two thousand of us?"

The response was a cacophony of laughter, hoots, and various scornful comments, and then the men became increasingly silent.

Husband said, "We must avoid any bloodshed, but it's time we had an understanding with the governor. Reverend Caldwell here has volunteered to take a message from us, declaring our peaceful intent but firmness in demanding our rights."

Within a half hour, Caldwell returned with Tryon's reply. He refused any compromise and said that any matters of substance could be addressed only after the "mob" dispersed and returned to their homes. He stated that his militia forces would move forward within an hour to arrest anyone remaining at the site.

This response resulted in a sharp division among the Regulators and other men. Henry and a dozen others surrounded Husband near the platform, and Ethan could see that they were engaged in a heated argument. The crowd became strangely quiet, and Ethan could hear Husband stating firmly that he would not participate in any act of violence. Henry and most of the others, confident of their strength, pledged to stand firm. A shock went through the onlookers as Husband mounted his horse and quietly rode away, and Ethan pressed forward to tell Henry that he had also decided to leave.

Before he could reach his brother, he heard the sound of approaching troops, and within a few minutes they could see Governor Tryon and several British officers, followed by a large contingent of armed militiamen. The leaders stopped at the edge of the clearing, turned to give apparently prearranged orders, and the military force deployed in a line abreast, partially surrounding the assembled Regulators.

"Look," said Henry, "they have two field pieces with them, aimed at us. They look very small, like half-pounders."

Tryon now turned toward the speaker's platform and shouted, "This is the governor speaking. Your assembly violates the laws of North Carolina, and I demand that you disband immediately and return to your homes."

William Butler, one of the Regulator leaders, responded, "Governor, we are law-abiding citizens, gathered here peacefully to plan how best to explain our grievances in petitions to you, the state council, the king, and the Parliament."

"I'm not here to debate with you, but to demand that you break up this unlawful assembly immediately. I'm not going to wait any longer."

One of the farmers on the edge of the crowd shouted out, "Governor, we ain't going nowhere. We're staying right here."

A shot rang out from a partially concealed militiaman, and the man fell, with a bullet through his thigh. There was a wild commotion, with most of the Regulators moving backward across the clearing. A rifle was fired from behind one of the trees, and a militia officer clutched his shoulder and slid from his horse. The governor and the officers moved back a few yards into the trees, and most of the crowd managed to scramble out of the clearing. Then Tryon shouted, "Open fire!"

Ethan and Henry had moved toward the edge of the clearing and only had to take a few steps further to be in the trees. They turned just as the two small cannon were fired into the hundred or so men still in the open area, from a distance of not more than fifty yards. The rattle of musketry followed from the militia, and more than a dozen men were left on the ground as the others quickly cleared the open area. A number of the Regulators, including Henry, took positions behind trees and began to return fire, while Ethan moved farther back into the woods with others who were unarmed. For more than an hour, hundreds of rounds were fired by both sides, with the members of the militia kept in order and therefore more exposed than the Regulators, who quickly hid themselves in the brush and trees. Finally, all the antagonists were well concealed, with human targets difficult to find. Only the dead and wounded were in the open area, and it seemed obvious that a number of the militiamen were also down.

The firing became spasmodic, and then Tryon's voice could be heard shouting, "Hold your fire! Hold your fire!" A few minutes passed until all firing ceased, and then the militiamen began to move forward cautiously. Most of the Regulators and observers had caught their horses and left the area, but a few hundred men remained in the immediate vicinity. Ethan noticed that Husband had returned and joined the other Regulators. Commanded by their experienced officers, the militiamen formed a rough circle around the edge of the clearing, in effect controlling the area.

Ethan found his brother and suggested that they go home, but Henry said, "I have to stay with the other Regulators, to protect our interests and to support our leaders."

As Henry, Husband, and others confronted the enraged Tryon and his militia leaders, Ethan joined a group of men who were caring for the casualties lying on the ground or leaning against trees. Nine of the men in the clearing were dead and more than twenty of those remaining were wounded. He heard one of the officers report that nine militiamen had also been killed and more than fifty wounded. The governor ordered the militia not to permit anyone else to leave the clearing and, in a surprising move, instructed his surgeons to care for the wounded Regulators.

For the first time, Ethan noticed that Judge Edmund Fanning was there. He and the governor consulted for a few minutes, looking from time to time at the men confronting them. Finally, Tryon called out sixteen names, including Henry Pratt, Herman Husband, and Silas Wythe, the man who had been shot first, through his thigh, and ordered them arrested. There was murmuring among the Regulators, and they moved closer to one another, but then Husband announced, "Men, we have nothing to fear from the law, and we want no more bloodshed. We'll go peacefully." The hands of the captives were tied behind them, and then the governor shocked the crowd by announcing, "Silas Wythe is guilty of treason and of instigating this tragic military action. He is hereby sentenced to be hanged."

The militiamen leveled their weapons at the Regulators, while Wythe was taken to a nearby tree, a rope looped and tightened around his neck, the other end thrown over a horizontal limb, and two soldiers pulled until his feet were two feet off the ground. Ethan watched the rough-hewn farmer with horror until his struggles ceased and his body hung suspended, oscillating back and forth a few inches like a pendulum.

Tryon then broke a deathly silence by saying, "The prisoners will be taken to jail in Hillsborough. All you other men are ordered to return to your homes."

The powerful Regulator movement was over. But its demise, in many ways, was a precursor of the greater war that was to come.

CHAPTER 8

Trial and Execution

Ethan stayed at home Sunday, but early the next morning he rode into Hillsborough to see what he could do to help his brother. The town was strangely quiet, with few people on the street. He rode to the courthouse and saw a few militiamen standing near the entrance, with a larger number around the nearby jail. In an open yard adjacent to the two buildings, he noticed a row of stocks and a permanent gallows, designed for the execution of two men at a time. He had seen both men and women in the stocks, guilty of what seemed to be minor crimes, including "malicious gossip," and knew that the death penalty was a common punishment not only for murder but for thievery and sexual misconduct. As he approached the jailhouse, a sergeant looked up and asked, "What do you want?"

"I've come to see my brother, Henry Pratt, who was arrested Saturday."

"My orders are that there will be no visitors, but a hearing, or trial, will be held in the courtroom this afternoon at three o'clock. Just one family member of each prisoner can attend."

"I'm his only relative, and I'll be there."

That afternoon, Ethan found a place in the courtroom, along with about twenty other family members. The rest of the space was filled with armed militiamen, except for a fenced-off area within which the court proceedings were conducted. The trial proved to be a farce, with one of the high-court justices from New Bern obviously having decided the outcome in advance.

With the bound defendants lined up in front of the bench, the judge announced, "This is a case with hundreds of witnesses, including the governor and a number of state militia officers. I have a deposition from Governor Tryon, who has had to return to New Bern. Judge Fanning and senior militia officers who are here in the courtroom have corroborated his sworn statement. There has been clear evidence against the defendants, some of whom are known to have participated in the disruption of this same court last year.

"We have testimony from many witnesses that Assemblyman Herman

Husband objected to the violence and even departed the clearing before the first shots were fired. He has been dismissed, but with a severe warning against further participation in assemblies that may lead to riotous behavior.

"The following named men have been found guilty of violating the Riot Act passed last year and are sentenced to be placed in stocks for two days, to be served only water and no food, and then to be given forty lashes."

Ethan was relieved when Henry's name was not called, but then noticed that some of the most widely recognized leaders of the Regulators had also not been sentenced.

The brothers exchanged glances while the eight men were led from the courtroom, and then the judge said, "These other six men have been proven guilty of sedition, of instigating violence that caused many deaths, and I must now close my afflicting duty by pronouncing on all of you the awful sentence of the law, which is that you, Henry Pratt . . ."

Ethan did not hear the other names, but held his breath until the judge continued, " . . . be carried to the place from whence you came, that you be drawn from thence to the place of execution, where you are to be hanged by the neck; that you be cut down while yet alive, that your bowels be taken out and burnt before your face, that your head be cut off, your body divided into four quarters, and this be at His Majesty's disposal, and the Lord have mercy on your souls."

There was an outcry in the courtroom, and the militia leveled their weapons while the judge pounded his gavel and shouted for order. When quiet was restored, he added, "The sentences will be carried out tomorrow at sunrise." Under heavy guard, the condemned men were marched back to the jailhouse, unable to avoid looking at the nearby gallows.

Ethan did not know what to do, except to remain near the courthouse and find companionship among the relatives of the other Regulators who had been sentenced. Late that afternoon, one of the bailiffs came to him, handed him a key, and said, "Your brother said to give you this."

The shoemaker's shop had not been disturbed, nor had the living quarters upstairs. Ethan found some cornmeal and salt pork and cooked his first meal of the day; then, after removing his shoes, he lay down on Henry's cot. He dozed fitfully during the night, rose long before dawn, saddled his horse, and rode to the town square, where about a hundred people were already assembled. He tied his mount to a small tree near the square and walked to within ten yards of the gallows, between it and the jailhouse.

Four large flambeaus were stuck in the ground and revealed by their flickering light that workmen were completing a modification that would now accommodate three victims at a time. As daylight came, a half hour before sunrise, so did the people. Ethan recognized many of the Regulators who had been at the Alamance assembly on Saturday, plus several hundred others. He sensed that most were like him: restless, angry, sullen, perplexed as to what could be done to prevent the execution.

He soon heard the sound of a drum and the barked orders of command, and a company of militia marched to the gallows, halted, and formed a ring around it facing outward. All had muskets, some with bayonets fixed. A captain mounted the gallows platform and shouted, "No firearms will be permitted in the square. Anyone who has a rifle or pistol must deliver them to the courthouse for safekeeping."

The crowd had become quiet, and attention was focused on men whose weapons were visible. Within a minute, most of them walked toward the courthouse, but a few others stood where they were, looking defiant. Small groups of soldiers moved among the spectators, surrounding those who still retained their guns, and forced them either to leave the square or turn in their weapons. By this time, the sky had brightened in the east, and the crowd looked toward the jail, where the sheriff, his deputies, and a platoon of soldiers stood near the door. Soon three of the prisoners emerged, their legs manacled and their hands bound in back.

Ethan saw that one of them was Henry, whose eyes were cast downward. They shuffled forward, tightly surrounded by the heavy guard. Ethan was taller than most men, and he stood near the direct line from the jail door to the gallows platform. As the men passed him, he called out, "Henry!" His brother paused, looked at him, and smiled. One of the militiamen prodded him and said, "Keep moving." This quiet exchange seemed to enervate the crowd, and a murmur of voices began to grow much louder. Then one man shouted "Freedom!" and soon there was a steady chant of "*Free*-dom, *Free*-dom, *Free*-dom." Ethan joined in as loudly as he could, and, for a few moments, his frustration waned and he had a transient feeling of achievement.

Once before, as a teenager in Philadelphia, Ethan had witnessed an official hanging, but under totally different circumstances. The condemned man had been convicted of murder, and the spectators were there to see justice done or just to enjoy a spectacle. This time, it seemed that almost everyone was there to condemn the injustice, and their very presence was a protest. Except for those guarding the prisoners and participating in the execution, he could see only a few whom he suspected of being opposed to the Regulator movement. They were better dressed than most, and included some well-known merchants and large landowners. Perhaps for their own security, they stood in a group together, on the edge of the crowd.

The procession by this time had reached the gallows, and the three men climbed the steps and took their places, abreast, facing the crowd and the center of the square. It was obvious that they were trying their best to appear impassive, but with only limited success. The strain on their faces was obvious, as each of them searched the crowd for their friends and relatives. Three hangmen placed black hoods over their heads and then adjusted nooses around their necks. The throng was momentarily quiet and then involuntarily moved toward the gallows. Some tried to begin a chant of "No—no—no," but it soon faded away. There was total silence when the trapdoors were released, and the men were hanged.

Ethan remembered the terrible sentence that the judge had read out in court, and wondered briefly if the convicted men would be drawn, quartered, and beheaded. With growing relief and some embarrassment for his thoughts, he realized that the words were part of an ancient condemnation designed to strike fear in those who heard it.

Then Ethan was almost overcome with nausea and with frustrated anger. His only brother was dead, and he had done nothing to save him. After a few minutes he walked toward the gallows, as most others withdrew and began to leave the clearing. A sergeant confronted him and told him to move back. "I've come for my brother," he said, and it must have been obvious that he would not be deterred. The sergeant said, "All right," and nodded to the hangmen still on the platform.

There was a wagon waiting to receive the bodies as they were brought down to the ground, but Ethan insisted that no one touch Henry except himself. He lifted the slight frame of his brother easily, carried him over to his horse, and draped him carefully across the saddle. He rejected several offers of assistance and then led the horse slowly to the shoemaker's shop, obtained a pick and shovel, and proceeded to the cemetery. He dug a grave alongside that of Henry's wife and buried his brother. He had been overwhelmed with a desire to be alone, but now he wished that Epsey could have been with him as he recited some verses from the Twenty-third Psalm and the Lord's Prayer as best he could. Later, he would bring her with him, when he erected headstones on the two graves.

Back at home, Epsey wept softly as Ethan described what had happened, fumbling with the words, as though he could hardly believe it himself. He struggled to hide his mixed emotions of grief, anger, and a sense of inadequacy, and soon left the house, saying that he was going to check on the cows and hogs. He returned well after sundown, nodded to Epsey, and sat down on his pallet, leaning back against the rough logs of the cabin's wall. Epsey moved toward him and saw that his eyes and cheeks were wet with tears. He seemed a hollow shell of the strong and self-reliant man she had always known, now almost childlike in his vulnerability. She reached out and touched the top of his head, not knowing what to expect. Instead of moving away, Ethan moved his hand up and clasped her fingers. Epsey sat beside him, and he put his head on her shoulder as she held him close. She was overwhelmed with a desire to nurture her husband. She soon bared her breast and held him close against it, and he responded eagerly to this unprecedented intimacy. She was surprised by his passion, and thankful that she could help relieve his torment.

After Ethan was sleeping soundly, Epsey returned to her own bed and lay awake the rest of the night, embarrassed about what they had done and wondering what they would do in the future.

In the morning, their relationship was as it had always been, except that Ethan was inclined to reveal his opinions more freely.

"The Regulators were mostly good men, and the cause was right—for freedom and against oppression. The problem was that there were too many leaders, and a few hotheads who violated the law and committed crimes against people and property. Their words and actions looked like an attack on the crown and not just against some local crooks. This turned many people against us."

Epsey noticed that he said "us." "What can you do? What can we do?" she asked.

"I just don't know. None of us ever thought that Tryon would go to such lengths against the Regulators, but it seems obvious that our strength has been concentrated in just a few western counties and there is less support than we thought in most of the colony. It may be that the king and Parliament will react against what Tryon has done and give another opening for citizens to take action."

In a few days, these opinions proved to be excessively optimistic. When Ethan and Epsey rode into Hillsborough to take care of what was left at the shoemaker's shop and to order a grave marker from the stonecutter, they found a group assembled around the public posting board. An official notice, signed by Governor Tryon, stated that pursuant to a ruling by the state council, every male inhabitant would be required to swear an oath of allegiance to the colonial government and to the crown. The penalty for refusal to do so would be arrest and trial for subversion. State and county officials would visit every home to secure the written pledges.

Back home, Ethan was now in a quandary. He had always considered himself to be a good British citizen, loyal to his king. Although the administration of Governor Tryon had proved to be abusive and many of the local officials were obviously corrupt, he had heard that a new royal governor was coming to North Carolina who would be representing the more moderate policies of the prime minister, Lord North. Rather than consider swearing allegiance to the government, several hundred of the more ardent Regulators were leaving Orange County and moving westward to a remote settlement area known as the Watauga Valley, which was almost completely independent of control by officials in New Bern. Ethan had no desire to join them, both because he preferred to stay where he was and because he had never felt at ease with the more militant Regulators. Finally, he told Epsey he would join most other citizens in confirming allegiance, and then await the arrival of officials who would seek this assurance.

When they came, almost two months later, Ethan was in the field plowing, and he noticed that one of the local lawyers was riding with the soldiers. Ethan didn't expect any trouble and was doubtful that his name was on the list of active Regulators, although he had been at Maddock's mill and at the Alamance confrontation. To his surprise, the lawyer asked him to produce the deed to his land and all his back-tax receipts.

Ethan unhitched his horse, climbed on its back, and the group rode to the cabin. As was the case with many of the frontier families, Ethan's land grant had been prepared by lawyers at the courthouse and witnessed and recorded by officials whom he now knew could not be trusted. It was generally assumed that the building of a cabin, clearing and cultivation of fields, and recognition of boundary lines by one's neighbors was an adequately binding title to land. Now that most of the Quakers had moved to Georgia, the judge and several of the other local officials owned their land.

The lawyer glanced at the papers produced by Ethan and said, "I don't see any deed here. There is just a letter, and without any stamps on it. I have looked at the courthouse records, and it's doubtful that you own the land you're plowing. All the property owners around you have clear and legal titles. It would pay you to clear up these questions."

The next day he went to the courthouse and produced the letter signed by Edmund Fanning, who at that time had the title of clerk, that confirmed a free grant of two hundred acres from the governor in 1766. When Ethan asked to see the records on his farm, he was told to wait and then told to come back late that afternoon. When he returned, the clerk of the court informed him that there was no record of any legal title to his land, but only entries of his payment of property taxes and his failure to buy adequate stamps for a license to operate a blacksmith shop. The clerk explained that what Ethan, the Quakers, and a number of other farmers had been issued was now interpreted by the government as a permit to examine the land, not to own it. Two lawyers were in the room, and they confirmed that legally he had been clearing and plowing fields that were not his. Clear title to land in this area was now being granted by the governor's council for £16 per one hundred acres, and, in fact, a buyer from Wilmington had posted a bond for £120 to buy property in the area, including Ethan's farm and some nearby land that was still occupied by four Quaker families.

Ethan walked from the room, stunned and angry, and decided to return home. Since it was not much out of his way, he rode by to visit one of the Quakers, whose name was Jonathan Mabry. When he recounted what had happened to him, Mabry responded, "We have had the same experience more than a month ago—all of us Friends—but we didn't know that any others were involved."

"I guess my farm is just in the wrong place. Have you decided what you are going to do?"

"We're going to leave North Carolina. I've just come back from Georgia, where I visited with Joseph Maddock. Our people there are getting along fine, and Brother Maddock has just obtained a grant of more land near their first settlement. My family and two others are planning to move

down there next month, and the other Friends will be going back to Pennsylvania, where they have relatives."

That night, Ethan and Epsey sat up late, discussing their future. Their
overriding sense of loss was still about Henry. In her quiet way, Epsey had
reminded her husband several times that he was not to blame, and that
there had been nothing he could have done. They shared the general realization that political and financial decisions in Orange County would be
made by people who would never accommodate their presence, at least not
on this land.

Ethan said, "I reckon the leather shop is ours, and the folks around
Hillsborough could still use a good shoemaker."

Uncharacteristically, Epsey spoke up strongly. "Ethan, you left Philadelphia because you didn't want to be shut up for the rest of your life in a
shoemaker's shop. It's farming, and being alone in the outdoors, where
you find happiness."

Ethan thought for a while and then replied solemnly, "We don't have
many choices. I'd rather stay here on our own place, but I've become convinced that this won't be possible. Even if I wasn't Henry's brother, our
land has been tied in with that of the Quakers, and there are powerful people determined to get it. We could move westward with some of the Regulators, but I've never felt at ease with most of those who have gone ahead.

"There are really just two more choices: to return to Philadelphia or to
move to Georgia with Mabry and his people. I guess it's Georgia."

CHAPTER 9

The Pratts Move to Georgia

1771

The next morning they began planning how best to make the move.
Ethan left home early for Hillsborough and loaded some of Henry's most
useful possessions on his animals. On the way back home, he stopped by to
tell Mabry that they would be going with him to join Maddock. The
Quaker was delighted and gave Ethan information concerning the trip.
They decided that they would try to leave in four weeks, giving them some

time to close out their business in Orange County. Since it was toward the end of the summer, the Pratts were able to harvest their crops and garden. They disposed of the produce, livestock, and furnishings that they could not carry with them, and worked out how to pack the remaining belongings on their draft animals, including two new packhorses purchased for a total of £7.

Without any problem, Ethan was able to sell Henry's property in Hillsborough to the merchant with whom he had done most of his trading. The agreed price was only about half what the lot, buildings, and furnishings were worth, but both men knew that Ethan was not in a good bargaining position. On the way home, he felt surprisingly relieved, and when he entered the cabin and embraced her, Epsey could sense immediately that her husband was happy and relaxed once again. Each day, as they prepared to leave North Carolina, the cabin and fields seemed less and less like their own.

One day, as Ethan was in his workshop replacing a broken spoke on their two-wheeled cart, he was surprised to glance up and find Epsey standing in the doorway, looking at him. She rarely approached him when he was working, and he waited for her to speak.

She finally said, "Ethan, I've something to tell you."

Somewhat abruptly, he replied, "Well, what is it?"

"I think I am with a child."

Epsey read her husband's look of astonishment as disapproval, and she took an involuntary step backward and lowered her face in embarrassment. Ethan dropped his drawknife, moved toward Epsey, and held out his hands to her. She slipped between his arms and placed her head on his shoulder, and he held her to him.

"I'm grateful, I'm grateful," was all he could say, but it was adequate for her.

They went into the house together, and she reported that she had missed two periods, had some nausea in the mornings, and that her breasts were sensitive. Ethan was pleased with the prospect of a child, hopefully a son, but concerned that the long trip to Georgia would be difficult for his wife. She assured him that she was healthy and that they would be at their new home long before the baby was due. She felt that it was natural for them to refrain from any physical intimacy, and this unspoken attitude caused a reversion to their previous celibate relationship.

. . .

Ethan met with the Quaker men to discuss the possible routes to Georgia. Mabry described how he had traveled on horseback and had followed the most direct inland trail, far from the sea and paralleling the coast. He had crossed the Haw and Deep rivers, then ridden along a roundabout trail west and then south to cross the Savannah River at Augusta. Maddock's settlement, which they had named Wrightsborough, was farther west. He estimated the total distance to be about 350 miles, and it had taken him twelve days to get there and, traveling light and without cargo, nine days to return.

"This is a difficult path, often through Indian territory, suitable most of the way only for unburdened horsemen who can move rapidly. It's not one we can follow with our families and livestock," he said.

He spread a rough map on the table and continued, "Here is the route that Maddock recommends for us."

The men gathered around and traced the path they would have to follow, much more southerly, and along the coast.

Ethan asked some questions but didn't argue with Mabry's experienced advice concerning travel arrangements. Their first day's travel would be to the banks of the Haw River, which they would ford southwest of Hillsborough. The trail then paralleled the Haw and Cape Fear rivers to Wilmington, and from there they would travel along the coast road on into Charles Town. Except when traveling along the established coastal route, they could expect only narrow trails first traversed by Indians. They knew from their own experience that these were mostly unmarked, frequently just wide enough for a horse and rider, but at least they provided a clear route to the best places for streams to be forded. Any possessions would have to be lashed onto the backs of their horses and oxen. On the wider and more heavily traveled trails they could use a travois, an A-frame platform made of two poles dragged behind a horse, with a load carried on hide stretched between the poles.

Based on what they had learned from the Quakers who had preceded them to Georgia, they figured they could travel fifteen to twenty miles each day on a good trail and half that when there were frequent streams to cross, if the livestock tended to wander, or when rain created bogs or flooded the lowlands. They hoped to make the trip in four weeks, with good luck and favorable weather, or a week longer if they were delayed.

Mabry said, "I've just got a message from Maddock, who has to go to

Charles Town to supervise a shipment of farm produce to the Bahamas and to buy supplies. He plans to meet us there, and we can accompany him to our settlement in Wrightsborough, either directly through Augusta or down to Savannah and back up the river. The choice will depend on whether we can make all the arrangements for our land with Georgia officials in Augusta or will be required to do this in Savannah."

Ethan asked, "How far is it from Charles Town to Augusta direct and through Savannah?"

"According to Maddock, it's about ten or twelve days for us by the more direct route and three days longer if we keep on along the coast."

"How about the Indians? Do we have anything to fear as we move southward?"

"We believe not, so long as we stay on frequently traveled traces and near the coast. It's only when a group turns westward, toward new lands, that the natives are likely to be hostile. Keeping together and showing our peaceful intentions is our best protection." He smiled and added, "Letting them see our hunting rifles may also be of help."

Late in September, the four families formed a caravan with their personal possessions, household furnishings, tools, food, and corn for horse feed lashed on or suspended from packsaddles on the backs of oxen and horses. Barrels or kegs were suspended on each side. A sturdy horse or ox carried from 150 to 250 pounds each, along paths sometimes only two or three feet wide. As many as a dozen animals were tethered together, each secured to the packsaddle ahead, with the lead animal controlled by a man or woman walking or riding. There was always a man leading the caravan and one following to keep an eye out for stragglers.

With some reluctance, the men had decided to sell their hogs, expecting to buy brood sows in Georgia, and they now formed one small herd of their best sheep and cattle. After a day or so of unpleasant experimenting, they identified the natural lead animals and put bells on them. Hickory hobbles minimized the chance of their wandering off while they grazed at night. The men, assisted by their dogs and sometimes other members of their families, rotated the duty of lead drover, each working for a day at a time to keep the herd moving along together. At least one watchman had to remain alert at night to keep the herd together. As the animals became accustomed to one another and to the daily routine, the drovers learned how to perform their tasks with minimal effort and maximum rest.

Although Jonathan Mabry had discussed the route with Maddock, he was sometimes doubtful about the way to be taken, so the other Quakers and Ethan helped make decisions when the trail forked or crossed another. The backwoodsmen usually carried a small compass, because they could be confused about directions even near their own homes. In the flat regions such as those in the creek swamps, without topographical landmarks, it was not possible to know directions when the sky was overcast and no heavenly bodies were visible.

On the long trip, Ethan and Epsey managed their own oxen and pack-horses and took their turn with the other families to drive the herd of sheep and cattle, each of which had its ears marked by its owner. The Pratts had two dogs, one a bluetick hound and the other a mixture of shepherd and terrier. The hound usually stayed close to the trail, almost always in sight. The other, named Squire, was much more energetic, and Ethan soon taught him to help with herding the animals. Within a few days, Squire became accustomed to this work and assisted each of the men as they rotated on the job.

Ethan was glad to do even more than his share of the common work required to assure the safe and orderly procession, which was not difficult as long as the group moved together on established trails. When not acting as a drover or off hunting, Ethan usually walked along the trail, and Epsey rode on their one saddle horse, leading the other draft animals. They were all docile and naturally tended to follow the animal in front of them, so when Epsey dismounted and walked, she needed to give them little guidance, only to yank on the halter when they tended to lag behind or paused to take a bite of grass. She was often nauseated, and felt better while walking and leading the animals with a short guide rope.

After ten days of slow travel, they camped for two nights near Wilmington, where the men went into the town to buy some supplies and to replace a packhorse that had wandered off one night and could not be found. They found the coastal road to be much more convenient, often wide enough for horses or people to walk abreast, but frequent ferry crossings were both time-consuming and relatively costly.

At the previously arranged place in Charles Town, they met Joseph Maddock, who first expressed his impatience with their late arrival, two days later than scheduled. Then he outlined for them his plans for the rest of the journey. They learned that they could make arrangements for their land grants in Augusta, but would still take a roundabout path. Their route would take them southwestward along the coast halfway to Savannah, and then westward, crossing the Savannah River at a shallow ford known as Pallachucola, and then up the west side of the river to Augusta. There was a more direct route, but it was not the one Maddock and the other Quakers preferred, since it incurred payment of more ferry fees.

They had traveled only a short distance before trouble arose. They all knew that Joseph Maddock was the acknowledged leader of the Quakers and that he had made the arrangements for the land in Georgia, so although there had not been any general agreement, no one objected when he assumed that he was the undisputed boss of the caravan. Ethan had known Maddock as an honest and hardworking miller who treated his customers courteously, but now he seemed to be excessively proud and domineering, not deferring at all to the family who did not share his religious faith, headed by a man who seemed so mild-mannered and obliging. One day, while Ethan was tending the herd of cattle and sheep, Epsey was alone with the draft animals. She stopped them and walked to a nearby tree, where she heaved with nausea for a few minutes and then walked back toward the lead ox. Maddock rode his horse back down the line, stopped in front of Epsey, and shouted, "Doesn't thou know how to handle oxen? Move up, or else let thy husband manage the team!"

Then he whirled and rode away, leaving Epsey with her face flushed, both in embarrassment and anger. She had never had anyone speak to her in this way. When Ethan returned, he walked beside his wife for a few minutes without speaking. He could see that she was distressed.

"Are you not feeling well?"

"I've been nauseated, but no more than usual. I'm just angry at Mr. Maddock."

She explained what had occurred, and Ethan handed her the whip and untied his horse. Epsey urged him to forget what had happened, but Ethan galloped forward and found Maddock.

"What have you said to disturb my wife?"

"Nothing. I only urged her to close the gap between thy wagon and the one ahead."

"It's not what you said, it's the way you spoke that I cannot accept."

"Cannot accept?"

"That's right. Don't you ever speak to my wife again."

"Mr. Pratt, I consider thee to be a guest in this caravan, and thou art welcome. But there can be only one trail master and I am that person."

Ethan struggled to control his anger. He knew that all the families had a collective voice, but he also realized that in a showdown, the Quaker families would all stand together. He saw no need to involve anyone else in the affair.

"I am not disputing that, Mr. Maddock, but do not forget what I have said. If you have anything to say to my family, let it be to me."

From then on, although both tried to forgive the other, there was a coolness between the two men.

CHAPTER 10

Life on the Frontier

In Augusta, with Maddock's help, the four families filled out the necessary papers and each obtained what seemed to be a clear title to a certain amount of land, but without the exact location specified. They learned that about twelve thousand acres had been granted for the entire Quaker community and that Maddock was in charge of allocating a specific tract to each family. This would be done for the newcomers after they arrived at their destination. They all made final purchases of supplies, camped one night on the outskirts of the small town, and the next day were eager to see their new lands.

They traveled northwestward for about forty miles and then stopped at what Maddock said was his land, where he had built a gristmill near the center of the land grant. He had a map on the wall, on which he pointed out that the Quaker tract was bounded roughly by Little River to the east, Briar Creek to the southwest, the Ogeechee River to the west, and on the north by Indian territory as defined by the treaty of 1763.

At the settlement area, the Pratts found the Quakers involved in establishing the small town of Wrightsborough, named for Governor James Wright, who had issued the land grant in 1767. The meetinghouse was located on the edge of a plantation owned by the governor.

Since the first group of forty families had come down from North Carolina with Maddock that year, some of the Quaker settlers had become dissatisfied with pioneer life, or were afraid of threats from the nearby Creek Indians. A few had already moved back to one of the northern colonies, and now about ten other families had decided to give up farming and seek a more close-knit community where security would be better, a permanent meetinghouse could be established, and tradesmen could capitalize on their skills. It was not difficult for the four newly arrived families to trade the packhorses they had purchased for use during the trip. Ethan swapped his four brood sows with one of the families who was leaving, and supplemented his woodworking and blacksmithing tools with a few purchases.

Maddock explained, "Georgia's headright system allows a maximum of one hundred acres of land to every head of family and fifty additional acres for all other members of the household, free or slave. In addition, the governor can sell up to one thousand extra acres of unclaimed land to a competent farmer, at a cost of one shilling for each ten acres."

He smiled and continued, "As seems to be his custom, Governor Wright has taken thirty-five hundred acres on the edge of Wrightsborough to be added to ten others he already owns nearer to Savannah, worked by more than five hundred slaves. His ownership here may be helpful to us in the future."

Mabry asked, "How far is it to Savannah?"

Maddock seemed pleased to give the answers. "The distance to the capital by land is about a hundred and thirty miles, but most of the travel is done on the river, which almost doubles the distance. A boat or barge downstream takes four days, but fifteen days to come back upstream. We ride horseback down easily in three days, and it takes about eight days to travel with oxen and driving a herd of farm animals. The first one hundred miles or so above Savannah are over flat, sandy land, mostly under big longleaf pines and with a goodly number of swampy areas to cross and streams to ford. Then, as thou hast seen, the land up toward Augusta changes to a richer soil, with a lot of small hills and valleys."

Ethan was surprised to see that Maddock had assigned property to the three Quaker families before they arrived, contiguous to land already occupied. He could tell from the map that a fairly large area was left on the extreme western border of the 1763 land grant, with a plot designated for him and Epsey. It was near the headwaters of Briar Creek, and he guessed that much of it was likely to be swampy. Apparently, Maddock noticed that

Ethan was displeased, and announced in an officious way that there would be no arguing, but that any two families could exchange sites if they mutually agreed. Ethan decided not to protest but to accept what was offered to him. By this time, fifty-seven families were in the area, and Ethan's grant was for two hundred acres, with an additional forty acres nearer the creek that was designated for use as a cowpen. The land grant papers were completed, with Ethan making certain that the legal deed clearly designated him as the permanent owner after he had paid the small surveying fee and agreed to build a cabin and clear a portion of the land.

The legal processes required several days, and during this time Epsey decided to raise again the long-dormant subject of their religious life. Since the first day of their marriage she had honored her commitment to study the Holy Scriptures each day. Ethan would listen quietly as she read aloud, but never took the initiative in either prayer or Bible reading. She remembered that one of her major hopes in moving to a frontier area was to minister to the heathen Indians, and she thought that now was a good time to pursue the same goal that had been the life's work of her father. She had planned her argument carefully and suggested to Ethan that, since they were surrounded by Quakers, they might attend some of the weekly meetings with the other families in Wrightsborough. If these sessions should go well, they might consider a religious affiliation.

Ethan listened respectfully, thought for a few moments, and then responded with finality: "Epsey, I believe in God, but there is no way that I could become a Quaker. I agree with their opposition to violence and to slavery, and I like their wanting to keep the government out of their personal business. But I can't abide their controlling each other. I've seen them punish both men and women for gossiping, having too much debt, or marrying too soon after a spouse died. I won't be a part of it."

This was an extraordinary speech for Ethan; obviously he had given the subject a lot of thought. Epsey looked directly at Ethan and responded, "I thought it might be good for us to be part of a group, but I agree with much of what you say and will let the matter rest."

Ethan and Epsey left Wrightsborough as soon as possible and followed the designated trail and landmarks that took them to their own land. They found the site without any trouble, made a small camp that afternoon, and

spent most of the next day searching for the corner markers and boundaries of their property. They became increasingly pleased, soon realizing
that the soil was rich, more than half the land was gently rolling and suitable for cultivation, water was plentiful, and—perhaps a mixed blessing—
there were no settlers on land adjoining theirs. North and west was Indian
territory, south was the broad swamp of Briar Creek, and the plot to the
east had been earlier assigned to a Quaker family who decided to leave
Georgia and move back to Pennsylvania.

Ethan had already noticed while in Wrightsborough that the settlers
seemed to have much more fear of Indians than back in North Carolina,
and he soon realized that their concern might be justified. Although British
maps showed Georgia's western boundary to be the Mississippi River, Indian tribes legally controlled all except a narrow strip paralleling the Atlantic Coast and the Savannah River, beginning just a few miles from his
assigned homestead. The terms of the 1763 treaty between Indian chiefs
and Governor Wright had not been approved by some of the young
Creeks, and a few braves had tried to intimidate the settlers whose homes
were established near the boundary of the ceded land. They would beat
drums at night and on a few occasions had stolen livestock and burned
some outbuildings. The king's Indian superintendent, John Stuart, was
competent and respected by most of the settlers and native leaders. He did
everything possible to prevent any altercations between the whites and the
Indians, and the older tribal chiefs joined in this effort to preserve peace.

The few British soldiers who served under Governor Wright were stationed in or near Savannah and played a small role in controlling the natives. Even more important to the Creeks and Cherokees than any military
threat was the possibility of an interruption in trade. The natives were fascinated with the goods of the white man, including salt, sugar, rum, blankets, and relatively worthless trinkets. Steel knives and muskets were the
most prized possessions. For all these they traded the cured hides of deer,
beaver, raccoons, and foxes—but because of the real difference in value and
the shrewdness of the white traders, the Indians slowly accumulated a substantial debt. In fact, the Indians owed so much and were so eager to continue trading that they were already exploring the possibility of ceding
more land in order to settle the back debts so that trade could continue.

Ethan had no fear of the Indians, but at the same time it was his responsibility to get to know them and for them to understand that he would treat

them as good neighbors. The nearest Creek village, he had seen from Maddock's map, was only five miles from where he intended to build his home. He knew from experience that his skill and his tools, particularly his forge and anvil, could be of great benefit to the Indians. Also, Epsey was familiar with the use of rudimentary medicines and was imbued with a genuine desire, derived from her parents, to be of help to the natives. Although these plans for building mutual trust and respect were limited, they contrasted vividly with the attitude of many of the settlers, who looked upon the Indians as subhuman and felt that they were inherently criminal in character. Pioneer farmers believed almost unanimously that the Indians should be pushed farther west, away from the land that they felt was ordained by God to be used exclusively by the colonists.

Since Ethan and Epsey had already been through the same process in North Carolina just a few years earlier, it was not difficult for them to select the best house site. The weather was temperate for October and they weren't concerned about keeping warm, but their household goods needed to be protected. Their first task was to build a small lean-to for shelter, with tarpaulins and hides stretched over saplings to form a roof and three sides. It was located on high ground in a grove of enormous chestnut, oak, white pine, and hickory trees, and with a spring not too far down the hill. It was likely that their permanent cabin would be in this area.

They laid out their fields and pastures, mostly where a thick stand of smaller trees had replaced many older ones blown down in a storm at least three decades ago, and combined the clearing of cropland with accumulating an adequate supply of logs for the construction of their cabin. Although pregnant, Epsey was as strong as most men and wanted to help in many phases of this work, even though Ethan cautioned her about her condition. Ethan worked from daybreak to sunset, usually seven days a week, although his wife never worked in the fields or garden on Sundays. She did not feel any religious restraint on housework, including carding, spinning, weaving, or other tasks that could have been postponed for a day.

They moved from the lean-to into the new shelter as soon as a roof was in place and then chinked between the logs with clay, hung the door and three windows, and completed the fireplace and chimney. The door, with a window on each side, opened to the south, and the other window was across from the door. The fireplace and chimney were on the east end of

the house. As soon as possible, Ethan built a shed about twenty yards behind the main building, with walls on three sides and open in front. Here
he installed his forge, anvil and blacksmithing tools, grindstone, and shaving horse, and built a shelf around two walls to hold supplies. He was especially proud of his extensive collection of woodworking tools, some of
which he had crafted himself. His field implements and a small supply of
iron pieces were kept on the ground, and seed and other items that might
provide food for rodents were contained in bags or wicker baskets and
hung by wire from the ceiling joists. A pole fence enclosed a small corral
around two sides of the shed, with a swinging gate that opened toward the
house. One corner of the corral was covered with poles and branches, to
give some protection to animals that would huddle there in severe weather.
The woodpile was quite close to the house and always contained some
saplings and trunks of larger hardwoods that Ethan cut and split into fireplace size during his spare time. This firewood was stacked neatly against
the side of the cabin, convenient to be carried inside for cooking and also
for heating during the cold months.

The cabin was in the center of a square cleared area, roughly 350 paces
on each side, which contained about twenty-five acres and was encompassed by a laboriously constructed split-rail fence. From the southeast corner, a narrow trail led through the woods toward the Quaker settlement at
Wrightsborough, six miles away.

Epsey's routine in and around the house was hardly disturbed during
her pregnancy, although she was sometimes concerned about a small issue
of blood. Ethan was not aware of the problem and discussed her pregnancy
only when asked if he had any suggestion for a name for the baby. He responded, "I've been thinking that if it is a boy we might call him Henry."
She agreed, and suggested Abigail as a possible girl's name.

When she decided that her time was approaching, Ethan went into
Wrightsborough and found a woman who had experience as a midwife,
and hired her to assist with the childbirth. The little boy was born healthy
and screaming, but Epsey bled profusely despite the best efforts of the midwife, and lay weakened and pale after the birth. Neither of the parents was
especially disturbed when the woman said, "I doubt that she'll have another one anytime soon."

After a week, Epsey insisted that the woman return to the settlement,
and Ethan finally acceded to her demands and assumed the role of nurse

for her and little Henry. Epsey was distressed by her inability to resume normal duties, but she had more than adequate milk for the baby and finally was able to sit by the fire as she nursed the child and directed her husband in performing his tasks as cook and housekeeper.

There was a limit to how much land they could cultivate with a pair of oxen and one draft horse, so Ethan had little need to expand the area of his fields. Their cattle, sheep, and hogs were permitted to forage freely on leaves, acorns, chestnuts, and hickory nuts, but it was necessary for Ethan to maintain contact with the animals in order to treat them for any injuries or diseases and prevent their wandering off his property. He observed them as much as possible during each day, and late every afternoon he would go to the edge of the woods and, with a series of shrill whoops, call the animals to him, where they were always rewarded with a few ears of corn or some small bundles of fodder or hay. They could always use more grazing, and he cut and girdled trees both for firewood and to expand the area where grass could grow. He fenced these areas for grazing, knowing that later this land could be cultivated. In other wooded areas, Ethan used carefully controlled burning to remove the thick layer of pine straw and leaves from the ground, permitting natural grasses to emerge that were tolerant of shade. Ethan had always looked forward to these times in the woods, but now he found every excuse to come by the house and hold little Henry, at least for a few moments.

One day after he had worked several hours and had come in for a late breakfast, Ethan said, "Epsey, now that you're able to walk around without any trouble, I'd like for you and the baby to go with me to the woods. I'm clearing off and fencing a little pasture for the milk cow, and y'all might enjoy being away from the house for a while. I'll be glad to tote the baby."

Epsey was surprised and delighted, and they began to look for opportunities for the three of them to spend time together. This unaccustomed relationship between Ethan and Epsey brought a degree of sustained familiarity and sharing that they had never known before. Both of them were completely fascinated with the baby, and Ethan was amused to find himself somewhat resentful as his wife regained her strength and was able to relieve him of his duties in caring for the child.

During most seasons there was little time for either of them to rest. Epsey restricted her time in the corn, wheat, flax, and tobacco fields, but she still called the garden her own and expected Ethan to break the land with his ox-drawn plow only when one crop of vegetables was harvested and it was time to plant another. She grew Irish and sweet potatoes, beans and peas, okra, onions, sweet corn, and greens. She carefully saved her own seed, bedded the sweet potatoes in a hill of alternating layers of pine straw and earth, and stored Irish potatoes and onions in a cool attic space above the ceiling joists. Her vegetable rows were well fertilized with animal manure and humus, and mulched to minimize weed growth and the time required for hoeing. She dried or smoked some of the venison and turkey that Ethan brought home from his hunting trips, and worked with him in butchering hogs and shearing sheep. Together, they tanned the hides of deer and cattle, rubbing them with salt and lime, and then completing the process with tannin obtained from oak and hemlock bark and chestnut wood. This final product prevented further shrinking and rotting of the leather.

After all the buildings and necessary fences were completed, Ethan dug a well in the yard, which obviated trips to the spring about one hundred yards from the cabin. It was now much easier for Espey to keep the garden watered during the hot and often dry summer season, by carefully ladling a cupful from her wooden bucket at the base of each young plant. Epsey had previously considered cutting firewood to be partly her job, but now Ethan insisted that, with the baby, this was his sole responsibility. She still helped care for the animals when they were in the fenced pasture or corral, and milked the two cows, or whichever one was fresh at the time.

Epsey tried to do most of this outdoor work during the cooler hours of the day, with her housework done in between. She often carried little Henry in an old shawl slung across her back, and Ethan built a small covered crib at the edge of the garden—on stilts, due to concern about snakes and rodents—where the baby could lie in the shade while Epsey worked.

One of her most time-consuming tasks was the making of garments, using the raw fibers of flax, cotton, and wool. Despite its tedious nature, Epsey enjoyed the work, which was completely compatible with caring for the child. The repetitive process did not require her concentration, and she was free to think about other things as her body rested from more strenuous labor. She and Ethan sheared their small flock of sheep just once a year, although some of the Quakers took the wool twice. The wool, about two pounds from each animal, was carefully washed to remove the excess oils and then dried before being stored. The flax plants were permitted to begin

rotting in piles, then pounded to remove the straight and strong fibers.
Most difficult and rarely used were cotton fibers, which had to be plucked
laboriously from each seed. Bundles of all these materials were stored in
the attic space and brought down for dyeing before being carded and spun.

Ethan thought often about his son, and during his frequent times alone
he was filled with an even stronger sense of anger and humiliation at the
death of his brother and having been cheated of his land. He was determined that it would never happen again, and that his son would be able to
work these fields in the future. When little Henry was older, they would begin to expand the cultivated land together, and he would apply for an additional land grant. Despite the apparent fairness of Governor James Wright
and his government, Ethan was distrustful of public officials and would always be careful in his dealings with them. At the same time, he had seen the
lawlessness of some of the Regulators who had violated the king's laws and
damaged the property of the courthouse workers in Hillsborough. All this
made him even more strongly inclined to live in relative seclusion, satisfied
to develop his farm, explore and hunt in the wilderness areas, and be alone
with Epsey and little Henry.

Ethan's life had always been one of hard work and rare moments of inactivity, but there were two things that he relished. Often with the baby's cradle nearby, Ethan took pride in making his own tools, furniture, and other
household furnishings, and enjoyed the hours in his workshop, mostly on
rainy days or when his other chores were not pressing. It was a special
pleasure to sit at his shaving bench, converting the split pieces from a recently cut white oak or hickory tree into hand rakes, hay forks, wooden
harrows, furniture, or household equipment for his wife to use. Some beautifully crafted chairs were a special source of pride. The clean splitting
of the straight-grained wood, the shaping of posts and rungs with his
drawknife and spokeshaves, the careful bending, fitting, and locking together of the pieces, and the final weaving of the seats were a pleasure for
him. There was always a sense of challenge and achievement, and a practical benefit when he loaded six of his chairs on a travois and dragged them
to the trading center, to be traded for supplies or some of the few pieces of
eight that he and his wife saved for future use.

The other great joy was his excursions in the wilderness with his two
dogs, his gun and traps, or just taking long trips, sometimes for a full day,

under the guise of exploring for future hunting or grazing opportunities. There were no game laws, but the frontiersmen knew about the habits and life cycle of wildlife, on which they depended for income and a major part of their families' diet. Ethan never shot a turkey hen from late March until the end of July, when it was laying eggs and raising the young poults until they could survive alone. During this time, Ethan knew that the gobblers still wanted sex, and he would conceal himself thoroughly and imitate the mating call of a hen by sucking on a hollow wing bone. When the gobbler came within range, he would harvest enough delicious meat to feed his family for several days. For the rest of the year, he took what turkeys he could find, and when he was lucky enough to kill more game than usual, Epsey would smoke the meat to preserve it. He wondered how soon his son might accompany him on some of these excursions, and planned how he would teach him the skills of a woodsman.

C HAPTER 11

The Pratts and the Morrises

1772

J oseph Maddock was an enthusiastic promoter and had many friends in the Northeast who spread the word about the availability of land in Georgia. More Quakers moved into the Wrightsborough area, so that within two years of Maddock's arrival there were almost one hundred families in the congregation. Now that the town was established, a larger portion of the new arrivals either decided not to farm or could not acquire suitable land, but they were quickly absorbed into the community if they had skills as blacksmiths, tanners, saddlers, shoemakers, or merchants, or were willing to work for hire. The moving water of the creeks provided the only power to be harnessed other than from draft animals. An invaluable service was provided by a sawmill, which substituted a waterwheel and a gear-driven saw blade for the backbreaking effort of two men who would cut boards by pulling an eight-foot-long ripping saw back and forth.

Ethan visited Wrightsborough as rarely as possible, usually just to trade his chairs and farm products for needed supplies. He and the Quaker

leader had never again mentioned their altercation during the trip southward, and Ethan took corn and wheat to Maddock's mill, where he and the
miller were polite to each other. On one visit there he noticed a slender
young man wading in the creek, scooping up dirt and sediment from the
bottom in a shallow pan, then examining it closely. As he bent over, totally
absorbed, his long black hair fell forward in front of his eyes, so that Ethan
wondered why he didn't tie it back in a pigtail. It was a bright late-winter
day, warmer than usual, but still too cold to be in the water, and after
watching for a few minutes, Ethan asked, "You found any color?"

The young man looked up, smiled, and said, "Hello. I'm not panning
for gold, but analyzing the crustaceans that live here."

Ethan was intrigued. "For what?"

"I'm hoping to identify and list all the living things of this area, both
plants and animals."

"How do you know what they are?"

It seemed that the man wanted to talk. "Oh, I have a few books that describe what grows in Europe, and if I can't find them I just write down what
they look like or draw a picture. Until I left Philadelphia last fall, I shared
this kind of information with a man named John Bartram, who is the king's
botanist in the colonies. His son is living on the Cape Fear River in North
Carolina and plans to come to Georgia next year. I have suggested that he
visit here in Wrightsborough."

The young man introduced himself as Kindred Morris and was eager to
show what he knew about the trees and shrubs around the creek and mill
house. Ethan was impressed to see him point to each plant and call out
both the common name and the Latin name. He asked about the strange
names, and Kindred explained that a Swedish professor named Linnaeus,
who taught at Uppsala University, had assigned the names.

Ethan asked, "And what was the professor's first name?"

Kindred replied, "Carolus," and then realized that Ethan was smiling
broadly at the excessively detailed lecture. He flushed with embarrassment, and then both men began to laugh. Ethan admitted that he had
never noticed most of the common varieties and thanked the young man
for the information.

He finally said, "My name is Ethan Pratt, and I live near here." Then
Ethan, who relished his privacy, was surprised to hear himself say, "You'd
be welcome to come out sometime and look at the things on my place."

"I know who you are, because I just got rights to the piece of land that lies east of yours. As you probably know, the family who owned it moved back up north and never built on it or cleared any land. My wife and I plan to move out there soon."

"I know the property very well. I figure you must not be a Quaker, if that's the land they gave you, that far from the settlement. But come on out, and we'll be glad to help you get settled. Sometime I'd like to look at your books. I know the animals fairly well but could use some help with the names of the plants and how they might be used." He didn't mention the similar books he had read in Epsey's Philadelphia home when he first met her.

Back home, Ethan mentioned the encounter to Epsey, who noticed that he was surprisingly enthusiastic about what he had learned during his few minutes with Kindred along the creek bank.

"Seems like looking at snails and crawfish is a waste of time, but it's all right if that's what he wants to do."

"Well, there's not much to be done this time of year if you don't have a place of your own. He and his wife will be moving out this way before long, to the place next to ours. I offered to help them get settled when they come."

Epsey was silent for a while and then said, "I guess that's the least we can do."

A few days later, Ethan began to hear the sound of an ax east of his farm. It was not his nature to take the initiative in an encounter and he refrained from investigating, but he found himself glancing down the trail each day, wondering when Kindred would appear. Fairly early one morning, he was under the lean-to astride his shaving horse, carefully fashioning staves that, after drying and planing, would go into the sides of a churn. He and Epsey already had one, and he was planning to make this one as a gift to the Morrises. He heard voices on the trail, young voices full of laughter, and looked expectantly toward the deep woods beyond his field of winter wheat, on which a few cattle were grazing for a few days before being moved off to let the crop mature. There were no leaves to impede his view, as the pine tree foliage began at least fifty feet up the trunk and the hardwoods were bare. Here on the high ground, only the beeches still carried last year's silvery brown leaves, not to be shed until the new leaves pushed them off the stems. The small limbs and leaves of all kinds had long ago been eaten as high as cattle could reach. Ethan finally glimpsed two figures moving toward his cabin and turned away, pretending a lack of interest in their approach. Only when they emerged into the clearing did he look up, express surprise, and move to his front door. He opened it and called softly to his wife, "Epsey, we've got company." She rose from her chair and joined him on the small porch, holding little Henry in her arms.

The first thing both of them noticed was that the young woman's bonnet was decorated with an elaborate pattern of lace, which would have aroused mild attention at a social affair when everyone put on their best, but was startling when worn in the woods or fields during the working week. She came forward without hesitation, almost skipping instead of walking, and greeted the Pratts.

"Hello, my name is Mavis. I guess you know that we'll be settling not too far up the trail toward Wrightsborough. I've really been wanting to meet our future neighbors, and especially since Kindred told me about Mr. Pratt's interest in trees and the things that live in creeks. We'll have a lot to talk about, won't we?"

She walked steadily toward Epsey and reached out for the baby, whom she was soon cuddling.

Ethan was somewhat disconcerted by her taking the initiative in the conversation, not giving her husband a chance to speak first, and looking directly into his eyes as she spoke, which was an almost unprecedented experience for him. After a few seconds, he turned to greet Kindred with a nod and a murmured welcome, while the two women began to exchange some polite words, mostly about little Henry.

Kindred said, "We didn't want to come over until both of us were here. For about ten days I've been living in a lean-to in the woods by myself, cutting some smaller trees and girdling the big ones where I'll be planting crops. But Mavis came out with me yesterday so we could pick out a place for our cabin. It's on a small knoll but near a spring so we won't need to dig a well. We've been working together gathering some flat foundation rocks and dragging the straight logs to the house site, but before we start to notch any out for the walls, we thought we'd best look and see how you did yours."

The two younger people had already spoken more words than the Pratts usually exchanged in an entire day.

Epsey finally said, "Well, we've been hoping for some neighbors, and we're glad to have you move out here. Come on inside and sit for a while."

The Morrises, particularly Mavis, were eager to talk and soon revealed a lot about themselves. They had both grown up in Philadelphia. Kindred had been born in 1752, was twenty years old when he married, but looked younger than his age. He was a small man, slender but wiry, with delicate features. Except for Mavis's bonnet, neither she nor her husband seemed to care about how they looked. Kindred's long black hair tended to fall forward in front of his light gray eyes, and he had a habit of brushing it back every few minutes.

Mavis was bright-eyed, talkative, and surprisingly frank with her comments. She was quite pretty, somewhat buxom but athletic, with curly yellow hair, disheveled and not quite encompassed in her bonnet. Mavis said that she was barely sixteen years old when she married. Her parents had died of typhus fever when she was twelve, and she was taken in by a relative and assigned to work in the home of Dr. John Bartram, under the supervision of a stern and dominant housekeeper. One day, she related with a laugh, Dr. Bartram had found her in his library making sketches of some of his specimens, and she was promoted "from sweeping floors to drawing bugs." She met Kindred when he came to the house to attend some talks on botany.

She paused for breath, and they all looked at Kindred.

"Ever since I was a child, I've been interested in plants and animals, and I saved up my money for the Bartram lecture series. He is the king's botanist, you know, and is famous both in the colonies and in England. I met Mavis there, and we got along well with each other. I like to study and also enjoy working outdoors, even including fieldwork. What I really want is to make enough on our farmland to let me concentrate on studying biology, both in books and in the woods—"

Mavis interrupted, as seemed to be her custom. "I was eager to find a husband who would take care of me and help provide for a life of our own. I liked Kindred when we met, and was able to talk him into getting married. Dr. Bartram didn't try to stop me when we made our plans to move away, but we agreed to continue with our nature studies and to send a copy of our journals back to him. He has traveled some in Georgia and Florida, knows Governor Wright, and helped arrange for us to get our land."

In a few words, Ethan described their background, including the fact that they also came from Philadelphia. He omitted any reference to the unpleasant events of their stay in North Carolina, just stating that they had decided to move to Georgia with their Quaker neighbors. Then he asked about their plans for the future.

Kindred replied, "Well, first of all we need to build a cabin, and then to establish a farming operation that will provide a living for us. We're already clearing some land, and we have enough money to start a small herd of cattle, sheep, and hogs. We'll be growing enough feed for them, will have a garden for ourselves, and will probably limit our cash crops to just enough to buy supplies."

Mavis said, "Our main interest is in biology, and we'll use our spare time to catalog as many specimens as possible. Kindred knows much more than I do, but I'll keep the journals and do the drawings. Dr. Bartram let us have some books that we're studying. I don't know why, but Kindred has a lot of interest in the natives, and we understand there's an Indian tribe near here."

Epsey looked at Ethan and said, "My parents had a great interest in bringing the Gospel to the Indians, but we haven't had much to do with them. A few come by here to visit on occasion, but mostly so Ethan can help them with blacksmithing or carpentering. We trade with them sometimes, and they haven't bothered us. It's too hard to exchange ideas, mostly by sign language. One of them knows a little English, but we haven't learned more than a few words of Creek, or whatever you call it."

Kindred replied, "I want to learn the language and also as much as possible about their way of living. Dr. Bartram has met some natives on his travels, but never learned much about them on his brief stops in the villages. He's interested in anything we can learn. As I told Mr. Pratt, I understand that his son William will be coming through Georgia next year, and we hope he will visit Wrightsborough."

Ethan asked, "What can we do to be of help to you?"

Kindred said immediately, "We want to look at how you built your cabin and outhouses, since this is our greatest need right now."

Ethan said, "You're welcome to look at our house. It's not much, but it keeps us dry and was simple to build. We corrected some of the mistakes we made on our first cabin in North Carolina. I thought I heard your ax a few times, and we were fixing to come over in a day or two, but didn't want to bother y'all."

The men began discussing, in general terms, some of the difficulties

Ethan had to overcome in building the cabin there and in North Carolina, while the two women went inside. Mavis still held the child as she politely admired the furniture, the spinning wheel and loom, the churn, and the fireplace fixtures, but after a few minutes she gave little Henry back to Epsey, excused herself, and went back out into the yard. She joined the men as they examined the solid rock foundation under the squared sills, and the logs, flattened on top and bottom, that made the walls. Ethan explained, step by step, how he had built the house, while Kindred and Mavis asked questions. It was obvious that she considered herself an equal participant in shaping plans for her home, and she did not hesitate in questioning some of the decisions Ethan had made in building his own. Their main discussion was how to notch the logs at the corners, and Kindred agreed with Ethan's rounding out a notch in each log to fit the contour of the one below.

They started to move on, but Mavis said, "Kindred, I think it would be better if the log ends were dovetailed, like in a cabin that Dr. Bartram built on his farm near Philadelphia."

Kindred was embarrassed by the implied criticism of Ethan's technique, and said, "But this is a simple method. Dovetails are much more complicated."

"No, in this way every curve is different, depending on the size of the log, and it's not easy to carve out a round shape with an ax. With dovetails, you can make a pattern, cut them all out on the ground exactly the same with nothing but straight ax strokes, and then just stack them in place. I liked the way Dr. Bartram had it done and made some sketches for him, which I still remember. The best thing is that it didn't take much trimming to make them all fit when they lifted the logs up. Here, let me show you."

She went to the wagon and got a notebook and pencil and quickly drew a sketch. Kindred didn't say anything, but Ethan examined the drawing and finally said, "I believe this would be better, and the logs would be locked in both directions."

Mavis took careful notes, jotting down the dimensions, sketching the construction details, counting the logs, and estimating the number of rocks required. Red clay, plentiful in the area, would be used for chinking between logs. With only one room, the main decisions to be made were whether to have a clay or a puncheon floor of split logs smoothed with an adze, and where to put the door and windows. For this discussion they moved into the cabin and sat with Epsey around the table. Like the Pratts,

Kindred and Mavis decided to use packed earth underfoot for the time being, but to leave the door, fireplace, and ceiling about a foot higher than was now needed, to accommodate a puncheon floor later on.

Mavis had a steady stream of questions and soon knew as much as possible about the Pratts' lives in Philadelphia, North Carolina, and there in the Quaker settlement. Epsey was more reluctant to pry into the personal affairs of the Morrises, but Mavis volunteered much of the information without being asked.

"Dr. Bartram suggested that we come to Wrightsborough because he was acquainted with Mr. Maddock and some of the other Quakers. When we arrived there and were waiting to get our land allotted, we lived in an attic room with a Quaker family named Fleming, and we took our meals with them."

Epsey asked, "Are you and Kindred of the Friends' faith?"

Mavis laughed. "Oh, no! We rarely ever went to church in Philadelphia, and never to a Quaker meeting. We attended twice with the Flemings, but those folks are too strict for me, and some of them made it plain that they didn't approve of my frivolous ways."

Epsey was somewhat disappointed with this answer and decided to change the subject.

"Do you have enough things to set up housekeeping?"

"Well, I didn't bring much with me, except a few cooking utensils, plus the quilts, sheets, and household linens that I reckon all young women are expected to make or buy before we get married. We're getting by, but we plan to buy some more things after our place is finished."

Ethan and Kindred soon turned the conversation back to the cabin construction. Epsey made a few suggestions on how their own fireplace and windows could be better located, and everyone agreed.

Ethan said, "I'll be over tomorrow to help you get the balance of the logs and rocks, and then we can put up the cabin together."

"No, I'd rather for me and Mavis get all the materials ready, which will give us a chance to train our two new oxen. Then I'll come and get you to help us put up the walls."

When they left, Ethan said, "He's not the kind of man I thought would be living way out here. He's still just a boy with bookish ways and doesn't look strong enough to cut down a tree. I doubt that he'll make a go of it."

Epsey noticed that he hadn't mentioned Mavis, but didn't comment on this. She replied, "Well, I think they'll be good neighbors. In any case, we need to help them all we can. I've got some things we can do without, and I'll get them ready to carry over when the time comes."

Ethan gave up his hunting for the next few days, ran his trapline as quickly as possible, and spent almost all of his time at his shaving horse and forge. Then, without waiting for a call from Kindred, he and Epsey loaded two new chairs, a small table, a churn, and a set of fireplace fixtures on their wagon and rode over to join their neighbors. They were surprised at how much work had been done and how precisely the rock foundation had been laid and the logs cut and notched. Even the ceiling joists and rafters were ready for assembly. Kindred was splitting three-foot-long pine shingles with a froe when they arrived, while Mavis was whittling locust pegs for fixing the joists to the top wall plate and tying the door and window frames to the wall logs.

Ethan said, "I don't see how you did this much in advance. I would have had to measure and cut the logs one by one as I put them up."

Kindred, pleased and somewhat embarrassed, replied, "Well, Mavis just made a careful drawing of what we learned at your house, and it was not hard to figure out what we would need. In fact, she cut all the dovetails, mostly with a saw and adze, while I dragged the logs up to the house site with the oxen."

Each day after that, Ethan rode his horse over to the Morris place and worked with them to erect the small house. It was finished within two weeks.

Ethan noticed with some bewilderment the relationship between Mavis and Kindred, which was quite different from how he and Epsey treated each other. They were more like a brother and sister, quite at ease, exchanging jokes and comments with complete abandon and arguing on an equal basis. On occasion, Mavis reached out with a feminine gesture, letting her fingers linger on Kindred's neck or pushing his hair back from his eyes, but her husband seemed almost unaware of her delicate caresses. These movements made a profound impression on Ethan, because Epsey had never taken any such physical initiative since they had known each other. He was the one who had reached out on increasingly rare occasions, and he had never expected Epsey to go any further than to fulfill her conjugal duties, which she did with minimal response or emotion.

They had been together only a week or so before Mavis felt enough at ease to make the same kinds of flirtatious gestures toward him. She seemed fascinated with the thick blond hairs on his arm and would stroke them on occasion. His arm jerked sharply when this first happened, but afterward he tried to ignore any physical contact between them, whether it seemed deliberate or accidental. On one occasion when the three of them were sitting by the Morrises' spring below the cabin for a noon rest and to eat, she looked up and caught his eyes on her. Her gaze never wavered and their eyes were locked for a few moments, and then he looked away and felt his face flush and his spine tingle. She gave a little laugh, and Kindred asked, "What's funny?" She replied, "Nothing, just a passing thought." For Ethan, the thought did not pass, but lingered.

To an extraordinary degree, Ethan had become the unshakable focus of Kindred's trust and admiration. Mavis assumed that this indicated a natural respect and admiration for a man who was older and who had become a teacher and a role model for them both as the couple set up housekeeping and established and assumed frontier life.

Solitude was what Ethan had always relished most, but now, for a change, he often asked Kindred to join him, and they formed a friendship that he had never thought possible. They hunted and trapped together for meat, skins, and for small animal and insect specimens, which they studied carefully. At first, Ethan waited impatiently when Kindred lagged behind to examine something along the way. Then Ethan became an eager student as his neighbor shared his knowledge of the growing things that surrounded them. The men discussed some of the generic relationships, and Kindred carefully preserved and made notations in his notebook about those that seemed to be new and different species.

As time went on, they shared more and more mutual interests. Ethan was familiar with the practical aspects of farming, carpentry, blacksmithing, and life in the forests and swamps, and took pleasure in teaching Kindred what he knew. They felt at ease, learning from each other. Ethan borrowed one of the Morrises' most treasured books, written by Linnaeus, whom Kindred had mentioned when they'd first met under the mill. Ethan tried to learn more about how plants and animals were named and related to one another.

Although she didn't say anything, Epsey looked forward to planting time, when she knew that Ethan would not neglect his duties in their own fields. On occasion, when the men were away and their own household chores were not pressing, the women visited with each other, always at the Pratt cabin. They found it pleasant to spend these hours together, with at least a small cooking fire going on the hearth, fed with more logs during cool or rainy days. Without prior arrangement, Mavis would walk the mile or so, usually bringing with her some of the raw materials used for making cloth.

Epsey was a skilled weaver, and Mavis asked how she had learned the craft.

"My mother had a loom in our house in Philadelphia and would sometimes weave as much as three yards a day. She taught me how to use it as soon as my feet would reach the pedals, and I've always enjoyed the work. Except for a little calico, I've woven almost all our cloth since I left home. The biggest job is the carding and spinning."

"I hope you will teach me how to do it all. What kind of fibers are your favorites?"

"I'll be glad to show you. Wool and flax are the easiest, and I mix in some cotton, but it's tedious to separate the seeds."

While the baby crawled around the cabin, they sat side by side carding fibers, and Mavis watched closely when Epsey was spinning or weaving, asking questions and trying to learn the techniques herself. Later, while Epsey was carding or preparing food, Mavis soon learned to turn the large spinning wheel with a foot pedal, leaving both hands free to spin the carded and rolled fibers into thread.

The crafting of a spinning wheel and loom required a lot of skill, and Epsey was especially proud that Ethan had made the one she used. He was now helping Kindred make another one for Mavis, using Epsey's as a pattern. Together, they had split out a thin piece of white oak eleven feet long and had it drying slowly in a circular shape, later to become the wheel itself. The wheel hub, spokes, posts, and spindles were turned on Ethan's lathe.

The fibers were dyed before carding, and Epsey shared her knowledge of the process while Mavis made notes. Except for indigo, the colors were somewhat drab, but better for normal wear than the dingy white of the natural fibers.

"We get most of our dye from walnut hulls, which give me shades of color from light tan to dark brown, depending on how long I boil it together. I can get it even darker by adding the bark from walnut roots. If I want black, I use witch-hazel tree bark. Yellow comes from the outer bark of hickory and oak, or from broomstraw. I get a clear blue from indigo, which almost everybody grows, or a lighter shade from the inner bark of maple. Red comes from madder, pokeberries, blackberries, or red clay, purple from pokeberry roots, and green from green oak leaves. When I have time, I get green by dyeing the fibers yellow first, and then blue. Then I use salt as a mordant, to set the color and make it permanent."

Sometimes they would blend wool with flax and perhaps some cotton to make a lighter material that was still warm and durable, called linsey-woolsey. The women developed an ease with each other, even when they remained silent for long periods of time, but they also discussed their common family affairs, garden projects, the drying, smoking, or salt-curing of meats, and always the status of the baby.

Although she was only a few years younger, Mavis treated Epsey almost with the deference of a child for a parent, and Epsey was drawn to the younger woman by this attitude and by fascination with her ingenuous attitude toward life. When Epsey seemed in the mood for conversation, Mavis bubbled over with unrestrained comments and questions, particularly about Epsey's earlier years, her marriage, childbearing, and almost every aspect of the frontier lives that they now shared. Perhaps without knowing why, Mavis refrained from mentioning the outings she sometimes shared with the two men.

Epsey enjoyed answering the questions and, on occasion, even asked a few herself.

"Why do you always wear lace around your bonnet, even out here in the backwoods?"

Mavis laughed. "I get a lot of comments or strange looks about my bonnets.

"I was twelve years old when both my parents died with typhus fever, and I was taken in by my father's cousin, who was a widow. She was good to me, but had very little, even for her own three children. She made lace for one of the shops in Philadelphia, and taught me to tat.

"About two years later, she realized that she could not support all of us, and arranged for me to go and work for Dr. Bartram, who was a famous lecturer in biology. Even after I left my cousin's home and took on this work, I would still make lace in my spare time and take it to her on my visits so she could fill more orders.

"When I met Kindred and we decided to be married, she called me in and wanted to add her own gift to the things I had made for my wedding chest. It was a box of the most beautiful lace, except for one strip, which I recognized as the first piece I ever tatted. I was surprised that she had kept it, and told her that I would wear some of her lace every Sunday. She replied that lace was not just for special occasions and she hoped I would remember her every day, so I promised to wear a piece of lace whenever I put on my bonnet. It's the only thing I have to remind me of those earliest days, of my own family. I still tat every now and then, and I've become used to wearing the fancy-looking bonnets. They last just as long as the plain ones, and Kindred doesn't seem to mind."

"Tell me a little more about Kindred."

"Dr. Bartram gave lectures in his large house, charging each of his students a small fee. One of the most eager learners was Kindred, who would absorb everything taught to the group and search for anything extra that was available concerning the flora and fauna of the colonies. He saw that I assisted Dr. Bartram by sketching some of his specimens and arranging the materials for his lectures, and began asking me questions. When I learned that he was thinking about finding some land for a farm somewhere in the west, I saw it as an opportunity to have a new life and maybe a family. I really took the initiative, but it just seemed that both of us decided at the same moment to be married and move off together."

She added, as though it was necessary, "I'm not sure about having a family, but we have a great time together. We love our biology work, and stay in touch when possible with the Bartrams. We've just learned for sure that William, the son, will be coming to Wrightsborough, and we are helping to make preparations for his visit. The farm is a real challenge for us, but we enjoy the hard work. Kindred is determined to do as well as Ethan, although both of us know this won't be possible. No one could match Ethan."

"Y'all do well enough. Kindred has taught as much as he's learned."

A long silence followed, and their next topic was about household duties.

Watching Mavis and Kindred having good times together, almost like children, Ethan considered his own personal habits and priorities with some embarrassment. He and Epsey had a mutually respectful relationship, each appreciating the good qualities of the other, willing to forgive or ignore habits that might be somewhat aggravating. In effect, they lived as partners, operating the farm and caring for household duties, each immersed in the hard work of frontier life. He spent almost all his time girdling more trees, clearing new ground, building fences, tending his beehives, and laboring almost without ceasing in the fields and among his hogs and cows. In the wintertime he worked in his shop, making and repairing the things he and Epsey used, and taking every opportunity to work his traplines and to hunt for deer, wild turkey, and an occasional black bear. She kept the house and small yard almost immaculate and took great pride in her large garden. In addition, she was always eager to hoe in the fields and to care for any sick animals that were confined to the lot, and was strong enough to do this while carrying little Henry. Although she offered, Ethan never permitted her to plow.

Ethan didn't worry much but had a constant commitment to produce enough surplus corn, wheat, tobacco, honey, and some cows and hogs to be traded along with his hides in Wrightsborough or Augusta. They needed salt, some cloth, powder and shot, rough iron that could be made into tools, and occasionally more frivolous things like rum and tea when the upriver price was lowered by a recent shipment into Savannah. He had never before felt guilty where his hard work was concerned, when he was away from Epsey, but now he realized that he was being selfish when he left his duties and spent a number of hours each week with the Morrises.

After each of those visits he would come back to his own cabin still filled with the wonder of some natural discovery, a new species they had found, or perhaps just a startling fact about one of the birds, animals, or plants that had long been part of his life. He would find himself in an effervescent mood, the excitement of his newfound knowledge and personal companionship not yet fully faded. It was obvious that Epsey did not have much interest in learning more about botany or biology, and after a few attempts to share his feelings he learned that it aroused in her a totally uncharacteristic resentment, and drove something of a wedge between them.

Epsey did ask a few questions about their experiences, apparently to be polite, and inquired a couple of times if Mavis had gone along with them. It made Ethan uncomfortable to report that the three of them had been together, and after that, by emphasizing the hunting and trapping and by other means, he tried to limit his brief report of the trips to include only the two men.

Somewhat against her will, Mavis was excluded from some of the men's forays, but she always joined in the discussions when they were in the Morris cabin comparing their notes with the texts and illustrations in the books. Having helped John Bartram for several years with preparation for his lectures, she was often more familiar with the specimens than Kindred, and it was she who tabulated the collected data and added the final sketches to the notebooks. She was always eager to teach Ethan when he lingered after an excursion in the woods and swamps.

As the spring progressed, much of Ethan's time had to be spent in his own fields and pastures, and his relationship with Epsey became more natural again as they shared common chores. There were times of excitement when their son stood alone, took his first steps, and finally began to say a few words. But during planting and harvest seasons, it was inevitable that the two families would find it convenient to cooperate in some tasks that related to their farmwork. The men shared a small still, which produced enough whiskey for their families' medicinal needs, and they planned to make a few gallons of wine each summer from the wild muscadines and fox grapes that were plentiful in the forest. They also worked together on the forge, where Kindred usually pumped the bellows and Ethan, at his anvil, would do the rudimentary blacksmithing jobs required on their farms. They shod their own horses, made and sharpened iron points to fit on the wooden plowshares, and crafted tools and a few other items, including the hinges and latches for the main doors of their two houses. They made andirons for their fireplaces, where they cooked all meals, along with fire pokers and tongs, iron hooks, ladles, and large forks.

During their visits together, Mavis was willing and even eager to discuss any subject with Epsey. Although Mavis had made some initial frank comments, she realized that the older woman was reticent to share information about anything personal except the achievements of little Henry.

One afternoon, however, while the baby was sleeping, Mavis surprised Epsey by asking, "Epsey, do you and Ethan sleep together?"

After some hesitation, she replied, "As you can see, we have separate cots."

"That's really not what I mean. As between husband and wife?"

Not wanting to discuss her most intimate affairs or admit how seldom they had intercourse, Epsey responded, "Well, how do you suppose we got little Henry?"

"Well, that's what I meant, but I don't know if we'll ever have children.

After we were married I tried everything I could—in a decent way, of course—but Kindred didn't seem to find me attractive in that way. Finally I got him to talk about it, and he said he looked on me more like his sister. I guess I'm just not physically attractive to him."

Not wishing to pursue this subject further, Epsey responded, "Well, I've never seen any husband and wife who got along better than you two. Y'all seem interested in the same things, and I don't remember ever noticing any anger between you."

"That's true, and I'm thankful for it. We have a lot of arguments, like how best to frame in a window or about identifying a bird or a flower, and I have as much of a voice in making decisions as he does."

While their thoughts and discussion turned to safer things, Epsey could understand exactly how Kindred must feel about the things that happened in bed. She had always felt that there was something wrong with "knowing" each other, as the Bible said, and had a feeling of guilt after she and Ethan acted in that way. God had blessed them with their baby, but now that another was unlikely, she could find no justification for further intimacy of this kind. She also felt that Ethan's dominant role in making family decisions was compatible with the teachings of the Holy Scriptures.

CHAPTER 12

The Neighboring Indians

The Morrises considered themselves to have a good life. They did not object to the hard work in the fields, relished the isolation of their homeplace, and neither they nor any of the other Wrightsborough settlers were abused by the colonial authorities in Augusta or Savannah. The white families also had the apparent goodwill of the neighboring Indians, most of whom lived peacefully across the Ogeechee River. There was one native village on the riverbank that was only five miles from the Morrises' farm, located on land that had been ceded previously. The Creek families had simply stayed where they were, since there had been no demand for this particular place from white settlers.

Kindred was fascinated with the natives, and as soon as their cabin was completed, he had begun to visit the Indian village as often as possible. He almost memorized the two books he owned about their culture, and tried in every way to be sensitive and respectful in his dealings with them. He was naturally kind and gentle, and made his Indian friends feel like superior instructors as they answered inquiries about their way of life and taught him their language. He quickly learned to converse with relative ease, using a combination of signs and, with every visit, more of their words.

Kindred soon knew almost everyone in the village, and some of them reciprocated by asking questions about the habits and motivations of the white settlers. He talked to men of all ages, but most often to one older woman called Soyarna, who was the chief's sister. The villagers turned to her for medical advice, and Kindred asked her a stream of questions about the plants in the forests and how different ones might be used for medicinal purposes. In return, he shared with her some of the knowledge he had derived from his own books and personal observations. Kindred was eager to please his new friends and sought every opportunity to bring them small gifts, to help solve some of their problems, to provide improved seeds, and he even did some simple blacksmith work for them, using Ethan's forge.

Kindred and Mavis kept a careful journal of this information, which at first he shared eagerly with Ethan and Epsey, but he soon saw that only Epsey showed any interest in what he was learning from the Indians. Although Ethan never spoke about the natives harshly and dealt fairly with those few he knew, his natural attitude was to let them mind their own business so long as they didn't bother him. He seemed to consider these activities of his neighbor to be a waste of time, taking Kindred away from his farm chores—and from Ethan, on days when it was too wet to work in the fields and the two could have been hunting, fishing, or exploring together. Kindred felt this disapproval from Ethan, but there was some consolation in being used as an intermediary when Ethan needed to trade with the Indians or communicate with them about something of common interest.

Kindred and Mavis tried to make a scholarly comparison between the settlers and the nearby Indians, and they found surprising differences between their living conditions. Kindred knew that some of the Indians near the older settlements in Pennsylvania had adopted improved agricultural practices of the Europeans and were planting the same varieties of corn, sweet potatoes, wheat, buckwheat, tobacco, and sugarcane. However, their Indian neighbors in Georgia still used traditional farming practices, what the Europeans called "swidden." They cleared small plots of cropland in an area by cutting through the bark layers of the large trees, removing smaller trees and bushes for firewood, and burning the remaining trash and ground debris. They were then free to plant among the dead trees and stumps by poking holes in the ground with a pointed stick and planting several seeds in the same hill, primarily corn and yams, but also beans, sunflowers, and even vines that produced pumpkins, squash, and gourds. This small area was cultivated the same way for a few years, until the soil nutrients were depleted and a new area had to be cleared. Usually, within five years or so, the soil around an entire village was no longer productive and, with the game and fish also depleted, the village had to be moved. One adverse consequence of this was to give proof to the Europeans' claim that the Indians were nomads and not fixed to any particular place, and therefore should not object to moving farther westward.

With few exceptions, the women did all the work in these small plots, which were mostly just large gardens. The crops were for their own consumption and were combined with roots and leaves from edible plants and meat from the animals and fish that the hunters brought home. Tobacco was also an ancient and important product, smoked for pleasure and in peace ceremonies.

Multicolored corn was the dominant crop, and the annual Green Corn Ceremony, or Busk, was the most sacred holiday. Men and women were separated, the village cleaned, the existing fires extinguished; then everyone bathed, the shaman relighted the sacred fire, and all crimes, except murder, were forgiven. Then the clan feasted, and women took coals from the central place and started new fires in their own wigwams.

Although Kindred denied Ethan's statement that the natives were inherently lazy, he had to admit that they were comparatively indolent when compared with the white settlers, with their long workdays and constant striving to produce as much food and fiber as possible for their own use or sale. While the Indian women tended the crops, cooked, or cared for children, the men spent most of their time hunting, trapping, sleeping, and training for combat. By the standards of the settlers, the natives paid little attention to comfortable or secure shelter. Even their more permanent homes were much smaller and more loosely constructed than those of the whites, little more than lean-tos made of limbs, grass, and deerskins. Kindred noticed that several times a year those closest to the river were flooded with water more than a foot deep.

The Creeks had a matrilineal society, with all members of a clan related to one ancestress through her female descendants, although on some rare occasions an outsider could be adopted. The clans were named for animals, aspects of nature, or even plants, such as Wolf, Turkey, Deer, Bear, Wind, Fox, or Potato. Loyalty to the clan, or family, was the most important aspect of life, more so than to the tribe, village, or anything else. Members of a clan lived close to one another, often within the same compound, and one of the Wolf clan would likely stay with his clan brothers when visiting in another village, but would be forbidden to marry a girl from a Wolf family. Children of both sexes were considered to be progeny of the mother and members of her clan, with sons trained by the mother's oldest brother. The husband and father, who was not a member of the clan, performed this service in his sister's family.

Among white settlers who were objective in their attitude toward the Indians, the Cherokee, Creek, Seminole, Catawba, and Choctaw people were known as the "five civilized tribes" of the southeast. This opinion was shaped primarily because they were less warlike and depended more on agriculture and the requisite permanence of village sites than the more mobile tribes of the north and west, who moved frequently to accommodate the changing hunting seasons. Few white settlers could detect any significant differences among the Indians, except for some minor clothing habits, and had little interest in learning more about the natives. The immediate neighbors of the Pratts and Morrises were Upper Creeks, whose lands were near the undefined border with the Cherokee nation that controlled most of north Georgia. Kindred learned that there had been a long history of military conflict between the Indians, but there was relative peace now as they faced a common enemy, the constantly encroaching white settlers.

One day, early in July, Kindred was examining plants alongside a small tributary stream of the Ogeechee when he smelled a foul odor and traced the scent to a growth of purple blossoms. He knelt among them and saw that they were trilliums, with their generic triple leaves and blossoms. As he examined them closely he felt that he was being watched, but could not see anyone when he looked around. Some minutes later he thought he heard a twig snap and quickly turned in the direction of some willow saplings alongside the stream above him. He remained still for a minute or two, examining the area closely, but could see nothing. Finally, he turned back and prepared to collect a sample of the plants so he could identify it from his books at home. A shadow fell across him, and he looked up to see a young Indian, not quite his age, who had approached silently and was watching with a slight smile on his face. He was taller than Kindred, with a slender waist and surprisingly broad shoulders. His hair was parted in the middle and tied in back. He was barefoot, his only clothing a leather strip between his legs, with each end tucked into a thong around his waist.

They examined each other carefully, and Kindred was determined not to break the long silence. The Indian seemed friendly and finally said, "If I was an enemy, you would be dead."

Kindred replied, not altogether truthfully, "No, you broke a stick and revealed yourself."

After a moment, the Indian asked, "Do you have a bad wound to cure?"

Kindred was perplexed by the question and assumed that his limited knowledge of the language had caused him to misunderstand.

"I don't know what you mean."

"This plant is sometimes used to treat rotting flesh, since it has the same smell."

"If so, I think it may be what we call *Trillium erectum,* which is found in the northern colonies and has been used for the same purpose, and also for the pain of childbirth. How do you know about it?"

"I am Newota, and my mother, Soyarna, uses plants for treatment of illness in our village. I am learning from her and from my uncle."

"My name is Kindred, and my home is two hours' walk to the east. I have an interest in all the living things in this area, including insects, birds, animals, and plants."

Newota was silent for a few moments and then said, "I know about you from my mother. You have been to my village several times while I was with my uncle in a northern tribe. Except for traders, you are the first white man who has done so. My mother says that you ask many questions, not just about plants and animals but even more about our history and customs. For what purpose do you study us? We have had only disease, cheating, and lies from those of you who have settled our land. And why do you examine these plants if it is not for healing or as part of your religion?"

These questions were difficult to answer, and Kindred had never addressed them even in his own thoughts. He finally gave an inadequate response.

"I try to learn about people and things for my own enjoyment and for knowledge, and so that I can share it with others who have similar interests. I hope to put this information to good use whenever possible."

Newota nodded and said, "I can understand your desire to learn, and perhaps you may be able to teach others when you are much older. My own purpose is to use plants to ease pain, which is also a path to manhood as a medicine man." He was surprised to hear himself add, "And perhaps a tribal leader."

Both young men were pleased with the ease of their communication and the personal revelation of their ideas and ambitions for the future. They walked over to a nearby fallen log, sat down, and continued to explore mutual interests. Newota made it clear that he also wanted to learn about living things that were not of immediate benefit, and about the culture and even the language of the white settlers.

"This would be helpful to my people," he said.

From then on, the two young men met frequently and visited each other's home. In order to become more proficient in the two languages, each spoke in the tongue of the other and they prompted with new words and corrected mistakes, often with laughter. Kindred discovered that the Indian "boy" was almost eighteen years old and was contemplating marriage. Newota explained the mating customs of both the Creeks and Cherokees, and the procedure that he would have to follow when he decided to take a wife. On his recent trip a girl had been indicated that he might want, who lived in his uncle's village and was of another clan. If he gave the word, the aunts or mothers of both would try to arrange a marriage.

Kindred asked, "How about the father?"

Newota replied, "A father would be kept informed but has no role to play in the process of mating. If the girl wants to indicate her consent, she will set a bowl of hominy outside her dwelling at a prearranged time. Then, if I want to proceed, I will ask for some, and she can agree or not. If the answer is yes, my clan will offer gifts to the girl, and sexual relations are then permitted."

He paused, as if pondering the prospect, and Kindred asked, "What is the next step?"

"I would have to prove my manhood and my seriousness by building a dwelling in her clan area and then by killing an animal for food. When we share the food, which she will cook, this is the wedding ceremony, but it is only a trial marriage for a year. If either of us finds it to be a mistake, the man will move back to his clan, leaving the woman with the house.

"I don't think this will apply to me, but if it proves to be a good marriage, the woman may give permission for the man to take other wives, who would most likely be the wife's sisters or cousins. If another woman is chosen, she has the right to have a new dwelling."

Kindred found that Newota did not share his embarrassment about discussing intimate issues. He explained, "Girls can have sex before marriage, but after marriage they are not expected to lie with any man except their husband. This is an act that can dissolve the marriage, still leaving a woman with the house but subjecting her to severe punishment by the tribe, such as the severing of an ear. A widow is expected to mourn for four years and not remarry, but can remarry earlier with permission of her husband's clan."

Kindred hesitated before asking, "And what progress did you make in this procedure?"

Newota smiled and said, "I decided not to eat the hominy."

During their subsequent meetings the two young men exchanged information about general tribal affairs and the botanical specimens. Although Kindred could identify them from his books and his own knowledge, Newota knew how each might be used to advantage. He wanted to be both a warrior and a medicine man and had learned about curing plants from his mother and also through disciplined training from an exalted medicine man, known as a *hillis haya*.

They enjoyed challenging each other with queries concerning the medicinal values and identification of plants. Kindred would mention fever, and Newota would name wolfsbane, woodbine, and willow bark, and tell him that some of these could also help with arthritis or pain. Wolfsbane root, he said, could be poisonous. Diarrhea could be controlled by ground pine, which looked like a vine with pine needles, and menstrual cramps were treated with black haw and spikenard. Eye diseases were treated with nightshade, which was also a strong narcotic. Kindred already knew this plant as belladonna. They laughed about some of the names and uses.

Puke weed was used to induce vomiting, and passionflower was effective against both depression and hemorrhoids.

Newota explained that it was the men's job to get meat, and they began learning the techniques of hunting and trapping at a very early age. Even little boys knew how to snare birds, squirrels, opossums, raccoons, and rabbits, and they soon learned to use blowguns and small bows and arrows to kill the quarry. After they were accepted as mature members of the tribe and given an adult name, they spent much of their time hunting the more elusive, larger game, especially white-tailed deer, turkey, and an occasional bear. Good hunters attempted to adopt the habits and even the character of their quarry, and to imitate the animal sounds as realistically as possible.

Kindred asked about the women.

Newota continued, "Our women are closer to the earth than the men and are taught to be self-reliant. They care for the crops and gather fruit, nuts, and edible roots. At childbirth, a woman is prepared in body and mind to be alone during this holiest of times, to deliver her baby and then to bring it back into the village as a gift. The young child is her responsibility. The new-born baby is rolled in snow or dipped in cold water, rubbed with bear grease, and bound to a cradle board for the first year of its life. Almost always held next to its mother, the child, especially if it was premature or weak, benefits from constant care, frequent feedings, and the mother's body warmth. She begins training her infant in the value of silence and respect for elders. Soon her brothers and sisters join in both instruction and discipline. Children are not to be noisy, must never interrupt an adult who is speaking, and are chastised severely if they walk between their elders and a fire or commit some other impolite act. As a youth, I could never join in a discussion unless questioned directly by one of the adults.

"As early as I can remember, I had to be learning. When quite small we were required to spend an hour or so without moving, just observing carefully the action of a hill of ants, a swarm of bees, birds building a nest, or fish guarding a bed where their eggs were laid. Later, we were expected to study other animals and were deliberately embarrassed if we could not answer questions about their habits. My uncle would recite long lists of things or events, and I was expected to memorize them without mistake. When sent to a destination, I had to describe in detail what I had observed, seemingly about the most insignificant things."

Kindred described his early life, including his timid attempts to protect his mother from the severe discipline of his father. He had been apprenticed to a merchant as a delivery boy, and his life had been changed when he'd called on Dr. Bartram, who introduced him to the study of plants and insects, primarily from books and preserved specimens. When not working, it seemed he'd spent much of his early life in learning to read and write. He was somewhat surprised to realize how much of his learning had come from books, and how little from personal observation.

As they moved through the forest, by day and night, Newota taught Kindred about the heavens. Even when the North Star was not visible, he could easily determine the direction of north by observing key constellations or individual stars, or by a glance at the moon at any time of day. Newota was always aware of the surrounding topography, the general slope of hills, the flow of even the smallest of streams, or the direction of prevailing winds. He knew that certain insects placed their cocoons or nests on the south sides of trees or rocks, where the warmth of the sun was most prevalent. When none of these indicators was immediately available, Newota could move in a straight line until he found one of them, avoiding the natural human tendency to travel in a circle. He always had a sense of belonging wherever he was and was confident of finding a destination, even when uncertain about his exact location.

Newota explained, "In peace or as warriors, success comes to those who are most completely at one with the forests and swamps. We learn the advantages of patience, how to wait concealed and without movement for hours at a time. As a baby we are taught to endure extreme cold or other pain without crying or flinching. When I was a boy my uncle required me to immerse myself daily in the creek, even when there was ice on the surface."

Kindred noticed that Newota would never hesitate to swim a stream even in the coldest weather, then emerge from the other side and continue on his way as though it were summertime. Newota criticized the settlers' constant grasping for ever more territory, and added, "Our people have never wanted to possess land as our own. I love the earth and all its creatures. I sit and lie on it to gain strength. I prefer bare feet to moccasins. Some of the older people consider it sacrilegious even to plow the ground. How can any person or even a tribe claim to own the earth? Can we declare exclusive right to the wind, the sunshine, or the flowing water?"

Kindred was sympathetic with these feelings and replied, "Well, it really amounts to the same thing if your tribes claim rights to hunt and fish in certain areas and reserve the use of some fields for growing corn and pota-toes."

Newota continued, "This has been our history, but we now face a diffi-cult future. My uncle explains what is happening. The great king across the sea has forbidden any settlement in Indian lands, but your people pay little attention to his proclamations. Our people are hungry for merchandise from Europe and are constantly outtraded. Some have quit growing our own food. They prefer to exchange deerskins and furs for corn and meat. The factor who comes to our village collects the cured skins, assures their quality, binds them into bundles, and then has only one buyer with whom to trade. We are always at a disadvantage when the traders reach an agree-ment, but the reaction of our people is just to be grateful when they can buy goods on credit, regardless of the cost. There is no doubt that your po-litical leaders encourage and even pay merchants to ensure that our people are always in debt. They know that we have only our land to repay what we owe."

Kindred intended to ask about trade with the Indians on his next visit to the town, but he didn't have to wait that long. One day he was working in the blacksmith shop and Ethan was giving him some advice on when the metal should be hammered, and how rapidly to quench its heat for maxi-mum hardness and strength. They looked up when a horseman ap-proached and saw that it was Reuben Starling, who represented the district Indian agent. He told them he was on the way to Indian territory and had stopped for a drink of water.

Kindred asked, "Mr. Starling, tell us how you came to be a trader, and something about how you do it."

Starling seemed glad of a chance to talk about himself. "Well, first of all, my license could only be issued by Indian Superintendent John Stuart, who directly represents the king. I had to show familiarity with some of the lan-guages, post a bond, and swear my own loyalty to the crown. I am really a part of the government and make my own reports on the situation among the Indians and spread whatever information is given to me."

"Are you free to trade where and how you wish?"

Starling laughed. "Sure, just as long as I stay in my assigned villages and pay the established price for pelts. I'm responsible for the quality and weight of them, and have a factor in each group of villages who collects the skins, makes sure they are cured right, weighs them, and binds them in bundles of about fifty pounds each, so I can carry three or four on a pack-horse. We want all we can get, so we will advance to a good hunter five pounds of powder, twelve pounds of bullets, and British goods equal to about thirty pounds of skins. I also have a list of prices for the goods we trade, but all of us consider them to be the bottom price, and we get all we can. Every village is pretty far in debt right now."

"Suppose another man comes in and offers the Indians a better deal?"

"We have our own villages and nobody else can trade in them. If any of us do illegal trades like this, the Indian superintendent will revoke our license and we'll be arrested."

"How about the people that work for you? Won't they trade on the side?"

"We can't hire a Negro, half-breed, or even a white man who has taken on Indian ways of living."

When Starling rode away, Kindred exclaimed, "It's a damned shame the way they cheat the Indians! Something ought to be done about it."

Ethan was surprised. "What do you mean? They don't have to trade if they don't want to. They're the ones who beg for the goods, kill the deer, and buy more than they can pay for. There's just one man that trades for the whole village and one man that sells to him. What's unfair about that?"

"But they are too ignorant to know how to trade."

"Kindred, you're wrong as hell. They're shrewd enough to make agreements and sign treaties that they don't carry out. You yourself are always telling me how smart your friend Newota is. Besides, they can always pay off their debts when they come to Augusta to work out a new deal on land."

Kindred decided not to reply, and went home as soon as his tools were repaired and sharpened.

Now when Kindred was with Newota, fishing, hunting, trapping, or exploring, they discussed the relationship between the Indians and the whites more than the characteristics of plants and animals.

Kindred said, "I know that some of your own people have lived with us and then come back to the tribes. Don't they learn how much we have in common and how to get along with each other?"

"Yes, a few have lived with white men and later returned to their families, but with little knowledge of the earth or forests. They cannot tell the simplest of odors, bear either hunger or cold, and cannot walk silently, kill a deer, or survive without assistance from others. They wish to wear heavy clothes and sleep under many blankets. Some have learned how to be good farmers, usually a woman's work, but they can run only a few miles and have no knowledge of how to hunt and defeat an enemy or even protect their own home and village. There is no swearing in our language, but they bring back filthy words. Like many of us have now become, they are obsessed with the love of possessions and an easy way of life.

"When white traders use them in negotiations for pelts, we know that their loyalty is to the one who pays them. We do not trust them, and they are ridiculed. One old man said that the Indian agent was so stingy that he carries a white rag in his pocket and blows his nose in it for fear that he will blow away something valuable!"

They both enjoyed the joke and continued their walk through the woods. Newota continued his discourse.

"There are other things that we find amusing. We eat in silence, perhaps smoke a pipe, nod to each other, and depart. Thus, we honor our host. Our leaders who have been to Savannah tell us that white men eat noisily, finding it necessary to talk constantly. A brief period of silence seems to be embarrassing. After the food and drink are consumed, the guests are expected to say foolish things before departing."

One day they discussed a belief in God, and Newota said, "We observe your religion and do not want it. For instance, we consider all days to be holy, and not just one out of seven. Your churches seem to teach people to quarrel about God. We never have disputes about the nature of the Great Spirit or how we relate to him. We may hear contrary opinions at different times, but we try to weigh the character of the ones who speak and keep our judgments to ourselves. The Spirit does not give us reasons for quarreling and divisiveness, but is a unifying life force that binds all humans together with each other, and with the animals, birds, the wind, and even the rocks and earth. Everything is connected. We respect the spirit even of the animals we kill for food, and seek their forgiveness when their lives are taken."

Kindred felt that he should defend his people, and said, "If your beliefs are so superior, then why are you afraid of the inferior settlers?"

"Well, you already know that your numbers are increasing rapidly, your weapons are superior, and your diseases are fatal to our tribes. I have heard my uncle and my mother discussing another difference between us that they consider to be most important. You white men, at least your leaders, are taught to look far into the future and make plans accordingly. These ideas are set down in writing so they can be shared with many others. Then it becomes a commitment among many people to pursue those distant goals. We don't think in this way, but are inclined to limit our planning to the hour, or at most to the few days that are required to complete a journey, to plant a garden, or to carry out a military operation against another tribe. This makes it difficult for our chiefs to comprehend the agreements that your leaders entice them to accept."

Kindred responded, "Most of what you say is true, but your chiefs enter into these agreements voluntarily and later blame the whites for the consequences."

"The fact is that none of our chiefs can speak with authority for more than a few villages. Your leaders exalt them with honors of leadership they do not deserve and bribe them with gifts so they betray their own people. They know that when they return home they have no power to enforce what they have promised, but the white men have a paper that was signed without our understanding what was in it. Even then, the white leaders only observe an agreement as long as it is to their advantage."

Kindred became increasingly concerned about the abuse of his new friends, and his animosity grew toward the white settlers who despised the Indians as savages and looked upon them as interlopers on lands that God had ordained to be occupied by white men. It was painful to Kindred, who was somewhat shy and inarticulate among relative strangers, to remain mute when he heard crude jokes about the stupidity or filthiness of the Creek men and the animal-like sex habits of the squaws. He also observed that what the Wrightsborough merchants charged for trade items was quite flexible, boosted substantially by even the reputable and trusted merchants when the natives were forced by urgent need to purchase supplies in the village.

He recalled the attitude of the Quakers of Philadelphia, who had prided themselves on treating the Delaware Indians justly, claiming that their agreements had never been violated although no papers were signed. They chortled, however, over one example of shrewd trading, when William Penn had concluded an agreement to acquire land between two rivers "as far as a man could walk in a day and a half." He had then hired a champion runner who traversed sixty-six miles in the allotted time.

One day, while returning from the town with Ethan, Kindred criticized one of the merchants whom he had observed trading with an old Cherokee, and was shocked by his friend's reaction.

Fully confident of his natural status as leader, Ethan said, "Kindred, you are being ridiculed by the folks around here. They see you as being totally misled by the savages and ignorant about what is going on. You have to realize that these people are just different from us. I agree with you that they should not be abused, and you know that Epsey and I have always been willing to help them when they were in need. But everyone knows that they're living on land that is going to be ours and will have to move beyond the Oconee River in a few years."

Kindred replied, somewhat angrily, "You're wrong about this. The Creeks and Cherokees have solemn commitments from the highest British officials, even including the king. Both Governors Wright and Campbell have made this clear, and right now our troops are removing some of the settlers who have cleared land in Indian territory."

Ethan replied, "British officials are not the same as us. Most of them that are shaping the treaties are Englishmen who look forward to going home someday. They don't need land over here and will give the natives whatever they want to get them to join in the wars against the Spanish and French and to let British merchants get rich from trade. We settlers are different. We are wedged in a tiny sliver of land between the Savannah and the Ogeechee, and we're usually victims in trading with the same merchants. There are vast areas of land west of here, with just a few redskin villages scattered around with little patches of good soil cleared for producing crops. They're too lazy to live any way except hand-to-mouth, dwelling in skin and mud huts, just barely getting by from one season to another."

Kindred had an uneasy, sinking feeling that the conversation was opening up wounds between them that would be difficult to heal, but he felt too strongly about the subject to remain silent or pretend to agree.

"The British are right, and the rest of us are wrong," he replied. "I know there are some bad Indians like there are evil white folks, but the vast majority are good people. They just want to live in peace, with the kind of life they've known for centuries, but they've almost been wiped out with our diseases and get cheated every day. Do you know how much they have to pay for a metal bucket or a yard of cloth?"

Ethan waved his hand dismissively. "Well, they surely don't have to trade if they don't want to. It's their own greed that will force them westward. I've been finding skinned deer carcasses with the meat totally wasted except to feed foxes and vultures. All they want these days is more and more hides to buy the kinds of goods you claim we're forcing on them. When they've killed all the deer this side of the Ogeechee, they'll have to move on, and we'll just move another step into their old lands."

Kindred admitted the truth of this statement and added, "Now when a bundle of hides is delivered to the trader, more than half are applied to existing debts, and the rest is not enough to pay for what they take home."

Ethan said, "You're right, and this is the best lever we have to use on them. When they run out of hides or credit, they'll just have one thing left, and that's land."

They were soon to part ways as they approached the side path leading to Kindred's homestead, and he tried to ease the obvious tension.

"Well, once we reach agreement with them and sign a treaty, it should be honored. If the Indians agree later to sign a new one, that's up to them, but they deserve to be treated right."

Ethan replied, "I can't disagree with being fair and keeping our word, and I also know that there are good and bad folks of all colors. But our first task is to take care of our families and ourselves, and this is the choice that we all have to make."

He hesitated a few moments and then added, "Maybe you've been spending too much time across the river, Kindred. Good day to you."

Kindred sat on his horse quietly, blaming the tears in his eyes on the glare of the evening sun and watching until Ethan's broad shoulders and yellow pigtail disappeared around a curve in the narrow trail. Something had gone out of his life. He realized that he had indeed been naive, at least in presuming that Ethan would share his concern about the plight of the natives. He didn't see how anyone could know how he felt about Newota.

After a day or so, Mavis asked, "Kindred, are you sick or something?"

He shook his head and replied, "Ethan seems to have changed since we first met him."

"I haven't noticed it. What do you mean?"

"Well, for one thing, he seems to want more and more land, when it seems to me that both of us have all we can use."

"Kindred, you know that we are different from him and almost all the other settlers. They see the size of their farm as a measure of success in life. Besides, Ethan probably figures that someday Henry will be needing more fields and woods than the Pratts have now."

She looked at her husband for a while and then asked, "Is that all that's bothering you?"

"I'm not sure Ethan feels loyal to the crown or to the British officials in the colonies, and he also seems unhappy with the Indians." He paused for a few seconds and then added, "He even fussed at me for visiting their village."

Now Mavis understood.

Although the two families were still polite and apparently friendly when together, Kindred's solo visits with Ethan became less frequent, and Mavis was pleased to become the primary focus of his philosophical musings and their discussions as naturalists. They did the necessary farmwork but were not trying to expand or even improve their homestead as were the Pratts. Kindred now almost invariably moved toward Newota and the Creek village to pursue his botanical studies. Mavis went with him a few times and came to share his deep concern about the increasing tensions that were developing between the Indians and the white settlers.

The Morrises summarized what they learned from Newota and sent the information to Dr. Bartram. Without their asking, Bartram sent them a small stipend on occasion, depending on his judgment of the effort they had expended and the value of the information to him.

One day, Kindred asked Newota, "How do your people go to war?"

"I've only witnessed preparations for a serious excursion on one occasion, when I was not yet a man. That day, I remember the group of warriors being led in single file by the chosen leader, who was my father."

He paused. "That was the last time I saw him alive. He and two other men were killed in that battle, but none of their bodies were taken. They were brought back to the village, and there was even some sense of pride and achievement, because their scalps were intact. The outcome of the battle was not clear, but the honor of our clan was defended. In an attack on well-known neighbors with whom we have had peaceful relations, our purpose is almost always to repay an insult or resolve a dispute over hunting

grounds. Usually little blood is shed, and both sides are likely to be satisfied if our integrity is honored."

Kindred said, "Europeans do the same thing in personal duels with
swords or pistols, many of which are not meant to be fatal."

Newota continued, "We announce our arrival back home with shouts,
songs, and whoops. The warriors will fast for three days to remove the pol-
lution of shedding human blood. Women always sing and chant in admiration. A few tribes have begun attacking others in order to take captives,
knowing that the British have been eager to buy them as slaves. But when
we have taken a mighty warrior whom we have feared and respected, he
may be scalped alive and tortured by fire, permitting him to show his brav-
ery and courage while singing a death song."

Kindred was silent for a while. "I don't see why you and the Europeans
can't live in peace with one another."

Newota replied, "My uncle tells me that we have good relations with
some foreign people. I have learned that along the Mississippi River and in
the northwest, the French have had few permanent settlements and little
desire for farming land. What they seem to want is trade, and in this they
have been in competition with the British. Also, both sides have used every
possible means to recruit our braves to help their army fight the other.
Some of the chiefs have learned how to play one white nation against the
other, to our maximum advantage, but the gifts and bribes they have received are seldom distributed among the villagers."

Kindred already knew most of this, at least as it related to the British
presence in Georgia and Carolina, but didn't understand how the Indians
assessed the other Europeans.

"What about the Spanish, who first moved into Georgia and Florida
and now have ceded the territory to Britain?"

"I only know what my uncle has told me. The Spaniards have been the
worst of all, looking upon those not sharing their religion as animals whose
lives are insignificant. They have been cruel and despotic. When they first
arrived in Florida and along the coast of Georgia long ago, there were
many thousands of Timucuas in Florida. Through disease, assassinations,
and starvation, the Spaniards almost completely wiped out the entire population. When the British took over Florida recently, the Spanish carried all
the surviving Timucuas back to Europe—in one ship! These were the
Christians, and there were less than one hundred of them. Now a number

of my fellow Creeks, Cherokees, runaway slaves, and criminals are moving southward to settle the abandoned lands. They are becoming known as Seminoles, which means 'wild ones,' or 'runaways.'"

Deeply troubled by all this, Kindred asked, "Don't your people see that relating to the Europeans is just bringing tragedy, and the eventual loss of your hunting grounds? You have brave warriors who know the forests, and who could band together and protect the land and your way of life."

Newota smiled and said, "You are speaking as an Indian, but as a foolish one. You have to remember that we are not united and never will be. Ours is a nation of small and independent towns, and the clans are not willing to accept orders from distant chiefs. Unfortunately, most of our fighting is done among ourselves, and not against a common enemy. When leaders come together, any decisions are made by consensus, after extremely long deliberations. This usually means that compromises wipe away any hope for strong or concerted action. In fact, the Indian superintendent knows much more about the individual tribes than do any of us, and he has paid spies among us who prevent any surprises.

"We have been defeated whenever we have opposed the settlers with weapons. The only successes are claimed by young men who go at night to attack the more isolated colonials, and these have been mostly north of here. They are the acts of cowards, without the honor of warriors, and almost always work to our disadvantage. Whites take retribution against entire clans for misdeeds of a few, so that our losses in property and lives are far greater than any harm inflicted. Our elders are then inclined to sue for peace, and almost always lose in the talks."

Without realizing it, Kindred placed himself in the position of the natives. "Newota, I know that some of these things can't be changed, but the situation is not hopeless. It's the British officials that try to protect your people, and the threats are coming from the settlers. They're still moving into Georgia and I hear them talking about driving the natives out by force, destroying villages and even killing your families."

Newota shrugged his shoulders. "Well, there is not much we can do about it."

"There may be," replied Kindred.

Kindred decided to try to help his Indian friends. Accompanied by Newota, he traveled to a number of villages west of the Ogeechee, learned of any homesteads being established near Indian villages, and secretly reported them to British officials. He soon learned that his only reliable allies were Indian Superintendent John Stuart and his subordinates, who were determined to honor terms of the treaties, to restrain the more militant settlers, and to maintain peace. Their ultimate goal was the highest possible level of lucrative trade with the natives. From these contacts, Kindred was able to learn in advance about the extremely rare occasions when mounted dragoons went into Indian territory to remove the illegal settlers, and he shared this knowledge with Newota. Because of this assistance and his knowledge of their language, the Indians began to look to him for advice and support on almost any issue that concerned them.

Pressure concerning trade was also building in London. By 1772, the Indians had accumulated such a large debt that white merchants threatened to cut off all trade. Some of the Cherokee chiefs were eager to pay debts with territory, but the 1763 land agreement involved all major tribes and required that British royal governors be parties to any further land treaties.

In Georgia, there was a growing division between British officials and relatively poor and land-hungry settlers, who began to infiltrate Indian lands, particularly north of Little River and westward to the Ogeechee. When British General Thomas Gage learned that Indians had attacked some backcountry settlers, he responded, "We ought to thank them for preventing these vagabonds from wandering where they don't belong."

Governor Wright was in London for meetings with Parliament and vacationing on his family's estate, but when he was informed that more than five hundred "Cracker families" had settled in Indian territory, he decided to return to Georgia. Back in Savannah, he and Indian Superintendent Stuart agreed that they would rather deal with the Indians than white trash, and would find a way to approve land grants only to "the middling sort of people, who can pay for land, and have families and a few Negroes."

Kindred now found that British officials were much more respectful to him and seemed to appreciate the information that he gave them about white intrusions into Indian territory, but he was careful to conceal his activities from Ethan.

Governor Wright wanted to preserve harmony in his colony and to meet the demands from local merchants and their associates in London, and he finally thought he saw a way to negotiate an acceptable agreement.

He called a meeting in Augusta in the summer of 1773, attended by royal officials and leaders of the Creeks and Cherokees. After several days of negotiation, the Indian chiefs were amply rewarded with gifts and honors, traders received assurances that their debts would be paid, and the British promised the Indians that they would prevent all illegal settlements on their remaining land. About 1,600,000 acres were ceded north and west of the 1763 lands between the Savannah and the Oconee rivers and northward from the headwaters of Briar Creek. This would be enough for about four thousand land grants, and all proceeds from selling the land, at a price ranging from two to five shillings an acre, would be applied to the Indians' debt of about £40,000.

CHAPTER 13

William Bartram Visits Georgia

MAY 1773

Seventeen seventy-three was a special year because of the new treaty between the British and the Indians, and for the Morrises it was a time of great anticipation and pleasure. They had a letter from William Bartram saying that he would be visiting Georgia the first week in June, and requesting that Kindred meet him in Augusta. Mavis and Kindred brought their notebooks and sketches up-to-date, packed them in saddlebags, and rode the forty miles at the appointed time. Bartram had arrived in Augusta shortly after the treaty was signed and made arrangements to join the British surveying team in Wrightsborough as they traveled north to mark the new territorial boundaries. He was delighted to see the Morrises, since he had known Mavis when she lived in his father's home, and Kindred had been one of the best students who attended lectures there. They spent several hours sharing information about their mutual discoveries in the field of botany, and were particularly intrigued by the customs of the natives. William reported that his father, John, was now seventy-four years old but in good health and still conducting lectures in Philadelphia.

Kindred and Mavis were amazed at the preparations that Bartram had begun in Savannah and completed after almost a week in Augusta. Using funds provided by an eminent botanist in England, he was beginning an excursion of four years in the southeast, with an entourage of about twenty men, mostly mounted on horseback, plus ten pack animals. His basic task would be to observe the flora and fauna of the area and to send to London written descriptions, sketches, and actual specimens. In addition, he would keep a journal during his travels, emphasizing his observations of the lifestyle of the inhabitants, both natives and the few whites who had decided to live among them.

After leaving Augusta, they enjoyed a day and a half of leisurely travel, during which Bartram exclaimed repeatedly about the size of the trees and stopped to measure the circumference of some of the larger specimens. He found one black oak that measured thirty-one feet, and insisted on sketching the entire tree, estimating the height of the first limbs and the extent of the leafed area. When they arrived in Wrightsborough, the seventy-year-old Joseph Maddock welcomed the famous botanist enthusiastically. Kindred and Mavis were standing by Bartram's side and instantly detected the warmth of this reunion of two men whose families had been quite closely related both in Pennsylvania and in North Carolina. Bartram expressed his pride in the Quaker settlement and asked Maddock to give him a report on its progress.

"We have a total of about forty thousand acres, lying mostly along the borders of the 1763 ceded area. There are already two hundred and eight families involved, most of them Quakers. Now, almost exactly ten years later, treaty terms will open another one to one and a half million acres to the colony, including a large area to the north and west. I have to admit that some of the settlers have already moved into Indian territory. This may precipitate some conflicts in the future, but so far we have gotten along well with the natives. We treat them right, and trade with them has continued to grow, even though we Friends have done everything possible to keep our exchanges on a current basis and not permit any appreciable debts to accumulate."

Kindred did not speak, although he knew that this was not true of some Quaker merchants who cheated the Indians. He had already shared this conflicting information with Bartram and decided that perhaps Maddock was speaking only of what was decided in the Quaker meetings.

Bartram congratulated the Quaker leader and asked, "Do you know any of the Indians personally, and can you communicate with them?"

"Yes, of course. Since we established the town of Wrightsborough, some of the clan leaders have been coming here to trade, and these particular ones have learned enough English words, along with signs, to conduct business. I have to admit that not many of us have bothered to learn their dialects, which to me seem almost incomprehensible. I understand that thy young friend Kindred is one of the few exceptions, having become quite fluent in the language of the Creeks."

They turned to Kindred, who replied, "Yes, I have a young Creek friend with whom I have spent a lot of time. We have shared some language lessons and are now able to converse quite easily in either English or the Muskogean dialect of the Creeks. We've both learned some of the Cherokee words, which, as you know, are derived from the Iroquois."

Kindred realized, to his embarrassment, that this was more of an answer than was expected, but found that Bartram was intrigued. He would be traveling within these two Indian nations and, as a scientist, wanted to learn as much as possible about them. He asked, "Do you think your Creek friend would be willing to travel with me for a few weeks, at least while we're in this territory? We'll be here in Wrightsborough four or five more days, which should give him a chance to respond."

Kindred promised to ask Newota about this, and Bartram turned back to Maddock.

"I observed on all the plantations around Savannah, and to some degree in other places along the river below Augusta, that many of the settlers have begun to depend on slaves, both blacks and Indians, as a way to operate and expand their farming operations. What is going on here in your region?"

With obvious pride, Maddock responded, "We Friends have no slaves and have passed a binding resolution at meeting prohibiting any ownership of another human being. We cannot enforce this ruling on those who are not of our faith or in the future, but at least until now I know of no slaves within the lands for which I received a grant and then apportioned to others."

"I'm glad to hear this. Now let me explain my tentative schedule, which of necessity must always be quite flexible. My primary purpose throughout my journeys will be to make scientific observations, but also to learn as much as possible about life in the southeastern colonies. I would like to spend a few days in Wrightsborough, with most of my time in the forest area with Kindred. Then the surveyor team is supposed to come here, and I shall join this British and Indian group, who will be establishing the boundary lines of the territory just ceded by the Indians in Augusta. Then we plan to return to Savannah, continue my examination of the coastal areas of Carolina and Georgia, and later go farther into the interior of northern Florida and southern Georgia."

Maddock asked, "How long will all of this take?"

"At least three and perhaps four years. I am obligated to send reports and specimens to London as frequently as possible and will need to make contact with a seaport on occasion."

"Well, we are pleased and honored to have thee with us. Is there anything we can do in addition to the housing and basic supplies that we have already set aside for thy convenience?"

"No, but I'd like to ask Kindred to contact his Creek friend, so that I'll know if we can depend on his services."

Newota was sitting on the riverbank, and his thoughts were drifting from one subject to another when he was startled by laughter, quite close to him behind a nearby tree. He recognized it to be Kindred's, who stepped out into the open and said, "If I had been an enemy warrior, I could have had your scalp before you knew I was here."

They embraced, and then Newota said, "Well, you have learned too much from me about moving quietly through the forest. We'll have to put bells on your ankles. I would have been more alert if I hadn't thought you were with your botany teacher, and didn't expect such a great warrior as you to be nearby."

"I've come back early just to see you and to share a great opportunity. Dr. Bartram wants to meet you and to ask that you accompany him for a few weeks when he travels from Wrightsborough northwest to the Broad River and then eastward to the Savannah."

"That sounds like Cherokee territory, and I do not know why he would want me unless you have given him some misleading information."

"He needs someone who can help him with the language, and a bonus would be that you know a few things about the plants he will be studying."

"Why should I go? I have my mother and my tribal duties to care for."

"First of all, you'll be paid for your services, and I'll make sure that it's in something of value and not just trinkets or rum. The best part will be what you can learn about the forests and its creatures from one of the wisest of men. At least come with me to talk to Dr. Bartram."

The gifts had not enticed Newota, and he shook his head with some regret and started to turn away.

Kindred said, "The great chief Emistisiguo will be disappointed. I understand that he had also mentioned your name."

Without hesitation, Newota said, "I'll be at your cabin at sunrise tomorrow."

Kindred smiled to himself, having fully anticipated that his trump card would be sufficient. Everyone knew that Emistisiguo had now become the principal leader of the Upper Creeks and was respected among both Creeks and Cherokees. He had a natural aversion to the avarice of colonial settlers and was shrewd and effective in utilizing his relations with the British to enhance the well-being of his own people. He was an honest man who could not be influenced with bribes, and he worked closely with Indian Superintendent John Stuart and also with various military leaders. With authorization directly from the king, Stuart had made Emistisiguo a "great medal chief," one of only five so honored in all of America.

Newota had always objected to trading with the white merchants, so this was his first visit to Wrightsborough. Before arriving, he and Kindred had discussed what would be a fair but advantageous arrangement and decided that Kindred should speak for him with Bartram. Newota preferred not to bargain, but before the negotiation was completed, Bartram insisted on talking directly to him, to test his ability to speak both in English and in the Creek and Cherokee dialects. For three weeks of his services as interpreter and assistant, Kindred arranged for Newota to receive a generous supply of iron cooking utensils, needles, two knives and some other tools, and a compass. Bartram also offered a small illustrated book, a copy already owned by Kindred, about the plants found in the colonies. Newota could not read it but hoped someday to learn.

Along with the biologist's group of about twenty men, there were an almost equal number of British surveyors, plus the Creek and Cherokee leaders and their attendants. Without any discussion, it was understood that Emistisiguo would be speaking for the Indians. After extensive discussions, spokesmen for the different factions had decided to proceed northward for about three days to a place known as the Great Salt Lick, a deposit of what appeared to be chalk, that was well known to all the tribesmen. Covering several acres, the place was heavily frequented by all kinds of wild animals, and both the Creeks and Cherokees came there to obtain the white earth, which they believed to have nutritional and medicinal benefits. Bartram wanted to obtain a sample of the material, and the Indians insisted on the place as a known point of departure for the survey.

The British surveyors also decided to establish the Great Salt Lick as a geographical benchmark from which other points on their maps could be determined. Kindred was interested in this process, and a young lieutenant named Craddock seemed eager to show off his knowledge of surveying. He was especially proud of a new sextant, with which accurate angles between heavenly bodies could be determined.

"To determine our latitude, or distance above the equator, we merely have to determine how high the North Star is above the horizon and make a small adjustment," he explained.

Kindred replied, "I understand this, but how about east and west?"

"You know the sun moves fifteen degrees westward every hour, so what we need is an accurate clock to determine how far we are from Greenwich, England. This is an almost impossible problem for ships at sea, but we can do fairly well on land, where our telescopes can be held without movement."

He paused, and Kindred nodded.

"We know about when the sun is passing us, but don't know what time it is. There are two heavenly clocks that we use. For centuries, astronomers have recorded in elaborate tables the movement of the moon across the heavens each month, and by measuring how far the moon is from certain stars, we can know the time anywhere on earth. Another way is to look at two of Jupiter's four moons, which rotate around the planet like an exact timepiece in the sky. With accurate observations and less than an hour of computation, we can know the exact time and then from the sun determine how far we are east or west of Greenwich."

The exact position was determined after several days of observations with astrolabes and the sextant, and a stone monument was erected at the site to be used as a starting point for their measurements and mapping. The Augusta agreement called for the new colonial boundaries to extend from the headwaters of the Ogeechee River northward to the upper fork of the Broad River, then directly eastward to the Savannah. The British had some earlier maps of the area, a large compass mounted in gimbals, and other surveying instruments to determine the location of boundary points. The chief surveyor was a British colonel, who was obviously impatient with the leisurely progress and had originally objected to any stop at the salt lick. Once the marker was erected, he was determined to press ahead rapidly to the Broad River so that he and his assistants could use another set of astronomical measurements to determine the corner of the lands granted to white settlers.

When the large caravan was finally ready to move, the colonel ostentatiously set up his large compass and indicated the course to be followed to the Broad River fork. After a brief conversation with the Cherokee chief, accompanied by Newota, Emistisiguo immediately stated, "We all know the North Star, but this is the wrong direction to the next point of reference, and a violation of the agreement made in Augusta. We will not proceed with you if you follow this wicked and lying needle. It cannot be used to trick us and to permit you to take our territory."

The colonel said, "This compass is an instrument used throughout the world for many generations, on land and on the sea. With known corrections, it always indicates the correct direction. It cannot be wrong, and we will follow it to the next point."

The chief moved close to the compass, drew his scalping knife from its sheath, and held it close to the instrument, which then swung far from its northern point. He turned and walked away, making a brief remark to Newota.

Newota then reported to the colonel, "The chieftains and all their men are going back to their villages, and you must not proceed further into their territory."

Both the Creeks and Cherokees returned to their tents and prepared to leave the camp. Bartram and the surveyors were in a quandary about what to do, and asked Newota to join them in inducing the Indian leaders to continue their joint effort.

Newota said, "They will not change. They know the correct way to the next place."

"Then what can we do?"

"You must follow them. If they do not arrive at the designated fork in the river, then perhaps they will agree to retrace our steps and give your instruments another chance."

The chief surveyor said, "This is a waste of time. We'll just be wandering around in the woods and swamps for a few days for nothing."

Bartram asked, "But what will it serve us to proceed without the natives, and into their own territory? It is obvious that they are preparing to leave us."

Newota added, "There are some other requirements. Emistisiguo has designated the Cherokee chief to be the expedition leader since we will be in his territory. The compass case is not to be opened, and some substantial gifts are expected because the little instrument has been used to imply that the Cherokees do not know their own lands. If we proceed, Cherokee scouts must always be in the forefront of the expedition."

This was not a decision to be made lightly; it would be a four-day journey before they reached the stream, to see how great an error the natives had made. But they finally agreed to the Indians' demands, and the group set out again in a northerly direction, led by two young Cherokees who moved forward with seeming confidence. Their general course was at least two points farther east on the surveyor's compass than the colonel had originally planned. The entourage now moved in a relatively straight line but at an excruciatingly slow pace, since the Indians knew they were being paid by the day.

Expecting to have to retrace their steps, the colonel instructed his men to make only light and infrequent trail marks, and he looked at the compass only inside his small tent when they stopped to camp. He compared it with the North Star and was absolutely convinced that, when just slightly adjusted for known deviation in the area, it pointed to true north. He shared this information with Bartram and with anyone else who would listen, but none of the Indians would speak about the subject. With growing impatience, the British surveyors were forced to follow the two braves along their obviously erroneous route.

Before noon on the sixth day, they arrived precisely at the upper fork of the Broad River. The Indians celebrated and jeered at the British surveyors, who, at first, were in a quandary about what had happened. Then they realized that the compass had, indeed, been correct, but their maps had been wrong. The headwaters of the Broad River and its tributary streams were several miles eastward of where they had been expected.

The promised gifts were delivered to the chiefs, and that evening a peace pipe and a few cups of rum were passed around. The next morning the Indians and survey team prepared to proceed directly eastward to the Savannah River, as prescribed in the text of the treaty. But Bartram, having seen enough of this region, decided to follow the Broad River more south-ward, which would bring him to Augusta almost two weeks early. Newota, eager to return home, was delighted with this decision.

The group proceeded down the Broad and Savannah rivers to the mouth of the Little River, where Newota was paid for his services and he and Kindred proceeded back to their homes, while the scientific party re-turned to Augusta and then Savannah.

BOOK II

1774–1777

CHAPTER 14

Stirrings of a Conflict

The Pratts and Morrises were still getting along well as neighbors, but they had something of an argument when the new treaty opened up lands farther to the north and west and extended all the way to the Oconee River. Ethan was eager to dispose of some of their present holdings and expand across the river, but the other three adults preferred to stay where they were, in an area that had come to be called Sweetwater, about six miles northwest of Wrightsborough. Ethan was determined to allow for his son's future, but finally compromised by putting in for additional grazing rights, bringing both families up to the maximum acreage permitted under the old head-right system. Their new property was in the rolling hills just west of their first farms, still in the area that drained into Briar Creek. They only had to pay the survey fees, plus three shillings an acre for their new land. With Governor James Wright and his council in charge, there was little speculation or fraud, quite different from what the Pratts had known in North Carolina. They and the Morrises helped each other clear some land and erect fences to hold the growing herd of cows and the hogs they had accumulated.

Just by observing developments within their own small community, Ethan and Kindred could understand the growing tensions among the British, settlers, and natives. It was clear that British officials considered it their duty to retain control of the political and military affairs of the colonies and extract maximum profit from trade, both with the Indians and the white settlers. The established colonists who had good property holdings supported this premise and wanted to live in peace on their farms or in their villages. Their commitment was to a life in America, with an assumed loyalty to the crown but a desire for minimum interference in their own affairs.

The vast majority of natives, British officials, and American settlers had much in common, including a strong desire to live as neighbors and to overcome difficulties peacefully. But there were strong and increasingly angry men with clear goals, and among them violence was preferable to patience and accommodation. There was an insatiable demand for more land from the stream of new settlers who moved south and west from the northern colonies or from Europe, and on this tide of immigrants into the frontier regions was a froth of indolent or unruly riffraff, often incompatible with established neighbors or unwilling to comply with the legal standards of any organized society.

Hannah Clarke stirred, dimly aware that something had disturbed her sleep, and then lay as quietly as possible, not wanting to waken her husband. Now wide awake herself, she listened intently and was then certain that she heard something moving in the yard. This was nothing new to her, or a cause for concern, since their North Carolina cabin and fields were in a small opening of less than forty acres surrounded by woodland and swamp, and deer and black bear were frequent night visitors. But then a light flickering on the oiled paper of the window caused her to sit up and shout, "Elijah!"

He jumped. "What? What in hell's the matter with you, woman?" Then he also saw the light, leaped from the bed, took his musket from the corner, and threw open the door. One end of the barn was in flames, and there was the dim outline of two mounted horsemen on the edge of the trees, a hundred yards from the barn. Elijah looked closely, and could see another man just behind the barn, in the small corral where his two horses were moving nervously. He leveled his rifle and fired at the figure, but was so careful not to hit his own livestock that he knew the bullet had overshot its mark. While he reloaded, all the men disappeared beyond the barn and into the woods, and then Elijah ran to the corral and opened the gate, knowing that his freed horses would not move far from the cabin. It was too late to save the barn and the hay, fodder, and ear corn—all that he had saved from a year of hard work in the fields. All he could do was curse bitterly.

He knew, even without having seen them clearly, that the thieves and arsonists were the damned Cherokees, and he shouldn't have been surprised by this tragedy. Last week, he had been dragging the last of the ear corn home on a sled from his most distant field when a group of four Indians emerged silently from the forest, sat on their horses for a few moments, rode forward, and then dismounted so as to intercept him as he moved toward the house and barn. Elijah dropped the horse's reins and held his gun in both hands, pointed at the ground a few feet in front of the Indians. The leader raised his right hand, palm forward, in a gesture of peace.

He recognized the group as coming from a village just five miles to the west. He had visited the village and a few others on several occasions to supplement his supply of animal skins before he went to Hillsborough to trade. Elijah was a shrewd bargainer and knew how to extract the maximum number of hides for whatever he had to exchange. His friend Aaron Hart was in almost constant contact with the natives, and Elijah absorbed and used the information he received about which village had a surplus of skins and which might be in need of supplies. He and the Indians could communicate with surprising ease, displaying their goods to one another and using sign language to make their bargaining proposals, supplemented by the few English words that the Indian traders knew. Elijah had refused to learn any of the strange-sounding Cherokee syllables, which he found distasteful.

The spokesman of those who stood in front of him in the pathway was an old man called Lone Tree, who spoke politely and with dignity, offering to exchange deer hides for corn. Elijah had never been friendly with the redskins and realized that they must be desperate to come to his homestead on such a peremptory visit. Although he had made a good crop, he knew he could drive a hard bargain, so he replied that he didn't have any corn to trade. Lone Tree continued to face Elijah respectfully, but the three younger men were looking closely at the large woven baskets heaped with well-filled ears. Their village was long overdue to be moved to a new site, as was evident to any knowledgeable visitor who observed the depleted soil in their garden plots. Winter would soon be coming on, and the visitors did not attempt to conceal their need for food. Even their original offer was far more than the normal value of a basketful of grain. Elijah could see a great advantage in waiting for colder weather, and rejected every offer. Lone Tree had even offered a good hunting knife in a beautifully decorated sheath, which Elijah had seen worn proudly by the village chief on his previous visit.

But he resented the savages coming to his homestead and was determined not to let them have any corn. He repeatedly told them that he had no grain to spare, claiming that he had come through the past season with a poor crop and needed all the harvest for his own family. He knew, as perhaps did some of the Indians, that there was one field of his corn, adjacent to the swamp, which had received plenty of rain and produced a bumper crop. He had enough to feed his own family and more, but a reserve supply was always a good idea, and if there was going to be a shortage this winter, he wanted to take advantage of it.

Then one of the young braves, his face disfigured by a deep scar that ran from his left eye and down across his mouth, so he seemed to have four lips, pushed forward and demanded that the white man accept their offer. His voice was harsh, and he ignored the seniority of the older man. Elijah refused to look at him or to respond, stating again to Lone Tree that, like the Indians, he lacked enough corn for his own family. The four men left the yard, moving westward toward their home village, except the young man turned and stared at Elijah for a full minute before following the others into the forest.

Now, watching the fire consume his barn, Elijah remembered the disfigured face and felt sure that he was the victim of animosity and tribal hunger. This was just one more personal disaster that had befallen him during the past year, the most tragic being the death of his and Hannah's youngest child, a two-year-old son. Hannah, now dressed in her loose-fitting dress she called a Mother Hubbard, came out of the house. She saw the expression of anger and despair on his face and approached him timidly. "We've still got a hill full of sweet potatoes and almost three bushels of meal and grits in the house," she said quietly. "We'll make out somehow."

He managed a small, sardonic smile. "Yeah, and we can eat more coons and possums, or maybe little Johnny will be more successful with his squirrel and rabbit snares." Elijah was barefoot and wore only a long homespun shirt, but this was how he was often clad throughout the day when he was working in his small fields or tending the animals in the woods. The soles of his feet were as tough as leather, and he put on his moccasins, linsey-woolsey underwear, and buckskin breeches only when it was cold or when he expected to meet someone other than Hannah and his son John. He caught and tethered the horses and, since there was nothing else to be done until daybreak, not more than an hour in the future, they moved back toward the cabin and lit a candle. It was not customary for the couple to talk to each other except concerning matters of the moment, but now seemed a good time to consider some more basic decisions about their future. They sat across the table from each other, and Hannah waited for Elijah to break the silence.

"Hannah, I don't know what we'll do now. We've both of us worked as hard as we could, and have nothin' much to show for it. I'm thirty-eight years old, don't have any learnin', tho' I've always thought I was a good farmer and had a way with animals. But two years of drought and now this fire has got me, and the heavy taxes of the damned governor are past due and we can't pay 'em. All we've got to sell is the few cows and hogs that are feedin' on acorns and leaves in the woods and swamps, and the market for them has almost dried up because farmers don't have any hay or corn for feed and everybody's tryin' to sell at the same time."

She had never before heard him speak so frankly about himself or share future plans with her.

"Well, we've had bad times before, and the Lord has always taken care of us. Don't you think we'll get any help with the taxes and some protection from the government?"

"Hell, no. That's over with. The Regulators was our only hope, and they was wiped out at Alamance and their leaders hung. Everybody's afraid to speak out against the son-of-a-bitch governor in New Bern. About all we're beggin' for now is to pay our high taxes in cows, hides, grain, or tobacco, but the only thing they'll take at the courthouse is hard money, and you know we ain't got it. All we had was this shack and a barn, and the barn's gone."

Elijah waited awhile, thinking, before he stood up. "Well, I'm lookin' for something but I don't know what. James Few and some of our other neighbors have been talkin' to me about how we can band together and maybe stay here where we are. Right now our land ain't worth nothin', even though every year more settlers are moving thisaway and wanting to buy. With the high taxes we owe and no crops, we ain't really in possession of what we're workin'. Some of my folks live over in South Carolina, and they've offered me some land. It's only about fifty acres, but it's at least enough to get started ag'in. I'm going to walk awhile, catch the horses, and check on the cows and hogs."

Hannah said, "Well, I don't want to move again."

As he walked out the door, Elijah said, "Me neither, but we may have to jes' move off and leave this place."

Hannah watched her husband leave and had a fleeting sense that she had made a serious mistake by joining her life to his. Her father, Anthony Reddick, was a successful mariner, having retired from the sea as a young captain who saw clearly that the profits from his voyages went to those who owned the ships. He moved first to a job with a shipping company and specialized in arranging transport of cargoes within coastal vessels so they could be unloaded expeditiously. He saved his earnings and eventually owned a substantial portion of several ships. His only daughter had grown up in relative affluence. She was completely dominated by her father, a widower, who applied his knowledge of women visited by sailors to his daughter's potential future and did everything possible to isolate her from the outside world. Her contacts with her peers, even other girls, were mini-mized, but private tutors gave her as good an education as was available to any other young people in the thriving seaport of Norfolk.

As a sixteen-year-old, she worked several hours a day in her father's of-fice, and it was there that she met Elijah Clarke. He had been hired by a sta-bleman to deliver twenty packhorses from Hillsborough to Norfolk, for shipment on to Newport. He was obviously confused when he entered the office, and Hannah soon realized that the young man could not read the di-rections he carried in his hand. She examined the paper, asked him a few questions, and told him to deliver the horses to the dock, have the invoice signed by the leading stevedore, and then return for payment. She was somewhat disconcerted because his eyes never left her face, and he seemed to have no embarrassment about his obvious illiteracy.

When he returned, Elijah began to tell her about his 150-mile trip from home and his prospective ability to acquire his own homestead and farm after he returned. Mr. Reddick came from his office after a few minutes and interrupted the conversation, paid what was due for the horses, and stood there until Elijah was gone. That evening, as her father was locking the door of the office, Hannah noticed the young man across the street, look-ing at her. As their carriage drove away, he casually lifted his hand in a slight wave, and she was relieved that her father had not noticed the ges-ture. The next day, a few minutes after her father left for the docks, Elijah entered the office and said, "I waited so as to see you ag'in."

"Why would you have wanted to do that?"

"I'm hopin' you'll go home with me."

Hannah turned away in deep embarrassment, but three days later she was behind his saddle as they rode westward to his future home, leading a packhorse that carried two bags containing her most precious possessions. She had never confronted her father, but merely left him a letter assuring him that she was well and happy and promising to write him after she was married and settled.

She had learned to love and admire her husband, even though he dom-inated her completely and made all the basic decisions about their family. She cherished the few books she had in the house and regretted that Elijah could not read them. Within a few months after their marriage, she had made a disastrous suggestion that she might teach him, and he had ex-ploded in anger at what he considered to be a personal insult. She was courageous and self-sufficient, learned to expand her own family responsibilities without discussing them with her husband, and made as many friends as possible among the other women in the settlement region.

They now had three children, but it was their oldest son, John, who was the focus of Elijah's interest. Hannah compensated by being especially attentive to the two girls. She had considered Elijah to be overly concerned about possible Indian attacks, but now appreciated his insistence that she and John become expert in the use of the family rifle.

Two weeks after the barn burned, their closest neighbor, John Dooly, came to visit and they naturally talked about Alamance and the hangings in Hillsborough.

"That's not the end of it," said Dooly. "Tryon has moved most of his militia into this territory and they are looking for anyone who has been active in the Regulators. Every man in this part of the colony is being ordered to come to his local courthouse and swear an oath of allegiance to the government."

"Well, I'll swear before God I won't do it," said Elijah, and turned to Hannah. "We'll just have to move."

A year later, the Clarkes were struggling to make ends meet on their small farm in South Carolina, still living in a tiny log cabin that was in no way equal to the one they had left behind. Elijah's kinfolks had not been generous, and gave him land in hilly country on weak and rocky soil. He and Hannah were quite discouraged and talked every now and then about returning to North Carolina, especially to the Watauga Valley in the far west, where many of their neighbors had gone.

Unlike his wife, Elijah didn't make friends easily. He was a strong-willed and confident man, seldom doubtful once he made up his mind, and not inclined to admit having ever made a mistake. Hannah had learned to accommodate these traits and to accept his making major decisions without consulting her, but other men preferred not to suffer his domineering attitude nor to be around him except for casual conversations. The one exception was Aaron Hart, who saw in Elijah the characteristics that he himself lacked.

Aaron was a trader who was constantly moving around a wide area of the Carolinas. He had bought a small cabin on the Haw River south of Hillsborough and soon established a travel route as far south as Savannah, with regular excursions into Indian territory. He rode mediocre mounts, followed by two to four tethered packhorses loaded with his merchandise of the moment. As everyone knew, he was always ready to trade any of the horses and even harnesses, as well as his constantly changing stock of goods. He liked to have one companion in his travels, usually a young man who helped him with his inventory so that Aaron could remain alert when moving along a trail that might be dangerous. Although mild-mannered, he was shrewd and resilient, and well able to protect himself. His services were appreciated among the white settlers' isolated homesteads, and were even more valuable in the Cherokee and Creek villages. He offered one of the few alternatives to the official British traders, whose terms were relatively harsh and rigid and whose demeanor was usually humorless. Aaron was as fluent in the native languages as any white man and seemed to feel at home among the Indians when he came to visit.

One product that the trader distributed freely was information. He loved to talk and prided himself on staying abreast of current events along his trade route and also news available from the latest periodicals published in Charles Town and Savannah. Although there was little profit from it, Aaron went out of his way to stop by Elijah Clarke's place whenever he was passing through. The big farmer would listen attentively to his every remark, ask endless questions, and then finally expound on whatever subject interested him most. He was harsh in his judgments, seldom failed to make a firm decision, and Hart would always leave the Clarke homestead with a renewed sense of his own self-importance and more certain of his opinions about complex issues. He was too malleable to take issue with Elijah, but mainly put forward contrary opinions by quoting others and then waiting to see what the farmer's reaction would be.

There were two issues on which he had to be very careful. One was how to accommodate Clarke's illiteracy without embarrassing him. The other was their sharp differences concerning Indians, who, in this cabin, were always called "savages" or worse. Aaron respected the natives whom he knew, trusted them more than he did most of his white customers, and usually remained mute or noncommittal when Elijah was attributing to them the characteristics of animals or vipers. He would never have admitted how much he enjoyed having sex with their women, and certainly not with one woman with whom he stayed several days at the end of each of his forays into northwest Georgia, despite the fact that he was married. She had already borne one of his children, and was pregnant again.

Late in seventy-three, on a visit to Orangeburg, Aaron had seen men gathered around a proclamation signed by Georgia's governor, James Wright. This was a notice that he had been expecting, to implement a new treaty that ceded a large tract of land northwest of Augusta and also farther south toward Florida. The governor was appealing for qualified settlers to move into the new territories, the only charge being enough to cover the cost of surveying, and a few shillings per acre to help pay off debts that the Indians owed to British traders.

On his next visit to the Clarkes, Aaron described the new opportunity to Elijah and Hannah. He was not surprised when Elijah made an almost immediate decision that was destined to change all their lives forever. He adopted the land grant opportunity as his own idea and began to announce his future plans as they formed in his mind. "This looks like what we been needin'. Some say Georgia even has an honest governor. I'm aimin' to go to some of our old neighbors back in Carolina and maybe a few around here to see who'll go with us. We'll be needin' to live close together, so we can protect ourselves against the savages. You cain't trust any damn agreement they make, and they'll be burnin' and stealin' just like they done in Carolina."

Aaron was pleased when Elijah added, almost as an afterthought, "Aaron, I hope you'll be with us, and that you'll help me pick out the right folks to go along when we move."

Hannah had some real doubts about moving again, but she could see that her husband had his mind set on it and didn't say a word. Elijah figured that he might get twenty families to join his group, but first the two men rode the eighty miles over to Augusta to confirm the accuracy of the information on the poster, and to learn how they could claim some land northwest of the town. Aaron went home to tell his wife about their new plans for the future, and Elijah went back to call out names of potential partners who might join in the new venture in Georgia. Hannah made out a list, and after almost two weeks of riding from one farm cabin to another, Elijah had persuaded a dozen families to join them. They all agreed to assemble at his place the first week in November, after their crops had been harvested and the surplus sold. In the meantime, Aaron had been down to the newly ceded land to locate a suitable area to be claimed.

Filled with his own importance, he made his report to Elijah. "The land agent in Augusta said there was a tract of land in the far north portion of the new grant still available, and he seemed eager to see it settled. I went up and rode over it as well as I could, and it looks like the best that's still available.

There's almost five thousand acres, and some of it's pretty hilly, but he'll let us divide it up the way we want, depending on the governor's rules concerning size of the families. I gave the agent a few nice things for his wife, and he said he would hold the tract for us, particularly seeing as how it's pretty isolated."

By early 1774, Elijah had induced sixteen families from North and South Carolina to join in the move to Georgia. He concentrated on men he knew to be staunch and reliable when lives or freedom were at stake.

Some of the more militant Creeks who lived across the Ogeechee River had been angered when the treaty was signed in 1773, claiming that the Cherokees had given away their territory, and when the settlers widened the Indian trail from Augusta to Wrightsborough that same year, they saw it as launching a flood of new settlers who would occupy their homeland. Since almost all available land had already been taken throughout the colonies, white settlers moved quickly into the more attractive new land. Much of it went unclaimed, however, because the British screened out "ruffian" settlers, and troops didn't provide enough safety for more responsible families. The granting of fewer official land grants than expected meant that less money was available to be applied to the natives' debts to white traders, and most tribes soon found themselves squeezed on trading values and denied further credit even when pelts were offered at a low value. Increasing animosity between white families and the Creeks was unavoidable, and some young militant warriors began making raids against white settlers.

The Indians knew that Kindred Morris was a strong defender of their interests and that his friend Ethan Pratt also treated them fairly, so the two families had no problems with harassment or threats. But in 1774, over the opposition of the Quakers, some of the other settlers decided to raise £50 to finance a fort just west of Wrightsborough. They decided that all families in the area would contribute a portion of the cost, depending on how far they lived from the fort. The argument was that even the more distant settlers might have to hide there in case of an all-out attack. Kindred refused to contribute either money or labor, but Ethan put in four shillings and spent a week with other men cutting logs and erecting the small barricade.

Even from the earliest days after they moved from North Carolina, the Quakers represented only a small majority of the total white population in northeast Georgia, although a few others of their faith moved down to join them. Governor Wright continued to arrange for more responsible families who arrived in Savannah by ship to pay their small fees and settle either in the newly ceded regions west of the Savannah River or inland from the southern coastal area. Many others, including those like Elijah Clarke and his friends, came to Georgia overland, mostly from the Carolinas. Few of these newcomers had any deep religious commitments, but had come to the region to escape the restraints of more orderly societies and to acquire new lands, whether or not they complied completely with the colonial laws.

Although Governor Wright was always loyal to the king and Parliament and tried to enforce even the unfair laws, he had a well-deserved reputation as a fair and honest man who was respected both by the colonists and by leaders of the Creek, Cherokee, Catawba, and other Indians, even while they were being forced farther and farther westward. He was also effective in obtaining special attention and some financial assistance from London for his young colony, which was seen as a valuable buffer between Spanish Florida and other colonies to the north. In general, there was a stable relationship among the British officials, white settlers, and Indian tribes in Georgia. It was becoming rapidly apparent that this mixture of positive factors did not exist anywhere else in America.

Early in 1774, Ethan and Kindred rode into Wrightsborough to sell three calves and to buy some farm supplies, and they found Joseph Maddock in the general store.

"Hast thou heard the bad news from up north?" he asked.

Ethan said, "No, we don't get much information out where we live. What has happened now?"

"Well, some of the Boston leaders objected to the price on East India tea, boarded one of the British ships, and threw the cargo over the side into the harbor. It was an open act of rebellion against the crown."

Ethan commented, "That's probably because of the special tax on tea that was levied against the colonies. Has it been removed?"

"The tax is still in place, but the British East India Company lowered the price to more than compensate for any tax that has to be paid. The cost of tea actually went down."

Kindred spoke up for the first time. "I don't understand why people would object to buying cheaper tea."

Ethan said, "I can give you one answer, and maybe another. Almost every merchant in the colonies has been bypassing Britain and getting tea from other sources. Now they have a pretty good inventory, and the new cut price is probably under what they've paid for the stock they have on hand. It's likely that the Boston merchants want to see British tea destroyed to keep the price up. This is all a matter of money. The other answer is that there have long been a few hotheads that just want to show disloyalty to the king. Many colonists became organized in years past to oppose the Stamp Act and the Townshend Act, which involved special taxes, and the one on British tea is about the only one still in effect. These hotheads have to have some reason for a crusade. They should be made to pay for the tea they destroyed, and that will be the end of it."

Maddock said, "Well, my hope is that there will be no violence."

Ethan responded, "It's just a brief skirmish and we'll hear no more of it."

Within a few months, the Pratts and Morrises began to hear about military clashes between colonists and the king's forces in the north, and the two families agreed that these were unfortunate and unwarranted acts of disloyal British citizens. The laws passed in London concerning trade and taxation had relatively little impact on them. They produced on their farms almost everything they needed and, like most other frontier families, their natural duty was to mind their own business, support the crown as they had always done, and express their views strongly but peacefully.

———

C H A P T E R   1 5

A Special Colony

G eorgia was a special colony. Europeans had first settled on the Georgia coast in 1565, almost half a century before the first British adventurers landed farther north at Jamestown in what was to be Virginia. Spanish explorers, traders, and missionaries flourished on the coastal islands and up the inland rivers for more than two decades, but persistent attacks by Creek and Cherokee Indians finally forced the Spaniards to withdraw southward into Florida. The British, French, and Spanish all attempted to use the native warriors as surrogates to control the territory between Charles Town and St. Augustine, but none was successful. Finally, as far as Europeans were concerned, Georgia became a wilderness dominated by natives and inherently hostile to white settlers.

In 1732, a group of twenty-two idealistic and ambitious Englishmen obtained a charter from King George II to conduct a kind of "holy experiment" designed to provide employment, religious freedom, democratic rights, and enlightenment to the natives, in an environment free of the curse of rum, slavery, or avarice among the trustees. In February of the following year, James Oglethorpe arrived with 114 settlers, of the 600 who had applied for the voyage. They landed in a place they called Savannah, on a high bluff overlooking a large river. A man not able to pay for his passage was promised fifty acres of land and a year's support for his family. The more affluent were promised five hundred acres of land, the right to bring ten servants, and no property taxes for fifty years.

As a trustee of the new colony named for the king, Oglethorpe was prohibited from holding office or owning land, but he assumed all the responsibilities of a leader and was soon busy assuaging the Indians with blandishments and bribes, establishing the town of Savannah as a permanent settlement, resisting the decadence of nearby South Carolina, where slavery was encouraged and rum was imbibed freely, and defending the colony from Spanish troops in Florida.

Three years later, Oglethorpe went back to London and secured the title of "General and Commander-in-Chief of the Forces of South Carolina and Georgia," along with authority to recruit forces to defend both colonies. By then, he could count 800 people in Georgia who had come from mainland Europe to seek their fortune or to find religious freedom. Forty-five of them were Moravians, 110 were German-speaking Salzburgers, and 42 were Jews, mostly from Spain and Germany, who had arrived in Georgia in 1733, just five months after the first settlers. The general was criticized for accepting this large Jewish settlement, but he was especially grateful to one of them, Dr. Samuel Nuñes Ribeiro, who provided invaluable services as the colony's physician. These earliest settlers were peace-loving, appreciated their grants of land, and were loyal to the British crown. Oglethorpe also welcomed a group of Highland Scots, who volunteered to serve under him in defending Georgia against the Florida Spaniards. They were given attractive landholdings on the coast sixty miles south of Savannah in St. Andrews Parish, well placed to obstruct any invasion.

After his mother died when he was nine years old, Lachlan McIntosh had come to Georgia with his father, Captain John McIntosh, an officer in the

Highland Scots Regiment. Just four years later, when the regiment was fighting the Spaniards near St. Augustine, Captain McIntosh was captured and taken as a prisoner of war to be confined in Spain. Now without parents, Lachlan was put in Bethesda Orphan House, an institution near Savannah that was run by Reverend George Whitefield. The good reverend believed that the best way to mold young men was with strict discipline and severe punishment, which young Lachlan suffered for two years before running away and joining the regiment of his father. Almost immediately after being assigned to an inferior post, he proved to be a hero at the decisive Battle of Bloody Marsh, which solidified Georgia's hold on the southern part of the territory. Lachlan served well as a cadet and then an officer, and showed extraordinary courage and a talent for military tactics.

Although they served General Oglethorpe well against the Spaniards, it was commonly known that the Scots felt little affection or loyalty toward the British government in London. Even before crossing the Atlantic to start a new life, both in the early days of Georgia's founding and during the later decades, the Scotsmen's relations with England had been strained because of opposition to the forced union of the two countries, the breakup of the clan system, and the forced change in their customs. The Highland Dress Act had prohibited the wearing of distinctive kilts, and many families could not afford to rent land after Parliament forbade their making payments by giving military service to the clan chief. Tenant families were forced from the homes of their ancestors, and independence of the clans was diminished. The British encouraged the more militant Scots to move to Ireland, where many of them became prosperous in the woolen trade. Parliament soon passed the Woolen Act to protect the industry in England, and the resulting depression in Ireland caused another wave of emigration to America, mostly to the southern colonies, where homesteads were plentiful.

AUGUST 1774

It was not surprising that the Scotsmen at St. Andrews were the first Georgians to condemn British violation of what they considered their basic rights. Overwhelmingly, they opposed taxes levied without representation, the blockade of Boston Harbor, colonial families being forced to provide housing for British troops in America, and the trial of colonists in British courts.

As a strong and serious man having passed his forty-sixth birthday, Lachlan McIntosh was head of his own family and the preeminent leader in the parish. Now he and the other men were assembled in the meeting-house in the southern coastal town of Darien, near the Altamaha River. Lachlan's brother George was there, along with his cousins and members of the Mackay, Dunbar, Cuthbert, and other clans, almost all of whose predecessors had served in the Highland Scots almost four decades earlier.

Lachlan was a tall man, robust but not obese, with strong, sloping shoulders and arms that seemed too long for his body. He had the bearing of a military officer and always dressed properly even in civilian attire. One not unattractive peculiarity in his appearance was that he had a widow's peak that was carefully brushed to the center to form a distinctive curl. He usually had a glint in his eyes and slightly smiling lips, but the expression of bemusement could change instantly into one of fury if his hair-trigger temperament was aroused. Even his family and closest friends were reluctant to precipitate this change, but they still respected Lachlan because he was a fair man, his judgments were sound, and he was dedicated to the basic principles of the Scottish community.

Lachlan looked around him at the men in the meetinghouse and said, "All of us were embarrassed when the folks in South Carolina called us cowards and traitors to liberty, and declared an embargo against trade with Georgia. As you all know, our neighbors at Midway in St. Johns Parish are the only ones who will stand with us for freedom, and are willing to join us in renouncing our ties with this colony and aligning ourselves with the pa-triots in South Carolina. As Puritans from up north, they still have strong ties to the colonies that are already at war. However, I have just been in-formed that the Council of Safety in Charles Town expressed their appre-ciation for our offer but, after some considerable debate, have rejected it because such a great distance separates us and they prefer not to fragment our colony. We have called a meeting for next Thursday in Savannah, at Tondee's tavern, so we can decide what we must do now in addition to sending useless petitions to Parliament about taxes and boycotting a few British goods that we don't need anyhow."

After some typically heated discussion, the group decided that Lachlan would continue to marshal and train volunteers from the two most radical parishes, who were already preparing to fight if necessary, and his brother George should speak for St. Andrews Parish in the Savannah meeting. There was a general but unspoken belief that Lachlan was not diplomatic enough to put forward the views of their parish without alienating other groups in Georgia who were known to differ widely in their degree of loyalty to the crown. Nevertheless, he was the one who took it upon himself to describe what was to be expected, summarizing what most of them already knew.

"The colony is divided, not based on principle but according to the self-interests of each group. The strongest loyalty to the crown comes from Anglican clergymen, from politicians who have been given leadership positions by the royal council, from merchants who have special permits to trade overseas or with the Indians, and from recent immigrants who still have strong family ties to the old country. There is also aversion to action among farming families in provinces up the Savannah River, where most of the settlers have not been affected by the various taxes Parliament has levied. British troops are considered to be their best defense against Indian attacks, and some families are grateful for the land they have obtained from Governor Wright. The German Lutherans at Ebenezer, most of whom don't even speak English, just want to be left alone, and the Quakers around Wrightsborough want to avoid conflict of any kind. Not many of these people from up the river are going to be at Tondee's tavern, but their Tory influence will be felt on those who do attend the meeting, and some of the others will be afraid of any kind of conflict."

Lachlan did not mention that one reason for the lack of strong voices in the colony was that Governor Wright and his personally chosen council members were deeply concerned about developments in the northern colonies and had done everything possible to meet the legitimate needs of Georgians.

When they assembled in Savannah the following week, George McIntosh found that Lachlan had sized up the situation accurately, with the attending group of critics almost evenly divided and only the representatives of Savannah's Christ Church and one other parish joining St. Johns and St. Andrews on most questions. Each issue was hotly debated, and the group finally proclaimed their general condemnation of the blockade of Boston Harbor, taxation without representation, and the carrying of Americans to be tried in England. But despite the most fervent effort by the McIntoshes and others, the group decided not to send delegates to what had come to be known as the Continental Congress, which was to be convened in Philadelphia the following month, in September 1774.

It was not surprising that when delegates from the other twelve colonies convened, they voted to "lament Georgia with resentment." Neither in Savannah nor in Philadelphia was there serious talk of a revolution or any breaking of ties with Great Britain. In fact, it seemed that the colonial delegates agreed more with the sentiments of the Quakers than with any other group in Georgia. Disappointing many of the more fervent colonists, the delegates almost unanimously preferred reconciliation with Britain, and sent an "olive branch" petition to London affirming their loyalty to George III and urging him to renounce the abusive actions of Parliament.*

Despite the moderate decisions of the Continental Congress, there was wide support in Carolina and even some in Savannah for much more confrontational action. A more radical group, the Liberty Boys, let it be known that they were prepared to act with violence. Fourteen Georgia Whigs were arrested when they publicly supported the scattered acts of rebellion in Massachusetts, and it was obvious that there were others like them in the community. As part of a wide-ranging effort to demonstrate loyalty to the king, Governor Wright sent messengers throughout the colony to request that Georgians sign a petition condemning the disloyal Whigs. Except for small groups of dissident settlers like those being influenced by Elijah Clarke, there was little condemnation of the British in north Georgia. Elder Joseph Maddock led almost all the Quakers in signing the paper and, despite Ethan Pratt's advice to stay aloof from these political struggles, Kindred Morris put his signature on the document, having no way to know how much grief this would cause him in the future.

Disgusted with timid leaders in other parts of the colony, Lachlan McIntosh and other Scotsmen called another meeting in Darien in early January 1775, where they equated current problems with justification for their ancient animosity toward the English as "such oppressions neither we nor our fathers were able to bear, and it drove us to the wilderness." There was enthusiastic support among the Scotsmen for Georgia's full association with the other colonies, and the group tried to sway opinion in Savannah by passing a resolution that approved the conduct of "the brave people of Boston and Massachusetts Bay to preserve their liberty"; endorsed "all resolutions passed by the American Congress"; condemned a series of unlawful acts passed by the British Parliament; and urged the appointment of two

---

*It was signed by almost every leader who would, in the near future, sign the Declaration of Independence.

delegates to the Continental Congress to be held in Philadelphia in May. They vowed never to become slaves of England, declared their "disapprobation and abhorrence of the unnatural practice of slavery in America," and urged the manumission of all slaves and compensation for owners. Lachlan was the first signer, and the others quickly added their names.

CHAPTER 16

Massacre of the Indians

Having experienced troubles with doubtful land titles in the Carolinas, Elijah Clarke and his neighboring families were careful to get the proper documents when they obtained rights to settle near the Savannah River along the northern border of the 1773 land grant. Elijah encouraged the other men to locate their homesteads so that the entire group could remain in close contact with one another. All of the cabins were soon connected with a spiderweb of trails. Elijah and Hannah decided to build a new cabin and barn that almost joined each other, and to accept the constant animal sounds and odors in lieu of risking another fire being set by undetected intruders. This proximate location made possible an additional safety precaution, as they spent weeks of hard work putting up a stockade of upright poles, just large enough to encompass the two buildings and a small yard. Except for slits left as rifle ports and the large swinging entrance gate, the barricade cut off their view of the surrounding woods, but they did not trust the Indians who lived only a few miles away, and felt that the increased safety was worth the trouble.

Aaron Hart and his wife had settled within a mile of the Clarkes, and within sight of where two major trails crossed. Maintaining his far-reaching trade route and not intending to farm for a living, Aaron decided to take a minimum amount of land, only fifty acres, which was to be used mostly for pasture. An extra shed was built on the side of the Harts' cabin as a storeroom for his goods, and he now cut off some of his former trading territory in North Carolina and added an equivalent area in south Georgia. When Aaron was away, his wife frequently spent nights with the Clarkes.

Their decisions concerning safety seemed justified toward the end of January 1774, when Aaron came home to report that a group of Creeks had burned a homestead fifteen miles to the southwest, and murdered and scalped a man named William White, his wife, and their four children.

Elijah said, "Damn the bastards! We've got to go teach 'em a lesson."

By the time Elijah and Aaron arrived at White's place, a dozen men were there, looking at the smoldering ruins and already having dug six graves for the scalped and mutilated bodies. Since no one else seemed to be in charge, Aaron asked Elijah what he thought they should do, and the others seemed willing to listen to his opinion. Naturally assuming the role of leader, he decided that they should follow the war party, which they assumed had crossed the Ogeechee River.

Clarke insisted that they examine the surrounding area carefully and report to him on all tracks left by unshod horses, which they followed carefully. After a day and night of tracking and examining the trail and campsites, they learned that there were about a dozen Indians, that they had two or three guns, and that they were moving fast and staying together as a unit. It was also clear that the Indians were skirting the towns of their own people, indicating a renegade group. When the trail turned north and then east, the settlers decided that another attack was planned, somewhere north of Augusta. One by one, the men announced that they were returning to protect their own homes, and Elijah was not able to dissuade them. Finally, he and Aaron were forced to abandon the chase.

Two weeks later, at about nine o'clock in the morning, what seemed to be the same band of Indians attacked a place known as Sherall's Fort, where there was a small commissary store. They had apparently watched David Sherall and the youngest of his three sons leave the area and then began firing on the fort. Mrs. Sherall, two adult sons, and a Negro slave killed three of the attackers as they attempted to scale the palisade wall. The others set fire to a corner of it and then backed off and continued the assault with their weapons.

Sherall had stopped to talk to his closest neighbor down the trail, and they saw the smoke from his homestead. The boy was sent to get help from Elijah Clarke, who lived just three miles away, while the two men rushed back toward the fort. As they drew near, they glimpsed flames through the trees and drew up their horses to assess the situation. The fire seemed to be confined for the time being to one corner of the stockade, and the men rushed forward to extinguish the flames. At that moment, an Indian on each side of the trail fired muskets at the settlers, and others followed this attack with arrows. From a distance of not more than ten yards, almost every bullet and arrow struck its target. The Indians moved in with their scalping knives, then dragged the two bodies off into the bushes and resumed their positions to guard the trail.

As Elijah Clarke approached the fort, followed by five other men and Sherall's son, he held up his hand to stop the procession.

"When savages are attackin' a place for a long time, they are careful not to be surprised and always leave an ambush party alongside the trails. Let's split up, stay a hundred yards back from the path, and move forward. We need to move fast and don't have to be quiet. If they hear us, they'll back up toward the stockade."

As they broke into the clearing, the entire party of Indians looked at them for a few seconds, sized up their adversaries, and disappeared into the woods. One of the men said, "That's Big Elk giving the orders. He has been to my place a couple of times to do some trading. He's devious, knows these woods and trails like the palm of his hand, and he's mean as hell."

After burying the dead, the men decided they would take the Sherall family to the Clarke stockade and then spread the word to as many settlers as possible to assemble there the following day to decide what they should do. There was little argument when the meeting was held.

Elijah Clarke explained, "If the nearby tribes see these bandits succeed and go to war, we wouldn't have a chance even if all of us quit farmin' and spent all our time huntin' the bastards. Our lives depend on most of the damned Indians stayin' peaceful, and only sure punishment will prevent a general uprisin'."

Aaron Hart said, "We need some help from British troops. Governor Wright is under pressure from London to keep up trade and bring settlers to the ceded land, and he's expected to maintain order in the colony."

"Yeah, but maybe Georgia is not as important to England as we think it is," someone said.

Aaron replied, "We don't amount to much as far as trade is concerned, but the British need this colony. We lie between the Spaniards in Florida and the Carolinas, and to some degree we also tend to hold off the French west of here. I agree that the best approach is to stamp out any renegade uprisings when they are just getting started, but there ain't three thousand white fighting men in Georgia. We've been lucky so far, but there's been a

lot of trouble with the Cherokee in the frontier areas of Carolina, and it's finally got here."

Clarke and two or three of the settlers wanted to go right after the Indians,
but a strong majority finally decided that there might be more than one group
of marauders and they needed to get more help before abandoning their own
homes to possible attack. Also, Aaron was convinced that British officials
should assume responsibility for overall peace with the natives. Aaron and
two other men would go to Savannah to inform Governor Wright that they
must have protection from some of the British troops, only a handful of
whom were in the ceded area. They would remind him in respectful but forceful terms that they had settled in this frontier area with the clear assurance of
protection, and a lot of families would have to abandon their claims and move
to a more civilized area if military help was not forthcoming.

The governor responded as they had wished, and within a week a Captain James Grierson arrived in Augusta with fifty men, obviously green
troops and all wearing newly issued militia uniforms, except for two British
sergeants. With great fanfare, they established a military camp at Sherall's
Fort, and after a few days Grierson dispatched twenty of his men, on foot,
to visit some of the nearby Indian villages to gather evidence so he could
make an official report to the governor. When they had been gone less than
two days, a small party of the renegade Indians ambushed the group, and
three of the militiamen were killed by arrows and bullets fired from the underbrush. Not knowing the strength of their attackers, the troop returned
to camp and refused to remain any longer in the "Indian-infested" land.
Without any further discussions with the settlers, the entire detachment returned to Savannah.

Governor Wright was deeply embarrassed and used the occasion to dispatch an urgent message to London, describing the incident in the most
compelling terms, emphasizing the seriousness of the threat, and requesting more British troops. What was more effective while the message was
making its slow way to London was that the governor had Indian Superintendent John Stuart condemn the tribal leaders in the area for violating
peace agreements and cut off all trade with them.

Finally realizing that they could expect no help from Savannah in the
near future, some of the settlers met again at the Clarke homestead. They
decided unanimously to assemble their families in safe places and to abandon their farms and homesteads long enough to punish the renegades. It

was assumed that Elijah would be their military leader. One of the Indian traders reported to Aaron that he knew where Big Elk and his group of mostly young Creeks had been camping, deep within Cherokee territory, and offered to lead them there.

Elijah said he would need at least one hundred men who were willing to go on what was certain to be a difficult and time-consuming mission, and Aaron suggested that they send riders to the different areas in the ceded lands to call for volunteers.

Clarke replied, "No need to go to Wrightsborough. The damned Quakers won't help with anything that might involve violence, and we sure as hell intend to be violent."

The men laughed, and then someone said, "They're not all Quakers. In fact, I think there's some Regulators that moved down there from Orange County in Carolina."

"Well, if so, they'll be good men. Try to contact them, and let them know we'll have to be leavin' from here in three days—early Friday mornin'."

Ethan was working in his blacksmith shop when Aaron Hart rode into the yard. Little Henry was playing nearby. After greeting each other as longtime acquaintances, from the Hillsborough days, Aaron said, "Ethan, I've come here with a message from Elijah Clarke."

"I know of him and understand that he and a group of his friends have settled north of here, in some of the new lands over near the Savannah River."

"That's right. In fact, I've moved into the same general settlement. Have you also heard of Big Elk's renegades attacking the forts just west of us?"

"Aye, that I have, and we regret the loss of lives and property. We hope the Indians have gone back to their villages after meeting with the militia."

"It was the cowardly militia that went home, back to Savannah, and the Indians are still a threat."

He went on to describe what had happened, and that all trade had been cut off between the British and the Indian tribes. Finally, he said that a group of settlers had chosen Elijah Clarke to be their leader and were deciding what to do.

Ethan could see the drift of the conversation and said, "Well, trade is important to all of them, and I reckon they've been forced to disband by now."

"That's what I've come to tell you. This is a group of Creeks that are outcasts from their own people and have been condemned as bandits. In fact, some traders reported that they have set up their tents in Cherokee territory, and they know about where it is. We realize you live among the Quakers, but Clarke suggested that you might join us for a few days to keep from having to face another raid. Next time it may be down here, as you also live near the edge of ceded lands."

"We know the Indians around here fairly well, and they've always been peaceful. I'm not much for fighting and would rather stay here to protect my own place. Besides, I've heard that Clarke is pretty well known as a wild man, inclined to violence."

"There will be several dozen of us going, and we just want to arrest Big Elk and his men to prevent more attacks on our families, and send a signal to others that might be tempted to go on the warpath. These few renegades are going against the treaty that was signed last year by both the Creek and Cherokee chiefs."

Ethan was still unconvinced. "I'll have to think on it. Where will the group be?"

"We'll be meeting two hours after sunrise tomorrow, where the lower Cherokee path crosses Rock Comfort Creek."

"I know where it is. I can't say now, but I'll be there if I can come."

"We've made a list of settlers, and Kindred Morris is on it. I think I'll go by and see him. Do you know where he might be?"

"There's no need for that. He'll not be wanting to go."

Aaron knew Newota well and was familiar with Kindred's involvement with Indian tribes. Aaron declined Ethan's invitation to stay and eat, but took a drink of water and rode off down the trail.

For a few minutes Aaron thought about how different Ethan and Elijah were and was somewhat pleased with himself for being able to forge a friendship with the two strong men. It was typical of him that he thought well of both men, and he also thought it would be good for them to get better acquainted with each other.

Aaron had visited the Pratts several times on his travels and knew that Ethan was committed to a peaceful existence for himself and his family, preferring to be alone except for an occasional visit with the neighboring Morrises. He respected the Indians who lived across the river, was seldom profane, and considered his earlier official oaths as a British citizen to be binding on him as one loyal to the crown. Quite tall and powerful, Ethan was at ease among other men and never felt any need to prove himself superior in any way or to exercise control over anyone. In a conversation, he preferred to listen rather than express his own views. Aaron was not surprised that Ethan preferred not to give an immediate response to his invitation, and was sure he would consider all sides carefully and make a sound and cautious judgment.

Except for his imposing size and intimate knowledge of the surrounding wilderness, Elijah Clarke was almost the opposite in every way. He seemed driven always to exert his superiority over others, and his natural leadership abilities permitted these efforts to be successful. Elijah liked to expound his views and to harness other men into some kind of alliance with him. He was harsh and immediate in his judgments of others and in decisions about his own life. Since his encounter with the royal governor in North Carolina, Elijah had never professed any sense of British citizenship and was always in the forefront of rebel discussions. In many ways, it was uncomfortable to be around this overbearing and opinionated man, who was often wrong and never in doubt, but there was an attractive vitality about him that brought a number of men to his side. He never liked to be contradicted, and Aaron was always careful to express contrary views cautiously or in private. Elijah despised all Indians as savages, was never willing to attribute to them any human characteristics, and this was one subject on which Aaron never expressed his real opinion. Elijah would have been disgusted to know that Aaron had consorted with an Indian "wife," considering that any sexual relation other than rape was ungodly with a squaw.

Ethan watched Aaron go, took Henry to Epsey, and then got his rifle and walked off into the woods, feeling that he should consider carefully this proposition to join Clarke. He was troubled about the prospect of increasing violence, and of becoming involved in it himself. Like all the settlers, and particularly those who lived on the outskirts of the ceded areas and nearest the Indians, he was acutely aware of the danger to his family if respected Indian leaders decided to approve raids on the remote settlements. At the same time, he considered it unlikely that they would renege on their commitments, forgo the advantages of peaceful trade, and attempt to take back the land they had ceded. An all-out war would undoubtedly bring trained British troops into the area, more than a match for the poorly armed natives. This was especially true because the Indians were divided, with only rare cooperation between the Creeks and Cherokees. But he trusted Aaron Hart and finally decided that it might be helpful to join in

punishing Big Elk's small group, who probably were outcasts and condemned by their own people. Another factor in his decision was that he
and his neighbors might very well need protection in the future, and the
newer settlers farther north would be valuable allies.

Before going to bed, he told Epsey that he would be leaving early the
next morning to meet some other men about an Indian threat. It was less
than twelve miles to the meeting place, and Ethan was there shortly after
sunrise. Neither Elijah Clarke nor any of his close friends had arrived, but
a few men had already gathered, mostly from the older settlements nearer
Augusta. They shared what information they had but knew little about the
latest developments or any plans for their mission. It was more than an
hour later when the others arrived, almost two dozen men who had obviously traveled together and seemed to know one another well.

Clarke was silent while he counted the group, and spoke first: "We need
three times as many men, but this will have to do. I believe we have enough
here to teach the red bastards a lesson they'll not forget."

He stepped down from his horse, and the others gathered around him.
Ethan examined him closely. Except for himself, Clarke was the largest
man there. He had thick black hair, cut in a rough fashion about even with
the lobes of his ears. His eyes were surprisingly large but squinted often as
he talked. His aquiline nose and somewhat protruding chin gave an impression of strength to a short upper lip and a soft-looking mouth. He had
prominent, yellowed teeth, and the upper ones were constantly in view
when he spoke. As the situation was explained to the newcomers, it seemed
to Ethan that Clarke was excessively presumptuous in his position as
leader, not acknowledging the voices of the other men until he had finished
his long and somewhat convoluted statements. At times he struggled for
the right word, and the man next to Ethan whispered, "He can't read and
write, but he's smart as hell."

When a few of the men began expressing their views, Clarke listened
for about five minutes and then held up his hand to demand silence. He
summarized, "Well, now we all know about the Whites, the Sheralls, and
others—the killin's and scalpin's of their women and children, and the
burnin' of their houses and barns. We're dealin' with a bunch of cowards,
who are despised by their own people. The only ones worse are the militiamen sent here by the governor, who messed in their pants and ran when
they heard the sound of the first bow twang."

There was soft laughter, and Elijah waited for it to subside.

"It's fallen on us to handle this mess, and we're gwine to clean it up. Big Elk and his men believe they are safe until they're ready to strike us again, and have set up camp about twenty miles across the river. Mr. Moses, who trades with the Cherokees, is with us and says he knows right where they are."

He pointed to a small and obviously nervous man near him.

"I reckon everybody brought enough to eat, and powder and shot to last us awhile. It might be important for us to know how to reload in a hurry. Also, you need a knife for close fightin', and I see some of you have a tomahawk. We ain't going to turn back until we find them and finish our business."

These comments were unnecessary, but no one objected. Most of the men were avid hunters and habitually carried a hunting knife and a musket or long rifle whenever they donned a hat and coat to leave their own cabin. On horseback and in the woods, a weapon was in their hands, and some even contrived ingenious ways to secure their gun across plow stock handles in the field. This permitted them to respond quickly if an enemy appeared or if they saw a deer, bear, or turkey within shooting range.

There were several questions about distances and directions, and then Ethan asked, "What are we going to do when we find them?"

Clarke appeared to notice him for the first time, although Ethan was a foot taller than the average man, and obviously strong and able.

"As I've already said, we know where they are. We'll use their own tactics, by surroundin' them at night and then movin' in at daybreak when most of them are still asleep."

Ethan, apparently quite at ease, persisted, "And then what will we do with the prisoners?"

"They'll not want to be prisoners and will probably fight to the end. I reckon we'll treat the bastards the same as they would treat us. Ain't that what the Bible says?"

There was a general murmur of laughter and approval, and Ethan decided not to pursue the matter further.

The men mounted their horses and followed in single file behind Clarke and the trader, who was consulted every now and then if there was a choice of trails.

Late in the afternoon, Clarke halted the group in a small clearing by raising his hand. When the others had gathered around him, he said,

"We'll stop here. We think they're only about two miles away. Stay quiet, keep your horses close, don't make any fires, and get some rest if you can. Later, a few of us will scout ahead on foot, locate the camp, and size up the situation. They's enough of a moon so we can see to get around. Then we'll come back here, work out some signals, and give everybody a rundown in time to line up for the attack."

After it was dark, Clarke chose a few of his closest friends and they moved off toward the northeast, easing along silently down a dim trail in their moccasined feet. They were back in about three hours, finding all the men sitting up and talking softly in small groups.

Clarke called them together.

"We located their camp, which looks almost like a permanent settlement. We saw two fires about burned out but didn't see nobody movin' around. They're on this side of a pretty good-sized creek that won't be easy to cross. We'll divide up into three groups. I'm puttin' Aaron Hart in charge of eight men, who'll go to the right. Micajah Williamson here will take the same number to the left side. We've already worked out where everyone will be lined up. I'll be with all of the rest of you to make the first and main attack in the middle. I figure there'll be twelve with me, and I'll want two to keep the horses quiet and close together. It's not a big place, so we ought to be able to see each other after we line up. When I think we're all ready, which'll be about first light, I'll signal by shootin' my gun. Then everybody goes in as fast as hell. If anything moves, shoot it, but be damned sure you don't kill me! Be careful not to waste your first shot, because after that you may have to depend on your knives and hatchets. I don't want anybody to get away."

Ethan asked, "What about the ones that give up?"

Clarke responded sharply, "I've already told you there won't be any, but you can capture one if you want to take a murderer back home to live in your cabin."

Ethan decided not to respond. It was a sober and somewhat frightened band of men who then moved down the trail together, until Clarke stopped and pointed to his left and right. They were still three hundred yards from the Indians. Ethan was one of those who went with Hart. As his group moved away, they could hear Clarke quietly directing the remaining men to their places.

Hart seemed to know what to do. When they were close enough to the creek to hear the water running, he stopped and motioned the men to come close to him. He whispered their instructions: to form a line almost perpendicular to the stream, size up the Indian camp, and make sure they all had their guns, knives, and hatchets ready for the attack.

Ethan found his place, checked the positions of his nearest companions, and decided that he would go straight for the lean-to nearest him. There was no immediate response from among the shelters when the signal shot sounded, but before the settlers could reach their destinations, the sleepy Indians were rising from their pallets and reaching for weapons. There was scattered gunfire around the periphery of the camp, screams from the victims, and then the grunts and curses as men closed in mortal hand-to-hand combat, all knowing that their lives were at stake.

The fighting was over within ten minutes, with Big Elk and every brave killed except two, who jumped into the creek. Hart ordered Ethan and two other men to follow them, and they moved almost one hundred yards downstream but soon lost sight of the Indians, who apparently swam to safety. As they stood still and listened quietly to detect any movement in the brush across the creek, Ethan heard Clarke shout for all his men to reload, and to search every hiding place for "cowards that refused to fight."

A few minutes later, the settlers were surprised to find a number of women and children, including three infants, huddled inside the shelters, all attempting to hide under or behind hides or blankets. They were brought into the center of the clearing, and crowded closely together, touching or embracing each other in fear.

Ethan heard Clarke order, "Kill them all!"

He ran back toward the clearing, shouting, "No! No!"

But it was too late. While most of the white men held back and a few protested, Clarke and several of the settlers moved in, and with their hatchets, soon killed all the survivors. When Ethan arrived, some of the Indians were being scalped.

He grasped Clarke by his shoulder and spun him around. "This is murder! You're no better than Big Elk!"

Clarke backed away and leveled his rifle at Ethan's chest. "Don't ever touch me again, Pratt, unless you're ready to die. These people are all guilty and they have to learn a lesson. I'd advise you to get your arse away from here and go back to your damned Quaker settlement. You had no business being here in the first place."

Ethan was furious and disgusted. He looked around at the faces of the other men and saw a clear distinction among them. He judged that at least a third of them agreed with him, but no one spoke. He turned and walked slowly out of the clearing, heading down the trail toward where they had left their horses. Only two other men followed him, and they were soon on their way back home. He tried not to think about the bloody scene he had left behind.

CHAPTER 17

Clarke Organizes a Militia

Aaron Hart was half-asleep as he held on to his saddle and swayed back and forth on his bay gelding. Day was just breaking, and he had already been riding for an hour and a half. He had to yank the reins several times to keep his horse from ranging up alongside the one in front of him, on which sat the much larger man who never wanted to be challenged in any way, not even as to who would lead the six-horse caravan down a narrow Indian trail. Elijah Clarke had always had a tendency to dominate other people, and since the group of men had, almost automatically, chosen him to be their leader, he was even more inclined to prove his authority at every opportunity. In many ways it reassured the other men to follow someone who was right sure of himself, but it had become increasingly difficult to have a give-and-take discussion about controversial issues or even to share in making the simple decisions necessary to forge an effective militia group.

Aaron's thoughts wandered idly over his relationship with Clarke, which had begun when they were neighbors in North Carolina. Beginning as a farmer, Aaron had accumulated a small string of packhorses and began trading in an ever-expanding area. Although profits were minimal, he enjoyed meeting people, sharing news and opinions, and being free of the drudgery of farmwork and the exclusive role of husband. It was his knowledge of the new territories that had influenced his small group of friends to move first to South Carolina and then to Georgia, and to settle northwest of Augusta near the Savannah River. From there he had established a new trade route through Wrightsborough, across the Oconee into Indian territory, and south to Savannah. Aaron had been one of the regular visitors in Henry Pratt's cobbler shop in Hillsborough and had known the Quakers and Ethan Pratt before they moved to Georgia. He was thoroughly familiar with their commitment to peace and their loyalty to the king. He felt somewhat guilty that he had recruited Ethan to participate in the raid on Big Elk three months ago and had not spoken out to let the other men know he shared Ethan's disgust with the massacre of the women and children. He rationalized his reticence by convincing himself that his loyalty to Elijah would let him restrain any future barbaric acts.

Aaron thought with some satisfaction about his secret, at least from white friends: that he had taken a wife in a village near Newota's, and she had borne him a second child. Although he spent only a few days there at a time, he had adopted many of the Indians' customs when he was among them, and his generosity had made him a favorite among them. He had also known Big Elk, whose village was a full day's journey to the west. He knew of the big Indian's hatred of the white settlers and his criminal habits, but despised him most because of his brutality toward his own family and those around him. It was Aaron who had located the trader who'd led them to the successful raid against Big Elk and the killing of his traveling party.

Except for his wife and especially his Indian family, Aaron Hart never had any intimate relationships, and now he found great pleasure in helping to form and train this motley group of recruits as members of his own militia platoon. It was like a new life for him, and he contemplated how he could best impress the men—not just in putting up a fence, caring for packhorses, or trading goods, but also in such things as marshaling a force rapidly, the use of secret signals, and how to improve accuracy with his gun and the speed with which he could reload it. Without telling anyone about it, he practiced in the woods behind his house and was glad that he could afford a good rifle and a plentiful supply of powder and balls. As Elijah put more responsibilities on him even during working days, he felt a pang of guilt when he walked by the barn and horse stalls behind his cabin and noticed that they were not as clean or meticulously maintained as he had always kept them.

Elijah Clarke had become something of a hero throughout north Georgia after the raid on Big Elk's camp, as accounts of the military success were repeated and exaggerated, but Aaron and the others all understood that no one was to mention the final slaying and scalping of the innocents.

It was only after that military operation that the men had decided to stay in close touch with one another, and the group was slowly developing into a close-knit militia force, preparing themselves for another fight with the Indians when it might become necessary. They enjoyed something of a conspiratorial alliance as Elijah called them together every week or so to share ideas on the best weapons to carry and ways to improve on the tactics they had used in the raid.

At first there were only sixteen of them, since Ethan Pratt and a few others would not have been welcome, and Clarke preferred to include men who lived within a few miles of his fort. From the beginning he divided them into two equal groups, requiring that they compete with one another in marksmanship and in simulated battle.

Without consulting anyone in advance, Clarke had announced at the first meeting, "I'll be figurin' out some plans on how we can work and fight together, somethin' like we had at Big Elk's camp. Aaron Hart and Micajah Williamson will be my permanent lieutenants, each one in charge of half the men." Without any orders or even unofficial directions, all the men began addressing Elijah as "Captain Clarke," and in almost every way this set him apart from the others, even from those close friends and neighbors who had spent their lives together with him. In the same subtle way, it was assumed that Hart was Clarke's aide-de-camp. In addition to delivering orders from the captain, Aaron had another important role: to accommodate and conceal as much as possible the fact that Clarke was illiterate. With some difficulty he could sign his name, but it was Aaron's duty to read news reports to his commander and to prepare written orders and even private messages, when needed, to his wife, Hannah. This was not a secret that was well kept, but it was one not discussed by any of those who served with the militia.

Like a blind man who develops other senses more acutely, Elijah Clarke was endowed with the extraordinary ability to assess a complicated situation and devise almost instantaneously the best means to take advantage of it. He was a stern commander but a fair one and was exceptionally sensitive to the needs of the militiamen's families. As his surrogate back home, Hannah considered it her duty to take care of the other wives and their children.

Now riding along behind the front horse, Aaron knew that this morning the captain's leadership abilities would be fully tested. All the men were challenged by the discipline of military service and proud of their progress in marksmanship and tactics, which most of them had assumed would be

used in defending their own homes and families against possible Indian attacks. Their ranks had grown steadily, and their commitments and political
attitudes increasingly unified, slowly changing under Clarke's strong influence and by the news they'd received from the northern colonies. Elijah
was always outspoken and would not brook any open dissent from his support of the decisions of the Continental Congress, including an embargo of
trade with both Britain and the Tory merchants in Savannah. It was obvious that the captain was becoming less interested in possible battles with
the Creeks and Cherokees and more fascinated with news about the growing armed struggle against the king's forces. Some of the militiamen also
shared the intense condemnation that Carolinians felt toward the "pacifists
and cowards" in Georgia.

This morning the men were assembling far to the southeast of their
homes, near the junction of Kiokee Creek and the Savannah River. This
was one of their favorite meeting places, on a high bluff overlooking the
water and far enough off the main trail so their campsite was not disturbed
by travelers who might be going to and from Savannah. Aaron had some
trepidation about the meeting, because Clarke had informed Micajah and
him the previous evening that he would require all the men to join him in a
commitment to support the revolutionary Minutemen in their direct opposition to British forces. Although he was loyal to Elijah Clarke and increasingly dominated by him in their common military commitment, it was not
easy for Aaron to accept this mandate to express disloyalty to the crown.
His father had come from Liverpool, and he had never before questioned
his own role as a British citizen. Not much of a religious man, he had always considered his first loyalty to be to the king. As had all the other men,
he had taken solemn oaths to that effect when they had signed land deeds
and various other official papers, and routinely offered toasts to "His
Majesty the king." It was easy for him and other Englishmen to condemn
Parliament and there were plenty of reasons to do so, but he had an uneasy
feeling that Clarke's present attitude bordered on treason.

When the men arrived at their camp on Kiokee bluff, they staked out
their horses, stowed their few supplies in the lean-to sheds, and prepared
for a two-day training session. This morning, however, instead of dividing
into platoons, Clarke had the men assemble in the open space for what
they assumed would be a lecture on military tactics.

When the men were gathered, all standing in a semicircle and facing

Clarke, he began with some humorous remarks. "We've come a long way in the last few weeks in findin' places without gettin' lost more than half the time, in movin' through the woods without runnin' all the rabbits out of Georgia, and loadin' and firin' our guns without killin' the other men in our platoon. I counted twenty-nine men here this morning—thirty if you want to count me—and I reckon most of you have something to eat, your rifles, powder, and balls—I'm talkin' about lead balls. For all this, I'm grateful."

He paused as the men laughed, but they grew silent as it became obvious that his demeanor had changed. "Up to now, we've all been lookin' back at Big Elk and gettin' ready for another fight with the damned savages that want to burn our houses, steal our livestock, and rape our women. I think the red sons of bitches remember the lesson we taught them, and Aaron and I have tried to make sure they also know about us preparin' for the future. Maybe we've already done a lot, even without a fight, to protect our families. I hear that the governor is goin' to meet with the Creek leaders to force them to stop their raids and help us capture the two buggers that escaped across the creek.

"Now, there's somethin' else that's a bigger worry to me, and I hope it bothers y'all too. We've all heard about what has been happenin' up in Massachusetts, where British troops have been attackin' people like us and tryin' to starve them with embargoes, heavy taxes, and such, if they try to protect themselves. I've been proud of the folks in Carolina that have supported the actions of the Minutemen around Boston, but except for McIntosh and a few others, I've been ashamed of the cowards in Savannah that are against freedom and citizens' rights and want to spend the rest of their lives kissin' the governor's arse. My wife, Hannah, has been wantin' to move across the river, but I don't intend to change farms ag'in durin' this lifetime, so we're stuck here in Georgia."

There was no clear response from the men, either supporting or disapproving, but they looked at one another as though to discern a common reaction. Clarke paused a few seconds and then added, "I don't claim to know what's goin' to happen, but when the time comes, I aim to be protectin' myself from the British bastards, and I hope all of you feel the same way."

Aaron was not surprised to see that some of the men were becoming uncomfortable with what Clarke had said. He knew the ones in his platoon quite well and had participated in conversations with them about the controversies that were arising in the north. He estimated that almost half of them would oppose any armed actions against British troops. He noticed some murmurs of agreement but decided that he would have to be the one to speak up so those in opposition would feel that they had a voice in the discussion.

"Captain, I feel the same way you do about freedom and our right to protect ourselves, but it seems to me that the British troops in Georgia are here to keep the Indians under control, and I think we're a lot better off under Governor Wright than Carolina has ever been under their royal governors. I'm ready to fight the savages, but I wouldn't feel right lining up to shoot one of the king's soldiers unless I thought they was planning to hurt me and mine."

Aaron had shared his views with Clarke privately the previous evening. Clarke had then made it clear to Aaron and Micajah that he was ready to draw a line between the militiamen, once and for all.

He looked at Hart, a strong man like himself and a good leader, and said, "Aaron, I hear what you say, but it don't suit me none. We all know that John Stuart stirs up the Creeks and Cherokee ag'in' us, tellin' them that all us settlers wants is to steal their land. The division is comin' or is already here between savages and settlers, our own freedom and being pushed around by folks in London, and between bein' a man and a coward. I know some of you feel different, but I don't think we can walk a fence rail no longer, and we'll have to take a stand one way or the other."

Clarke was a shrewd leader and didn't want to lose any more men than necessary. He looked around and continued, "We ain't fightin' the Redcoats yet, so y'all will have a chance to decide that later. You've probably been knowin' how I feel. I want to keep us all together, irregardless of how you might be headin' now, and I'd like for all of us to keep on learnin' how to fight as a group, even if it turns out to be ag'in' the Indians. For now, let's just say that we'll be protectin' our women and chillun against whoever might bother them. Anybody who don't agree on this is welcome to leave."

The men looked at Hart, who finally said, "I'm hoping I'll never be aiming at another white man, but I admit we can't see what might be coming later on. Most of us know how to shoot, but we don't yet know how to fight, and we need to learn. I reckon I'll be staying, at least for the time being." Clarke nodded, and they turned their attention to weapons and tactics.

Aaron hoped he had helped avoid any kind of rebellion, but he could pick out at least five loyalists among his men who rejected Captain Clarke's attitude and would soon find themselves incompatible with the majority.

Although they were now unwilling to confront Elijah with their concerns about what seemed to be treason against the crown, Aaron knew they would simply stay at home instead of responding to the next call to assemble. Yet, while Clarke's clear commitment to the rebel cause would eliminate some of his potential recruits, men had a natural inclination to identify and despise an enemy, and Aaron reckoned that the militia would more than compensate for their reduced ranks with their growing willingness to practice for war, even against Britain.

Two of the older men had served as soldiers with the British army, and Clarke told them to describe what they had learned. They began their instruction with close-order drill and marching abreast, then kneeling in a solid rank to face an enemy. Clarke was expecting this discourse and let them go on for about twenty minutes before he exclaimed, "That may be a good way to fight a French army on a battlefield, but here in the Georgia woods it's a good way to get killed! We ain't in the bloody army. What the hell do you think these trees and bushes are for, if not to hide behind and catch the bullets comin' our way? We'll move like the damned Indians, quiet and fast, and we'll spread out so we're just close enough together to know where the next man is. Later, we'll have to know about bayonets, artillery, and stuff, and your learnin' can help us then."

This was typical of Elijah's training technique. The captain would set up a dispute, quarrel with the conclusion of the others, and his final word would prevail. It didn't matter that the retired British soldiers were embarrassed and perhaps angry.

Although there had been no concerted attempt to do so, the men were dressed in a surprisingly similar fashion, with the dominant feature of their clothing being long-sleeved shirts that came down almost to their knees, usually worn outside whatever trousers were underneath. Later, both the British and regular Continental troops would come to call them Shirtmen. When they were not barefoot they wore Indian-style moccasins, mostly for warmth during the colder months. They had broad sashes or leather belts around their waists, inside of which they carried either a knife or a tomahawk, and a powder horn and a roomy pouch were slung over their shoulders to hold parched corn or other food, plus spare flints, bullets, patches and grease, and sometimes a bullet mold. Blanket rolls and other supplies were carried on their horses, which were always kept close at hand. As was the custom of those who lived in relative isolation, most were armed with the long rifles they used for hunting or protecting their families and property. Others, who lived in settlements, had brought various kinds of guns, including smoothbore muskets or shotguns.

Hoping to redeem themselves, the two men with British army experience demonstrated their muskets, and their ability to attach bayonets to the barrels. The men could see that this was a formidable weapon at close range against an enemy struggling to reload weapons, but most of them had never had a use for bayonets and still believed that their long rifles gave them adequate protection and hunting skills.

The group spent two days together, first in general discussions of weapons and in target practice, and finally the two platoons actually maneuvered against one another. Before returning to their homes, Clarke assembled the men for a final summary of what they had learned.

"Y'all can see that we ain't much of a company of fightin' men. If the barrels ain't wore out to smoothbores, most of you riflemen can hit what you're aimin' at up to two hundred paces or so, which is farther than we're apt to see anything in the woods where we'll be fightin'. The muskets ain't very accurate beyond sixty yards, but they're lighter and shorter, and the rifles take a lot more time to reload, maybe a full minute. An enemy can be on us in this time, with a bayonet in our guts. The best thing I've seen is our guns shootin' at different times, so anyone comin' in on us is always facin' a bullet. We'll have to use whatever we have for now, but we'll improve over time. I've seen the need for a bayonet, and I want all of us to have one. When you get home, you might whittle and grind down the handle of a good butcher knife, so it will fit in or around your gun barrel, to use if someone comes on you right after you shoot."

Before disbanding, he instructed the men always to have plenty of powder and balls, and to practice at home, both in marksmanship and in improving the speed with which they could reload and fire. Although there were some holdouts, most men began to like the muskets, with their smoothbore and three-quarter-inch-round balls, which, with intense practice, they were able to fire at least three times in one minute, and some of the more proficient could get off four shots. Each man carried cartridges, called "cottages," which were the projectile and a charge of powder wrapped in paper. To load, they tore off one end of the paper, poured the powder in the barrel, and then rammed the paper and ball down into the barrel. In rainy weather, with powder inclined toward dampness, the first firing of either type gun was uncertain, and the men would usually wait until the weapon was needed be-fore charging the flintlock with powder to complete the load. Clarke eventu-ally urged most of his men to shift to muskets, like all other militia in the colonies, but he retained some riflemen in each squad who were attached to their long guns. Their sharpshooting ability was invaluable, especially at longer range, since the group was unlikely ever to have cannon of any cal-iber. Clarke taught all his troops to fire in sequence so that, when possible, adjacent men were never reloading at the same time.

The two British veterans taught the militia how to deal with incoming shells, which had fuses that burned several seconds, and sometimes longer, after the projectile had landed. They were to shout "Shell!" and throw them-selves prone or behind a protective barrier until after the explosion. One of the most helpful drills was when Clarke would assign these same experienced men to lead one of the platoons at a time in the British manner, where all troops in line would fire simultaneously and then reload, which made them vulnerable in woodland combat. They found that the Indian style of fighting was almost always superior, but the Redcoat teams presented a formidable threat when they turned to the use of bayonets. It became increasingly obvi-ous to the Georgia militiamen that in actual warfare a forceful charge with bayonets was the most effective way to dishearten and rout an inexperienced and uncertain enemy force. The stiff blade, whether at the end of a gun bar-rel or just lashed to a stout wooden shaft, was fearsome in its savagery and superior to a sword or other close-order weapon. Long before being engaged in actual combat, they learned to fear the bayonet while fumbling helplessly to reload their own gun under the intense pressure of combat.

Captain Clarke's men agreed on certain rendezvous points if they were lost or separated, and each man knew which others to notify if the word was given to assemble for a simulated drill or a military operation. They had sim-ple signals for communicating with each other, mostly using cow horns, which could be heard for more than a mile if the wind was still. Their meet-ing places for training were changed almost every month, and Elijah had Aaron prepare simple maps of their operating areas, mostly along the west-ern side of the Savannah River, all oriented around the tributary creeks and ancient Indian trails. The men knew that their knowledge of the terrain would be a crucial factor in almost any battle. They learned how to move rapidly, on foot, horseback, or canoe, and to converge at a meeting place.

One of the most difficult of Hart's recommendations for Captain

Clarke to accept was the advantage of retreating in the face of a superior force. He reminded the captain repeatedly that the militia numbers would almost always be small and their troops scattered over a wide area, and that it was no disgrace to leave the enemy in charge of a small plot of contested ground if the militiamen could survive to fight again. Their advantage would almost always lie in mobility, concealment, and flexible tactics. Eventually, even before these tenets were proven in battle, they became accepted among the men.

Seven of the assembled men failed to report back after Clarke's comments about opposing the crown, but there were no defectors among the group who had moved with Clarke from Carolina into Georgia. It was interesting to Aaron that Clarke never mentioned the defectors, either in private or public discussions, but there was no doubt that their names were engraved in the captain's mind as traitors.

CHAPTER 18

Peace in Georgia, Fighting in the North

Newota stood just inside the meetinghouse, not qualified to sit with the assembled chiefs but knowing that his presence was as necessary as any except that of Emistisiguo, their great leader. Since he would be the one who would interpret what was to be said if they decided to confront the white officials, it was important that he understand the nuances of the seemingly interminable discussions. Knowing the chief of the Upper Creeks well, he could already predict what decision would be made, but the talks had to complete their course because it was necessary for all the lesser chiefs to feel that they had been personally involved in shaping the consensus.

He watched their leader with close attention and admiration. For more than a dozen years both Creek and Cherokee had respected him because of his natural aversion to the ambitions of colonial settlers, who always wanted more land, and his shrewd utilization of his relations with the British to enhance the well-being of his own people. To obtain this goal, he worked closely with Indian Superintendent John Stuart and also with various military leaders. The king of England had made Emistisiguo and four other leaders "great medal chiefs" in 1765, and this honor gave him special status with the British and his own people.

The young Indian almost dozed off when the lesser chiefs were talking, but he snapped back to attention when Emistisiguo said, "Let us review what has happened. Some of the outcasts from our villages violated our decision and my pledge to refrain from attacks on peaceful white settlers living near the Oconee. All but two of the raiding party were killed at Big Elk's village, including their families. Since then, the murderer Elijah Clarke has begun training others to make further attacks on us, and they have convinced Governor Wright to stop all trade with our villages. Some of our people are starving, and our braves have stopped hunting because cured skins have no value."

Several of the chiefs stirred and one of them indicated that he wished to speak. Newota saw that he was Big Elk's uncle, White Fox. Emistisiguo looked at him sternly and said, "You have made it clear to all of us how you feel, but time for punitive action against the whites has passed. We have lost the support of both the governor and John Stuart, who tell us that war must end."

White Fox lifted his hand, palm outward, indicating that he still had a comment to make. "I have come to agree with this. All my people insist that trade be resumed, and there is little doubt that continuing warfare is against our best interests. The renegade whites are being brought together as warriors, and this has given more of them the excuse to cross the river into our territory. Even the British troops are protecting them, and we are becoming estranged from our friends. But we must have retribution against those who killed our women and children, since the British have ignored this terrible crime. It is a matter of honor."

Emistisiguo was obviously impatient to end the discussion, but White Fox was an influential leader and his villages were on the forefront of Creek territory, bordering on land held by the whites to the east and the Cherokees to the north. He was a warrior by inclination, but known to be a good and honest man, embarrassed by the criminal actions of his nephew.

"White Fox, there is reason in what you say, but we must take care of our present needs and also plan how best to strengthen our hand for the future. I suggest that we meet with British leaders, attempt to negotiate the resumption of trade, and decide how best to punish those who destroyed Big Elk's village. Some British officers have made it clear to me that these white murderers may soon be fighting against the British, and that the Redcoats will need us to join forces against them. That may be the time for retribution."

Newota could see that a decision had been made, and the council soon decided to send a message to Governor Wright agreeing to a meeting to resolve the mutually damaging impasse. Emistisiguo had full confidence in the young man and said, "Newota, you have heard our talk and understand what we have decided. Tell the governor that we will come to Savannah on the full moon after the Green Corn Dance, and that we will be prepared to resolve all our differences."

Having been thoroughly instructed during his years with Kindred, Newota was as eloquent in the English language as were his British counterparts. Although some of the white traders spoke the various Indian languages and dialects, Emistisiguo trusted only Newota to be both accurate and honest in the long exchanges, and to relay the nuances and proprieties of their positions.

When the appointed time arrived, the British and the Indian chiefs had completed all the basic arrangements, and Newota and the governor's aide-de-camp had agreed in advance that the leaders would meet for at least three hours each day, beginning two hours after noon. There was some argument about who would speak first, which might indicate that one side was the supplicant. Eventually it was decided that on the first day the governor would welcome the group, Emistisiguo would respond with a general discourse on the Creeks' habitual desire for peace and good trade, and then there would be an exchange of appropriate gifts. On the second day, the substance of the issues would be presented, beginning with Emistisiguo making tangential comments and then both sides moving step by step to the heart of the issues that needed to be resolved.

Twenty-two chiefs accompanied Emistisiguo to the meeting, along with Newota as interpreter and a large entourage of tribesmen and women, who camped near the town during the discussions. Governor Wright headed the British contingent, and he was supported by three army officers, a number of subalterns, and Indian Superintendent John Stuart. Another man was introduced as "Elijah Clarke from Augusta, accompanied by his aide, Aaron Hart." The Creeks glanced at one another. This was the first time they had ever seen the militia leader face-to-face, although their scouts had observed him and his men often during their training exercises.

On the second morning, Newota knew in advance what the governor would say, having been thoroughly briefed by one of the Creek leaders who worked closely with the Indian superintendent. Elijah Clarke had presented the settlers' most important demands: that no native villages be established on or near the Oconee River, and that the two escapees from Big Elk's band be found and delivered to the settlers for trial and execution. After Governor Wright proclaimed the settlers' ultimatum as his own proposal, the Indian leaders repaired to their own settlement and discussed the matter for the remainder of the day. The next morning, Newota interpreted Emistisiguo's response to the entire assembly as the chief stood erect, with arms folded across his chest:

"We will honor the agreements made last year with our British brothers regarding territorial boundaries. There have been violations on both sides, but I will guarantee our commitment provided the governor gives an equal assurance that his troops will prevent illegal settlements on our land. It will not be possible for the two braves of Big Elk to be delivered to white men for trial and punishment. We acknowledge that they have been guilty of serious crimes and, although your people have also committed murder against innocent people, we ourselves will punish those of our own tribes. I will deliver their scalps to you before the next full moon."

The chief paused and then added his crucial element as an apparent afterthought. "We know that the British need to obtain skins and hides from our people, and we are willing to resume trade without further delay."

The governor glanced at the faces of his associates, and all the British officials indicated their agreement with the proposal. However, Elijah Clarke would show no flexibility in the matter.

His face was flushed and his voice somewhat strident when he glared around and said, "We ain't goin' to agree to any Indian settlements near the Oconee. Our people have suffered too much from murder, rape, and the burnin' of our homes. We demand the right to cross the river, both to hunt and also to defend ourselves. Also, we're the ones who suffered from Big Elk's renegade attacks, and it's our right to give them the punishment they deserve."

There was an uncomfortable silence, and the governor motioned for Clarke and Hart to follow him and John Stuart into a back room. They had a heated exchange, and Aaron finally helped convince Elijah to accept the overall proposal, with the understanding that the natives would be forced to move from all territory ceded by them in the Augusta agreement of 1773. Furthermore, if the scalps were not delivered as offered, British troops would join the militia in a search party to find and punish the two braves who escaped from Big Elk's camp. Elijah also agreed to permit the governor to speak for the entire group in the presence of the Indians, so that it would not appear that the whites were divided among themselves.

The assembly soon reached an agreement, and after another exchange of gifts the Creeks went back to their camp and departed the following day for their villages. They agreed that a death sentence be issued for the two criminals, and three weeks later Newota was sent to deliver the two scalps to Governor Wright, with a solemn statement from Emistisiguo that they were from the renegades.

All the white leaders marked the chief as the unquestioned leader among his own people, and a man who could be trusted to honor his commitments. The chiefs had also learned a lesson that would have profound consequences as tension increased between the British and the militia forces: in the long run it was undoubtedly better to cast their lot with the Redcoats, but to remember that the whites were divided. Both sides, in a dispute, would be seeking their favor and services, which could be sold to one or the other—or sometimes to both.

Although Aaron Hart was spending more time in military training, he and all the other militiamen, most of them farmers, had to continue with their normal work. As a trader, he was better able than most to discern the changes taking place among those with whom he was doing business. He could see that there was a growing alignment of Georgians into two camps, Tories against Whigs—those loyal to King George against others who were beginning to favor increased independence from the unpopular British Parliament. There was a larger number who refused to take sides but who supported the boycott of Savannah merchants, were openly antagonistic toward the neighboring Creeks, and felt that the British troops did too little to control the Indians. Many of the settlers criticized Indian Superintendent John Stuart, and some accused him of inciting the Indians against the more militant colonists. There was no doubt among the militiamen that Emistisiguo and other shrewd Indian leaders were using these troubled times to strengthen their ties with the British, who had trade goods to offer and were not eager to take their land. Aaron had mixed feelings about these growing divisions, but he was proud of his new authority and was increasingly loyal to Elijah Clarke, who relied on him for both information and advice.

CHAPTER 19

The Georgia Navy Strikes

MAY 1775

Although Governor Wright was able to marshal enough Tories to block Georgia's support of the northern colonies, the Liberty Boys and the coastal parishes remained active in their opposition to British policies. The focus of the struggle for power was in Savannah, where the Whigs steadily increased their authority through the congress and the new Council of Safety, whose members were elected directly by the people. Month by month, the council asserted authority to control militia groups, choose military commanders, and even propose negotiating trade agreements with Indians. Governor Wright retained his high and influential office, but complained to his superiors in London about the rapidly growing usurpation of his authority. His royal council continued to meet in Savannah, but their main role was to lament the improper activities of the rebels. Secretly, the British government instructed Wright to abandon his post whenever necessary for his own safety.

Lachlan McIntosh was spending more time in Savannah, looking for additional ways to strengthen opposition to England. He and George felt that it was their responsibility to keep this goal alive, but they deplored the criminal activities of the Liberty Boys, whom they considered to be irresponsible hoodlums.

One afternoon in May, George came to Lachlan's room at Tondee's tavern, accompanied by a man named Backmon from Charles Town. After they exchanged pleasantries, Backmon said, "There is a British ship, the *Philippa,* in Charles Town and we have learned that it will be loaded with powder and lead to be delivered to Savannah for the Indian trade, or perhaps to be used against anyone supporting action against Parliament. It would be difficult for us to interrupt this process, but we have been thinking about capturing the ship and its cargo after it is loaded."

There was no response, and Backmon began to fear the reaction to his bold proposal.

Then Lachlan asked quietly, "How long before the ship will be ready to sail?"

"At least two weeks, perhaps more."

"Are you positive that its destination will be Savannah?"

"Yes, our source of information is authoritative and dependable, and we will know if there are any future changes in the plans."

"Why do you come to us?"

Backmon now hesitated and then responded, "There are those of us who think that if we move in Charles Town, the ammunition may just be returned to safekeeping or to its former owners. Also, British troops will be guarding the ship closely."

After a moment, he looked from Lachlan to George and continued, "We are also interested in seeing some activity in Savannah that will demonstrate opposition to London's abusive policies and help solidify Whig strength in Georgia."

He looked directly at Lachlan and added, "We thought you might consider taking the *Philippa* after it arrives here."

George spoke for the first time. "Lachlan, I have learned that there is a small but adequate vessel already completed by a shipbuilder on Daufuskie Island, and that its present owners are merchants who are now concerned that the trade embargo will prevent its proper use."

It was soon agreed that close cooperation among the men would be maintained, and that the Georgians would proceed with an effort to arrange for a surprise when the loaded ship arrived from Charles Town, either from land or perhaps by acquiring and outfitting the merchant vessel.

The next day Lachlan and George went to Daufuskie Island to see the ship and were pleased with what they found. It was a schooner, somewhat roughly built but strong, entirely of oak, with a fifty-foot keel and twenty-two-foot beam, designed to hold three hundred barrels of rice. The two masts were lying alongside on sawhorses, ready to be stepped. A small sign tacked to the hull proclaimed that the ship was the *Elizabeth,* and the shipwright said this was the name of the owner's wife. When Lachlan questioned him closely, he admitted that the merchant financiers had begun to have doubts about its value and had been reluctant to make the final payment and accept delivery.

Back in Savannah, Lachlan quickly raised funds adequate to purchase the *Elizabeth.* He then returned to Daufuskie, swore the shipbuilder to secrecy, ordered places made for five carriage guns and notches for small arms, and changed the ship's name to *Liberty.* A crew was employed and rudimentary training commenced on the use of the weapons.

It was inevitable that Governor Wright would hear rumors of their outfitting a small warship, and in June he dispatched a report of this activity to
General Gage. He was uncertain about sending mail through his own seaport and transmitted the messages through Charles Town. They were intercepted and forgeries were forwarded, stating that there was no cause for
concern or assistance but that the governor was aware of "some little alarm
about two or three armed canoes from South Carolina." HMS *Philippa* had
decided to sail soon after receiving word about the bloodshed at Lexington
and Concord, and its captain, Richard Maitland, anchored off Tybee Island, where he expected a warm welcome from British authorities for his
four and a half tons of gunpowder, seven hundred pounds of bullets, bulk
lead, guns, and other gifts for the restless Indians.

The inexperienced Georgians sailed out near the other ship but decided
to permit it to get under way into Savannah Harbor before showing her
weapons and identifying themselves with a flag inscribed "American Liberty." They both anchored, at which time Captain Maitland, still convinced
that the British controlled the colony, left his ship to report the threat to
Governor Wright. The Whigs arrested Maitland as soon as his boat
reached the dock, boarded the unsuspecting *Philippa,* and unloaded the
powder and ammunition. It was clear that the provincial congress had almost full authority in Savannah and that the governor was something of a
prisoner himself. After a few days, Maitland and his ship were permitted to
leave Savannah, a good bit lighter than when they had arrived.

Now emboldened, the Council of Safety decided to send sixty-three barrels of rice and £122 in currency to the boycotted Bostonians, and a few
days later, on July 4, 1775, there was a meeting of the provincial congress at
Tondee's tavern, with all districts and parishes represented. Lachlan McIntosh and four other of his clansmen from St. Andrews were among the
most militant. After electing Archibald Bulloch as president of the Council
of Safety and George Walton as secretary, they resolved to join all other
colonies in restoring American liberties and in healing the unhappy divisions between Great Britain and her colonies, but made it clear that their
loyalty was to the king and not the Parliament. They framed a new government for the colony, voted to create an army and navy, raise money,
and set other policies for a people struggling for liberty. They also named
four delegates to represent the colony in Philadelphia and to bring back decisions and recommendations to their fellow Georgians. The four Georgia

delegates, including the Reverend Zubly, were seated in the Continental Congress, two of them wearing homespun. Given Zubly's strong and vocal support of the crown, however, he was soon forced to leave Philadelphia under a cloud, but the others remained, and the colony continued to be represented by Lyman Hall, George Walton, and Button Gwinnett.

With little opposition, the leaders in Savannah approved all recommendations of the Continental Congress, including a total boycott of trade with Great Britain and Ireland and an end to all slave trade from Africa or anywhere else, which they presumed would be damaging to the British slave-trading economy. They pledged to act with frugality so as not to need the boycotted goods, including refusing to wear any adornments other than just a piece of black crepe or ribbon at funerals, to horserace or game, or to attend shows or plays. They also advocated severe punishment for any merchant who might violate these restraints. The boycott against British goods hurt Georgia more than any other colony because she had no currency of her own, produced only rice, lumber, indigo, and skins, manufactured hardly any necessary items, and had long been heavily dependent on imports from Britain. All these announced actions were focused on the Parliament, with the presumption of continuing loyalty to the crown.

The Sons of Liberty, however, were determined to precipitate confrontations with any authorities, Whig or Tory, who were not in favor of full independence for the colonies. The actions of these militant young men were often illegal but their leaders were well known, and they had considerable support among the populace and even from some members of the Council of Safety. Toward the end of July, a British mariner named John Hopkins proposed a toast among his fellow sailors that included the words "Damnation to America!" The next night he was taken from his bed in a cheap lodging, carried to the town square, and tarred and feathered. Crowds watched and many cheered his ordeal, and no one attempted to intercede on his behalf. He was threatened with hanging unless he drank a toast, "Damnation to all Tories and success to American liberty," and he did so. He survived the torture but was scarred for life.

As far as Georgians were concerned, their provincial congress soon rejected any authority of the British governor and his ministers, began dealing with Indians, controlling trade, and cautiously taking over the judicial system.

In November, the Continental Congress voted to raise three battalions of troops for South Carolina and one for Georgia. When the word reached Savannah, the provincial congress elected Lachlan McIntosh as commander, with the rank of colonel, and Major Samuel Elbert as his deputy.

CHAPTER 20

Does God Approve Revolution?

In June 1775, Aaron Hart rode hard from a visit to Charles Town directly to see Captain Clarke. Hannah told him that her husband was out back, probably near the creek, looking for a cow that was overdue to drop a calf. The two men finally met after an exchange of signals on cow horns, and Hart blurted out, "'Lige, fighting has broke out in Massachusetts, and the colonists in Philadelphia have decided to form an army to protect themselves from the British."

"That sounds good, Aaron. Jest tell me what you know."

"Well, I brought a newspaper that's got the story." Instead of handing it to Clarke, he said, "Let me read it."

The article described how the British had learned that Minutemen had munitions stored in Concord, about twenty miles from Boston. Lord North had ordered General Gage, commander in the northern colonies, to move in with troops to seize them. A local silversmith named Paul Revere had detected the troop movement and spread the alarm in the countryside. There was a military confrontation in Lexington on April 19, and eight Minutemen were killed. This caused an uproar, and when about two thousand British troops later moved toward Concord, militia companies from two dozen towns met and defeated them, killing 273 Redcoats and forcing the invaders back to Boston. There they were being besieged and, without relief from a strong British force, would soon be forced to evacuate the city.

Clarke was very excited, and said, "If folks in Savannah don't help out now, I'm movin' across the river where the people want freedom."

Aaron replied, "Well, at least Georgia will be well represented when the Continental Congress convenes again. This paper says that Lyman Hall and Archibald Bulloch will be in Philadelphia, and we know that Hall feels about the same way we do."

. . .

Lachlan and George McIntosh were approaching Darien on the coastal trail from Savannah, letting the horses move at their own pace, which was their customary fast walk. On occasion, one of the men would give an almost undetectable movement with his military spurs, and almost simultaneously both mounts would break into a slow, rolling gallop. This was a traveling routine the brothers had followed for years, and they passed the vistas of longleaf pines, live oaks, marshland, and occasional glimpses of the inland waterway with little notice. In the late August afternoon they could still enjoy the relatively pleasant weather of the south Georgia coast and the cool and wistful nature of the gentle breeze from the sea that barely disturbed the leaves and grasses.

George broke a long silence. "Lachlan, how do you think the king and Parliament will react to the olive-branch message from the Continental Congress?"

"Well, it depends on whether the submissive document gets there before the news about British losses at Bunker Hill, how well the patriots fought there, and how much backing they seem to have from the countryside. My guess is that London will decide to stamp out the rebellion with harsh measures, taking the weak action of our delegates as encouragement."

George replied, "According to the report that Lyman Hall gave us two days ago, it wasn't very weak."

Lachlan had little patience with his brother and said, "Just to declare that we are 'united colonies' and appoint George Washington as commander of the Minutemen doesn't amount to much when at the same time they rejected any move toward independence and pledged our continuing loyalty to the crown. Their final statement could at least have included the demands that we Scotsmen have been putting forward in Georgia."

George decided not to pursue the discussion, and the two men rode on in silence.

Shortly before reaching their home, Lachlan said, "We'll be convening our own congress here in Georgia, with a few leaders having the power to make and enforce decisions."

"Similar to what's in South Carolina, with a council of safety?"

"Yes."

"Will you be a member?"

"I reckon that's a possibility."

. . .

When Aaron Hart informed Elijah Clarke about the action of the Continental Congress, Elijah directed the members of the militia group to assemble at his house the following weekend. When they did so, they also brought news of Bunker Hill. The men discussed these developments with different reactions. Elijah said, "Shit, we've taken all we can and it's time we got out from under the Redcoats once and for all. All the bastards in London want out of us is taxes and profits from trade with the damned Indians."

Aaron Hart, who was reluctant to contradict Clarke, replied, "As our delegates said, it's not King George that's at fault, but the Parliament and the ministers he's put in power. What we need to do is convince him that we have good reason to be dissatisfied. Besides, who is going to rule in the colonies, the French and Spanish? They're already doing everything they can to take over and are sure to move in if the British leave. A few Minutemen won't be able to fight them off."

"Well, I reckon we can give the king one more chance, but in the meantime we need to get ready here and in all the colonies to help the patriots when the time comes."

In Wrightsborough, the discussions had a different focus. There was almost total loyalty to the crown and to Parliament, and a condemnation of the colonists in Massachusetts for resorting to violence. In Quaker meetings, the custom was that any man could state his views without interruption or time constraint, and Joseph Maddock voiced a common opinion.

"Like all of us, the people up north pledged or affirmed before God that they would be loyal to the crown, and this means to the entire government in England. We can never forget that it was the royal governor who granted us this very land, and we know that British troops are protecting us from both the Indians and also from a possible invasion by the French from the west. The king has called on people in all the colonies to help pay the expenses of these efforts to protect us, but it's well known that we have not paid our share. There's never been an example in history where a colony has broken ties with a mother country and benefited from it. I agree that the Parliament has made some mistakes with the Stamp Act and the Townshend Act, but they repealed them when made to realize their errors through peaceful persuasion.

"To resort to violence is a sin. It will bring suffering and death to many innocent and peace-loving people. The Holy Scripture has given us guidance in how we should deal with authorities, when we are disappointed or even angry. The apostle Peter, who suffered from Roman persecution, said it well. I have found his advice and would like to read a few verses from the second chapter of First Peter:

> *"As free, and not using your liberty for a cloak of maliciousness, but as the servants of God. Honor all men. Love the Brotherhood. Fear God. Honor the King.*

> *"Servants, be subject to your masters with all fear; not only to the good and gentle, but also to the forward. For this is thankworthy, if a man for conscience toward God endure grief, suffering wrongfully. For what glory is it, if, when ye be buffeted for your faults, ye shall take it patiently? But if, when ye do well, and suffer for it, ye take it patiently, this is acceptable with God.*

> *"For even hereunto were ye called: because Christ also suffered for us, leaving us an example, that ye should follow his steps: Who did no sin, neither was guile found in his mouth: Who, when he was reviled, reviled not again; when he suffered, he threatened not; but committed himself to Him that judgeth righteously."*

Maddock stood erect, with bowed head, as he closed the Holy Book. Then he looked around him and said, "It seems that Peter is speaking directly to the people in every colony when he says, 'Honor all men. Love the Brotherhood. Fear God. Honor the King.' What could possibly be more clear? We are told to submit ourselves to those who have rule over us, with a specific reference to the king."

There was a general murmuring of approval, and no voices were raised in opposition. In their further discussion it was obvious that their sincere desire was to avoid armed conflict, not only with British troops but also with the heathen natives and the militant colonists.

At about the same time, the Reverend John Zubly, a fiery Presbyterian minister in Savannah, preached a sermon from a text different from that chosen by Joseph Maddock. Taking a verse, James 2:12, somewhat out of context, he read, "So speak ye, and so do, as they that shall be judged by the law of liberty." Although he was a strong monarchist who advocated total loyalty to the king, the people distorted his views as though he had quoted God as elevating the law of liberty above those passed by Parliament. His sermon was repeated for days and distributed in print throughout the colony. He was even put forward as a delegate to the Continental Congress.

CHAPTER 21

Thomas Brown, British Spy

The horseman appeared somewhat ill at ease as he approached the settlement of Orangeburg. It was late afternoon, and despite being extremely weary after a two-day journey from Charles Town, he tried to sit erect in the saddle. He appeared to hold his head proudly, facing straight down the widening trail, but his eyes shifted uneasily from side to side. His clothing, somewhat mixed between that of an English gentleman and an off-duty military officer—which is what he was—contrasted sharply with the homespun shirts, leather trousers, and bare feet or Indian-style moccasins of the men whom he saw in the fields or near small cabins. All of them looked at him closely, more than the normal perusal of a stranger coming into Orangeburg from the southeast. Since all of them were somewhat familiar with weapons, they noticed the good quality of his musket and the sword by his side. His mount was superb, a roan stallion, and the man rode him with ease. He was aware of the eyes on him and responded to remarks of welcome, mostly "Ev'nin'," with a polite nod of his head.

Although he was only sixty miles east of his home, he had never taken this route before. There was a small fort and only a few houses in the village, so he had no trouble finding the tavern, which he approached with studied nonchalance. A little stream ran one hundred feet in front of it, coming from a spring that seemed to be the watering place for the dozen or so families in the village. He stopped his horse well below the boarded-in pool, dismounted, removed the somewhat ornate saddle and bridle, and led the animal to the stream by the halter rope. After the horse had its fill, the man tied him to a low bush, removed a silver cup from the saddlebag, and drank several drafts from the spring. Only then did he turn toward the tavern.

Six men were on the front porch, now speaking softly or in whispers, their normal conversation quieted by the horseman's arrival. Although they were ordinarily somewhat crude, were not especially hospitable to strangers, and enjoyed ribald jokes at the expense of others, there was something about the approaching horseman that kept his observers quiet and seemingly respectful, or at least wary. They noticed that, although it was early August and their shirts were damp with sweat, the man seemed to be impervious to the heat. He stepped on an adze-flattened log and then onto the low porch, and looked coolly at each of the men around him. They were not accustomed to looking directly at anyone for more than a moment, but none of them could fail to notice the strange intensity of his gaze. His face seemed to be expressionless, but his eyes, almost completely devoid of color, had a disturbing effect, as though they penetrated what they observed.

He nodded, seemed to recognize one of the men, and said, "Good evening." They replied, almost in unison, "Ev'nin'." He disappeared through the front door, and they could hear him talking to the tavern owner. One of the men, a herdsman named Simon, made a motion with his head, and they all left the porch, walked out of earshot, and turned to one of their group, a visitor from Augusta, who had exchanged glances with the stranger. "That's the king's man, who's been moving from one place to another in this area, mostly trying to convince folks to kiss the governor's ass. There's all kinds of stories about him, none of them good. He's just a damned lieutenant in the British army, but they say he's the bastard son of Lord North and has more pull with the governor than a bloody colonel. My cousin went to his house across the Savannah River a few days ago, to where the man has been given five thousand acres of land that he's working with indentured servants he brought over from England about a year ago. I hear he pulled a pistol and shot at one of his neighbors."

"Then what's he doing here in Carolina?"

"He's been debating a man named Drayton, who seems to be a revolutionary, and trying to get people to agree to be loyal to the king, claiming to be speaking for the governor. Some believe he's trying to find them that's disloyal to the crown, and particularly to learn if the Liberty Boys have any supporters. Maybe he's learned that some of them was here last night. Most folks around Augusta just laugh at him, because he don't seem to know what he's doing. Governor Wright made him a magistrate, but so far all he's done is sign a few papers and wander around in Carolina."

"What's his name?"

"His name is Thomas Brown."

The tavern owner came out and called from the porch, "You men come on inside. There's free drinks for you."

This was an invitation not to be refused, and they entered the familiar room, glanced at the Englishman standing at the counter, and took their customary seats at a long and crudely built table. This was their territory, and they felt at ease. Without asking, the innkeeper brought each of the men one of his largest tankards, taking full advantage of the opportunity to make a maximum sale. Simon picked up his ale, glanced at the lieutenant, nodded slightly as a sign of thanks on behalf of all of them, and drank. The other men then followed suit, but no words were spoken among them. Finally, after about ten minutes of silence except for an undercurrent of soft remarks and some quiet laughter around the table, Brown said, "Pour another round." When the big mugs were refilled and partially drained, Brown finally broke the uncomfortable silence with a polite inquiry.

"Gentlemen, how are the crops this year?" He had a low-pitched voice, quiet but clearly understood even with the modulations of someone recently from London.

Simon answered, "The corn is middling, but the tobacco don't amount to much. A late frost killed most of the plants, and we still need some rain."

"Yes, I observed this along the trail from Charles Town. Maybe the thunder and lightning in the west will bring some rain. Has there been any trouble around here from the Indians?"

"Not here in Orangeburg, but there was some raids west of here last March, across the Savannah in Georgia." Simon waited to see if there would be any expression of knowledge about the region around where he thought Brown's land might be located, but there was none.

So far, the questions were polite and predictable, but the next one put the Carolinians on guard.

"What kind of job is John Stuart doing?"

Everyone knew that Indian Superintendent Stuart represented the king directly in dealing with all the tribes along the Atlantic Coast. There had been intense arguments about his performance in this same tavern. The point of view about him was the best indication of a man's attitude toward the officials in Charles Town and Savannah, even though Stuart represented the crown directly and governors could not tell him what to do. Last night, one of the hotheaded young men from Augusta had claimed that

Stuart was stirring up the Indians and encouraging them to attack any settlers who were publicly critical of London's policies or who expressed approval of the Minutemen, who were confronting British troops in New
York and Massachusetts. Although there were differences among them, the
local men in the tavern were all British subjects, and most of them just
wanted to take care of their families, work their land, sell their produce, live
in peace, and avoid any direct involvement in the increasingly intense disputes between the Tories and Whigs. They were uncomfortable, but somewhat intrigued, when any of the radical and sometimes violent Sons of
Liberty paid a visit to the community.

Simon, although one of the more militant local citizens, thought it was
best to be cautious and comply with what Brown wanted to hear. "There
are some that think Stuart stirs up the savages, but others feel that he is doing a fair job. In any case, he helps us with our trade."

Brown nodded and said, "Peace is what we want, for the Cherokees and
Creeks to leave us alone and for us not to fight our neighbors."

The men seemed to agree but did not reply.

He decided to give a better indication of his own sentiments. "I've just
come from Charles Town and am glad to see Parliament resolving the
problems with the colonies. Closing the seaports in the north was a bad
move, and the king is very anxious to have full trade and to give all British
subjects equal treatment."

With the passage of the ale pitcher, the men were becoming more inclined to talk freely and to agree with the generous visitor.

"Yes, a little corn went from South Carolina to Massachusetts last year
when Boston was put under quarantine for destroying the tea, but what we
want here is to be treated proper and left alone."

Brown was quick to respond, wanting to carry out his somewhat sensitive assignment but without starting an argument with the men. "It's just a
few radical Whigs who are causing the problem, wanting to resolve misun-
derstandings with violence and even murder. I've heard tell of cases where
some young hoodlums have attacked their own neighbors who remain
loyal to the crown."

The men glanced at each other, knowing that for several months they
had not been free to express their frank opinions in a community that was
becoming increasingly polarized.

The Englishman continued, "My hope is that the people of Carolina will help maintain order, increase trade with the Indians, and build up good markets for what we produce. The governor wants to improve the roads and ferries, and see that we obtain some more land in the west that will be made open for settlement. He has asked me to come here and then go to Augusta to see if there is anything he or the state council can do to help your communities."

They continued the conversation for a while, speaking mostly of crops and the supply and latest prices of rum, sugar, salt, and other commodities that were brought in from the port of Charles Town. They heard raindrops on the roof, and one of the men said, "Well, maybe you brought us a shower." Brown nodded, smiled slightly, and said, "I hope so. How far is it to Augusta?"

"It's about a good day's ride, including the river crossings."

"Well, I'll stay here tonight, and go there tomorrow."

There was no spare room in the small building, but the innkeeper said there was a shed behind his house where guests stayed every now and then, and he agreed to provide a meal and some feed for the man's horse.

Now, in the tiny shed room, Thomas Brown's primary task was to get comfortable enough to sleep. He had not yet extinguished the sputtering tallow candle and could see the water beginning to flow under the door and form rivulets on the uneven earthen floor. Other than his low cot with its corn-shuck mattress, the only piece of furniture was a three-legged stool. He stepped carefully on still-dry places and placed his belongings on a slab-board shelf that extended across one end of the room, then blew out the candle, crawled onto the cot, adjusted the blanket around himself, and prepared to sleep. But a kaleidoscope of images of the last few days remained vivid in his mind despite his efforts to think only of benign and peaceful things.

His memory of the Charles Town visit was pleasant. The governor had treated him warmly, welcoming him into his private office and even offering him a cup of tea. Brown realized the political overtones of this relationship. He was aware of the prevailing rumor that he was the bastard son of Lord North, now prime minister, and that his presence in the colonies had been arranged at the highest level in London. He had not tried to correct the mistake. Brown felt that some enemies of his had spread the lie when he had received such a large land grant, but he felt that it might be to his advantage not to dispute the rumor of his personal ties to the highest official in London, save the king himself.

What South Carolina's governor, Lord William Campbell, knew was that Brown had been given a lieutenant's commission despite not having any military training, and that the young man had been dispatched to America with a shipload of covenant servants. These families were bound to work for three years to pay for the cost of their transportation and would then be allotted enough land to start a small farming operation. The governor had heard, and believed, that this special treatment was designed to remove Brown from England: either a rich family was making a major financial investment in the future of a son, or Brown was a potential source of embarrassment to the most influential politician in the kingdom.

The young man seemed to be ambitious and had offered his services to the governors of Georgia and South Carolina, just to "promote loyalty to the crown." Like Governor Wright, Campbell was willing to allot a few minutes of his time every month or so to have this small addition to the intelligence gathering he desired from around his colony.

Thomas Brown was actually a native of Yorkshire, born in 1750, and the eldest son of Jonas Brown, a prosperous shipowner. The grandfather of Thomas's mother was Sir Isaac Newton. Taking full advantage of his father's wealth and influence, Thomas combined a good education with a life of debauchery with his friends. His father was an ambitious man, who soon realized that some of Thomas's escapades were bringing discredit on the family. The young man was sent on an extended sea voyage in the Caribbean on one of his father's ships and then, through an arrangement that he never fully understood, Thomas had been placed in charge of a group of indentured servants on the *Marlborough,* a three-hundred-ton round-bottomed ship in which his father owned an interest. For this trip, from Whitby around the Orkneys and then to Savannah, he was promised a portion of land and the services of any six of the men whom he might choose, each of them obligated for three years of service on the farm.

On the same ship was a man named Michael Herring, who paid his own passage and was looking for employment in the new country. He was an Irish farmer who had left home because his older brothers had priority as heirs of the family land. He and Brown met early in the voyage, and knowing that he was almost completely ignorant about agriculture, Brown arranged for Herring to be the overseer of his new farm, with a place to live, an annual salary of £25, and the promise of one hundred acres of land. Herring's first task was to select the six men who would be working for Brown, and by the time they reached America he had made his choices.

When Brown arrived in Savannah, he delivered a sealed envelope to the governor, who was informed in the document that the newly commissioned lieutenant was well educated, proficient with guns and the sword from their use in his hunting and dueling activities, had never had any real military train-ing, and was apparently averse to taking orders. What he had was a sharp in-telligence and total loyalty to the British government, and he was to be treated with respect and consideration during a stay of at least four years in the colonies. He was to be introduced to top officials in both Georgia and South Carolina.

Without further instructions, the governor did not know what to do with him, but after a brief conversation he found that Brown was thor-oughly familiar with the steps being taken in the Parliament to address some of the legitimate complaints of the colonists, and was an enthusiastic supporter of the government's policies. After some consideration, Gover-nor Wright decided that Brown should be encouraged to live in northeast Georgia, where almost unlimited land had become available under the In-dian treaty of 1773. He gave Brown twelve contiguous land grants totaling 2,600 acres, most of which were above the Little River, an area still dis-puted by some of the young Creeks. A nearby fort protected the southern portion, and this is where the first development was begun, to be named Brownsborough. It lay in the confluence of Kiokee and Greenbriar creeks, about twenty miles northwest of Augusta. Because of Brown's good educa-tion and "gentlemanly bearing," Governor Wright decided to appoint him magistrate, the governor's official representative in that remote area, and Brown volunteered to make a confidential report from time to time on the attitude of the people along the upper Savannah River. Brown was at-tracted by the somewhat clandestine nature of his assignment, but he had no desire to create trouble or to endanger himself. After claiming his prop-erty, he assigned Herring and the indentured men to clear and work almost two hundred acres of open cropland and to care for a small herd of sheep, cows, and hogs. Brown soon learned that his overseer was a competent and honest manager, and although he maintained an interest in the land as a place to hunt and a source of income, he took temporary lodgings in Au-gusta while the plantation was being developed. He spent most of his time visiting taverns in a wide area, where he could enjoy himself and also as-certain the opinions of his neighbors.

. . .

In Georgia and South Carolina, the governors now had to deal with provincial congresses that professed continuing allegiance to the crown but were known to be supporting the American cause as expressed, sometimes violently, in the north. In both colonies, real power was vested in the councils of safety.

Thomas Brown followed these developments closely, always looking for an opportunity for advancement and to ingratiate himself with British leaders. It soon became obvious that his chances were much better in South Carolina, where the governor had already found his intelligence reports more welcome.

Governor Wright was still personally popular and there was little disaffection toward the king in Georgia, but political power in Charles Town was centered in wealthy rice barons who were eager to control the colony and whose first loyalty was to their own enhanced wealth and influence. Although they only represented the coast, where just one-fourth of the population lived, and had always scorned, ridiculed, and alienated the settlers in the backcountry, the support of those "commoners" had become crucial in the struggle for political dominance over the monarchists.

In his wanderings around western Carolina, Brown became aware of the activities of William Henry Drayton, whose main purpose was to arouse opposition to Governor Campbell and the royal council. Drayton was also spreading the false report that the British were planning to recruit Indians and black slaves to help in controlling any moves toward independence by the colonies. The threat of an Indian war was bad enough, but the prospect of an insurrection was much worse, especially in the low country of Carolina, where there were five black slaves for every white person. As soon as he had as much information as possible, Brown made arrangements to meet with the governor.

After making his report, Brown waited for an approving response but was disappointed when Governor Campbell, seeming to be speaking more to his aide-de-camp, a young man named Knapton, than to Brown, said, "I have long been familiar with Drayton's efforts and have been trying to assess all the factors involved among the hill country families. Some of the farmers, particularly those from central Europe, will be afraid that any disloyalty might cost them title to their land, which has been allotted by grants from the king. Even more of them have always despised the large plantation owners and Charles Town merchants, who have cheated them whenever possible and deprived them of fair representation in political affairs of the colony. The political situation is complicated, and it will be difficult for them to determine the origin of most of their grievances, so their inclination has been to mind their own business and avoid taking sides. It is important that we maintain this situation.

"As is well known, we have British militia in the backcountry, led by Colonel Thomas Fletchall, whose task is to protect the frontiersmen from Indians and to preserve loyalty to the king."

Then the governor addressed Lieutenant Brown directly: "Your report confirms what we have heard before, and indicates more boldness on the part of Drayton. I would like for you to follow Drayton and members of his so-called secret committee and refute his lies. You and Mr. Knapton can repair to his office and prepare a script to follow, based on all the false claims being promulgated. From time to time hereafter, you can make your reports through him. You may call on Colonel Fletchall for any assistance needed, and I will inform him of this conversation. Thank you, Lieutenant, for your good service."

Brown mumbled his respects and followed Knapton down the hall, where they prepared speaking points to be followed. He was to refute any derogatory statements about the royal government in Charles Town, emphasize that the British military was strong, that beneficial trade was to be had with England, that a war might bring a slave revolt, and that the king was determined to resolve differences with the colonies through peaceful means. They agreed that his most effective argument was that Drayton's sponsors, the merchants and rice barons on the coast, were already enslaving the backwoodsmen. If necessary, he could accuse Drayton of gathering guns and ammunition and forming a military alliance with the Cherokees.

On the way back to Augusta, Brown ignored the governor's bypassing him to talk to his aide, and convinced himself that all the good ideas had been his, that the governor was greatly impressed with his report, and that his new assignment would place him at an exalted level of influence. He had flickering concerns about his own safety, which he was able to dispel by recalling the presence of Colonel Fletchall's Redcoats in the area.

It was not difficult for Brown to arrange for his participation in debates with Drayton. His new adversary was completely self-confident, and the local audiences always seemed to relish the direct verbal confrontations. The meetings became increasingly heated, and on several occasions Brown and Drayton almost came to blows. Results were mixed, but there was no doubt that the lines between the two active sides, Whigs and Tories, were being more sharply drawn.

Although he had no real authority from the Council of Safety, Drayton assumed an increasingly fervent attitude. Finally, in late summer 1775, Drayton returned from Charles Town with a dozen Carolina militia and stated that Brown would be arrested and that the governor and other British officials should also be imprisoned. Brown called immediately on Colonel Fletchall and some of the king's troops to accompany him to the next confrontation with Drayton, in the town of Ninety Six, shortly after noon. There was another sharp debate, with neither side taking any military action. Afterward, Brown began the journey back to his Georgia plantation, but Drayton and his associates invited Fletchall to join them in the tavern. During the night they flattered him—bragging on his leadership capabilities, plying him with whiskey, and finally inducing Fletchall to sign an agreement that neither side would give aid and comfort to any British troops opposing Americans nor would they dispute the authority of the Continental Congress.

Brown was furious when he learned of Fletchall's betrayal. Drayton returned to Charles Town, where he proudly displayed his "treaty" and urged the Council of Safety to arrest the royal governor and others who were still publicly supporting the Tory cause. The council members were not inclined to take such bold action, but gave Drayton a carefully worded order that was almost indecipherable in its meaning. Drayton, however, interpreted the directive as authority to act. He worked closely with the Sons of Liberty and urged them to assist in the moves against Thomas Brown and others in the backcountry.

Brown had been proud of his recent actions, really the first that had any substance to them, and hoped that the governor would acknowledge his successes in the public meetings. During his first months in Georgia, he had never had cause to conceal his personal ties to high officials in London and his loyalty to the crown. His large grant of land from the governor of Georgia and his easy access to top officials in both states seemed to be adequate assurances of his status and safety. But now, after the debates with Drayton and the apparent yielding of Fletchall to rebel pressure, Brown began to have his first feelings of insecurity. The provincial congresses were assuming more authority in both Georgia and South Carolina, and the royal officials themselves seemed to be under duress. He was not surprised when he began to receive direct threats, obviously from some ignorant and disreputable scoundrels.

First he had found a crudely written note on the front door of his plantation cabin, warning him that his opposition to freedom would result in "dier sirkumstanses." It was a shock to know that the intruders had singled him out, but when he shared the message with farm supervisor Herring, he attempted to treat it as something of a joke, not wanting to acknowledge any degree of personal unpopularity or vulnerability. The next Saturday night he heard some horses come into his yard, and a few minutes later Herring opened the back door of his cabin.

"I'm afraid we may have some trouble, Mr. Brown. There's a group of men outside, and I think I recognize some of the horsemen as having been around here before. They may be the ones who left the note."

Brown slipped on his trousers and replied, "I'll take care of it, Herring. I'm sure there's nothing to fear."

He checked his two dueling pistols to be ready to fire, opened the front door, and stepped aside quickly into the shadows, letting the dim light from candles in the house illuminate five young men in the forefront of the group who were facing him, sitting on their horses.

They shifted uneasily, and then the leader of those in front, a burly man with bright red hair, dismounted and took two or three steps forward, still holding his bridle reins in his left hand and a long rifle in his right. The muzzle was pointed at the ground. He said, "Mr. Brown, my name is Chesley Bostick, and these are my friends, who believe in liberty. We've heard disturbing things about you. It's said that your Georgia land was given to you directly from London, through influence of the governor of South Carolina, and that your ties are to Charles Town, not Savannah. Some of the men on your place here have heard you defend the unjust laws imposed on the colonies and criticize those of us who are for freedom. We've come to make sure that you agree with us that folks here in Georgia should enjoy the same rights as them that live in London."

Brown was surprised at Bostick's eloquence and relieved by his relatively moderate words. The last thing he wanted was a physical confrontation with the young toughs, who carried knives and some hatchets in their belts and had at least two muskets that he could see. They had obviously

been drinking. Trying to appear at ease, he responded that Governor
Wright in Savannah had approved his land grant in accordance with existing laws, and that all British citizens should be treated equally. He did not
add what he really thought, that many of the ungrateful colonists were
guilty of treason if they condemned the king's policies and espoused the
proposition that they could establish their own independent laws.

The leader said, "Well, that sounds all right, but we want you to know
there ain't any room in this colony for those that don't believe in the kind
of liberty we're demanding."

Herring and several of the plantation's men stepped out of the shadows,
on each side of the porch, with guns raised. Emboldened, Brown brought
his pistols into clear sight of the intruders and said, "You men are on private property and I have heard what you have to say. I suggest that you
scoundrels get out of my yard."

One of the men reached for his musket, and Bostick dropped his reins
and moved both hands toward his rifle. Brown was as surprised as anyone
when one of his dueling pistols discharged, hitting the ground very near
the young leader's foot.

The intruders all looked at Bostick, who retained his composure but
backed away, limping as he went. His horse had tossed its head but was still
in place, and he mounted quickly. He glanced at the others, and they rode
away without further incident. Brown decided to stay close to his home
and directed that some of the workforce remain on guard. Herring reported later that Bostick's foot had been badly bruised and that there was
talk in Augusta about the possibility of the Brownsborough homesite and
crops being burned if its owner didn't change his ways. Brown wanted to
avoid any trouble and felt that he needed some advice about how he
should react to the physical threats and to the growing displeasure about
his activities in the area.

After a few days, Brown decided to visit Governor Campbell in Charles
Town to report what he considered to be increasing militancy among his
Georgia neighbors. Sharing his plans only with Herring, he bypassed Augusta, traveled down the river almost to Savannah, and then took the
coastal trail to Charles Town. He was reassured when the governor welcomed him to his office and informed him that King George and Lord
North were taking major steps to ensure that the legitimate complaints of

the colonists would be answered. He emphasized that the policy throughout America was to preserve peace with the Indians, to increase trade, and
to reward and protect those whose loyalty to the crown was staunch.

The governor added, "Despite these generous decisions, we're having
trouble here in Charles Town from Drayton and the Council of Safety, who
have even demanded that I surrender my office and leave the colony. Also,
there are some hotheads in the northern colonies who are resorting to
armed insurrection, but our troops will be able to handle them easily. I receive reports from all over the southern region and can assure you just a
small group is trying to stir up trouble. They are mostly isolated bands of
cowards, whose bark is worse than their bite. I trust you will not be intimidated by their threats."

"I am not afraid," responded Brown, attempting to sound convincing.
"But I thought you should know about the rumors and reports I have
heard and my own personal encounter with some brigands who call themselves Liberty Boys. I'll be going back home and will continue to do what I
can to assess the situation in the countryside and to strengthen the resolve
of loyal British subjects."

"I'd like you to go back through Orangeburg, if you have the time. This
is in an area where Tory support is quite strong, and you might be able to
observe what's happening there. I've sent my own representative, William
Thompson, on a tour along the Savannah River farther south to perform
the same tasks, and he is due to arrive in Augusta on the third Tuesday in
this month. I'll send him word that he should get in touch with you, and
you can share what you learn. You will find that he is a well-informed and
prudent man. He'll be reporting back to me, and you can send any information by him, either verbally or in writing."

After Brown's departure, it was good that he did not hear the governor's
remark to his aide: "The lieutenant was more frightened than he let on,
and I don't believe we can depend on him in any kind of physical confrontation. I'll want a personal assessment when Thompson returns to
Charles Town."

Now, in Orangeburg, Brown was wakened by relative silence when the
fierce rainstorm changed to a slow patter of drops, and by the realization
that his blanket and legs were soaked from a leak in the roof. He was instantly under the impression that one of the men in the tavern had been in

his yard when the Sons of Liberty had threatened him, even though it had been difficult to see most of them in the dark and shadows. But after a few moments he was reassured by recalling the relatively harmonious conversation at the tavern, and he was relaxed when he lit the candle, dressed, and gathered his belongings. By sunrise the rain had stopped completely, and he was already on the trail to Augusta, thinking about what his future plans might be.

With difficulty, he had restrained his own feelings of contempt for the loungers at the tavern, an unkempt and ignorant lot. He could tell that they were not being honest or frank in their restrained comments, and suspected some of them of disloyal tendencies toward the crown. He had received reports that several Liberty Boys had frequented the public place in Orangeburg, and he knew he was supposed to identify any citizens who supported their acts of treason so that the officials could stamp them out. Brown had been willing to repeat a prepared speech in his public debates with Drayton, but he had to admit that, as was the case last night, he had tried to avoid specific confrontations and deal in generalities. He had always felt that being cautious was the best way to enhance his effectiveness as a spy, or a secret agent of the king. It had been something of a game for him, but one that was becoming more of a challenge. The visit of the militants to his plantation had been a great shock, and he was relieved that the governor had described the Liberty Boys as a small and inconsequential group of radicals.

This adventure in the colonies was not to the lieutenant's liking and, in effect, had been forced on him. His ultimate goal was to return to London, or at least to England, as soon as he could dispose of his landholdings and obtain permission from the authorities. He was, after all, a man of the city and intended to be gone from his homeland just until his friends sent word that some personal problems there had died away with the passage of time—not more than two or three more years under the worst of circumstances. His thoughts were focused on what sort of report to the governor might minimize the value of his service as a so-called protector of the king's business in this godforsaken part of the world.

This was his first trip directly from Orangeburg to Augusta, but he was confident that he could follow the directions he had received at the inn. He hardly noticed his surroundings during the first few miles, but as the sun rose he became more aware of the narrow trail and the heavily wooded countryside. He moved along as rapidly as his fine horse could carry him during a full day's ride, trotting on occasion or maintaining a rapid walk. It was easy to follow the clear path through the thick woods and brush, usually not more than a yard wide. But it became more difficult, just a slightly trodden way, under the enormous trees that shaded out any undergrowth except for dogwoods and a few other shade-resistant species that he did not recognize. At times Brown had to search for the too infrequent blaze marks on trees to stay on the main trail, and he referred to his compass frequently to assure that he was always traveling westward.

He was always alert to the danger of a possible Indian attack. He had never seen one of the savages but had heard many reports of the murders, involving scalping, mutilation, and burning of bodies, by renegade savages along the western frontier, and he tried to convince himself that he was far from that dangerous region. Still, he was glad no one could observe how he leaped in the saddle and almost lost his hat when a startled doe or even a squirrel made a sudden noise in the nearby brush. More than anything else, Brown wanted to be out of the woods before dark caught him, and he pressed on, not even tempted to stop at any of the few homesteads he passed on the way. He had never spent a night without a mattress under him, except on a few hunting excursions in Scotland and Ireland when he and a group of his companions had chosen to sleep on folded blankets in canvas tents.

At one of the sandy places at a creek crossing, he noticed hoofprints, indicating that another horseman had preceded him down the trail since the rain had stopped, and after that he looked carefully ahead as he rounded each curve. Around noon, he stopped beside a small stream to eat some of the parched corn and dried beef he had bought at the inn, but quickly resumed his journey. According to the governor, his rendezvous with William Thompson was scheduled to take place in four days, and he wanted to visit his farm before returning to Augusta.

Brown crossed the Savannah River just after sundown and decided to spend the night in the inn where he had been instructed to meet Thompson. He had been there a few times and knew that the innkeeper, James Jarvis, had a reputation as an honest and competent manager. With a generous tip, he arranged to have a cot of his own, and also made arrangements for accommodations for the evening of the third Tuesday before proceeding twenty miles farther to his home. He was reassured when overseer Herring reported that there had been no other threats while he was away. Despite having been through an entire year of farming, Brown still did not know much about the process and had little interest in learning more. He was always uncomfortable in the swamps and forests except along well-known hunting trails and in an area near the cabin, and arranged in subtle ways for Herring to be with him when he had to travel far from the clearings.

After a weekend of rest and a brief examination of his livestock and crops, Brown rode into Augusta and found Thompson at the tavern, as the governor had arranged. After exchanging cautious greetings, the two men walked down a narrow and muddy street toward the river so they could discuss their assignments and observations privately. They noted a large, ornate white house and observed with scorn that the other forty or so structures were crude homes and storage sheds made of logs. Their overnight dwelling was the only inn in the town, except for a crude shed near the river that had no official permit but sold cheap rum and other strong drink to anyone who entered, and was rumored to serve even Indians through a back window.

Thomas Brown assumed naturally that he held seniority and waited for his companion to report on circumstances in the community. Instead, Thompson said, "I've just come from Savannah, where there are at least two dozen licensed taverns, and I've seen another half dozen on the road between here and there. This is a hellhole, with almost a complete disregard of the law."

Somewhat abruptly, Brown said, "Well, we'll have to put up with it just for one night. What do you hear on your travels?"

"For the past two weeks, I've been from here to the coast, on both sides of the river, and have been very discouraged about what is going on. As in Charles Town, the provincial congress has taken control of most affairs, and there are a group of ruffians who are causing a lot of trouble in Savannah, openly bragging about insulting Governor Wright and professing support for a revolution against the crown. Shortly before I arrived in Savannah, a large group of criminals almost killed a British seaman named John Hopkins just because he gave a toast condemning disloyalty to the king. They put hot tar and feathers on him, and a rope around his neck, and would have hanged him if he hadn't recanted."

Brown said, "Yes, I heard about this in Charles Town, but didn't learn what the British authorities did to the malefactors."

"Nothing at all! The governor and his council are left with little authority, much of which has been taken by the Whigs."

Brown remained silent, and Thompson finally said, "It's the damned Liberty Boys. I personally saw three of them night before last in the inn where we are staying, physically abusing a frontiersman from the west who refused to join them in a toast to freedom. He insisted that all he wanted was to mind his own business and live in peace, but he finally drank with them."

"Did the man not have any support from others?"

"After the radicals left, some of the people in the tavern seemed to agree with him, but there was a lot of fear, or at least reluctance to take sides in what could have been a violent confrontation."

"The damned cowards!" exclaimed Brown. Observing the intensity of his companion's feelings and sensing that the remark may have been meant to include him, Thompson decided not to comment further on the incident as they returned to the inn. He wished that Brown could have been present to experience the intimidation that had kept him and the others quiet in the presence of the abusive group, whom he hoped would not return.

Back at the tavern, they ordered some ale and then a meal of venison and coarse bread, which they ate at a table in the corner of the room. Eight or ten other men were also eating supper, most of them choosing fried fish from the river. Along the narrow end of the room was a chest-high counter with a door behind it, apparently opening into the living quarters of the proprietor. Directly opposite was a narrow stairway going to the second floor, where four small rooms could house paying guests. Brown and Thompson shared one of these. Above this was a long and narrow attic with a ceiling not more than four feet high, containing a row of crude mattresses, let out to paying guests, with everyone expected to accept just half a bed for the standard fee. On the ground floor, where people ate, a door in the middle of the long wall opened onto the street, and to the right of the door was a window, with its wooden shutter propped open to encourage some stirring of the humid air. A sputtering lantern was hanging from the ceiling, and a tallow candle burned on each of the several tables to supplement the dim light.

As Brown and Thompson finished their meal and decided to retire for the night, five men stepped through the open door and looked around the room. Brown saw immediately that four of them were the same men who had visited his farm less than a fortnight ago, and one was obviously their leader, a large young man wearing a wool hat that partially covered his red hair. It was Bostick, the man whose foot might have been hit by a round from Brown's pistol.

"Have you seen that son of a bitch who was here last night and was against freedom?" he demanded of the innkeeper.

"No, he has gone back to his home in Wilkes County, I reckon."

They demanded a bottle of rum, threw a coin on the counter, and stood while they drank. Then Bostick looked at Brown and Thompson in the corner. Brown's eyes were on him for a brief moment, and then he looked away as though he was disinterested. The man whispered to his companions, and they all focused their attention on Brown.

There was silence in the tavern for a short time, and then came the rough voice: "Mr. Brown, we meet again."

Brown waited a few moments and then responded calmly, "So I see."

"I want to know what your business is."

Brown's face flushed, despite his effort to remain calm, and then he surprised himself by saying, "To mind my own, and I advise you to do the same."

There was total silence in the room, as attention was focused on the face under the wool hat. He raised his glass and said, "To the Liberty Boys of Savannah!" His companions and a few others took a sip of their rum or ale, but neither Brown nor Thompson responded. Everyone was uneasy, and several of the customers quietly left the tavern. Others watched closely as tension rose in the room.

Brown was extremely uncomfortable, with his spine tingling and something clutching at his heart, but he made every possible attempt to conceal his feelings. He did not know how to deal with the situation, here in this strange environment. Many thoughts raced through his mind. If he were confronting adversaries in a tavern in London, he could depend on a general respect for law and propriety, or for spectators or the proprietor to call officials to preserve order. A personal slight or insult between two gentlemen could often be handled by seconds so that the outcome would be the saving of honor without serious bloodshed.

He rationalized his present caution by the thought that his and Thompson's overall mission of promoting loyalty to the crown could best be achieved without public altercations with radicals. A political dispute with ruffians in a tavern was certainly not the best tactic. At the same time, a profession of disloyalty would be an unthinkable admission of cowardice that would arouse considerable attention, and was certain to be reported by Thompson to Governor Campbell and then, perhaps, back to his friends and benefactors in London. His best approach would be to avoid any specific response and to finesse the present confrontation. He turned back to his meal, attempting to ignore his hecklers.

"Give the men in the corner a drink from Chesley Bostick," the wool hat ordered the innkeeper, who quickly placed two small glasses on the corner table and filled them with rum.

"Now, I want to propose a toast to freedom, and a curse on cowardly bastards!" he said. All eyes turned toward the two men in the corner, and especially to Thomas Brown, the obvious leader of the two. Hardly realizing what he was doing, he stood, raised the glass in front of him, and poured its contents on the floor. "I will buy my own rum and drink a toast with all those loyal to the king," he said.

No one noticed when Thompson eased out from the table to stand near the open door, while Brown gazed back and forth at the five men a few steps in front of him. He was unarmed, having left his gun and sword in the room upstairs, and he was acutely aware that his adversaries carried knives and tomahawks in their belts. He could not believe they would actually attack him, with so many witnesses in the tavern. Everything seemed like a dream, happening in slow motion. As the men moved forward, he thrust his table toward them, leaped toward the stairs, and then saw one of the heavy chairs swinging toward his head.

When he regained consciousness he was lying facedown on the rough and filthy floor covered with blood, and his hands were tied behind his back. Thompson and most of the other patrons had disappeared.

CHAPTER 22

Tar and Feathers

Bostick was seated on the edge of a table, just one of the blurry-looking faces that Brown could see around him. The contents of his pockets were on the table, and Bostick, sneering at the prostrate man, said, "Well, Mr. Thomas Brown, I see from this paper that you are a lieutenant in His Majesty's service. Please explain to us what your duties are here among us and where your uniform might be."

When there was no response, Bostick directed that Brown should be pulled to his feet and said, "I'm still waiting for you to pledge your support for liberty and an end of tyranny directed from your friends in London."

Brown refused to speak, and when Bostick nodded, one of his men struck the helpless man just above his ear with the flat side of a tomahawk, knocking him to his knees. With his left eye temporarily blinded and blood running from his scalp and the corner of his mouth, he considered his predicament and could see no way to escape from this incredible situation. He could only hope that some commitment to the law and to proper conduct would prevail, or perhaps the awareness of future punishment would deter the gang of thugs.

Bostick said, obviously for the benefit of his audience, "I am hereby convening an official session of the Sons of Liberty, and we will give this scoundrel a fair trial for insulting the revolutionary cause. I have heard that Captain Elijah Clarke is in town with a few of his troops, and we are sending for him to serve as judge. While we all have another drink, will someone please place the accused in a chair, in a more respectable position that this distinguished courtroom deserves."

There was some mandatory laughter among Bostick's associates and a shuffling among the remaining spectators, but no one made a comment, everyone obsessed with the drama developing before them.

The helpless man was lifted back into a chair, where he sat erect with difficulty. Someone tied a rag around his scalp to staunch the fresh bleeding. After everyone had a drink together, Bostick continued, "Mr. Brown, we heard several days ago that you were heading our way, coming back from Charles Town, and we also had reports that you have been making false promises and threatening people to get them to support the Tory cause and to stamp out freedom. We planned to meet you across the river in South Carolina, but you arrived earlier than we expected. We came here tonight to welcome you back to Georgia. Our hope is that you will see the error of your ways, and we're waiting to hear from you."

There was a commotion at the door, and a large man entered the room. Brown had never seen him before, but knew who he was from many conversations that he had overheard during the last few months. Captain Elijah Clarke was about forty-five years old, impressive in size and demeanor, and obviously respected by Bostick and the other ruffians. Brown's spirits lifted, as he anticipated Clarke's bringing an end to this embarrassing charade.

Clarke looked around the room without speaking and then looked at

Bostick, who began talking rapidly. "Captain, as you know, this here is Thomas Brown, who is a Tory spy for the governor of South Carolina but lives up near Kiokee Creek on a big plantation that he's working with indentured slaves. Some of them complained about their treatment, and we went to see him up there last week, peaceable, just to ask him to understand how the folks around here was being hurt by folks like him and by the oppression of Parliament. Instead of listening to our message, he pulled out a pistol and shot at us, hitting me on my foot."

There were some snickers from the other men, and Bostick silenced them with a frown and a threatening move of his hand.

Finally, Clarke spoke for the first time. "I already know of these activities and also know his farm manager. Mr. Brown, what have you got to say for yourself?"

After an uncomfortable silence, Brown finally decided to reply, "I am a Georgia citizen, a landowner living on a legal land grant from Governor James Wright. I am also a personal friend of Governor William Campbell, and I request that you release me immediately or take me to the legal authorities of this state."

He was vaguely aware that he had misspoken and finally decided that it was the use of the word "request" instead of "demand."

"Mr. Brown, you are lookin' at the legal authority, a citizens' jury, and you are accused of denyin' justice, participatin' in the abuse of the free and peaceful citizens of Georgia and South Carolina, and attackin' one of your neighbors."

Then he ignored Brown and turned to the accusers. "Mr. Bostick, y'all don't need me here, and I've got other things to do. Just see that justice is done."

Clarke then left the tavern, and all eyes turned to Bostick, who consulted briefly with his companions and then announced, "We'll call our first witness, Mr. Leander."

The herdsman whom he had seen in the tavern in Orangeburg stepped forward and said, "This man was in a group of us good citizens last week, trying to tell us that only loyal Tories would be able to sell their goods in Charles Town, and others might even be subject to Indian attacks on our homes. He also spoke as a friend of John Stuart, who we know to be stirring up the savages against us."

Brown said, "That's a lie," and decided not to speak further.

Relishing his position as presiding officer, Bostick asked, "What do you have to say in your defense?"

When there was no response, he added, "I find you guilty as charged, and this jury will now decide on a sentence."

After a brief consultation with his cronies, Bostick announced, "We have decided to give you the same sentence as was awarded to a traitor last month in Savannah. You are to be tarred and feathered, and dragged around the street until you confess to your crimes and pledge not to repeat them. Is there any objection from other members of this legal and respected court?"

There was no response.

"If not, you will stay under guard here tonight, and we'll reconvene at sunrise to execute the sentence. In the meantime, Mr. Jarvis will put a bandage on the little scratch on your head."

One of the men said, "Most of the tar is going to stick in his long hair with all that blood. Shouldn't we scalp him first?"

Everyone laughed, and Bostick said, "No, but take a sharp knife and relieve him of that tangled mess so the bandage will do more good."

His almost bald and badly aching head now bandaged, Brown lay in the corner of the room, on his side and with his hands still bound. He could see that at all times one of the men was there guarding him while the others moved in and out of the tavern, drinking, telling jokes, and laughing. He cursed the day he had come to this lawless country. It was inconceivable that such a thing as this could happen, and he was quite sure during the long night that local officials would hear of what was happening and come to release him.

However, as day began to break outside the tavern, he heard a cart drive up, and voices laughing and talking about how much better use this would be for tar and feathers than caulking the bottom of boats and making featherbeds. It wasn't long before rough hands grabbed him and dragged him outside, and supported him until he was able to stand erect. On the cart he saw a large iron pot of wood tar with a blackened broom handle sticking out of it. Alongside was a hemp bag tied at the top with ends of feathers protruding through the rough interwoven strands of the fabric.

Bostick was there, still in charge, and asked, "How hot is the tar?"

"Hot enough to flow, but not so it will kill him."

"Mr. Brown, are you ready to confess, and pledge your support for the freedom of all colonists from oppression?"

Still half hoping that this was a local farce and that the ridiculous sentence would not be executed, Brown shook his head. He was deathly afraid and would have cried out for mercy if there was any hope of succeeding. He looked around him, his senses now as alert as ever in his life. He attempted to memorize each face. He tried to speak but was unable to think of what to say.

"Then untie his hands, strip off all his clothes, and proceed with the sentence. Let him keep his boots."

The lieutenant was soon naked, and some of the men hooted and made ribald comments about his shriveled privates and his almost snow-white skin. Then one of them took the dripping broom out of the kettle and began to cover his body with the almost scalding pitch, beginning at his neck and working downward. The pain was excruciating, as was the torment of his frustrated anger and shame. The men surrounding him seemed to enjoy the spectacle, with those who had previously been silent becoming caught up in the enthusiasm of the mob. Only a thin coating of the hot tar adhered to the vertical parts of his body, but it puddled on top of his shoulders and in his boots around his feet, where the heat did not dissipate and the pain intensified.

He groaned as quietly as he could, barely restraining himself from crying out in anguish. Carrying out Bostick's order, the other men opened the bag, picked up handfuls of the feathers and threw them on Brown, and then turned the bag upside down over his head and body.

"Now we want everyone in Augusta to see this frizzled chicken!" Bostick shouted, and his audience laughed. He secured a rope loosely around Brown's neck and tied the other end to the back of the cart. "Let's take him for a tour of the town."

Several men took the tongue of the cart and began to move, looking back to see how fast the tethered prisoner could walk. The hundred yards or so around the few stores seemed like an eternity to Brown, and when they returned to the front of the tavern, he heard, as at a distance, Bostick ask, "Do you confess and pledge your loyalty to our cause?"

Brown stood mute, not knowing how to reply, and Bostick said, "Take him around again." When they returned, the captive could hardly walk, but still refused or was unable to respond. His heart was pounding with fear and anguish, but his mind was dulled and somehow he could not acknowledge what was happening. As the third circuit began, he fell to the ground, and the rope tightened around his throat. He lost consciousness.

"He'll soon be dead," said one of the men.

Bostick thought for a few moments and then said, "That is not what we want. Throw some water on him."

When Brown regained consciousness, Bostick said to him, "You're a dead man if you don't confess. I'm going to ask you once more: Do you admit your crime and pledge to support freedom?"

Brown was resigned to his fate and felt that the unconsciousness of death would not be as unpleasant as his present plight.

Then, like a miracle, it seemed that there was a profound transformation deep within his very soul. All at once, he was obsessed with hatred instead of fear, and he didn't want to die. Should he give his life now and permit his despised enemies to be forever triumphant? It was as though his own destiny became remarkably clear: ultimate revenge. He looked around him, his pulse pounding in his temples and the faces of his tormentors partly obscured by what seemed to be a veil of red. He delayed no longer in making his decision. He nodded his head. "I confess," he said, and the bystanders cheered. Then he repeated what Bostick commanded.

"Take off the rope and untie his hands," Bostick ordered. He turned to the innkeeper and said, "Mr. Jarvis, you can clean him up and give him his clothes. We left his money, so he can pay you."

A few hours later, after the innkeeper had obtained a bottle of turpentine from the boatbuilder, Brown and Jarvis had removed most of the tar. The exhausted man lay on the cot in the tiny low-ceilinged room, his entire body a dull red, with many blisters rising in the places where the hot tar had accumulated. Some of his toes were badly burned and had no feeling in them. The innkeeper returned his purse, in which Brown was surprised to find all his papers and his money.

"I need to stay here until I am able to travel. Get me some grease or ointment for these burns so that we can treat my worst places, and be sure to take care of my horse. You will be well paid, and I will not forget you in the future, when I return."

The innkeeper merely nodded, certain that the man would, for the rest of his life, stay as far from Augusta as possible. He couldn't know that within the befouled and pitiful man there was an obsessive hatred and determination to repay his tormentors, and that it would be the all-pervasive commitment of his life.

After two full days of fitful rest, with his head pounding and his vision blurred, Brown notified Jarvis that he would be leaving early the following morning. The innkeeper suggested that he hire someone to accompany him to his homestead, but Brown declined, not revealing that he had decided instead to make the journey across the Savannah River to Ninety Six, the nearest post where a contingent of British troops were stationed. Despite the need for further treatment of his lacerated head and the burns over his body, his immediate priority was to find his way back to British authorities, where he could marshal support for a forceful return to Augusta. Even though it would mean penetration by Carolina troops into a different colony, he was sure that responsible officials in Georgia would welcome any punishment that could be inflicted on the traitors who had attacked him and had perpetrated a similar crime in Savannah.

Brown could hear rain pounding on the roof a few inches above his head, and the murmur of sounds of tavern customers downstairs, with his name mentioned every now and then, but Jarvis provided food and other services in his room and carried out orders that he not be disturbed.

Early the following morning, he struggled into his cleaned clothes, leaving them as loose on his body as possible and not worrying about stains from the grease that still covered his most badly burned places. He could not put any weight on his right foot, which was afflicted with deep wounds, so that he could almost see the bones in two of his toes. Still two hours before daybreak, he had the innkeeper fill his saddlebags with provisions and obtain a crutch for him to use. There were difficult choices to be made, particularly concerning his foot and his buttocks. Finally, he spread the thick folds of his blanket across the saddle, placed his musket in its scabbard, put his empty right boot in a bag suspended from the saddle, and had the innkeeper help him onto the horse. He guided his mount through the empty street to the river and finally succeeded in rousing the ferryman, who was excited and nervous when he recognized his customer. After paying what amounted to a small bribe, Brown crossed the river alone, still in the saddle, and then walked his horse slowly northward toward his destination. He had to obtain assistance before proceeding on to Ninety Six. After just a short ride he desperately needed to rest but felt that he could not dismount and then climb back onto his saddle. With difficulty, he was able to urinate, but not without wetting his trousers and the side of his horse. After riding just a few hundred yards, Brown realized that he was increasingly dizzy and could go no farther without falling from his horse.

When he heard a stream gurgling off to his right, he rode alongside it until he located a fallen log as high as his stirrups, eased off his horse, tied the rein where the animal could nibble grass, ate some food beside the stream, and then lay on the ground and slept fitfully. After taking a long drink, he led the horse back alongside the log and eased himself onto the padded seat. He found the pain to be bearable and proceeded for a couple of hours before coming to a small clearing with a log cabin, a lean-to behind it, and a few acres of crops and pasture.

Before he arrived at the front door, a farmer came out on the porch to meet him, a rifle held in the crook of his arm. Brown decided to address the man forthrightly and said, "I have been burned and can hardly travel, and I need to get to the fort at Ninety Six as soon as I can. I know that all your crops are not yet harvested, but hope that you can help me with my journey. I'll pay you for your time and trouble, and will be deeply grateful."

The man helped Brown from his horse and into the cabin, where his wife and two children had been peeping through the door. "My name is Jason Turner. It's too wet to work in the field, and this afternoon I will be glad to go with you to the settlement. I've been needing to do some trading and don't require any pay."

The family members were polite and somewhat timid, and they observed Thomas Brown with great curiosity, while attempting to conceal their interest. They could see that he was quite weak and feverish, and that he did not wish to discuss his circumstances any more than necessary. He seemed to be obsessed with his own thoughts and eager to recommence his travels. He accepted some warm water and managed to bathe and rewrap his right foot, which was badly swollen.

That afternoon Turner helped Brown onto his horse, and the two men rode for only a half mile before the injured man began swaying in the saddle. After a brief conversation, Brown agreed to go back to the cabin to spend the night. After eating a few bites of cornbread and drinking some milk, he lay down on a pallet and slept soundly, rising sometime during the night to relieve himself outside. The next morning, Brown and Turner proceeded as rapidly as possible to Ninety Six, where they entered the big gate of the fort. Brown insisted that Turner accept a sovereign for his trouble before they parted company. Then Brown hobbled into the clapboard command post, had the duty officer close the door, showed him his papers from the governor, and asked to see the commanding officer, a Captain Whitman. The captain knew of Brown as the "governor's man," had seen him during one of his encounters with Drayton, and had already heard a report of the incident in Augusta. The captain was a professional soldier, completely loyal to the crown, and treated the lieutenant with sympathy and respect. He arranged for a curtained-off bed and some rudimentary medical treatment from the apothecary assigned to the fort. Brown asked for paper and writing materials, and spent as much time as possible composing a report of the disgraceful attack on himself. He finally decided to abbreviate the written account so that he could describe all the facts directly to the governor. After two days, Captain Whitman assigned a dependable man to accompany Brown to Charles Town, a long trip of about 175 miles.

Brown knew that his experience in Augusta was an extremely serious development, indicating a level of insurrection that no one in the government had expected or been willing to acknowledge. What the lieutenant wanted most was to lead a large group of horsemen back to Augusta, to arrest the perpetrators of the crime against him and the crown, and to see them hanged. He decided to report first to his military commander, Colonel Ezekiel Hawkins, to whom he would deliver his abbreviated written report, wanting to make a full account only to the governor, who would be the one to authorize a full-scale military operation. He was pleased to be ushered immediately in to see the colonel, who knew of his mission across the colony and understood the necessity for his traveling out of uniform. Brown noticed that the colonel seemed somewhat discomfited as he accepted the folded report and nodded for him to be seated, assuming that he was concerned about his obvious injuries. The colonel spoke first.

"I've had a report about your misfortune, Lieutenant, and hope your injuries are not too serious."

"No, sir, except for the scalp wounds and my right foot being badly burned."

"From what I've heard, this has been an unpleasant incident, and I am

pleased to receive an explanation of your actions. I have already had one
from Thompson."

"Thompson! The scoundrel! He abandoned me at a critical moment,
leaving me at the hands of the hoodlums and traitors in the Augusta inn.
He deserves severe punishment."

"This is not a decision for you to make, Mr. Brown. I understand that
he had the good judgment to avoid a direct confrontation with the ruffians
and to handle the unfortunate situation with diplomacy. He also reported
that you were well cared for by the innkeeper, and only then did he leave
Augusta to bring me as early an account of the affair as possible."

Brown could not believe what he was hearing and started to reply angrily, but the colonel raised his hand with his palm outward, a clear signal for
silence. He sat behind his table for a few moments and then said, "The governor is deeply concerned about what has happened and has instructed me
that neither you nor Thompson may speak of this to anyone. He has seen
the other report and would like your fuller explanation as soon as possible."

"Sir, I prefer to see the governor in person so that I can discuss the matter with him fully before a decision is made on retribution for the criminals
who attacked me."

"I've given you the governor's request for a full written statement, and
tomorrow morning I shall send a messenger for it. In the meantime, you
are to stay in your quarters within the military compound. An orderly will
be at your disposal, and my personal physician will call upon you promptly
so that your wounds can be treated properly."

Brown started to protest, but the colonel picked up papers from his desk
and ostentatiously demonstrated that the conversation was over. His brief
written report was still folded and unread. The lieutenant stumbled as he left
the room, almost forgetting the pain in his foot as he left the building. What
could Thompson have said? Why were not the military and political officers
in an uproar, already planning how best to address the insults that had been
leveled against the crown itself? He would write a full account, indeed, and
would include his own recommendations on how best to take retaliatory action. He would also insist on supplementing the document with a personal
visit with the governor, despite the ridiculous instruction to remain in his
quarters. Surely this was because they had overestimated the seriousness of
his burns and felt that he was not able to move about.

For now, he saw no alternative except to return to his room and await his call to see the governor, who had always treated him with respect, knowing of his possible relation to the prime minister. The physician appeared within an hour, examined his head and burned body with few remarks or questions, and finally said, "I believe you have had a concussion, but there is not much to be done about it. Except for the toes of your right foot and a few burns on the tops of your shoulders, the other wounds should heal in a few days if they do not become infected. You will have some scars, but they will be superficial. Do not break the blisters or cover them with grease or oil. You must keep the burned surfaces as clean as possible. I shall do my best to treat your toes, but I am afraid that you may lose at least two of them, and perhaps more."

Brown listened impassively, even to the last remark. He was obsessed with anger and consternation, and when the doctor left he began writing furiously, filling sheet after sheet with his description of the seditious actions of which he and the royal government officials had been victims.

That night, Brown was aroused by a knock on his door and found the governor's secretary, Mr. Appling, standing there. Still walking with a crutch, Brown invited the man to come in and sit down.

"When can I see the governor? I have some very important information to give him."

"The governor has already received a full accounting from Mr. Thompson and only needs a written report from you so he can conclude the matter."

"The hell you say! I have been seriously insulted and injured while on a personal mission for the governor, and I insist on being given an immediate opportunity to inform His Excellency and to join in the expedition to find and punish the hoodlums who committed this crime—not only against me, but against the crown itself."

The secretary remained silent for a moment or two and then said, "Lieutenant, this is an incident that is regrettable and, as you say, deeply insulting. Jokes are already making the rounds of the city about what happened to you, and Mr. Drayton and the Council of Safety are calling for your arrest. This is damage that has already been done to you personally, and this cannot be undone." Appling paused for a few seconds and then added, now in a more confidential tone that indicated he was speaking for himself and as an objective observer, "The governor is determined to minimize the tainting of himself or anyone in London, including His Majesty."

As the secretary left, Brown was incensed. He concluded his document with the words: "Any failure to punish these scoundrels will, in effect, reward them for their actions and indicate that their own influence is greater than it actually is. These radical Whigs with their treasonous ideas are a tiny minority of the population and need to be stamped out as quickly as possible. This is a good opportunity to take strong action to demonstrate the authority of the crown."

Early the next morning, he could hardly wait for the earliest opportunity to have his horse brought around, and then set out for the governor's office with his report. Only an orderly was there when he arrived, and he dismounted and seated himself outside the locked door of the government building. After about an hour, which seemed much longer, Mr. Appling arrived and seemed startled to see Brown.

"What can I do for you?"

"I've come to see the governor."

"The colonel has informed us that your statement would be in writing and that you would be remaining in your quarters for a few days of medical treatment."

"I'm quite able to move about, as you can see, and have brought my report, but wish to supplement what I have written and to answer any questions the governor might have. Also, I have some suggestions on what specific action might be taken that I believe should be shared directly with him."

"The governor will not be available this morning, but I will relay your report to him and bring his response to you."

Brown had reached the end of his patience and refused to leave until the governor arrived even if ordered to do so by other top officials in the government. He waited almost two hours before Governor Campbell rode up, seemed startled to see Brown, accepted the envelope, and disappeared. A half hour later, Brown was invited into his private office. After the two were alone and with the door closed, the governor turned to his visitor.

"Sit down, Lieutenant. I have read your statement and received reports from other sources, with amazement and deep concern. I prefer that you not speak for a few minutes while I explain the very disturbing situation that exists in South Carolina. This will demand your mature judgment concerning the overall state of affairs in this colony. At least for the time being, I am faced with a council of safety that is strongly influenced by William Henry Drayton, whom you know only too well. Until the king's authority can be clearly reestablished, they have taken the debates in which you have participated to imply disloyalty to the Continental Congress. The fact is that at Ninety Six he has seduced Colonel Fletchall–"

Brown interrupted to say, "Sir, I can tell you that when Fletchall betrayed us to Drayton, he was drunk as a coot!"

The governor motioned for silence. "Let me continue. The fact is that Fletchall, claiming to speak for all Tories, signed a treaty there that promised, in effect, that any Tory who proposed helping the British army was subject to severe punishment. Since then, Fletchall has tried to deny his signed agreement, but Drayton has convinced the Council of Safety to arrest as treaty violators anyone accused of opposing the so-called provincial congress. They are demanding that you be arrested, along with Moses Kirkland, who has already found safety on a British ship, and a motion was even made in the council for me to be placed under house arrest. I am sure the situation will change, because Drayton's influence is shaky, with most responsible people thinking he is too radical and trying to start a war. But for now, I am afraid there is no way for us to give you assistance, and it may be best for you to leave South Carolina for a while."

The governor again raised his hand as Brown opened his mouth to protest, and continued, "The situation is not much better in Georgia. I have just learned that anyone opposing the crown has been officially declared to be a traitor and has lost protection of His Majesty's government. His property will be confiscated, and he will face execution. However, Governor Wright has informed London that the laws of Parliament can't be enforced, and he has just asked me to support his request to General Gage for more British troops in Savannah. They will not be forthcoming, and it is likely that the governor is under the same duress as I."

The lieutenant was devastated, and speechless for a few minutes. He was inclined to dispute the governor's assessment but quickly remembered his own personal observations and various bits of information that he had received lately. He had to admit that the royal military forces in Georgia and South Carolina were minuscule compared with the demands on them. Most of the able-bodied men had been sent either northward to serve with General Thomas Gage, who was under pressure in Massachusetts, or down to St. Augustine to help defend Florida against threatened attacks from Georgia. At the same time, South Carolina's provincial congress had recruited three regiments of volunteers, so far not involved in insurrection but pledged to "resist force with force."

Without further response, he took his leave of the governor and returned to his room in the barracks to consider what he should do next. His own pain and embarrassment were proof of growing rebel sentiments in the backcountry, but he had had no idea that the Tory cause was even weaker on the coast. Still, he had sworn to avenge himself, and this was by far the overriding commitment of his life, regardless of personal danger. What could he possibly do under the circumstances?

That afternoon, Colonel Hawkins came to see him, asked how he was feeling, and said, "The governor suggests that you leave South Carolina immediately, in order to recuperate from your injuries, and that you make your departure with little public notice."

"Sir, this is a suggestion that I do not intend to accept. I will wait here until I can talk to him about a further assignment in His Majesty's service, and am sure that I can make a convincing case."

"Let me rephrase his message: this is not a suggestion, but a direct order. In fact, there is a brig leaving in two days bound for St. Augustine, and your passage on it has been arranged."

"But, sir, I know nothing of St. Augustine and have no business there."

It was only the lieutenant's well-known lack of military training and his possible high connections in London that allowed the colonel to be patient. He explained, "We have had control of Florida now for two and a half years and consider St. Augustine to be an important bastion in our defense forces in the east. Also, there is considerable military activity in north Florida, where we are working very closely with our Indian allies. The governor feels that you can be quite useful there. I will return tomorrow with your written orders, and to make more detailed plans for your departure."

Brown was distressed at what was happening and decided to play what he thought might be his best card in this verbal contest.

"Sir, my personal honor is at stake. Because of a statement I was forced to make under threat of death, it is believed in Augusta and the surrounding area that I am disloyal to the king and a supporter of insurrection. I cannot accept this situation, even in the face of severe punishment. My intention is to send a copy of my report to London, where, as the governor knows, it will be received by high authorities. I am willing to be moved to Florida, but regardless of what else happens, I request that my good name be cleared. I hope you will relay this message to the governor."

The colonel gave a polite nod and left the room.

It was an hour or two before Brown's anger cooled enough for him to think rationally. Faced with the inevitability of his transfer, and without any conscious decision, he began to relate his disgrace in Augusta to the disturbing orders he had just received. As he sought an explanation for the governor's decision, he slowly came to realize that high British officials might well be in agreement with the governor, because a test of strength with the revolutionary forces would have a doubtful outcome. It was better to ignore the tavern incident than to acknowledge that the Sons of Liberty could perpetrate such a crime with impunity. As far as the authorities were concerned, even in London, Brown was best assumed to be a foolish, naive, and perhaps drunken rowdy rather than someone who was actually representing the crown. It seemed clear that officials were letting it be known that they had no interest in his case and wanted to minimize any public knowledge of it.

His next questions were about his own future. What was he going to do? How much of his official status as a lieutenant could he retain? What did he really have to contribute? The last question was the most difficult to be faced. He lay on his bed and, in one of the rare times in his life, made an increasingly frank assessment of his own capabilities. It was difficult for him to acknowledge that his rank of lieutenant had not been earned through any appreciable military competence, but had come to him through his father as benefactor, and partially as a means of removing him from London. Even now, he knew little about the land in which he was living, or of its inhabitants, either the colonists whose families had immigrated from Europe or the natives who still occupied and controlled most of the territory in Florida and all of Georgia except a narrow strip of land along the Atlantic Ocean and just west of the Savannah River. In fact, he had never seen an Indian except around trading posts, nor desired to do so.

The following day Brown decided to remain in his quarters, both to save himself further embarrassment and also to comply with the governor's directive to avoid any public notice. The physician came with an assistant, examined his foot carefully, and announced that two of his toes would have to be amputated to avoid the spread of gangrene. Brown had to accept this decision, and suffered through the brief operation, which he found no more painful than what he had already endured. In fact, after the bleeding was staunched and his foot bandaged, it felt better than before.

It was midafternoon before the governor's secretary returned.

"I have brought your orders and a response from the governor. He agrees fully that any doubts about your loyalty must be fully addressed, and I await your suggestions on how this might best be done. However, it is important to Lord William that this matter be handled here in America, between you and him. I must have your assurance about this."

Brown nodded and handed over an additional statement he had drafted, expressing his condemnation of the malefactors and their treasonous acts and expressing his full and unequivocal loyalty to the crown. It also included his promise that he would return to Augusta and seek full and personal retribution. "I want this posted in Augusta, Ninety Six, Fort Granby, and in Orangeburg. If this is done, I see no need for any correspondence with London."

The secretary read the statement through several times and then said, "This will be done, but it must be clear that it comes from you personally and that this is not an official document that has the approval of the government."

Brown agreed. The secretary placed two packets on the table and said, "The ship has completed loading and will sail tomorrow at daybreak. The captain is prepared to receive you and your horse late this afternoon."

He then departed without another word. One envelope, addressed to him, contained twenty pounds and his orders, on a single sheet, to embark on the schooner *Moriah,* to proceed to St. Augustine, and to report to the senior military commander. The other, much thicker packet was addressed to Colonel Augustine Prevost and marked "personal and confidential."

Brown followed his orders and found the *Moriah* to be quite different from the large square-rigger on which he had come to America. It was a small ship of about seventy tons, with a square stern, two masts, fore and aft sails, and a long bowsprit that carried a surprisingly large jib. His horse was placed in the hold with some cattle, and he was assigned to a small cabin with the first mate. Except for brief introductions, they hardly spoke during the short voyage. It seemed obvious to Brown that the ship's officers were uncomfortable with him, probably familiar with his circumstances. He regretted having to use a crutch but was glad that bandages concealed his shorn head.

Among the supplies Brown had the orderly acquire before leaving Charles Town was a standard manual that was used in the combat training of British infantry, and on the overnight trip down the coast he devoted his time to studying the intricacies of military tactics. He was somewhat disappointed that the text had nothing to say about what he might expect to encounter either in Florida or in any other colony in the New World. In fact, it was dated 1730 and only covered the rudimentary handling of weapons, close-order drill, and the type of attack with fixed weapons, abreast of other soldiers, that had been used almost since Roman times in European combat. However, he was able to learn some of the military terms and to extract some tidbits of advice, which he memorized and attempted to apply mentally to the swamps and forests through which he had passed on his trips from Charles Town to and from Georgia. He was thankful for his good horsemanship and that he was proficient in the use of his sword, musket, and pistol, but remembered with concern and curiosity the long rifles, tomahawks, and knives that the well-armed men on the frontier seemed to favor.

CHAPTER 23

A Rebirth at St. Augustine

OCTOBER 1775

When Brown arrived at St. Augustine, he was surprised and impressed with the fortifications that had been built by the Spaniards thirty-five years earlier to protect their forces from a British sea attack. But he soon learned that although there were about 150 well-trained troops present and British ships were dominant in the Caribbean, the primary defense of the fort came from its geographical location. To the west and north was the St. Johns River, and farther north the wide St. Marys River flowed eastward to form Florida's boundary with Georgia. St. Augustine was almost impervious to attack, except from a formidable force at sea, which the French and Spanish could most certainly not deploy. In fact, the British had not gained Florida from Spain in 1763 by any military attack in the area, but by the terms of a general treaty signed in Paris that ended both the Seven Years War in Europe and the French and Indian War in the New World.

As a result, St. Augustine was now a secure military base of the British government, from which the defense of eastern Florida was assured, and forays might even be launched northward into Georgia. Its primary vulnerability came from its being surrounded by water and thin, sandy soil, making it difficult for settlers in the region to produce enough food to support the army detail and the few civilians who lived there. Recently, with Whigs becoming more dominant in Georgia and the Carolinas, there were a growing number of loyal Tory families moving to Florida to avoid harassment from the American rebels.

It soon became obvious to Brown that Governor Patrick Tonyn and the military commanders in St. Augustine had great influence in London, far exceeding that of the royal governors in either Charles Town or Georgia. In the continuing competition for troops and supplies, the Florida post always seemed to prevail. It seemed that London authorities had relegated the two other southern colonies to a low priority, and that the days of Lord William Campbell and Sir James Wright might be numbered. Except for sporadic Spanish threats to Pensacola, in western Florida, British control of the colony was not seriously challenged, even after fighting had broken out in the northern colonies and radical groups, with which Brown had become all too familiar, were threatening the peace in the southern colonies.

Here, also, the British were able to have friendly and mutually supportive relations with the Indian tribes along the coast, whose influence extended all the way northward to Virginia and westward to the Mississippi River. In all the coastal regions, there was a constant pressure on the American settlers to move westward, always arousing the animosity of the native tribes. The British officials, and especially those in Florida, were not considered guilty of this obsession with new lands, since their duty assignments in the colonies were relatively brief and their homes and families remained in England.

When Brown reported to the headquarters of Colonel Augustine Prevost, Major Howard Furlong met him and took the envelope into the colonel's private office. Brown was deeply concerned about the possible contents of the message and waited impatiently until the major reappeared and led him down the hall to his own room. Brown hoped the man was well aware of the rumor that his father was the prime minister.

"Lord William has given us a brief report of your unfortunate experience in Augusta and has informed us of your limited military experience and your eagerness to be of service. The colonel doesn't have time to meet with you, but I have set aside time to hear your own, more complete description of what happened."

Brown recounted the events in Georgia, struggling to control his almost overwhelming feeling of anger. The major asked a number of questions, and Brown was impressed with his personal interest and obvious intelligence. Here was a man who seemed to have all the attributes of a competent field commander and was the first person who showed Brown the respect of discussing in any depth what had happened.

Furlong said, "You have to understand the need for you to leave Carolina, and to minimize public knowledge of what happened in Augusta. We don't have enough military forces in either Savannah or Charles Town to move into the backcountry with any hope of success. Such an effort, as desirable and justified as it might be, would be unlikely to succeed. It is better not to reveal this weakness of our troops or the extent of the building rebellion. The top officials decided, I think rightly, that it is better to let this be treated as your personal problem, and not as an official incident that would require retribution. As unpleasant as it is, you must accept the responsibility for what happened, although I have to add that I do not hold you to blame for the confrontation. I hope that I would have acted similarly. The next decision to be made is what you shall do here in Florida."

Brown restrained himself as he considered what Furlong had said and then, with an intensity that surprised and somewhat concerned his new superior, he replied, "Sir, I shall soon be adequately healed of my present injuries and ready for any assignment that you might give me. I have never commanded men and have little actual military training, but I am willing to do anything to correct these deficiencies. If you will give me the opportunity to learn how to be a soldier, on my own time, I will also perform other regular duties to the best of my ability."

"Come back tomorrow at this time, and your assignment will be ready."

As he emerged into the brilliant Florida sunshine and walked haltingly back to his assigned quarters, Thomas Brown realized that, for the first time in his life, he had established a definite and exalted ambition. He was obsessed with the commitment to master the art of combat, specifically that designed to accommodate the peculiar circumstances of the woods and swamps between him and Augusta, Georgia. During the night, he tried to resurrect memories of the wilderness and was disgusted with himself that the images were still alien and fearsome. He had a hazy realization that he would need British tactics correlated with those of the native Indians, and it was clear that he had neither. He was hardly aware that his former fear and timidity were being replaced by hatred, vengeance, and a lack of concern for his own safety.

The following day Brown returned to the office, attempting to conceal his limp as much as possible. Major Furlong looked at the young lieutenant for a while and, apparently having made a decision, leaned back to indicate that he had an extensive statement to make.

"I have consulted with Colonel Prevost, and we have decided to describe our situation to you and then make an assignment. One of my responsibilities is to collect and assess intelligence from every available source. We have some problems north of here. As you know, the Whigs and revolutionaries have put enough pressure on the port officials in Savannah to prevent their shipping supplies here to us. This requires us to import goods from much farther away or to go directly into south Georgia to purchase corn, potatoes, cattle, sheep, and other produce directly from settlers who are loyal to our Tory cause or who are willing to sell at a good profit. In addition, we must maintain the front line of our defenses at or beyond the St. Marys River against periodic excursions made against us from the fumbling militia forces of Georgia, who are also harassing Governor Wright enough that he may soon leave Savannah and return to London.

"In all these efforts this far south, we cooperate as closely as possible with the Creeks and Seminoles. Authorities in London permit Governor Tonyn to keep Indian Superintendent John Stuart stationed here or in Pensacola so that he can assist us with both trade matters and maintain an adequate military liaison with the natives. The fact is that Stuart has enough influence to ignore the governor's directives if he disagrees."

Brown was intrigued with this report, some of which was not generally known, and considered the major's frankness to be a compliment, but he did not know how to guess what was coming next. He sat on the edge of the chair as he heard the major's words.

"With permission of Colonel Prevost, I have decided to make you my personal assistant, with the primary duty of representing me outside this office and gathering whatever intelligence is available. My other duties do not permit me to leave St. Augustine except when there might be a military emergency, and this seldom happens. I need someone with unquestioned loyalty to the crown, and the memorandum you brought me from Charles

Town emphasizes this as one of your unquestioned attributes, and you have some knowledge of Georgia and South Carolina, which I lack."

Brown's face flushed with pleasure and excitement, and he eagerly accepted the assignment. "I will never disappoint you, sir. During the last year I have acquired some experience in gathering information and relaying it to Governor Campbell. I will carry out this duty to your satisfaction, will demonstrate my complete loyalty to His Majesty, and devote myself to ensuring that the traitors and criminals are identified and brought to justice. To speak with complete frankness, however, I must state again that I know little about how to prevail in combat, either in an open military confrontation or in the wilderness. With your permission, I would like to learn as much as possible." And then he added, "Always subject to serving well in my primary duties, of course."

With a smile, Furlong added, "What you learn about military matters will be up to you. First, your wounds must heal and during this time I want you to learn as much as possible about the political and military circumstances that affect our duty. Later, I will assign one of my most competent sergeants to accompany you, and he can recommend, perhaps, one or two Indians as well. You must remember that the loyalty of the redskins is to whomever they consider to be best for them at the time, but you can depend upon their personal courage and knowledge of the wilderness."

Ten days later, as Brown was studying documents and maps in Furlong's office, the major came in and said, "I have some information that might be of concern to you. The brig *Hinchinbrook* is coming to St. Augustine within a day or two, and Lord William Campbell will be on board. Under threat of being arrested by the radical Whig faction in Charles Town, he traveled to Savannah and boarded the ship."

Brown was surprised, and also disappointed, but he had an immediate hope that having a respected former advisor nearby might be helpful to him personally. He asked, "Sir, if I may ask, how will another governor fit into the situation here?"

Furlong thought for a few moments and then replied, "It will depend on whether Lord William stays here or is soon to be returning to London for another assignment. Of all the leaders I know in this region, he has the most influence with General Clinton. I have heard that he is a special friend of Governor Tonyn, but has had some differences with Colonel Prevost in the past. It may be just that the colonel is Swiss, or that so many of the

Prevost family have been given positions within this military command. As you may already have learned, he has two brothers, a son, and several cousins serving under him."

Soon after arriving in St. Augustine, Governor Campbell sent for Lieutenant Brown, who was surprised to find Governor Tonyn also present. Campbell seemed somewhat aggravated when he learned that Tonyn had not seen the written report he had sent with Brown, and proceeded to give a brief but complimentary account of Brown's activities along the frontier. Brown assumed later that this was a way for the governor to compensate for his peremptory handling of the situation in Charles Town. It was the first time since he had been in St. Augustine that the lieutenant had met anyone more senior than Major Furlong, and he was pleased to have his activities in South Carolina described to Tonyn in positive terms, without any reference to his abuse in Augusta. The two senior officials pretended not to notice that he still walked with a limp, had bruises from the rope around his neck, and his hair was embarrassingly short. Brown was soon dismissed, after a brief meeting.

Brown's burns healed rapidly in the Florida climate, and he soon learned to pack cotton or soft rags where his toes should have been and abandoned his walking stick; despite the pain, he was able to walk with only a slight limp. As the head wound healed, he had his hair trimmed neatly and then obtained Major Furlong's permission to let it grow back to shoulder length so that, as an ostensible civilian, he could better perform his duties in gathering intelligence. For a month, he spent much of his time in Major Furlong's presence or directly under his supervision, eagerly learning everything possible about the local military situation, reading all the standing orders from London, memorizing the deployment of men in the entire Florida command, including Pensacola, and studying relationships with merchants who had contracts to supply food to the fort.

Brown was pleased to learn that the British navy was more than equal to those of the French and Spanish combined, and the major reminded him that control of the sea from Canada to Florida would ultimately bring about the end of the mutiny against England. This advantage would bring supplies to the fighting forces and opportunities for trade with Europe. There was little doubt that if the rebellion was prolonged, the revolutionaries would eventually recruit more men than Parliament could spare to send to America, even if the Redcoats were supplemented with German Hessians and other mercenaries. However, there was also little doubt that the superiority of the British fighting men would be overwhelming.

Although Brown had never been involved in regular service, he knew that British infantry, once committed to the army, had to remain in service at the pleasure of the crown. These boys from poor families, often Scots and Irishmen, made the military a career and were proud of their regiments, which became their family and their home. They were forged into a cohesive fighting force by strict discipline and intense training, with almost constant battle in Europe providing experience in strategy and tactics that ensured their superiority in any theater of war. Their infantry units were exceptionally fearsome, led by ambitious young officers always eager to prove their gallantry. They lived with the fact that their standard muskets were inaccurate except at relatively close range, but when their ranks held solid even after accepting casualties from enemy fire, they knew they could rely on the devastating use of bayonets in hand-to-hand combat.

Brown had to decide how he could be most helpful without having any real military training. By examining records of previous purchases, he was able to gather personal knowledge of farm families who produced the meat and grain for the British so that, when necessary, he might deal directly with them. It was a surprise to him how great a geographical area had to be covered to obtain enough food for the fort, and how high were the prices. One problem was that many of the Whig farmers refused to permit their produce to be consumed by the British.

His mind turned more and more toward the possibility of combining the military efforts of regular British forces and natives in the interior. In the broadest sense, he saw the advantages of massive movements of British forces into the southern colonies while Creek, Cherokee, and Coweta braves were marshaled to move on a broad front against disloyal Whigs. On the other extreme, Brown envisioned small groups of natives and Redcoats being used to cover south Georgia, to intimidate individual settlers, and to secure supplies for the growing population of St. Augustine.

Brown rarely left the fort during these early days in St. Augustine and was relieved that no others in his rank or below seemed to know about his embarrassing experience in Augusta. He saw Colonel Prevost only rarely, and felt uneasy with him, sensing that his presence might be resented. Although he had been introduced briefly to Governor Tonyn, his subsequent response was mainly just a momentary glance at the scars left from the rope around Brown's neck and the burns on his hands. He had a good relationship with the major and finally asked if he might begin his military training. Furlong seemed to relish the prospect and said, "You are in for an adventure. I will have Sergeant Alonzo Baker report to you Saturday morning."

When the time approached, Brown sent word to the sergeant that he preferred to meet in a local pub instead of in the officers' quarters or the major's office. He arrived early and took a table in the corner so that he could observe those who entered and left the tavern. At the appointed hour, the door was thrust open by a brute of a man, no taller than Brown but fifty pounds heavier. His considerable paunch went relatively unnoticed, as an observer's eyes were drawn to his great shoulders and bull neck. He glanced around the room and then moved gracefully to where the lieutenant was sitting.

He saluted and said, "Sir, I've been ordered to report to you."

Brown returned the salute without rising and said, "Sergeant, please have a seat, be at ease, and share an ale with me."

Baker was surprised by these opening remarks and sat stiffly in the chair opposite Brown. He was not accustomed to being offered such an invitation, although, like other experienced enlisted men, he shared the conviction of innate superiority over junior officers whose rank exceeded their capabilities.

When their drinks were served, Brown began with a statement that he had carefully prepared. "Sergeant, it is my understanding that you are the most competent and experienced fighting man on this post. I have to state that I stand at the other extreme, having had little training and no experience except in the use of a sword and pistols, almost exclusively in personal contests. My primary duties now are to serve Major Furlong as an assistant and to concentrate on gathering intelligence. However, I have a desire, approved by the major, to learn as much as possible about military skills. My hope is that you will be willing to assist me as my instructor. When we are together, at least for a few months, there will be no consideration of relative rank, just as you have related to officer trainees who are seeking their first commission."

The sergeant was silent for an uncomfortable period of time and then asked, "Am I permitted to speak frankly, sir?"

"Yes, of course."

"Then let me say that I don't like the proposal, sir, or the decision. Why should I assume the role of a drill master in addition to my other duties, and what is the reason for your request to the major?"

Brown replied, "Let me answer your second question first, by describing the circumstances that brought me here. I have some influence in London, which permitted me to be given a commission and then sent to South Carolina and on into Georgia, where I was deeded a large landholding and enough indentured servants to work it. As a special representative of the governor of South Carolina, I was asked to assess the loyalty of citizens in the region around the upper Savannah River. One night in Augusta, I was surrounded by a large group of brigands and traitors, humiliated in a mock trial, and severely abused by these criminals—in fact, covered with tar and feathers—because I professed my loyalty to the king. When I reported this tragic event to authorities, it became clear that they were not prepared to acknowledge the crime publicly, most likely because of inadequate means of contending successfully with the men who had abused me. It is for that reason that I was asked to leave Carolina. Now I have only two purposes in my life: to preserve the authority of the crown in the colonies and to seek vengeance against those who have wronged me."

He paused for a few moments and then continued, "The answer to your first question is that the major has decided that I should become proficient in combat and has suggested that you might fulfill this role. Let me add that if you object, I will ask him to name another person."

The sergeant was impressed with the intensity of Brown's demeanor and the simplicity and obvious truthfulness of his words. He asked several more questions, until he was satisfied that he understood enough about the incident to sympathize with Brown's anger and determination. He was especially impressed by the anguish with which the lieutenant used the words "tar and feathers," and wondered if he could have described such an embarrassing experience if it had happened to himself.

Brown then added, "I won't be a burden to you, and Major Furlong has granted me the authority to shift some of your responsibilities to others, to ensure that your overall duties are not increased."

There was still some obvious hesitancy from the sergeant, and Brown added, "Let us give this proposition a trial for a month. At the end of that time, I will leave the decision about its continuing for you to make."

Sergeant Baker finally nodded, and Brown immediately asked, "Then how shall we begin?"

Baker then spoke, almost as an equal. "It will take me a few days to shift my duties to others. In the meantime, let me give you the same assignment as for the other young officers I have trained, sir. Except for the marching and close-order drill, you must master the parts of the manual that pertain to the handling of weapons, transmission of commands, and basic infantry tactics. In addition, it's the physical strength and endurance that's important. It won't be easy with your sore foot."

Brown didn't say that he had already begun studying military tactics, but just nodded at the sergeant's preliminary suggestions on both the texts and physical exercises. By the time the two men had shared a beef stew and several more tankards of ale, the earlier strain between them had dissipated.

During the following weeks, Brown exceeded in every instance the assignments that Baker gave him, and even surprised himself with the rapid recovery from his burn injuries. In addition to rigorous exercises in the privacy of his quarters, he found that long walks in soft sand just above the packed-sand beach were easy on his right foot, calmed his troubled and impatient nature, and added rapidly to his stamina. Brown was also impressed and pleased with the sergeant's eager desire for information about political circumstances, both in England and in the colonies. They soon realized that their new partnership was mutually advantageous, and at the end of a month there was no consideration of terminating the arrangement. They were developing a sense of partnership and mutual respect, and a growing sense of purpose, almost without need for spoken words.

Brown was fully occupied with both his official assignment as an assistant intelligence officer and the development of his prowess as a soldier, and began to see that the two might be increasingly intertwined as his skills evolved. Sergeant Baker responded favorably to Brown's suggestion that they recruit an Indian warrior as an additional instructor, and agreed to join Brown in wilderness training. It required several weeks of interviews and trials before they finally decided on a middle-aged Seminole named Sunoma, who spoke the language of the Creeks and was also somewhat familiar with English. He had been the leader or chief of a town on the Ogeechee River but had decided to move to Florida for reasons he declined to give. His breechcloth, which was all he chose to wear in the woods, revealed a repulsive scar across his upper abdomen, which he said came from a spear thrust in battle. Although somewhat skeptical of his veracity at times, both Brown and Baker were soon impressed with the Indian's knowledge of the forests and swamps.

Sunoma seized upon the authority the two white men granted him and demonstrated the characteristics of a leader of men, but one with a sense of humor. He insisted that the men wear moccasins and light clothing, and criticized them severely when they made excessive noise, became confused about directions, or failed to detect things of interest as they passed or approached. One of his favorite exercises was to permit them to choose a location in the wilderness and then to approach them within easy arrow range before they knew he was in the vicinity. Then he would sit in a location known by the two white men and see how early he could detect the approach of either one of them. When they failed by moving a bush, snapping a twig, or disturbing a bird, he would howl with laughter and tell them they could move more stealthily if mounted on an ox or an alligator. In fact, Sunoma was inclined to be arrogant and domineering, and the sergeant had to remind him on occasion that he was being amply rewarded for working for the British, and that their failures were proof of his inadequacy as an instructor. Slowly, the lessons with Sunoma had some impact, and both men learned to shift their identities from European soldiers in an alien environment to native woodsmen with increasing abilities.

Brown began to monitor the activities of the existing trading forays into western Florida and southern Georgia, and observed that these were often relatively fruitless. When he quietly suggested to his superior that his small group might increase the acquisition of food and other supplies, he was quickly given permission. This was to be the beginning of a series of remarkable experiences.

Major Furlong had never known any other officer whose zeal exceeded that of his assistant. During the first few months, Brown mastered the relatively voluminous documents that related to the history, geography, and people of the southern region of America, accumulated maps of the south Atlantic Coast and data about military installations, and studied the parliamentary laws and directives from London, many of them signed by Lord North. He succinctly outlined the pertinent interrelationships of all this material and quietly laid his report on the desk of the major, who shared much of it, to his own great advantage, with his superiors.

His aide, Sergeant Baker, grew to respect the lieutenant and to confide in him. Brown learned that he had earlier been stationed in Georgia and assigned as leader of a small group of dragoons who patrolled the outer boundaries of the colony west of the Savannah River. Disgusted with what he considered to be revolutionary sentiments, he had killed a prominent

Whig settler in St. Johns Parish who publicly supported actions of the Continental Congress and then resisted an arrest ordered by Governor James Wright. Although his superiors determined that Baker had only been performing his duty and was not at fault, he became the target of abuse by Georgia Whigs and, after an appropriate interval to show that the military commander could not be intimidated, had been transferred to St. Augustine.

The lieutenant could now ride and walk without serious discomfort and increasingly was away from the military base. Usually dressed in civilian attire, he and the sergeant consulted with Indian leaders and visited the scattered settlements above and below the Georgia–Florida border, where he traded goods or exchanged British currency for supplies needed by the troops and civilian inhabitants of St. Augustine. With a friendly attitude and quiet inquiries, he soon accumulated a great deal of knowledge about the families whom he visited on his journeys, and recorded in meticulous detail in his logbook every comment that indicated the political preferences of each family. He was careful not to express his own views, except as a somewhat ignorant subordinate officer who was performing his assigned duties. During the long hours of their excursions, he was an avid student of military matters and constantly questioned his British and Indian companions about the environment within which they moved, and how they could make better use of it, especially the rivers and their tributary streams.

From a retired naval officer, Brown learned the rudiments of mapmaking, how to use an octant, and the observations of heavenly bodies that were useful in navigation. He carried a slim packet of available maps in his saddlebag and constantly corrected the errors he found in them.

CHAPTER 24

The Florida Rangers

DECEMBER 1775

One day, late in December 1775, Brown asked for private time with Major Furlong, and brought him some disturbing information.

"Some of my men have just come from Savannah and report that the Whigs are taking over the streets there. Some claim they want to continue as

British subjects and just redress their imagined grievances, but the cursed Sons of Liberty are publicly calling for total independence and acting as criminals and traitors with relative impunity. It is my opinion that Governor Wright will soon be forced to leave America and return to London."

Major Furlong responded, "Yes, we have seen this coming for some time. For all practical purposes the Savannah port has been closed to us, and you know we have had to depend on imports either directly from England or from the West Indies. What we lack is enough food for our one hundred and fifty troops and the growing number of Tory families who are moving here because of fear of what might happen to them in the future."

"Sir, you've wisely identified a growing problem. As the Whigs become stronger in Savannah and other parts of Georgia, the settlers in the southern region are less willing to trade with us. But, with your permission, I would like to propose a possible solution. The Tories who are coming here now for their own safety don't have anything to do. I would like to gather a few of them who have their own horses and weapons, give them some military training, and have them join me and Sergeant Baker. Then we'll visit the settlers, buy what we can from loyal Tory families, and take what we need from the disloyal Whigs."

Furlong's response was instant, and negative.

"Governor Tonyn could never be responsible for any actions such as those you have described. There would also be no way to ensure that we do not abuse families who are loyal Tories. And besides, it would not be easy to recruit men away from their families unless they are given the full pay and privileges of military service."

Having anticipated these concerns, Brown hastened to say, "Sir, respectfully, please permit me to respond. This would be a matter completely removed from official status. Both Sergeant Baker and I would take a leave of absence, and you, Colonel Prevost, the governor, and all others could disavow any connection with our activities. At the same time, what we collect in goods or intelligence would be placed at the disposal of whomever you designate to receive it. I will be personally responsible for its proper handling. Here in my hand is a dossier of every family within fifty miles of the Georgia border, with full information about their political loyalties, or, in some cases, a lack of any interest in politics. I will leave it here, with your permission, for you to examine. I can assure you of its accuracy. Our efforts among the settler families could, if desired, be restricted to those designated by you. The recruitment, training, and equipping of our associates would be my full responsibility, and I would assure that their recompense would be both adequate and no burden on the treasury of our government."

"Lieutenant, I see that you have given this proposition your full attention."

"Yes, sir, but I have taken no action on it and have only discussed it in quite general terms with Sergeant Baker."

"I'm still concerned about the proposal but will present it to both Colonel Prevost and Governor Tonyn, and will try to have an answer the next time I see you."

At the suggestion of Sunoma, Brown departed on a tour of Indian territory in the western part of the colony, primarily canoe trips along the Flint and Chattahoochee rivers. He had accumulated a small quantity of goods that he left behind as gifts to the chiefs of each village and kept meticulous records of each visit. He also corrected errors in the rudimentary maps of this broad area. As expected, he found the leaders to be strongly inclined to support the British forces, wary and fearful of the land-hungry settlers, and shrewd enough to play one side against the other for their own advantage.

When Brown returned to St. Augustine after being away for almost a month, he was summoned to the office of the major, who used careful, diplomatic language to give Brown his response.

"Colonel Prevost has deep reservations because of the uncontrollable nature of your proposal, and also because it gives you direct authority to work with the natives. This is a duty that is supposed to be exclusively performed by Superintendent John Stuart, who is now spending most of his time in Pensacola. In fact, Stuart has already registered a strong complaint about your recent foray through Creek territory without his foreknowledge or permission. The colonel wants nothing to do with your proposal and is not disposed to receive your reports that I have offered to him. However, I must say that Governor Tonyn has found some merit in your proposal about recruiting a few assistants to expand the trading policies that have long been pursued by this command. He seems to be intrigued with the information that you gather, but he wants absolutely no responsibility for your so-called trading operations."

The major paused and looked at Brown, smiled slightly, and almost winked. They both realized that their relationship in the future would be directly with the governor, but always so that any official responsibility could be denied.

"To summarize, you may continue your trading activities, and have my permission to use your own judgment about how individual transactions are concluded. I realize that it is probably inevitable that those known to be loyal to the crown will be given superior treatment. Although I wish to be provided information important to our command, there is no need to make official reports about the details of your activities. Do you understand my comments?"

"Yes, sir. I understand the unofficial nature of my work, and I shall be responsible for the success of this effort."

"Your request for an extended leave of absence for you and Sergeant Baker has been granted. Also, with your experience and new responsibilities, it has been decided that, before you take leave, a promotion is in order. Congratulations, Captain Brown."

After saluting and expressing appropriate thanks, Brown asked for and received permission to respond frankly.

"Sir, I am honored, but really prefer not to have a specific military rank, except what I already have. Since our organization will be completely unofficial in nature and consisting of a wide mixture of men, including natives, the sergeant and I had thought that I might be known simply as the commander of the group. I will, however, defer to your judgment."

Major Furlong paused and then replied, "Captain Brown, it may be a good idea to have any promotion entered only in the official records and not through insignia to be viewed by the public. Since you and the sergeant are on a leave of absence, it may also be best to refrain from wearing your uniforms, except when you consider it necessary to impress the natives with your British credentials."

Brown saluted once more and responded, "Yes, sir, I understand." He didn't add that this was already his established practice.

The major prepared to dismiss Brown but then added one comment: "As you know, we are relatively isolated here in St. Augustine, except when a ship comes in with supplies. Even then, the reports are highly unreliable, depending upon the limited knowledge and political biases of the vessels' captains. One of the things we most need is information. I would like for you to give me such reports in writing, and I shall share the appropriate ones with the governor."

The reply was immediate: "Sir, I will do whatever is possible to collect intelligence from as wide an area as possible and will make every attempt to strengthen my circle of informants. We already have some informants throughout the Indian lands, westward beyond Pensacola, and eventually I hope to develop some opportunities all the way to New Orleans. There are a number of people in both Savannah and Charles Town who remain loyal to the crown. I realize that there is no regular courier service between our northern commanders and St. Augustine, and we can, perhaps, supplement reports that you and the governor will receive through official means. With your permission, I shall make brief assessments that present this information in perspective."

Major Furlong nodded. "Perhaps you could begin with just a summary of how settlers have reacted to the so-called revolution to date, and it may be better that your submissions be signed with a pseudonym." He thought for a few minutes and added, "Your reports should be to the governor, who will always appreciate them, and can come through me. When advisable, I'll summarize them and share information with the military leaders. I suggest you refer to yourself as 'the governor's agent.'"

Having achieved much more than he had anticipated, Brown took his leave as soon as possible. He was extremely pleased with the new operating freedom that was now his. Sergeant Baker was waiting outside, and the commander of the newly authorized force said quietly, "Our entire proposal has been approved, but we will be standing alone if we fail. One thing on which we need to concentrate is the collection of information from as many sources as possible." The prospect of promotion had been insignificant to him, and he did not mention it.

It required less than a week to have ten men ready to ride, with promises of adequate adventure, the pride of service, and the knowledge that Brown had authority to reward them properly. Calling themselves the Florida Rangers, they began what would be, in effect, armed raids on settler families who had shown the slightest inclination to support the Whig cause. There were thousands of cattle and hogs, with their ears marked to indicate ownership, roaming in the swamps and woods of a geographical area that covered more than ten thousand square miles of north Florida and south Georgia. In the best of cases, the Tory farmers and ranchers were eager to sell their goods at a reasonable price, and Brown made certain that they were always treated with an acceptable degree of fairness.

As planned, Brown implemented three different approaches to the settlers, depending on their political inclinations. Those loyal to the king were treated with deference and respect, and their sales were all voluntary and for a fair price. To those whom he knew to support the Whig cause, he soon proved the error of their ways. The settlers in this region were isolated and completely helpless to resist demands of the visiting Rangers for their produce, often at prices far below market value. In addition, the farmers and ranchers rarely detected most of the Rangers' secret depredations until they would discover at some later time that stocked animals and stored produce were missing. A few confronted those who were taking their property, but this was a fruitless response, and several of the more militant and obdurate men were killed. What Brown wanted was for the word to spread, so that it became clear to the settlers that their expressions of political allegiance were a substantial factor in how they fared. A few of those with strong revolutionary sentiments abandoned their property and moved to Savannah, but over the months others shifted strongly toward the Tory cause. A few of them even volunteered to ride with the Florida Rangers.

Within a month, Brown submitted his first report to Major Furlong, primarily comprising three lists. One was of settlers who had proved themselves to be completely loyal to the crown, listed under the heading "Tories." The second, a somewhat shorter list, included the names of Whigs, who by their actions or reported words were known to support the revolutionary cause. The longer column of names was of families who were known to have little interest in political affairs or who had expressed equivocal opinions concerning events in Charles Town or Savannah. Although the Ranger commander did not reveal his intentions, he was determined to increase the first list at the expense of the other two.

In St. Augustine, the results were all good. There was an unprecedented influx of produce, and the surplus provided substantial income when exported to the West Indies. Although Thomas Brown and his renegade group were at first ridiculed, the Florida Rangers became well known as the months passed, acknowledged as a source of satisfaction among British officials, at least during their more private moments. The number of Rangers continued to expand, with groups roaming an ever-larger area. The major never accepted offers of an accounting of all the goods seized, but Brown kept detailed records in case they were ever wanted. He was able to keep his volunteers well pleased with what they were able to take home. He himself showed no desire for income above his army pay, and he forbade any stealing of seized goods by Rangers.

Commander Brown was satisfied to direct the operation, assure its success, and make plans for an expanded future. He was a rigid disciplinarian, brooking no disloyalty or questioning of his final decisions, but he understood the need for consulting closely with his immediate subordinates and particularly with the leaders of returning groups. He worked closely with Sergeant Baker and Sunoma, from whom he constantly sought advice on tactics, knowledge about the countryside, and intelligence about every family in the territory. Sergeant Baker was adept at extracting information about the raiding parties themselves, and it was not difficult for him to compare what was taken with what was delivered to the fort. Two cases of thievery resulted in a hearing before Brown at one of their outposts near the St. Marys River, and the guilty men were promptly hanged.

These actions established the character of the Florida Rangers and the primary duties of their commanding officer. Whenever possible, he left Baker in charge of acquiring supplies for St. Augustine and spent his time among the Indian tribes, learning about them and, with a portion of spoils secured from Whig settlers as gifts, securing their trust and friendship. Working closely with Indians on both sides of the Chattahoochee River and with Tory sympathizers throughout Florida and along the Atlantic Coast, Brown was developing an intelligence system that provided him information almost as soon as it reached the commanders of the Continental forces or the Georgia militia.

Increasingly, St. Augustine was becoming a focal point for British information and strategy as colonial forces assumed political control in Georgia, the Carolinas, and Virginia. Thomas Brown felt that the future of the Rangers would depend not only on the supplies that they continued to collect, but even more important, on intelligence that he was able to provide for Governor Tonyn. He was intrigued to hear about developments in Virginia that added an exciting new dimension to his long-standing scheme of harnessing natives with regular British troops and decided it was worthy of a brief assessment for Governor Tonyn.

Your Excellency:

I am emboldened to give this Assessment of the rebellion to date, encompassing well-known events and some personal Opinions. You are well aware of the Situation in our region. The traitors have made little if any Progress in the Northern colonies. Despite General Benedict Arnold's taking of Mon-

treal, and Fort Ticonderoga in northern New York, his forces have now been Repulsed at Quebec and destined to Withdraw at an early date from all of Canada. Their men have been no match in a Sustained battle with British forces and have either fled or deserted after being away from their homes for a few weeks. General Sir William Howe is holding firm in Boston, and it is generally believed that he is assembling a Force to take New York and perhaps Newport. There have been a few Skirmishes in Virginia and the Carolinas, and a small group of radicals have been Successful in inducing Lord John Dunmore to transfer his office in Virginia from land to a small British fleet, operating in the Chesapeake, from which he has led Attacks on rebel shore positions with two Regiments. It is interesting to note that one of them is composed of former black slaves, whom he has recently Declared to be free of Bondage if they take up arms on Behalf of the King.

I have just learned that Dunmore took a number of slaves and Indentured servants from the huge Plantation of George Washington, who has declared publicly, "If that man is not crush'd before spring, he will become the most Formidable enemy America has. His strength will increase like a rolling snow ball." Although these new troops were afflicted with the Pox and other diseases and Lord Dunmore could not prevail militarily, his Blow to slavery is a threat to the rebels and to the established way of life in all the Southern Colonies, and particularly in the Carolinas.

Although not all our early Efforts have been successful because of the time and expense required to move Military forces from England to this land, let me point out that the Inherent advantages are with us. Our nine million people are confronting a mere two million colonists, with decidedly less than half of them willing to Support the insurrection. As is well known, our army is blessed with a Heritage of courage and experience, while their foe is a Rabble of temporary recruits, largely untrained. Our dominance on the seas is Unchallenged, which offers great future advantage all along the Atlantic coast.

Another untapped Potential is that most of the Indians are well aware that their Wellbeing is with the Crown, and they are ripe for recruitment to our cause, an Endeavor in which I remain involved.

Respectfully submitted by
the Governor's agent

While the main work of the Ranger groups continued to be buying or confiscating cattle and other produce, Brown began to concentrate his personal attention on military matters. There were a few skirmishes, with settlers who banded together to protect their property from the Rangers and with Whig forces in more challenging military excursions launched south and eastward from Savannah. After each engagement, he carefully analyzed what had happened and how the best of British army tactics could be melded with the wilderness skills of the Creek warriors.

Some of Brown's successes contributed to increasing divisions among British officials. On one side was John Stuart and Augustine Prevost, newly promoted to brigadier general, the first determined to retain his unique role in dealing with all the Indian tribes, and the latter wanting to control all regular military personnel, having nothing but scorn for the irregular volunteers and natives. Both of these powerful leaders resented the activities of the Florida Rangers and were also contending for influence with Governors Patrick Tonyn and James Wright and former governor William Campbell. The governors had become intrigued with Brown's ideas about regaining British control of Georgia and South Carolina with coordinated attacks from regular troops and Indian recruits and had shared the plan with British General Henry Clinton. At the same time, Stuart and Prevost were using all their influence to restrain any involvement of the Rangers among the Indians or in military actions.

Despite all his activities and growing influence, Brown rarely forgot for as much as an hour his humiliation in Augusta and his ultimate and overriding ambition for revenge. After a year in Florida, he received a letter from his plantation manager, Michael Herring, who informed him that he was returning to England, to rejoin his family in Yorkshire. His reason for leaving Georgia was that Chesley Bostick had been commissioned as a captain in the Georgia militia, and his first act had been to plunder Brownsborough. He had transferred the cattle, hogs, and sheep to Augusta and given the plantation workers an option of either prison or service in the revolutionary forces. Herring had been able to escape and had found his way to Savannah. He also informed Brown that Bostick's first permanent military assignment was to command Fort Howe, on the north bank of the Altamaha River. This was information that Brown had already received from his own sources.

CHAPTER 25

"Common Sense"

1776

The activities of the outside world had hardly touched the daily lives of the Pratts. Ethan continued his quiet and fulfilling life as a farmer and herdsman, concentrating not on further expansion of the fields and grazing areas but on the improvement of those already in use. He rotated his crops as best he could to maintain soil fertility and control erosion, and to take maximum advantage of potential marketing opportunities, mostly through merchants in Wrightsborough. He deliberately limited the size of his swine and cattle herds but attempted to improve the quality of the breeding stock. Somewhat to his surprise, when he had tallied up the records in the winter of 1775, his income from the products of his woodshop almost equaled that of his entire farming operation. Designing and making furniture were where he found the most pleasure.

Ethan was very proud of his son, Henry, now four years old, and had already made a number of toys with which the boy played while his father was immersed at the forge or in the woodworking shop. He was pleased that the boy was always eager to accompany him to the fields and woods; Henry was already learning the rudiments of farming and the life of a trapper and hunter. His constant stream of questions sometimes taxed Ethan's ability to explain some of his own innate knowledge and basic decisions. For some reason, he was more inclined to share Henry's more interesting inquiries with the Morrises than with Epsey.

It was a Sunday in March 1776, too early in the year for demanding field-work but another opportunity for Ethan to perform some of his never-ending chores. This morning he was splitting shingles, surrounded by round sections of a large red oak tree, each carefully sawn two and a half feet long. The grain was almost perfectly straight, and it was a pleasure to divide each section down the middle with a blow of his ax and then, if needed, his chisels. He would then separate the two halves, then the quarters, and continue until each bolt of wood was about two inches thick. He removed the relatively soft heartwood in what had been the center of the tree and then, with his froe, he divided the bolts until he had a surprisingly large pile of shingles, about six inches wide and none more than a half inch thick. There was a rhythm to his work, which included placing the shingles into neat piles until he was ready to install them as the roof of a new cattle shed. With his strength and skill, this kind of work took little more effort than breathing, and he had plenty of time for his mind to wander from one subject to another.

Now, though, he was deeply troubled, feeling somehow that his entire way of life might be changed. He and Epsey had spent several hours during the previous afternoon and night reading a pamphlet called "Common Sense" that Aaron Hart had brought to their cabin. He said that the treatise had been distributed widely throughout the colonies and had created a furor. Militants had been delighted, monarchists were filled with condemnation, and most other citizens had been amazed at the inflammatory language used. Aaron added that almost every household in Charles Town and Savannah had purchased a copy.

Ethan realized that no longer could there be a moderating distinction between unrestrained condemnation of Parliament and statements of continuing loyalty to the crown. King George III was attacked personally in the pamphlet as "the Royal Brute," monarchy was denounced as an unreasonable form of government, and there was an open call for complete freedom from British rule. These words were a shock, almost a sacrilege, to many people in the colonies who were loyal British subjects, and this included Epsey and Ethan. He had an uneasy memory of the hours he had spent in his brother's shop in Hillsborough, when similar rhetoric was used to condemn the government and policies of Governor Tryon, and he could not erase the image of Henry's lifeless body swinging at the end of the executioner's rope.

Aaron had hurried on to visit other families, but his final comment was that never again could the Continental Congress send a conciliatory message to London, pledging to remain loyal to the king. He added that within a few months every colonist would be faced with a clear-cut decision. Ethan recalled Epsey's comment afterward, with which he agreed: "We'll just have to stay here and mind our own business."

Most people in Georgia would have agreed with the Pratts. Except in Savannah and a few settlements along the coast, the movement toward possible independence had little effect on families in the colony, which had been settled less than forty-five years and still had strong family ties with the mother country. The earlier settlers had always been loyal British subjects, and they cherished their ownership of the land granted by the British government. The young colony had received more financial assistance than any other, and most Georgians had not been dissatisfied with the honest and beneficent administration of Governor James Wright. The Stamp Act, Townshend Act, and Intolerable Act had little effect on them, and most were put off by the relatively violent and sometimes brutal activities of the Sons of Liberty. Although few citizens were deeply religious themselves, they were often in contact with the Anglicans, Salzburgers, Quakers, and other Christian groups, who were outspoken in their loyalty to England or their condemnation of any acts of violence.

Settlers on the frontier feared that rogue Indians would attack their relatively isolated farms, and a major factor in determining loyalty was what force could best guarantee safety from the marauders. There was increasing justification for this concern as the war gained momentum in the north. Actions of the more militant separatists increased animosity between the natives and some of the ne'er-do-wells who resented not having more land of their own and were determined to do everything possible to drive the Indians ever farther westward. They considered any abuse of the Indians to be justified, and retaliation by the natives was easily blamed on the cowardice of the Redcoats or as having been deliberately instigated by Indian Superintendent John Stuart.

CHAPTER 26

Georgians Expel the British Governor

MARCH 1776

Colonel Lachlan McIntosh had followed closely the progress of the Continental army under George Washington, but was frustrated by its limited role of merely protecting the rights of the northern colonists as part of the British Empire. He was delighted when, in February 1776, Washington put Major General Charles Lee in command of the Southern Military Department, covering Virginia, the Carolinas, and Georgia. He had met him briefly in Savannah and knew that Lee had spent several years as a plantation owner in Florida and realized the importance of protecting the colonies from a British northward thrust. Lachlan hoped that some regular Continental troops might be coming to Georgia, and that a successful strike against St. Augustine might now be possible. Thoroughly familiar with the coastal area and having been involved since boyhood in conflicts with Spanish troops operating out of Florida, Lachlan knew how difficult such a military operation would be. Only the deployment of a large contingent from the Continental army could make the attack successful, and special influence by Lee would be necessary to induce General Washington to spare an adequate number of troops from his own beleaguered force in the north. An official military operation against Florida would encourage the Council of Safety to give McIntosh the support he was still lacking in his new position as commander of its militia.

The provincial government in Savannah had cast its lot completely with the revolutionary cause by naming Lyman Hall, Button Gwinnett, and George Walton as delegates to the Continental Congress. Both collectively and individually, these men were outspoken advocates of independence and they were given a free hand to vote accordingly. Their simple instructions were to protect the interests of their remote and beleaguered colony.

The most intriguing news in Savannah was that Gwinnett had expressed his strong preference to stay in Georgia and made it clear to everyone that he was distressed and infuriated to have Lachlan McIntosh as the state's military commander, which had been his own ambition. He finally agreed to go to Philadelphia in May only with the understanding that he would be deputy to the president of the Council of Safety and therefore second in command of the colony's government. He was determined to reverse the appointment of McIntosh, and he believed that this high political position would open opportunities to reach his goal of taking over command of Georgia's troops. Lachlan McIntosh was well aware of Gwinnett's comments and was somewhat amused by them. He was completely confident that his lifelong commitment to military service ensured his position, but within a few days of his appointment he was faced with a more immediate challenge: a military engagement with British forces.

Emboldened by its new authority, the Council of Safety ordered a total embargo on trade that would benefit British forces in the north. The British fleet, however, was still dominant and exerted unrestricted influence over all the waterways. After being denied rice in Charles Town, the British dispatched four warships and a transport to Savannah, with a detachment of the king's troops. The small fleet anchored below the city, and an emissary was sent to make a purchase. The Council of Safety directed that sixteen rice barges be moved farther up the river and that Governor Wright and his council be detained to prevent their aiding the British forces. Colonel McIntosh ordered a young major, Joseph Habersham, to take the governor, and the twenty-four-year-old youth entered the mansion alone, recited his orders from the Council of Safety, and Wright acquiesced without a struggle to being placed under house arrest.

Early in March 1776, when the Georgians refused to sell rice to the British, the men-of-war began to move up the river to take the grain by force. The Council of Safety announced that it would burn the rice barges and even the warehouses along the shore "rather than suffer the British to possess them." South Carolinians applauded this heroism and sent a small detachment of militia to help defend Savannah. For Georgians, this would be the first armed conflict of the Revolutionary War. Spasmodic gunfire was exchanged during the next few days as the warships proceeded upriver toward Savannah with fitful winds, and the council finally ordered as much grain as possible to be offloaded and the remainder to be destroyed. Lieutenant James Jackson set afire two small Tory-owned vessels, loaded with rice and deerskins, and let them drift down to the barges. Two of them burned, but the British were able to seize ten others, holding 1,600 barrels of rice. One of the warships ran aground near Hutchinson's Island while the others anchored just opposite the town.

Colonel McIntosh and 250 men threw up breastworks and mounted three four-pounders to bear on the vessels, and his riflemen drove British troops from the upper deck of the grounded vessel. Some Georgians were captured when they went aboard one of the rice barges to attack Redcoats, and several men on both sides were killed during these exchanges. The British naval commander, Captain Barclay, invited three Georgia deputies to meet under a truce flag to negotiate a solution to the impasse, and had them detained and held as hostages.

When the British refused to release the three men, the Georgians decided to arrest all the members of the royal council who were still in Savannah. There was a stalemate until three weeks later, at the end of March, when the British freed the Georgians and paid for the rice taken from the barges. The ships withdrew and Governor Wright and the council members were put on parole, based on their pledge that future transactions would be peaceful, that Savannah would not be damaged, and that they would not leave the city.

Thomas Brown considered it an appropriate time for a brief assessment:

Your Excellency:

I regret to inform you that, because of Insults, physical abuse, and actual threats on his Life by rebellious Whigs, Governor James Wright has departed from Savannah and embarked on the British frigate Scarborough. *The Traitors have gained control of the harbor and trade, the Courts, the Militia, and all other aspects of Governance. The so-called Council of Safety has announced an independent effort to deal with the Indians, in direct competition with Indian Superintendent John Stuart. As Your Excellency knows, this is a more blatant act of Rebellion than has been perpetrated in any other Colony, but I can assure you that it has been confined almost exclusively to the immediate Environs of Savannah. Loyalty to the Crown is firm in all other areas of the Colony. Our Rangers will continue to strengthen Loyalists in Georgia and to monitor developments closely.*

To conclude my previous report regarding Virginia, British officers reported that Lord Dunmore's black troops served Heroically, but their services were short-lived. They were heavily afflicted with Smallpox and Coastland fevers, and the Regiment dwindled during the early months of this year. Each of the former slaves who deserted or was discharged from the Ethiopian Regiment was encouraged to return to his former Master, which, tragically (?), may have spread their infections within the colony. I have been informed that Lord Dunmore plans to leave his Base on Gwynn's island in the near Future and sail with some of his survivors to Saint Augustine. My suggestion is that, if this occurs, the ship be Quarantined, supplied with food and water, and sent on to some Island in the West Indies.

You may be interested in knowing that this same Disease played a major role in General Howe's wise decision to abandon the port of Boston. The Pox had swept through the city, and the General ordered all his troops inoculated and permitted diseased Citizens to depart. It seems that soldiers from Europe suffered little, but many British troops who had lived in the Colony were lost. There has been no explanation for this Distinction. It is believed that with most of his troops now in Halifax, an Attack on the much more valuable New York may be a prospect.

Respectfully submitted by
the Governor's agent

Georgians were proud of their newly claimed freedoms and not prepared
to accept any further dominance from London. The state congress sent additional instructions to their delegates in Philadelphia that the colonies
should be treated on a continental basis and not as individual provinces,
and declared that all government actions would be in the name of the people of Georgia and not of the king. Colonel McIntosh was praised for his
forthright stand against the British ships and was further honored when he
was directed by General Washington to report to General Lee in Charles
Town on the status of military forces in the region.

The colonel took John Houstoun with him, a friend who had been a
delegate to the Second Continental Congress in July 1775 and was known
to both Washington and Lee. Riding side by side up the coastal trail, they
discussed the impending meeting. In order to supplement his own knowledge, Lachlan asked, "John, what do you know about the general?"

Houstoun replied, "Lee is the most interesting leader in the Continental
army. He's an Englishman, and no relation to the Lees of Virginia. As a
young British officer, he was captured in the French and Indian War, and
while being held as a prisoner near the Canadian border he fell in love with
a Seneca princess and married her. Later, he was wounded at Fort Ticonderoga and returned to London as a hero. His reward was a large plantation in Florida and he moved there a few years ago. He began to condemn
actions of the British Parliament and wrote some pamphlets strongly supporting the American side, so when he resigned from the British army last
year and bought land in Virginia, the Continental Congress commissioned
him as a major general, second in command only to Washington. He
knows the British, the culture of the Indians, and he knows how to fight."

Houstoun paused and then asked, "What do you intend to tell him
about Georgia?"

Lachlan said, "Here are my notes for the report."

He handed John a sheet of parchment on which he had written a very
discouraging assessment:

> *Ga. is just a narrow settled strip about 40 miles wide just west of the
> Savannah River and 100 miles along the seacoast. 8 rivers separate about
> the same no. of islands; there are not more than 3000 Ga. men able to bear
> arms (most still loyal to the crown), and the Creeks alone have more warriors
> than this, not counting at least an equal number of Choctaws and Cherokees.*

The Indians are inclined to support the British, who now have 580 regulars at Saint Augustine and an unchallenged fleet making constant raids on our shores. 15,000 sometimes restless slaves along the coast produce 35,000 tierces [barrels] of valuable rice. There is plenty of food in Georgia, but never enough ammunition.

After discussing this information, they decided that Lee already knew a lot about Georgia, at least from a Florida perspective, and that their verbal presentation could be relatively brief.

The general greeted the two Georgians somewhat stiffly and asked them immediately to give a report on the military situation in the colony. Lachlan gave a summary while referring to his notes and then added, "General Lee, I have little good to tell you. Despite my best efforts, I am not having any success in recruiting men to defend the colony. I wanted at least a thousand, but so far only two hundred and thirty-six have signed up, and most of them will agree to serve only six months."

Lee seemed surprised. "Why can't you get more?"

"In the first place, very few of the good men are willing to leave their farms and jobs, and they fear Indian attacks if they are not protecting their own homes. Also, as you know, there is still a great deal of Tory sentiment, and a feeling among many Whigs that a few political leaders have taken all the top positions in government and are helping their friends in business and other ways. Another serious problem is that the Continental Congress doesn't seem to look on Georgia as very important. Let me give you an example: the recruitment bounty in South Carolina is twenty-five pounds, but I've been given only six pounds, which is not enough to pay for uniforms and food. There are just twenty-seven officers in service, and more than half of them have to work continuously to recruit reluctant citizens. Despite our best efforts, I figure we have about one hundred troops that are reasonably able to fight. This does not include some armed militia along the frontier west of Augusta, whose main goal is to fight the Indians and who have never shown any willingness to accept outside direction."

Lee asked, "Is this the report you wish me to give General Washington?"

"No, sir; there is more. I figure that we have three or four main points to make, and you are familiar with them. The first is that Georgia is the largest colony and has plentiful supplies of rice, cattle, and horses, which are already badly needed by the Continental troops and may be even more valuable if farming is interrupted in the north and additional men leave their homesteads to take up arms. As you know from living in Florida, many of these supplies are along the coast, vulnerable to being taken by British forces from the sea, as they've done recently with some of our rice in Savannah. Except for the sloop *Liberty,* which is now in Charles Town, there is not an American ship of any kind to protect what we have."

Lee seemed somewhat impatient and did not respond.

McIntosh continued, "The next point concerns the strong British forces in Florida, and especially in St. Augustine. So far they have been relatively dormant except for raids to secure supplies, and these seem to be increasing lately. We have information that the British are discussing a joint attack by Indians and regular forces, perhaps supported by liberated slaves, first against Savannah and then the Carolinas. Our main protection now comes from the relatively impassable territory of swamps and rivers between Savannah and British territory, with which you are familiar. We need some fortifications at key points, which we could establish at very modest cost.

"As you may know, this is an area within which I have spent my life. The Creeks are prevalent in this area, and it would be dangerous if the British ever recruit them, as they would be strong and active allies. We need trade goods to keep them at least neutral."

General Lee looked at both men, thought awhile, and then said, "Colonel McIntosh, I know of your father's military service since the colony was first founded, and of your own heroism in battle. Also, it has been brought to my attention that you were one of the foremost leaders in St. Andrews Parish in promoting support for the colonies' rights in the face of Parliament's oppression. In fact, I quoted you in some of the treatises I published. Your report is sobering, but your requests seem reasonable. I just have one question to ask. What can be done to improve the spirit of your fellow citizens?"

Lachlan was pleased by the general's comments and decided it was time to make his main request.

"General, almost all of our concerns could be addressed by a preemptive strike against the British forces in east Florida. This would help establish some fortifications to protect our coast, let us prove the seriousness of Georgia's commitment to the Continental Congress, demonstrate to the Creeks the advantage of supporting us or staying neutral, and give our patriotic citizens some motivation to volunteer for military service. We would need your full support, with both leadership and troops, and I believe this would be a good investment of your time and effort."

General Charles Lee felt responsible for reassuring Georgians that Continental leaders recognized their importance. He could also see the necessity of preventing any moves by the British farther northward from St. Augustine, perhaps even into the Carolinas and Virginia. After some further discussion, it was agreed that the general would marshal a force of at least 450 men and come to Savannah to join McIntosh and other Georgians in planning an excursion against the British in Florida. They set a goal of launching this effort within three months.

At that time, none of the three men had heard of Thomas Brown or the Florida Rangers, but a few days after they began issuing orders, Brown was thoroughly familiar with their plans. After sharing his intelligence with Governor Tonyn and Colonel Prevost, he immediately assumed as his own responsibility the marshaling of Creek Indian attacks on a few settlements, which greatly reduced the recruitment of frontiersmen into the Georgia militia. As usual, he was able to furnish a complete report of these preparations to his superiors and to prepare his own forces for a confrontation. One of his agents in Savannah obtained a copy of a message from Lee to his superiors, which proved to be quite amusing to Governor Tonyn and the military commanders:

> *The people here are if possible more harum skarum than their sister colony of South Carolina. They will propose anything, and after they have propos'd it, discover that they are incapable of performing the least. They have propos'd securing their frontiers by constant patrols of horse rangers, when the scheme is approv'd of they scratch their heads for some days, and at length inform you that there is a small difficulty in the way; that of the impossibility to procure a single horse. Their next project is to keep their inland navigation clear of tenders by a numerous fleet of Guarda Costa arm'd boats, when this is agreed to, they recollect that they have not a single boat. Upon the whole I shou'd not be surpris'd if they were to propose mounting a body of Mermaids on Alligators . . .*

Still somewhat skeptical, General Lee came to Savannah in August and, despite the terribly hot and humid weather, began preparations for an invasion of Florida, designed to break up the settlements between the St. Johns and St. Marys rivers, to punish the Florida Rangers and stop their raids into south Georgia, and then to take St. Augustine. But after only a few days in the town he confirmed the colony's vulnerability and expressed deep concern about bitter divisions among the leaders. Lee even recommended abandoning all land south of the Altamaha River and expending all their effort in defending the rest of the state, but Georgia leaders unanimously rejected his proposal and he finally agreed to join in an attack on east Florida. As the general commented, "This is the only issue on which the leaders in Savannah can agree."

In September, before a common force could be marshaled in Savannah, the British attacked New York and Lee was ordered back north with all his troops, leaving the colony defenseless except for the Georgia troops and a few from Carolina. Acting independently, McIntosh took his small force southward in September and was able to penetrate as far as the St. Marys River, but all he could do was lay waste to some of the Tories' crops and then withdraw with a number of casualties, mostly inflicted on the close-ordered troops by stealthy flank attacks from the Florida Rangers.

Thomas Brown was amused by this failure, which created no problems for his operations in the territory south and west of the Altamaha River. He directed his Rangers to incur as much support as possible from the natives, to retain the loyalty of Tory families, and to make it difficult for McIntosh and militia groups to recruit volunteers. It was gratifying to him to learn that the Whig and Continental leaders were well aware of the Florida Rangers and that McIntosh had issued a command that all Whigs, both military and civilian, should obtain as much information as possible about them and, especially, their commander.

CHAPTER 27

The Struggle for Indian Allegiance

With only a few mounted units, McIntosh was limited to isolated patrols along the border areas where most of the loyal Whig families lived. Brown had no desire to confront these troops but was able to monitor their movements, either through intimidated or loyal settlers or with his Indian allies. Each time the Georgia troops completed their patrol and withdrew, the

Florida Rangers immediately moved into the abandoned area, and finally established control over south and west Georgia. Brown worked like a man possessed, organizing sporadic raids near Savannah just to harass the Whigs, and having some of his men make forays into north Georgia, even above Augusta and across the river into South Carolina. The Chattahoochee and its tributaries became one of his favorite water routes, providing easy access to every important Indian settlement in the western part of the colony. He also extended his scouting activities into Pensacola and westward along the Mississippi River. His protector and confidant was Governor Tonyn, who shared selected intelligence information with Colonel Prevost. It was well known in Florida that the two leaders were highly competitive, struggling for authority at home and for favor in London. Brown was adroit in capitalizing on this disharmony by giving every credit for the Rangers' exploits to the governor.

Although Indian Superintendent John Stuart pledged repeatedly to restrain any warlike activities by the Indians against white settlers, it became increasingly obvious to both Tories and Whigs that the natives were alienated from the Americans and supportive of the British cause. Stuart was spending most of his time in Florida, either in St. Augustine or Pensacola, but his deputy, Alexander Cameron, lived in a mansion in western South Carolina, not far from the Savannah River, and in Stuart's absence was inclined to act more boldly and independently than was warranted. His other base of operations was west of the Chattahoochee in Tallassee, on the major Indian trading route from Mobile to Augusta. Perhaps more than any other British official, he had an intimate personal relationship with the Cherokees in the southeast.

Cameron had taken an Indian chief's daughter as a mistress, and they lived as man and wife. Instead of being at all ashamed of his native spouse, he delighted in having his "Indian princess" preside over elaborate parties, dressed in the finest and most stylish attire that could be bought in Charles Town. During their years together, she bore him three children, two of them boys. Over time she cast aside her earlier subservience in the presence of her husband. She was a beautiful and strong-willed woman called Blue Star, and much of Cameron's effectiveness in carrying out his duties was dependent on her relationship with the native leaders. To enhance her influence, she was permitted to travel to the key villages, with an appropriate entourage, to distribute presents—ostensibly from her and Cameron but made available by the British government (often without its knowledge or approval)—to keep the Cherokees friendly and loyal.

One August morning in 1776, Blue Star walked into their mansion's library and told her husband, "There is a scout from the Florida Rangers here to see you."

When a Creek warrior was ushered into the house, he had a brief message for Cameron: "Commander Thomas Brown plans to visit you tomorrow, at midmorning." Cameron was intrigued with the news, because he had known of Brown as a relatively timid and inept agent of the governor of South Carolina, later the disgraced "Burnfoot" Brown, and, during recent months, the bold and remarkably successful leader of the Florida Rangers. He couldn't imagine the purpose of Brown's visit.

The next morning, Brown arrived at Cameron's home as scheduled, accompanied by almost a dozen men, three of them Indians. When Cameron invited the group onto the porch, Brown responded that he wished to speak privately to their host. As the other men tied their horses and were ushered into the kitchen area for some coffee and sweet cakes, Brown and Cameron entered the library, and Cameron closed the door. He noticed that his guest walked with a slight limp but exuded the aura of a natural leader, sure of himself and obviously speaking with authority.

After a brief exchange of greetings, Brown said, "I come to you from St. Augustine with full approval of Governor Tonyn. All of us realize that John Stuart retains the title of Indian superintendent, but he is confining his personal movements to Florida, seems to be in ill health, and is no longer as vigorous in the pursuit of his duties as has been his custom."

Cameron, who had long chafed under the distant command of his superior, found these first words encouraging but was careful not to express his own opinion except to nod as a signal that he understood what had been said.

Brown continued, "As you know, the rebellious Whigs seem to have made progress in both Savannah and Charles Town in taking almost all power from the officers of the king, and they are now trying to induce the backwoods families to follow their lead in this treasonous activity. But the fact is that British troops dominate Florida in its entirety, and my men and I control almost all of Georgia south and west of Savannah. However, the settlers around Augusta seem to be moving toward support of the Whigs, and some of their militia leaders have even been joining in the fruitless forays toward Florida. We need to move against them."

Naturally cautious, Cameron asked, "How can this best be done?"

"Of the two hundred Indians who serve under my command, a number are Creek and Cherokee from this area. They tell me of the constant encroachment of these same settlers into their native lands, and seem certain that many warriors would like to protect their families."

"After the terrible Cherokee war, what can they do?"

Despite his normal impatience, Brown decided to share some information that he had accumulated about the status of the native people. He wanted to demonstrate to Cameron his interest and involvement with the Indians, and also make a strong concluding argument.

"It is very interesting how many Indians there are in the region of the southern colonies—a total of about forty thousand. My best estimate is twelve thousand Cherokees, two thousand Chickasaw, twelve thousand five hundred Choctaw, and fourteen thousand Creeks, with a few other scattered tribes. As you know, the greedy leaders of the Cherokee, Chickasaw, and other natives have swapped most of western Virginia and the Carolinas for a few wagonloads of trade goods. It is obvious to the Indians that the British have attempted to protect Indian lands, and that greedy settlers are always pressing westward, convinced that they are superior to the natives both in law and in the eyes of God. With so few white men prepared to fight, the natives hold in their hands the balance of power. With proper encouragement and leadership, they are too powerful a force to remain dormant."

Cameron asked another question: "What can I do?"

"We all see you now as the real leader of the Indian tribes, representing the interests of His Majesty's government. It is time for the natives to protect their property and to keep the Georgia and Carolina militiamen nearer their own homes so they can't join the rebel forces. A show of strength by the natives would be very helpful. My hope is that service with the Rangers can provide them a way to fight the despised settlers without drawing a destructive reprisal against their people."

Cameron was shrewd enough to detect the subtle promise of increased personal authority if he accepted the basic premise of Brown's words, but he also recognized his own vulnerability in the upper Savannah River area from Elijah Clarke and an aroused militia if the frontier families learned that he was involved in fomenting what might be called another Indian war. He also knew that ultimate legal responsibility for dealing with Indian tribes still rested with Superintendent John Stuart, and that a decision to change this fact could be made only in London, and certainly not by Governor Tonyn or Thomas Brown. He wanted time to consult with his wife, both on whether to act and how to keep any positive response from being subsequently revealed. It was Blue Star who could provide the best answers to these questions.

"Commander Brown, I understand your message and agree with its import. It seems to me that this could not be done successfully without extending the operation along a broad frontier, and surprise would be crucial. I would request a few days to explore the attitude of the Creek and perhaps Cherokee leaders toward the possibility of their taking up arms."

Brown agreed to this proposal and promised to send a scout to receive Cameron's reply a fortnight from that day. Without remaining even for an offered meal, the Florida Rangers departed. Since Chief Sunoma had already discussed the matter with Blue Star several days before this visit, Brown had every confidence that the response would be positive.

Within an hour, Cameron and his wife had explored all the potential challenges and consequences of inciting the Indians, and had decided that the effort should be mounted.

Despite the severe punishment of the Cherokees farther north, Cameron and Blue Star expected to find a more willing response among the Creeks. Any punishment from the white community would be limited to raiding parties of militia groups, whose numbers, weaponry, and time of service would all be limited. As a personal precaution, however, they decided to move their family, slaves, and a small herd of livestock about sixty miles to the west, into the heart of the Creek nation and among Blue Star's relatives. Next, they sought a meeting with Chief Emistisiguo, and within a few days they were ushered into his camp. They were surprised to find him alone, except for a young man who was identified as Newota.

Cameron and Blue Star had decided in advance that he would be the only one to speak, and that his presentation would be cautious and designed to solicit the opinions of the great chief. After exchanging the proper courtesies, Cameron said, "As you know better than I, our brother Cherokees to the north have suffered greatly after they rose up against the settlers, and the king who has honored you as a great medal chief is determined that a similar situation does not occur in Georgia."

Emistisiguo did not respond, but merely nodded, almost as though he were preparing for sleep.

Then, somewhat hesitantly, Cameron continued, "The Cherokees in

Carolina acted alone, and without any involvement with their British friends."

The chief smiled wryly and responded, "It may be more accurate to say that they were abandoned by your people, and left to be massacred."

Cameron decided to get directly to the point. "There are now opportunities for some warriors to give support to our common effort and to be associated directly with the British."

"How is this to be done?"

"With the king's Rangers."

The chief glanced at Newota, who exchanged a slight smile with Blue Star. She realized that Cameron was now the only one there who did not know that this proposal was one long discussed much more directly between Thomas Brown and Emistisiguo.

The chief said solemnly, "It seems to me that this possibility may be promising at this time. I will have Newota pursue it further."

After his visitors had departed, Emistisiguo said, "This is the commander's way of letting me know that he has received permission to expand the role of the Rangers with the participation of more of our young men. You may discuss the terms of their service with Sunoma and ascertain how many are needed, what their compensation might be, and the rules under which they will operate. I would like to give final approval to the proposal before it is initiated."

Newota felt bold enough to ask, "Why has Commander Brown proceeded this way?"

"Because he desires to have a British government official involved and knows that John Stuart opposes everything he is doing. To recruit the deputy to his side is a second but beneficial choice. Furthermore, he realizes that there are many young Creeks who would not be free to participate without my tacit approval. Now there may be an effective but fragile coalition that extends from London through the governor of Florida, and from Brown to Sunoma and our warriors, without bypassing me."

"What about Cameron?"

"Henceforth, he can be bypassed."

CHAPTER 28

Florida Rangers Versus Georgia Militia

A week later, Newota was standing before Emistisiguo, who was seated on a folded blanket in his dwelling. They were alone, and the young Indian had just returned from a visit with Chief Sunoma, designed to build upon the initiative from the Ranger commander through Cameron and Blue Star.

"I seemed to be expected and was well received. Chief Sunoma was informed about the issues and prepared to respond satisfactorily—"

The chief interrupted him with a slightly uplifted hand. "It will be helpful for me to know in more detail what was said. There is nothing else that awaits my attention."

Newota thought for just a few moments and spoke again: "Chief Sunoma first wanted to give me his analysis of the current situation. He pointed out that the British and even most of the rebels want peace and trade, but some frontiersmen want no trade and welcome armed conflict with all our tribes. After a few encounters of the Rangers with white settlers, some angry Georgians and Carolinians have urged their political leaders to declare an all-out punitive war against us, as was done against our Cherokee brothers in Virginia and the Carolinas. They claim that any Creeks who give comfort to the British are to be treated as defeated enemies and have forfeited possession of our land.

"He emphasized how different Georgia is from the other colonies, where our people have been forced far westward by military pressure and insignificant rewards for more than a century. In this colony, because of the benevolence of the king, we still inhabit all the land except for a small strip along the coast and just west of the Savannah River. He realizes that this policy in Georgia has formed a natural sense of trust and cooperation between the British and our tribes. Creek and Cherokee leaders have been wise in granting allegiance where the natural advantages exist. He acknowledged that both American and British forces are now seeking the support of the Middle and Lower Creeks since effective control of Savannah and Charles Town has given the rebels a temporary advantage in trade opportunities. Chief Sunoma was careful not to criticize Superintendent

John Stuart, who is attempting to overcome this handicap by using overland routes from north Florida and the Flint and Chattahoochee rivers to move goods into the interior of the colony."

Newota paused for a moment, but he continued when Emistisiguo did not choose to respond. "It was about this time in our meeting that Thomas Brown joined us, and he was the one who now spoke. He said he realized that native leaders must strive to do what is best for their own people, always considering current circumstances and not looking back on past obligations or agreements. He said that the British offer our people reliable trade, no encroachment on our land, maximum enforcement of previous treaty terms, and a cooperative relationship, with mutual respect. The commander made it clear that there are many young men willing to join in Ranger operations, but it is important to him and them that the great chief not disapprove.

"When I questioned him, he responded that John Stuart is not involved in his proposal and may even disapprove if questioned directly, but has been aware for many months of the Creeks who have cooperated with the Rangers. Increasingly, Governor Tonyn is making overall decisions, as Stuart has become relatively inactive and somewhat isolated in Pensacola from the contested frontier areas. Since the departure of Governor James Wright, the colony of Georgia is in the hands of the revolutionaries, and he used Elijah Clarke as an example of their attempt to frighten and control the Creeks by the threat of terrible destruction of our villages and people. The commander considers any peace or trade proposal by the rebels to be by 'rum and false words.' He summarized by saying that he desires to expand the participation of natives in a much wider geographical area, can guarantee adequate compensation, and will be glad to meet with you personally or to communicate through Chief Sunoma and me."

Emistisiguo nodded and then said, "The commander's talk is good, for what he and the governor want, and much of it is true. John Stuart is also eager for our help, but he and the British military leaders oppose our working with the Rangers. None of them can be trusted to fulfill promises made to us. I will continue to communicate with Stuart, who also speaks for Prevost. Regardless of what I say, Brown will continue to expand the Rangers, dealing directly with local tribes over which I have little control. You may tell Sunoma that I want local villages rewarded for their help and protected from retaliation. As Brown knows, this is the only response I can give."

As he departed with his predictable message, Newota knew that

Brown's influence among young Creeks was now greater than that of the great chief. In the tribes' relationship with white people, they had found that only among the Rangers were they always treated with respect and as equals. There was firm discipline, but adequate praise and loot, which the participating braves shared generously with their home villages. His thoughts turned to the conclusion of his mission, and a return to his home village, and Kindred.

As Brown fully realized, the level of combat would soon increase. Within a few weeks there was an adequate reserve of young Indians, almost all Creeks, who were available to perform assignments as prescribed by the Ranger commander. He gave the new recruits as much freedom as possible regarding their activities, but insisted that their attacks be strictly limited to those geographical regions and families approved by him in advance. Although some fragmentary information about their increased activities reached the frontier, most families assumed that these were just more of the constant rumors of impending Indian attacks that were a natural part of their lives.

Clarke and his militiamen realized that the reports were true and that they were likely to be targeted. Since their homes were concentrated in a relatively small area, they were able to herd the most exposed families into small forts, where they could best defend themselves. As soon as possible, Clarke marshaled a group of Georgia and South Carolina militiamen, and they methodically attacked Indian villages and crops in a wide swath east of the Appalachian Mountains. The Indians were also prepared, and they and the entire Ranger organization did their best to monitor the militia movements. Most Indians were able to vacate their homes before the militiamen arrived. Clarke's policy was to burn all dwellings and to execute five men in each Indian settlement if they could be captured, as a warning against further predations against Georgia settlers. Long before Clarke reached Blue Star's home, Cameron and his family had moved once again, to join Stuart in Pensacola.

These military skirmishes, over several months, were damaging both to white settlers and Indian tribes, but they accomplished Brown's purposes of keeping the militia occupied, discouraging settlers from leaving their homes to join the revolutionaries, and driving the Creeks and Cherokees increasingly toward alignment with the British troops. The effectiveness of the Florida Rangers created consternation not only in south Georgia, but throughout the southern colonies.

Brown knew how favorably Governor Tonyn now looked upon his performance. Aware of the well-known competition between Tonyn and Prevost, he was emboldened to express a higher ambition to the governor. Brown let it be known that there were several majors serving under the general and in South Carolina, and he did not want to be officially subservient to them. Tonyn responded by using his authority to give Brown a provisional commission as lieutenant colonel, which was readily accepted since he now saw the advantages of military rank. Prevost was furious when he learned of this decision, but his command was restricted, by regulation and his own choice, to regular British forces, and Brown now had the authority and rank that he desired as commander of the Rangers. He began to expand his activities far beyond the original purposes of his irregular forces, with his ultimate, personal ambition still focused on Augusta.

Brown knew almost immediately when the Americans moved into an area to recruit white families that had ties to the Tories. He made it clear to those who were inclined to be neutral and mind their own affairs that the Rangers would continue to be dominant and would penalize or reward them according to their political inclination. To increase the value of intimidation, he ordered the Rangers, including Creek warriors, to commit well-publicized acts of robbery and arson against certain settlers who were known to support the rebel cause.

In January 1777, Thomas Brown submitted this assessment to his superiors:

Your Excellency:

I realize that, with favorable winds and available Couriers directly to Florida, your information from the north will be much superior to my own. But since my Rangers have several sources of intelligence from land, along the Coast, and down the Mississippi River, I will, on occasion, give you a brief Summary of what we have learned, even though I fear that you will find it to be old news.

Although Washington assembled a Force of 30,000, equal in number to that of the British, General Sir William Howe has Prevailed with superior strategy and force of arms in taking New York. My information is that the high Commanders of the rebels had strong disagreements, with Charles Lee advocating a Withdrawal to save their forces and Washington insisting on a defense of the almost surrounded City. Washington prevailed, and the rebels lost 4,000

of their men before Retreating into New Jersey. In effect, the Confrontation
was between Generals Howe, Clinton, and Cornwallis and the rebel com-
manders Washington, Charles Lee, and Nathanael Greene. General Clinton
had little Trouble in taking the other important Northern port of Newport.

One of the most amusing Developments was the capture of General
Charles Lee, who was caught last month Sleeping in a New Jersey tavern
and captured by four of our officers and less than two dozen men. He was sec-
ond in command of all rebel Forces, but by far the more Capable. It is safe to
say that their troops are both Dispirited and in Disarray, and Plagued with
widespread desertions.

Respectfully submitted by
the Governor's agent

By this time, several hundred Georgia men had volunteered for training as
militiamen, mostly under the general supervision of Elijah Clarke but always
directly commanded by leaders of their own choice. They knew one another
intimately and were able to magnify their strengths and compensate for individual weaknesses. Most of these men were farmers, whose primary goal
was to protect their families. They served as guerrilla fighters only episodi-
cally, while attempting to keep their land producing. Within their own local
regions, they devised an intricate system of intelligence to monitor the movement of British and Indian marauders. On rare occasions they were able to
capture much-needed supplies from the British. Although Continental army
leaders acknowledged their value and legitimacy, the militiamen were given
little support or assistance. They furnished their own weapons, dressed in
homespun clothes, and rarely expected any pay for their services. A few families from the northern part of Georgia had moved into peaceful areas in the
Watauga Valley region of western North Carolina, but those who remained
were highly motivated partisans, many of whose farms had been ravaged,
and whose families were often huddled in a few small stockades or secure
hiding places in their own woods and swamps.

Increasingly deprived of normal lives and facing constant threats, men
on both sides of the Savannah River found safety and purpose by joining the
militia units. They felt that the best way to defend themselves against Indian
marauders was to respond without mercy, destroying entire villages and
killing all the savages who were suspected of harboring the raiding parties.
The strongest among them were usually successful because of their own

prowess and their reputation as unrestrained retaliators. They themselves could strike with stealth and speed, and most of their women were trained in the use of weapons. Regular troops who joined the Continental army were mostly single men who enlisted for three years. The militia rarely signed up for more than three months, and they were apt to depart at any time regardless of enlistment agreements if they received a message from home calling for their return, even just before a major battle. They were not amenable to discipline, except from their own elected officers, and usually preferred to retain their own accurate rifles instead of shifting to the musket/bayonet weapon. Both they and their commanders were averse to rigid battle lines. Although the regular Continental troops were still given training to array themselves in line as did the British, they had learned from experience that it was better to yield the field of battle, preserve their strength, and then to fight again against a weakened or exposed enemy.

A small group of the militia in Georgia and South Carolina, whose farming interests had faded into relative insignificance or who had nothing of their own left to protect, were free to follow Elijah Clarke and others in maintaining a permanent core around which other, more transient volunteers could rally. The revolution in the southern states was initiated by wealthy and influential political leaders along the coast, but the responsibilities for combat were shifting to these backwoodsmen, some of whom would never yield even when their plight seemed hopeless.

CHAPTER 29

Georgia Remains Independent

1777

Sitting in the main room of Clarke's cabin, Elijah Clarke and Aaron Hart listened intently to their visitor from South Carolina. There was a small, rough wooden table between them, with a jug of corn whiskey and three tumblers on it. The man was William Henry Drayton, and they had been expecting his visit. With little regard for small talk, he presented his case without delay, deigning only to swallow half a tumbler of moonshine to cut the dust of his long ride that morning.

Drayton was well known in north Georgia as the radical South Carolinian who had debated with Thomas Brown and, in effect, come to control the state's Council of Safety. It had surprised no one when this firebrand, who despised Georgia's relative neutrality, initiated an effort in Charles Town to form a union of the two colonies. Since Elijah Clarke and other settlers who lived in north Georgia were closer to their South Carolina neighbors than to the merchants and political leaders in Savannah or Augusta, many of them supported this effort to "strengthen Georgia's backbone."

The visitor was speaking. "It's time to get off our arses and let everyone know that South Carolina and Georgia are working and fighting together on the side of freedom and independence. All the other colonies have already taken a stand. The problem is in Georgia, where a group of weak-kneed cowards act like they want an independent country but would really rather stay part of the British Empire. There is no way to change the situation as long as the damned Whigs in Savannah are divided and the rest of the state is afraid to take a stand."

Aaron saw that Elijah was nodding in agreement, and hastened to respond, "Mr. Drayton, there are a lot of Georgians, not only up here but also in Savannah and along the coast, who have made it plain that we support the Continental Congress."

"That's just the point I'm making. The people are for freedom, but there are too many rich merchants in Savannah still in bed with the king's men, and there ain't no way to change them. All they want is to protect their property, play with their little, selfish government, and let others fight the British. London has bribed this colony since it was set up over forty years ago with handouts and special privileges that the rest of us have never seen. The only way left is to bring the people of our two states together under one government. Then we can speak with a clear voice, defend ourselves better from savages, and form a fighting force that will run the British out of both east and west Florida."

Elijah was obviously excited when he said, "I feel like you do. There's no reason for the river to keep us apart no longer. The folks up here already feel a lot closer to Charles Town than we do to Savannah. All they do down there is talk and talk and then back away from whatever calls for guts."

Aaron had heard Drayton's proposition discussed in Savannah and many other places, both by Tories and Whigs, and knew that most Georgians, on both sides of the arguments with London, looked on any union with South Carolina as effective annexation of their colony. He decided to be cautious.

"There are a lot of good men in Georgia that are wanting to give full support to the Continental army, and they are gaining strength in Savannah. Even though Button Gwinnett and Lachlan McIntosh are at each other's throat, both of them have made it plain that they agree on what Georgia ought to do. But I don't believe they'd ever want to see Georgia become just a part of South Carolina."

"That's not the way it would be, man. The two states would go into an equal partnership, not with one over the other. We don't give a shit who's trying to dominate any state government right now. Once our people are united, we'll have things our way. Besides, McIntosh hasn't been able to recruit an army that could defend a chicken house, much less fight the British."

Elijah said, "Well, you can count on us militiamen in this part of Georgia."

Drayton responded, "Captain Clarke, I'm proud to hear you say that. We know lots of people in these parts look on you as their leader. I'm going from here down through Augusta and then to Savannah, where I intend to present an official petition from the South Carolina Assembly calling for a union of our two states. I feel pretty sure it will be well received."

Aaron didn't say anything more, knowing that Drayton was headed for a disappointment.

The preeminent leader of Georgia's opposition to "annexation" by South Carolina was Button Gwinnett. He had been born in Gloucester, England, accumulated a small fortune in Charles Town, and moved to Georgia in 1765. Familiar with sentiments in both states, he saw South Carolina's attempt to merge with Georgia as a threat to his dream of military leadership, and public confrontation as a way to increase his political influence. After failing as a merchant in Savannah, Gwinnett had planned his political career carefully. He bought St. Catherines Island off the coast of Georgia and was soon elected to the provincial commons. He represented St. Johns Parish, whose mainly Congregationalist citizens were, along with the Scots farther south along the coast, in the forefront of opposition to British policies. Gwinnett had little interest in legislative matters, but he cultivated friendships with every leader in Savannah whom he believed would ultimately choose the state's military commander. He failed as a planter and was plagued with an increasing load of debts, which he paid by selling off portions of his island.

He was vituperative in his criticisms of Lachlan McIntosh, from nearby Darien, whom he had always seen as his primary rival. The two men had become bitter personal enemies who operated in different arenas. Gwinnett concentrated his efforts on the political scene in Savannah while McIntosh, confident of his military credentials and his support from General Washington, had always confined his political interests to leading his fellow Scotsmen in St. Andrews Parish. Nowadays, he was fully occupied with raising as strong a colonial military force as possible, to be used mostly in skirmishes with the Florida Rangers, who continued their raids into Georgia.

Gwinnett was a powerful man of average height, with broad shoulders and a slight paunch. He always disdained a wig and combed his hair straight back so that it hung below his collar. He was a solemn person, and although his receding chin and slightly pouting mouth gave a first impression of weakness, his brilliant mind, intimate knowledge of the political currents in Savannah, and his accurate assessments of his peers made him a formidable politician. He never forgot a slight or a favor and was able to accumulate an intimate cadre of supporters who were almost fanatic in their loyalty to him. He was somewhat reclusive in his personal habits and withdrew to his isolated home on St. Catherines Island whenever there were no political decisions to be made in Savannah. Gwinnett was a superb marksman and recorded in a journal the long distances at which he killed deer. Only on rare occasions did he invite any guests to join him, such as when his faction was called to make political plans for the future. The intensity of his commitments was the basis of his political influence, which had been enough to make him a natural choice as a delegate to the Continental Congress.

With the return of the three delegates to Georgia following their signing of the Declaration of Independence, they had been treated as heroes and Gwinnett was elected to be one of the thirteen permanent members of the Council of Safety, second in authority only to Archibald Bulloch, who was given the title of president.

When Drayton arrived in Savannah, he made his presentation to a reasonably polite state congress and was then excluded from the proceedings while Gwinnett gave the response. He condemned the proposal as Georgia's absorption by South Carolina, questioned Drayton's motives, and made the conclusive point that any such union would be a violation of the Continental Articles of Confederation, which both states had recently accepted.

After hearing that his plan had been unanimously rejected, Drayton

continued the unification effort in some Georgia settlements by condemning the state's leaders, comparing them with the worst of the Stuart kings in
their despotic rule over an oppressed people. He accused the Georgians of
wanting to abandon their colonial government altogether and return to direct British rule. Several months later, after Georgia had adopted a new
constitution and elected John Adam Treutlen as the state's first governor,
Georgia officials finally issued a warrant for Drayton's arrest and put a
£100 bounty on his head. Protected by Elijah Clarke's militiamen and
South Carolina friends, Drayton was never caught, and he returned to
South Carolina as the primary leader in promoting the rebel cause.

Almost a year after the thirteen colonies had declared their independence,
Lieutenant Colonel Thomas Brown was lying in his hammock in a small
room, formerly one of the prison cells of Fort Matanzas, completed about
thirty-five years earlier on the banks of the Tolomato River to protect St.
Augustine from any possible sea attack. He should have been enjoying the
slight breeze from the Atlantic Ocean, but he was restless and ill-tempered.
Despite having been on horseback for almost twenty hours the preceding
day at the end of a 450-mile trip from Pensacola, he had slept little during
the night. His scouts had been waiting for him when he returned to St. Augustine to report that the American cavalry of General McIntosh were
again active south of the Altamaha. They were apparently planning another of the endless military excursions of Continentals into what Brown
considered to be Ranger territory. With almost six hundred British troops
now stationed in St. Augustine, any predictable foray into Florida could be
repulsed, but he was still rankled and embarrassed because combined Continental and militia forces had crossed the St. Johns River in September and
threatened British installations in the south. It was ironic that the successful
repulsion of the invaders had caused increased tension in St. Augustine between British troops and the Rangers, with Governor Tonyn congratulating Brown's forces and the general giving full credit to regular troops
serving under his brother, Major James Mark Prevost.

Sergeant Baker had twice warned Brown about the disturbing rivalry,
which resulted in almost nightly brawls in the local tavern and around
campfires. The rigid discipline imposed on the Redcoats was in sharp con-
trast to the relative flexibility in the Ranger organization, and exaggerated
reports of valuable loot secured on their forays aroused envy among the

regular troops. The Rangers' loud claims of military invincibility had been vividly disproved when McIntosh and his American forces had operated for several days with relative impunity in a region that the Rangers had claimed as British territory and under their complete protection. It was not possible for Brown to explain even to some of his own men that the woodland tactic of the Rangers was to fade away in the face of concentrated force in order to return and triumph later by stealth and surprise. Neither side was in the business of occupying territory in southwest Georgia.

Some of the Tory settlers who had come recently as refugees from north Georgia had brought distorted accounts of Brown's humiliation in Augusta and the truth about his lack of formal military training. He noticed an increasing inclination of regular British officers to shun him in any public encounter, and he concentrated ever more time and attention on his forays into Georgia and on maintaining close relationships with Sergeant Baker (who refused further promotion), Chief Sunoma, and a growing cadre of Indian and Tory militia whom they had recruited and trained.

One of Brown's key aides was Daniel McGirth, an American deserter who had been a loyal and effective scout and guide and extremely helpful to the Continental troops and Georgia militia in the coastal area near his home in Darien. His driving interest before the war had been the breeding and racing of fine horses, and he rode a superb iron-gray mare named Gray Goose. A wealthy young militia lieutenant named Clarke Christie, stationed at Fort McIntosh, was determined to acquire the horse, but McGirth would not sell her for any price. After he also refused to swap his mare for a commission as lieutenant, Christie began to abuse the scout, and one evening called him "a stupid son of a bitch." They exchanged blows, and McGirth prevailed in the brief fight, leaving Christie nursing a bloody nose. McGirth was amazed a few hours later to be arrested and courtmartialed for striking an officer. He was given ten lashes in front of the Darien courthouse and confined in the local jail. A sympathetic guard gave McGirth a broken trowel, and after loosening some window bars, he found Gray Goose and fled to St. Augustine. His intense hatred of the American rebels made him a natural recruit for the Florida Rangers, and he was soon one of Thomas Brown's most valuable men.

Brown now thought of McGirth, rolled out of the hammock, dressed quickly in his cool, spartan room, and within an hour was with Sergeant Baker, who was never surprised at these impromptu tactical planning sessions.

"I think it's time for a direct confrontation with the rebel military forces in Georgia."

The sergeant realized immediately that this proposal represented a radical departure from their previous policy, based on hit-and-run tactics when dealing with Continental or organized militia forces. Any direct confrontation had always been the role of British regulars, but Baker was not surprised by the proposal because he also felt the need for revenge and for the restoration of the reputation and morale of the Rangers. He was familiar with the constant concoction of plans in Savannah to launch another invasion of Florida, and the self-congratulations of the rebel leaders about the establishment of a remote outpost south of the Altamaha.

"Yes, sir, it may be advisable to show who controls south Georgia. Where do you think we might make a move?"

"This time it should be against a military installation and not just some settler outposts. We need for our men to gain this experience and at the same time demonstrate to Governor Tonyn that we are capable of more ambitious military operations. What do you know about Fort McIntosh?"

The sergeant smiled as he looked at some notes in a ledger. "I like the name as a target. General McIntosh is a favorite of Washington, and an attack here would wake up the Georgians. Also, I'm sure McGirth would welcome an opportunity to visit a certain lieutenant. Sunoma had three of his men in the fort last week, trading venison for some knives, which was all the Continentals had available. According to their report, there was a Captain Winn in command, and he has just a few troops under him, all infantry, including Lieutenant Christie and one other, and three sergeants. They seemed fairly well trained, but not very alert inside the little fort after they closed the entrance for the night. I've heard that Captain Winn is a nephew or cousin of Governor Bulloch."

"Send a couple of our good men back in there, preferably settlers who can pose as loyal Whigs. Let them take some of our best food supplies as though they were on the way to Savannah and need to stay overnight for safety. They're willing to sell to the fort to save the long trip. Let them know what information we need, but don't share our plans with them."

"When do you think we should make our move?"

"Well, I don't want to fail. We'll have to train our men on how to take a fortified military post. Do you think we can gather information and train a hundred men within a month, say by the middle of February?"

"Yes, sir."

It was decided, and Brown was soon thoroughly familiar with the fort, which was about one hundred feet square and located on a small hill near the northeast bank of the St. Illa River, which he learned was defended by seventy men, mostly Georgia recruits but including more than a dozen Continental regulars who were thought to be well trained and competent. Captain Winn was young, but obviously eager to make a name for himself. His instructions were to limit forays outside the fort and to concentrate on self-defense. Maintaining a permanent military presence so far south in Georgia was, in itself, an important symbolic victory.

Brown imposed a close observation on the activities of the fort, and also in Savannah within the Continental command. There was no real attempt to conceal intelligence either within the military offices or in the taverns where officers and men gathered to drink and exchange rumors and information. He was soon rewarded with a report that food and ammunition would be delivered to Fort McIntosh by barge, down the inland waterway and up the St. Illa River to the fort.

Brown decided that he would let Sergeant Baker and Lieutenant McGirth lead the expedition, while he stayed behind in St. Augustine. Their plan was to intercept the shipment at the mouth of the river, replace the crew and escort troops with Rangers, and take the fort after the gates were opened to receive the much-needed supplies. A force of about ninety men would be deployed close enough to surround the fort at the crucial time and ensure that the operation was successful.

A courier informed the Ranger commander as soon as the shipment left Savannah on the slow-moving barge, and the plan was put into effect. It was implemented without a hitch, and the fort was taken with minimal loss of life on either side. As was customary, Captain Winn and the other captured defenders were released on their personal guarantee of no further military service, but McGirth insisted that Lieutenant Christie be taken captive to St. Augustine as a guarantor that the noncombatant pledges would be honored. Two experienced Tory volunteers and four Creek braves guarded the prisoner. There was confusion among the group as they crossed the St. Marys River, and Christie was killed as—according to his captors—he attempted to escape. Before the white Rangers could restrain them, the Creeks scalped the dead Georgian, and after a brief discussion, his body was buried near the river.

Brown confronted Lieutenant McGirth, who denied that he had incited the attack. Although the denial was not persuasive, Sergeant Baker convinced Brown that an attempted escape was their best explanation of the event. There was no way to conceal what had happened, and the colony was aroused as never before by the capture of one of their few forts and by the unprecedented "execution" of a hostage. Archibald Bulloch reported the savage incident to General Robert Howe, in Charles Town, and asked him to send a force to defend Georgia. Troops were dispatched but did not arrive until after McIntosh had moved south and the invaders had faded away into the swamps and woods of west Georgia and north Florida. The Georgia troops found that their fort had been ransacked, burned, and abandoned shortly after its capture by the Rangers.

C H A P T E R   30

A Deadly Duel

April 1777

Georgia political and military leaders realized that their real authority did not extend far from Savannah, with most of the settlers in the south intimidated by the Rangers and those farther up the Savannah River reluctant to give any support to the revolution. It was truly a divided state. Archibald Bulloch, as president and head of the Council of Safety, was the most revered man in Georgia, and the one person who was able to coalesce almost unanimous support among the otherwise sharply divided political factions. He was given almost dictatorial powers to recruit and deploy a strong militia, but he died suddenly and mysteriously a few days after taking office, and the Council of Safety promoted Button Gwinnett to succeed him. There was some trepidation about this decision, but Gwinnett had a few fervent supporters who refused to consider any other choice.

One of Gwinnett's earliest official acts was to have George McIntosh, Lachlan's brother, arrested on charges of violating the embargo against trade with the British, and placed in irons in the common jail. In fact, a

Tory factor had changed the shipping papers and surreptitiously sent the ship to St. Augustine, delivering the rice to British buyers. The entire Scottish clan deeply resented the insult that had been aimed at them, and as soon as possible, while Gwinnett was visiting Augusta, the Council of Safety released McIntosh on bail and ordered him to report to Philadelphia for trial. The Continental Congress considered the case and determined that there was insufficient evidence for a trial.

Button Gwinnett was furious when he returned to Savannah and learned that George McIntosh had been set free, but he placed most of the blame on Lachlan and the Scots clan from St. Andrews. After only a few days, he decided that it was time to fulfill his ultimate ambition: to assume command of the state's military force as the acting president and lead another invasion of Florida.

Thomas Brown quickly learned of these plans, but was unconcerned. With 350 Florida Rangers, Brown felt equal to the challenge of facing 600 Continental troops and perhaps 1,000 Georgia militia, both groups dispirited by a lack of unified leadership and with their first duties considered to be protecting their families and operating their farms. Backed by more than a thousand British regulars stationed in St. Augustine and a fleet that controlled the sea, Brown was delighted to give Major Furlong an account of what he considered to be ludicrous activities around Savannah, expressing himself in the slang expressions of his own Rangers. He presumed that the informal report would be widely distributed.

> The leaders of the rebels are like dogs in a pissing contest. The Georgians despise each other, and the so-called Continental commanders have little control over them. General Charles Lee was disgusted when he was in Georgia, and requested a transfer out of the Southern region. General Robert Howe replaced him and is visiting Savannah, but will not be able to referee successfully between President Button Gwinnett, a traitor who signed the Declaration of Independence, and Brigadier General Lachlan McIntosh, who is the most able military commander in the colony, but has few forces and limited authority. Not only do the two compete for control over their incompetent forces, but they hate each other and struggle for political and military power. The only thing on which the two Georgia leaders agree is not to submit to the command of a Continental officer.

After a few days in Savannah to explore plans for a possible attack on Florida, General Robert Howe returned to Charles Town in disgust, leaving a few of his troops in Savannah. After Howe's departure, Gwinnett assumed that his political title empowered him to move against the British, so he planned another Florida excursion. Despite the urging of his closest associates, Gwinnett refused to notify Continental Commander Lachlan McIntosh of his plans. Few recruits came forward when Gwinnett attempted to put together a force of militia, and an aggravated Council of Safety made a last-minute call to McIntosh for help with the expedition.

In April 1777, the forces finally began moving toward Florida, but a new argument broke out before they were halfway to the Florida line. The intense animosity between Gwinnett and McIntosh made it impossible for either to take orders from the other, or even for their subordinates to cooperate in planning or executing the military operation. Both Gwinnett and McIntosh refused to move their forces farther southward unless the other would submit to his own leadership. Finally, the council ordered the two leaders and their troops to return to Savannah, where each man marshaled political supporters and attempted to justify his actions.

In May, Gwinnett lost his campaign for governor to John Adam Treutlen, after holding the state's top office exactly two months. Almost immediately, Brigadier General McIntosh filed a charge with the general assembly that Gwinnett had been disloyal, had refused to accept legal orders, and therefore had caused the expedition to fail. As expected, Gwinnett denied all the charges and claimed that McIntosh was to blame. After a hot debate, a bare majority of the divided parliament voted that Gwinnett had not acted improperly in the campaign. When he heard of this decision, McIntosh called his adversary "a scoundrel and lying rascal." As was expected, Gwinnett's seconds delivered the inevitable challenge that evening.

It was still dark the next morning when Brigadier General McIntosh and his second, Colonel Joseph Habersham, arrived in a meadow near Savannah, on a plantation formerly owned by Governor James Wright. There was an early fog, but it was thin enough for the assembled men to see their carriage at a distance of at least thirty yards. Habersham moved around restlessly, but McIntosh seemed perfectly at ease as they listened to the first twittering of songbirds and watched the sky begin to brighten in the east. A quarter hour later, former president Gwinnett and his political ally George

Wells arrived. As an apothecary who practiced medicine, Wells could play a double role in also caring for either combatant who might be wounded. The seconds consulted with the two duelists and then met with each other.

Dr. Wells said, "President Gwinnett has decided to let the general name the distance."

When Habersham walked away and presented the question to McIntosh, his response was, "I propose three paces."

Both seconds protested strongly that this would leave little chance for survival, so after some discussion they settled on four paces, still a deadly range for two skilled marksmen.

Gwinnett immediately accepted this proposal, and after checking their pistols, the two principals approached each other without speaking, turned, and waited until the signal was given. They took the prescribed steps, turned, and fired. Both were wounded, with bullets in McIntosh's thigh and near Gwinnett's groin. Gwinnett was on the ground, but McIntosh did not fall. The general looked down at his despised adversary and coldly asked, "Another shot?"

Gwinnett, whose right hip appeared to be fractured, replied, "Yes, if someone will help me stand erect."

The seconds interceded, and Wells examined both of the men's wounds. McIntosh's leg was soaked in blood, but he refused any treatment from his opponent's second, managed to apply a tourniquet, and was able to climb into his carriage without assistance. After he and Habersham departed, Wells and Gwinnett followed them back to Savannah. Three days later, Gwinnett died from "mortification of the wound," perhaps because of inadequate treatment. Even Mrs. Gwinnett blamed her husband's death on the "unskillfulness of his doctor," but Lyman Hall, Gwinnett's friend and executor, filed official murder charges against McIntosh. The general surrendered, requested an immediate trial, and was acquitted. Gwinnett's supporters mounted a campaign throughout the state, urging Georgians to refuse service under "the murderer." The rancorous arguments persisted, so in October, five months after the duel, McIntosh left a bitterly divided Georgia, reported to General Washington, and on General Charles Lee's recommendation was placed in command of the western districts of Virginia and Pennsylvania.

Despite news of military action in the northern states and some attacks by the Florida Rangers, most north Georgia families were relatively untouched by the revolution. This was especially true among settler families, many of whom lived on isolated homesteads and felt that their first responsibility was to protect their families and property. Deep south Georgia or Florida was an ultimate destination for the most dedicated Tory supporters, while Whig families felt secure along the coast near Savannah and in some areas around Augusta. Even in the coastal region, the British government still had quiet support from former members of the governor's council, Anglican clergymen, some of the wealthy Savannah merchants, Indian traders, and recent immigrants from Britain who retained close ties with their families back home.

Settlers in Wilkes County were even more divided than others in the colony. The fighting farther south and along the coast had hardly touched the lives of the Pratts and Morrises. Although Ethan did not share the pacifism of the Quakers, his hope was that political differences might be resolved peacefully, and he was determined to remain aloof from military action. Kindred was fervently against any combat that indicated disloyalty to the crown or might impact adversely on his Indian friends. There was a stark difference in actions and basic philosophy between the Quaker-dominated community around Wrightsborough, who were inclined toward the Tory cause but were deeply religious pacifists, and the militants who followed Elijah Clarke and were closely aligned with the most radical Whigs in Savannah.

At the same time, Elijah Clarke was in a quandary. He was a proud militiaman, completely committed to independence for Americans but with an abhorrence of serving under any governing authority that he did not respect. He and his neighbors considered themselves removed from the political debacle in Savannah, where the leaders were an embarrassment and considered unworthy of their support. The death of Archibald Bulloch, president of the Council of Safety, and the assumption of authority by Button Gwinnett had confirmed their belief that Savannah was a nest of fruitless intrigue and a breeding ground for corruption. Elijah was familiar with General McIntosh's lifetime of military service, and respected him as a courageous and competent leader. The militiamen celebrated both Gwinnett's political defeat and the news of the fatal duel.

With the election of Treutlen as governor, the militiamen began to consider a change in their own role. Their inherent desire was to remain as independent as possible, relying on their own weapons, training as their duties at home permitted, and making collective decisions about when to assemble for military excursions within their own community or as partners with militia groups in western Carolina. At the same time, they saw the failure of combined expeditions against Florida and the successes of the Florida Rangers as a clear indication that they could be helpful as the struggle for independence progressed.

In June 1777, Aaron Hart brought an invitation from Governor Treutlen to Elijah Clarke for a meeting in Savannah. Clarke took Aaron and militia leaders John Twiggs and John Dooly with him, and within a few days they were in the governor's office.

After an exchange of greetings, Treutlen said, "Gentlemen, I want to express my thanks for the good support I received from your county in my campaign for governor. What I want to do is to serve as well as Archibald Bulloch, and to pull all Georgians together in the same spirit of harmony and cooperation that he experienced."

Clarke replied, "Well, there ain't no doubt that you'll be a big improvement over the man you beat, and those of us who live up the river will be willin' to help you whenever we can. I guess you have other things in mind as the reason you asked us to come here."

Treutlen could see that idle conversation was not appropriate and decided to get to the point of his request.

"I want to see the different Georgia militia units strengthened and organized as much as possible into an effective fighting force. We don't even know how many Continentals General Washington will send down here, and we have to let the British know we are able to defend ourselves. I know you men have been operating some in the Carolinas, and we also need you to help out in our own state."

Elijah responded, "Governor, we'll be glad to help as we can, but there ain't many of us. All we have to fight with is our own weapons and mostly on our plow horses. We been up to Watauga Valley twice, but mostly we stay ready to protect ourselves against the savages. I could bring some men down here to help when we're needed."

Dooly then spoke up. "Gwinnett didn't seem to need us, even though we could have helped in going down against Florida. After what happened, it's likely now that Burnfoot Brown will be moving farther north, and he's got to be stopped. But most of us need to stay as close to home as possible."

Treutlen said, "Well, it seems that we have a lot in common. Although we can't seem to get more troops from the congress, they have given us some money to be used for our militia. I asked you to come down here to see if we can provide you with some military supplies."

Clarke responded, "I reckon we can use some help, but what would we have to do for it?"

"The military commander would have to sign a personal bond that the provisions would be properly used, only for the direct requirements of the troops he leads. What we have to offer is some muskets and bayonets, powder and ammunition, a few horses and harnesses, blankets, and some tents. We also have a few pairs of boots."

Clarke thought a few seconds and asked, "I reckon I'd be the one to sign. How many men could you supply?"

"How many do you have?"

"About a hundred and twenty have come forward on occasion to volunteer, but less than a hundred have stuck with trainin'. We could probably call out about eighty right now if we needed them."

"How many could you get if supplies were available?"

Clarke, Dooly, and Twiggs mumbled a few words to one another, and Clarke said, "Maybe two hundred, and mostly from Wilkes County."

Treutlen said, "There is a limit of twenty-three pounds per man, so you'll have to find the best bargains for everything. Also, you'll have to make this amount last for at least a year, and maybe longer."

Clarke asked if some of the supplies could be bought in Augusta, nearer their homes, and the governor approved this request.

After a couple of hours of careful figuring among all four men, Clarke finally agreed to sign a personal bond to the colonial government for £4,560. Aaron assured him that he would not have to repay this enormous amount, but that all of them would be responsible for the proper use of the money. It was more than a month later before they finished supplying the militiamen who were already under their command, and they found it surprisingly easy to expand their force with the offer of adequate supplies.

In early November 1777, Brown submitted another account to his superiors:

> *Your Excellency:*
> *Since you may not yet have received this information, I feel that I should report the first rebel victory of the Insurrection. I have just been informed by*

courier that a greatly superior rebel Force of 17,000 under Horatio Gates surrounded General Burgoyne with less than half as many men at Saratoga, in New York, and more than 5,000 of our troops were captured. Prior to this, British forces had taken Fort Ticonderoga and were moving Southward with ease. Although we can easily overcome this temporary military Setback, news of it might be interpreted in Paris as Encouragement to the French in giving Support to the rebels. As we all know, they still resent having lost Canada almost fifteen Years ago, and have been looking for some excuse to give Assistance to the rebellion in order to strike back at us.

There is also a believable Report that General Sir William Howe is planning to take Philadelphia, either moving his Forces by land or sea. An adequate fleet of more than 200 vessels has been assembled near New York to Transport either troops or supplies when the time comes.

*Respectfully submitted by
the Governor's agent*

Almost three months later, there was another submission:

Your Excellency:

This is a brief and general Report, much more Encouraging than my last. With our taking of Philadelphia, the Continental Congress was forced to flee to York, Pennsylvania. The British are spending the Winter in comfort, well supplied in Philadelphia, while the often-defeated Rebels huddle in misery somewhere further west. They have no funds to pay the troops, no clothing to be issued, and a great sense of Malaise prevails among them. There has been a ridiculous effort by them to exaggerate minor Skirmishes at Trenton and Princeton in New Jersey, which is understandable since these are the only Victories that their so-called commander-in-chief can claim.

*Respectfully submitted by
the Governor's agent*

Thomas Brown was aware of major changes being contemplated in British strategy, and he and Sergeant Baker discussed the relationships among the British leaders in Florida. As was the case in Savannah, divisions and confusion had evolved among them, and Thomas Brown and the Florida Rangers were the focus of the disputes. Because of jealousy and their relative inactivity, most regular British officers and men despised

Brown and the Florida Rangers. Despite this, Brown had the full support of Major Furlong, his original sponsor, and of Florida Governor Tonyn because they could take credit for his successes and utilize the intelligence information derived from his British and Indian scouts.

On the other side was Swiss colonel Augustine Prevost, the rigidly formal Florida commander who was closely associated with other officers in the regular British forces, notably including his brother George and his son James Mark. He deeply resented the unstructured operation of the Florida Rangers and had objected officially and strenuously when Governor Tonyn had given Brown a provincial appointment as lieutenant colonel. Prevost had never acknowledged any accomplishment of the Rangers and had failed to forward to Brown a commendation that had been received from General Sir William Howe. Instead, he reported to Sir William that "there are now four companies of Rangers, but they are of little service and without any control or regulation."

Governor Tonyn obtained a copy of this message and hastened to assure Sir William that Brown was a gentleman of education and from a family of reputation and fortune who led the Rangers effectively and in almost constant danger to himself. He reported that these raiders, fully authorized and supported by him, had supplied St. Augustine with food and other supplies, including more than three thousand head of cattle, and had been extremely successful in recruiting Indians into the service of the king. He added, erroneously, that Brown had personally led in the capture of Fort McIntosh. Overall, Brown was pleased with his status and was looking forward to an increased role for the Florida Rangers in the future.

BOOK III

1778–1785

CHAPTER 31

The British Southern Strategy

1778

Early in the spring of 1778, there was a meeting of unprecedented importance in St. Augustine, and carefully chosen officials occupied the six available chairs around the small table in the governor's private anteroom. There was a brigadier general named McPherson from General Sir Henry Clinton's headquarters, Governor Tonyn and his chief political aide, newly promoted Brigadier General Augustine Prevost, and two of his deputies, one of whom was his brother George. Thomas Brown sat by himself, in a corner of the room, having been invited by the governor but forbidden to bring any other members of the Florida Rangers.

It was now almost two years after independence had been declared, and everyone in the room was aware of the discouraging developments in the colonies. Although the British had taken New York and Philadelphia, they had been defeated at Saratoga, failing to cut off New England from the rest of the continent. In addition, royal governors had been forced out of Norfolk, Savannah, and Charles Town, and their efforts to retain the loyalty of citizens were doubtful at best.

Governor Tonyn was presiding, and everyone became quiet when he stood at the end of the table and cleared his throat.

"Gentlemen, let me report first of all that I have exchanged several messages with General Sir Henry Clinton, who will now be the supreme commander in America. He has suggested that we assemble here to review the situation in the colonies and receive some information about decisions that have been made in London. I need not remind you of the sensitivity and the need for absolute confidentiality concerning these reports.

"You are all aware that we have had notable successes in the northern colonies, but we must also acknowledge that something of a stalemate has now developed there. The recent alignment of the rebels with France has complicated the situation, and it may be that active French involvement will be forthcoming. I have already discussed the strategic decision with

General McPherson, who has arrived here this morning from New York, and I would like to summarize it for you."

The governor was obviously enjoying his role. He paused to sip from a silver tumbler of water, while the others waited with different expressions. McPherson had a self-important air as the one who had brought the important message, and Prevost was impatient at the drawn-out ceremony. He had made clear his disapproval of Brown's presence and was only partially assuaged when his aides were permitted to occupy the last two chairs at the table. Subordinates mirrored the demeanor of their superiors, while the Ranger commander tried to ignore the secondary position of his own location.

Tonyn looked around and then continued, "This frustrating situation is about to change, and we are likely to play the major role in ensuring a rapid and inevitable British victory. A decision has been made in London that we will hold New York as our primary base in the north, defeat the revolutionaries in that region whenever possible, retain our control of the seas, and continue to convince citizens of the advantages of loyalty to the crown.

"The force of the British Empire will henceforth be focused on the southern colonies, a decision that I have long advocated. This position has been strongly supported by both Governor Wright and Governor Campbell, who are eager to return to their former posts. Our first thrust will be to recapture Savannah, providing a base for the taking of Charles Town. We will then be positioned to move against Washington's forces simultaneously northward from the Carolinas and southward from New York, while preventing the rebels from receiving any supplies from overseas. In very general terms, this describes the strategy of our government. If there are any questions, either General McPherson or I will be prepared to answer them."

Without acknowledging Tonyn's leadership, Prevost addressed his question directly to McPherson: "Sir, to what extent is General Clinton willing to assign naval and ground forces necessary to take Savannah?"

"His Lordship has assured me that adequate power will be exerted to accomplish this goal. This will be done even if it requires a temporary holding action in the northern colonies. We assume that many loyalists will rise up to assist us when we prove our strength. We have estimated that it will require about two thousand troops to capture Savannah and five thousand to take Charles Town, and more will be assigned if later intelligence indicates their need."

"What role will be expected from the limited troops now in Florida, who have, on occasion, been hard-pressed to defend our own territory from rebel attacks? Our regular troops have performed heroically, but I have to state that the lack of a unified command by our adversaries has been a major factor in their repulsion."

"The major thrust against Savannah will be from the sea, but this in itself will be an impossibility with rebel troops marshaled to oppose us in the marshland approaches. It will be necessary for all available forces to make a simultaneous attack by land. I have brought you orders from General Clinton and would like to return to him with an assessment from you about your additional needs. There are a few other military units in the Caribbean which might be available."

Brown had noticed that Prevost did not mention the involvement of the Rangers in defending Florida, but he decided not to comment. In his mind was a map of the torturous channel from the sea to Savannah, with a latticework of tidal creeks that would have to be crossed. A concerted defense of these crossing points would make an attack very costly, provided the rebel forces were forewarned about the invasion.

There was a pause in the conversation while everyone contemplated the ramifications of the news, and finally the governor nodded to Brown. "Commander, do you have any comments or questions?"

"Yes, sir. To what extent will we be free to recruit assistance from the native tribes, and with what rewards can we entice them to play a significant role?"

Tonyn said, "Let me attempt to answer that. This issue has not been addressed in the instructions I have received, but I shall recommend strongly that we capitalize on the natural friendly relations that exist between His Majesty and the aboriginals. If they see that their own best interests will be served by cooperation with us, then they must be welcomed to this partnership."

Brown chose not to pursue the subject of rewards, but addressed an additional question to General McPherson. "Sir, what tentative plans have been made concerning Charles Town?"

"We contemplate bypassing the city for the time being, concentrating on Savannah, and then launching a subsequent attack from sea and land, with a much heavier dependence on our army forces on this second phase of the military operation. A prolonged siege may be necessary, which will require substantial forces to seal off Charles Town from the mainland."

Brown could envision a greater role for the Rangers in the Carolina operation, with a need for maximum native support. His thoughts were immediately focused on the importance of Augusta, but he decided not to speak further. His best opportunity to expand his ideas would be in more private discussions with Governor Tonyn, who obviously had a direct and personal relationship with General Clinton.

The men continued their conversation for an additional hour, which gave General McPherson an opportunity to go into some detail about current plans. General Clinton, in New York, would remain in overall command, and dispatch a force by sea from New York to attack Savannah. Realizing that the timetable for the invasion was still being considered, everyone urged that it be delayed until at least October, when the southern weather would be more cooperative and military operations in the north less likely. Brown could see these intervening months as necessary in recruiting Indians, intimidating doubtful settlers, and preparing his Rangers for operations farther north than had been customary.

Early in 1778, Captain Chesley Bostwick was commissioned in the Continental forces and assigned for service at Fort Howe on the Altamaha River. Thomas Brown was aware of the appointment even before Bostick arrived at his post. He called in Sergeant Baker for a private consultation.

"Sergeant, I am giving you the strictest orders that a man named Chesley Bostick, now a captain in the Georgia militia, is not to be killed. I can tell you that he is devious and a coward, and has been ordered to Fort Howe for duty. If you learn his exact whereabouts, I want to be told. If he should be captured, I want him brought to me immediately. Do you understand?"

Baker understood more than he acknowledged, having long ago learned of Bostick's role in ordering the torturing of the commander. This was a story frequently told by the people around Augusta, often with hilarity, but it was a subject that was never discussed in Brown's presence.

"Yes, sir, I'll relay these orders to our people."

Within a few days, Sergeant Baker was informed that Bostick had assumed command of Fort Howe. Brown immediately decided to make a preemptory strike against the fort, and he and 110 Rangers and Indians crossed the broad Altamaha River upstream, careful to avoid detection. He ordered his troops to surround the small fort at night, and his Indians then gave loud war whoops as the other Rangers fired their muskets over the barricade, careful not to kill the troops within. They succeeded in the surprise attack within an hour and captured twenty-three prisoners, but somehow the commanding officer and a few men escaped. The Rangers spiked the guns, took the ammunition, set fire to the fort, and withdrew. Bostick later reported that they had skirmished with the "greatly superior forces of 'Burnfoot' Brown." At the same time, Brown's agents spread the word in Savannah that Bostick had retreated in terror, abandoning both the fort and his men to just a handful of the enemy. A court of inquiry was ordered, and Bostick was demoted to lieutenant and fined £10.

Predictably, Prevost discounted the importance of the action, while Tonyn asserted that the destruction of the fort would discourage American recruitments and military operations along Georgia's western frontier and would enhance British operations all the way to South Carolina.

In March, Thomas Brown submitted another report:

Your Excellency:

The rebels' effort to form an Alliance with France is generating proof of Subterfuge and Artifice on both sides. It is obvious that the rebel Army is both unwilling and unable to fight, and the French are merely dreaming that a Miracle will give Canada back to them, along with some territory east of the Mississippi River. Faced with our superior fleet along the Atlantic coast, their navy has had to confine its activities to attacking a few small islands in the Caribbean. As I reported earlier, our well-supplied troops spent the winter without challenge in Philadelphia, New York, and Newport, and there is little prospect of another foray toward Montreal or Quebec. Washington is fully occupied with sustaining his few remaining troops and attempting to minimize the increasing Desertions, while John Adams and others, now back in Philadelphia, are criticizing him as a timid and ineffective Commander.

As we take the South and move northward, hopefully with full involvement of our Indian friends, this will cause a Diversion of troops from the north, dividing and further weakening the rebel Force.

Respectfully submitted by
the Governor's agent

In the spring of 1778, American leaders both in Philadelphia and in the southern states began to realize that the stalemate in the north might lead to increased British activity in the south. The depredations of the Florida

Rangers had become almost unbearable to the Georgians, and the revolutionaries were additionally concerned about continuing activities of British ships along the coast of Georgia, where they frequently sent raiding parties ashore to take food supplies and slaves from the defenseless villages and plantations. Georgia leaders saw the recent destruction of Fort Howe as proof of their own weakness and perhaps the first phase of a broader military operation by the British.

Hearing persistent pleas for more protection from Savannah and having observed naval movements out of New York perhaps toward the south, General Washington finally became convinced that the long-rumored British attacks on Charles Town and Savannah might be coming. Georgia would undoubtedly be the first target, from the British stronghold in Florida. He sent General Benjamin Lincoln to replace General Robert Howe as southern commander of the Continental forces and ordered Howe to Georgia to co-ordinate the defense of the state. In an attempt to strengthen Whig support, Washington further directed that anyone who could marshal fifteen or more volunteers was free to plunder Tory property in Florida at will, and would be given at least a sergeant's commission in the Georgia militia. He also offered five hundred acres of free land to any family that would settle south of the Altamaha River or in east Florida, but there were no takers.

As an additional response to British threats, Washington sent a few hundred more troops into Savannah to serve under General Howe, making a total of two thousand Continentals, joined by South Carolina militia under Colonel Andrew Williamson and a Georgia contingent under newly elected Governor John Houstoun. There were also several naval units under Commodore Oliver Bowen, including five galleys, two sloops, and eight smaller ships manned by rowers. In all, it was a formidable force, but General Howe reported that many of the revolutionaries lacked shoes, blankets, and adequate shelter, and most of them carried only the weapons they had brought from home, with little ammunition. For the past eight months there had been no money to pay troops, but now the Continental Congress made $600,000 available to the Georgia militia. Although the inflated currency made minimal purchases possible, this was a welcome recognition of their importance as a buffer between the British forces in Florida and the northern colonies.

The British knew that morale throughout the Continental forces was poor, with frequent desertions. Punishment for the many malcontents was increasingly severe. Brown reported that on one day there were ten convictions for desertion, with seven sentences of death by firing squad, one of hanging, and two of one hundred lashes. One sentence of four hundred lashes was administered to a farmer who had deserted and returned to his family. There was an outcry among the troops when he died because of this whipping.

Elijah Clarke and his militia now considered themselves to be well organized and trained, and they were eager for a taste of combat. Elijah came to Savannah with two hundred volunteers, who were outfitted with adequate supplies and ammunition. Then he volunteered for service, preferably in one of the forays into north Florida. The Georgia state council decided to avoid the previous political-military competition among their officials and placed Governor John Houstoun in full command of its combined force. Although the governor had no military training, Elijah Clarke was willing to serve under his command in order to be directly involved in real action against the British.

When Clarke met with Governor Houstoun and his Georgia detachment, he found that his troops were the only ones outfitted either for combat or for survival in the hot and malaria-infested coastal region. Ten men were assigned to each small tent; there was just one canteen issued for every six men, and a camp kettle for every fifteen. Few of the troops had adequate ammunition, there was practically no medicine available, and a sense of despair was prevalent. Elijah was determined to show the superiority of his fighting force and began to argue for more direct action instead of waiting in Savannah to respond to some future attack by the British. He convinced the other Georgia leaders that Savannah would be easy to defend with proper placement of no more than one thousand troops. The city was nearly surrounded by swamps and marshlands, making a land attack almost impossible, and entrance by sea could be prevented by well-placed artillery and, if necessary, by sinking ships in the main channel.

A consensus soon evolved that the best strategy was to launch a concerted attack against Florida. All of the leaders realized that throughout the earlier months of the war and even with twice as many men as the British, the Continentals had never been able to cross the St. Marys River into Florida, much less take St. Augustine. Nevertheless, there was a general belief among Georgians that the mistakes of the past could be corrected and that this time the unprecedented American force would prevail.

Perhaps predictably, the old debate about ultimate command was resumed between General Robert Howe and the provincial leaders. Immediately after his arrival in Savannah, General Howe infuriated the Georgians by refusing to participate in any meetings with them in uniform, insisting that he would only consult with them as a civilian. Emphasizing his own military career and status as Continental commander, General Howe claimed the right to overall command and refused to serve under the youthful and inexperienced Governor Houstoun. Meanwhile, Commodore Bowen insisted that his galleys were a naval force and therefore under his exclusive command. Colonel Williamson, leading the South Carolina militia, refrained from participating in the debate, but refused to agree that he would accept orders from other leaders. In order to resolve the impasse and minimize past mistakes, they all finally decided to retain their independence but to consult closely with one another and to clarify responsibilities before the major strike was launched.

Having full information from Brown about these discussions and aware of the formidable size of this force of Georgia militia and Continental troops, Governor Tonyn was concerned that some of the settlers south of the Altamaha might shift their allegiance and join a victorious force of invaders, and he was not at all certain of the loyalty of the Creeks and Seminoles. The governor's main commitment was to defend St. Augustine, and he issued instructions for the Rangers to stay in contact with the enemy's troops, skirmish to delay their progress, but avoid a pitched battle. This was, in fact, Brown's standard and preferred tactic.

Governor Tonyn had rarely had to call on the regular troops stationed in St. Augustine. In almost every case, he had been able to defend Florida and to harass the local Whigs with only the Rangers and a small group of loyalists from Georgia and Carolina, almost all of whom had been recruited and led by Thomas Brown. This relatively cautious and dormant policy was completely compatible with the character of General Augustine Prevost, who never came forward to demand a more vigorous role for his Redcoats. Now, however, the situation was about to change.

CHAPTER 32

Last Invasion of Florida

MAY 1778

The Altamaha was a mighty river as it approached the sea, and as Elijah Clarke and Aaron Hart sat on its southern bank they discussed the regions of the state that were drained by its two main tributaries, the Ocmulgee and the Oconee. The stream's multiple sources were 250 miles northwest of them, extending more than one hundred miles above Augusta, and the slow-moving waters that flowed past them had drained only lands still controlled by the Creeks and Cherokees. Permanent white settlements existed alongside the stream for less than thirty miles, from their present location to the sea. They hated to admit how small a portion of the state they actually controlled.

Clarke said, "It really gripes me to know that we've let the bloody Rangers control almost all our Georgia territory between here and the Florida line, and it's time we pushed them out once and for all."

Cautiously, Aaron responded, "They've never operated much right along the coast, but if this expedition fails, we might see both them and the Redcoats in Savannah."

"Well, now that General Howe finally got here with his one thousand Continentals and if Houstoun and Williamson ever come with the other militia from Georgia and South Carolina, we'll have enough strength to go all the way to St. Augustine."

With approval from the Georgia council and the governor, Elijah Clarke and his two hundred mounted militia had moved down to the north side of the Altamaha, where they had waited until the last week in May, when General Howe and his Continentals joined them at the site of the destroyed fort named in his honor. Then they had crossed the river without opposition and were waiting again, this time for almost another month, for the arrival of Governor Houstoun and Colonel Williamson, each of whom was supposed to bring about five hundred state militia. The Georgia contingent finally appeared across the river on July 4, and the South Carolinians arrived a week

later. Now all of them had crossed the river and were bivouacked along its
southern shore.

At the invitation of General Howe, the other leaders and their top aides
were assembled in his large tent. He was the first to speak.

"I would like to welcome Governor Houstoun, Colonel Williamson,
Colonel Clarke, and others. Now that we are all together, it is imperative
that we understand what collective forces we have and how best to coordinate our movements southward. I must say that I have never participated
in a military operation with four independent commanders, but this is the
arrangement and I am willing to honor it.

"As all of us will remember, our agreed plan has been to assemble at Fort
Howe with expedition, then to move southward and take Fort Tonyn, just
across the St. Marys River in Florida. With our combined strength, this
should not be a major obstacle. Our next move will then be as directly as
possible to St. Augustine, which we can expect the British to defend strenuously. If we can inflict serious casualties on them in advance and also
demonstrate our own strength and capabilities, it is quite likely that they
will capitulate without a major engagement. We will be supplied by boats
from Charles Town and Savannah, using the inland waterway."

Elijah raised his hand and began to speak without being recognized.

"General, we all remember our plans, but I can already see some problems that we have to face. My men and I have been here for six weeks,
waitin' on everybody else to arrive. We've just about eaten up all our food,
and I understand that the others don't have much to share. Mine are
fightin' men that have been trainin' together for three years, and we're eager for our first fight with the British, but we're not used to this country and
a lot of us are already sick. We can get our own food or eat grass, but I'd
like to know about the medicine."

Howe responded, "I have the same problem with my men, who have
been dropping like flies. Let's let my regimental physician give us a report
before we continue with the military discussion. Dr. Masterson, please."

Dr. Masterson stood, cleared his throat, looked at some notes taken
from his pocket, and said, "We have been terribly disappointed by the
nonarrival of supplies that were supposed to come by boat from Savannah,
including ipecac, jalap, calomel, and other purgative medicines for the
treatment of malaria, typhoid, consumption, yellow fever, and other inca-
pacitating diseases. Now we understand that the newly arrived troops have

not brought what we need. There is a new group of sick soldiers every day and we have little medicine to treat them. We've had new promises from Savannah that medicine is on the way, and I don't know what we shall do if it does not arrive. I apologize for this negative report."

After the doctor sat down, there was a general discussion, with all four leaders participating. The final conclusion was that they would adhere to the plans made in Savannah and move forward, in the meantime sending an urgent message back to Savannah with instructions on delivering the medical supplies up the St. Marys River for their use after their capture of Fort Tonyn. Houstoun and Williamson announced that they would need several more days of preparation, but Howe and Clarke stated that their men had waited long enough and would proceed immediately to take Fort Tonyn, then wait for the others before advancing further.

Thomas Brown had operated in this region for three years, with a highly trained and disciplined force, and he and his men knew every trail and stream. His information about the planned invasion of Florida had been shared between the governor and General Prevost, and there was a struggle over who would command and ultimately receive credit for another expected expulsion of American forces. Most of the British regular troops stayed near St. Augustine to guarantee its defense while others were sent to strengthen Fort Tonyn, where the Americans were first to be confronted. Without specific orders to the contrary, Brown decided to ignore the decision of his superiors to yield to the Americans while they were still in Georgia. The Rangers, using tactics of the natives, harassed the invaders at every opportunity as they moved through the swamps and pine forests and eventually crossed the St. Marys into Florida.

Brown followed General Prevost's orders that Fort Tonyn be burned and abandoned, leaving the American forces with a hollow victory, and then placed his three hundred Rangers in direct line of the rebel's advance. The governor had earlier requested that Brown's forces be given supplies and military support, pointing out that the Rangers had been the ones who had gathered the available provisions. General Prevost refused, unless Brown and the Rangers were put under the direct military command of his son, Major James Mark Prevost. Tonyn, having exhausted all his authority, asked Brown to "waive every punctilio" and agree to serve under regular military officers. Without leaving his post, Brown submitted his resignation, explaining that this was a severe censure upon his service as an officer and a gentleman and that he could not betray commitments to his Rangers and "serve under every British subaltern." He reminded the governor that the king had personally approved the independent status of the Rangers. Tonyn forwarded Brown's response to General Sir Henry Clinton, who was sure to rule against Brown. Not receiving any supplies from the British main force, Brown issued instructions to his men on how to subsist on the leaf buds of palmettos, which the Rangers soon said were "better than cabbage."

Major Prevost deployed his men fourteen miles farther south of Brown on Alligator Creek, a site well known to the Rangers. Never having been welcomed into Fort Tonyn, the Rangers had used this crossing point as a campsite, and had deepened some finger lakes to enclose a raised mound of earth that the men named Brown's Battery. Major Prevost now sent word for the Rangers to retreat and join his forces, but Brown dispatched only half of his men to Alligator Creek to improve its defenses and led the rest to harass the invading force on its flanks and rear.

After the Americans discovered the charred remains of Fort Tonyn, Elijah Clarke announced to his men, "This reminds me of Burnfoot Brown's foot!"

There were peals of laughter, and then he added, "Now we'll show him how real woodsmen fight."

Clarke obtained permission from General Howe to drive southward with his well-organized and competent cavalry, to reconnoiter, and to round up the scattered Rangers. The main force of Continental troops would follow, and the combined force would then attack the British, whom Clarke's scouts soon discovered to be deployed at Alligator Creek. Fighting a rearguard action to delay the American advance, Brown withdrew his forces to the southern bank of the creek, where Major Prevost's Grenadiers were occupying the well-fortified Brown's Battery, just behind a tangled obstacle of underbrush and a number of pointed saplings, forming what they called an "abatis."

About nine hundred Redcoats were waiting for the charge, and Brown sent a company of Rangers out wide around each flank of the Americans. It was with great difficulty that the Georgia horsemen fought their way through the intertwined logs and brush, and when Clarke ordered them to jump the creek, they found it far too deep and wide. Under heavy fire and wild whoops and yells from the Indian and British defenders, the almost drowned horses stampeded and the cavalry fell back. Clarke took a bullet through his thigh, and a number of American troops were killed and wounded. Howe and his Continentals never charged, and he quickly ordered a general retreat. Major Prevost began pursuit but turned back when his troops had a brief skirmish with Captain James Jackson and a small detail, and ordered a total withdrawal south of Alligator Creek when he realized that British troops were too scattered throughout the swamp to be marshaled for any concerted attack on the Americans.

At a council of war back at Fort Tonyn, General Howe informed the group that primarily because of sickness, only 350 of his original troops were still fit for action, and that he lacked both dependable military support and an adequate number of horses to carry ammunition and supplies. He stated that the long delays were not his responsibility, and he carefully prepared a document listing eight reasons for the failed mission.

After all his subordinate officers agreed and signed the paper, General Howe ordered his forces to withdraw back up the Georgia coast. This was to be the last of the ill-fated and often ludicrous attempts to attack the British in eastern Florida, but it was only the first encounter between Thomas Brown and Elijah Clarke. More than one-third of the invaders were dead or incapacitated, and this failure during the summer of 1778 spread despair throughout American forces and, at the same time, encouraged the British to expedite preparations for major invasions of their own.

It was important to recapture Savannah and Charles Town for two strategic purposes: to convince European leaders that Britain was crushing the revolution and to provide bases from which to destroy all revolutionary forces in America before they could benefit from the treaty that had been signed with France in February promising money, weapons, and soldiers. By taking Georgia and then South Carolina, they would be cutting off vital food and other supplies that had been moving northward to the Continental army. It was logical to begin with Savannah, because of the invulnerable British base in Florida, the effectiveness of the Rangers, and the apparently tepid support for independence in the backcountry of Georgia. Victory would be inevitable if Britain controlled the seas.

The British realized that Savannah was almost invulnerable to an invasion from the sea and could be taken only after a tedious and costly siege, but they were prepared to make this sacrifice in time and casualties because of its importance. The final plan, evolved during the summer months, was for Prevost to attack through southern Georgia with two thousand ground troops while General Clinton would send a large additional force by sea from New York, commanded by Lieutenant Colonel Archibald Campbell. At the same time, Indian Superintendent John Stuart and Thomas Brown would arouse the Creeks and Cherokees to support the British cause. Whigs were not to be punished or abused, but offered complete amnesty if they would only profess their loyalty to the crown and forgo support for the Continentals.

General Prevost insisted that Brown, as merely a provincial officer, not be included in this detailed planning, but Governor Tonyn invited the Ranger commander to each briefing because he had been advocating the same plan for at least a year before it was adopted in London. Furthermore, Brown's intelligence information was excellent, and he had become much more effective in dealing with the Indians than Stuart, who had lost much of his former vigor and was inclined to remain close to his office in Pensacola.

By this time, General Sir Henry Clinton's long-delayed instructions had been received that "provincial" Lieutenant Colonel Thomas Brown and the Florida Rangers would be under the direct command of General Prevost, but Brown soon learned that his superior officers rarely exerted any real authority except in an organized battle. Knowing that Elijah Clarke was still in Savannah with his militia, Brown decided to send a Ranger strike force 150 miles up the river into Wilkes County, instructing them to let their movements be known as widely as possible. The property of twenty loyal Whig settlers was destroyed and several were killed in attacks on their homesteads, which created consternation among militia members who had been recruited into the Georgia forces. Many of them either insisted on being relieved of their duties or simply deserted and returned to their farms and families.

This action was reported to officials in St. Augustine, where General Prevost received them with strong condemnation and, once again, interceded with General Clinton. Major James Mark Prevost was promoted to lieutenant colonel and Clinton ruled that senior provincial officers, including Thomas Brown, would be placed under all regular officers of the same rank. Brown's days of almost complete operational freedom were over. He decided to stay aloof from General Prevost during the prospective attack on Savannah and to assist Colonel Campbell and the troops coming from New York by sea.

On September 8, Thomas Brown provided an assessment to Governor Tonyn's aide-de-camp:

If His Excellency already has this information, please do not bother him with this report. In my previous message, I speculated on an Alliance between the revolutionaries and the government of France. That illicit Agreement has been reached, and for several weeks we have been notified of French supply ships delivering small quantities of guns, ammunition, tents, clothing, and money through Ports in New Hampshire, but the so-called Continental Congress has now realized that little will come of it. Last month, there was a joint Attack on Newport by the rebels and a large French force under Count d'Estaing, but the commanders quarreled, the British Fleet arrived, a storm brewed, the French withdrew to the West Indies, and the rebel land Force was almost destroyed. It is interesting to note that some French officers have also been Authorized to join the rebels, but their quality is doubtful if not Ludicrous. One is a child soldier, the Marquis de Lafayette, who has been given the rank of major general at the age of nineteen! Another is a German mercenary who calls himself the Baron von Steuben, but is little more than a drill Instructor.

Since General Clinton assumed overall Command, he has abandoned Philadelphia, to concentrate his strength in New York, and to use this strong position as a Base from which Canada can be defended and the rebel forces can be attacked. Although I rarely comment on matters in this Region, with which you are thoroughly familiar, let me add the speculation that our Forces may very well decide to move from Pensacola against New Orleans.

Respectfully submitted,
Lieutenant Colonel Thos. Brown

Thomas Brown was delighted that bold action finally would be taken against the rebels and concealed his disagreement with British higher authorities concerning amnesty for the Whigs. He had an extensive dossier that included almost every frontier settler family in Georgia and felt that it was his responsibility, and not London's, to determine their fate. His Rangers were the king's men, who would be riding into the yards and fields to confront the settlers, and no superior was likely to learn the exact result of each encounter. Brown's raids became more aggressive than ever, and many loyal Whig families decided to abandon their homes and move to

Savannah or farther into the pioneer areas in north Georgia, where rebel strength still prevailed. By October 1778, Georgia Whigs controlled only a narrow area extending along the west side of the Savannah River and down the coast, in most places not more than thirty miles wide.

CHAPTER 33

Quash Dolly, Slave Woman

It was in late November that Colonel Augustine Prevost started northward from Florida by land, and Lieutenant Colonel Campbell sailed from New York at the same time with seven warships and several transports carrying 3,500 men to join in the attack on Savannah. American leaders were thoroughly informed about the impending assault on Savannah but were confident of its defense, depending primarily on its natural protection of marshland and water. General Howe was now in overall command of about five hundred Continentals remaining from the recent incursion into Florida, supplemented by about 150 South Carolina troops who had not returned home. In addition, Captain Elijah Clarke returned to Savannah with his militia, and Governor Houstoun marshaled other available Georgia militia. These were considered more than adequate, since Savannah was impervious to a quick attack and General Howe had assurances of strong support from Charles Town if a tedious siege operation was begun.

Because of the doubtful loyalty of so many people, military decisions on both sides were hardly made before being widely known, both among the revolutionaries and the British. The problem was in interpreting accurately the plethora of information that was available.

The Florida Rangers were ordered to collect as much intelligence as possible about Whig strength and deployment. Brown had a number of informants in Savannah. Some were members of the American military and others were merchants or other private citizens whose secret loyalty to the crown had never wavered. He was able to provide British authorities with descriptions of the various military units, and reported that the defenders were perfectly confident of the invulnerability of the city. He knew the Savannah area well and was quite worried when he considered how easy it would be to defend. The only encouraging news was that the three Georgia commanders had, as always, failed to accept any one as leader and each was acting as an independent command.

The first certain reports Brown had was that a small but determined detachment in some of the coastal forts had stopped Prevost's advance and forced him, at least temporarily, to turn back. Brown had mixed emotions when he received the news: gratification that his political and military adversary in Florida had failed, but deep concern at this omen that with Prevost's delay and the well-prepared American defense of Savannah, the entire British "southern strategy" would be frustrated. Brown was, in effect, an independent operator and decided to remain in the vicinity of Savannah and do whatever was possible to assist the British fleet sailing down from New York and scheduled to anchor off Tybee Island, about fifteen miles from the main settlement.

Quash Dolly tried to hold back tears and to ignore the intense pain that, in unpredictable waves, wracked her body. What she wanted most was to put down the brush broom and go back to lie on the pallet in her cabin down the white sand path below the big house. But then she realized this was not the supreme desire of her life: it was a mixed yearning to avoid any other beatings from the overseer and, in some fashion, to see him suffer as she had. Despite the rags tied at her crotch, she could still feel the fresh blood on her legs and knew that the other women could see the dried remnants of it on her bare feet. What they could not see were the stripes across her back.

It was difficult for her even to remember when she was known as Quanimo and, although a slave, had lived in relative luxury. Her family had belonged to a widower, Quintus Swanson, who was a teacher in England in his earlier years until he agreed to move to Savannah to serve as secretary for Governor James Wright. Slavery had been illegal in Georgia when the colony was founded, but it soon became apparent that plantation owners in Virginia and the Carolinas had a huge competitive advantage in using slave labor. Under intense pressure, Georgia's royal government finally legalized slavery in 1750, and the trade built up rapidly. Within a few years, the Savannah slave market was auctioning as many as 260 newly arrived slaves in a day.

When Mr. Swanson arrived in Savannah in 1766 and reported to Sir James for duty, he was surprised and disturbed to hear the governor announce proudly that he would furnish him a small cottage east of the town and that two African adults had been assigned to care for his personal needs. The governor brushed aside his quiet demurrals about the servants, but Swanson had actively condemned slavery while he was in England and was determined to grant manumission to the black couple as soon as possible.

He was delighted with his tabby cottage, which reminded him in many ways of those along the coast in England. Its thick walls were made of lime and seashells, and helped provide a cool interior. It was one of those farthest from the center of Savannah and backed up to the open marshland, which looked like a huge sea of waving grasses but hid a web of streams, deep and uncrossable at high tide, in which he could easily catch a mess of sea trout and an occasional flounder.

Within a week, a soldier delivered the man and woman to Swanson's small home, and he was surprised to see that a girl child was peeping out from behind her mama's skirts.

The soldier said, "I see on this paper that their names are Cato and Phebe, and the pickaninny ain't got no name yet. They belonged to a man named Joseph Dolly on Ossabaw Island who died owing some taxes, and the governor picked them up at the public sale. They been over here about six years and can speak some words."

Quintus was somewhat embarrassed after the soldier left, but realized that he was expected to give the Negroes a place to stay and something to do. As a benevolent gesture, Quintus decided that he would assign them the last name of Dolly and instruct the couple in how to use the King's English, discover and enhance whatever talents they might have, and learn the proper legal procedure for releasing them from a life of slavery. He soon learned that they called the girl Quanimo, the name of her father's mother.

Perhaps to assuage his conscience about owning other human beings or just to exercise his talent as a former teacher, Quintus decided that Quanimo would be given an education, since she was about six years old. As the governor's personal assistant, he felt that he could ignore the colonial law that prescribed a penalty of £15 for anyone who taught a slave to read and write. He had a small library of which he was very proud, and he enjoyed teaching the girl for an hour or so each day when he was not traveling with the governor. He was surprised and delighted at how eager she was to be with him, and how rapidly she learned. After a year or two of enjoying their services, Mr. Swanson no longer considered freedom for his slaves. It was a source of pride to him that Quanimo was reading the books and papers in his library.

Quintus Swanson died in March 1775, and the property of his modest estate was sold at a public auction. To their distress, the slaves were sold individually. They were torn apart tearfully, with hopes that someday they could be reunited. At the auction, Quanimo noticed that most bids for the men were about £45, for women £25, and £10 for children old enough to be separated from their parents. She couldn't tell if the same man bought both of her parents, and she wept silently when she realized that she would never see her mother and father again. When she was led to the center of the platform, she could hear some ribald comments from the men—that she wasn't old enough to do much work but would be good for other things. She couldn't understand the exact amount paid for her, because the auctioneer's words were a cacophony, but the length of the bidding indicated that it was as much as an adult price. Quanimo decided then that she would never reveal her familiarity with the English language.

Although it was not necessary, an iron bracelet was put on her right arm and she and three black men were secured to the back of a two-wheeled cart and instructed by their purchaser to follow it. They soon arrived at dockside and were herded aboard a large flatboat, about twelve feet wide and thirty feet long, containing a number of empty hogsheads. From the scattered grains of rice on the bottom, she surmised that this crop had been brought to market in Savannah. There was a square sail furled near the bow, and she soon counted eight slaves carrying supplies onto the vessel, obeying the unequivocal orders of another black man.

As soon as the loading was complete, the boat was shoved away from the dock, and the men rowed it clumsily to the middle of the stream, where the outgoing tide helped with the movement of the vessel. The men rowed steadily, except when the fitful westerly wind permitted the sail to be used. The four newly acquired slaves were used to spell the crew when they were tired, but Quanimo was never asked to do anything. She sat near the stern leaning against a barrel and listened intently to her new owner, Mordecai Singleton, talking to the black "driver," whom he called Big William. Their destination was Hopewell plantation, on the north bank of the Ogeechee River. She stayed in her place, except when she moved behind the pile of hogsheads and squatted to urinate. She watched the men drink dipperfuls of water from a barrel near the mast, but refrained from doing so herself, since she was not working.

When the boat finally docked late in the afternoon, it was met by several other slaves, the owner's wife, Elizabeth, and a white overseer named Andrew Perkins, who was quite deferential to the owner and seemed to be a polite and gentle man. Mr. Mordecai pointed out the five slaves to Perkins, assumed that the supplies would be properly unloaded, and walked to the big house with his wife. Perkins immediately changed character, cursing the slaves, giving excessive orders in harsh terms, and then ordering the new slaves to step forward.

He walked slowly around them, prodding each one with the butt of his riding whip. Finally, he asked, "What are your bloody names?" One by one, the four men responded, and when Quanimo gave hers, he shouted, "What the hell kind of name is that?"

She mumbled, "Dunno, sah, jes muname."

Perkins thought for a minute and said, "You need a short one, like ever'body else. From now on, your name is Quash."

Later, Quanimo learned that this was the way it was entered on the plantation's books, and what her white masters and the other slaves would always call her.

Quash quickly learned the Georgia laws and plantation rules designed to control slaves: they needed a written paper to leave the plantation; no more than seven males could travel together without a white to accompany them; they could not carry a firearm, purchase liquor, or buy or sell anything; large assemblies were prohibited, as was the playing of drums, horns, or other loud instruments that might call slaves together. Some of the prohibitions were ignored, such as assembling and playing music, but they could be imposed at any time and the slaves were made to feel that they had special privileges when the laws were not strictly enforced. Also, some of the best slave musicians were ordered to play for plantation owners' parties.

Quash was assigned to one of the smallest shacks, where she found two women and five small children living. Her part of the space was four nails on the wall, and a place on the floor large enough for a tick filled with rice straw. There was a small clump of palmettos behind the shack, where all of them relieved themselves. Sarah, a middle-aged woman, was from Sierra Leone, and Ida, a few years older than Quash, thought she was from

Ghana. Both had been on the plantation for four years and had never worked anywhere except in the fields or in the large garden.

Quash decided to conceal her previous experiences even from the other women and to blend in as much as possible with them. Their native languages had been different, but they now conversed easily in the Gullah dialect that had become common to all slaves along the coast. It was a language in its formative stage, with slaves from many West Africa regions using it as a lingua franca. Gullah was a mixture of English, a few words of French, and a conglomeration of the most convenient expressions from their native lands. Included were an increasing number of English words, but with a singsong inflexion that made them almost incomprehensible to white people. It interested Quash to hear the African words spoken by her masters and their guests, especially those who worked closely with the slaves. Many words like "tote," "goober," "gumbo," "yam," and "cooter" were often substituted for "carry," "peanut," "okra," "sweet potato," and "tortoise."

Illiteracy prevailed among the common laborers, except for one elderly man who could read (or recite from memory) a few passages from the Holy Bible. Big William was able to write, laboriously inscribing names and work records in a journal provided by the plantation owner.

For the first time in her life, Quash tried to become familiar with the culture of her race. She knew that her parents, like Big William, had come from Senegal and she had spoken their native language as a young child, but later her mother had encouraged her to rely on English whenever possible. Quash learned immediately that the women despised and feared the overseer, but respected Big William and depended on him to protect them and to meet their basic needs. Their advice was that she remain as unobtrusive as possible whenever she was in the presence of white people.

Big William was a constant subject of conversation among the other slaves, because he controlled almost every aspect of their lives. Because of the similarity in production techniques in Africa and Virginia, and down through Georgia, rice growers could estimate how much land an able-bodied worker could plant, or cultivate, or harvest in a day. Such a worker was called a "full hand," a designation given to about eight out of ten adult slaves. The system was somewhat flexible, but Quash was told that a full hand was expected to work a specific square area, whether planting, weeding, or harvesting rice. Smaller tracts were assigned to children and to adults who were old or weak. Depending on their strength and dexterity, they were expected to do three-quarters, half, or just one-quarter as much work. Well-behaved slaves were free of work when the daily or weekly task was done and approved by a driver. Slaves worked in larger groups in such common tasks as clearing new ground, digging canals and ditches, threshing rice, and cultivating corn.

The first morning after her arrival, Quash accompanied the other women to work in the rice fields. It was planting time, which they told her would run from March to May. Big William was waiting for her, asked to see her palms, said they looked like a baby's ass, and stated that she would be classified as a half-hand because of her apparent weakness and inexperience. It was backbreaking labor, wading barefoot through ankle-deep water and transferring the rice shoots from a flat bag on her back into the soft bottom.

The main rice fields were in a big bend of the Ogeechee, and salt water never intruded. At high tide the still-flowing fresh water was above where the rice was planted, permitting the two main canals to be filled twice a day. Heavy wooden gates controlled the flow of water from the river to and from these canals, and smaller gates or piled-up dirt were used to plug the ever-smaller channels leading to different areas. The river water was used both to nurture the growing stalks and to drown emerging grass and weeds. At times, the fields were permitted to dry so that surviving weeds could be pulled up or chopped with hoes. Each plot in a rice field became the personal responsibility of a particular worker, so everyone could tell whose fault it was if there was a poor stand or a weedy area, and Quash soon felt a sense of ownership for the area under her care.

Big William had two other drivers working under him, each in charge of half the field hands. The other men were used in clearing land, digging irrigation trenches, plowing furrows in dry rice fields, sawing lumber, caring for the livestock, cultivating corn, potatoes, and other crops on the plantation's high ground, or serving as carpenters, blacksmiths, or leather workers.

For the first few days Quash worked between Sarah and Ida on an area half as large as theirs, and even then they helped plant some of the plot assigned to her so they could move abreast up and down the field. She had to stand erect frequently to ease the pain in her back, and was afraid that the driver or even the overseer would notice that she was not working steadily.

Sarah was talkative and inclined to answer a steady stream of questions, mostly about other women. Quash learned that two older women were caring for the thirty-two small children, three were responsible for cooking the slaves' big evening meals and enough bread, potatoes, rice, and sometimes meat for mornings and at noontime, two were assigned to help the male gardener, three worked in the big house, and four women were now too old to leave their cabins and perform any useful tasks.

Quash was somewhat surprised when she learned that a doctor and his assistants from Savannah provided the same medical care for the owner's family and the slaves, but later she came to understand that his slaves were Mordecai Singleton's most valuable possessions, the source of his income and the measure of his wealth and social prestige. In fact, the slaves were usually worth about twenty times as much as the entire plantation on which they lived and worked.

The planting season continued for the next two months, as the crew moved from one field to another. Within two weeks, Quash could stay abreast of the other women and paused no more often than they to get the kink out of her backbone. She was proud when Big William met the group of women early one morning, looked at her, and said, "You be a full hand now." From then on, her plot was the same size as that of the other women.

Quash Dolly was a slender girl of medium height, as black as her grandparents in Africa, always quiet and modest, and unaware that her posture and demeanor somehow set her apart. She seemed to retain her dignity even when she was wading barefoot in water and muck with her long skirt pulled up between her legs and tied around her waist. Although relatively young, a few months past seventeen, she did her work well and was respected by the other slave women.

One day, she and the other workers noticed Master Mordecai and his wife, Elizabeth, riding their horses near the field and stopping to talk to Big William. They seemed to be looking closely at the women, all of whom paid special attention to their work and refrained from glancing toward their owner and supervisor. As they were leaving the field that afternoon and walking toward their quarters, Big William motioned for Quash to come to him. Her mind quickly reviewed the status of her work plots, trying to remember if there were any that would warrant his criticism.

He said, "Quash, the missus want a worker in de big house, and you maybe can do it."

She tried to think of a reply but realized that none was necessary. He had already made the decision. She had never been near the big house but had exchanged a few words with Maggie, the mulatto slave who was in charge of cooking and cleaning for the master's family. She was treated with great respect, as one who had lived on the Hopewell plantation for more than twenty years and had personally served Mordecai's parents before his father, Archibald, had died and his widowed mother moved to Savannah.

Maggie sent for her late that afternoon, shortly after sundown, and made it plain that she had been involved in choosing Quash to serve under her. She explained that three women usually worked in the house, cooking, cleaning, and caring for the personal needs of the family. Recently, the young couple had been entertaining more guests, and Miss Elizabeth had decided that they needed extra help in the kitchen and serving meals.

Maggie asked if she had any clothes other than those worn in the field.

"Yes'm, I hab a few, but some may be too little."

"Fetch 'em."

When Quash unwrapped her small bundle of clothes, Maggie looked up in surprise.

"Did you steal these?"

"No'm, my master give me them fo' I come here."

"Put'm back. I get you sum mo' fo' de kitchen."

Maggie thought for a few moments, and decided not to ask any more questions.

Quash's work, mostly in the kitchen, was less strenuous now, but she missed being out of doors during the changing seasons, the more unrestrained camaraderie among the workers, the rhythmic songs that helped pass the time, and the days when her tasks in the fields were completed early enough to enjoy fishing in the river or large canals. Now she had to be in the big house seven days a week, at least an hour before the family was expected to need attention, and to stay there until after all the supper dishes were washed.

In a short time, comprehending the English language perfectly, she understood much of what was happening on the plantation. Such information was freely available, as Singleton and his family discussed almost every subject with little restraint when the slaves were present. She wondered about this at first, but soon realized that they assumed that black women, except for Maggie, were too ignorant to understand words of more than one syllable, could not comprehend complicated issues, and that it really didn't matter in any case if a mere slave knew things about their personal affairs.

Mordecai Singleton had recently inherited this seven-thousand-acre plantation by the river, accumulated from his late father's political influence and an early land grant formula designed to encourage maximum settlement and utilization of land, especially along the Georgia coast.

Mordecai obviously had many friends in Savannah, who welcomed his frequent invitations to dine and spend the night on the plantation, one of those closest to the town. They enjoyed riding horseback along the trails and through the woods, and hunting deer, turkey, geese, duck, and quail during the fall and winter months. There was good fishing throughout the year, and for large banquets Big William was asked to net mullet, to gather bushels of oysters, and to prepare a part of the meals over coals on outdoor grills.

The more interesting events to Quash were when smaller groups assembled in what was called the great hall, which had an expandable table that could seat from eight to sixteen diners. She served often at these affairs and was impressed by the diversity of Singleton's guests. She overheard the young master reminiscing about past experiences on the plantation, and how his father had been loyal to the crown and deeply concerned about growing Whig strength in the coastal area. She was intrigued to hear her young master joking about condemnation of the Sons of Liberty in Savannah and the enthusiastic toasts to the king that had formerly prevailed in the dining hall. Nowadays, it was customary for her to serve groups of young men from Savannah who proposed different toasts—to some heroes who had thrown British tea into Boston Harbor, to General George Washington, and to independence of the colonies.

Because of a sense of duty to other slaves and her own personal interest, Quash attempted to overhear the owner's specific instructions to the overseer about affairs on the plantation. Singleton did not seem to be very interested in the details of crop production and the management of individual fields, which everyone knew to be the responsibility of Big William. But the colony's law required that a white man had to be in charge of any group of Negroes, and Perkins had to fulfill that role. It was he who made ultimate decisions about such things as the slaves' housing, food allocation, rewards and punishment, and access to medical care. Quash noticed that Singleton kept careful records of overall expenses and income from the farm, liked to demonstrate his knowledge of field operations, and demanded strict accountability from Perkins. The young master seemed to know the exact yield that was expected and realized from each of his fields, and one overall standard that he mentioned often was that the average amount of rice produced per slave should be ten barrels. Earlier, she had heard him receive almost the exact same information from Big William.

One of Singleton's primary regrets, expressed often to his wife, was the departure during the previous winter of William Overton, the dependable overseer who had served his father for fifteen years and had finally saved enough to buy his own small farm down near the Florida border. The new overseer, Andrew Perkins, had already been caught lying on two occasions and was suspected of some petty thefts, the most serious of which was an old pistol that had vanished from the owner's saddlebag after a hunt. Quash was almost certain that this would be the only crop season over which Perkins would preside, before being discharged after the rice harvest was completed in September.

Perkins was shrewd and devious and seemed to have two almost completely different characters. He was quiet, well mannered, deferential, and addressed the slaves firmly but politely in the presence of the owner's family. But even with these best efforts to make a good first impression, he was a decidedly unpleasant man. Tall and thin, he had a long, aquiline nose that hooked down over a straggly and drooping mustache. His most unattractive feature was his mouth. He had obviously been struck a severe blow in his earlier years, and his upper lip was thrust to the left side and greatly enlarged, which made the lower part of his face seem strangely diminished. Perkins was acutely aware of this defect and had an acquired habit of keeping one of his hands in front of his mouth, ostensibly to rub his nose or to stroke his mustache. This also helped to conceal his crooked and blackened teeth, discolored by a lifetime of chewing tobacco and a habitual lack of cleanliness.

When away from his employer, Perkins almost constantly abused those under his direction, apparently convinced that they would be more productive if afraid and intimidated. Slaves on the plantation were disturbed and resentful of the changes that Perkins had brought. The one among them who was most knowledgeable and personally involved was Big William. A slave himself, he had earned the confidence he enjoyed by hard work, intelligence, and an ability to perform his duties harmoniously with others in the closed plantation community. Perkins had been there only a few weeks when Mr. Singleton abruptly rejected his request to choose another slave as the work supervisor. The response was clear. "William will be head driver as long as I own this land. You'll have to get along with him."

Quash was satisfied with her work in the big house. Hopewell plantation was known to produce as much of the slaves' rations as possible, and adequate cropland was set aside for this purpose. Unlike most other plantations, Hopewell had a cane mill where a large quantity of molasses was distilled, and enough sweet potatoes were grown and carefully stored to last almost the entire year. Everyone on the plantation knew that the basic weekly quota for each slave was a peck of corn, a quart of molasses, and at least two pounds of pork, with twice as much beef sometimes substituted for pork. In addition, turnips, sweet potatoes, okra, and peas were grown in the large central garden, and extra rice during harvest season. The key to their diet was pork, which provided grease and was used to flavor the vegetables, and Quash had recently overheard Singleton tell Perkins to increase the pork allotment to three pounds a week. Instead, the slaves were still being issued only two pounds.

While Quash was washing breakfast dishes one morning, Perkins stepped inside the kitchen door just in time to overhear a remark she made about how she and other slaves were being shorted on the allocation of food. Their conversation was in Gullah, but, having been raised on the coast, he knew the dialect as well as Quash knew the language of the young master at the dining table. She was not surprised when, late that same afternoon, he sent for her to come to his cottage.

She was relieved to see that Big William was also in the room. Perkins said, "You bitch, you been accusing me of stealing food, and in the big house where anyone can hear you."

"No, sir, I ain't done that," which, to an uneducated ear, would sound like "Nosah ain dunat."

"You're lying now, and I've noticed how biggety you've been getting with the other niggers. I can't abide anything like this, and you need a lesson you won't forget."

He turned to William and said, "Put ten stripes on her back that she'll remember."

Quash had been whipped only once before, as a child by her father when she had stolen some paper and writing materials from Mr. Swanson's library. This was done after a severe lecture, and with a loving investment in her own maturation. Big William never carried a whip like the drivers who served under him, who draped one over their shoulder as a symbol of authority. They were permitted to inflict a lash on occasion, to drive home a point to a reluctant or inattentive worker, but more formal floggings had to be authorized by the overseer. Quash knew that Perkins ordered several slaves flogged each month, with ten or more lashes, and was always there personally to observe the punishment. Other penalties ranged from deprivation of privileges after tasks were completed, the wearing of chains, incarceration under harsh conditions, and even hanging. In the latter case, almost always for serious crimes against white people, colonial funds were used to compensate the owner for the loss of his property.

Quash had never known Big William to whip anyone, but now he told her to turn around, drop the calico shift down to expose her back, and put her hands against the tabby wall. She flinched as the leather whiplashes came, but moaned aloud only once when the thong tip wrapped around her side and popped on the nipple of her right breast. Even though Perkins was watching close enough for her to hear his deep breathing, she had a feeling that Big William held back on the strength of his blows. When the punishment was over, she untied the clothing from around her waist and pulled up her dress before she turned around.

Perkins said, "Don't forget to keep your mouth shut, or you'll get worse."

Quash assumed that she was being dismissed. She didn't lift her eyes from the floor or speak, but nodded her head, moved through the door, and returned to her cabin. As she left, she heard raised voices behind her. She felt better the next week, when Perkins directed that all slaves receive their three pounds of pork.

There was a general knowledge on the plantations that some of the young women, especially those who did housework, would be expected to have sex with owners or their grown sons. In return, some favors would usually be granted—either extra food, better living quarters, or perhaps even a trinket or two. Young Singleton, however, had never been known to take advantage of this opportunity, either before or after his father's death. Even Quash, who would be attractive to a man of any race, never felt that he wanted her.

After her whipping in Perkins's cabin, she was consoled by Big William, and lay several times with him, usually in a storage shed behind the blacksmith shop. She was attracted to him but realized that he would not have a permanent relationship with her. Although still childless, he and his wife had been together for only a year and were believed to be close and compatible. There would not have been any real stigma if Quash had delivered a child, but she was relieved that she did not become pregnant.

One afternoon, while the Singletons were visiting in Savannah, she was thumbing through a book in the library and glanced up to see Perkins watching her. She pretended to be dusting the bookshelf, then arranged the books neatly and turned to leave the room. He was blocking the door, and she could only stop and wait for him to move. He leered at her and said, "You trying to pretend you know how to read?"

She replied, in the Gullah dialect, that she was just cleaning the house.

He looked at her for a few moments. "You come by my house when you leave here."

She looked down at the floor and didn't respond, and he turned and left the room. Quash considered her plight. It was inconceivable that she could disobey directly an order from the overseer, and she doubted that she should consult them even if her mistress or Big William were available. She worked later than usual and then walked down the path. Perkins was in a chair on the porch, and when she looked at him he beckoned her toward him. By the time she got there, he had gone inside, leaving the door open. She heard him say, "Come on in," and proceeded into the cabin. He shut the door, and they faced each other. She noticed the short whip in his right hand.

She finally asked, "What you want wid me?"

In a somewhat strained voice, he said, "I want some of the same cunt that Big William's been getting in the storehouse."

She shook her head and moved toward the door, but Perkins grabbed her forearm and forced her to her knees, then knocked her down as he brought the butt of the whip against her face. He grabbed her before she could move, dragged her to his bed, and raped her with brutal thrusts of his body. From his actions and epithets, his excitement seemed to come from the suffering he was inflicting. Strangely, even more unpleasant than the intense pain of his blows, her twisted arm, and the sexual attack was the smell of his fetid breath in her face. When he crawled off the low bed and picked up the whip, she turned on her stomach and locked her fingers behind her head. He finally tired of beating her and slumped in a chair in the corner. Perkins made no attempt to stop Quash when she stood, with difficulty, adjusted her shift, and left the cabin.

Back in her quarters, the other women helped her clean and dress her wounds and quickly surmised what had happened. They called in one of the midwives, who ordered Quash to stay in bed for at least a day after the bleeding stopped. When Mrs. Singleton returned, the midwife told her that Quash had some kind of malady and shouldn't be near the children, and Maggie arranged for her to do light work in the yard and garden until her external wounds healed and she was again presentable enough to work in the big house. Now, though, she was still weak, and the flow of blood resumed each time she spent several hours on normal work in the yard. She was still afraid of the overseer, who was often on his small front porch and seemed to be leering at her when she walked by on the way to or from the big house. One afternoon, Big William was waiting for her and expressed his regret that she had been ill. She was surprised and somewhat disappointed that he had not learned more specifically about her problem, but remembered that this was threshing time, and that he was fully absorbed with the work of the field hands.

As she approached him, he smiled and said, "I'm glad you're better, and back in the big house."

She replied, "Yes, I'm better."

"After dark, you be wid me?"

"I cain't do it right now."

"If it's de rag, I can live wid it."

Quash decided to tell Big William what had happened, and she was concerned about his reaction.

He finally said, "Nudder tam, 'em be ded."

Quash didn't think Perkins would actually be killed, but she wasn't sure. She was concerned about Big William, knowing that the entire community would be aroused against a slave who physically attacked a white supervisor, regardless of any extenuating circumstances or the reputations of the men involved. She tried to dissuade him, and he finally said, "He be knowing."

Within a few days, Big William assured her that she would not be assaulted again, and she noticed an intense strain between him and Perkins.

When Quash was once again able to return to the big house, her interest increased in what was happening beyond the plantation. Mr. Mordecai
began to entertain more of the young men from Savannah, who were never
circumspect in their comments, especially after a number of toasts at the
conclusion of their meals. While serving the table or lingering just outside
the door, she was completely ignored as she listened attentively to the conversation. It became clear to her that the Americans were expecting a
British attack on Savannah, but were supremely confident that they could
repel any foray from the sea. They compared the marshlands and deep
sloughs as a natural defense similar to the swamps and rivers that had
helped to make fruitless all attempts of the Americans to attack St. Augustine. She could envision every detail of the marsh near Savannah as the
men described the placement of guns and troops to block any movement of
British troops westward from Skidaway Island. She began to wonder if she
could exchange this special knowledge for her ultimate goal in life.

When Big William arrived, the others left, and she told him about the
British armada approaching Savannah and reminded him of having lived
in the marsh.

He listened and said, "De British be better."

There were few plantations south of Savannah with which Thomas
Brown and his Florida Rangers were not thoroughly familiar. A number of
his men were former slaves who had moved down to St. Augustine with
their masters and had been granted manumission by British law. Brown's
subordinate officers were always eager to find good men, and those familiar with plantation life were especially valuable as collectors of intelligence
information. He had relatively easy relationships with the slave population,
and they helped keep him abreast of the situation on the larger plantations
along the coast, some of which had several hundred slaves. Using these
and other sources, Brown was able to maintain a careful record of the Tory
owners who supported the crown, and his men had strict orders not to
abuse them. The others were increasingly mistreated, so that they soon
learned to restrain or conceal their support of the Whigs and to avoid any
contact with those who opposed British rule.

Hopewell, which was very near Savannah, had never been targeted by
the Rangers' raiding parties. The elder Mr. Singleton had been a close
friend of Governor Wright and a helpful source of information for the

Rangers even after the Whigs gained control of Savannah. But the situation had begun to change after his death, and one of the Negro Rangers brought word to Brown that young Singleton had been consorting with members of the Sons of Liberty. On his next visit to the coastal area, Brown decided to visit Hopewell, and he and about twenty of his Rangers camped on the riverbank several miles upstream from the plantation.

It was a week before Christmas, and Brown was sitting near a small fire in front of his tent, eating some venison that had been roasted for his traveling party. Just at dusk, one of his men walked to within a few yards of the commander and waited to be recognized. He was an older Negro who had adopted the name Liverpool, from the home port of the slave ship that had brought him to America. Having worked for several years in the local rice fields before he and his former master had moved to St. Augustine, he had many friends among the slaves near their present campsite. Brown finally looked up and asked, "What is it, Liverpool?"

"De head driver from Hopewell want to see you."

"What does he want?"

"Don't know, sah, but he be a good man, name Big William."

"Let him come, then."

"He be here now."

Liverpool turned and beckoned with his hand, and Big William stepped from the shadows. He approached Brown and informed him without preliminary discussion that he had some information that might be useful.

Brown decided to ask a few questions, to assess the intelligence and reliability of the man.

"Do you know how many slaves are on the plantation?"

"Yassuh, they's one hundred twenty-eight right now, able to work."

"How much rice do you produce?"

"This year, better'n fifty bushels to the acre on 'bout three hundred acres."

To test the slave, Brown asked, as though he didn't know, "And how many pounds to a bushel?"

"Forty-five, sah."

Big William was not at all uncomfortable, answered without delay, and was obviously familiar with the farming operation on the plantation.

Brown then asked, "And do the Singletons have many visitors at Hopewell?"

"Yassuh, mostly in the wintertime, with hunting good."

"Who comes?"

"Wal, de governor have been, and other mens from Savannah."

"Do they come together, at the same time?"

"Nosah, they mostly comes separate."

There was a long pause, and then Brown asked, "What brings you to see me?"

"A woman work in de big house, heard de British come to Savannah."

"That may be right, but what's that got to do with me?"

"You works wid the British, and she may help."

Brown was skeptical but decided to waste a few more minutes.

"What in hell could a slave woman do?"

"She raise in de marsh, and know de way fum de ocean to de town."

Brown was instantly alert, well knowing that confident American forces were prepared for a British invasion and had deployed both troops and artillery along a slough two miles east of the city, covering the main route that would have to be taken by any force that attacked Savannah from the sea. Although he could not be certain when they would arrive, he and everyone else knew that Campbell's forces had left New York six weeks ago, and that Colonel Prevost was supposed to be moving north from Florida but had been held up near the St. Illa River.

Brown said, "Bring her to me."

Without any reticence, Big William replied, "She want sump'n."

"What is it, for God's sake?"

"Freedom."

CHAPTER 34

The British Take Savannah

Slavery had never been an easy subject for the Florida Rangers to address. Brown realized that on all plantations in Georgia and many in Florida, slaves comprised more than half the total value of the owners' holdings. Although the British government had long ago passed laws outlawing the slave trade either from Liverpool or from Africa, it was not illegal for the colonists to keep any slaves they owned and to buy and sell them as desired. If it was known that he helped to free a slave even from a Whig owner, many of the most prominent Tories would condemn this as a threat to their own economic existence.

Brown finally responded, "If she is helpful, she'll be free, even if I have to buy her myself. Let Liverpool bring her to me, and don't let anybody else know about this."

Quash met Brown before sunrise the next morning, and the commander immediately asked what information she had to offer.

She put aside all restraint and amazed Brown by saying, in perfect English, "My parents were owned by the governor's secretary, Quintus Swanson, whose home was east of Savannah near the road to Tybee Island. I grew up there, was educated by Mr. Swanson, and spent my youth in the marshes. I have never spoken English like this after I was sold to Mr. Singleton, but work in the Hopewell big house with three other women. I was serving dinner this past Sunday and heard some young men from Savannah talking about the same marsh areas where we lived. They ignore us slaves when they talk, and I listened carefully. The revolutionaries know the British are coming, and General Howe is defending the main road, which they believe to be the only one. I know a way around it."

While she spoke, Brown examined her carefully. Although her face was bruised, she was a beautiful black woman who stood erect, proud, and was more self-assured than any Negro he had ever seen. Her extraordinary appearance and demeanor increased his natural caution, and he asked, "Why do you tell me this?"

"Because of my good treatment by Mr. Swanson and my need to escape from the Hopewell overseer, Mr. Perkins. When I told Big William what I had learned, he urged me to talk to you."

Brown had Sergeant Alonzo Baker bring a chart of the coastal area. They could see that there was an almost impregnable bridge crossing where the main road was traversed by a deep waterway, only a half mile from the town. This crucial point was about ten miles from the open sea but only a fourth that distance from the nearest site where the British might land, and there was no other route into Savannah. When shown the map, Quash said that her previous home was near this defense point but that there was a back path, not used by white people, that could bypass the bridge and provide access to Savannah if the streams were crossed at low tide.

That night, Brown arranged for a large and fast canoe to carry himself, four oarsmen, and Quash Dolly down the Ogeechee and then up the inland waterway to Tybee Island. There, they hoped to meet the British forces and share their information with Colonel Campbell. Brown instructed Quash to lie in the bottom of the boat and not glance at Hopewell plantation as they passed. For the rest of the trip she kept a shawl around her head, concealing her face and even turning away from any shore area where observers might be present. They all knew that it would be only a few hours before an alarm was raised about a slave having escaped, and the system for capturing a runaway was highly organized and rapidly implemented.

Quash had no compunction about the action she was taking. Regardless of the character of plantation owners or their treatment of Negroes, there was almost unanimity among slaves that their lot would be improved if the British could prevail in the ongoing war. She tended to draw a general conclusion from her own comparison of treatment by Quintus Swanson with what she had recently experienced at the hands of Andrew Perkins. She knew that former slaves now in St. Augustine and up the Atlantic Coast had been well treated by the British, and that some had even been given uniforms and weapons so they could engage in combat. More important, of course, was this unexpected chance for complete manumission, as promised by Thomas Brown.

As he waited in a small encampment on the beach, hidden by an overhanging bluff, Brown sent a few men toward Savannah to explore the marshland and observe the deployment of American forces. It was cold, and a light rain was being blown into their sheltered area by a strong wind. These men were experienced in infiltrating loosely structured military lines, disguised as farmers, fishermen, tradesmen, or even as militia or Continental soldiers. As a former slave, Liverpool was one of the Rangers' most effective spies. Shrewd and eloquent, he was equipped with a standard pass used by trusted servants to go on errands for their masters. By the time the British fleet was sighted, two days before Christmas, Brown had a complete report awaiting its commander, Colonel Archibald Campbell.

Their plans succeeded far beyond any expectation. The British forces landed on December 29, and Brown provided a thorough assessment of the deployment of Whig forces under General Robert Howe, Governor

John Houstoun, and Colonel George Walton. The British launched a mock raid against the main American forces, while the real force waited for low tide at night and followed Quash Dolly quietly along a narrow and little-used path through the palmettos and across the tidal streams. And then the British troops moved quietly and unimpeded into the town.

At daybreak, panic seized the citizens of Savannah and the forces that were supposed to defend it. Many officers and men deserted their posts and attempted to escape. Neither General Howe nor any of his subordinates really knew what had happened, but the word spread rapidly that a slave woman had guided them across the marsh. The British captured 423 Americans, killed nearly 100, and more than 30 others were drowned when they tried to cross the waterways as the tide rose. Only 7 British troops were killed. Everything in the city was taken, including 45 cannons, 637 rifles and muskets, and a large supply of powder, shell, and shot.

Despite his best efforts, Colonel Campbell was unable to control his own forces as they swept through the defenseless city. They pillaged the stores, raped some of the women, and disemboweled some of the captured soldiers even after they lay down their weapons. General Howe, with his few remaining troops, retreated northward along the Savannah River, crossed the stream into South Carolina, and issued an order for his surviving Continental troops to reassemble.

Brown was deeply disappointed by the atrocities of the victorious Redcoats. Although not especially concerned about the suffering of the Americans, he realized that recruitment of the survivors to the British cause would now be much more difficult. He remained close to Quash Dolly and kept her apart from any conflict. He made certain that everyone knew of the crucial contribution of the slave woman, and she was soon being treated as a heroine. Colonel Campbell ignored any compensation that might be due her master, Mordecai Singleton, and made arrangements for her to proceed on the first British ship sailing from Savannah to Nassau, along with a reward of £50 pounds and official papers certifying that she was a free woman.

British commander Campbell found Thomas Brown's assistance to be invaluable, as he provided a remarkably complete and accurate dossier of merchants and plantation owners, describing their holdings and their degree of loyalty to the king. Not without some degree of personal prejudice, he also advised his superiors as to the honesty of loyalty pledges from many of the more prominent colonists. Brown examined the list of captured Georgians and advised who should be either released on parole or imprisoned and their property confiscated. He also named a few who had violated previous oaths of allegiance to the king and were to be executed for treason. While he performed these pleasant duties as a supreme judge in Savannah, he was contemplating plans for the British to move 150 miles up the river to Augusta.

Recruited by General Howe to join in what was expected to be its easy defense, Elijah Clarke and sixty of his militiamen had been camped on the north side of Savannah, near the river. As surprised as anyone when gunfire broke out in the center of the city, Elijah roused his men and charged in to join the battle. It was obvious that the British were in control, but the Georgia militia engaged in the fruitless defense long enough for Elijah to see three of his men killed and nine wounded. Then they managed quite easily to escape capture and joined other Americans in what was at first a frantic retreat.

The British chose not to pursue General Howe or his troops, so there was an orderly crossing into South Carolina at a place called Sister's Ferry. Captain Clarke and his men were requested to stand guard, and they watched the big ferry make repeated trips across the river, loaded almost to the gunwales with troops, horses, and what was left of their arms and ammunition. He thought about just taking his men home but decided to seek official permission and also to learn what plans General Howe had for the further defense of Georgia. He found the general alone in his tent, surprisingly attended only by a lieutenant and two sergeants. After the lieutenant obtained the general's permission, Elijah approached the tent, letting his boots make as much noise as possible so Howe could hear him as he walked near the closed tent flap.

He said, "General, permission to enter?"

He heard a muffled voice say, "Enter."

The general was sitting on a campstool, with his elbows on his knees. His face was ashen, and his eyes were red as though he had been weeping. He looked up without speaking, and Elijah had a feeling that the general did not recognize him.

He said, "General, this is Captain Elijah Clarke, and I've come for further orders for my men."

General Howe looked at him dully and finally said, "Just get the hell out of Georgia."

"Sir, our families are all up the river, and we can't afford to leave them and the others. We seen what the British done to the people in Savannah."

"What do you want, Captain?"

"To go back home, sir, and to keep on fightin'."

"You can go where you wish, but the British are too strong for us to fight them anymore. I've sent orders down to Sunbury for all the troops to join me in Carolina."

"Well, General, I figure we might have enough men up the river to give the Redcoats some real trouble around Augusta."

"I've also ordered all my troops in Augusta to cross the river."

Clarke's face flushed in anger and disgust to know that the entire colony was being abandoned, and after a few moments he was glad that the general was looking at the ground and that he hadn't expressed his feelings.

He took a step backward. "Thank you, sir. We'll be goin' home."

Aaron Hart was waiting nearby and quickly joined Clarke.

"What's wrong, Cap'n?"

"That bloody general has lost Savannah, and now he's givin' up Georgia."

He went on to recount the conversation and finally said, "Howe and his Continentals was in Savannah for more than three months and never knew as much about the marsh as what Campbell learned from one nigger woman in two hours."

"What are we going to do now, Cap'n?"

"We're goin' home. I ain't never goin' to fight ag'in under a politician or an officer without guts. I believe me and Dooly and Twiggs together can hold on to at least two hundred men that will keep on fightin', and I don't believe any Redcoats or Burnfoot's Rangers can tangle with us in our own hills and swamps."

What was left of a Georgia government convened in Augusta to face the prospect of a total and permanent loss of their state to the British. An executive council condemned General Howe, expressed confidence that recently appointed General Benjamin Lincoln would serve well as commander of the Southern Department of the United States, adopted a site in Wilkes County as the state capital, and made other rudimentary decisions. In reconstituting the state's defenses, they commissioned Clarke as colonel, and both Twiggs and Dooly as lieutenant colonels, with the militia in Burke and Wilkes counties under their command.

The British found little opposition in the state. Colonel Campbell's troops waited a month and then pushed all the way up the Savannah River to Augusta without the loss of a single soldier. British dragoons were ordered to scour the countryside within thirty miles of the river to confiscate as many supplies as possible and to enforce loyalty to the crown. Campbell issued a stern and binding order that the Quaker settlement be spared as an example of benevolence, and expressed confidence that the Indians and the loyalists in the backcountry of Georgia and South Carolina would rally to the British flag if they were treated well and that all opposition to the king's forces would disappear.

More than 1,300 new loyalists came out of the farms and woods of north Georgia and swore allegiance to the king, and were formed into twenty militia companies for the protection of British-held Georgia from South Carolina raids. For all practical purposes, there were now only twelve states. British officials honored Colonel Campbell as the first military commander to have "taken a stripe and star from the rebel flag of Congress." It seemed obvious that the Redcoats would soon take Charles Town and control South Carolina, and the British commanders were confident that only a mopping-up exercise would be necessary to assure a solid base for military moves northward into North Carolina and Virginia.

They considered themselves to be embarked on the final stages of the war.

CHAPTER 35

The Hornet's Nest

1779

Ethan Pratt had seen the Quakers, Morrises, and many of his other neighbors swear allegiance to the crown, believing that the war was over and that the Declaration of Independence had been in vain. Along with a few other families along the more remote frontier, the Pratts still tried to avoid an alignment with either Whigs or Tories.

Knowing that Campbell had moved up the river with more than five hundred troops, the Georgia militia leaders had to face reality and made no attempt to defend Augusta. From his home in Wilkes County, however, Elijah Clarke assembled as many men as possible, using lists that had been carefully maintained by Aaron Hart. With about 180 men gathered, Clarke nodded to Dooly, who spoke first.

"Men, all the Continental troops have left for South Carolina, and we hear that General Howe has resigned in order to defend hisself against a court-martial. General Lincoln is in command of what troops warn't killed or captured, and has set up headquarters in Purysburg."

Someone shouted out, "Where in hell is Purysburg?"

Dooly replied, "It's across the river in South Carolina, about thirty miles above Savannah. He's put out a call for militia from the Carolinas and Virginia to join in keeping the British from moving north toward Charles Town."

"Why don't we join up with him?"

Elijah Clarke spoke for the first time. "Bullshit! We ain't ready to give up Georgia, and I sho' as hell won't put my men under another general that don't know his arse about fightin' in the woods."

There was a general murmur of agreement, and Dooly continued.

"We've got two things to do now. One is to convince all our neighbors that we're going to fight on, and not to give up to the British. The other is to divide up into small groups, guard every trail coming into the back-country of Wilkes and Burke counties, and kill as many Redcoats as we can."

Elijah said, "What we need to do is carve out some territory here where we feel the most at home. All of us needs to study it and figure out how to guard every trail against any bugger that tries to come in without our permission, jest with one or two men."

Aaron Hart said, "You mean a sanctuary."

"I don't even know what that means. I'm talkin' about like bein' inside our own hornet's nest so anybody that messes with us will live—or die—to regret it."

The men were excited by the idea and began to look at some of the maps they had prepared and used for military training. Within a couple of hours they had identified an area big enough to include several separated forts with good trails connecting them, with maximum natural protection from impassable creeks, swamps, and hills. Just by felling a few trees, it would be easy to close any of the old trails they would not be needing. Elijah summarized these decisions and added, "This has got to be our special place, but there's two things to remember. We've got to let Redcoats, Thomas Brown and them other savages, and everybody else know, by God, that if they come in here ag'in us, they'll be dead men. There cain't be no exceptions. The other thing is that this is not just for hidin'. It's for attackin' as long as we're able to fight. Mine and Dooly's farms happens to be on the edge of this area, and my fort will be useful sometimes as a meetin' place. We'll be able to move out fast, to our own farms or toward Augusta or across the river to Carolina, and to come back—sometimes in a hurry!"

It was inevitable that the protected area would be called the Hornet's Nest.

Georgia's leaders began rallying supporters in the backcountry region. Their first efforts were to convince as many settlers as possible that the revolution was not lost, and to use either promises or intimidation to secure their support. The militia commanders issued edicts in north Georgia that all property owners had to swear allegiance to the Continental government or lose their estates, and a few settlers began to reject their recent oaths of allegiance to the crown. This was not enough for Elijah Clarke and his most militant followers, who wanted to give a vivid warning to those who remained subservient to the British.

One of the defecting Whigs was a prominent landowner, Zachariah Timmerman, whom John Dooly had warned personally to renounce his oath of loyalty to the crown. He immediately went to Augusta and surrendered to Colonel Campbell. The British spread the word about Timmerman's wise action and placed him under the care of a corporal named MacAllister, a favorite of the colonel. Within a week, an American raiding party entered the compound, attacked MacAllister, killed, disemboweled, and decapitated him, and took Timmerman just outside the town, where he was hanged, with a note pinned to his chest that said, "Justice." This was a harsh reminder to doubtful Whigs, but MacAllister's name became a battle cry for the furious British troops.

General Prevost, now occupying Savannah and serving as acting governor, seemed to have little interest in Augusta. Knowing of Brown's intense interest in the area, however, he directed that the Florida Rangers refrain from any movements northward along the Savannah River, and Brown was forced to comply. This meant, in effect, that few if any Creeks or Cherokees were available to join the British in the region, despite the earlier arrangements that had been made with Emistisiguo and even John Stuart. All British efforts would now be focused on Charles Town. Deprived of any dependable assistance except for his own troops, it was clear that Colonel Campbell and his five hundred men would be hard-pressed to hold Augusta against a concerted attack from the west.

Colonel Clarke was eager to retake Augusta but realized that Georgia's combined militia were not adequate. He sent Aaron Hart with a request to General Lincoln for assistance. The predictable reply was that holding Charles Town was his preeminent goal, which would require all available troops when the time came for its defense. However, he recognized the tactical importance of Augusta as a staging area from which the British would surely move by land toward the South Carolina coast, and promised to send 1,200 troops from Charles Town toward the Georgia city, commanded by a general named John Ashe, from North Carolina. The general was inexperienced but politically influential in his home state, and eager to demonstrate his military effectiveness.

These plans had to be delayed when British Lieutenant Colonel John Boyd moved from Carolina into north Georgia with seven hundred men, reported his presence to Colonel Campbell, and began to terrorize Whig families in the area. The written intelligence report to General Lincoln stated: "Like plundering banditti, they appropriate every species of property to their own use, abuse the inhabitants, and wantonly butcher anyone who opposes their rapacious demands."

Lincoln sent orders to Clarke to rally all the Georgians possible, and sent South Carolina's Colonel Andrew Pickens to help the Georgians defend themselves against Boyd's predatory troops.

When Campbell ordered Boyd and his seven hundred men, many recruited from among local Tories, to concentrate on destroying the few remaining Georgia militia, the British forces camped at a farm on Kettle Creek to rest, slaughter some cattle, and graze their horses. It was a prosperous farm, with canebrakes and a swamp on two sides. Colonels Clarke, Dooly, and Pickens, with 350 men, found Boyd's campfires from the previous day and closed in to within a mile of the farm. Dooly was on the right flank and Elijah Clarke was on the left, each with 100 men, and Pickens was in the center with 150. At daybreak, the Americans launched a simultaneous attack. Boyd fell, mortally wounded, and the remaining British troops fled across the stream. Clarke forded the open creek under fire, and his horse was shot, falling on him. He narrowly escaped drowning but was able to join in mopping up the battlefield and in the subsequent celebrations.

Following the debacle in Savannah, Kettle Creek was one of the most startling victories of the war, and news of it swept through the colonies. The psychological impact was enormous, coming at a time when the general presumption had been that the British were invulnerable and the revolution in the south was doomed. Many Whigs renounced their oaths of allegiance to the crown and returned to their homes, and a greatly encouraged General Lincoln dispatched General Ashe on to Augusta and even began preparations to retake Savannah.

Most of Boyd's men went back home to North Carolina, but two hundred reached Augusta, where Campbell's regular troops treated them with contempt. One hundred British had been killed and seventy-five taken prisoner, five of whom were former Whigs whose names were known by Colonel Pickens. They were hanged as traitors. The Americans suffered nine killed and twenty-three wounded and captured, including a small man named Stephen Heard, who had been a large landowner and a prominent Whig politician in Savannah. When Colonel Campbell heard about the hangings at Kettle Creek, he decided to execute Heard as a public demonstration of British justice. Heard had a giant house slave called Mammy Kate, who learned that he was in Augusta and sentenced to be hanged. She filled a large basket with clothing and some pies and cakes as gifts for the British guards, entered the compound, and got permission to visit her master so that he could dress appropriately during his last hours of life. Wanting as much of a pageant as possible for the public execution, the British agreed. Mammy Kate went into the guardhouse, put Heard in the basket, arranged the pile of clothes under a blanket on his cot to resemble a sleeping man, placed the basket on her head, and carried him out of Augusta. Back home again, he set her free and gave her a home and a surrounding tract of land on his small plantation.

After a few days, General Ashe arrived across the river from Augusta with his large North Carolina army, and Colonel Campbell abandoned the town and moved down the river to Hudson's Ferry to join troops of the main British force. He was surprised to learn that they faced a dangerous situation. The British still held Savannah securely, but General Prevost had sent most of his men back to St. Augustine, and their upriver forces were now almost surrounded by General Lincoln's troops across the river in South Carolina and Ashe's army to the north.

Although welcomed to the region by the Georgia militiamen when they met briefly after his forces crossed the Savannah into Augusta, General Ashe quickly made it obvious that he resented any suggestions from Elijah Clarke and John Twiggs about how his troops should be deployed and used. Looking at rudimentary maps, Ashe's staff decided that an open meadow on high ground north of Briar Creek would offer them every advantage. Enemy troops would have to cross the creek to reach them from the south, the Savannah River provided protection from the east, and there were relatively flat fields and woods to the north and west that would provide access for supplies and give the Americans plenty of room for maneuvering.

When Colonel Clarke sent an offer of assistance, General Ashe replied flatly, "Tell Clarke that I'll take my position upriver from the British, which will prevent them moving back toward Augusta. I've studied the maps and am familiar with the area we'll be occupying, so I can handle any developments. The militia forces can come in to join me if they wish. I'll let them know when I decide to move south to take Campbell's army."

It was obvious that Ashe and his staff were supremely confident of their ability and wanted to have a direct confrontation with the despised British. His ambition was to equal or exceed what the militiamen had done at Kettle Creek.

In the meantime, Colonel Campbell learned that Thomas Brown was in the area and, without consulting General Prevost, sent for the Ranger commander. They discussed alignment of military forces, and Campbell asked for advice. It had been raining for several hours, and Brown replied, "Colonel, my men and I know this region well. There is a ford near Ashe's camp that I'm sure is well guarded, but it can't be used except when the water is low. If this rain sets in, the lower reaches of Briar Creek will be flooding. Give me a chance to assess the situation, and I'll be back with you tomorrow morning."

As soon as their meeting was over, Brown sent for Newota.

The heavy rains continued, and when Briar Creek began to rise, General Ashe was even more convinced that the British would not be likely to make any troop movements during the inclement weather, much less to cross the swollen stream.

CHAPTER 36

"Take No Prisoners!"

MARCH 1779

Ethan Pratt awoke from a fitful sleep in his narrow cot in one of the corners farthest from the fireplace. In the dim light from the still-glowing embers he could see his son, Henry, on a pallet on the floor almost under his own cot, and his wife sleeping near the far wall. It was hard to remember the last time he had crossed the narrow room to join her there. The heavy rain had stopped, but he could still hear a few drops hitting the roof. He moved quietly, trying not to wake anyone. Epsey had returned home after sundown the previous evening after spending almost a week with a woman who lived halfway to Wrightsborough, who had finally delivered a baby after several days of difficult labor. There had been little opportunity for her to sleep while taking care of the woman and fulfilling all her duties in a home with a husband and six children. This had been the first occasion that Ethan and Henry had been alone together for such a long time, and the pleasure had been balanced against Ethan's greatly restricted activities. During the last two days, mostly confined to the cabin because of the downpour, both of them had been equally eager to have Epsey return.

As Ethan walked across the cabin floor toward the fireplace, the hard-packed earthen floor again reminded him that he had never really finished construction of their home. He punched up the fire, laid on three small logs to relieve the cold of early March, and sat down at the table to watch the flickering of the first small flames. Now he was fully awake, still dressed only in a long shirt, and thinking about the chores that would occupy his time during the day. He had finished breaking all his open land and decided to go over it with a drag harrow and a leveling log to smooth the surface before laying off rows for planting. For a few more days, while the fields dried, he would be free to spend time in his woodshop, which he always anticipated as something of a vacation.

The table at which he sat was five feet long, crafted beautifully from hard maple, with only the top and edges of the boards planed smooth, but each fitted so snugly into its neighbors that no cracks could be seen. Six chairs stood around the table, the number decided more from a desire for symmetry than the needs of his family. Ethan was always pleased when one of their rare visitors commented on the workmanship of his furniture. The chairs were made entirely of white oak, including the seats, woven from strips of inner bark, now hardened and polished from several years of use. All pieces had been smoothed with a spoke shave and then a scraper, and were locked inseparably by driving them together while they still contained different degrees of moisture so that the drier rungs and curved back slats would expand and the relatively green legs and high-back frame would contract as the moisture equalized.

A shallow-lidded bowl of grease was on the table, with a wick protruding from inside. Either this crude lamp or candles made of beeswax or tallow provided a local source of light when Ethan and Epsey needed to supplement that from the fireplace. They usually went to bed before it became dark outside, and even in the daytime there was no source of light unless the door or outside shutters were opened, and even then little sunlight could penetrate the greased paper that was tacked inside the window openings as a cheap substitute for glass. A spinning wheel and loom now stood in a corner, and along the wall on one side of the door were a number of pegs driven into the middle of a log at about head height, on which he and Epsey usually hung most of their clothing. Those nearest his cot held a long black coat, a buckskin jacket, a coonskin cap, a broad-brimmed hat with a flat top, and a spare homespun shirt, long enough to reach down to Ethan's knees.

The large stone fireplace filled more than half the wall, which visitors would see to their right on entering the cabin. All the cooking was done there, mostly on two swiveled hooks that could be easily swung inward near the flame or out into the room over the hearth. There were four spikes on each side of the hearth, which Ethan had imbedded into the mortar between rocks, on which iron utensils could be suspended. There was a bellows, a flatiron, a gridiron, tongs, a frying pan, an iron skillet, a pot, a coffeepot, a basin, and two pewter candle makers. A board for baking bread leaned against the wall, scoured clean, and a shelf extended along the wall on each side of the fireplace. One held a dozen books, arranged neatly in four piles of three each, with a large family Bible on top of one pile. Epsey thought it was sacrilegious for the Holy Scriptures to be placed under another volume. There was a long-unused lamp on this same shelf, which had burned sperm oil when they had first bought it in North Carolina. A few heavy white cups, bowls, and plates were on the other shelf.

A churn, made of wood, sat on the floor near the fireplace. This was a cylinder that held about two gallons of milk, mounted on a cradle so that it could be turned end over end with a hand crank. Ethan had also brought his shaving horse and a few woodworking tools into the cabin so he could work more comfortably during the cold days of winter. His cobbler's bench was a permanent fixture in the room, sometimes used as a seat when he was not making or repairing shoes.

The Pratts' home had changed very little since it was first built and furnished, when he and his wife considered it to be just a temporary shelter and expected soon to have a larger home, one with floors of split logs, glass windows, a broad front porch, and another room just for sleeping, with this original building to be used for storage or a shelter for their animals.

Shortly after dawn, Ethan carried some bread and meat from the hearth to the table, with a glass of milk, but he had not begun eating before he heard the sloshing of a horse's hooves entering his yard. The trail ended at his house, so Ethan always knew that his home was the destination of anyone who came here. He blew out the small flame on the table and, as silently as possible so as not to waken Epsey and Henry, he reached for his long coat and slipped it on. Except for the flickering fire, the cabin was still dark inside, which was how he now preferred it.

He slipped his always-loaded rifle from the deer-antler rack on the wall and slid back the small board that opened a crack in his door. He was relieved to see that his visitor was well known to him, a sergeant named Randolph who served as an aide to Colonel Elijah Clarke. Ethan was surprised to see him, since he and the militia leader had rarely even seen each other since their confrontation during the attack on Big Elk. Ethan had volunteered to join several search parties following Indian raids, but always under either Twiggs or Dooly as leaders. Although he was now inclined to support the revolution, he had refrained from signing up as a militiaman and had continued to work on his relatively isolated landholdings. He stood his rifle against the wall, opened the door, and stepped out on the small porch, hardly large enough for the two straight-backed chairs that he and his wife would sometimes bring out from alongside the table during the hottest afternoons.

Ethan said, "Welcome, Randolph. Are you looking for some home cooking, or just a place to get out of the rain?"

The other men liked to tease Randolph, who was not very bright, never participated in any kind of levity and seemed puzzled but good-natured about it, and always tried to extract the exact, serious meaning from any statement of his compatriots. His life was devoted totally to serving Elijah Clarke, and he was very proud of this relationship.

"No, I et already, and I'm used to the rain. The colonel wants me to git back as soon as I can."

"Then what brings you here at this ungodly hour?"

"They had a meetin' last night, and want you to carry a message to General Ashe, who is camped with about two thousand men just this side of the Savannah River. We got word from someone at Burton's Ferry that the British might be movin' north, and some of their troops have been seen along the trails."

Ethan could tell that Randolph was eager to leave.

"Why do Clarke and the others want me to deliver the message?" he asked. "Why couldn't you go yourself?"

"Well, they think all the men they got needs to stay around Augusta and up the river since Ashe moved south, and he didn't leave any of his men behind that could carry a message. The main thing is that you're one of the few that knows Briar Creek and the swamp all the way to the river, and understands how fast things can change with the risin' water. We don't think the British can cross the creek now, but maybe you can tell the general about the Redcoats we already seen on this side and how they might be plannin' to come down on him."

Ethan asked several other questions and then said, "Tell the colonel that I'll soon be on my way, and I'll get Kindred to go with me."

The sergeant thought for a moment and finally blurted out, "From what I've heard that he's been sayin' around Wrightsborough, I'm not sure which side he's on."

Ethan was sometimes short-tempered, and now he spoke angrily. "Kindred would never betray us. He did sign the paper criticizing the Boston Tea Party and expressed his concern about disloyalty to the crown, but that was a long time ago. Now he knows as well as any of us what the British troops and their Indian allies have done to our families and our homes. I'm taking Kindred."

Ethan went inside the cabin and brought out a handful of corn cakes and some fried pork, which the sergeant took, then whirled his horse and rode toward the nearby forest. He turned, however, and came back to give a final message.

"The colonel says the information is to go direct to the general, and nobody else. The password is 'high spirits.'" Then he moved out of sight down the trail.

By this time, Epsey was up and Ethan explained that he had to take a message to the Continental general who was camped farther down the creek that ran through their farm. As Ethan dressed, prepared a small packet of food, and checked his rifle and ammunition, he thought about Kindred and could understand the derogatory comments of the sergeant. He, too, had been concerned about the excessive time his neighbor had been spending among the Indians. On more than one occasion, Kindred had expressed his criticism of the settlers' encroachment on the native lands and what he called mistreatment of the Indians by Wrightsborough merchants. He recalled riding to Kindred's home one day and meeting three British mounted soldiers on the narrow lane. When questioned, Kindred gave a somewhat confused explanation about the soldiers being lost and looking for the best way to get back to the main trail going south to Savannah.

Within an hour, Ethan had saddled his horse and ridden a mile to the Morrises' farm, anticipating the eagerness of his young friend to join him in what would be an interesting and important adventure. But when he found Kindred and explained their assigned task, the response was somewhat surprising: "I've got a lot to do, and I doubt if you really need me to go with you."

Ethan replied, "Kindred, you don't have to go if you don't want to, but I need someone along just in case we need to send a report or message back to the militia leaders in Augusta."

Kindred spoke with Mavis and finally agreed, still without enthusiasm, and the two men were soon on their way through the woods, moving in a southeasterly direction. It was unlikely that any other white men used this route, but it was their preferred way to the river and then on to Savannah. They followed the narrow trail that roughly paralleled the creek, always taking the correct fork to avoid going to the stream or northward toward other homesteads in the area. Formed over a period of generations by Creek Indians, these trails could not have been laid out better if done by expert surveyors. Mostly on high ground, they avoided thickets and descended to cross a number of small tributary streams at the shallow, fordable places. The men moved forward as fast as possible, keeping their horses at a trot or a fast walk. At best, they could not reach Ashe's outposts before midafternoon.

As they began their ride, Ethan had backed off to let Kindred go first down the narrow trail, thinking that the younger man would appreciate knowing that he was trusted to take the lead. Ethan was a natural leader, broad-shouldered and strong, blond, ruddy-faced, quiet and self-possessed until aroused. He was at ease exchanging frontier stories, often arousing laughter as he described his own mistakes and foibles, but the other men were cautious about going too far to make him the butt of their own jokes. They also knew that, around Ethan, his young friend was also within this protective shield, so their sly comments about effeminacy and friendship with Indians were not made in his presence. Kindred's admiration for Ethan was obvious to everyone.

Kindred rode his horse with complete ease, permitting the animal to accommodate the changing characteristics of the trail with an almost imperceptible shift of the reins or a murmured word. Ethan noticed the fluidity of his movements, similar to those of Newota, who had sometimes joined them to hunt for turkey or deer. Ethan was also impressed with Kindred's knowledge of the forest, which included not only the common names of major trees but also those that most frontiersmen ignored and just called bushes and weeds. He was modest about displaying what he knew, but when any question about plants or animals came up naturally, he and Mavis were always ready to share their knowledge with the Pratts and other neighboring families.

Despite their close relationship, there was a slight strain that had developed between the two men. When he first arrived, Kindred had become closely associated with some of the nearby Quakers who lived in their own settlement at Wrightsborough. His own first name was an indication of the influence of these early settlers who were prevented by their faith from taking a human life, a fervent belief that he shared. Neither Kindred nor Ethan had much time for religion, although they shared the undefined religious heritage of their ancestors who had come to the new lands from England and Scotland. With some reluctance, Ethan had been willing to take up arms, but only after he had seen the atrocities committed against their neighbors by some of the renegade Creek braves.

Ethan and Epsey had discussed Kindred's relationship with Newota. Both of them were younger than the Pratts in age and attitude, they shared an interest in the outdoors, and were fascinated with each other's culture. During the few times he had been with Newota, Ethan had also been interested in learning about the lifestyle of the Creek families, and was impressed with the young Indian's woodland skills. Newota was well behaved and respectful, highly complimentary about Ethan's farming and woodworking skills, and eager to learn as much as possible about the use of a white man's tools.

There was one concern that troubled Ethan, however, and he and Kindred had previously discussed it in general terms. Only recently had their views diverged. Although Ethan had decided that full independence for the colonies was the best choice, Kindred was still unconvinced that the ultimate goal of the Continental forces should be a separate and independent nation. He seemed certain that reconciliation was possible, once the colonists achieved permanent and legal relief from the punitive taxes imposed on them from London, along with fair representation of the Americans in colonial parliaments.

They were now riding side by side under enormous trees, mostly oaks, pines, poplar, and hickory, with just a few dogwoods and other shade-tolerant species interspersed in the relatively open spaces below the solid canopy of branches. At Ethan's suggestion, they dismounted to relieve themselves. When they remounted, Ethan decided to clarify the issue that had bothered him.

"Kindred, Sergeant Randolph seemed to doubt your loyalty when I told him you would be going with me. He had overheard one of your conversations in Wrightsborough and didn't understand some of the things you said."

There was a long silence as their horses moved down the trail. It was the first week in March, and only the conifers and a few water oaks had green foliage, while the beeches were still retaining the light brown, dry leaves of the previous season. Some of the trees were more than four feet in diameter, with an occasional giant half again as large. The sound of the horses' hooves was almost completely muted by the sodden bed of leaves and needles. Ethan had drawn slightly ahead and did not notice for a few seconds that he was riding alone. He looked around to see that Kindred had stopped twenty yards behind him and was sitting quietly on his horse, looking down.

He called out, "Hey, what's wrong?"

Kindred didn't respond, but just shook his head slightly. Ethan rode back and asked, "Don't you feel well?"

"I feel all right, but I have to tell you something."

"What is it? We need to be getting along as quick as we can."

Kindred looked up, a stricken expression on his face. "I knew the British were coming, but I wasn't going to warn Ashe."

"How did you know, Kindred?"

"Newota left his village two days ago to lead Prevost and his troops to Ashe's camp."

Ethan was shocked and angry.

"You knew this and didn't tell me or anyone else?"

"It's not my responsibility to protect these people. It's the British who have tried to work with the Indians, and to protect them and their lands. Newota asked me to go with him, but I refused. I promised to stay quiet about what he was doing."

"Damn it, Kindred! What are you going to do now?"

"I don't know. You practically forced me to come with you. I guess I'll go back home."

There was an uncomfortable silence and then Ethan said, "No, you'll have to come along with me. I can't have you finding Newota and the British and getting us in worse trouble. We'll have to work this out between us when we get back home. For now, we'll just try to hold down the bloodshed. You stay right with me, and when we get there I'll do all the talking."

Kindred finally spoke. "Ethan, I wouldn't try to find Newota, but there is no reason for you and me to talk about this anymore. You know what I think. I can understand how some of the northern colonies might feel betrayed and abused by the king. Their royal governors were corrupt and abusive, but you know that Governor Wright always treated us well. When the Whigs forced him out of Savannah, our lives became even worse than before. Now the fighting is all around us, and our own neighbors have become alienated from each other. All that most settlers want from the Indians is more and more land, and will cheat them in any way to get it. What I want is to live in peace and to see our young people grow up without having to kill the Indians and Englishmen around us."

Ethan had realized that his neighbor was loyal to his Indian friends and was peaceful in nature, but was surprised to hear such a long statement from Kindred about any subject other than plants and animals.

He started to reply, but Kindred continued, "I'm grateful that you understand my concerns and still trust my loyalty. To be frank, I don't really think this trip is necessary. You and I know the region almost as well as Newota. There is no way Colonel Prevost can bring his troops up the Savannah and cross Briar Creek with it flooding like it is. The water is probably four feet above normal level at Ashe's camp. I think he has chosen a good place."

Ethan couldn't dispute much of what Kindred had said, and he chose not to repeat their discussions about the long-term goals of the colonists. They simply had a genuine difference of opinion about the ability to live under leaders chosen by the authorities in distant London. Also, it now seemed impossible to restrain the more militant commanders, since many of them on both sides in this frontier area had witnessed and even perpetrated the most despicable atrocities against innocent and defenseless people. He would never forget what he saw Elijah Clarke do to the squaws and babies in Big Elk's camp, and he had buried some of the mutilated bodies of wives and children of settlers whom he knew well.

"Well, you may be right about Ashe's judgment, but it's obvious that Colonel Clarke is concerned. Also, as you and I know, our militia forces can't get to Ashe from upriver, since that trail is now flooded. This general route we're taking is about the only way that anyone could reach the North Carolina troops. Although Ashe is relatively isolated from our militia, he's surrounded on three sides by water, so you may be right about the safety of his troops."

They rode on without speaking, and after a few hours they heard loud talking and the noise of a large campsite. As they approached, Ethan was prepared to call out the password that would gain them safe passage through the outpost guards. They were soon surprised to see the tents ahead of them, without having been challenged as they approached.

The general's location was obvious. One tent was noticeably larger, having a sheet of canvas stretched horizontally over its entrance flap to provide protection from the sun and rain and a group of soldiers lounging in its vicinity. These men looked up as the two horsemen approached, dressed in their rough, homespun clothes and slouched hats, wearing nothing that would provide any military identity.

Ethan spoke first. "We have a message from Colonel Elijah Clarke for General Ashe."

A noncommissioned officer with two stripes on his sleeve approached them, reached out his hand, and said, "Give it to me and I'll deliver it to the general."

Ethan said, "There's nothing in writing, and our orders are to relay the information directly to your commander." He had a momentary feeling that he was being prodded, or even insulted. It was generally known that his own leader was almost illiterate, barely able to write his own name. For those who served with Clarke, this soon became an insignificant fact, but they were accustomed to implied insults from some of the other troops, who shared the inevitable feeling of competition that existed among the militia forces. He was acutely aware of a disdainful attitude among the half-dozen troops who now surrounded the two horses, but decided to sit patiently until the silence was broken. He noticed that the soldiers in the camp were not armed; their guns were stacked neatly in a line in front of the tents, and five small cannon, lined up adjacent to each other, had been hauled in and left wherever the draft horses were unhitched from the guns' carriages.

The corporal finally said, "Wait here," and walked away, not to the commander's tent but to the third one down the line. After a few minutes, a lieutenant emerged from the tent and approached Ethan and Kindred.

"Tell me what the message is, and I'll inform the general when he is disposed to receive it."

Ethan did not consider violating Colonel Clarke's instructions and replied with complete composure that although the message was urgent, he would wait for the general. Finally, the lieutenant nodded curtly and entered the commanding officer's tent. He soon returned and told Ethan, "Wait over there under the tree." The two men rode over, dismounted, and sat on some large roots near the tree trunk. They waited for more than an hour, and the sun was setting before General Ashe finally came out. He was wearing a woolen undershirt with long sleeves and blue military trousers, held up with leather suspenders. He was hatless, and Ethan noticed that his hair was long down the back of his neck and quite thin on top, brushed over in an ineffectual effort to cover his balding pate. It was obvious that the sun rarely reached either his head or face, and he even lacked the sunburned neck of men who spent their days outdoors. Ashe made it clear that he didn't welcome this intrusion by farmers on his military encampment.

"What does Clarke want?" he demanded.

"Sir, he only wants to give you information received from a trusted source that British troops are moving toward your location and may try to cross the creek."

"That's ridiculous," replied the general. "Even if they had such plans, they could not cross either the Savannah or Briar Creek with the lowlands flooded as they are."

Ethan informed the general that British forces had actually been sighted the previous day above Burton's Ferry, more than thirty miles from their base camp and moving to the northwest. His remarks were interrupted by a dismissive wave of Ashe's hand and a comment that seemed to be directed mostly at his own men.

"Now I understand your commander's problem. My own men have detected movement of enemy troops just across the swamp to the south, but there is no way they can cross to attack us. It could only be a few of their scouts, and I'm sure they have reported to Prevost that we are too strong and well placed to be assaulted. As a safety precaution, we have able lookouts posted to watch in that direction.

"You men can spend the night here and then go back tomorrow to inform Colonel Clarke that we are secure in our present position, fully capable of performing our duties, and waiting for the rest of the army to join us, as directed by General Lincoln."

"General, we'll obey your orders, but I would like to add that the normal route down here from up toward Augusta is under at least five feet of water. The only way to attack this position is from upstream on the north side of the creek, in general following the route we have just taken."

"This only confirms what I've been telling you. Our position is invulnerable to attack." The general turned away from Ethan and Kindred, ending the conversation. They watched him reenter his tent, and then they watered and fed their horses, and lay down for the night, wrapped in blankets that they always carried lashed behind their saddles.

They were up at dawn, soaked with falling rain, and decided to share some breakfast with the Carolina troops before heading back up the previous day's trail. As they put bridles on their horses and prepared to saddle them, they heard drums beating in the forest upstream from their position. Both they and the troops looked around in wonder, and the general and other officers emerged from their tents.

"Who in hell is that?" shouted a colonel. There was no answer, as everyone looked up the trail. Soon a flash of red clothing could be seen, then another and another.

"It's the British!" someone screamed.

There was a mad scramble, first toward their stacked guns and the cannon, and then, with the realization that it was too late to defend themselves, toward the forest and swamp away from the charging troops. With their horses saddled and ready, Ethan and Kindred waited to see if they could be of help, but soon realized that the situation was hopeless. The general and other officers made no attempt to rally the men to face the Redcoats, but joined in the completely disorganized rout. The commanders had a decided advantage, in that they were familiar with the rudimentary maps they had studied in their earlier planning of the campsite.

A hail of bullets whistled by Ethan and Kindred as they leaped on their barebacked horses and dashed toward the thick forest, leaving their blankets and rifles behind. Ethan shouted for Kindred to stay away from the nearby creek, where most of the escaping troops were heading. They were soon alone, several hundred yards from the campsite, but close enough to hear a constant volley of gunshots behind them and the shouts of the exuberant British. They also heard the screams of those struck by saber strokes and musket balls or carried away by the stream in which many of the Americans sought safety. The two men soon reached what seemed to be deep and still water far from the creek channel and saw that they could go no farther on their horses, which they released. Both men were strong swimmers, and Ethan began to wade out into the water to swim to some higher ground that he could see in the distance. He could hear the British coming toward them but noticed that Kindred did not follow. He turned to urge his friend to join him.

"Ethan, I'm sorry, but one of the shots hit me in my right leg, and it hurts too bad for me to swim," he said. "I'll hide here in the brush and you can come back and get me when they're gone. If I'm discovered, I'll just surrender and take my chance as a prisoner. I know Colonel Prevost, and Newota will put in a good word for me."

Ethan examined the wound, which was bleeding only slightly, and saw that the bullet had punctured the upper thigh and had not emerged. He thought the bone was broken and was doubtful that Kindred would be able to move.

"Come on," he said, "I can help you through the water. It's not too far to that big tree over there on the hummock."

"No, I'm staying here. We both can hide better if we're separate. I'll be all right."

Ethan had to make a decision and soon realized that he had no alternative except to continue on his own. Not only was he well aware of Kindred's stubbornness once he made a decision, but it was highly likely that they would both be joining the other prisoners if they didn't move quickly. He helped Kindred move under the low-hanging limbs of a young magnolia, which, even now, the wounded man called a "grandiflora." After he partially covered Kindred with dead leaves until he was well concealed, Ethan eased into the water and breaststroked to the small island, where he crawled up on the land just as the Redcoats came into view. He lay flat on the ground, partially concealed by some fallen limbs. With mounting concern and uncontrollable guilt, he watched as the British approached Kindred's hiding place. He prayed that they would not find him.

Then he was stunned to hear Kindred's voice as he dragged himself out of the covering leaves and put his hands in the air. "I surrender. I am not armed. Just take me to Colonel Prevost." The leader of the triumphant troops grabbed Kindred, pushed him down on his stomach, and tied his hands behind his back, where he lay without moving or speaking further.

"You're one of the few left," he said, "and we'll soon have all the others who haven't drowned themselves."

One of the other men, who seemed to be in command, pushed forward. He said in an angry voice, "Corporal, have you forgotten what the colonel ordered and what I made clear to you? We are not to take any of these rebel bastards as prisoners. Anyone who forgets McAllister and brings one in alive will lose his month's ration of rum."

He kicked Kindred in his side and then thrust his bayonet deep into the captive's back, put his boot between his shoulder blades, pulled the weapon free, and then plunged it even more deeply where he thought the heart would be.

Sickened, and flinching as though the blade had penetrated his own bowels, Ethan dropped his head to the ground. He felt physically unable to move. Then he heard orders being issued: "Search all around here. Look in every hiding place. If you find rebels or see any swimming, shoot them." Still at least partially concealed, he wiggled around to the other side of the huge tree, out of sight of the British. There, he found a hole at ground level, about three feet high and half as wide, through which he was able to squeeze his body.

Ethan Pratt could still see the British bayonet penetrating the back of his helpless friend, who had been lying on the ground, his hands tied together. Now Ethan lay shivering uncontrollably, his long and muscular body curled up in a hollow black oak tree, fearful of his own life and wondering how he could have left Kindred behind, wounded and defenseless under the magnolia leaves. Had he not known that he was trusting and naive, with confused loyalties that might cause him to reveal himself and surrender?

Despite his grief and guilt about what had happened and how it might have been prevented, he could not forget his own danger, and how easy it would be for him to face the same fate within the next few minutes. He had no rifle or pistol, only a knife that he always carried at his belt—an insignificant weapon if he was forced out of his uncomfortable sanctuary to face the well-armed dragoons who seemed to be motivated, even obsessed, with hatred and a desire to obey their commander's orders without mercy.

He knew that his trail to the water's edge was clear enough to be followed by a Savannah barrister, never mind men who had spent months in the Georgia woods and swamps when every day their lives depended on vigilance and the interpretation of sights and sounds. From their vantage point, where his tracks had entered the slowly swirling swamp water, they would soon know that he would be either on the hummock or still swimming downstream. If he, himself, were tracking a wounded animal, he would almost surely pinpoint its destination as the small island he had reached.

Water ran from his long hair down the back of his plain buckskin coat. He had lost his hat but was thankful that the leather thongs had kept his moccasins on his feet even during his escape through the water. The rough, homespun shirt provided no warmth but now seemed to wrap an icy blanket around his body. His right hand rested on a small pouch, attached with a loop around his neck, which contained his flint and steel and some now worthless black powder and balls for the rifle he had left behind.

The last stages of the late winter storm still surged around him at intervals, with flurries of light rain stirring the surface of the swamp water. Even the enormous tree seemed to groan as the gusts of wind struck its upper branches. It was relatively dry inside, because the tree was perched on a hummock, its roots locked deep within an ancient mound of earth that protected them from the soddenness that would not have let this species survive. Year after year over the past three hundred years, the tree's fallen leaves and shedding limbs had added increments of humus to the ground, steadily increasing the height of its own island. These subliminal thoughts were like breathing to Ethan, who lived and worked and hunted along and within this exact same stream and swamp that formed the southern border of his own farm.

Inside, the space was not quite as large as in the two-man canvas tents—small enough to be carried in a backpack—issued to well-supplied soldiers, but the shock of Kindred's murder and Ethan's resulting fear of the Redcoats had made his usual preference for clean and open spaces fade into insignificance.

For some reason, he had another concern, something in his subconscious that slowly penetrated his more acute sorrow and fear. The water around him was at least five feet above that of Briar Creek at its normal stage, when its flow consisted only of that which rose from the underground aquifer through the multiple springheads that fed trickling streams that would eventually flow into the Savannah River and then the sea. Even though they could all swim for short distances, the nonaquatic wild animals had to survive these periodic floods by finding a relatively dry haven. Possums, raccoons, bobcats, and squirrels found shelter in the treetops, deer habitually bedded down in the high places, and rabbits and foxes always built their dens where they would not drown and had plenty of time to return to them as the waters rose. His list narrowed, as his eyes became more accustomed to the dim light. He could see the rough inner bark, the darkened strands of fiber that still carried moisture and nutrients from the ground to the upper limbs, all disappearing in the intense darkness above. His eyes wandered over all these surrounding walls, covered with an interlocking mass of cobwebs, seemingly impenetrable. He heard a slight movement on the floor of his sanctuary, and then a shock went through his body, his spine contorted, and he involuntarily pushed back toward the narrow opening through which he had entered. Ethan was a brave man, familiar with the wilderness and its creatures, but he was instantly injected back into one of the few recurring nightmares he had experienced since childhood. Not four feet from him was a huge cottonmouth, which he knew to be the most dangerous snake in this region—always given a wide berth if possible.

This was one creature that would not usually move to escape an approaching human, but would sometimes move forward to attack. Ethan knew them well, from his own observations and because they were a favorite subject of frontiersmen's stories, mostly true but sometimes exaggerated, of their size and the dramatic nature of their encounters. The snakes were easily identified. The cottonmouth, to which Kindred liked to refer in exaggerated tones of foreboding as *Agkistrodon piscivorus,* was the only water snake that swam with a few inches of its neck in the air. It had a broad head, and its eyes were not round like those of other water snakes but catlike, vertical slits, a pair of which now fixed on him. He knew there was a small heat-sensitive pit between the eyes and nostrils, with which it could locate its prey. So far, the reptile seemed to be relatively dormant, not yet recovered from its months of winter hibernation and not disturbed enough to give the warning signal of a wide-open mouth that exposed the cottonlike interior surrounding the glands of poison, much more lethal than that of copperheads and rattlesnakes. There was nothing within the hollow with which he could defend himself, so his only choice was to be still and quiet, fortunately the same tactic that was the best defense against his other enemies with the bayonets, who were not more than fifty yards away.

Ethan attempted to control his pounding heart, at first presuming that the roaring in his own ears might be reverberating around him, enough to arouse the cottonmouth. He soon realized the foolishness of this assumption and was relieved to observe as the seconds passed that the snake remained still, coiled in a depression in the rotting wood particles that seemed to be its habitual resting place. Ethan began to assess his other chances for survival, attempting to put himself in the position of his British pursuers. He knew from his own experience a few minutes ago that it was extremely unpleasant to wade and swim through the slowly moving water, in some places more than chest deep, between his hummock and the high ground where Kindred's body lay and where his assassins still lingered and argued among themselves.

Neither the Redcoats nor the revolutionary soldiers had boats, since the colonists had certainly not foreseen a military engagement in the middle of an enormous lake, and the British had made a forced march of more than forty miles before launching their surprise attack. Only the local militiamen, who lived and farmed in this area, seemed to know how to accommodate, like the wild animals, the streams' transformation into a tremendous current that spread over a hundred square miles just a few hours after a heavy downpour upstream. It was this knowledge of the local terrain that had brought Ethan and Kindred from their homes to the unanticipated battle site.

"Look here, Sergeant, you can see the tracks where another one of these scum went in the water." The sergeant ordered two of his men to go as far as possible to the right and left, and to move out into the water far enough to see clearly behind the big tree. When they reported no one on the small island, the sergeant said, "Well, he's either drowned or we don't need to worry about a coward like him, willing to leave this other fellow in order to save his own hide. There's no need to swim around searching for him. We're wet enough already. Let's spread out and maybe we'll find some more of the bastards hiding between here and the camp."

The patrol group moved back toward the other troops, and there was no remaining sound except the gurgling of the slow-moving stream.

Ethan hid on the hummock for almost four hours, waiting until the last British troops had moved downstream toward the Savannah River and a triumphant return to their base. Then he waded back to the higher ground, noticing that the water level had dropped almost six inches. His first task was to carry Kindred's ravaged body to a place well above the flooded ground and to bury him. He dug the grave with a broken bayonet, laboriously chopping through the nest of roots and removing the sodden earth with his hands. Throughout more than an hour of labor, he mumbled something of a prayer, mixing words of anger, sorrow, and mostly guilt. He could not forget the words of the British sergeant as they gave up their hunt for him. Then he searched the devastated and abandoned campsite where he had attempted to warn General Ashe and tried to ignore the dozens of bodies of Continental troops that were lying where they had fallen. He had a brief feeling of obligation to cover them in some way, but realized immediately that this would be an impossible task. He did, however, make sure that none of them was still alive, and felt a strange and somewhat embarrassing sense of relief that the British had been so thorough in their efforts to decapitate or disembowel their fallen or captured foes.

He found some hard, dry biscuits under a collapsed tent, its sides ripped by sword or bayonet thrusts, but despite his hunger he couldn't eat there among the dead. He wrapped a supply in a piece of canvas and began his long walk home, which would be more than twenty miles. After he was well clear of the battle area, he sat down by a small stream and ate exactly half of his food.

Ethan felt like a coward and a criminal as he resumed his walk, following the same general route that he and Kindred had used only a day earlier. He was surprisingly weak and confused. Everything looked different now and he found it difficult to recognize even the obvious landmarks that any outdoorsman would store automatically and indelibly in his memory. The strangeness even applied to a stream crossing, a large fallen tree across the trail that had to be circumnavigated, a muddy slope where footing was difficult, a singular rock formation. At first he thought it might be the change in perspective of a man on foot instead of horseback, and then that he was moving in the opposite direction. But even when he turned around to imitate his earlier view, the scenes were hardly recognizable. It required a great deal of mental discipline to convince himself that he had not taken the wrong route. He looked at his pocket compass to double-check his general direction and had to acknowledge that there was no other trail that paralleled the north bank of Briar Creek. He felt that a different person inhabited his body.

Now, as he trudged homeward, his mind cleared and he realized that the trail had, indeed, been changed after he and Kindred traversed it, now trampled by hundreds of British troops who had followed its general direction. When he had walked about ten miles, he saw where Newota had obviously led them to the trail after crossing Briar Creek, and had then turned toward the campsite of the Continentals. From this point on, Ethan recognized the undisturbed path with which he was familiar and felt that he was regaining his equilibrium and his sense of judgment.

But he was filled with conflicting emotions, some of them pent up from the past. He deeply resented the brutal murder of Kindred and reluctantly concluded that he could no longer remain passive in the growing conflict. A major impediment to this decision had always been the necessity of serving under the direction of Elijah Clarke, a man with whom he was naturally incompatible and who might very well not accept him as a volunteer militiaman. He had been surprised that Clarke had asked him to deliver the warning to Ashe, but realized that it was because of his unique familiarity with the lower reaches of Briar Creek, and possibly the influence of Aaron Hart and John Twiggs. Also, there had been no way to anticipate how important the message would prove to be.

Ethan moved forward at a steady pace with his long and effortless stride, stopping just once in the night to doze for a few hours under a rock outcropping a few feet from the trail. When he reached the Morris homestead he started to turn in toward the cabin, but stopped and then proceeded to his own place. He would come back when he was better prepared to tell Mavis what had happened. He was not surprised that Epsey detected his approach from a distance and was waiting in the front yard when he arrived. She looked at him closely but waited for him to speak first. He sat down heavily on one of the chairs at the table, and she sat across from him. Ethan described the events of the past two days since he had left the cabin. She cried out softly when he told her of Kindred's death, asked if he had stopped to tell Mavis, and offered to go with him to share the bad news.

After Ethan had bathed and changed clothes, they walked to the Morris cabin, and Ethan told Mavis what had happened. She was stunned and began to weep softly. He had a strong urge to take her in his arms and console her, and was relieved that Epsey moved forward to fill this role. After a minute or two, Mavis asked Ethan a few questions about her husband's death. He replied as well as possible, not mentioning their conversation on the way and saying that he should have ignored Kindred's objections and insisted on carrying him through the water to possible safety. He ended his comments with assurance that Kindred was properly buried.

Mavis was silent for a few moments and then said, "Maybe you all realized how close he and the Indians had become."

She paused, glanced at both of them, and then continued, "I heard Kindred and Newota discussing the presence of the Continental troops, and Kindred encouraged Newota to guide the British to a crossing place over

Briar Creek, but he chose not to become involved himself. He was increasingly unhappy with the way things were happening in the war, but wasn't strong enough to make a clear choice. He was torn in several directions, wanting an end to the violence, feeling protective of the natives across the river, having strong personal ties with Newota, but overwhelmingly filled with admiration and respect for you, Ethan."

Epsey asked Mavis to gather her things and move in with them for a while, but Mavis immediately rejected this invitation. "I've always felt at ease here by myself, and now I'd just rather be alone for a while to decide what to do next. I'll let y'all know if I need anything."

Ethan and Epsey walked toward home, and when they approached their first field, Ethan said he was going to check the livestock. He walked almost all the way around the periphery of his land, moving slowly past some of his favorite places as he thought about recent events. He tried to strip away some of the self-deluding premises of his life and found this to be very difficult.

Ethan had always been a methodical man, proud of his logical approach to challenging and complex issues, reticent about revealing his inner feelings or the process by which he made decisions. Not even Epsey ever felt that she understood what he was thinking when they faced changing circumstances and had to formulate new ideas. Over their years together she had learned that he would listen to her preferences, but her first indication of what he was thinking was usually when he revealed his final conclusions. There was no way that she could know how careful he was to conceal his uncertainties from others, and how he valued his reputation for self-confidence and calmness during times of crisis. He was innately inclined to limit his ambitions, so that a possible failure would not indicate weakness or inability. He approached challenging tasks in incremental steps, and only after careful assessment of all the eventualities. Ethan was uncomfortable when he felt that his own independence was restricted, and he had a natural aversion to close associations with any other person or group. Although he had little interest in their religious beliefs, he had felt compatible with the neutrality of the Wrightsborough Quakers concerning the increasing conflict between Whigs and Tories. He realized now that he had used his proximity to the Quakers to justify his reluctance to become completely committed to either side, and to be left alone with his farm and his own affairs.

As his thoughts were permitted to roam, they focused increasingly on the words of the British sergeant: "a coward like him, willing to leave this other fellow to save his own hide." Ethan tried to recall the reasons for abandoning Kindred, and rejected the excuse that his friend had insisted on being left alone. There was no doubt that he had pushed off into the water with a sense of personal relief, falsely convinced that Kindred would stay hidden under the leaves so that both could escape capture. He could have pulled the injured man with him across the stream, with the broken leg immobile and buoyed by the water. He could easily imagine both of them hiding inside the hollow tree until the patrol had examined the shore and departed. They would not have been impeded by the British on their return home.

Finally, Ethan was able to consider his current situation, and what he should do in the future. By the time he returned to his cabin, long after sundown, he had decided on the unpleasant prospect of traveling to Augusta, which was now the Georgia militia headquarters. He was ready to report for service under Elijah Clarke. The memory of the British bayonet in Kindred's back had overshadowed the slayings and scalpings in Big Elk's camp.

CHAPTER 37

Ethan Pratt Goes to War

Back home, Epsey was surprised when Ethan told her that he was going to talk to Elijah Clarke about serving with the militia. Her husband knew how opposed she was to violence and that she considered the killing of another human to be a mortal sin. She could tell that Ethan was also troubled about the prospect of violating what had been a basic principle of life for both of them but, typically, she decided not to comment.

Early the next morning Ethan mounted their remaining horse and went to Wrightsborough, where he learned that Clarke was still in Augusta. He rode the thirty miles with some trepidation, not knowing what to expect when he offered his services to a strong-willed man with whom he had an unforgettable confrontation when they had last been together. He knew of Clarke's growing reputation as an effective military commander, and of his demanding and officious attitude toward the men who served under him.

Ethan was willing to accept his subordinate place in the militia ranks, but there were limits on personal subservience. When he arrived in Augusta he was directed to the most prominent dwelling in town, known locally as McKay's Trading Post. It had become the center of what government Georgia still had remaining, and Clarke and other militia leaders used two rooms in the large white building as their headquarters when they were not in the Wilkes County forests.

There were several men lounging on the porch when Ethan arrived, and he nodded to some whom he had met before.

He asked, "Where can I find Elijah Clarke?"

One of the men responded, "I reckon you're looking for Colonel Clarke. If so, he's inside, in the back room."

Ethan entered the building and walked in to where Elijah was seated behind a table, talking to John Twiggs and another militiamen named William Few. Clarke looked up and seemed surprised to see Ethan. He didn't rise, but leaned back from the table and said, "I guess you were at Briar Creek."

Ethan had the impression that Clarke was blaming him for what had happened and didn't respond until the commander continued, "I've had a little information about the bloody battle, but not from anybody that was there. Ashe and most of his top staff escaped to Matthew's Bluff and took a boat across the Savannah that same night. Now he's makin' all kinds of excuses, but the fact is that about half the men in his camp were drowned or killed."

Somewhat surprised that Ashe had survived and not knowing what he had reported, Ethan gave a fairly detailed description of what had occurred, including the general's rejection of the warning, his nonexistent defense, the wild retreat of his Continental troops, and their terrible casualties. He mentioned that Kindred had been one of many who had been murdered after surrendering, and said that he had escaped by swimming through the swamp.

Clarke remained silent during the vivid description of the greatest defeat the colonists had ever experienced in the region. Finally, he responded, "Well, we did the best we could to tell Ashe what we knew. I suspicioned that he was lyin' about what happened. The bastard has wiped out all the gains we made at Kettle Creek and our chances to move down toward Savannah. It won't be long before Prevost will move into Augusta."

He shifted in his chair and added, mostly to his two friends, "We've been fightin' the war almost three years, and I don't think Washington has won a battle. The British control New York, Philadelphy, and now most of Carolina and all of Georgia except right here where we are."

Twiggs added, "Also Canada and Newport."

There was an uncomfortable silence, and then Ethan looked directly at Clarke and said, "I'd like to talk to you awhile."

Clarke didn't respond, but Twiggs and Few left and closed the door, and Elijah waited for Ethan to speak.

"I've decided to join the militia if you need me."

The two men looked at each other, with neither willing to avert his eyes. Clarke broke the prolonged silence. "Mr. Pratt, I don't have no doubt about your ability as a hunter, a woodsman, a horseman, but there are some other things that bother me. I've never had any showin' that you're willin' to fight the British, and I seen myself that you don't like bloodshed or takin' orders."

Ethan's face flushed as he struggled to control his temper. He finally said, "There's a difference between fighting enemy soldiers and killing women and children, but let's put the past aside. I want to help run the British out of Georgia and protect our families from them and the Indians. As for taking orders, I'm willing to be treated like any other militiaman, and you have my word on it."

The colonel was at ease and spoke as a superior to a new recruit. "Pratt, I ought to tell you that on both sides of the river we don't have more than two hundred men who are willin' and able to fight. We're facin' strong British troops downriver and northward in Carolina and have an even worse problem with the son of a bitch Brown and his Rangers. We spend most of our time either at home protectin' our families or hidin' in the woods, and we're still learnin' how to fight."

"Well, I'm willing to learn like the others."

The colonel made Ethan wait for an answer. Finally he said, "You can report to Captain William Few, and I reckon he'll be glad to have you."

The two men didn't shake hands or come in contact, but nodded to each other as a sign of mutual agreement.

Ethan found Few and reported as directed by Clarke. Unlike the colonel, Few was an educated and well-mannered man, soft-spoken and polite, who drove his men by his own example. Few loaned Ethan a British infantry manual, which contained many marginal notes and stricken-out sentences, mostly related to close-order drill. He then told Ethan he could return to his homestead, gather personal belongings, take leave of his family, and then plan to spend what time he could spare with the militia unit.

"Like you, a few of our men still have homes and stay there when they can. Most of these are within this small area above Augusta that we're able to defend. You'll be the only one from the Quaker settlement. It is important to have some outposts intact to demonstrate Whig strength to the Indians and to settlers whose loyalty wavers, to provide information from as wide an area as possible, and maybe even to produce food to be shared with those who are committed to full-time military service. Unless we're assigned a mission, these part-time men in our company will get together two or three days a week for training and so we can share information with each other. The next time will be early Saturday."

"Well, I've come prepared to stay and will not be going back home for a week or so. My intention is to spend all my time in the company while I'm studying the manual and learning what else I can on the job. I have a good rifle and ammunition, and expect to trade for a better horse when I can find one. My land is all prepared and ready to be planted, and my wife can take care of the livestock until I can sell most of it. I'll come on the assigned days, do the cultivating in between, and you can call on me whenever I'm needed."

Captain Few seemed pleased with Ethan's response and said, "With as few men as we have left, there is more than enough for us to do. Maybe you can spend some days with me, just to see what is going on, and to learn how the different units work together. The colonel can provide some help if you need it, both in finding a good mount and helping to pay for it."

"I'm grateful but plan to take care of my own needs."

The original government grant had long ago been spent, and new recruits were expected to furnish their own blankets, clothes, horses, saddles, weapons, and ammunition. Ethan soon learned that each man scouted for perishable food to supplement small allotments of tobacco, sugar, salt, and dried corn and meat. They would have to travel fast and light, and didn't carry tents or any but the most rudimentary cooking utensils. Commanders usually parceled out powder, which was often scarce, while the men tried to furnish their own bullets, usually molded from a mixture of lead and pewter melted from candlesticks, dishes, utensils, and any other scraps of soft metal they could find. Militia on both sides of the war were dressed alike (and often confused with each other), and most of them left their homes and families for relatively brief periods and received little if any pay for their military service. In the past, many volunteers who wanted service for longer enlistments had been incorporated into regular Continental troops in Georgia, and now served under Generals Lincoln and McIntosh. Elijah Clarke and other militia commanders knew that their companies were subject to orders from these senior officers, but the individual militiamen did not consider themselves bound to carry out orders with which they disagreed. Their military service was a fragile relationship that might be broken by family responsibilities even if their unit was facing combat.

Ethan went out of his way to learn what he could about the customs and tactics of the Georgia militia, and was surprised at the loosely structured organization of the group. Captain Few seemed to enjoy giving Ethan special instruction, and was pleased at the enthusiasm and rapid progress of the frontiersman, who was larger and stronger than any other man in the company. Ethan learned to work closely with the other men in the swamps and forests, and to participate in the communication network that ensured rapid marshaling of the militia when they were needed.

Under Captain Few, he found that the company's primary goals were to improve their fighting skills, consolidate remaining families and possessions within their protected area, strike with deadly force against any intruders who dared to enter, and make some outside raids against the British who were downriver from Augusta. These responsibilities fell on the few beleaguered militia troops who remained in north Georgia, since all organized Continental troops were concentrated across the river in South Carolina. During his days with the militia, Ethan rode, camped, and helped to plan tactics with all his ability and skill as a woodsman. He became a dedicated warrior but joined the other men, including Clarke and Few, who took advantage of dormant times to return home for brief visits with their families. He volunteered to join in a long foray to the south, part of a futile but symbolically important attempt to harass the British around Savannah.

Ethan did not see Mavis during the next few weeks, nor did he spend more than a few days at his own cabin. He had not been able to talk further even to Epsey about what had happened, and had been unable to describe his emotions during or after the military engagement. He knew he should have visited Mavis as soon as possible and offered his help in arranging for her care, but he never really considered doing so. Some of his reasons were rational, including the need to give Elijah Clarke an immediate report on what had happened in the disastrous battle and then to join in military operations. This had not, however, prevented his visiting his own homestead, where he came when possible to care for his crops and livestock. After all, Epsey had agreed to take care of Mavis and to help make arrangements once she decided whether to stay at home or go to Wrightsborough to stay with friends. Another reason for his reluctance was that he did not want to learn that she shared her husband's antagonism toward the American militia. He was more concerned about her future plans. Now as a widow, would she stay in northeast Georgia or move to Savannah to seek haven among the loyalists— or move back to join the Bartram family in Philadelphia?

She was almost constantly in his thoughts, and not just questions about her political attitudes or future plans. He repeatedly and methodically remembered almost every encounter with her during the last few years. His heart had leapt the first time he saw her, as she almost seemed to float down the path toward his cabin. The intriguing confluence of youth, naïveté, acute intelligence, eagerness to learn everything about frontier life, carelessness about her own appearance, and apparent lack of awareness of her extraordinary beauty had been almost immediately apparent. Soon thereafter had come ingenuous and unabashed intimacy as she had talked frankly about her private feelings, and her amusement when she had looked directly at him until he invariably turned away. His body still tingled when he recalled a warm spring afternoon as he had lounged on a creek bank with her and Kindred. Mavis had reached out, touched his forearm, and commented about the thick blond hair, which she stroked with her fingers. She and Kindred had both laughed at his muscle spasm and his blushing embarrassment.

Subsequently, Ethan had tried to minimize such opportunities for direct contact with her, but some were inevitable as the three of them rode horseback, explored the swamps and woodlands, and shared family meals and farming projects. He felt certain that neither Kindred nor Epsey would have had any concern or even awareness of the intensity of his feelings toward Mavis or her apparently innocent flirtations with him.

Ethan's visits to his home became more infrequent, as he always found Epsey unharmed and apparently satisfied and happy with little Henry. In addition to giving necessary care to the foraging animals, she had even made one trip into Wrightsborough to trade corn and the last two of Ethan's chairs for some needed supplies. Both of them realized that they had been fortunate in the early choice of their homesite. Not only was it in a remote area through which there were no passersby, but it was considered to be part of the original Quaker community, which both sides in the war had decided to exclude from their more brutal forays. Even during this time of the state's sharp division, no families in the Wrightsborough area had been injured in any way, and he was not surprised that his wife was quite self-sufficient.

Late in June, after a discussion of their present circumstances, Ethan asked Epsey about Mavis, and Epsey responded that she had decided to move into Wrightsborough to stay with one of the Quaker families who had offered her room and board for her services as a house servant.

He didn't comment, and managed to conceal his disappointment by coughing and turning away. He did not stay for the night, but he said that his services were needed, and began the long journey back to his militia unit.

CHAPTER 38

The British Take Georgia

JUNE 1779

Elijah Clarke overestimated British strength and ambition following Ashe's defeat at Briar Creek. Both London and the Continental Congress were satisfied to stabilize the military situation in the state, with the remaining Georgia politicians and militiamen able to remain in and around Augusta, and with Savannah and all the rest of Georgia under British control. Lieutenant Colonel Prevost established headquarters at Ebenezer and commanded British troops in the field, while his cautious father served as acting governor of the conquered state during the few months that it took Governor James Wright to travel from London back to Savannah.

. . .

The Georgia militiamen were given intense military training, sent out on frequent patrols, and educated through formal and informal sessions about the British enemy. They learned that the formidable core of the Redcoat armies was a highly trained professional infantry and cavalry, only a few of whom were yet deployed to fight in the interior of Georgia or the Carolinas. The American militia commanders were almost always elected by the troops who served them, and the units were bound together by mutual admiration, trust, and common purpose. They were surprised to learn that British officers were assigned to command even local militia units, comprising Americans who remained loyal to the crown—men who were either recruited for an extended period or who volunteered for relatively brief tours.

Ethan realized that the southern countryside had become almost completely divided, often with brothers enlisted in opposing militia forces and fathers fighting their own sons. There were different degrees of fervor for either cause. Many just wished to be left alone to pursue their own interests, and were swayed by an inclination to get along with the most powerful force—military or economic—in the neighborhood. Like himself, some of his new companions had little interest in political affairs, but had been alienated by atrocities committed against their homes, friends, or families, and had joined the other side for revenge. There was no doubt that any opportunity for neutrality was waning as the war continued in the south, and all militiamen knew of families who were leaving their homesteads and moving to a geographical area where neighbors would share their political commitments.

The men in Ethan's company were amused and somewhat disgusted at the politicians who hung around Augusta and the military camps, attempting to use their popularity or even bribes to gain an advantage within the remnant of a state government. Election to political office seemed to Ethan one of the most worthless goals imaginable. He was only a little more tolerant of the Quaker merchants in Wrightsborough, who sought every opportunity to benefit financially from the conflict, knowing that their own lives or property were at little risk. Even within his small sphere of knowledge and influence, it had become clear to Ethan that those who were to determine the outcome of any military struggle were the relatively few who were willing to fight and, if necessary, sacrifice their own lives to prevail. He had already decided that he would be one of these.

The militiamen had little information about the broader aspects of the

war, but understood hazily that there was a relatively dormant standoff in
the northern colonies, that the British controlled most of the seaports, and
that a very important contest for Charles Town was imminent. Aaron Hart
told them that the professional British and Hessian armies, superbly
trained to use the weapons of their day, usually prevailed in battles against
Continental troops. George Washington had apparently decided to preserve his army and avoid any direct engagements, an approach that was
also advisable for the militia when they faced a superior military force. Although they agreed that self-preservation was vital for their small group,
the most dedicated militiamen were eager to lash out at personal enemies,
to defend their home territory, and to demonstrate their personal courage
and military prowess. They learned that their role would be to strike
quickly, to orchestrate successful ambushes of moving enemy troops, to
stand and fight until the battle was decided, but then to fade away to harass
the British and fight again when surprise or circumstance was favorable.
Some of the well-mounted militiamen who served under Clarke had already proven themselves equal to any warriors of the day—tough, daring,
fast-moving, having lived with their weapons throughout their adult lives,
and closely bound to their fellow horsemen by kinship or long friendships.
Mounted on good horses, they were almost completely mobile, their movements and future locations often unpredictable even to themselves.

News about any kind of victory by the rebels made a resounding impact
on the citizens of the area, as had Washington's victories in brief skirmishes
at Trenton and Princeton two years earlier. The general support of the populace gave the rebel militia one of their greatest advantages: intelligence
about the enemy. Their victory at Kettle Creek had been a crucial factor in
shaping the transient loyalty of wavering settlers, although this was largely
wiped out at Briar Creek.

Never forgetting the example set by Lord Dunmore in Virginia, Thomas
Brown encouraged his superiors to call for the release of all Africans who
would agree to fight with the Redcoats. In June 1779, General Sir Henry Clinton offered freedom "to every Negroe who shall desert the Rebel Standard,"
which aroused anger and despair among all the plantation owners, even those
who were supporting the Tory cause. Many of the slaves responded and began moving from the coastal plantations toward Savannah to offer their services as soldiers or just to become dependents. Although some of them would

fight heroically, they were ill-equipped to take up arms and, usually crammed into Negro camps without the medical care they had enjoyed on the plantations, were remarkably susceptible to "white folks" diseases. Thomas Jefferson estimated that 90 percent of those who escaped from Virginia owners died of smallpox, syphilis, or typhus fever. Governor Dunmore in Virginia and General Sir William Howe in Boston had realized as early as 1775 that the Europeans were relatively immune to smallpox, and encouraged infected people to leave British posts so they could carry the disease to the more susceptible Americans, who had never been exposed during childhood. In fact, the Americans also used slaves to send smallpox to the enemy, as plantation owners gave freedom to black people with the disease and encouraged them to flee to enemy strongholds carrying blankets and clothing saturated with the virus.

When William Few assembled Ethan Pratt and other platoon members near Wrightsborough late in June 1779, he gave them some bad news, directly from Savannah. Indian Superintendent John Stuart had died earlier that year, and Governor Wright and leaders in London had decided to appoint Thomas Brown as superintendent of the Creeks, Cherokees, Catawbas, and a few smaller Indian tribes along the Atlantic Coast. There was little doubt among the British or revolutionary leaders that Brown was the most knowledgeable and influential white man among the Indian tribes and had long advocated their recruitment in the king's service.

The militiamen had intercepted a message, assumed to be authentic, indicating that Brown's first action in his new position was to orchestrate Creek attacks against Whig settlements, offering cash payment and prizes for scalps. Elijah Clarke immediately announced that they were going to destroy an equal number of Tory homesteads, but in fact the message proved to be fallacious and there was no evidence of a widespread crusade against settlers' homes or families.

Aaron Hart gave the best assessment: "Most of these folks have tried to stay out of the fight, guessing who will finally win and let them keep their property. British leaders have announced an official policy to treat the undecided settlers well, and Brown is forced to obey orders. The best thing we can do is recruit the ones we can and leave the rest of them alone."

Although the Morris and Pratt homesteads were in a remote area, everyone in Wrightsborough knew that there had been no Indian or Ranger attacks on any settlers within the Quaker community. The devout Friends assumed that this was in answer to their fervent prayers, but some of their leaders knew that they were protected by a special order from Governor Wright, who was soon to return from London. Mavis had been working as a house servant in the town since her husband was killed, and was surprised one morning to meet Epsey and seven-year-old Henry on the village street. Mavis was impressed with how much the boy resembled his father, and had difficulty looking anywhere except at the tall child with long blond hair, tied like Ethan's in a ponytail down his back.

Almost apologetically, Epsey said, "For several months, Ethan has been spending almost all his time on his military duties and has had little opportunity to care for growing crops or our cattle, hogs, and sheep. I've sold all I could round up, except our milk cow, and plan to move into town here until the fighting's over."

Mavis concealed her surprise and replied, "I'd be very glad to be of help until you get a place to stay."

"Oh, I've already visited Brother Joseph Maddock, and he has promised to arrange with one of the other Quaker families to accept me and Henry as boarders until my husband decides to come back home."

Mavis asked, "Have you already moved your things?"

"I've brought my spinning wheel and loom and stored them in Maddock's barn, and we'll go back home to get the rest of what I'll really need. I've hired a man to do the hauling."

When Mavis casually asked about Ethan, Epsey just replied that he was off somewhere in the Carolinas, fighting along with some other men from Georgia. She said that he was with Captain William Few but did not add that she had not heard from him in several weeks.

Although they had lived as neighbors for almost seven years, the two women were strangely ill at ease in each other's presence and rarely saw each other thereafter.

Back home on the farm, Epsey began to prepare for her planned move to Wrightsborough. In her mind, she had already divided their possessions into three categories: those that would be left behind and abandoned; more valuable things to be hauled to Wrightsborough and sold; and personal belongings that she and Henry would retain while living in someone else's house. For a substantial fee, Joseph Maddock had agreed to send a waggoner to help with the move. All the livestock had already been sold except the saddle horse and their best milk cow, which had recently calved. Epsey had decided to carry the cow and calf to Wrightsborough to be sold and to keep the horse in the town stable so she and Henry could visit the homestead when possible in the future, and to have it available when Ethan came home after the war.

Henry was excited about going to a new home in town and insisted on helping as their belongings were divided. As the appointed time approached for the wagon to arrive, Epsey decided to go to the woods corral and bring the cow to the house so it could be tied behind the wagon.

"Henry, I'm going down in the woods to get the cow. Would you rather go with me or stay here and continue piling up your father's tools? I'll be back inside of an hour."

"I'll stay here, Mama. I think I know what Daddy will be needing when he comes home."

Epsey smiled and began the long walk past the fields and then several hundred yards farther to a fenced area of about two acres, which included an open grassy knoll and some shade trees. This was the same place where she and the baby had accompanied Ethan when he'd cleared the area for a small pasture. She remembered how compatible they had been, both with each other and in their basic attitude toward life. Now he was a different man, obsessed with killing. Almost by habit, she prayed that God would change her husband by reminding him that their Savior was the Prince of Peace. She saw no justification for the terrible violence that had so changed their lives.

Although the cow was quite tame, she was reluctant to be roped and taken to the barn lot, where she would be kept separate from her calf while providing milk for the family. Epsey attempted to hem the cow into a corner but was never quite able to slip the rope over her sawed-off horns. As she chased the cow around the corral, she heard voices coming from the direction of the cabin. She assumed that the waggoner and an assistant had arrived early, but after a few minutes she became alarmed, as it was obvious to her that there were several voices, some apparently raised in anger or excitement.

Epsey abandoned her effort to catch the milk cow and began to move down the wooded lane toward the open fields and the cabin. She heard the sound of horses departing and then saw a column of rising smoke. She was terrified and ran as fast as possible, with her long skirt pulled up between her legs and clutched against her stomach. She could soon see that the cabin and outbuildings were all in flames, and she could not detect any movement around them. She glimpsed a small group of horsemen disappearing along the trail leading toward the Morrises' cabin, and it seemed that there were at least two white men and the rest Indians. Epsey soon found the body of her son near the woodpile, horribly mutilated and scalped.

For a long time she sat on the ground, holding Henry's lifeless body, hardly aware that she was drenched in his blood. She was overwhelmed with grief, which slowly changed to bewilderment and then anger, at the war and everyone who was responsible for the violence. She was embarrassed to realize that she had even included Ethan among those who were committing the repulsive acts.

Finally, she was able to control her grief and rise and consider her own responsibilities. Almost everything that could be of value had been taken, and the men had rifled through all the personal belongings that had been neatly piled in the yard waiting for the waggoner. First she found a blanket in which she tenderly wrapped Henry's body. Then she used an old shovel blade and dug a grave, deep enough to avoid any possible violation by scavenging animals. After a prayerful burial and the erection of a small marker, Epsey considered her plight and decided that she must go to Wrightsborough as quickly as possible, for her own safety and to warn others about what she considered to be a war party. She walked carefully around the still-smoldering cabin and tried to identify as many different footprints as possible. She was certain that there were at least three different white men and a much larger number of Indians, whose moccasin prints were indistinguishable from one another.

Since they had taken her horse, she had no way to carry anything except on her back. Then she thought of the cow, returned to the woodland corral, soon had it roped, and brought it back to the cabin. She packed her most urgently needed things, draped them across the cow's back, and began the six-mile walk toward town.

A week later, Ranger Captain James Grierson arrived at British headquarters in Augusta and went to Colonel Thomas Brown's office to give an account of the patrol under his command. Brown confronted him before he could speak.

"I've had a report that you have attacked and destroyed homesteads in Wrightsborough, which you know to be a direct violation of directives from London and also my own personal orders to you."

Grierson was taken aback by this unaccustomed condemnation and replied, "Although I've always disagreed with this policy, my best efforts have been to keep our men out of the Quaker area."

"Do you deny this information that I have received directly from Joseph Maddock?"

"Sir, there was one exception just east of the Ogeechee River, and it involved a non-Quaker named Pratt who is a full-time militiaman that is right now fighting with Elijah Clarke against our troops in Carolina. I was just going to burn the buildings, but some of the Cherokees got out of hand and killed a boy that was there. We searched the place, and no one else was around."

"That's the same name Maddock gave me, but I didn't know anything about him. I'll have to make a report to the governor, and what you told me had better be right."

After Grierson left, Brown felt that his general policy of harassing only members of the American militia had not been violated. It was his purpose to punish both the traitors and their families as severely as possible, but always to draw a line between the committed revolutionary militants and others who might be forced or enticed to join and support the loyalists. It required only a few minutes with his notebooks for him to confirm the information about Ethan Pratt, and he felt certain that he could assuage the concerns of the Quaker leader and that there was no need for a report to Savannah. In fact, he decided to let it be known that the Rangers had been responsible for the incident, in order to send a clear message of intimidation to still-doubtful settler families.

It was not in Epsey's nature to remain idle, and she soon rented a small shack near her new home, in which she placed her spinning wheel and loom and began weaving cloth and making women's dresses and men's shirts. She had no trouble selling everything she produced, but her even more attractive items were soft and pliable leather goods, as she resurrected the skills she had known when working in Henry's cobbler shop in Hillsborough. Epsey fitted easily into the religious life of the Quaker community and was active in the community projects of the other women. She grieved over Henry, was concerned about her husband, and prayed with equal fervor and devotion that his life would be spared and that he would not be guilty of taking the lives of others. She had written him a letter telling him about their son's death, including the report that the raiders had been members of the Rangers.

Almost six weeks later, Ethan arrived in Wrightsborough, and he and Epsey greeted each other with a brief embrace.

Ethan said, "I came as soon as I could. We were in North Carolina when I got the message."

"Well, there was nothing that could be done, once it happened."

"How have you been?"

"As well as could be expected. I've managed to stay busy with my spinning and weaving, and the Friends have been very nice to me."

Ethan said, "I'm grateful to them." After a moment he added, "Have you been back out to our place?"

"No, there wasn't much need, and I didn't want to go by myself."

"I'd like to see it, and hoped you'd go with me."

They went together to the homestead, and Epsey immediately showed Ethan the undisturbed grave. They covered it carefully with stone and erected a more permanent marker, on which Ethan chiseled Henry's name and age. Although he was gentle with her and seemed eager to ascertain her needs, Epsey hardly recognized this to be the same man she had known before Kindred's death. Even his appearance seemed to have changed, from that of a relaxed farmer into an intense, wary, and dedicated militiaman. He was hardened and tough, completely unforgiving now as he swore revenge against Brown's Rangers, even using a few shocking words that grieved her deeply. Ethan was obviously impatient to return to his company in the battle area, and he left her in Wrightsborough and departed somewhat abruptly, before sundown.

She rarely heard directly from Ethan after this brief visit, but she could follow his general movements from occasional news that came to the Quaker settlement about the activities of Captain William Few. Epsey learned from one such report that Ethan had now received the rank of lieutenant and was Captain Few's aide-de-camp.

CHAPTER 39

Americans and d'Estaing
Attack Savannah

In July 1779, Thomas Brown sent a report to Governor Tonyn:

Your Excellency:

After our feint toward Charles Town, almost all the Rebel troops were pulled back into South Carolina, but the so-called Government of the Georgia rebels is still in Augusta. They are Divided and the two sides are almost at war with each other because General Washington has transferred Brigadier General Lachlan McIntosh back to Georgia to serve under General Lincoln. The Continental Congress ignores the Politicians and deals only with Lincoln, who remains at his home in Purysburg, S.C. He is said to weigh almost Thirty stone, almost too Fat to move around on foot or on a poor horse.

The Rebels are trying to show some Benefit from their new agreement with the Europeans. A Polish Count has reported to Charles Town and is moving around in western Carolina, and Count d'Estaing has been landing some French raiding Parties along the Southern coast, but all of this will end as soon as our fleet moves South again.

I have learned that Governor Rutledge has Appealed to French Vice Admiral d'Estaing and his fleet to attack Savannah, stating that the City is defended by only 1,000 British troops, who would probably surrender if faced with a Superior force. However, d'Estaing has been ordered to Concentrate his efforts in the West Indies, and the coming winter and the needs of his ships and men Require that he soon return to France for Reconditioning and Replenishment. I believe we have little to fear from the French.

> *Respectfully submitted by*
> *the Governor's agent*

It was two hours before daybreak on the fourth of September, and Lieutenant Colonel Thomas Brown was asleep on a narrow bed in the officers' quarters, which was a two-story house in the center of Savannah. He had been up until almost midnight, meeting with Sergeant Baker and three of his Ranger leaders. One of them was Chief Sunoma, his most trusted Creek warrior, an older man of forty. The Rangers were assigned the boring and fruitless responsibility of surveillance along the sea approaches to the city. He was instantly wakened by an almost inaudible creak of a floorboard, saw Baker approaching, and asked, "What is it?"

"The French fleet arrived off Tybee Island just after dark last night and have already sent a few men ashore. Our small contingent abandoned their post and moved back toward the city. We've only sighted eight warships, including one frigate, but we all know that d'Estaing has a very large naval force under his command, with a number of troopships carrying ground forces."

"Well, d'Estaing must now have changed his mind. He's a proud man, looking for glory. General Lincoln will surely move down on us from Charles Town, and if they are able to join forces and mount a sustained siege, it is unlikely that we can defend the city. We'll have to double our watch all the way down to Ossabaw Sound, to make sure where the French will be landing their main forces. Bring your reports directly to me."

Within a few minutes Brown had informed General Prevost of the French landfall and was pleased by the calm and respectful reaction from a man who had always despised him and derided the Florida Rangers. He presumed it was because of Governor Wright's moderating influence.

Prevost said, "There is still a possibility that this is a feint, and that d'Estaing intends to proceed northward to assist George Washington in Virginia or New Jersey. However, we'll have to be prepared, first for a well-planned siege and then a concerted attack from the French and Continentals. What do you think will be their next move along the coast?"

Brown was surprised and again pleased to receive a question of this importance.

"Sir, I believe this is their target, but we will not know until after a few hours. They'll have to deploy around the city to cut off our supplies and prevent reinforcements from joining us, and then wait for Lincoln and his Continentals before making their final demands. This will give us a few days, but the fact is that we are not prepared to repel an all-out attack."

Prevost was an intelligent man and a shrewd tactician, who had one major decision to make.

"When the time comes, we'll either have to fight or surrender. As you know, at this time we have less than a thousand men and the city is relatively defenseless once the marsh is penetrated. Together, d'Estaing and Lincoln can marshal more than four times our number and still leave Charles Town defended. In the meantime, we must make the best of what we have. We can begin to concentrate our artillery accordingly, but we have few entrenchments or abatis to protect these positions."

Prevost had been talking quietly, as though to himself, but now he turned directly to Brown, and the unprecedented sense of relative familiarity vanished. He ordered abruptly, "We'll meet in the morning at eight, and I'll want an up-to-date report from you about the French fleet."

Before landing his first troops, Count d'Estaing had sent word to General Lincoln by fast cutter that he would be moving to take Savannah in less than a fortnight and had suggested, almost as an afterthought, that the American forces from Purysburg and Charles Town might wish to join in the operation. Thomas Brown had a reliable spy named James Curry in Lincoln's headquarters, just twenty miles from Savannah, who immediately sent a written message describing this plan.

Brown was prepared the next morning, and he shared the sobering news with Governor Wright and the array of senior officers, with whom he felt decidedly ill at ease. He had always known that they did not consider him to be an equal. General Prevost and almost all other British military officials had made it clear that he was considered to be a disreputable officer and a reprobate who built his reputation on savages and militiamen more interested in looting than in conducting themselves as proper Englishmen. He was glad to be called on to speak first.

Brown looked around the room and then said, with a studied calmness, "We have now sighted at least three dozen French ships, including two with fifty guns, and eleven frigates. Several troopships are as close inshore as possible, and shallow draft cutters are approaching them, apparently sent down from Carolina. There is no doubt that Savannah is their goal. We also have reports that General Lincoln and the Continental army are preparing to move this way."

Governor Wright did not respond, but nodded to General Prevost, who was well prepared. Looking at some notes, he spelled out his orders with a reassuring clarity and confidence.

"I want you to close down the shore batteries. Spike the guns in permanent emplacements and transfer all the other cannon and ammunition into the city. Move our four small gunships upriver, where we will remove their weapons and men and then sink the stripped craft just below the town. We also need a boom and other barriers established upriver, to prevent any effort to float fire rafts down on us. I want all buoys and other markers removed so the French won't know where the channel might be. I have prepared a map that shows where your troops will be stationed, all within the town and facing the river toward Carolina."

The officers bent over a table and received their specific orders, somewhat surprised when the general prescribed the exact number of men for each position and seemed to assume that they would be protected by defenses that did not exist. Prevost then turned to Chief Engineer Moncrief.

"Major, each cadre of men will cut fascines and pickets and build their own protective abatis. I hold you responsible for the digging of adequate trenches for the men and redoubts for the cannon."

Moncrief's face drained of color, and he stammered out a reluctant response: "But, sir, I have only thirty men assigned to me."

Prevost looked up at Brown. "Colonel, how many slaves can you bring in within the next two days?"

Brown thought for only a few seconds before responding. "Sir, with authorization from you and the governor, I can conscript every one living near here on the rice plantations, not less than four hundred."

"Get them in here, then, and have them bring shovels and mattocks."

Still addressing Brown, the general added, "Colonel Maitland has eight hundred men at Beaufort. Send one of your best men to acquaint him with the situation here, the likelihood of Lincoln's moving south, and direct him to join us as expeditiously as possible. If he can do so before his path is closed, this will almost double our forces."

"Sir, I'll have a messenger there tonight, who will be well acquainted with the route along the coast that is least likely to encounter the Continental army."

As they prepared to leave, the general held up his hand and added, "You all know the serious straits in which we find ourselves. Even in the best of circumstances, with cannon mounted, entrenchments completed, and Maitland's troops with us, the enemy forces will more than double our own. D'Estaing is an able and ambitious man, who has been remarkably successful in the West Indies. The taking of Savannah will give him worldwide fame, and he will make great sacrifices to achieve this goal."

The general paused long enough to permit other comments, and then added, "I want my orders carried out thoroughly and quietly. This will not be the first time that British and Hessians have beat a greater superiority of both French and Americans. I rely firmly on the spirit and steady coolness of you and the troops we have the honor to command."

Brown was impressed by the thoroughness of the general's preparations, thrilled by his final words, and honored to be treated equally with the other officers and entrusted with major responsibilities in their presence. For some reason, the general's words about d'Estaing's ambition and desire for glory remained with him, and he hoped that the French general would not wait to form a true partnership with the American forces moving down from Charles Town. He would not be surprised if the French demanded surrender as soon as their troops were ashore.

Within a few days after the arrival of the French fleet, they had heavy artillery in place to begin a long-range bombardment of the town, and zigzag trenches were beginning to move out of the marshlands and toward the British defenders. When American troops reached the river and completed the encirclement of Savannah, the British realized that their situation was hopeless.

In a meeting of the leaders, Brown was able to report from his informant that a hot debate had erupted between the Americans and French. Indicating the character of the two leaders, Lincoln favored the slow and methodical tightening of the noose with a classical siege until the British were forced to capitulate, while d'Estaing was increasingly insistent on marshaling all their forces and taking the city by storm so that he could make an early departure for France. The initiative and final decision rested with d'Estaing, and he was strongly supported by the flamboyant Polish general Count Casimir Pulaski.

What the British needed was time, and Wright and Prevost began a series of delaying tactics while implementing their original plans. Brown got word to Maitland in Beaufort, who began moving along the coast toward Savannah. Four hundred and twenty slaves were taken from nearby plantations, delivered to Moncrief, and began digging the required entrenchments. Almost a hundred cannon, ranging from six to eighteen pounds in caliber, were removed from ships and downriver emplacements and mounted on bluffs overlooking the river, and defenses against direct attacks were hastily erected around each battery. Despite all this activity, it was inevitable that the American and French forces would prevail just by using the long-established technique of a persistent siege. Lincoln crossed the Savannah at Zubly's Ferry and Lachlan McIntosh joined him from Augusta, prepared for a joint American attack. Colonel Elijah Clarke and one hundred militiamen, including William Few's company, were eager to fight and volunteered to serve under McIntosh.

D'Estaing's expected surrender message was arrogant in tone, in effect both bypassing Governor Wright and derogating the Americans: "Sir: Count d'Estaing summons his Excellency General Prevost to surrender to the arms of the king of France. He apprises him that he will be personally responsible for all the events and misfortunes that may arise from a defense, which, by the superiority of the force which attacks him, both by sea and land, is rendered manifestly vain and of no effect."

He went on to remind the general of the glorious achievements of the French in the Grenadas, and warned him of the same fate, especially if anything was done to destroy the city or British vessels in the harbor.

The British leaders huddled and decided to prolong this process as much as possible by waiting a few hours and then sending an evasive reply:

"Sir: I am just now honored with Your Excellency's letter, containing a summons for me to surrender this town to the arms of His Majesty the king of France, which I had just delayed to answer, till I had shown it to the king's civil governor. I hope Your Excellency will have a better opinion of me, and of British troops, than to think either will surrender on a general summons, without any specific terms. If you, sir, have anything to propose that may with honor be accepted by me, you can mention them, both with regard to civil and military, and I will then give my answer. In the meantime, I will promise, upon my honor, that nothing, with my consent or knowledge, shall be destroyed, in either this town or river."

In d'Estaing's response on the same day, he included these key words:

"Sir: You are sensible that it is the part of the besieged to propose such terms as they may desire; and you cannot doubt of the satisfaction I shall have in consenting to those which I can accept, consistent with my duty. I am informed that you continue entrenching yourself. It is a matter of very little importance to me; however, for form's sake, I must desire that you will desist during our conferences together."

He added a postscript: "I apprise Your Excellency that I have not been able to refuse the army of the United States uniting itself with that of the king."

The British marveled at these last words, knowing full well that d'Estaing would have to rely heavily on the Americans during a final attack. Prevost's reply was designed to gain further time, as Maitland was at this time crossing the river, under cover of dense fog and undetected by the French.

"Sir: The business we have in hand being of importance, there being various interests to discuss, a just time is absolutely necessary to deliberate. I am, therefore, to propose that a suspension of hostilities shall take place for twenty-four hours from this date; and to request that Your Excellency will direct your columns to fall back to a greater distance, and out of sight of our works, or I shall think myself under the necessity to direct their being fired upon."

Having nothing to lose and certain of success, d'Estaing granted the delay. Now, with Maitland's eight hundred troops deployed and most of his defenses arranged, Prevost notified d'Estaing that he would have to defend the city and that the evening gun fired an hour before sunset would be a signal of the recommencement of hostilities.

The French and Americans now moved forward their mortars and light cannon, and for two weeks extended their siege trenches toward the town. They commenced a strong barrage the first week in October, and Prevost requested from both Lincoln and d'Estaing that women and children be permitted to leave the town. This was refused by another message from the French: "It is with regret we yield to the austerity of our functions, and we deplore the fate of those persons who will be the victims of your own conduct, and the delusion which appears in your mind."

D'Estaing's fellow naval officers put great pressure on him to conclude this adventure, based on an engineer's estimate that it would require ten more days for the siege trenches to reach the British lines. The French general had long overstayed his time in the western Atlantic, was expecting the inevitable approach of autumn hurricanes, and had received warnings of a possible British naval attack from the fleet stationed in New York.

Thomas Brown and fifty men were assigned an area on the extreme right of the line facing the enemy troops. He was pleased that in the written directive, his group was called "the King's Rangers." Brown had lost touch with his key informant, a former clerk of Charles Town named James Curry and now a sergeant major on General Lincoln's staff, who was always familiar with plans at the top level of command. Now, at about midnight on October 7, Curry reported personally to Brown, having left the American lines and traversed the heavily defended approaches to the city. He relayed the complete plan of attack, as agreed between d'Estaing and Lincoln, and said it would commence in exactly forty-eight hours, at daylight, with three thousand troops engaged. There would be a feint by the Americans, and Count d'Estaing would personally lead the main attack.

Because of confusion and delays when the time came, the massive assault was not launched until well after sunrise, when morning fog had cleared and the American and French troops were in plain sight. The British had focused the aim of their cannon fire so as to repel troops, with canister, grape, and chain, and this barrage was strengthened by the muskets of skilled Hessian soldiers. D'Estaing was seriously wounded in the withering fire, and Count Pulaski left his own troops to lead the faltering Frenchmen. He was stricken from his horse almost immediately after he arrived at the front of the battle line. The Americans charged all along the front as planned but were not able to penetrate the British defense.

Finally, after an hour and a half, the allies requested a cease-fire to bury their dead and remove the wounded from the battlefield. It was granted, and during this time a general retreat was ordered. The British had achieved a total victory. Generals Lincoln and McIntosh returned to their former posts, the twice-wounded D'Estaing took his fleet to France after weathering a severe hurricane within a week after sailing, and the heroic Count Pulaski died at sea of gangrene soon after a grapeshot was removed from his groin.

Thomas Brown quickly gathered as much intelligence as possible and reported to his superiors that this was the most costly battle of the Revolutionary War. Of the 1,200 killed or seriously wounded, 469 were Americans and 640 were French, while the British had only 100 casualties. He also learned that, with full approval from George Washington, General Lincoln would now devote all his efforts to the defense of Charles Town.

The Ranger commander had special reason to be exuberant. Not only had the British won a great victory, but for the first time he had been accepted and treated with respect as a vital element in the defense of Savannah. The stream of intelligence information that came in through his militia and Indian Rangers had proven to be reliable, and the revelation of the enemy's battle plans by his spy, James Curry, had been the crucial factor in the final battle. Now he anticipated relatively unimpeded British forces moving up the river to Augusta, and he hardly needed to state again his own personal desire to command the northeast Georgia region.

Among the Americans, it was a time of discouragement and the casting of blame for the unexpected defeat. With Augusta now defended by just a handful of Continental troops and General Lincoln's move of his major forces to Charles Town, rebel resistance within Georgia was almost nonexistent. Fewer than 150 American militia remained in their small pocket of territory in north Georgia, ceding the rest of the state to Tory forces. There were six small forts in the area, which the militia used or abandoned as needed. At each, they paid close attention to the placement of outposts and the ability to use their limited number of armed men to the greatest advantage in repelling incursions. The detachments of roving scouts and several hundred Indian braves under Brown's command all decided to concentrate their efforts in other areas, largely undefended, where spoils of war were available and weak or more accommodating settlers could be induced to support the Tory cause.

The secluded region of the Hornet's Nest was the only site where Georgia political leaders could assemble for brief sessions and maintain a revolutionary presence in the state, but their primary efforts were to remain alive and to protect whatever they still owned from Brown's Rangers and their loyalist neighbors, who were increasing in number as hopes for the revolution had faded. The politicians were bitterly divided into two camps, still based largely on their previous support of either Button Gwinnett or Lachlan McIntosh, resulting in what Aaron Hart called a political comedy.

George Walton and other Gwinnett loyalists forged a letter to the Continental Congress purporting to be from the state assembly demanding that McIntosh be withdrawn from the state and assigned to another area. The forgery was discovered, and Walton was publicly censured by the Georgia assembly—and appointed chief justice the following day by the same body. Dr. George Wells, who had been Button Gwinnett's second in his duel with McIntosh, was elected by the assembly to be "fully competent to the transaction of all public business, as effectually as though the Governor was in the state." These political altercations precipitated another fatal duel, this time between McIntosh's friend Captain James Jackson and acting governor George Wells. After Wells was killed, Stephen Heard was appointed governor. He was the same man who had been sentenced to be executed in Augusta and saved by Mammy Kate, the large house slave who smuggled him out of prison in a clothes basket on her head.

Thomas Brown summarized the events of 1779:

Your Excellency:

The few reports from me during the past Year are indicative of the relative lack of Activity in the Northern colonies. One assessment that was made by Sir Henry was the absence of strategic Advantage in holding Philadelphia, which our forces wisely abandoned. It seems that the rebels have not learned the same Lesson about Charles Town, which they seem determined to hold although its Harbor is of doubtful value, vulnerable to tides, shallow . . . and [with] . . . few guns.

Washington remains huddled in Camp, apparently inclined to wait upon the French armies and navy to provide any Challenge to our forces. Although d'Estaing's fleet has cruised along the coast, his only real action was the Debacle in Savannah, which was reminiscent of his earlier Failure to take Newport. The rebel commanders are merely Conserving their limited military strength and looking anxiously toward the South—and, I believe, with good Reason.

Respectfully submitted by
the Governor's agent

CHAPTER 40

New York to Savannah

This was a rare occasion in the Hornet's Nest, with rebel militia leaders Elijah Clarke, John Twiggs, John Dooly, Benjamin and William Few, and James Jackson all in the same place. Usually, they were scattered throughout the region, in which they could still move with reasonable security. Elijah had sent out word that all those available should meet to consider a request from General Benjamin Lincoln, and was somewhat surprised when they all appeared. Now, seated on stones or stumps under a huge red oak, they were facing Colonel Andrew Williamson, a respected South Carolina militia leader who had brought the general's message. As everyone expected, Aaron Hart was sitting close but slightly behind Colonel Clarke.

Williamson said, "Gentlemen, General Lincoln sends his regards to you, his thanks for your help against Savannah, and his admiration for what you have done to hold on to this portion of Georgia."

Elijah, wanting to draw some distinction between them, interrupted to say, "Colonel, didn't none of us do well in takin' Savannah, where we lost twenty-three good men. And you'll remember that the general was wantin' us to abandon the state completely just a few months ago, and gave us hell for stayin' here."

"Well, what he wanted then and still desires is for all of us to work together fighting for freedom, and not divide up our forces so they'll be weakened."

Elijah said, "What's the general wantin' to do now?"

Williamson responded, "We have good information that Clinton has already left New York with a fleet of ships and at least three thousand infantry and cavalry on board. He seems to be heading to Savannah, with plans to move up and attack Charles Town. If he succeeds, the British can put all the Redcoats they need down here in the South, take the territory we're holding, and then move north through the Carolinas and Virginia. We must hold Charles Town, and we need all the help we can get."

James Jackson lifted his right hand, and Clarke nodded for him to speak.

"General McIntosh has already talked to us about this, and we agree with what he has had to say about this strategy. It seems foolish to have all our Continental troops bottled up in Charles Town instead of fighting to hold on here and in other parts of the Carolinas where we can face the British on our own ground."

Williamson already knew both sides of this debate, which had been going on for days in General Lincoln's headquarters. He decided to end the argument and move on to his specific mission: "General Washington has issued orders that we hold Charles Town, and General Lincoln agrees with him."

Elijah stood, took a few paces back and forth, and responded forcefully, "I don't give a damn if every officer in the army agrees. We ain't goin' to move our militia out of the hills and swamps and away from our homes and families to huddle down with a few thousand Continentals in the streets of Charles Town. This looks like just another way for Lincoln to get us to abandon Georgia."

After waiting a second or two to be sure Elijah was finished, Aaron Hart said, "It seems that Washington would have learned something from the British when they moved out of Philadelphia even while they control the ocean. Charles Town is even more useless. I've waited sometimes for a week or two for a shipment of goods to come in across the sandbars and shallow water. What we need to do is hold on to Augusta, Ninety Six, and other places like them, and meet the British on dry land. They'll have to fight like hell just to take what we've already got."

Williamson responded, "We're going to hold Augusta, because General Lincoln sees it as a possible staging point for the British to use in attacking Charles Town. In fact, he has ordered me to be in command there, and I'll be bringing extra troops to hold it."

Jackson asked, "What about the smallpox?"

"What smallpox?"

"We hear that there's a lot of pox and other diseases in Charles Town, and that people are already leaving."

Williamson replied, "There have been a few cases, but nothing to worry about."

Elijah responded, "That ain't what we heard."

Williamson had done his best, but could see that further discussion would be fruitless.

"Colonel Clarke, let me leave General Lincoln's request with you and the other commanders. He would like for you to call for men to come and help defend Charles Town, either to join up with the Continental army or to serve as volunteers. This is the only way we see to keep the British from taking both states. Once they're able to move in several thousand more troops, the balance will swing in their favor, and they'll be moving west to take this territory and then north into Virginia."

Elijah said, "We'll think on it, and we'll see if any of our men wants to spend Christmas in Charles Town. They'll be free to go. In any case, we'll be helpin' you if they's any move ag'in Augusta. You'll be welcome to Georgia, and so will the troops you'll bring."

All the men laughed politely, and Williamson soon departed.

At the same time, Lieutenant Colonel Banastre Tarleton was standing on the quarterdeck of General Sir Henry Clinton's flagship, a formidable man-of-war that he presumed was rolling and tossing less than most of the smaller vessels in the armada.

Nevertheless, he had been violently nauseated for the last two days and was now sitting on a coiled line at the base of one of the masts, with a half-filled bucket of vomit between his knees. He had left his cabin and come topside with hopes that the cold wind and spray in his face would alleviate his malaise, but his ability to look around at the white-capped sea and to anticipate when the next surge of the deck would come had increased the churning in his stomach. At least his relatively secluded place would minimize the number of people who could observe his embarrassing state.

A severe winter storm had greatly delayed the voyage from New York, and they were only just now approaching a landing near Savannah, almost three weeks later than they had anticipated. The captain of the ship had informed them that the barometer was rising, so the miserable army personnel were waiting impatiently for the seas to calm. Their thoughts had not been on the future military engagements, but on their present personal plight. It had seemed almost impossible that the ships could survive, and they were amazed at the self-assured manner of the naval officers and men, who went about their tasks as though the vile weather was of no concern. During brief times of visual clarity, messages had been sent to ensure that the ships were not permanently separated, and the fleet's common destination had helped to maintain them in a reasonably compact array. The most serious news to Tarleton was that most of his cavalry horses had been lost, with their legs or necks broken as they were tossed about in the holds of the cargo ships or washed overboard if tethered on the upper decks.

The young officer took deep breaths and tried to think about more pleasant and interesting times, notably his recent experiences. He had been born in 1754, the son of a wealthy merchant in Liverpool, England, and spent his early life as a student with no apparent purpose in life. When he'd learned about the stirrings of rebellion in America, he'd decided to embark on a military career, and his father had bought him a commission as a cornet, the lowest officer rank in a cavalry unit. Early in 1776, he had volunteered for service in the colonies under Lord Cornwallis and soon distinguished himself with his personal prowess, daring exploits, and intense ambition.

In a bold raid late that first year in America, he had been instrumental in capturing Major General Charles Lee, who had been one of the most notable defectors from the king's service to assume a command in the revolutionary forces, second in rank only to George Washington. Emboldened by this success, Tarleton later attacked General Lighthorse Harry Lee in a tavern near Valley Forge, and this famous American leader narrowly escaped capture. It was obvious to everyone that Tarleton had become one of the favorites of Lord Cornwallis, who recognized these exploits by skipping the rank of lieutenant and promoting the young man to captain and only eight months later to lieutenant colonel, when he was not quite twenty-four years old. He could hardly believe his rapid advancement, but felt that he had fully deserved it.

After an hour or so topside, he saw an orderly emerge from below, and Tarleton rose to his feet, kept one hand on the mast to steady himself, and revealed his presence. He was told that the senior officers were assembling in the general's quarters. After standing for a few moments, he felt well enough to walk unsteadily to the leeward side of the ship, where he looked around to be sure he was not observed and then emptied the bucket into the sea. Back in the general's quarters, he found General Sir Henry Clinton, Lord Cornwallis, and others gathered around a small table, examining a chart of Savannah and its sea approaches. Cornwallis was speaking:

"We will disembark most of our troops at Tybee Island, and others will use convenient beaches in the same vicinity. Smaller vessels can proceed up the river to Savannah, where the governor and General Prevost will welcome us. Because of the long delays in our voyage, there is no doubt that the rebels have been fully aware of our movements and our ultimate goal, but there is little action they can take. As all of you know, I consider Charles Town to be quite vulnerable to a simultaneous attack from sea and land. It is well defended, but we have plenty of time to conduct a patient siege operation that will inevitably prevail. My surmise is that Lincoln will acknowledge this fact and will abandon the city in order to save his army, which will make them vulnerable to our forces as they move to the west and north.

"It will be important for us to encircle the area as early as possible to minimize the number of rebel troops that escape. I shall want Lord Cornwallis to orchestrate the attack from the south and west, and Tarleton's dragoons to move across the Cooper River to cut off supplies, reinforcements, and escape, to and from the north. I know you are already familiar with these plans that you have helped to devise. Are there any questions?"

Tarleton waited for the more senior officers to speak, and after a long silence he said, "Your Lordship, it has been reported that most of my horses have perished during the storm, and it will be necessary for me to acquire additional trained mounts before we are prepared to carry out your instructions."

"I am aware of this problem, but we cannot tarry in executing this operation. You can confiscate what horses are available from the British and irregulars in Savannah, and acquire others as we move into South Carolina. It will not be just horses we will be confiscating. We can be prepared for Governor Wright and General Prevost to explode with protests when they learn what men and supplies will be leaving their city for our use against Charles Town."

"But, sir—"

"Colonel, this will not be the first time that cavalry have gone into battle on plow horses. It will be a good way for your men to begin the new year."

Tarleton made a feeble attempt to join in the general laughter, and decided not to pursue the matter further.

CHAPTER 41

Brown Returns to Augusta

MARCH 1780

Thomas Brown was proud of what his Rangers had been able to accomplish, especially since he could now use his influence as Indian superintendent to expand the participation of native tribes. During recent months he had been able to send eight hundred Creeks to help defend Pensacola against the Spaniards and at the same time help coordinate the activities of northern and southern Indians through his communications link with the British at Fort Detroit on the Great Lakes. On one occasion, his men had intercepted a message from Virginia's Governor Patrick Henry to the Spaniards in the Gulf of Mexico that led to a notable victory for the British fleet. Meanwhile, in Florida and Georgia, Brown was now the undisputed leader of Tory militiamen, including commanders James and Daniel McGirth and James Grierson. They all understood the importance of Clinton's move against Charles Town, but Brown's top personal goal was still the taking of Augusta. Lincoln's most recent decision to strengthen this post with troops under Colonel Andrew Williamson was proof enough that the rebels also recognized its importance.

In March, Colonel Brown was surprised and intrigued to receive a sealed message from Williamson in Augusta, asking for a private meeting. It was hastily arranged, and the two men met secretly, and alone, a mile north of the tavern at New Goettingen, a hundred yards from the main trail on a bluff overlooking the Savannah River. There, Williamson expressed his belief that the British would soon control all of Georgia and the Carolinas and said he wanted to see them join Florida as part of Great Britain even if the northern states should become independent.

Brown was astonished, but he nodded and murmured that such a victory in the south would lead inevitably to control of all the colonies, though he shared Williamson's hope that, under the most adverse of circumstances, England and the deep south would be united.

Williamson shuffled his feet, looked at Brown, and finally stated that he had always had a natural loyalty to the crown and suggested that he might deliver Augusta to the British under the proper circumstances.

Attempting to conceal his excitement, Brown asked, "What do you consider to be the proper circumstances?"

"I would like to be in a position to serve the king," he said, then added after some hesitation, "but not in a subordinate position."

"Sir, what is your present rank in the militia?"

"I am a colonel."

Brown looked the man in the eye and then replied, "Let me see what can be done."

Within a few days, Brown had approval from General Prevost and offered Williamson his requested rank in the British infantry, knowing that he was actually a lieutenant colonel. The traitor accepted the offer, Augusta was abandoned, and Lieutenant Colonel Brown, with four hundred men, took the town without resistance. Now thirty years old, he had realized his utmost ambition. It was almost exactly five years ago that he had been tarred and feathered. Williamson reported that John Dooly was also ready to surrender his militia troops, and Brown and even the usually pessimistic Governor Wright were convinced that resistance was over. Cornwallis was so sure of Georgia that he sent some of the few remaining troops from Savannah down to St. Augustine.

. . .

With the Georgia militia now squeezed into the northwest wilderness area and all possible rebel volunteers marshaled to defend Charles Town, Thomas Brown was free to begin his long-awaited retribution against anyone in north Georgia who might have been associated with his torture and humiliation in Augusta. He was well aware of Governor Wright's directive concerning humane treatment designed to encourage loyalty to the crown, but claimed that he was seeking the same goal by intimidating the unrelenting revolutionaries.

Brown's first act as commander of the northern region was to declare that all Whig property be confiscated and to order that anyone who had supported the revolution must leave the state or lose his freedom. He organized raids against all families known to be supporting independence, concentrating especially on those who were supporting Clarke's militia. The one exception was that the Wrightsborough settlement was still sacrosanct, as it was inhabited mostly by Quakers committed to peace, who had named their village in honor of the governor. James Grierson, however, had a deep hatred for any Georgian who supported the revolution, and it was only with difficulty that Brown was able to restrain his ferocity in attacking them. Grierson sometimes violated his instructions and joined the Indians in their torture and abuse of the wives and children of disloyal settlers, and it was only with reluctance that he spared families who lived in the Wrightsborough settlement.

The Rangers arrested adult males, interrogated them severely, and carried forty-two of the suspected revolutionaries to be imprisoned in Augusta. At the same time, marauding bands of outlaws roamed throughout the south and western part of the state and took whatever they could find, claiming it was partial recompense for what the conflict had cost them. A few of them had been forced from their homes, but most were vagabonds who had never owned any property, and few had been willing to serve in the militia on either side. Despite entreaties from Governor Wright and the fragmented remains of the Georgia Whig government, absolute lawlessness prevailed, with atrocities a daily fact of life. All but the most stalwart families abandoned their homes, and women and children of Whig families either assembled in the scattered forts of the Hornet's Nest or moved into the western Carolinas.

CHAPTER 42

The Fall of Charles Town

MAY 1780

With George Washington's forces still dormant and New York apparently secure, the British were now free to take Charles Town. They had assembled more than six thousand troops, while General Lincoln's urgent appeals even northward throughout Virginia had failed to bring in any substantial reinforcements to protect the patriots' last remaining stronghold in the south. There was widespread knowledge of the smallpox epidemic in Charles Town, and few militiamen were willing to obey orders or honor appeals of a northern general to enter the city. Even some of the regular Continental troops deserted, leaving a large but dispirited force behind and taking the pox to spread it among their home folks. Lincoln wrote to Washington: "We have only a handful of militiamen here on duty. I am much surprised to find them so unreasonable as to wish to avoid this town. There is nothing to apprehend from the small-pox."

General Clinton was very pleased with progress and fully confident that overall British strategy was sound and assured eventual victory, with the taking of Charles Town setting the stage for the final months of the war. The holding of New York would ensure continuing dominance in the north, and a push by Major General Lord Charles Cornwallis and the entire battle force of Great Britain through the Carolinas and into Virginia would force a final confrontation with the Continental army. At the same time, he could depend upon Lieutenant Colonel Banastre Tarleton to inflict maximum punishment on the fragmentary rebel militia forces that still roamed through the southern area. The capture of Charles Town was the immediate task of all British forces under his command.

With written authority from General Clinton, Tarleton and his men went quickly through Savannah and the surrounding territory and began to confiscate all the horses they could find. This was soon known, and their efforts were largely frustrated. Horses were inherently mobile, and their owners quickly hid them or rode them to isolated places outside the city.

When the British army began moving slowly northward along the coast to initiate the attack, many of Tarleton's dragoons were poorly mounted or still on foot. They fought two skirmishes on the way and were able to confiscate enough draft horses to mount themselves. Lord Cornwallis gave Tarleton a daunting task: close off all remaining access by the Americans to the mainland north of the Cooper River—their only chance for supplies, reinforcements, or eventual evacuation from the besieged city.

Even before General Clinton sailed from New York, George Washington had become deeply concerned about the prospective loss of Charles Town. He and his aides studied their best charts of the harbor and decided that a maximum effort should be made to prevent British ships from approaching the city. The Continental Congress was able to dispatch four frigates with 112 guns to report to General Lincoln for his defense. This squadron arrived late in December, and the French soon added two ships mounting 42 guns and South Carolina four ships with a total of 106 guns. The naval commander was Commodore Abraham Whipple, from Rhode Island. The primary military maneuvers were verbal sparring matches between the commodore and his own commanding general, and no effective plan was ever evolved to utilize the formidable firepower of the fleet.

A British force of three ships of the line and four frigates unloaded all their guns on barges and managed to cross the shallow bar offshore from Charles Town, then reloaded the artillery and entered the deeper channel that led to the city. Rather than face what he considered to be an invincible approaching foe, Commodore Whipple decided to move two of the American frigates to the inner harbor, transfer guns to shore batteries from the other ships, and then sink them all in an effort to block the channel and force the British vessels to sail close under the guns of Fort Moultrie in their approach to Charles Town. This is what the British did on April 8, and their fleet passed the shore batteries with only twenty-seven men killed or wounded and minimal damage to the seven ships. That same night, 750 American troops completed a five-hundred-mile march from Virginia, crossed the Cooper River, and joined Lincoln's forces. There was great celebration among the local citizens as all the available southern troops were now assembled to defend their city.

When the British forces arrived from Savannah, General Clinton ordered his ground troops to encircle the city and make the major attack from the west against the strong fortifications. The Americans still had access to the mainland by crossing the Cooper River. On April 1, the British began the slow, tedious, and inexorable process of breaching the city's defenses by using ancient siege techniques. This was a procedure that could have let d'Estaing and Lincoln take Savannah had the French not been so impetuous in making the disastrous frontal assault. The siege was simple in its execution, but costly in time and casualties. First, a deep, wide trench was dug parallel to the main fortification, just outside artillery range, at about eight hundred yards. The excavated dirt was thrown forward, creating a breastwork that protected men and weapons in the trench. Next, one or more narrow ditches were dug back and forth in a zigzag pattern toward the target fortifications, but always at an angle to the defending guns. The forward points of these ditches, or saps, soon became the focus of mortar and cannon fire, so the "sappers" were always in great danger.

After fourteen days of zigzag ditching, work was begun on a second parallel trench, dug at a range of about four hundred yards. Like the first, it was wide, deep, and protected by the parapet of excavated earth. Now, in closer range from the defenders' guns, the sappers' work became even more difficult, and every effort had to be made to keep the points of their ditches deep, narrow, and protected by frames of logs or thick timbers that were pushed ahead to absorb the hail of incoming bullets and shrapnel. As much of the work as possible was done at night. The British maintained a strong body of infantry and artillery in the closest parallel trench to repel any American sorties against the sappers.

The Charles Town city fortifications were protected by a wide moat, eight feet deep, fed by a small stream and kept full of water by retaining dams. The primary target of the sappers was to breach these dams so the moat would drain and permit the attackers to use it as their final parallel trench. Despite the utmost concentration of musket, grape, and mortar fire on the British, this goal was reached on May 6, almost a month after Clinton had first demanded the surrender of the city. Three days later, they began a heavy bombardment, and perforated rounds filled with burning materials set fire to several houses. The Americans issued an official protest, and a British admiral's aide sent an unauthorized note to the gunners: "The admiral and I begs their compliments to you and begs you will burn the Town as soon as possible, and send 24-pound shot into the stomacks of the women to see how they will deliver them." The insulting message was widely quoted on both sides, and General Clinton apologized and stopped the bombardment, stating to his subordinates, "It is absurd, impolitic, and inhuman to burn a town you mean to occupy."

General Lincoln was relieved that the flurry of smallpox cases had dissipated, but he was faced with a much more serious and immediate dilemma: whether to stay and defend the city or save what was now the only American army in the south. Lachlan McIntosh insisted that the troops be moved across the Cooper River immediately, but the lieutenant governor and other political leaders objected strenuously, aroused the other occupants of the city, and threatened to destroy all the boats and open the city's gates to the enemy. Lincoln decided to postpone a decision, but within a few days the question was moot, as the British cavalry went into action.

Two weeks after the siege was begun, Lieutenant Colonel Banastre Tarleton made plans to cross the Cooper River. He received word that the main American force responsible for protecting Charles Town's supply routes was stationed at Monck's Corner, thirty miles due north of the city. Joined by Major Patrick Ferguson and his Tory troop, called the American Volunteers, Tarleton decided to attack. Moving rapidly at night and in complete silence, the British force located the Americans, commanded by General Isaac Huger. Although the Americans were preparing to march, they were completely surprised by the assault and offered little opposition as they fled through the swampland. Fourteen Americans were killed, nineteen seriously wounded, and sixty-four captured, along with fifty wagonloads of weapons, ammunition, and supplies destined for Charles Town. Tarleton's prize possession was enough trained horses to replace the embarrassing mounts on which he had joined the battle.

In the flush of victory, he paid little attention to the actions of his men, who slew some of the wounded and raided nearby plantations owned by prominent Whigs. The dragoons looted them and even abused some of the women, including Lady Colleton, the mistress of one of the largest and most beautiful homes. Major Ferguson was so irate and disgusted that he ordered the guilty dragoons to be lined up and executed, but Tarleton interceded and the guilty men were, instead, arrested and sent to Charles Town, where they were publicly whipped. This incident drove a wedge of rivalry and animosity between Tarleton and Ferguson, two young and extremely ambitious officers.

An expert on promulgating news of his exploits, Tarleton was soon known among the British and Americans, based on his daring adventures, his intrepid leadership in battle, his surprisingly rapid and sustained movements, and the brutality with which he permitted his dragoons to treat adversaries. He and Ferguson received reinforcements and moved rapidly to occupy both sides of the Cooper River, closing Charles Town's last access to the outside world.

General Clinton could hardly believe that the Americans would permit themselves to be taken, and had been certain that Washington would send a large army from Virginia to relieve the encircled city. He ordered Cornwallis to scout the approaches to Charles Town, and Banastre Tarleton was given this assignment. Sure enough, a Continental force under Colonel Anthony White had joined 350 other troops commanded by Colonel Abraham Buford, and the survivors of Monck's Corner, under Colonel Jamieson and Colonel William Washington, a cousin of the commander in chief. This combined force captured an officer and seventeen men under Tarleton's command, camped at a place called Lenud's Ferry, and prepared to force open a pathway for the relief of Charles Town.

Tarleton had only 150 men under his immediate command, but he never hesitated when he learned of the location of his captured men. Moving swiftly, his dragoons attacked immediately, once again catching his adversaries by surprise. He later described the action:

"The Americans were totally unprepared, resistance and slaughter soon ceased. Five officers and thirty-six men were killed and wounded. All horses, arms, and accoutrements of the Americans were captured. Colonels White, Washington, and Jamieson, along with some officers and men, availed themselves of their swimming to take their escape, while many who wished to follow their example perished in the river. The British dragoons lost two men and four horses in the action, but returning to Lord Cornwallis's camp the same evening, upwards of twenty horses expired with fatigue."

The next day, May 8, Clinton called for the unconditional surrender of Charles Town, but Lincoln insisted on retaining all military honors. Instead, the British commenced a massive bombardment with almost two hundred cannons, some firing incendiary shells. On the twelfth, Lincoln sued for a cease-fire and agreed to surrender. He and his most senior officers were to be accepted as prisoners, with the opportunity to be treated well and exchanged for British captives of similar rank. All other captured men, more than 3,300, were to be imprisoned on British ships, with a good prospect of dying of exposure and disease. About one thousand civilians, including volunteer militiamen from Virginia and the Carolinas, would be put on parole, their names recorded, and released on their word of honor that they would not again take up arms against the crown. This was the greatest defeat of the Americans and the supreme British victory of the war.

General Sir Henry Clinton sailed for New York after turning over authority to Lord Cornwallis, with instructions that he was to hold Charles Town at all costs, and not let excursions farther northward put the city at risk. He also announced unilaterally that all those on parole were to be released, their names recorded, and that they would be required to swear allegiance to the crown and actively support the British cause. To this, many Americans swore falsely and later joined the revolutionaries, realizing that they would be executed as traitors if subsequently captured by the British.

CHAPTER 43

Cornwallis Triumphant

MAY 1780

After Charles Town fell and the large rebel army surrendered, Lord Cornwallis was confident that all doubtful citizens in the deep south would acknowledge the inevitability of his ultimate victory and support the British cause. He instructed his force commanders to offer amnesty to any family that made this reasonable decision, but to be harsh with those not willing to take an oath of support or at least neutrality. This was a wise policy, but not one always followed by troops in the field, who had to obtain sustenance by force from homesteads in the area and were often interested in the spoils of war or the settlement of grievances against their former peacetime neighbors. Banastre Tarleton made little effort to control his men's harsh treatment of captured or wounded enemy or their families, and in Georgia, there was a parallel conflict. Governor Wright attempted to carry out London's orders to woo settlers back to the crown, but Thomas Brown and his Rangers were now in command in Augusta, and privately ridiculed Wright's order for clemency toward Georgia settlers. Brown assumed that he and his men were under the command of General Prevost, who had now returned to St. Augustine and had little interest in north Georgia.

Despite the uncertainty of surrender terms, many citizens came to Augusta to swear allegiance to the king, including Henry Laurens, president of the First Continental Congress, and two South Carolina regiments, with all their men. Brown granted them parole, with a promise of hanging if they violated it, and their names were sent to Charles Town, along with the weapons of those who refused to join British troops for active combat.

For all practical purposes, the American congress wrote off Georgia and South Carolina. What was left of the South Carolina government met in a wilderness hideaway and chose a merchant named Thomas Sumter, with limited military experience, to be "commander in chief" of an almost nonexistent armed force. Sumter began to recruit men to follow him, with the understanding that each one would have to provision himself with a horse, weapons, clothing, and food. He was a proud and ambitious commander, whose militiamen would soon remind the British that South Carolina had not given up all hope.

Captain William Few, Lieutenant Ethan Pratt, and about twenty other men were bivouacked in one of the more remote small forts within the Hornet's Nest area, discussing news of the surrender of Charles Town. They had carried out orders to assemble all the men possible and to report to Elijah Clarke. Their recent call had resulted in only a limited response, and they soon realized that a number of their men had either joined the British or sworn to forgo further revolutionary service. Their motivations were easy to understand, because there was no logical prospect of further resistance. When Few and his troops proceeded to the central campground at Freeman's Fort, seventy miles upriver from Augusta, they found the other companies to have had the same experience as their own. There was a total of only 140 militiamen present, dispirited as they faced Colonel Clarke to discuss the future.

Clarke looked over the small group and said, "It looks like we got a lot of men sick or still in bed with their wives."

There was a scattering of mandatory laughter, and then the commander continued, "Why the stupid general would hide in Charles Town and give up all his men is beyond me, and we would have been there with them if we'd followed his orders. It may be that the fat bastard has lost the south, and now we have to decide what to do. I'm proposin' that we cross the river and join the Carolinians that are still goin' to defend the western part of their state."

There was no response, only a nervous murmur and some shuffling of feet. Clarke looked from one of his company commanders to another, and finally James Jackson responded, "Colonel, as you can see, we don't have many men left, and most have brought their wives and children into the protected area. These are the ones that are not ready to give up, but what's going to happen to the families if all the men take off up north?"

Clarke was obviously aggravated as he responded in a low but intense voice, "Shit, we can leave enough here to guard the entrances to our places, and take the rest to fight the damned Redcoats."

He looked around for a while and then asked, "How many of you will go with me to Carolina?"

Ethan immediately raised his hand and then looked around to see that the company commanders and only about thirty others had joined him. Few of them had families to protect.

Aaron Hart attempted to salvage what he could from the embarrassing response. "It's clear that all of us are ready to continue fighting, but there's a question whether to do it here or in Carolina. The other questions are what to do about our families and whether we want to split up or stay together. I'm trusting the colonel to make these decisions, and I'm ready to follow where he wants to go."

After a few moments, Clarke said, "I ain't changed my mind about protectin' Carolina, but that don't mean we can't protect ourselves at the same time. I'll send a few men up to the Watauga Valley to see what plans they have and how we can help them, but most of us will hunker down here together till we see what's best to do, bring our families in close, and be strong if Brown tries to attack. I'm really pissed at the men who didn't show up when I called them, and we'll spread the word that anybody caught in Georgia that won't join us will be considered a traitor to the revolution and will be hanged."

As quickly as possible, the British fortified Charles Town, Savannah, Augusta, and Port Royal, so that Florida and the two southern colonies were effectively incorporated as British. General Clinton moved to New York and Cornwallis replaced him in Charles Town. He ordered Major Patrick Ferguson and Banastre Tarleton to crush any remaining rebel activity, without restraints. Georgia and Carolina militia leaders decided not to oppose the main British forces, and to remain in the distant west.

Cornwallis gave Tarleton permission to pursue Continental Colonel

Abraham Buford and his American force, with instructions to abandon the mission if the pursuit seemed fruitless. Typically, Tarleton considered only one option: a forced march at a maximum pace. He had 270 troops and one three-pounder, and they accepted a constant loss of exhausted horses. On May 29, when the British forces were within twenty miles, Tarleton sent a message demanding that Buford surrender, falsely claiming that a greatly superior force was surrounding the Americans. Buford rejected the demand and formed his 450 men for battle just a few miles from the North Carolina line in a place called the Waxhaws.

Although the British force was strung out for miles and the cannon's horses and many others could no longer move forward, Tarleton never hesitated when the Americans were sighted, and ordered an immediate attack. Tarleton's horse was killed and he was wounded and lost consciousness. Believing him to be dead, his infantrymen proceeded to slaughter all the wounded Americans with their bayonets. Three hundred twenty-six Continentals were killed or captured, while Buford fled. Only five British were killed and twelve wounded. Tarleton soon recovered and now became Britain's greatest hero, and the villain of America. Thereafter, "Tarleton's quarter" would be the American battle cry as conquered or wounded British troops were slain.

This abandonment of the normal rules of war was especially notable when it is remembered that, except for British officers, most of the Redcoats were actually Americans who had maintained their loyalty to the crown and had offered their services as the British became dominant in the south. They were as deeply and sincerely wedded to their homes and families as were the revolutionaries who opposed them, and they despised the Continentals and Whig militiamen as traitors. The mutual condemnation was intense, and over months of bloody skirmishing, the robberies and atrocities in the south built up an almost uncontrollable hatred between Tories and revolutionaries, so that all restraints were abandoned in the heat of battle or in dealing with wounded men following an engagement.

Thomas Brown had James and Daniel McGirth and James Grierson assigned to his command, but his most active fighters were the Creeks and Cherokees who roamed the frontier areas and preyed on the remaining settlers. Brown was not well trained to command forces of such diversity, and made no real effort to control the violence he unleashed.

The British Parliament adopted an official Disqualifying Act that required their own troops to protect surrendered Whigs who honored their parole pledges, and Cornwallis reluctantly complied with the decision. The general soon learned that Thomas Brown was demanding active cooperation by surrendered Whigs, not just passive neutrality, but decided not to interfere. Many of the parolees left in Georgia considered Brown's policy to be a violation of their surrender terms, and Clarke tried, through persuasion and intimidation, to recruit them to join his forces. Ethan Pratt, all the commanders, and a core group of American militiamen under Clarke's command had never surrendered, and now they were even more tightly organized, constantly alert, and almost always aware of what the Tories were planning.

This was a strange fighting force, operating on its own and having little if any relationship with George Washington's Continentals. As a rule, the regular American commanders knew nothing of their actions until after they were over, and with few exceptions Congress never supplied the militia leaders with any weapons, horses, uniforms, or other supplies. These southerners met their own needs from the territory where they happened to be operating. Most of the time they comprised small groups and were able to come forward to fight or to disband and reassemble in the hidden and well-protected recesses of the Hornet's Nest. Their greatest asset and most precious possessions were superb horses, from which they were seldom distant more than a hundred yards.

Believing the war in Georgia to be over, Cornwallis ordered Brown to relinquish his military duties and concentrate on being Indian superintendent. Brown was distressed, and sent the general a letter exaggerating the Georgia militia's continuing threat and embellishing his past exploits in combat and in securing intelligence. He claimed to have raised more Indian fighters in his brief tenure than had John Stuart over many years, and pointed out that his good relationship with the natives was largely predicated on his military command. Cornwallis replied that he needed no justification for his previous order, but he finally relented and decided that Brown could retain his military duties and help eliminate the remaining American militia.

Feeling himself to still be vulnerable, Brown gathered as much information as possible about the relative strength of Whigs and Tories in the southern states, and shared the assessment with his superiors in Savannah and St. Augustine. In Virginia, influenced by proximity to the northern fighting forces, Whigs far outnumbered Tories, and there was almost an equal division of loyalties in North Carolina. With British forces rapidly expanding their hold on South Carolina, Tory loyalty was surpassing that of Whigs and, as usual, Georgia's overwhelming loyalty was to the crown. In London, British leaders planned for future peace talks with the assumption that the two southern states were joined to Florida as an integral part of Britain and, at the same time, the Continental Congress considered omitting Georgia and South Carolina from those still defending independence.

In July 1780, while returning from one of their forays against the Indians and Brown's troops in upcountry Georgia, Clarke and Dooly decided to call another meeting at one of the forts in the Hornet's Nest to decide how they might be more effective in opposing the forces of Lord Cornwallis. While the word was being spread for the men to gather, they decided to visit their wives and families.

Thomas Brown had posted one of his most skilled Creek warriors to watch the small cabin that housed Dooly's family, and he hastened to report the colonel's arrival. The second night he was home, five Tories entered the home, caught Dooly in bed, and hacked him to death. They were under orders not to harm his wife and family, but they were permitted to ransack the house. They found a jug of whiskey but no food except some cornmeal, and decided to go to a nearby cabin to celebrate their successful mission and to assuage their hunger.

Unfortunately for them, they chose the cabin of Nancy Hart and demanded that she prepare food for them. Nancy and her husband, Benjamin, had moved from Carolina to Georgia with the Clarkes, and she had proven to be quite self-sufficient after her husband was killed on one of the militia raids into Indian territory. She was a rough frontier widow with two daughters and had joined Hannah Clarke in organizing the safest life possible for the frontier women, who were often left behind to care for themselves. They devised a system of communication so they could share warnings when danger was approaching, and decided which cabin would be chosen as a common home until their husbands could return. Nancy was an expert with a rifle and insisted that all the women who remained in their homes should become familiar with firearms. She liked to join the men in telling ribald stories, and delighted in incorporating her own flaming red hair and crossed eyes in some of the jokes. She had long been a fervent revolutionary, and at every opportunity she dressed in men's clothing and joined the militiamen in their forays against the enemy.

After barging into the ramshackle cabin, the Tories stacked their rifles in the corner and began drinking their jug of corn spirits. At first Nancy claimed that she had no food, but then she said, "I do have one old gobbler left, but he's too tough even for Tory teeth." One of them shot the turkey and ordered that she clean and prepare it for a meal. Nancy agreed and told her daughter, with a secret wink, to go to the spring for water. The Tories ignored the woman, who soon learned from their bragging that they had murdered her neighbor. The men became suspicious when the girl did not return with the water, and demanded that Nancy call her daughter.

She put them off as long as possible, and finally backed into the corner, picked up one of the rifles, and told the Tories not to move. One of them laughed and started toward her. She coolly shot him between his eyes and picked up another rifle. She was so cross-eyed that no one could tell where she was looking. Her daughter soon returned, shouting that the neighbors were on the way. When another Tory bolted through the door and ran across the yard to escape, Nancy killed him also, with a bullet in his back, and then forced the others to lie down on the floor to avoid further trouble. All three were immediately hanged when the Whigs arrived.

CHAPTER 44

Georgia Militia to Carolina

After attending a simple burial ceremony for John Dooly in his yard, Elijah Clarke proceeded with his plan to muster all Georgians, and about two hundred men assembled. Despite Clarke's request for men to go to western Carolina, just a few were willing to respond.

Lieutenant Colonel Thomas Brown despised Elijah Clarke, seeing in him a formidable foe and one of the last remaining threats to British dominance in the deep south. It was Clarke who was actively seducing released Whigs to violate their oaths of neutrality and take up arms against the crown. Brown had never been able to secure a reliable spy within the Georgia militia, but his Indian scouts were able to report their general movements. As soon as the Georgians crossed the Savannah River, Brown sent word to Lord Cornwallis that Clarke was traveling toward the western mountains of Carolina with a "motley crew," and urged his destruction.

Now secure in Georgia and in most of the Carolinas and preparing to move into Virginia to attack George Washington's army, Cornwallis had already dispatched Major Patrick Ferguson to protect his western flank. He forwarded Brown's request to Ferguson with instructions to intercept Clarke's small force and then to concentrate on the backwoodsmen of the Watauga Valley, who had come to be known as Over Mountain men.

While Elijah Clarke had been struggling to scrape up a few dozen men willing to support the revolution, Major Ferguson was overwhelmed with American volunteers who wanted to join the winning side, and selected two thousand of the best of them to serve with him. Ferguson was a brave and arrogant young man, already famous for having invented an improved breech-loading rifle that could be loaded and fired several times a minute. Twice wounded, he was a favorite of General Clinton but was not liked or trusted by Cornwallis, who preferred to depend upon Banastre Tarleton. Cornwallis assigned Ferguson to the thankless job of inspector of militia in May 1780, with instructions to concentrate his efforts on the frontier regions of the Carolinas, an area of little importance. Thereafter, Ferguson struggled to train and command the almost uncontrollable Tory militiamen, who expected that the purpose of each order would be explained to them by their commanding officers. They knew that the rebels chose their own officers, while the Tory commanders were always selected from within the army hierarchy. Ferguson was a strict disciplinarian and was often frustrated with the refusal of his troops to accept British military customs, but perhaps in one of his more sanguine moments he described his men accurately as "excellent woodsmen, unerring shots, careful to a degree to prevent waste or damage to their ammunition, patient of hunger and hardship, not obsessed with blankets, clothing, rum and other indulgences." He cultivated a reputation of being willing to listen to his back-country men, but he never really understood them and was not able to form them into a cohesive fighting force.

The Over Mountain rebels were fiercely independent pioneers, unwilling to accept any restraints on their personal freedom. They were creatures of the woods and hills, and more familiar with aiming their rifles at bear, deer, and turkey than at other men. Their first inclination had been to remain aloof from the mounting conflict between Whigs and Tories, but now, as Cornwallis began to expand control of western Carolina, they had to consider how best to respond to the eastern, or "flatlands," conflict. They were determined that the Redcoats would not control their region, and were pleased when Elijah Clarke, who was originally from that region of the Carolinas and knew the Watauga people well, sent word to Colonel Isaac Shelby that he and his militiamen would like to join forces.

Publicly and privately, Major Ferguson often expressed disdain and contempt for his rebel adversaries in the west. Now moving to carry out his responsibilities in that region, he committed a serious mistake by sending a foolish warning to the men of Watauga Valley that "if they do not desist from their opposition to British Arms, I shall march my army over the mountains, hang their leaders, and lay waste their country with fire and sword." The Over Mountain men heard the message, and there was no longer any doubt about their course of action. They and the Georgians would join forces near Ninety Six, harass the Redcoats, and prove to their countrymen that the war was not lost.

Lord Cornwallis had enough control over the Carolinas to receive regular intelligence reports, and he knew that Major General Horatio Gates was approaching South Carolina with a small Continental army. The American commander had not won much loyalty from his subordinates when he declared publicly that he had inherited "an army without strength, a military chest without money, a department deficient in public spirit, and a climate that increases despondency." Gates had won the respect of the British as the American military hero of Saratoga, and his movements were their major concern.

At the same time, Ferguson was hunting the combined force of militiamen under Elijah Clarke and Isaac Shelby, and had little doubt that the Redcoats would prevail in any possible encounter with this local rabble. Early in August there was a skirmish at a place known as Cedar Springs, where about two dozen Redcoats were killed. Shelby and Clarke followed their adopted strategy of inflicting maximum damage and embarrassment on the enemy and conserving their highly mobile force to fight again.

Emboldened by the brief encounter at Cedar Springs and determined to show once again that British forces were vulnerable, Clarke and Shelby began to seek another engagement. Within a few days they received word that a force of about two hundred Tories were at Musgrove's Mill, to protect a ford over the Enoree River, and decided to attack with two hundred hand-picked militiamen on horseback. Unfortunately, their scouts were detected and the British were aroused. At almost the same time, a local partisan informed them that three hundred additional mounted troops under Colonel Alexander Innes had arrived to strengthen the British forces. Clarke and Shelby knew that their troops could not confront a force almost three times as large, with two hundred of them well-trained British regulars. With their horses exhausted, neither could the two commanders retreat.

In desperation, they settled on a classical ruse: to entice the British to their defensive position. The rebels hurriedly erected breastworks of logs and brush in an arc of about two hundred yards along slightly elevated ground, and deployed Shelby's troops on the right and Clarke's on the left, with eighty men placed in reserve behind the front line. One of the Georgia veterans, Captain Shadrach Inman, took two dozen men and crossed the river, appearing to have stumbled on the British camp, and then retreated in stages to draw the enemy into the trap. The British were exulting as the rebels yielded before their muskets and bayonets, and never knew of the main force until the Georgians and Over Mountain men opened fire at a range of seventy yards. The British regulars held despite heavy losses and attacked with bayonets while the militiamen were struggling to reload their rifles.

Shelby's line started to yield, but Clarke ordered forty reserve horsemen to support his position, and the mountain men and Georgians gave their Indian war cry and charged. Although Clarke's horse was killed and he was severely wounded by sword slashes to his shoulders and neck, he never fell to his knees.

Of the five hundred Tories, sixty-three were dead, ninety wounded, and seventy were taken prisoner. Only four rebels were killed and seven wounded. The militiamen grieved when they found the body of Shadrach Inman pierced by seven bullets. Shelby said later that he was amazed at the wild and screaming charge of Clarke and his troops, which forced the remaining British to fall back.

Almost immediately thereafter, while celebrating their victory and planning an attack on Ninety Six, the rebels were advised to leave the field of battle and assure their own safety. The British had won one of the greatest victories of the war at Camden, North Carolina. With two thousand men under his command, Lord Cornwallis had attacked Major General Horatio Gates and mostly inexperienced militia from Virginia and North Carolina. Of the three thousand Americans who went into battle, most of them fled when attacked, without ever having fired their weapons. Two hundred and fifty were killed, eight hundred wounded, and one thousand taken prisoners. In fact, Gates and seven hundred survivors abandoned their women camp followers and wounded and fled 180 miles northward in only three days until they arrived at Hillsborough, North Carolina, the longest and fastest military retreat in history.

After mopping up the battlefield at Camden, Banastre Tarleton and his dragoons learned that General Sumter was nearby with eight hundred troops, most of them experienced Continentals who had captured some British troops and supply wagons. Tarleton immediately commenced a hot pursuit, with about a hundred light infantry accompanying his mounted dragoons. The two military forces proceeded on parallel paths on opposite sides of the Catawba River, with the British about ten miles behind. When Tarleton finally crossed the river on confiscated boats, his infantry were too exhausted to proceed. Typically, the British cavalryman refused to slow down. He picked the best of the foot soldiers, permitted sixty of them to double-mount behind his dragoons, and continued the chase. Believing himself to be completely safe, Sumter encamped at a place called Fishing Creek, permitted his men to go swimming and even visit nearby plantations, and went into his tent for a long nap.

Tarleton did not hesitate to attack, even though his 160 men faced five times as many experienced American troops. Once again, the British gave no quarter. The rebels lost all but forty of their five hundred men, who were either killed or captured, while General Sumter managed to escape, half-clothed and on an unsaddled horse. After the heartbreaking defeats at Camden and Fishing Creek in August 1780, General Washington ordered all remaining American forces to protect themselves from the advancing British.

Major Ferguson was eager to equal Tarleton's achievements, and he swore to his men, before God, that he would find and destroy the forces of the Georgians and the Over Mountain men. The militia commanders were equally determined that their troops would survive, and they disbanded and returned to their home bases in the Watauga Valley and across the Savannah River into Georgia. Now that he was back in the familiar region of the Hornet's Nest, Elijah Clarke's primary responsibilities were to avoid a military encounter between his few men and Thomas Brown's Florida Rangers, to protect their hiding places, and to dress his serious wounds.

Knowing of Clarke's return to Georgia, Brown decided to mount an attack against the militia stronghold. For a week, his best Indian scouts attempted to penetrate the area of the Hornet's Nest, with some success. By quiet and persistent observation of human traffic, they were able to ascertain most of the multiple routes that penetrated the wilderness, and learned where the lookouts were located. Three Ranger squads of twenty-five men each were chosen and given intense training, including familiarity with the maps that had been prepared. In the meantime, Aaron Hart had also received some intelligence from his common-law Indian wife, who knew only that some of the Indian scouts had been given this special assignment.

Alerted to the potential threat, Colonel Clarke posted additional guards at the key entry points, the normal lookouts supplemented by skilled marksmen who had been deployed along the trails to ambush any intruders. They remained in this alert status for six days, without incident, and began to assume that Hart's information was faulty. But before dawn on the seventh day, a Sunday, all three Ranger squads moved simultaneously to enter the protected area, with devastating results. Eighteen of them were killed, twelve were severely wounded and captured, and the others barely escaped with their lives. After a perfunctory trial, Clarke ordered the captured men to be hanged.

Thomas Brown abandoned any further plans to invade the Hornet's Nest and never mentioned his personal desire for revenge even to his closest military associates, but Alonzo Baker (whose official rank was now warrant officer) had long known the eagerness with which his commander received any news of the Sons of Liberty or their families, which was recorded in cryptic terms and carried always in the slit compartment inside Brown's wide belt. Brown had analyzed each of their military engagements, studied the reasons for success or failure of the military leaders, and learned how to share this knowledge with his superiors without arousing their resentment.

The primary source of Brown's effectiveness was the Rangers' network of intelligence agents, who were just as interested in what was going on among the Redcoats as in the inner councils of the Continental forces. James Curry, who had betrayed General Lincoln and whose information was crucial in the defense of Savannah, had not been his only spy in Charles Town. He also had loyal people who sent him regular reports from within the top command echelon in British headquarters. Increasingly, Brown became aware of a serious personal problem that he had with Lord Cornwallis, who had rescinded one decision to remove the Ranger commander's military authority but was well known to be committed to British military proprieties and to have little respect for irregulars.

With a complete military victory assured, Cornwallis believed that the best strategy for concluding the war in the south was to convince any doubtful families that loyalty to the king was advantageous to them. On this, he and Brown had no differences, but the two men disagreed strongly on how best to convince the potential rebels. Cornwallis was already stretching the policies of higher authority to require active support of the crown and not just neutrality, but the Rangers' additional abuse of settlers had aroused the attention of London. Brown was convinced that rewards should be restricted to Tories who were loyal enough to take up arms against the revolution, and that all others should be intimidated by fear and the certain prospect of brutal punishment. There were some blatant and well-publicized cases of abuse, and no one believed Brown's claims that he could not control his own men. Without consulting the Ranger commander, Cornwallis issued an order that no Indians could be engaged in battle or in any action that might inflict damage on a white settler.

Warrant Officer Baker brought the information to his commander, along with a spy's report that Cornwallis was reconsidering his previous decision to leave Brown with a military command in Augusta. The Ranger commander immediately decided to go to Charles Town, where he requested a meeting with the general. He was made to wait two full days before an aide came to his tavern room and invited him to headquarters. There, he introduced Baker as his aide, but was told that no one could accompany him during his "interrogatory." Brown contemplated the meaning of this word as he was made to wait again. He was finally admitted to a large and ornately furnished room that, Brown knew, had also been used by General Benjamin Lincoln. Two other high-ranking officers and several aides were with Lord Cornwallis, who merely nodded at Colonel Brown without rising from his chair. Brown saluted and remained erect, attempting to maintain dignity in spite of his discomfort at being examined by the entire group as though he was a curiosity.

Cornwallis broke the uncomfortable silence: "What can I do for you, sir?"

Everyone, and especially Brown, noticed that the word "colonel" was not used in addressing him.

"Your Excellency, I have come to pay my respects, to report on circumstances in Georgia, and to offer a brief description of the work of the King's Rangers."

"As you know, I receive regular reports from Governor Wright, whom I presume is familiar with circumstances in his own state. Also, I must say, I have received a number of reports about what I consider to be lawless activities of your men, as they attack helpless families in both Georgia and South Carolina. These brutalities are in violation of my own official directives and the universal laws of God and man. It would, indeed, be interesting to hear your explanation of what is happening under your command."

Although Brown had heard that Cornwallis did not look with favor on him as an irregular officer, he was taken aback by this direct and personal accusation in the presence of so many witnesses. For a few moments, his self-confidence was replaced by the same sense of inadequacy and uncertainty with which he had first left this same city and embarked in disgrace for what was to be a new career in St. Augustine.

At first in a fumbling way and then with increasing confidence and fervor, Brown described the organizational structure and more notable accomplishments of the Florida Rangers. He was careful to be brief, to minimize his own role, to refer often to General Prevost, and to mention the wide intelligence network that extended southward throughout Florida, westward to the Mississippi, and north to the Great Lakes. He mentioned as one example, almost in passing, his providing the detailed plans of the French and Continental forces, which frustrated their attack on Savannah.

He could tell that his words had a strong effect on his listeners, and there was no response when he paused for a moment. Brown decided to continue: "All my men are volunteers, having left their families and always having served without pay. Many of them have had their homes burned, their wives abused, and their property stolen by rebel criminals, sir, and I have to admit that it is difficult to control them in their desire for retribution. Another serious problem that I have to face is that even the slightest skirmish among the frontier settlements is deliberately and greatly exaggerated by the disloyal Whigs, who always want to discredit the king's men and hope to convince the Continental commanders to concentrate more attention here in the south."

This report was fairly accurate in its general terms, but Brown didn't hesitate to add a deliberate lie, which he rationalized as being necessary under the circumstances and because he believed strongly that his own policies in the backcountry battleground were a correction of the ill-advised directives of Parliament.

"The Rangers have strict instructions to comply fully with your orders in refraining from abuse of any settler family that renounces the rebellion and demonstrates loyalty to the king. We consider it very important to convince the doubtful ones of the lawful nature of British citizenship and the inevitability of our victory. Our policy is that only men who reject this opportunity may be punished in any way. I have prepared a complete listing of every family in the northern region of Georgia and a substantial number in Carolina, and my own personal assessment of their loyalty, which I will leave with subordinates for possible examination by Your Lordship. Furthermore, sir, we do not permit any Creek or Cherokee to participate in battle, but restrict their services to the delivery of messages, the collection of information, and efforts to prevent Indian support for the rebels."

Even Lord Cornwallis was favorably impressed, especially by Brown's fervent commitment to the loyalist cause and his seeming acquiescence to some of the general's most hotly debated decisions about humane treatment of Whig families. All of his subordinates in the room knew that the general had been convinced that Brown was a loose cannon who excessively persecuted settlers and had recruited Indians, prisoners, and other reprobates to serve in the Rangers, and that a few weeks earlier he had planned to have Brown stripped of his military command and replaced in Augusta.

There was another period of silence, and Brown made his final point.

"Your Excellency, it is well known that the superb British forces have had notable success throughout the Carolinas, but there are still a few irritants remaining on the scene in north Georgia and in the Watauga Valley. I realize that Colonel Tarleton and Major Ferguson have primary responsibility to chase them down, but I feel that my Rangers, especially the Indian scouts, can be of assistance in providing information about the whereabouts of the cowardly rebel commanders. Almost all the settler families are living peacefully on their farms and are restrained by their parole oaths or natural loyalty to the crown, but Elijah Clarke and a few other outlaws are hiding in the woods and swamps now. Many of these men are violating their paroles, and my men are hunting them relentlessly. Your Lordship, I pray that you will not decide to disassemble what I humbly consider one of the finest sources of military intelligence ever devised. I shall, of course, accede to your directives."

Cornwallis was convinced. He rose from his chair, walked around the large table in front of him, nodded in a friendly fashion to the Ranger commander, and said, "Colonel, let me thank you for this helpful report. I feel confident that the few remaining rebels will soon join our forces as we move northward to end this abominable revolution against the crown."

Brown made a proper exit from the headquarters, smiled and nodded at the waiting Baker, and the two men were soon on the trail back to Augusta. They were accompanied, always at some distance, by two white and two Indian scouts. Baker didn't break the silence, but waited respectfully for the colonel to describe the encounter. He did so in glowing terms.

"Lord Cornwallis treated me with great respect, and none of his top staff ever dared to speak while I was in the room from which he commands his forces. It was clear that he wanted to hear our report, and was very complimentary about the role our Rangers played in the Savannah victory. He was especially pleased to hear of our determination to root out the few remaining rebels in the vicinity of Augusta."

Baker assumed that the colonel had not mentioned the recent costly effort to invade the home base of the Georgia militia, and asked, "What did he have to say about his orders not to abuse them in any way, and to prohibit our Indian Rangers from joining us in military action?"

"Well, I'm not sure we saw completely eye to eye on these subjects, but he certainly understands my position."

It was clear to Baker that this was a subject not to be pursued further, and they began to discuss how best to end threats from the remaining rebel militiamen, some of whom were still active west of the Savannah River.

"We've learned the hard way how difficult it is to catch a coward like Elijah Clarke, who lacks the courage to stand and fight. He and his bunch of rogues only know how to fight from ambush, and to shoot any adversary in the back."

The sergeant nodded in agreement, having heard this discourse many times in the past. Now Brown added a new dimension.

"The first loyalty of those outlaws is not to the revolution and certainly not to any superiors. What they want is to protect their own property and steal from others. We can't stop them from robbing defenseless Tories, but we can make damn certain that everything they own is gone the next time they visit their homesteads."

Baker rode silently for a few minutes and finally asked his question: "But how about the general's orders against attacking civilians?"

"Hell, they're not civilians, and it's obvious to everyone that their families are just as guilty of treason as the men that are fighting us. When I was with him in person, I didn't find Lord Cornwallis all that eager to protect people like these. I'm sure those were instructions forced on him by people in London who don't know a damn thing about what's going on over here."

Despite his glib answer, the question had made an impact on Brown, and he considered how he might make his plans more acceptable to British authorities. Then it came to him.

"What we'll do is demand a declaration of loyalty from the entire family of every one of Clarke's militiamen. Even though the men may be off fighting or hiding, we'll direct that the wives or adult sons can speak for the family. If any of them refuse, then we'll just sequester their property."

Baker asked, "What does this mean?"

"It means to confiscate the property of a person for nonpayment of debts or for treason against the crown. As the commanding officer in north Georgia and as Indian superintendent, I will issue the order myself, couched in terms that will be approved by His Lordship. Then we can act accordingly, so as to accommodate each individual circumstance."

He thought for a few moments, smiled to himself, and added, "A number of the militiamen's homesteads are outside their so-called protected area, and we'll pick a few of those families and get some of our Indian scouts to help us teach them some unforgettable lessons that the others will be sure to remember. As you know, we have the name of every one who has taken up arms against us, and we'll just have to decide who will make the best examples."

After riding for a few miles in silence, Brown added, with a slight glance at the sergeant, "The life of a Georgia planter won't be bad after the war is over. I think I'll revisit Brownsborough and see if I can get the place back in shape."

Back in Augusta, Brown moved rapidly to implement his plans, but he had made too good an impression on Cornwallis. The general was convinced that the Rangers were a strong fighting force, especially in the wilderness areas of the few remaining rebel militia, and he was also reassured that these revolutionaries in the deep south were dispirited and would end their fruitless rebellion. He ordered that all regular troops be dispatched from Augusta to his forces in the Carolinas. The Ranger commander protested vigorously, but with no effect.

CHAPTER 45

Attack on Augusta

SEPTEMBER 1780

Despite the dismal situation from Virginia down through the Carolinas, Georgia, and Florida, Clarke and his key men were not prepared to accept defeat. They continually discussed how effective they and the Over Mountain men had been, and slowly developed among themselves a sense of invincibility, at least if they could fight according to their own rules and tactics. Although Clarke's neck and shoulder wounds had not healed and he was physically incapable of personal combat, he became more determined to orchestrate an attack on Brown's forces in Augusta. From two men in the town who remained loyal to the revolution, he received word that all the British regulars had gone and there were only 150 Rangers and a few Creeks to defend the town. Realizing his own vulnerability, Brown had sent his scouts to recruit a contingent of Indians, with promises of almost unlimited presents.

Clarke decided that it was time to strike and that he would need a maximum force to prevail against the fortifications. He could not afford a long siege like the one the British had mounted around Charles Town, which would deplete their meager supply of ammunition and permit rescue teams to be sent in from Ninety Six and other British strongholds. His intelligence was at least equal to Brown's concerning the innate loyalty of those militiamen who had offered their lives for independence in the past. He knew who had been paroled under oath and which men had never been captured by the British. He sent out word to carefully selected families that any

Whig who failed to come to Soap Creek in Wilkes County would be put to death. To preserve some secrecy, the purpose of the assembly was not revealed until almost two hundred men had assembled in mid-September.

Easily learning of Clarke's efforts to marshal a large force, Thomas Brown was glad when his Indian scouts reported that one thousand Creeks and Cherokees had been recruited to join him in Augusta and would be accompanied by David Taitt, the longtime deputy Indian superintendent who had spent most of his career operating out of Pensacola under the direction of John Stuart. Although many of the recruits were more interested in robbing settlements than in fighting the Georgia militia, Taitt was loved and trusted by the Creeks, and they felt that his presence was a good omen. However, when the large group was still a three-day march from Augusta, he became ill and seemed to be deranged. The Indians decided to return to Coweta Town in southwest Georgia, where they remained after Taitt died and was buried. Most of them went home, and only about 250 braves decided to report to Brown.

Clarke, who was weak from loss of blood and exhaustion but still able to remain astride his horse, harangued the assembly of Georgia militiamen and a few additional recruits from South Carolina.

"Men, we've got the son of a bitch where we want him now, bottled up in Augusta without any British regulars to defend him. They don't have no idea about our strength, but seem to think we're all cowards who have slunk off to hide. We'll not only be riddin' the world of Brown and Grierson, but we'll be savin' our own arses as well, because we're all livin' under a death sentence if the Tories or their savages can catch us asleep like they did John Dooly. They's another reason for us to take Augusta, and that's the big storehouse of guns, clothes, knives, household goods, and rum that Brown's usin' to pay the savages to attack our women and children. It's all there for the takin', and I'm sayin' it's time for us to go get it.

"Let me tell you two things. First, I won't be able to join in the fightin' but I can set on a horse and I'll be there with you. Second, we ain't aimin' to hold the town after we take it. What I want is Brown and Grierson strung up for their crimes, to prove to Cornwallis that the fightin' ain't over, and to see all of you enjoyin' whatever we find in the storehouse. Colonel Cruger is now in command at Ninety Six, and he'll be coming down after a few days. We'll be leavin' Augusta to see if he can defend both it and his own town."

Colonel Clarke believed every word of his speech and was euphoric about their prospective victory over his hated enemy. They then began their forty-mile ride over well-known trails toward the town. When they arrived two hours before daybreak, without being detected, Elijah divided his forces into three groups and caught Brown's 250 troops, mostly Rangers, by surprise. There was massive confusion, because these men had never before defended a stationary position and had no idea that the scattered and demoralized rebels might organize an attack. The Georgia militia had the first encounter with some Creek Indians camped two miles from the town. The Indians fired a few rounds and then hurried to McKay's Trading Post, where they knew most of the Tory troops were bivouacked.

When Colonel Brown heard the gunshots, he ordered seventy American prisoners and a storehouse of Indian presents placed under a strong guard, and then he and Major Grierson rushed to the trading post. When he realized that he was facing a strong force of Georgia militia, he dispatched a courier for help to Colonel Cruger in Ninety Six, forty-five miles away, but his pride, confidence, and expectation of impending Creek support prevented a real sense of urgency in the message. Brown's core of defending troops were soon surrounded by their enemies. The Rangers were crack shots and courageous men, and they were able to fight off the attackers throughout the day. The trading post building was too small for the combined Tory forces, so Brown ordered shallow earthworks thrown up around it and that night he enforced them with brush and sharpened tree trunks facing the enemy. Fifty of the Creek Indians, armed with muskets, were placed behind the barricade.

By midmorning, militiamen had reached the center of town, overpowered the guard, released the Whig prisoners, and captured the Indian gifts and weapons that were stored there, including two small artillery pieces. Since no one among them was familiar with "fort guns," they were to prove practically useless. During the night the rebels surrounded the building with their own trenches. The trading post was cut off from all water and other supplies, and Clarke's troops poured steady musket and rifle fire into the trench and the building. The Indians were forced out of the breastworks, and the survivors crawled up into the building to join the already overcrowded British. On the first day, casualties were great on both sides, and a single rifle bullet passed through both of Brown's thighs. Firing died down during the night, as both sides assessed their positions and planned strategy. The Rangers pried loose all the boards they could spare and wedged them, blankets, and mattresses in the windows, leaving small cracks through which their guns could be fired. The best Ranger sharpshooters were ordered to conserve their ammunition, but to kill any Whig who could be seen from their second-story vantage point.

The following morning, the attackers backed away to attend their wounds, leaving just enough troops to maintain the siege, and this arrangement of sporadic gunfire continued throughout the day, with an attempt by both commanders to minimize their casualties. A skillful British doctor dressed Brown's wounds, but he kept his boots on until his swollen legs became too painful to bear. Although in intense pain and propped in a corner, Brown refused to let his men consider surrender and he prepared for a long siege. He ordered that all men save their urine in earthen vessels. Once it cooled, he supervised its rationing, and even took the first measured drink himself, pronouncing it satisfactory. Some of the men insisted that they drink only the excrement from their own bodies, but Brown held firm and all of them were soon taking a cupful from the common pots.

The siege continued, and late on the second day, hearing the terrible cries of suffering men and seeing the piles of dead bodies pushed out of the fortification during the night, Clarke called on Brown to surrender. He refused, calling Clarke a bloody traitor who would be held responsible for this illicit attack using militiamen whom Brown had paroled with their solemn pledge to fight no more. Clarke had his own serious problems. By now, some of his men had broken into the storehouse, and they began dividing up the valuable stocks of Indian presents and imbibing freely of the rum, while Clarke struggled to keep the others at their posts. Not knowing that Brown was in desperate straits, Colonel Cruger had been in no hurry to relieve him, but he finally left enough troops to defend Ninety Six and took five hundred men with him to Augusta, including one hundred mounted dragoons, and was approaching the town from the east side of the river.

Clarke had already lost twenty men, killed and wounded, plus an almost equal number who had simply left the battle and defected with stolen goods. He counted only 140 men left, while Brown had more than 100 Florida Rangers, about the same number of Indians, and would now be supported by the large force under Colonel Cruger. When Clarke sighted them, he was forced to order the siege lifted. He paroled his Tory prisoners and began to withdraw, but a contingent of Cruger's men had crossed the river upstream to encircle the town from the west, and they, the Indians, and the Rangers attacked the Georgia militia simultaneously. Cruger said, "I am sending out patrols on horse to pick up the traitorous rebels, who will be roughly handled, some very probably 'suspended from trees' for their good deeds. We can end this rebellion by hanging every parolee that has taken protection and then acted against us." Twenty-three of the Georgia militiamen were captured, including Chesley Bostick.

Brown was unable to move from the pallet where he was lying in the trading post, but he now had an opportunity for revenge against some of those who had tormented him five years earlier, not more than a mile from this same spot. He examined the list of prisoners and carefully selected thirteen of them, whose names he had long ago memorized. Claiming that he was following the policy of Cruger and Governor Wright, he declared that all of these were men who had been captured and paroled, violated their oaths not to take up arms, and had already been sentenced to death. Warrant Officer Baker received the list and examined it closely. He could see that several of the men had never before been captured and were not violating parole. He was not surprised at this but was amazed that Bostick was not included. When Baker left to separate the condemned men, Brown sent for Chief Sunoma and gave him a folded slip of paper on which was written one name.

The Ranger commander lay on his back and watched without comment or a change of expression while, one by one, the condemned militiamen were hanged from the banisters of the stairwell. When later informed of the event, Governor James Wright said that the hangings should "have a good effect." These men actually turned out to be the fortunate ones. The Indians had lost seventy men and demanded control over other prisoners. Sunoma delivered one of the white men to them, and Bostick was slowly tortured, then killed and scalped.

A week after Colonel Cruger helped Brown save Augusta, the two leaders finally resolved differences in the wording of their report to Lord Cornwallis, by accepting the most glowing exploits of both men and exaggerating the formidable nature of their adversaries under Elijah Clarke. Now, with the report completed and signed by both men, they were sharing a bottle of good rum on the veranda of the trading post where Brown had been under siege.

This was the first time that Cruger had spent any time with the Ranger commander, and he found him to be one of the most interesting men he had ever known. Still unable to walk without crutches because of the wounds in both thighs, Brown received a steady series of reports from his men, both white and Indian. Cruger had listened to some of the conversations, and respect for their leader was obvious. Brown had a remarkable rapport with them, habitually asking about previous injuries, the well-being of their families in south Georgia or Florida, and always congratulating them on a thorough report. Cruger was intrigued with Brown's detailed knowledge of the region around Augusta. He seemed to know the name of each settler, the status of his family, the degree of his loyalty to the crown, and whether he had ever been captured by loyalist forces and put on parole. The latter settlers were considered to be in a special category, with an automatic death sentence if they were found bearing arms or supporting activities of the Whig militia, as Brown claimed to be the case of the twelve prisoners who were hanged after the unsuccessful siege. Brown looked over his glass of rum, which he was drinking sparingly with small sips, and said, "Colonel, I really appreciate the close cooperation we have enjoyed between our men and yours. It was particularly gracious of you to permit me to coordinate our joint operations against the rebels."

Cruger, who had been surprised at the obvious breeding and gracious manners of his companion, responded, "It has been a pleasure for us to join forces with you, and natural for you to be in charge of matters in this territory with which you are so familiar. How do you assess the present inclinations of the remaining families?"

Brown was eager to demonstrate the effectiveness of his intelligence operations. He could have given Cruger an almost equally detailed report from the region around Ninety Six, but he decided to restrict his answer to the Georgia side of the Savannah. He pulled a folded sheet of paper from his pocket, examined it for a few moments, and gave this reply:

"On the entire Georgia side of the river there are a total of five hundred sixty-four males whom we have been tracking for a couple of years. Two hundred fifty-five of them are serving with me or are in other loyalist forces, there are forty-two prisoners in Charles Town and twenty-one being held as hostages in Savannah, forty-nine are rebels with no families who are too cowardly to fight in any cause, and we have lost contact with fifty-seven others, who may be dead or have left the country. The other one hundred forty men are loyal to Clarke and must be captured or killed. Most of them have families of some sort, but our British forces are forbidden—by both Lord Cornwallis and me—to harm them severely."

He glanced at Cruger, who had something of a smile on his face, and added, "Of course, we can't always control what the Creeks and Cherokees do to the people who have been trying to take their land."

Cruger asked, "How many of Clarke's men have been given parole?"

Brown hesitated and then replied, "Only a handful of them have ever been caught by any British force, so most of them are not parolees. However, I have declared that they are to be treated as convicted traitors to the crown, and each of them is subject to being hanged if caught—and they know it. It would be rare for one to surrender."

Lord Cornwallis was angered by the attack on Augusta, mounted by some of the same men he had paroled after the siege of Charles Town. Although the rebels were repulsed with heavy losses, they demonstrated vividly that they had not accepted his presumption that the war in the deep south was over. The general now abandoned all restraints in dealing with Georgia and Carolina citizens. In effect, he authorized his field commanders to adopt the policy that he knew Brown was still following, the forced induction of Tory troops. He issued a blanket directive that "every militiaman who has borne arms or been paroled and later joins the enemy shall be immediately hanged." Also, passive neutrality for parolees was no longer acceptable; they had to cooperate with the Tories.

CHAPTER 46

Four Hundred to the Watauga Valley

SEPTEMBER 1780

Elijah Clarke had reached the low point of his life, with his men having suffered an embarrassing defeat and, for the first time, their enemies perhaps strong and emboldened enough to penetrate their hiding places. He was personally weakened, still suffering from his saber wounds, some of which had become infected once again.

After retreating hastily from Augusta, Clarke and his core militiamen reassembled in a place called Dennis Mill, where they had arranged for their women and children to join them. Although distressed to hear about the recent battle, the family members surrounded Elijah as a savior. He didn't know what to do with them, knowing that the few remaining revolutionary homesites were certain to be attacked, either by hostile Indians or Tory troops. Cherokees were to the north, Creeks westward across the Oconee, and Brown and his Rangers would be raiding from the south out of Augusta. With total savagery prevailing in northeast Georgia, Brown's Rangers seeking retribution, and with no possible support available from any Continental troops or other militiamen, Clarke consulted with his key lieutenants about how to deal with their desperate situation, and they decided unanimously to abandon all their property and possessions. Clarke dispatched a few dependable men to visit the settlements whose families were missing, with instructions to have everyone join them immediately, not to reveal their destination, and to bring tents, blankets, and all the food they and their animals could carry.

Ethan offered to go to the Wrightsborough settlement and bring back his own wife and any others who were willing to come. When he arrived in Wrightsborough, he paid a courtesy call on Joseph Maddock, whom he found at his home. Instead of inviting him into the house, Maddock joined Ethan in the front yard, in the shade of an enormous magnolia tree, where several chairs were arranged in a semicircle.

Maddock said, "Here is where I usually meet with other Friends who come to discuss the business of our town. Tell me, Brother Pratt, how is it with thee? I understand thou hast been involved in some of the fighting further north."

Ethan responded, "I am doing well and have been fortunate myself, but have seen many others suffer. I understand that this settlement has been spared the worst of the war."

"Yes, we have been fortunate. A number of our families have already left for Savannah, most of them hoping to reach Pennsylvania in the future. Only half as many Friends now attend the weekly meetings as before the war began. The British leaders seem to recognize that our faith prevents involvement in violence, and the governor has directed that we be spared.

Thy homestead is the only one that has been attacked. Once more, let me express my sorrow over the loss of thy son. May I ask what has brought thee back to Wrightsborough?"

"I have come to visit with my wife, and the wives of two other men who have been with me, Mrs. Hume and Mrs. Houstown."

"And not Mrs. Morris?"

"No, only the ones whose husbands have sent messages."

Maddock told Ethan where the women were living and offered to accompany him, but Ethan preferred to visit them alone. First, he found Epsey, and they greeted each other with a brief embrace.

"Ethan, it is good to see thee—you," Epsey said, smiling at her use of the Quaker pronoun. "Tell me how you are doing, and what brings you here."

"You seem to be doing well, Epsey, and so am I. We have been in the western Carolinas much of the time, and most of us are back in Wilkes County now. I have come to see you and the two other good wives to describe the situation and to learn what your desires might be. Colonel Clarke and the other officers have decided that we should move all our families to the Watauga Valley area in the western mountains, to stay there until the war is over. We will be assembling the entire group and moving together."

He paused to see if she had any reaction, but she was obviously waiting to hear him first voice his opinion.

Ethan continued, "Richard Hume and Bryan Houstown have asked me to give the same message to their wives. They asked me to recommend that they and their children join the group, and I will carry them back with me if they choose to go."

She noticed that he had not included her in the recommendation, and still waited.

Finally, he said, "I would like for you to go with us unless you feel that staying with the Quakers would be better for you."

Since the death of their son, Ethan had wondered about Epsey's feelings toward him. Her aversion to war and violence had always been obvious, and he could understand that these commitments could only have been strengthened during her stay in Wrightsborough. He had wondered at times if he was somewhat to blame for their family tragedy, and fully expected her to find some reason to remain here until the war's end. He would certainly not blame her.

She was quite self-possessed and responded calmly, "The Friends are good people, devoted to peace. Despite this, my preference is to be with the other wives and children. It may be that I can be of help with some of them on what may be a difficult trip."

Ethan reached for her hand and said, "I am grateful for this decision."

Epsey accompanied Ethan to visit the other two women, who took the suggestion from their husbands as a firm directive. Ethan spent the night in the tavern, and the small group, including four children, departed early the following morning to join the other families. There was no mention of Mavis until after they had left the village, when Epsey said, "Mavis has been getting along well here and joins often in the affairs of the Friends."

Within three days there were almost four hundred family members assembled in the Hornet's Nest, most of them children, and the militia leaders tried to assure them that there was hope of survival. Their only chance was to travel almost two hundred miles through Tory-dominated territory and cross the mountains into the Watauga Valley. Clarke explained that this was an area in western North Carolina that had been somewhat neutral in the war and so far impregnable to British and Tory intrusions. Before moving to Georgia, he had considered moving his family there, and was certain that Colonel Isaac Shelby and his Over Mountain men would welcome the Georgia refugees.

Since Epsey was one of the women in the group, Ethan received approval from Captain Few and volunteered to accompany Clarke. It was the first time he had served directly under the colonel, and he was somewhat ill at ease. His best approach was to stay as aloof as possible from the commander, which was not difficult as the long file of women, children, and militiamen crossed the Savannah and moved through western South Carolina. There were a limited number of horses, almost all of which were used to carry supplies, with only a few of the weaker women and children mounted. The militiamen who were leading and following the bedraggled crowd remained on horseback, attempting to minimize straggling and prepared to fight off any attack. Since the movement was at a walking pace, the horses were not overtaxed, and their forage from grazing soon became superior to the dwindling supply of food for humans.

Within a few days, Brown's ubiquitous scouts reported that the group had moved across the river, apparently abandoning their property in Georgia, and he was obsessed with their capture or destruction. However, his assigned duty was to protect Augusta and deal with the territories to the west and south, and his raiders were more interested in collecting spoils from the abandoned settlements than in confronting Clarke and his experienced fighters. He sent a message to Lord Cornwallis, urging him to have his forces in western Carolina find and destroy what Brown described as Elijah Clarke and his formidable militia. The general immediately assigned this task to Major Patrick Ferguson.

Although hunted by British troops and Indian scouts, the patriots and their families evaded them by using backwoods trails leading northward into the mountainous region, where they soon encountered an unseasonable winter storm. The group was running out of food with the high mountain range still to be traversed, and Clarke ordered that all the remaining corn was to be given to the children and that adults would have to depend on roots, acorns, and nuts gathered from the forest. As they entered the mountainous area and were wading through several inches of snow, they met a small group of men under Captain Edward Hampton, who offered some of their food and informed Clarke about a Carolina force that was being assembled to attack Ferguson.

With his wounds still festering and realizing that he was the only one who knew the best routes to the Watauga Valley, Clarke decided to continue with his group. They were no longer threatened by British troops, so he decided to dispatch Captain William Candler and thirty men, all on horseback, to join the Over Mountain men. Lieutenant Ethan Pratt immediately volunteered to be included in the group. He had performed well during the brief siege of Augusta and was ready for his first taste of actual combat against British regulars since the rout at Savannah, and it would be a relief to be out from under Clarke's direct command. Having spent several hours with the Georgians, Captain Hampton was eager to proceed without delay, so Ethan asked one of the remaining militiamen to inform Epsey that he was leaving.

After having traveled eleven days and two hundred miles, Clarke led the women and children across the mountain range through Sam's Gap and they finally saw the peaceful and fertile valley. Epsey and some of the other women insisted on pausing for a prayer of thanksgiving before they proceeded on to the banks of the Nolichucky River and were taken in by the host families. Shacks and tents were erected quickly for those who could not find shelter in existing homes. They were to remain there until peace returned to their north Georgia homeland. The escorting men planned to stay for two weeks to help with the housing arrangements, and then to join the Over Mountain militia in their western Carolina forays.

Colonels Brown and Grierson, who had been at least slightly restrained in their previous behavior, were now free to carry out their total domination of north Georgia. The only exception was the Quakers residing in the town of Wrightsborough, still protected by direct orders from the governor. As Indian superintendent and undisputed military commander of the region, Brown ordered the countryside to be ravaged, burning all the still unharvested fields on more than a hundred plantations owned by the men who were believed to have attacked Augusta. The buildings, land, harvested crops, and livestock were officially confiscated and given to his Rangers, stretching a somewhat equivocal order that had been issued by Cornwallis concerning a few special landholdings in the immediate vicinity of Charles Town. Rangers executed three militiamen who were captured, and the Indians were free to scalp and desecrate their bodies without restraint.

Now with strong support from all British officials in the southeast, Brown received another adequate storehouse of gifts for the Indians, who streamed into Augusta, and he gave supplies to his own supporters to rebuild and furnish their newly acquired property. He had undisputed control over the expanding force of Rangers and Indians, and relished his vast communications system, which was still expanding in geographical range and effectiveness.

CHAPTER 47

The Over Mountain Men

SEPTEMBER 1780

Lieutenant Ethan Pratt and the other Georgians were gathered around Captain Hampton after eating an early supper at the foot of a mountain range in western South Carolina. They were eager to learn all they could about the military situation in the Carolinas, and Hampton was proud of the progress that had been made in marshaling patriot troops.

Ethan asked a logical question: "Who is the overall commander of the Over Mountain men?"

After some delay, Hampton replied, "Well, we really have three different groups, and each has its own commanding officer, elected by the men."

"Then who are they?"

"Colonel Shelby, Colonel Sevier, and Colonel McDowell, and we have a total of about seven hundred men. This is about all of us except for those we left behind to defend our families against the damned Cherokee."

Lieutenant Pratt continued with another question, "And how do they decide who makes a final decision?"

Captain Hampton replied, somewhat testily, "They all have the same goal, they're close friends, and they make their decisions together. One thing they've decided is that we're moving early in the morning to meet some men from North Carolina and Virginia. This should give us more than enough to whip Ferguson's ass."

Two days later, at a place called Quaker Meadows, they joined Colonel William Campbell, with 400 Virginians, and Colonel Benjamin Cleveland, with 350 men from North Carolina. One of the first things the five colonels decided was to contact Continental General Horatio Gates to request that he send a general as their commanding officer. Without waiting for this request to be answered, they agreed to meet each day to decide on tactics, and set out late in September 1780 to find Ferguson.

Ferguson had been searching for Elijah Clarke, but now he received word that the Georgians had reached their destination and that a large force of Over Mountain militia were prepared to drive him from western Carolina. He sent a message to Lord Cornwallis requesting support and decided to move closer toward the general's encampment at Charlotte. In an attempt to recruit more Tories to join him, he issued a public appeal to the men of Carolina:

Unless you wish to be eat up by an inundation of barbarians, who by their shocking cruelties and irregularities give the best proof of their cowardice and want of discipline; I say, if you wish to be pinioned, robbed, and murdered, and see your wives and daughters, in four days, abused by the dregs of mankind—in short, if you wish or deserve to live, and bear the name of men, grasp your arms in a moment and run to camp.

The Back Water Men have crossed the mountains . . . so that you know what you have to depend upon. If you choose to be degraded forever and ever

*by a set of mongrels, say so at once, and let your women turn their backs upon
you, and look out for real men to protect them.*

> Pat. Ferguson,
> Major 71st Regiment

Copies of this obnoxious notice were passed around the patriot troops, and
they were both infuriated and amused. At first, Ethan and the other Georgians could not understand why the men were addressing each other as
"barbarians" and "mongrels," and asking if they were ready to join the
other cowards in attacking innocent ladies. While the men joked, the
colonels were busy selecting their best riders to move against Ferguson.

There were two other southern military commanders who were engaged
in a political struggle for command. South Carolina militia leaders had already elected Thomas Sumter as their commander in chief, with the rank of
brigadier general. A few weeks later, North Carolina Governor John Rutledge gave a political appointment of the same rank to James Williams, who
was distrusted by many troops because of his use of authority for financial
gain and his false claims of heroism. When Williams claimed his first command with the new commission, a large delegation of officers went to the
governor in Hillsborough to inform him that their men would not serve under his appointee. Under pressure, Rutledge announced that Sumter had the
same official commission, with command of all South Carolina militia.

Now, as the assembled Georgia and Carolina troops searched for Ferguson, Brigadier General Williams came to camp and insisted that he was the
senior officer, that only militiamen from Virginia and North Carolina should
follow the British force, and that all the others would proceed with him to attack Ninety Six, where everyone knew that he had financial investments. After a squabble and accusations that he was trying to gain spoils and avoid
combat, most of the men chose to go with the combined troops against Ferguson. When Williams was able to recruit just sixty men, he decided to tag along
with the larger force. The colonels met at Cowpens on the Pacolet River,
about one hundred miles north of Augusta, and had a planning council from
which Williams was excluded, but he was finally permitted to join the army
on an equal basis with the other leaders. Over their strong complaints, Captain Candler and his thirty Georgians were ordered to serve under the disgraced Williams. In order to preserve some semblance of a military structure,
General Williams gave a field promotion of one rank to both Candler and

Pratt. At Ethan's suggestion, a vote of all the men in the small detachment confirmed this decision. There were 910 men in the total rebel force, including 50 on foot. Still without a clear ranking leader, the other colonels deferred to Shelby as the overall commander of the 440 Over Mountain men and 470 other militia from Virginia, the Carolinas, and Georgia.

In October, Thomas Brown delivered what had now become a valuable report to Governor Tonyn on activities in the northern colonies.

> *Your Excellency:*
>
> *I am constrained to report, once again, that little has happened in the Northern colonies. One Disappointment, which has been easily overcome, was the taking of Newport by a French army of 5,000 under General Jean Baptiste de Vimeur. In fact, my information is that General Clinton had previously decided not to defend Newport, in order to utilize New York to the utmost. This also released additional troops to be placed under the Command of Lord Cornwallis. His Lordship was quite gratified to rout the Forces of General Horatio Gates at Camden in August, who had earlier taken Saratoga in the rebels' only Northern victory. I have had one Report that General Benedict Arnold has decided to abandon the hopeless Cause of the revolutionaries and to honor his lifelong commitments to Britain. If true, this will bring one of the most Successful military leaders to the service of the King.*
>
> *I am sure that His Excellency shares my Pride in our glorious achievements in Georgia, both Carolinas, and now in Virginia. If we can retain Control of the sea, there is no way that the rebels and their French allies can avoid total Defeat.*
>
> *Respectfully submitted by*
> *the Governor's agent*

CHAPTER 48

Ethan at King's Mountain

OCTOBER 1780

The rebels knew Ferguson to be one of the finest marksmen in the British forces, and he had publicized the fact that he was the inventor of a remarkable breech-loading "rifle gun" that was rugged, impervious to moisture, and could be loaded quickly even from the prone position. The Americans hoped that they would not face it on King's Mountain. What they did confront was a determined leader, small in stature, but proud and overconfident to such a degree that he exposed himself unnecessarily in combat. He was a famous and charismatic Scotsman and, as the major commandant of loyalist militia in the southern provinces, had little trouble in recruiting Tory volunteers to join his ranks. He had been determined to confront Elijah Clarke and what he considered to be other scattered remnants of despicable traitors, but he went into a defensive mode when he received an inaccurate and exaggerated report that he now faced three thousand Georgia militiamen, Over Mountain men of the Watauga Valley, and other troops from Virginia and the Carolinas. He decided to turn back toward Charlotte and General Cornwallis, from whom he had requested reinforcements.

When Ferguson's troops reached the base of King's Mountain, he ordered them to stand at ease while he and his aide, Captain Abraham DePeyster, rode to the top. There they found a narrow rocky area shaped something like a footprint, relatively bald, extending about a quarter of a mile east and west, and almost surrounded by steep wooded slopes.

Without waiting to be asked, DePeyster said, "According to the map, we're just inside North Carolina and about thirty-five miles from Charlotte. We can make it there in a long day."

Ferguson responded with a touch of ill humor: "We're not going to Charlotte. We'll remain here on top and see if the rebel riffraff are foolish enough to try to climb these steep slopes to attack. I have now received a late report that they have not many more men than we, and there is no question about the training and courage of the two forces. They are known to retreat rapidly when facing firm resistance and are especially fearful of bayonets. We have plenty of supplies to last another four or five days, and I've sent a message by two couriers to Lord Cornwallis asking for additional troops, who should be here before we need them. Then we'll hit them from all sides, with the goal of annihilating this last remnant of opposition in the south. In the meantime we'll rest and prepare for what I hope will be a decisive engagement."

DePeyster started to express some reservations about this decision, but he knew that Ferguson was eager for a victory and not inclined to order what would seem to be a retreat to a safe and protected position under Cornwallis's wing. Everyone in this western force knew and shared the intense competition between their commander and Lieutenant Colonel Banastre Tarleton, who had won some significant engagements and earned an enviable reputation as a successful commander, with far-reaching notoriety for the brutality of his treatment of the revolutionaries. The captain proceeded to implement the movement of the men to the mountaintop, where they were soon encamped, with a good, panoramic view of the surrounding countryside. The first tent erected was Major Ferguson's, where Virginia Sal, one of his several mistresses, soon joined him. As usual, there were a lot of ribald jokes among the men, but most of them were somewhat proud of their commander's prowess with women.

When questioned by DePeyster about erecting defensive breastworks, Ferguson responded that they would repel any attacking forces before they reached the crest of the steep slopes, but the men could begin collecting stones and logs, which they could arrange the following day. Although he had no expectation of a military engagement on top of the hill, this would keep their troops occupied during slack time as they awaited reinforcements and prepared for the coming fight. He was supremely confident that the invulnerable site would provide a good encampment within which to observe the countryside and prepare for their coming victory as they awaited the arrival of reinforcements from General Cornwallis. It was obvious that Ferguson sincerely disdained his adversaries.

That same day, October 7, the rebel colonels were confused about which way to go, and their exhausted men were getting restless, with some of them threatening to return home to care for their families. At Cowpens, they found a wealthy Tory, threatened his life, and finally compromised with him by slaughtering his cattle and harvesting an entire field of corn, which the men quickly consumed. Fortunately, as the force proceeded eastward toward Charlotte, they intercepted two other Tories, who reported that they had been with Ferguson and that he was on the way to join Cornwallis and his main force.

Shelby gave the captured men a simple choice: either immediate execution or truthful information about Ferguson's whereabouts. Their lives were spared when they said, "He's only a few miles from here, probably having arrived at King's Mountain, where he plans to camp."

The Tories, who seemed to have mixed feelings about Ferguson as a commanding officer, also said that the major wanted to stand out and was easy to identify. He liked to wear a multicolored hunting shirt over his tunic, and to give orders by blowing a silver whistle that he wore on a thong around his neck. They also revealed that there were about 1,100 men in Ferguson's force and that he had announced to them, "I will be on King's Mountain. I will be king of the mountain, and God Almighty cannot drive me from it."

They added with some relish that he also had more than one beautiful mistress traveling with him. The colonels also learned that Ferguson was really a Scotsman and that he was the only British citizen on the mountain. Known as the American Volunteers, all the troops were colonists who had remained loyal to the crown and were eager to fight against their neighbors and kinsmen whom they considered to be traitors. This was going to be a battle of brothers against brothers.

Some of the rebels were familiar with the site as a popular place for hunting and family outings, and described the topography of the mountaintop in some detail. Knowing that King's Mountain was less than six miles away, the Virginia colonels proposed that they rest and feed their horses, but Over Mountain leaders insisted that they move forward immediately and at top speed. Now commanding almost nine hundred eager riders, they pushed their troops forward without rest, concerned that Ferguson might actually be planning to join Cornwallis as quickly as possible. They did not have a wagon, cart, or any beasts of burden carrying equipage, but each man had with him what he required. At noon, the rain ceased and visibility improved. When they were about three miles from King's Mountain, the colonels were surprised to see that it was just a low hill, not more than sixty feet high, surrounded with a thick growth of trees but with a bald area on its top. They could see its general shape, and some local men were able to describe its exact configuration on the opposite side, which was not in view.

Not needing to devise a complicated strategy, each of the colonels was assigned a portion of the mountain, and all the troops were instructed to proceed to their place, at a distance from their target, and then move to the base of the mountain, making every effort to avoid Tory pickets. They were to remain absolutely silent until within gunshot range of the enemy troops, and hold their fire until Colonel Campbell and his men initiated the attack. Then everyone would fight like Indians, remaining concealed behind trees but advancing steadily up the steep incline. As had become standard practice for experienced riflemen, their primary targets were to be Ferguson and Tory officers.

On that Saturday afternoon a final offer was made for any cowards to leave, all guns were freshly primed after the rainy weather, and the patriots were told to put a piece of cartridge paper in their hats to distinguish themselves from the Tories, who were known to wear tufts of pine straw in theirs. General Williams and the Georgia men were assigned to the north side of the mountain, and Ethan's only additional order to his men was that they move up the steep slope as nearly abreast as possible, try to remain concealed, and commence firing only after they heard gunshots coming from the south side of the mountain.

While moving around to his assigned position, Ethan was torn by conflicting emotions. He still blamed Governor Tryon for the unjustified execution of his brother, Henry, remembered vividly the disemboweling of Kindred, and, more bitterly, condemned Thomas Brown and his Rangers for murdering his son. At the same time, he was objective enough to realize that this should not be an indictment of all British officials or of the government in London. The deaths over which he grieved had been tragic blows, but he could not avoid comparing British barbarism with the summary hanging of British prisoners and what had happened to the innocent squaws and their babies at Big Elk's camp. Both Whigs and Tories were guilty of atrocities, and he knew from recent conversations around campfires that his fellow militiamen had no intention of sparing the life of any Tory whom they might confront during the next few hours.

Being loyal citizens of Britain in Georgia had brought security and pleasure to him and his wife, and he was not especially motivated by a burning desire for "independence" or "liberty," since he had always considered himself to be both free and independent. None of his individual experiences or discussions had been enough to prevail on him to make such a firm commitment to fight as a revolutionary, but his earlier desire for neutrality had become impossible, and he had no doubts that he had made the right decision. He had committed his life to what was an unpredictable fate, so that his death was in some ways a sacrifice already made. He felt that each additional day of life was a gift.

Other thoughts raced through his mind. Although he had been involved in a few skirmishes, Ethan was still uncertain about what his reaction might be to his own, personal danger and the impending assault on the British. He had leveled his rifle and fired at Redcoats at Cowpens and in the brief Augusta siege, but those had been relatively impersonal encounters, where he had been arrayed with other riflemen shooting into an unidentifiable group of the enemy. This next confrontation would be him against specific human targets, with little likelihood that both could survive. Although a desire to compensate for his cowardly abandoning of Kindred and to demonstrate personal courage in the face of danger were probably his preeminent motivations as he moved up the steep slope, he removed any personal guilt about killing other men by deliberately relegating all British troops to subhuman status, undeserving of mercy. He was confident that he could squeeze the trigger without hesitation or a feeling of guilt. In any case, there was no way he could back down now from what everyone expected to be a bloody battle with large casualties on both sides.

Brigadier General Williams, perhaps attempting to redeem his reputation, was in the forefront of his small contingent as they crept up the side of the small mountain. Trying to keep an interval of three or four paces from the men to his right and left and slipping from tree to tree, Ethan approached the rounded brow of the hill. He and the others stopped when they could just see the heads of the British troops. Only a few minutes later, they heard the first rebel rifles fired to the south, and Ethan was amazingly calm as he and the other men moved farther up the slope and prepared to begin shooting at British troops, still at an extreme range. At first, there was little return fire except for a few indiscriminate shots by the confused troops, and most of their bullets seemed to be hitting the trees high above his head. He was behind a tree when he reloaded, and he could see that there was little danger to himself or to his fellow Americans; most of the British efforts to counterattack were on the other side of the mountaintop.

Although it did not seem necessary, General Williams was moving about and shouting orders to his troops. He was less than twenty paces from Ethan when a bullet blew off the top of his head. The surrounding men restrained their first impulse to go to their commanding officer, realizing that they could not help him. As next in command in the area, Ethan shouted, "Let's move up," and climbed the few yards to the next tree nearer the top of the hill.

Major Ferguson, who had been dallying in his tent with Miss Sal, was caught completely by surprise when the simultaneous attacks came, having been certain that another full day would be required before the rebels could reach the area, make their tactical plans, deploy troops, and launch an actual assault. He saw that the assembled piles of logs and stones would provide minimal protection with bullets coming from all sides, and recalled commenting to his subordinates that courage and the cold steel of sword and bayonet would be an adequate defense against the despised militiamen who might challenge him. Now his men were crouching behind the piles while he rushed to take charge and rally his troops. He shouted for them to return fire, and they launched bayonet charges over the southern lip of the mountain and down the slopes, forcing the Virginia troops to retreat entirely from the mountain. Twice more, Ferguson's American Volunteers drove some of their attackers partially down the slope, but each time they returned to the hilltop when Ferguson blew his silver whistle in response to rifle fire from a different flank.

When one group of Redcoats was forced back with heavy losses, they tried to raise a white flag, but Ferguson galloped over and tore it down. Finally, troops along the northern perimeter broke from the heavy foliage into the cleared area on the lip of the mountain. Ethan was in the vanguard, and saw Ferguson and a group of his officers and troops assembled in the center of the camp, gaining some protection from carts, wagons, and the piles of logs and stones. Ferguson seemed to have no fear, but dashed about on his horse rallying his men with shouts and his shrill whistle. When he saw the rebels emerge from the forest, he charged forward with his sword raised, leading about a dozen other mounted Redcoats. Now seeing the British commander clearly, at a distance of about sixty yards, Ethan knelt in the open and leveled his rifle at the commander's chest.

Ferguson was killed instantly, and his right foot caught momentarily in its stirrup, causing his body to be dragged across the rough stones before falling to the ground. Ethan could see the lifeless corpse twitch as a fusillade of other rifle bullets found their mark.

Now in command, Captain DePeyster saw that the situation was hopeless and raised a white flag, but it had little effect on many of the attacking troops. They either did not know the meaning of surrender, remembered the slaughter of their own families by British troops and their allies, or despised the Tories too much to be chivalrous in victory to a commander who had called them "barbarians," "cowards," and "a set of mongrels."

DePeyster threw his sword on the ground and shouted to Colonel Campbell, "This is damned unfair!" Campbell, now obviously in command, replied that DePeyster should dismount, his men should sit on the ground, and everyone who surrendered should remove their hats.

A group of Over Mountain men surrounded Ferguson's body, and it was soon stripped of pistol, sword, silver whistle, hat, and all clothing. Even some of the officers participated in this desecration of a man whose rash words had aroused their intense hatred. They learned that he had two mistresses in camp with him, one of whom was found dead in the commanding officer's tent, killed by a stray bullet. After some shouted arguments and ribald jokes, her body was wrapped together with Ferguson's in a raw beef hide, facing each other, and buried in a shallow grave. The militia released the other woman, along with nine other camp followers who had been traveling with Ferguson's army, claiming to be wives of officers and other men. Some of the favorites had ridden the best horses, sidesaddle, and had received fancy women's apparel that the soldiers had plundered from the local inhabitants.

The Americans killed 323 Tories, some in cold blood after they surrendered, severely wounded 163 others, and took 698 prisoners, while reporting only 28 killed and 62 wounded. Ethan and his compatriots were unaffected by the knowledge that, except for Ferguson, all the casualties were doubly despised Americans who supported the Tory cause. After searching through the woods to find their own casualties, the patriots left the dead American Volunteers for the hogs, wolves, and vultures to eat. The next morning, a Sunday, the families of some of the local Tories arrived at the site and were overwhelmed with horror as they drove off the animals and searched through the dead bodies for their husbands and sons.

Leaving behind a small contingent to complete the burial of their own dead, the Over Mountain men and other militia began marching with the prisoners up the Broad River toward Gilbert Town, which was on the way to their homes in the Watauga Valley. A special squad executed those who were too weak or wounded to proceed. When they came to a sweet potato patch, the rebels stripped it and ate the potatoes raw, the first food they had had in three days. There was not enough to share with the prisoners, but the next evening some raw corn and pumpkins were thrown to the Tories.

Under pressure from the more militant rebels, Colonel Campbell ordered a court-martial to be held six days after the battle, and thirty-six of the accused prisoners were found to be guilty of murder and other high crimes. In a driving rain, ten of them were hanged before Sevier and other Over Mountain leaders stopped the executions. One of the spared men stated that Tarleton had been expected to join their forces, and the rebels resumed their march northwestward until they crossed the Catawba River, which was rising rapidly following the heavy rains. Bone-tired and worried about their families, the Georgia and South Carolina militiamen had no desire for another military engagement, and decided to return to the Watauga Valley, while a few Over Mountain men delivered the remaining prisoners to Virginia. Neither Ethan Pratt nor any other junior officers raised any objection about the harsh treatment of the captured men.

The bloody victory at King's Mountain was a turning point for American forces in the Revolutionary War. When General Cornwallis received word of the King's Mountain battle, he realized that he was not able to protect his flank in western Carolina and could not make a rapid advance into Virginia. He decided to withdraw southward to Winnsboro and eventually camped near Ninety Six. His message to London described Ferguson's defeat as "not by soldiers but by savages."

Ethan Pratt and other members of the Georgia militia accompanied Colonels Sevier and Campbell back to the Watauga Valley, where Colonel Clarke met them as they approached. The Georgia men were surprised and concerned when they saw that he was very weak and pale, and that his right shoulder and upper arm were still bandaged. Elijah claimed that he was doing well and recovering nicely, but Aaron Hart, slightly behind him, shook his head with concern. When dismissed, Ethan went to find Epsey, who was living with two other women and three children in one of the tents that had been erected to supplement the overcrowded cabins of the Watauga Valley families.

Epsey was relieved to see Ethan and happy when she found that he was well and uninjured, but she showed little interest in the combat experiences of the militiamen.

She asked, "What will you be doing now, Ethan?"

"I reckon I'll have to carry out my orders, but we'll probably be staying on in the Carolinas. My understanding is that the British are in control of everything in Georgia."

As a statement of fact, she said, "This means that the families will have to stay here, I guess."

They bid each other good-bye, and Ethan started back to his unit. Epsey called to him and he turned around.

"Ethan, I'm always worried about you and pray that you'll be safe and we'll soon be going back home."

He came back, took her hands in his, and said, "Epsey, I miss you, and have the same hopes for our future."

CHAPTER 49

General Nathanael Greene

The Georgia militiamen moved around in western Carolina, seemingly without purpose, never spending more than one or two nights in any camping place. They were always eager to learn about military activities in the southern states, and their commanding officers shared what news was available. General Horatio Gates, ridiculed by many for his rapid flight after being routed at Camden, moved south to Charlotte, where, early in December, he awaited relief from his command. Colonel Sevier visited the Continental headquarters and came back to western South Carolina with what appeared to be a mixture of fact and conjecture about the overall strategic situation.

He commented to his listeners that General Washington had two serious problems: defections in the north and battle losses in the south. He had to stop the massive and almost unpunished desertions, which had become a way of military life among his discouraged and relatively inactive troops. After some New Jersey militia actually mutinied, Washington decided to set an example of stern discipline: he forced the top leaders to draw lots, and the winners shot the losers.

So far as the southerners knew, the opposing forces in the north continued their stalemated confrontations, and neither the British nor American commander in chief seemed to have any plan to change this strategy. It seemed that almost all action had shifted to the south, and here was where the best Continental commanders were needed. Washington was faced with a dilemma: General Howe had yielded Savannah, General Lincoln had surrendered at Charles Town, and General Gates at Camden had now lost South Carolina.

It was a source of great pride to the militiamen that their own victory at King's Mountain was the best military accomplishment in many months. Perhaps regular Continental troops could do something to match this success. Sevier said that what the commander in chief would want from the next southern commander was not a major victory, but just to keep Cornwallis occupied and discouraged from moving north to join Clinton's forces, holding in New York.

Within a few weeks, the militiamen learned that Washington had surprised his own closest advisors by turning his attention to Nathanael Greene, who was a Quaker and former blacksmith and merchant from Rhode Island. In 1775, the state assembly had utilized its provincial authority and promoted Greene from an inexperienced private to brigadier general. He had quickly become a favorite of George Washington, and both the military leaders and their wives were close friends. During the repetitive American retreats from New York, New Jersey, and Philadelphia, Greene learned how to move troops rapidly and to salvage an army even though the battleground was lost. For two years he had served as quartermaster general, bringing order out of chaos in providing supplies for the Continental army. He had then requested duty as a field officer, and Washington approved and recommended him as commander of the southern army. Greene resigned his commission in protest when Congress insisted on the appointment of Gates to this active command. Now, instead of accepting Greene's resignation, Washington ordered the thirty-eight-year-old general to proceed to Charlotte and replace Gates, and the Congress accepted this decision. The commander in chief told Greene, "There is an army to be created, the mass of which is at present without any formation at all."

When General Greene assumed command, he invited the militia commanders to meet with him, and they were favorably impressed with him personally and aware that he faced a formidable challenge. Gate's defeat at Camden had been devastating, with many of the survivors having deserted and returned to their own homes. Only 90 cavalrymen, 60 artillerymen, and 1,480 infantry were available for duty, fewer than 1,000 of whom were Continentals. The rest were unreliable militia who chose to serve and perhaps fight only when they pleased, and felt that their primary compensation was to be obtained by plundering the countryside. Greene said that the militiamen's victory at King's Mountain was the only encouraging news for a demoralized Continental army, and he hoped to follow up with some achievements of his own.

The assembled commanders assessed military alignments in the southern states. The British held heavily fortified Charles Town, and had established strong inland positions to protect their dominance along the Atlantic Coast, through Savannah and St. Augustine. They had at least 8,000 troops stationed in the southern states, 2,500 of whom were veterans under Cornwallis at Winnsboro and capable of forming a superb striking force. They controlled the Santee River and its tributaries, and forts in Orangeburg, Ninety Six, and Augusta seemed secure, but a substantial portion of British troops were required to defend these important positions.

War in the rest of the south would be a game of hide-and-seek, with taking and holding territory of minimal importance. Intelligence about enemy movements was crucial, as was secrecy for the smaller forces. As Cornwallis's British troops moved northward from Charles Town, their supply lines became longer and more vulnerable, and they had to compete for diminishing supplies of food. They all understood that any farm production was limited by repetitive raids on settler families by both Redcoats and Continentals; these families had learned to hide whatever they possessed and found it fruitless to plant new crops. The local military commanders commented to Greene that hatred had become more intense, with the most vicious fighting between former neighbors and often within families—father against son, brother against brother. The earlier policy of parole—releasing prisoners on their pledges of neutrality—had been abandoned, and future survival had come to depend on the killing of adversaries.

General Greene seemed eager to learn what he could from the militia commanders, since his overall tactics would be the same as theirs. His men would be quite mobile, seldom camping twice in the same place, and mostly moving at sundown and traveling through the night. Greene soon found that he had to depend upon the local militia, who, often on their own, continued to harass the Tories in the Carolinas and Georgia. So many deserters shifted from one side to the other that Greene said, "We fight the enemy with British soldiers and they fight us with those of America." He decided to remain in the upper reaches of the rivers, where the water was shallow enough to ford, and to send the experienced General Daniel Morgan with most of his troops southwestward across the Broad River and toward Ninety Six and Augusta. Morgan's instructions were to give spirit to the Whigs, to harass the British, and to minimize his own losses, which Greene had adopted as his general strategy. General Francis Sumter was pouting because he had been bypassed for command, and Morgan decided to operate without him. The winter of 1780 to 1781 were dark days for the revolutionaries.

Ethan Pratt was only dimly aware of these developments, but he tried to learn all he could about the progress of the revolution, and to understand his small role in the effort. He was somewhat surprised at how much he enjoyed his service in the militia. He cared well for his mare and his weapons, and learned how to use them to the fullest. The relatively idle physical life was combined with a sense that he was doing everything possible to achieve his current goals and without any responsibilities for a farm, a family, or earning a living. The camaraderie among the troops was gratifying, and he found that he was respected by his superior officers and also the men who served under him. There were moments of danger, times to travel rapidly and secretly, and a much greater number of days of relative idleness.

With Clarke still partially incapacitated with his wounds, unable to lift his right arm, no overall leadership had existed among the Georgians since the battle at King's Mountain. Desiring to continue fighting against the British, Ethan volunteered to serve under Major James Jackson. His new commander was only twenty-three years old, but he was ambitious and cool under pressure. He had already proven himself to be a fervent patriot and courageous warrior in the first military action in Savannah involving the rice barges, and later in the southern swamps of Georgia.

Along with other Georgia military leaders, Jackson received a message in January 1781 from General Daniel Morgan, who was encamped at Cowpens:

> *To the Refugees of Georgia*
>
> *Gentlemen: Having heard of your sufferings, your attachment to the cause of freedom, and your gallantry and address in action, I had formed to myself the pleasing idea of receiving in you a great and valuable acquisition to my force. Judge, then, of my disappointment, when I find you scattered about in parties, subjected to no orders, nor joining in any general plan to promote the public service. The recollections of your past achievements, and the prospects*

of future laurels, should prevent your acting in such a manner for a moment.
You have gained a character; and why should you risk the loss of it for the
most trifling gratifications?

You must know that, in your present situation, you can neither provide for
your safety, nor assist me in annoying the enemy. Let me then entreat you, by
the regard you have for your fame, and by your love to your country, to repair
to my camp, and subject yourselves to order and discipline. I will ask you to
encounter no dangers or difficulties, but what I shall participate in. Should it
be thought advisable to form detachments, you may rely on being employed on
that business, if it is more agreeable to your wishes; but it is absolutely neces-
sary that your situation and movements should be known to me, so that I may
be enabled to direct them in such a manner that they may tend to the advan-
tage of the whole. I am, gentlemen, with every sentiment of regard, your obe-
dient servant, Daniel Morgan.

Emphasizing the phrase "advisable to form detachments" and reserving
the right to act independently when they chose to do so, Major Jackson's
men and a number of other Georgians heeded this call and reported to
Morgan. Jackson's men and others who were well mounted were ordered
to serve under the commander in chief's cousin Colonel William Washington, who had been twice wounded in previous engagements with Banastre
Tarleton, but without having been involved in a victory. He was eager to
prove himself capable in battle.

The Georgians soon reported to their new commander that 250 rough-
neck militia had been recruited by Thomas Brown from their home state
and about 100 of them had been terrorizing the countryside near Ninety
Six. They were reported to be a motley group, only a few of them with
horses, and extremely brutal in their treatment of the families who were
their victims. Colonel Washington prepared to find and attack them, and
scouts familiar with the territory soon led his 280 horsemen to the camp of
the unsuspecting Tories near Hammond's store. Washington permitted
Major Jackson and the Georgians to be in the vanguard as they savaged
their hapless victims. Jackson imposed little restraint on his men, and
Ethan joined in the attack with fervor and without compunction. Their
foes were considered to be outlaws and criminals, not worthy of treatment
as respected combatants. Only a few escaped as the others were killed,
wounded, or captured, without a single casualty among the patriots.

Prodded by Elijah Clarke, the Georgia militia leaders urged Morgan to send an expedition southward into their own state, but Greene ordered Morgan's command to stay close enough so the two small patriot armies could join if threatened directly by a strong British force. At the same time, Cornwallis wanted to advance northward into North Carolina to attack Greene but could not afford to leave his southern flank exposed to Morgan and the militia forces in South Carolina. He dispatched Tarleton to defend Ninety Six and to attack Morgan's force, while he moved northward toward Charlotte. Tarleton was so serious about a victory that he issued the startling order, "No women present in camp." Eleven days of rain made it very difficult for troops to cross the rivers or their commanders to communicate. Typically, Tarleton risked his men and horses by crossing the flooding streams and moving toward Morgan, who saw the danger of being caught between Tarleton and Cornwallis. Still encamped at Cowpens, he prepared to move upstream to seek a place to cross the Broad River the next day, but he decided to stand and face Tarleton's troops when Major Jackson and his experienced militia rejoined him after their fight at Hammond's store.

Morgan had been a militiaman himself and understood their strengths and weaknesses. They were expert marksmen with the ability to reload rapidly, but they had no willingness to stand firm in an orthodox line of battle in the face of Redcoats with bayonets. He placed his 600 regular troops in formal battle array and then amazed James Jackson and the other officers by ordering 300 Georgia and Carolina militiamen to take positions one hundred yards in front, and another 120 of the finest marksmen even farther forward, to be the first to face Tarleton's dragoons. He gave all the militiamen one order: to "fire twice at officers and sergeants when they are within range, then fall back behind the other troops and remain as reserves." Morgan wanted them to know in advance that they would not be expected to face a bayonet charge.

Lieutenant Ethan Pratt was in the second line, with Jackson in command of about half the Georgia and Carolina militiamen. The others of their force were seventy-five yards in front of them. They watched as General Morgan rode the front two battle lines in the frigid early morning of January 17, beginning with the militia, who would see the first action within the next hour. To the men he shouted, "Let me see which are most entitled to the credit of brave men, the boys of Carolina or those of Georgia." Then he rode back and exhorted the regular troops to live up to their reputations for courage.

Tarleton attacked; his cavalry charge paused and withdrew temporarily when they met a strong volley from the forward militia as they came into range. Then the British infantry formed a battle line and advanced, firing their muskets with little effect. Their main desire was to make a bayonet charge, which wavered as the Georgia and Carolina riflemen in the front rank fired their second round and began an orderly withdrawal. The British suffered a substantial loss, but thought the American ranks were dissolving and drove forward, only to be met by rifle fire from Ethan and the others in the second rank. They quickly reloaded, fired again at the confused Redcoats, and withdrew. Tarleton's men then launched a more concerted charge forward, permitting Colonel Washington to begin firing at their exposed flank. The British broke their lines and rushed forward, to be faced by patriots who were standing their ground with discipline and complete effectiveness. The Redcoats broke and ran through the woods to safety, while some of Tarleton's reserve cavalry refused to obey his orders to attack. Georgia militia under James Jackson now joined the Continentals to face some heroic Scottish Highlanders, who fought until their plight was hopeless.

The Americans won a great victory, with 110 British killed and 702 taken prisoner, along with 60 Negro slaves. Twelve Americans were killed and 60 wounded. Cowpens was a crucial battle in which Cornwallis had lost one-fourth of his troops, and led to the end of the long deadlock between the two primary armies. Greene withdrew his combined force across the Dan River into Virginia, leaving Cornwallis in the Carolinas with a badly damaged army.

In February 1781, Thomas Brown assessed the overall battle situation:

> *Your Excellency:*
>
> *I would like to report that General Nathanael Greene has used every cunning Device to escape the efforts of Lord Cornwallis to destroy the rebel army, and has finally left no Continental troops South of Virginia. After a number of Costly engagements with the fleeing rebels, my best estimate is that Greene now has about 2,500 men under his command, 600 of them poorly Equipped militia, and Lord Cornwallis the same number, of whom 2,000 are experienced regulars.*

*Rebel General Daniel Morgan has had some Success against our forces,
but he has now retired to his home in Virginia. One of his aides, now our prisoner, reported that the old man is recuperating from an attack of Sciatica and
Hemorrhoids. There is much devastation, and supplies are very scarce for
both sides, now Forced to consume draft oxen or anything else they can find.
The same man stated that the irregular militia are especially in Need, with
many walking barefoot and leaving bloody tracks on the frozen trails, and
forced to eat hides, bones, and offal in order to stay alive.*

*His Majesty's army is now encamped in Hillsborough, North Carolina,
and our forces remain Secure in Charles Town, Augusta, Ninety Six, and any
other Stronghold that we desire to occupy, while some rebel militia under
Francis Marion, Thomas Sumter, and Andrew Pickens roam around the
Countryside as irritants. Leaders of the Georgia and Carolina militia, mostly
riff-raff, have urged Greene to return South, but I believe we have seen the
last of the rebel army in this region.*

*Respectfully submitted by
the Governor's agent*

CHAPTER 50

Georgians Turn to Combat at Home

After a few weeks in Virginia, the Georgia and Carolina militia commanders were becoming restive, and finally convinced their senior leader,
General Andrew Pickens, to meet with General Greene and urge him not
to abandon their states to the British. Their most convincing argument was
that the British army was facing starvation, having consumed all the provisions that could be taken from the surrounding territory. Strengthened by
an additional two thousand men, mostly Virginia militia, who reported in
early March, Greene decided to move back into North Carolina and to advance toward Cornwallis's army in Hillsborough. Cornwallis saw that he
could remain dormant no longer and prepared to launch an attack on
Morgan's former troops, now commanded by Colonel Otho Holland
Williams and comprising about a third of Greene's force.

There was increasing disharmony between regular Continental troops and the militiamen from the south, who had admired Morgan but found Williams arrogant, insensitive to their needs, and lacking any understanding of their proud status as volunteers. Knowing of the prospective engagement, Williams decided that he needed more foot soldiers instead of cavalry, and ordered the South Carolina and Georgia militia to send their horses home. They immediately threatened to resign from service, and the colonel was forced to cancel his order for them to dismount. Two days later, to avoid confronting the superior British troops, Williams rushed to ford Reedy Fork Creek with his regular forces, and ordered the already aggravated militia and some Virginia riflemen to cover his rear, where the British attack was focused.

When Williams's troops were safe, General Andrew Pickens went to headquarters to inform General Greene that he and his men would be returning to their homes farther south. They had served unfailingly for two months, during the most challenging times and far beyond their original expectation. Since the Continental force had now received a substantial increase in troops, to almost 4,500, General Greene agreed with their decision. He suggested to Pickens that the Georgia and Carolina militia might consider concentrating on taking Ninety Six.

Cornwallis had less than two thousand men in his army now, all of whom had been on short rations for the past six weeks. Still, both sides were ready for a showdown, and Greene decided to deploy his force at Guilford Courthouse on terrain with which he was thoroughly familiar. He remembered Morgan's strategy at Cowpens and put the North Carolina militia in the front line, with orders to his seasoned troops in the second and third ranks to shoot them if they fled. Some did fight, at least to fire one round from their muskets, but the British pressed forward as one thousand militiamen dropped their weapons and all other impediments and ran away. Cornwallis pressed forward through thick woods and, when the most vicious hand-to-hand fighting was at its peak and the outcome for his men was in doubt, ordered the firing of grapeshot into the general melee.

The British ultimately prevailed, as Greene withdrew in order to save the remainder of his Continental army, the only one in the south. However, the British also suffered heavy losses. A London commentator said, "Lord Cornwallis has conquered his army out of shoes and provisions and himself out of troops." The British troops moved slowly back to Wilmington and then to Charles Town, where they received food and other supplies from British ships, and then headed, once again, for Virginia. At the same time, Nathanael Greene moved his troops, almost unopposed, back into the south. The two forces passed each other, with the Continentals farther west.

Elijah Clarke was lying on a cot in a small cabin near the North Carolina line, his face drenched with sweat despite the coolness of the day. His wife, Hannah, was sitting in a nearby chair, watching him anxiously. She stood, walked over to the cot, and reached down to adjust the pillow under his head.

He exclaimed, "Dammit, woman, leave me be!"

"'Lige, you been mighty sick, with a high fever, and we are glad to see you doing better, even if it don't improve the way you talk and act."

He smiled slightly and said, "I reckon I ain't been a very good patient, but I cain't stand being flat on my back when there's so much to be done. How long have I been here now?"

"It's been a long time since your arm was almost cut off, and you been here going on two weeks. Your fever's broke, but your shoulder never has been healing right and it's much worse than it was at first."

"Well, I'm gettin' up in a day or two, no matter what you have to say."

Hannah saw that it was a waste of time for her to argue with her husband, so she gave him a drink of water and left the cabin. She found Aaron Hart and reported the conversation.

"Aaron, he's going to have to get some rest."

"Is he able to ride a horse yet?"

"No, but he could travel in a travois if he had to."

"General Andrew Pickens sent us word that the colonel is welcome to use his home in South Carolina, where there are servants, and it's a long way from any fighting that we know of. Maybe we can talk him into going there, and I'll go with him."

Hannah thought for a few moments. "The only way he might go is if we make it seem like he'd be doing General Pickens a favor by keeping an eye on his place. Even if he don't believe us, it might give him an excuse in his own mind."

Within a week they had made the journey, and Elijah was receiving good care and plenty of rest. For the first time, the inflammation left his wound and it began to heal.

. . .

When Thomas Brown learned about Clarke's location, he called in Tory Major James Dunlap, assigned seventy-five experienced dragoons to serve under him, and ordered them to proceed as rapidly as possible to the Pickens plantation with orders to capture Clarke and bring him to Augusta for public execution.

As the weather warmed, Elijah began feeling better and he decided to return to his men on the Carolina side of the Savannah River before Easter Sunday. The first information he received was that Dunlap had been assigned to conduct a pillaging operation against any Whigs who were still operating against the British. He did not know Dunlap's specific destination. After a few days with his men, Clarke decided to go to General Pickens's headquarters to thank him for his hospitality, report that he was ready for duty, and to suggest that the Georgia militia might hunt down Dunlap and his dragoons.

When Clarke arrived he found Pickens fuming with anger and despair. Before Clarke could utter a word, the general shouted at him, "The son of a bitch has burned my house and everything else I own!"

His overseer had reported to him that morning that Dunlap had come to the plantation, demanded Clarke's surrender, and had become enraged when informed that he had departed. He permitted his dragoons to loot the buildings and then ordered that everything be burned to the ground. Despite his best efforts to reassure Clarke that he did not hold him responsible, both men knew that the destruction was a result of the personal animosity between Thomas Brown and Elijah Clarke.

Certain that Dunlap would be returning to Augusta to report to Brown, Clarke sent pickets to monitor all the trails and soon learned that Dunlap and his men were encamped at Beattie's Mill. Shortly before daybreak, Clarke's militia surrounded the mill house and began steadily firing at their quarry. At about noon, a white flag appeared, and Dunlap shouted that thirty-four of his men were dead and he and the others were ready to surrender. When they walked out into the open and threw their weapons on the ground, Clarke had them lined up alongside the mill house and then ordered that they all be executed. Although Clarke was still not able to engage in hand-to-hand combat, he had directed the fight from his saddle, and both rebels and loyalists equated him with the massacre. From then on, loyalists understood that a "Georgia parole" meant death.

CHAPTER 51

A Victory at Augusta

JUNE 1781

As the Continental and British armies maneuvered farther north, near Virginia, the Georgia militia leaders realized that their fighting should now be concentrated nearer their own homes, and the scattered groups of militiamen began to reestablish a strong camp in the relatively secure area of the Hornet's Nest. With their families safe in the Watauga Valley, the defense of their own area would be much easier. Cornwallis had pulled all available men to support his move against Greene, and Elijah Clarke was convinced that Augusta was vulnerable if he could marshal enough support. He sent James Jackson, accompanied by Ethan Pratt, to present his proposal to General Greene.

They found the Continental army headquarters about fifty miles inland from Charles Town and were ushered in almost immediately to see General Greene, who had invited General Pickens to attend. Pickens strongly supported Clarke's suggestion, and after some hesitation Greene agreed that a genuine threat to Charles Town and Augusta would confront the British with a difficult choice. He would keep his troops at their present site, but sent Pickens and Lieutenant Colonel "Light-horse Harry" Lee to join the Georgians, with Lee to be in command of the actual move against Augusta.

Ethan Pratt tried to conceal his excitement about the prospect of attacking Augusta, which was occupied and defended by the Florida Rangers. Colonel Thomas Brown was in command, with Major James Grierson as his deputy. Ethan was not the only Georgia militiaman who was determined that the two notorious leaders would not survive the patriot attack, and a small group made plans to ensure that no quarter would be given them if the British force was defeated and the two taken prisoner.

After Pickett and Lee arrived at the Hornet's Nest, they and the Georgia militia leaders agreed on a strategy for the siege of Augusta. In order to block reinforcements that might be sent out of Savannah northward, they first took Fort Galphin, twelve miles below the town, and captured a large cache of badly needed supplies. When all roads and trails to Augusta were blocked, Lee sent word to Thomas Brown of the formidable patriot force and demanded his surrender. Colonel Brown refused to reply or even to acknowledge the message.

Brown's home base was Fort Cornwallis, in the center of Augusta, which was now well fortified: 250 Florida Rangers, 250 Creeks, 50 Cherokees, and about 200 slaves defended it. Knowing of preparations for the assault, Brown had sent for reinforcements from both Savannah and Ninety Six, but Georgia militiamen intercepted the messages.

On May 22, the Americans concentrated their first attack on an insignificant outpost a half mile upriver and named for its commander, Major Grierson. It was finally breached after a spirited engagement, and Grierson and most of his men escaped down a ravine to Fort Cornwallis. Forty-five wounded Tories were taken prisoner, and Lee could hardly restrain Clarke's men from killing them. The Americans then turned on Fort Cornwallis, having only an old five-pounder and a six-pounder taken at Grierson, while the British had eight good artillery pieces. Major James Jackson and his men moved in from the south, and Pickens and Clarke from the northwest.

Not being able to damage the fort from ground level, Lee decided to build a tower designed to elevate his six-pounder so it could fire down onto the British defenders. A square wall of long interlocked logs, hidden behind some buildings, was filled with dirt and stone, and then another square was built atop the first and filled again. At the same time, Lee ordered that his troops begin digging classic siege trenches toward the fort.

Lee again demanded Brown's surrender. This time the refusal was immediate and polite, and included an apology for not having answered the earlier demand because Brown thought it had come from Elijah Clarke, for whom he had no respect. Lee informed Greene of this exchange and indicated that he agreed with Brown, whom he described as "a vigilant, resolute, active, and sagacious officer." He reminded Greene of the murder of Major Dunlap and his men by Clarke's militia, an act of "plunder, murder, and iniquity."

After a week of being besieged, Brown began nightly raids against the Americans, but these efforts were repulsed. Finally, on June 2, the six-pounder was hoisted to the top of the completed tower and began to fire directly down into the fort.

Brown sent a Scot "deserter" with instructions to gain the Americans' confidence and then to burn the tower, but Lee was suspicious and had him detained. Brown had secretly dug a tunnel under the houses between the tower and fort, and now he burned all the buildings except one, under which he planted a huge explosive charge. Lee sent a small detachment of inspectors into the building, and they reported no reason why the building had not been burned with the others. Still, Lee was reluctant to occupy the house fully and stationed only a few men in it. That night, when Brown thought the house would be full of Americans, he blew it up, but only six men were inside. Lee once again called on Brown to surrender, and Brown's reply was to parade American prisoners along the parapet of the fort to show that they would be killed during any final assault. One of them was the aged John Alexander, whose sons James and Samuel were militia captains in the besieging force and who had been plotting with Ethan Pratt and others to kill Brown and Grierson.

Now Brown had no further options except to negotiate favorable terms of surrender. He chose a beautiful and talented young woman named Sophronia Cowan, gave her his optimum proposal, and late in the afternoon sent her under a flag of truce with instructions to speak to no one except Colonel Lee. To the Rangers' surprise and over the furious objections of Georgia's militia leaders, Brown's entire offer was accepted shortly before daybreak the following morning, fourteen days after the military engagement had begun, with Colonel Lee's words, "The judicious and gallant defence made by the garrison entitles them to every mark of military respect." The agreement quickly became known as Sophronia's Peace (Piece).

All British officers would be sent to Savannah on parole, accompanied by their Indians, with the troops to be considered prisoners of war. British and American doctors would treat the sick and wounded on an equal basis. The fort's defenders would have the honor of marching out with drums beating and their arms shouldered. The Scot "deserter" was to be treated as a loyal soldier and not executed as a spy. A special arrangement was made concerning Colonel Brown and Grierson: they were to be treated with respect and given personal protection under armed guards, and neither they nor their men would in any way be placed under the control of Elijah Clarke.

While Grierson and the others marched out and stacked their arms, Brown was taken directly to Lee's quarters, where the two men first exchanged comments about the current engagement and implementation of the surrender terms. Lee stated that Miss Cowan was resting in an adjoining room, having been awake throughout the previous night. Twenty-three Americans had been killed and twenty-eight wounded, while the British casualties were twice as great and their entire force were now prisoners. The two men then began a lengthy discussion about the overall conduct of the war, including past engagements and present circumstances. Lee was amazed at Brown's knowledge of details concerning events throughout America, including the personal relationship and even some supposedly secret communications between himself and General Nathanael Greene. With some pride, the Ranger commander described the extent of his intelligence network, which still extended from New Orleans to the Great Lakes and from Canada to Florida.

Just as they were concluding their meeting, a captain rushed in and informed Lee that Major Grierson had been taken, tortured, forced to sign a lengthy confession, and then hanged, apparently by a group led by the Alexander brothers, and that they and their father had disappeared. Lee was furious, and deeply embarrassed that his surrender terms had been violated. Brown was placed under a strong protective guard adjacent to Lee's personal quarters and the following morning was dispatched downriver to Savannah with a troop of men under the command of a trusted colonel. His written instruction said that if any harm came to Brown, "the laurels acquired by the arms of America would be stained by the murder of a gallant soldier who committed himself to his enemy on their plighted faith." When General Greene heard of Grierson's death, he wrote Lee that it was "an insult to the Arms of the United States and an outrage upon the rights of humanity," and offered a reward of one hundred guineas for the capture of the guilty parties.

Since almost every militiaman despised Grierson and Brown as despicable criminals, the reward went unclaimed, and within a few days Grierson's confession was delivered to James Jackson, but both Lee and Pickens refused to accept it and ordered Jackson not to share its contents with others. A later embarrassment for the patriot force was that all the slaves and presents for Indians were entrusted to a rebel captain named John Burnet for safekeeping, and it was later learned that he marched them over the mountains, through Kentucky to the Ohio, and down the Mississippi to Natchez, where he sold them all and disappeared.

Within a few days, Lee and Pickens were ordered to join Greene near Charles Town, and James Jackson was left in command of the forces in Augusta. The men were not surprised when Sophronia Cowan accompanied Colonel Lee to his new post. The British now held only Ebenezer, Charles Town, Savannah, and the coastal regions between there and Florida. Within three months Jackson's troops surrounded and occupied Ebenezer, with few casualties on either side. The Alexander brothers soon rejoined Jackson's troops, and Ethan Pratt and the other Georgians treated them as heroes.

When Brown reached Savannah as a parolee, he went to Charles Town and negotiated a swap for a patriot of similar rank so he could continue fighting. He was also able to secure the exchange of Warrant Officer Alonzo Baker, who had always been his preeminent confidant and advisor. While there, he learned that Cruger's orders to help him had been intercepted, that several hundred Creeks had been just forty miles away when he surrendered Augusta, and that the British had now decided to abandon Ninety Six without a fight.

His spirits were boosted when he returned to Savannah and Governor Wright told him that the emperor of Austria and the empress of Russia had offered to mediate the end of the war. A legal principle known as *uti possidetis* might result in Georgia and South Carolina joining Florida as British colonies if a peace agreement was reached with Savannah and Charles Town still in British hands. Wright had demanded that British forces retake Augusta so that the entire state might remain with Britain, but they now decided to concentrate on holding the port cities as adequate proof of Britain's claim on the states. Optimistic as always, Wright maintained that there were 7,800 inhabitants in the state, almost all of them either presently or potentially loyal to the crown. Brown knew better but did not express his contrary views when he received orders to continue fighting against rebels along the frontier and was given £10,740 to support his Rangers.

George Washington had the same information about the offer from Austria and Russia, and ordered Greene to use every means of establishing some form of state government as proof in Paris that the British hold on Savannah did not signify control of Georgia. Major James Jackson had made a fine impression on General Greene, and he now promoted him to colonel, to be commander of an official Georgia state legion that would include the Georgians who had fought under Greene in the Carolinas, some militia groups, and other soldiers who could be induced to transfer their allegiance from the British. Jackson recommended that Ethan Pratt be promoted to captain, and the request was approved.

Using the constitution of 1777 as a guide, superficial elections were quickly organized in the regions controlled by the American forces, and the delegates soon met in Augusta. This solidified a permanent shift of political

influence away from the more sophisticated elite on the coast to the
frontiersmen in the interior regions. They named Augusta as their capital
and chose a former delegate to the Continental Congress, Dr. Nathan
Brownson, as governor. Elijah Clarke was an elected delegate and was
given a choice committee assignment and designated to handle the disposi-
tion of confiscated estates. With both Creeks and Cherokees still on the
warpath and strongly supported by Brown and his Rangers, Clarke decided that it was best to defend the frontier against depredation, and only
later to offer his services to Colonel Jackson's militia or to General Wayne's
Continentals.

Knowing that the main threat was the Creek Indians, Governor Brownson sent a message to Emistisiguo, the Raven, and "The Beloved Men of
the Creek Nation," telling them how the British had been defeated, and
asking them not to be "perswaded by Brown's lying talk to engage against
us—our Brothers of Virginia have heard that your Tomahocks have drank
our blood—They have sent us a talk that they had whet their swords and
cleaned their riffles and only waited for us to give the word and they would
come and make your women widdows and your Towns Smoak—We have
sent them a talk and told them we believe the Creek Nation still wish to be
our friends and Brothers and what Blood was spilt was done by Mad
Young Men, set on by Brown's lying people among them." He asked that a
treaty be made, but the bond between Thomas Brown and the Indians was
too strong to be weakened by strange messages from Georgians whom
they had known only as enemies.

CHAPTER 52

Ethan and Mavis

AUGUST 1781

In Ebenezer, Ethan Pratt approached Major Jackson and requested leave
to return to Wrightsborough.

"Captain Pratt, you know that you are free to return to your home at
any time, but what would be the purpose of your visit?"

"Quaker leader Joseph Maddock has sent a message to me and to the families in the Watauga Valley stating that Governor Wright has protected the entire settlement from both Redcoats and Brown's Rangers. Few of the homesteads have been damaged or destroyed, and he wants me to review the status of the property owners who are not Quakers, and let him know whether we wish to retain our land. There are three others besides me who are in the militia, and they have asked that I represent them and ensure that their titles to the property remain intact. In addition, my wife has sent me notes from two widows to be delivered to Maddock."

"I don't see how your claims will make much difference. The governor authorized Brown to take all the property owned by any of the militia families, and he's turned most of it over to his Rangers. Only the outcome of the war will determine who the owners might be."

"That's true in most areas, but Maddock says there has been a special order protecting Wrightsborough, provided the owners make a claim with him. I believe that my homestead is the only one that has been destroyed."

"I don't blame you for going, but if the British hold Savannah and keep Georgia, I doubt if any of us wind up owning our land."

"You're probably right, sir, but I'm a messenger for five other people and need to go. I'll be back in a few days, well before we are ready to make a move against Savannah."

Now approaching Wrightsborough late in the August afternoon, Ethan was questioning his decision to return. It seemed that his laying claim to a homestead separated him from most of the other members of the militia who had lost theirs, and also indicated a lack of confidence in their ultimate victory. At the same time, he didn't wish to make a gift of their property either to the Quakers or to Thomas Brown and the Florida Rangers. He tried not to think about Mavis but couldn't avoid wondering if she was still with the Friends or had gone to Savannah during the extended period while the British were in full control of the state. In any case, his business with Maddock would be brief, and he wanted to return to his military duties as quickly as possible.

This was one of his rare visits to the town since the war had begun, and as he approached the settlement he was surprised at how little it had changed. It was an oasis in a state that had been devastated by raids from military units of both Whigs and Tories and by irresponsible and uncontrollable groups of white and Indian bandits. He planned to stop at the only tavern, spend one night, see Maddock in the morning, and begin the return journey. He was hoping for a mug of ale and whatever food they had to of-fer, but when he came in the door and identified himself, the tavern keeper handed him an envelope, saying, "I have been holding this for several days."

Ethan looked at his inscribed name and recognized Mavis's neat, back-slanted handwriting at first glance, having read it on hundreds of pages of the nature journals she had prepared for Kindred. He forgot about ale and supper, left the tavern, and walked off to be alone as he opened the single folded page. Although it was after sunset, there was still ample light. His hands trembled as he read the simply written note.

> *Ethan, Brother Maddock said you may be coming here. I know that your cabin was burned but Newota has told me the Indians put some kind of mark on Kindred's home and it has been protected. I would like to go back and get some things, including the spinning wheel you made for me. I am staying with the Flemings but they do not have a cart. I do not want to be a burden to you, but hope you can carry me. Gratefully, Mavis*

He tried to control the thrill that went through him, and deliberately thought about Epsey, still living in the Watauga Valley with wives and chil-dren of the other active militiamen. He was sure that she would approve his providing this assistance to their former neighbor. Ethan arranged with the innkeeper to care for his horse, to notify Joseph Maddock of his presence, and to reserve the use of a small two-wheeled cart, which he would use for the trip to the homestead the following day.

The next morning, Ethan went to Maddock's home as early as he thought it appropriate, knocked on the front door, and was ushered into a front room that was obviously used as a place of business. A large rolltop desk was covered with neat stacks of papers, and the contents of the cub-byholes were carefully arranged. It seemed to Ethan that his host had pros-pered during the war, both financially and in his role as a favorite of the governor. The room was the most elaborately furnished he had ever seen in a Friend's home, and Maddock was self-assured and somewhat conde-scending as he motioned for Ethan to be seated.

"Brother Pratt, I am pleased to see thee well. I presume that thou art here in response to the several messages I have sent to men with property in our settlement."

Ethan was relieved that the focus of the conversation was immediately on business and responded, "I appreciate this opportunity to see you again, and I have come in response to your inquiries, which several of my fellow militiamen have also received. Here are brief notes from three of them, and one from the widow Abrams, as you will notice, who hopes someday to come back with her children. I would like to inform them of their status when I return. There is one other widow, now in western Carolina, who desires to give up any claim to her former home, as stated in her note."

Maddock nodded his head, examined the memoranda, and responded, "These will be adequate, and we have decided to honor any claims from widows who intend to return to their homes. Please express my personal condolences to all of them. I have been especially grieved by the loss of your son. The governor will decide on ownership of any abandoned property, but he has asked for my recommendations. I doubt that there will be compensation for any who choose to move elsewhere."

Ethan expressed his thanks and prepared to leave.

Maddock asked, "Will thou be visiting thy homestead?"

"Yes, although I know that the cabin has been burned."

Maddock nodded without further comment, and Ethan took his leave.

At the livery stable where he had reserved a cart, Ethan chose one that was low-slung and with the wheels as close together as possible to accommodate the narrow trails. It had a seat on top and a relatively long body. Then he mounted the cart and drove the horse to the Flemings' home.

When he was still fifty paces from the front door, it was flung open and Mavis burst out, ran to him, grasped both his hands, looked into his eyes, and exclaimed, "Ethan, this is the best thing that has happened to me in years! I was praying that you would come. Have you brought the cart for my use? Can we really go to the farm? I'll be so glad to see it again! Ethan, why are you blushing so?"

He realized that his heart was pounding and his face was flushed, and he finally stammered, "Yes, I got your note and was wanting to see my own place, so it's no trouble to take you."

He looked around to see if anyone had observed her outburst and then asked, "Should I speak to the Flemings?"

"They've gone to the meetinghouse, but I stayed here because I was hoping you might come. I'll be ready when I get my bonnet and shawl."

In a few minutes they were on the way. Mavis was still bubbling with excitement and proceeded to ask a never-ending stream of questions about every aspect of Ethan's life since she had last seen him. Ethan was surprised at her knowledge of the war, but recalled that Joseph Maddock was thoroughly informed and that he relished sharing news with the Quaker families at their regular meetings. He soon realized that he was doing most of the talking as the cart bumped along the rough trail. He had not been so relaxed and happy in years. Only once did he mention Epsey, to say that she and the other women were doing well with the Over Mountain people, but that three of their husbands had been killed. In what seemed to be a comment of equivalent importance, Mavis said that Newota had been to see her several times, and they had a way to exchange messages. He was spending most of his time with Chief Emistisiguo, who communicated regularly with an Indian named Sunoma, who was with the Rangers.

Ethan's face flushed again, this time with anger as he recalled what Thomas Brown's Rangers had done to his son, Henry.

As they approached the Morris homestead they could see that all the fields had grown up in weeds, but the cabin had not been harmed. Ethan saw a small bundle of feathers and fur attached to the door, and presumed this to be the Indian mark that had prevented its destruction. Almost like turning a switch, their conversation was now focused almost exclusively on Kindred, and there was no reluctance or morbidity in their remarks. As they loaded the undamaged spinning wheel, the fireplace equipment that Ethan had made, a few notebooks, and some other items that she had left behind, Mavis seemed to recall only the delightful and interesting things the three of them had done together. Finally, as they closed the door and started walking toward the loaded cart, she grasped Ethan's hand and stopped him. She looked up into his eyes and said quite seriously, "You know that he was like a brother to me."

He had thought about going to see his own homestead but decided to wait until a later time, when he would be alone. Now, as the cart swayed and bounced along the trail, he glanced down at the fringe of lace on her simple bonnet, the cheap but sturdy printed cloth of her dress, her scuffed shoes, her long eyelashes, and the outline of her face. Mavis felt his eyes on her and moved nearer him. He was overwhelmed with a feeling of tenderness, and was also aroused sexually, which his tight trousers made obvious to both of them. Mavis was not naturally shy, and she looked up into his eyes without attempting to conceal her desire. It seemed that the years of mutual attraction could no longer be suppressed. Neither of them had ever made love to anyone other than their spouse, nor had their feelings toward each other ever been expressed. Now a lightning shock seemed to go through him as she let her left hand fall lightly on his knee. Ethan pulled up on the reins and said "Whoa" to the horse, louder than he had intended. Without speaking, he stepped down to the ground, walked around the cart, and held up his arms to her. He hardly felt her weight as he carried her a few yards from the trail. He found a place under a large white pine and lowered her gently onto its deep bed of fallen needles. It was softer than the corn-husk mattresses in their cabins, and much larger.

Later, they walked back, hand in hand. When they arrived at the trail, the forgotten horse was grazing quietly. Mavis looked up at Ethan and said, "I'll never forget this place."

"I'm still remembering it now," he said with a smile, as he carried her back into the woods.

CHAPTER 53

Cornwallis Moves North

SEPTEMBER 1781

As requested by Governor Tonyn, Thomas Brown assessed the overall war situation in September 1781.

Your Excellency:

I am exceedingly Honored that I have been asked to summarize reports received from the Colonies to the north. If I may be so bold, and again forgoing any comment on the Southern states with which perhaps you are more Familiar than I, let me report that there has been some debate among our Commanders about the proper placement of the extremely successful but somewhat depleted Army of Lord Cornwallis. General Clinton believes that all our forces should be concentrated for a major Confrontation with the rebel and French forces, which are apparently being led by French officers. We have a large army of 5,500 in the Chesapeake area under the Command of General Benedict Arnold (who now honors us with his Service) and with troops from New York, and those in Virginia joining him would ensure a Victory. With

Charles Town and Savannah secure, Lord Cornwallis prefers to join with Arnold and face the rebels in Virginia. Having had some Skirmishes with the boy general Lafayette, he is now in Williamsburg, but my latest information is that he contemplates moving to the Peninsula of Yorktown, where he can defend himself from land and be Protected and Supplied by the British fleet. There are some reports from the West Indies that Count de Grasse may move his large Fleet northward, but all past experience has shown that the French are giving top Priority to the Caribbean. In any case, we have a superior Naval presence in New York that can be utilized if needed.

It will be interesting to see if Washington is finally prepared, after almost three years of Dormancy, to risk any of his northern troops in battle, even though most of the officers and fighting men will be French. The Americans still prefer to Concentrate on New York and the French on the Chesapeake, both guessing what De Grasse might do if he moves his formidable Armada. It seems that, on land, the French wish to move south and fight, the Americans to refrain.

Respectfully submitted by
the Governor's agent

With the struggle for final control of Georgia intensifying, frightened and defenseless people moved to areas controlled by the military troops. Those Georgians inclined toward the Whigs felt safer in the vicinity of Augusta, and Tories were forced into the Savannah area. A few went to live among the Quaker families in the Wrightsborough community, whose settlement was still spared despite resentment of their neutrality by strong partisans on both sides.

While attempting to encircle Charles Town with his main army, General Greene decided that James Jackson should begin marshaling additional Georgia troops and then move downriver from Ebenezer to plan for a future effort to take Savannah. Jackson still had only a few troops and minimal supplies, while British General Alured Clarke defended the city with seven hundred loyalist militia, two hundred Hessians, and one hundred British troops, assisted by four hundred slaves, some provided with weapons. Brown and his five hundred Rangers were ordered to help defend the outskirts of Savannah, to keep the city supplied with food, and to harass rebels wherever possible. It was obvious that, with both their forces outside Savannah, the primary active conflict would be between Brown and Jackson. Having been frustrated in his plan to kill the Ranger commander in Augusta, Ethan saw this as a special opportunity to realize his goal.

In November 1781, after receiving a dispatch from General Nathanael Greene, Lieutenant Colonel Jackson assembled his key officers and enlisted leaders to share the news. Captain Ethan Pratt was pleased to have been given a preview of the general's report. Referring frequently to the message in his hand, Jackson reported that the French fleet under Admiral de Grasse had arrived in the Chesapeake Bay in September, had fought off a British naval force from New York, and then landed 3,500 troops, who reported to Lafayette. Within two weeks, the allied forces surrounded Yorktown and began an intense bombardment. Without support from the sea and facing a combined force of sixteen thousand French and Americans, Cornwallis and his seven thousand men had surrendered on October 19, 1781.

The Georgia troops cheered when they received this information, but Jackson cautioned them that the British still held New York, and they all knew that the war was not over in South Carolina or Georgia, where the British controlled the port cities.

General Greene felt that the battles that had been fought by him and others in the south were crucial in the final defeat of Cornwallis and his British army. To a friend, he wrote, "We have been beating the bush, throughout the Carolinas and Georgia, and General Washington has come to catch the bird." The commander in chief sent a message to his Quaker general in South Carolina: "General Washington wishes not only from his personal regard to General Greene, but from principles of generosity and justice to see him crowned with those laurels which from his unparalleled exertions he so richly deserves."

Thomas Brown felt constrained to explain the defeat at Yorktown, and sent this report to Governor Tonyn:

> *Your Excellency:*
> *The rebels are attempting to present events at Yorktown as a decisive Victory of their military forces. This is a false claim, as is clear to any careful Analyst. It is a small defeat of one of our armies, but not by the rebels. After his forces completely dominated their troops in the Carolinas, General Cornwallis concluded his repeated Victories with a decision to establish his winter base*

on a defensible Peninsula at Yorktown, protected on the seaward side by the British fleet. Although Washington preferred an attack on New York, Rochambeau insisted on moving against Lord Cornwallis. Unfortunately for His Lordship, Admiral Comte de Grasse decided to Abandon his efforts in the Caribbean, agreed with Rochambeau, and moved his entire Fleet (at least two dozen warships) to the Chesapeake Bay.

Early in September, there was a naval battle, and when Admiral Thomas Graves decided to Withdraw our fleet to New York to repair battle damage, this left Lord Cornwallis without necessary protection. A land force of overwhelming size, mostly of French troops and major armaments, then laid Siege and the relatively small British force had to yield. General Clinton still holds Firm in New York, and it is likely that French ships will leave and our naval forces will soon regain control of the Coastal regions, from Halifax completely around to Pensacola.

I have honored your Instructions by sending a large force of Indian Rangers to Pensacola to attack the Spaniards, who are being starved by our naval Blockade.

Respectfully submitted by
the Governor's agent

The analysis that Brown gave to Warrant Officer Alonzo Baker was quite different: "The loss of Cornwallis's army was a greater political than military blow. Although King George has stated that it would have no effect on his conduct of the war, Prime Minister North and others are facing the heavy cost of the greater conflict with France and Spain. George Washington deserves credit for the survival of the Continental army, and his ties to the French have proven to be of great mutual advantage. London has already begun negotiations with all their adversaries in Paris, and the control of Canada, Florida, Gibraltar, and the western portions of America are all on the table as stakes. We will fight to hold the seaports and offer to exchange New York for Charles Town and Savannah. They are the key to the final annexation of these two states."

For fighting men in the south, both British and American, little had been changed at Yorktown.

CHAPTER 54

Mavis Goes North

Mavis was standing at the window when she saw Newota in front of the Flemings' home, sitting bareback and leading another Indian pony. It was clear and chilly, with less than a quarter of a waxing moon. She had been watching since shortly after midnight, and it was still at least an hour before first daylight. Dressed warmly, she picked up a small bundle of possessions, slipped through the door, and joined the young Indian. Without a word, he took the bundle and helped lift her onto the small pinto. There was a serape of muted colors draped around his shoulders, but she could still see his bare legs and thought briefly of Kindred's unsuccessful efforts to demonstrate an equivalent immunity to the cold of winter.

She had been in a quandary since learning that she was pregnant. At first she was filled with joy, knowing that she might bear Ethan's child, but then she was flooded with apprehension about the inevitable reaction of the Quakers to a woman obviously guilty of adultery. The mildest punishment would be public humiliation and hours or days in stocks in the public square. She knew of others who had been whipped or held underwater until unconscious. Miscarriages were a common result of such abuse and were considered to be a proper retribution of the Lord. There were no friends to whom she could turn, and she had finally remembered Newota. Perhaps he would take her to his village until after she gave birth.

They moved westward through the deserted streets of the town, not stopping until they were clear of any houses. Then she called softly to him. He stopped and she let her pony join his.

"I am grateful that you have come for me."

"I am thankful to be of service, but need to know where you wish to go."

In her usual frank manner, she replied, "Newota, although I am without a husband, I am going to have a baby, perhaps in five months. I cannot stay with the Quakers, and need to go where I can be safe until then."

"You would be welcome with my people, but the village no longer exists and there are constant raids that drive us from one place to another. My mother has been killed, and my own duties require that I stay with Chief Emistisiguo, who also travels often. I could take you to Savannah, but it is increasingly under siege. St. Augustine is another option. You may make the decision and I will comply."

Mavis had been considering her choices for three or four weeks and had decided on Newota's village as her preference. St. Augustine was extremely distant and under British control. Although she knew no one there, however, that might be an advantage under the circumstances. Then, almost without thinking, she asked, "Do you know the Watauga Valley?"

"Yes, I have carried messages to that area several times to Indian leaders."

She dismounted and walked a few steps back along the trail. She preferred to be an American and knew that she would be welcomed, although some of the women might know that her child was a bastard. She would not be physically harmed and could withstand the personal embarrassment. When the war was over she could find a place to stay, perhaps using her talents as an artist and writer who was familiar with the field of biology. She could always work as a housemaid. In any case, her child could have a good life.

She returned to Newota and said, "That is where I wish to go."

He nodded and turned his pony northward at the next trail.

After having led some Pennsylvania troops at Yorktown, Brigadier General "Mad Anthony" Wayne had been appointed Continental commander in Georgia in January 1782, with all regular troops and half the militia under his command. This didn't amount to much because the enlistments of all his South Carolina troops expired within two weeks, and Elijah Clarke and most of his Georgians were away on one of their continuing raids against the Indians. Clarke now had a strong force with him and had destroyed most of the Cherokee villages east of the Appalachian Mountains. Wayne concentrated on securing deserters, arming slaves, and marshaling any Tories who would convert to the Whigs. He made a special effort to induce the German mercenaries to desert from the British, and a few of them responded to his offered bounty of two guineas. Still, Wayne had only 130 troops under his command, and all his small force could do was intercept Indians and others trying to go to Savannah with supplies.

He wrote: "The duty we have done in Georgia is more difficult than that imposed upon the children of Israel. They had only to make bricks without straw, but we have had provisions, forage, and almost every other apparatus of war to procure without money: boats, bridges, etc. to build without materials except those taken from the stump: and, what was more difficult than all, to make Whigs out of Tories. But this we have effected, and have wrested the country out of the hands of the enemy, with the exception only of the town of Savannah. How to take it without some additional force is a matter worthy of consideration."

The Creeks were looking for survival as allies of the British, and a small party of them on the way to Savannah ran into a troop of Americans under Major John Habersham. He pretended that he led a troop of Rangers, captured the Creeks, tied the leader to a tree, and slowly cut him to pieces. He released the others to go westward, to spread the word that access to Savannah was closed, but the Indians were not deterred. A few weeks later, Chief Emistisiguo and three hundred Creeks, at the end of a five-hundred-mile trek, attacked General Wayne and his forces. The battle was a standoff, but the chief and seventeen others were killed and twelve prisoners were captured. Some of those who escaped returned to their homes, but Newota and most of the others proceeded on to Savannah.

General Wayne turned the Creek prisoners over to some of their Cherokee scouts and the next morning had a report that ten of them had been slowly executed and two released, having provided information about their plans for a rendezvous with Thomas Brown and a small party of Rangers at a crossing of the Ogeechee River. The scheduled time was an hour after sunrise, two days in the future. Wayne immediately sent for Colonel Jackson, shared the information, and ordered him to trap Brown.

"Our information is that he only has about a dozen men with him, but I want you to have at least three times that many. He'll be approaching the river from the west and will be wary when he realizes that the Creeks are not there. You'll have to take him by surprise and let the Rangers know from the beginning that they are surrounded by a far superior force."

"General, I have a Captain Pratt with me who is knowledgeable about that area, having homesteaded not far from there."

"I'd rather capture Brown than kill him, but if he provides a danger to your men, you can act as you must."

Ethan was excited when Colonel Jackson briefed his troops on their assignment. He confirmed his knowledge of the particular crossing, and immediately drew a sketch of the trail that would most likely be used as the Rangers approached the river. He remembered his rifle shot into the chest of Patrick Ferguson and hoped that he would be the one fortunate enough to end the life of the despised man who had been the last white man to see his little son alive.

He was taken aback when Jackson said, "General Wayne wants the Ranger party taken alive if possible. We need to get all the information we can from them about Savannah's defenses, and to use Brown as a bargaining chip with the British. We'll surround them and expose our total force at my signal to show that their resistance would be suicide."

Ethan objected, saying, "Sir, these are the same people who have never shown mercy even to the most innocent of their victims. I urge you to let our men have retribution."

Jackson said, "I know that you and your men feel the same about Brown as you did Grierson, and we will have to kill them if they don't surrender."

After Ethan and the others nodded, he added, "Brown and his men are skilled woodsmen and will be alert to any danger. When we deploy, I don't want any tracks left on the trail to indicate our presence."

The Rangers approached the river at the appointed time, with Colonel Brown leading only eight other men, five of whom were Indians.

Jackson shouted, "Halt! You are surrounded on all sides, and we have thirty rifles on you."

As previously ordered, the Georgia men all let themselves be seen, but with their bodies partially concealed by a tree or other means of self-protection. Brown looked around quickly, saw that half the rifles were pointed at him, gave a low-pitched order, and raised his hands.

Within a few minutes all the Rangers were disarmed, had their hands trussed behind them, and were standing in a group, surrounded by vigilant and distrusting troops, still with their rifles leveled. It was with difficulty that Jackson restrained his men. Brown looked around coolly, with little expression on his face, apparently expecting no quarter.

Colonel Jackson confronted him. "What right do you have to bear arms, since we all know that you were placed on parole in Augusta?"

"I have complied with my pledge to Colonel Lee and General Pickens. I went from Savannah to Charles Town, where I was exchanged for Brigadier General Felix Thompson, who was captured at Guilford Courthouse. I have the official papers here in my saddlebag if you wish to see them."

Jackson consulted with Ethan and his other officers, and asked Brown,

"How do you explain your personal crimes against innocent women and children during your raids against settler families?"

Brown replied, "Colonel, you know that there have been despicable acts of violence committed by both sides during the war. I have attempted to comply with the basic orders received from my superiors, almost always having originated with the king and Parliament."

Unable to restrain himself, Ethan moved forward, looked directly into Brown's eyes, and asked, "Did these instructions authorize you and your men to attack a homestead in the Wrightsborough settlement, burn all the buildings, and savagely murder a little boy?"

Although Ethan had never discussed his personal loss with Colonel Jackson or the other men, everyone realized that this was more than a general question, and there was complete silence as they awaited Brown's answer.

"I have never approved or had any part in an attack on any person or property within the Quaker settlement."

Ethan drew back as if to strike Brown, restrained himself, and said, "You're a damned liar, and deserve to die!"

Brown momentarily lost his composure, as his face flushed and he struggled fruitlessly against his bonds. He finally said, "I have spoken the truth. You may do with us as you will."

With some reluctance, Jackson said to Ethan, "I seem to remember that Major Grierson mentioned a Quaker homestead in his confession." He turned to Brown and asked, "Are you aware that Grierson made such an attack?"

"Colonel Lee informed me that Major Grierson had signed a written confession while being tortured and before he was summarily executed as a helpless prisoner. I have not seen his confession but can affirm that our forces were under strict orders from both military commanders and Governor James Wright not to violate the Quaker settlement. I will only say that I have never violated these instructions or authorized any of my subordinates to do so."

Ethan looked directly at Brown, who returned his intense gaze without flinching. Finally convinced that the man was being truthful, he shrugged and turned away, both frustrated and also relieved of a burden of hatred that he had borne against the Ranger commander, along with a personal obligation to kill him.

Still with great care, Colonel Jackson and his men escorted the Ranger group to the Georgia military headquarters, where Brown was taken at gunpoint to General Wayne.

Except for the brief verbal exchange beside the river, Brown had not spoken and seemed completely subdued, but he had been considering how he might save himself and, at the same time, enhance the seemingly hopeless plight of British forces in Savannah. He was familiar with recent decisions made in London to stop funding the war against American troops, and he knew that the new British commander in chief, Sir Guy Carleton, had received secret orders that both Savannah and Charles Town be abandoned. He could only hope that the rebels were not aware of these strategic decisions.

Using all his persuasive powers, Brown gave an exaggerated account of Savannah's defenses, his own belief that the Americans could prevail after a long siege, and eventually induced General Wayne to release him on parole near the town, with a pledge that he would attempt to arrange for its surrender. Back with Governor James Wright and Colonel Alured Clarke, he described what had happened to him and informed the British leaders that the Georgia rebels, at best, were anticipating a long and costly siege in order to prevail. They were ignorant of orders that the city be surrendered. Together, they tabulated their most generous demands for the protection of themselves and the loyalists, and Brown carried them back to Wayne and some Whig political leaders who were assembled in their headquarters. Believing that they had prevailed in a shrewd bargain and that their major goal would be achieved without further military losses, the Georgia leaders agreed to the extraordinarily generous surrender terms. In addition to wanting to end the conflict, they knew that almost every merchant, financier, and most of Georgia's wealth were all located in Savannah, and their hope was that generosity would induce most of the Tories to remain and be loyal to their new nation.

Merchants who chose to leave were given six months to close their inventories, and the Georgians were disappointed when about 3,100 whites and 3,500 Negroes departed, mostly to Jamaica or St. Augustine, including the slaves of Governor Wright and other large landowners. Colonel James Jackson and his Georgians accepted the surrender of the city in July 1782, and most of the British troops departed for Charles Town or New York.

CHAPTER 55

Georgia Finally Secured

DECEMBER 1782

Leaving only a force of two hundred men under Colonel Jackson to defend Georgia, General Greene ordered Wayne and all his regular troops to report to him near Charles Town, and the American army finally moved into the city in December 1782, fourteen months after Cornwallis had surrendered at Yorktown.

Although having been forced to comply with orders from London, Thomas Brown remained deeply resentful of Georgia's surrender. In order to discourage American movement into the area near Florida and to solidify the British relationship with the indigenous tribal leaders, he used every opportunity to make threatening statements about retaining a strong force of Rangers in the region south of the Altamaha River. Because of these threats, Jackson was reluctant to release any of his troops, but after a few months all the Rangers and Indian warriors were ordered back to St. Augustine, and Governor Tonyn sent an official message to Savannah that there would be no more British attacks on the territory of Georgia.

When Thomas Brown finally returned to St. Augustine, Governor Tonyn honored him with an official welcome and reminded him that he was still the Indian superintendent and faced many challenges. He produced a tally sheet indicating that there were 2,400 whites and 3,600 blacks in the area, and several thousand Indians were following them into this haven, having placed their trust in the Rangers and regular British troops. For years, Brown had visited their villages, dealt fairly with their leaders, and convinced them that he was preventing further encroachment of American settlers on their land. Now he met with delegations of Creeks, Cherokees, Choctaws, Mohawks, Senecas, Delawares, Shawnees, Manjoes, Tuscaroras, Tatanous, and other tribes. They paid their respects to him, and he and other British officials gave them proper honors, thanked them for their loyalty, tried to reassure them about their future, distributed some gifts, and urged all of them to return home and unite forces to protect their hunting grounds. They were promised the permanent protection of the king, who would retain St. Augustine as the American capital of his vast kingdom.

Now secure in their control of Savannah, Georgia's newly elected governor, John Martin, met with Colonel James Jackson in Tondee's tavern, where they examined their best map of south Georgia.

The governor said, "Although we have assurances from British officials that the border between Georgia and Florida will be respected, we know damned well that Thomas Brown cannot be trusted. There is still no telling what he and his renegade Indians will do, including raids against our people right up to the edge of Savannah."

Jackson replied, "Well, now that all the regular British troops have left, I'm sure my men and I can handle any scattered marauders. I'd like to take fifty good men and make a tour all the way down past the St. Illa River, to make sure everything is peaceful and to send a clear signal about who controls the state."

Two hours later, Lieutenant Ethan Pratt was one of those assembled in front of the troops' barracks. Colonel Jackson first announced that some of the troops who desired to return to their homes would be free to leave, but stated that he needed a few men to accompany him on an excursion to the south that might take as long as three weeks. Knowing that Epsey was still in the Watauga Valley and not daring to see Mavis again in Wrightsborough, Ethan immediately volunteered.

Although their excursion along the Florida line proved to be uneventful, the leaders thought it was an ominous sign that they did not encounter any friendly Indians along the way. The tribes obviously considered the Americans still to be their enemies. After consulting with his subordinates, Colonel Jackson decided to return to Savannah.

CHAPTER 56

Ethan Returns to Augusta

Back in Savannah, the cavalrymen learned that the women and children were returning from the Watauga Valley to their homes in north Georgia, and Colonel Jackson directed that men with such families were free to meet them in Augusta, where all were scheduled to assemble.

Ethan Pratt had mixed emotions when he received permission to leave his post. He was grateful that the fighting was over, that the Americans had prevailed, and that he would soon be going back to his own property, but now he was faced with a different life. His challenging and gratifying service as an active militiaman would be replaced by the mundane duties of a farmer, almost penniless and with a cabin destroyed and crop and livestock operations to be begun once again. He was now a changed man, no longer compatible with the pacifist commitments of his wife and his Quaker neighbors, but he presumed that he could accommodate a peaceful life and relegate to a distant memory the extreme savagery of the battles in which he had fought.

Relieved of his military duties, Ethan rode with a dozen other men up the trail on the west side of the river. Now thirty-seven years old but feeling much older, he tried to focus on what his life would be as he took his wife back to their homestead and began rebuilding everything that had been lost. He could see little joy in his future. He owned as much land as two people could manage but had no money with which to buy livestock or equipment. Although slaves would be available in Georgia, he had neither the desire nor means to own them. There would be two potential sources of financial assistance, but he didn't relish the thought of turning to them. Joseph Maddock would certainly help to outfit his farm in exchange for a binding mortgage on the property. The other option would be assistance from Georgia's government leaders, who would be devising ways to assist thousands of potentially productive citizens as the state struggled toward a new life of independence. There was little doubt that James Jackson was destined to play a major role in these decisions, and he had already offered to help Ethan in the future. As usual, Mavis intruded into his thoughts, and he decided to give Wrightsborough a wide berth, knowing that he could not control his emotions if he and Mavis were together. In his own way, he prayed—without much fervor—that time would assuage his hunger for her.

When the men arrived in Augusta they found Elijah Clarke's wife, Hannah, in charge of the women and children. With the town almost completely destroyed by the repetitive battles and with only six houses still standing, most of the men's families were living in tents or other temporary shelters. Some of them had already been united with their husbands and had returned to their former homes, but there were still almost fifty women waiting, with their children. When Ethan asked about Epsey, Hannah replied that she had not chosen to come with the group and had sent him a letter that would presumably explain her absence. Ethan walked off by himself and began to read the brief letter.

> *Dear Ethan: With a heavy heart and after much prayer, I have decided not to return to Georgia. I have learned that my father has passed away and that my mother is ill and needs my help. I presume that you know Mavis Morris birthed a boy a few months ago. I have no condemnation in my heart, but do not believe we should be together in the future. I wish you well. Epsey*

A cold chill shook him, and his hands trembled as he read her words once more. He had an overwhelming sense of embarrassment, guilt, and remorse. As Ethan walked along a path beside the river and looked down into the water, he was in a quandary about what he should do. His mind was flooded with conflicting images—of his wife back in Philadelphia, Mavis somewhere attempting to care for a baby that was his son, a homestead where he would be tilling the land alone. He had no one with whom he could share his uncertainty or obtain advice. Eventually, he realized that he needed more time to make any binding decision, and that he was still needed among the small group of men who were responsible for the protection of the newly liberated land. Although released by Colonel Jackson from his military duties and realizing that it was late afternoon, he mounted his horse and headed back toward Savannah.

When Ethan reached Briar Creek near its junction with the Savannah River, he turned upstream on the well-worn trail that led to a place shallow enough to cross on horseback. Approaching the site of General Ashe's catastrophic battle, he was flooded with memories of his last day with Kindred, when the water level was at least six feet higher than today and the presently dry pathway through the woods was covered by a muddy torrent. At the turnoff to the crossing, he realized that he could proceed to his homestead without approaching Wrightsborough or likely seeing any other person. He knew that his cabin was gone, but having no urgent need to return to Savannah, he decided to make a brief visit, just to see how his fields and fences had survived the war.

Without touching the reins, he let his horse proceed down the trail.

Only then did his thoughts turn to Mavis, whom he had assumed was still with the Flemings in Wrightsborough until he'd read the shocking note from Epsey. Knowing Mavis, he was not surprised that she had concealed her condition from him, and could understand why it was not possible for her to remain with the Quakers. There was no way for him to understand why or how she had gone to the Watauga Valley.

He was now on the main trail that approached their two homesteads and, almost against his wishes, he recalled times when Epsey could have known of his interest in Mavis and her almost worshipful but still comfortable attitude toward him. Even then, during the relatively happy and carefree days of their early friendship, he should have known that the innocent interchanges between their two families had sometimes been painful to his wife. Lost in reverie, he was suddenly aware that he had just passed the huge pine tree that had played such a profoundly important role in his life.

He bypassed the Morris homestead and went directly to the remains of his own cabin. After visiting Henry's grave and wandering around the yard, he sat on a large stone inside the foundation and thought of his youth in Philadelphia and the first time he'd ever seen Epsey, as he had been cleaning the debris from the burned shell of their neighbor's home. With his eyes half closed, he could envision his own cabin exactly, with their beds separated and the boy on a pallet between him and his wife. He unsaddled his mare, rubbed her down as best he could, and carried his belongings to where his blacksmith and woodworking shop had been. The anvil, forge, and tools were gone, but the broken grindstone was lying on the ground. Exhausted, he unrolled his blanket and lay down on the ground.

Ethan slept fitfully, and the next morning he was awake before daybreak and began to walk around his own land. Although the fields were overgrown and some of the fences in disrepair, it was reassuring to see that the woodland and swamps were almost exactly as he remembered them. As the day wore on, Ethan's thoughts became clearer. There was no doubt that his natural place was here on this land, but he had gained a greater vision of what life could be in the newborn nation and he wanted to help shape its future.

The decision about his personal life was not so easy. He sat on a fallen log alongside Briar Creek, and could see Mavis clearly in his mind, a vision of youth, beauty, and exuberance. He tingled with vivid thoughts of the earlier and innocent flirtations that had led almost inexorably to the passionate consummation of their love under the pine tree. He had a strong desire to see his son and to share the responsibility for his care and nurture. He stood and began walking home.

But he was flooded with memories of Epsey and their life together as he passed the woodland pasture. He recalled nothing but good things—her patience, honesty, ability to withstand hardship without complaint, and her hard work in the cabins and fields they had shared for almost ten years. He thought of how close they were drawn together by the birth of their only child, and now admitted that in many ways she had been stronger than he during times of crisis and personal tragedy. There had never been any doubt about her loyalty.

He paused, bowed his head, and said a prayer for wisdom and judgment. After a few moments, he returned to the cabin site with renewed vigor, packed his gear, saddled and mounted the mare, looked around with satisfaction at his property, and rode down the familiar trail. He was no longer doubtful about his future as he traveled northward to find the woman who would share it with him.

Epilogue

The Treaty of Paris was signed in September 1783 and ratified the following May, bringing peace between Great Britain and America, but it was not until the end of November that American troops finally replaced the British in New York. This was almost ten years after the first shots of the revolution were fired at Lexington and Concord and three years after Cornwallis surrendered at Yorktown. In all, 100,000 Loyalists left America, most believing themselves to be abused and blameless, and moved to Canada, England, Florida, or the Caribbean.

Not realizing that there were also great issues at stake among the Europeans, people in the former colonies were amazed when the British agreed to surrender Florida to Spain. In June 1784, Colonel Brown and Governor Tonyn welcomed Spanish Governor Vicente Manuel de Zespedes to St. Augustine. There was almost inevitable tension between the two political leaders, but the new governor extended every courtesy to Brown, who became a personal friend and confidant of the Zespedes family. It is likely that the Ranger commander made his most damaging blow to Georgia's progress during those final months of 1785 when he was the last British warrior to leave America. During their long conversations and through direct intercession, he convinced Spanish officials that they should give full support to the Creeks and Cherokees in Georgia in resisting the western movement of the newly independent Americans. The most effective Indian leader was a mixed-breed chief of the Upper Creeks named Alexander McGillivray, who despised the white Georgians and had proven to be a master at forming strong alliances with the British.

Thomas Brown helped arrange binding trade and military agreements between the Indians and Spain, overcoming the best efforts of American leaders to take advantage of this economic opportunity. He also discouraged Spain from granting free navigation of the Mississippi River to anyone doing business with the state. Part of his motivation was the knowledge that Elijah Clarke had become one of the business partners of Georgia's governor, Samuel Elbert. The government of Georgia issued an official complaint to London about these activities of Brown, but this only intensified his efforts to align Chief McGillivray and his other Indian friends with Spain against any cooperation or agreement with the new nation that called itself America.

The Spaniards gave the British a gracious eighteen months to leave Florida, but Tonyn and Brown only moved from St. Augustine to St. Marys when the deadline came in July 1785, and they didn't leave America until November of the same year. It was now ten years since the Sons of Liberty had tarred and feathered Brown in Augusta. The British government had earlier granted Thomas Brown title to ten tracts of Florida land totaling 100,000 acres, which he never saw or claimed. He also received an annual pension of £500 for the rest of his life, and a large plantation on the island of St. Vincent, eighty miles west of Barbados. It is quite likely that Brown smiled with pleasure in 1812 when another war erupted between America and Great Britain.

Having suffered through continuing warfare since before the Declaration of Independence was signed in 1776, and with almost complete control of the state changing three times, Georgia was devastated. The governor reported to the Continental Congress that Augusta was completely destroyed and the formerly thriving Savannah was left with only eight hundred inhabitants.

Although there was little money and few goods available, men who had performed well during the revolution were rewarded with plentiful land that the Tories had abandoned. Colonel Clarke considered America's victory to give Georgians the right to disregard the restrictive British-Indian treaties of the past, and began to expand the state's settled territory at the expense of the natives. Restrained by national policies of the Continental Congress, he attempted to negotiate new treaties with the Cherokees and Creeks, putting pressure on the tribal leaders while claiming that the victorious Americans had built great ships and would soon have the trading items the Indians wanted. The Creeks were especially suspicious, but two of the chiefs, Tallassee King and Fat King, were richly bribed with presents and promises and signed away large land grants. Although all other Georgia chiefs renounced the agreements, state officials claimed the treaties were legal.

Still on the state lands committee and an active military leader, Elijah Clarke and his son John received more and more land, eventually paying taxes on 19,100 acres in Wilkes and Washington counties. The committee tabulated the certificates issued to returning veterans, each of whom received grants of at least 187½ acres. Two thousand nine hundred and twenty-three had stayed in Georgia and fought; 694 had left Georgia and fought in some way; 555 were never in service but had enrolled as Minutemen; 200 Continental soldiers had come from other states to help Georgia; and 9 received land because they had served in the navy. Most of the revolutionary soldiers simply moved westward, and Colonel James Jackson directed that the state build forts even on unceded lands to protect the settlers. In 1838, the last twelve thousand Indians were rounded up in Georgia by federal troops and forced to leave, with the survivors of the long "Trail of Tears" ultimately settling in Oklahoma.

When Ethan Pratt returned to Wrightsborough, he was asked to meet with his commanding officer, and Colonel Jackson urged Ethan to move to Savannah and continue to serve with him in the military and in other public and private endeavors. It was obvious to everyone that Jackson had a bright future in mind for him, but Ethan was determined to return to his homestead, expand his landholdings as much as possible, raise a family, and perhaps participate in the political development of north Georgia. The two men continued a close friendship, of great mutual benefit. As Jackson became a U.S. congressman, senator, and then governor of the state, Ethan expanded his landholdings beyond the original combined Morris and Pratt properties, and also served as a member of the Georgia House of Representatives.

It was a matter of some comment in the Wrightsborough community when he decided to replace his burned cabin with a stone structure, using native rocks from one of the hillsides. The house was patterned after some of those he remembered from Pennsylvania and was made to accommodate his large family. It served several generations of his descendants, eventually becoming the oldest dwelling in the state.

Within a few years, almost all substantial landowners were dependent on slave labor for their economic survival and growth. Slavery was perpetuated and confirmed as a national institution, with slave owner Thomas Jefferson declaring that it was a "necessary evil" for ensuring the superiority of whites and the continuation of the American way of life. For the next half century, legal and military battles would be fought over the conflicting claims for land, and the ravages of slavery and its aftermath would affect the nation for another 150 years.